IN THE LAND OF THE LONG WHITE CLOUD

IN THE LAND *of the Long* WHITE CLOUD

SARAH LARK

TRANSLATED BY D. W. LOVETT

amazon crossing

The characters and events portrayed in this book are fictitious. Any similarity to real persons, living or dead, is coincidental and not intended by the author.

In the Land of the Long White Cloud was first published in 2007 by Verlagsgruppe Lübbe GmbH & Co. KG as *Im Land der weißen Wolke.* Translated from German by D.W. Lovett. Published in English by AmazonCrossing in 2012.

Published by AmazonCrossing
P.O. Box 400818
Las Vegas, NV 89140

ISBN-13: 9781612184265
ISBN-10: 161218426X

Library of Congress Control Number: 2012940831

Contents

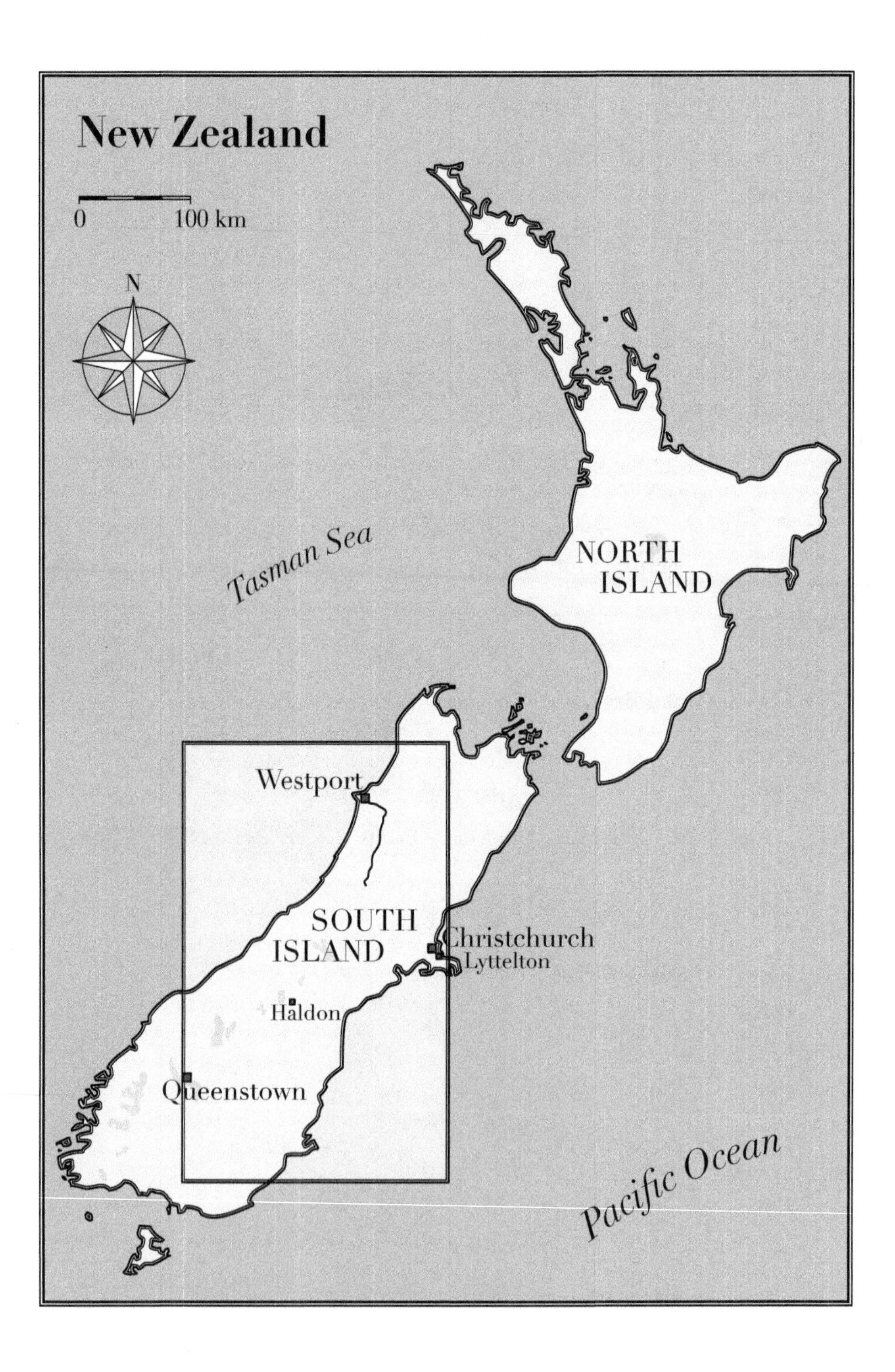
New Zealand
0
100 km
N
Tasman Sea
NORTH ISLAND
Westport
SOUTH ISLAND
Christchurch
Lyttelton
Haldon
Queenstown
Pacific Ocean

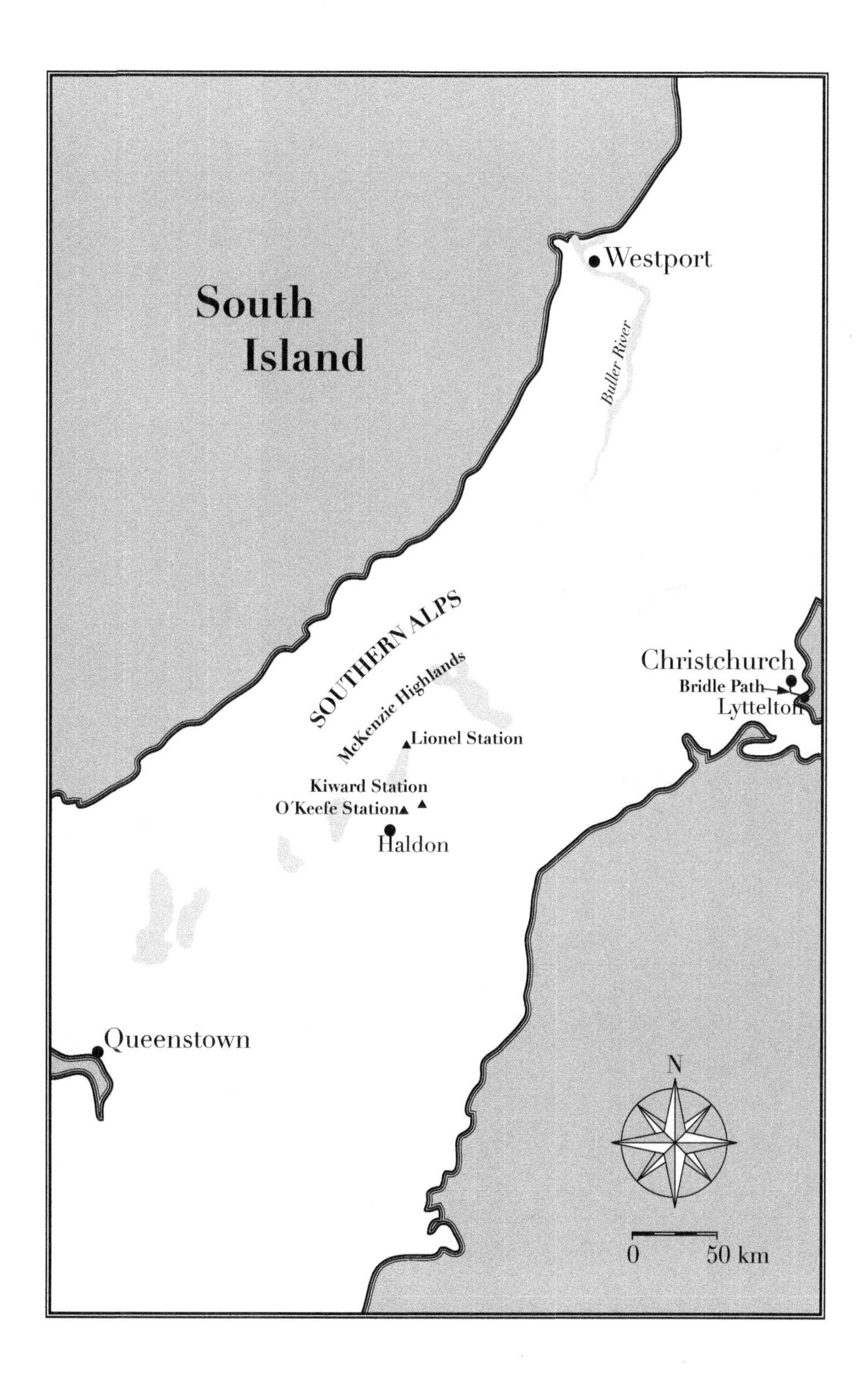
South Island
Westport
Buller River
SOUTHERN ALPS
McKenzie Highlands
Christchurch
Bridle Path
Lyttelton
Lionel Station
Kiward Station
O'Keefe Station
Haldon
Queenstown
N
0
50 km

Setting Out

London, Powys, Christchurch

1852

1

The Anglican Church in Christchurch, New Zealand, is seeking decent young women, well versed in housekeeping and child rearing, interested in entering into a Christian marriage with highly esteemed, well-situated members of our congregation.

Helen's gaze fixed briefly on the unobtrusive advertisement on the last page of the church leaflet. The teacher had browsed through the booklet while her students worked silently on a grammar exercise. Helen would have preferred to read a book, but William's constant questions broke her concentration. Even now, the eleven-year-old lifted his brown mop top from his work.

"In the third paragraph, Miss Davenport, is it supposed to be *which* or *that*?"

Helen pushed her reading aside with a sigh and explained to the boy, for the umpteenth time that week, the difference between definite and indefinite relative clauses. William, the youngest son of her employer, Robert Greenwood, was a handsome boy, but not exactly gifted with a brilliant intellect. He needed help with every assignment and forgot Helen's explanations faster than she could give them; he knew only how to gaze with touching helplessness at grown-ups, roping them in with his sweet boyhood soprano. Lucinda, William's mother, fell for it every time. Whenever the boy snuggled up to her and suggested they do some little project together, Lucinda scrapped the after-school tutoring that Helen had arranged. For that reason, William still could not read fluently, and even the easiest spelling exercises were hopelessly over his head. Attending a university like Cambridge or Oxford, as his father dreamed, was unthinkable.

Sixteen-year-old George, William's older brother, could not even be bothered to feign patience for his younger brother. He just rolled his eyes and pointed to the spot in the textbook where the exact sentence that William had been puzzling over for half an hour was given as an example. George, a lanky, gangling boy, had already completed his Latin translation assignment. He always worked quickly, although not always flawlessly; the classics bored him. George simply could not wait to join his father's import-export business. He dreamed of travel to faraway lands and expeditions to the new markets in the colonies that were opening rapidly under the rule of Queen Victoria. George was without a doubt a born merchant. He already demonstrated a talent for negotiation and knew how to use his charms to considerable effect. Now and then he even succeeded in tricking Helen into shortening the school day. He made an attempt that day, after William finally understood what he was supposed to do—or at least, where he could copy the answer. When Helen reached for George's notebook to check his work, the boy pushed it aside provocatively.

"Oh, Miss Davenport, do you really want to bother with all that right now? The weather's far too lovely for school. Let's play a round of croquet instead...you need to work on your technique. Otherwise, you'll just have to stand around at the next garden party, and none of the young chaps will notice you. Then you'll never get lucky and marry a lord, and you'll have to teach hopeless cases like Willy for the rest of your days."

Helen rolled her eyes and cast a glance out the window, wrinkling her brow at the dark clouds.

"Lovely notion, George, but the rain clouds are rolling in. By the time we've tidied up here and made it to the garden, they'll be emptying themselves out over our heads, and that won't make me any more attractive to the young nobles. How could you even think such a thing?"

Helen attempted to assume an emphatically neutral demeanor. She was quite good at it: when one worked as a governess to high-society Londoners, the first thing one learned was to master one's facial expressions. Helen's role was neither that of a family member nor of a common employee. She took part in the communal meals and often in the family's leisure activities but took care not to offer any unsolicited opinions or to otherwise draw attention to herself. In any case, she would never have found herself casually mixing with the younger guests at a garden party. Instead, she generally stood off to the side, chatting politely with the ladies while surreptitiously keeping an eye on her charges. Of course, her gaze occasionally alighted on the younger male guests, and then she would sometimes indulge in a brief romantic daydream, in which she strolled with a good-looking viscount or baronet through his manor house's park. But there was no way George could have noticed that.

George shrugged. "Well, miss, you're always reading marriage adverts," he said cheekily, indicating the church leaflet with a conciliatory grin. Helen berated herself for leaving it lying open next to her lectern. Naturally, a bored George would steal a glance at it while she was helping William put his thoughts in order.

"And you're very pretty, miss," George tried sweet-talking her. "Why shouldn't you marry a baronet?"

Helen rolled her eyes. She knew that she should chide George, but she couldn't help but be amused. If the boy kept it up, he'd go far; at least with the ladies, and in the business world people would appreciate his talent for flattery too. But would it help him at Cambridge? Besides, Helen believed herself immune to such silly compliments. She knew she wasn't beautiful in the classical sense. Though her features were symmetrical, they were rather ordinary; her mouth was a bit too thin, her nose too pointy, and her calm, gray eyes gazed too critically on the world to arouse the interest of a rich, young bon vivant. Helen's most attractive feature was her long, straight, silky brown hair, tinged with red, which fell to her waist. Perhaps she could have turned heads with it if she had let it blow freely in the breeze, as some girls did at the picnics and garden parties that Helen attended with the Greenwoods. The more brazen among the young ladies might declare all of a sudden while strolling with their admirers that it was too hot and remove their hats. Or they pretended that the wind blew their little hats away while a young man was rowing them across the pond in Hyde Park. Then they would shake down their hair, freeing it as though by accident from the constraints of bands and barrettes and letting the men marvel at their luxurious tresses.

Helen could never bring herself to do that. As the daughter of a pastor, she had been raised strictly and worn her hair braided and pinned up since she was a little girl. She had had to grow up early, as her mother had died when she was twelve and her father had placed Helen in charge of keeping house and raising her three younger siblings. Reverend Davenport had not concerned himself with problems in the kitchen and the nursery. Instead, he had immersed himself in his parish work and the translation and interpretation of religious texts. He had paid attention to Helen only when she kept him company while he worked—only by fleeing into her father's attic study could she escape the chaotic tumult of the family's apartment. Which was why Helen could already read the Bible in Greek when her brothers were still sloughing their way through their first reading primers. In her beautiful, needle-sharp handwriting, she transcribed her father's sermons and copied his article submissions for the diocese of Liverpool's newsletter. There was little time for diversions. While Susan, Helen's younger sister, took advantage of charity bazaars and church picnics to get to know the parish's young notables, Helen helped with the selling of goods, baked cakes, and poured tea. Unsurprisingly, Susan married a well-known doctor's son as soon as she turned seventeen, while Helen had been forced to take a position as a household tutor after her father died. Furthermore, with her earnings she supported her two brothers' law and medical studies. Their inheritance from their father had not been sufficient to finance a proper education for the boys—nor were they making much effort to complete their studies in a timely manner. With a flash of anger, Helen recalled how her brother had barely scraped through yet another exam just last week.

"Baronets normally marry baronesses," she finally replied curtly to George's question. "And as for this..." she pointed to the church leaflet, "I was reading the article, not the advertisement."

George said nothing but grinned knowingly. The article was about applying heat to arthritis, surely of interest to the older members of the parish, but Miss Davenport clearly did not suffer from joint pain.

Nevertheless, his teacher looked at the clock and decided to end the afternoon lesson after all. While George needed only five minutes to comb his hair and change for dinner, and Helen hardly more than that, it always took quite a bit longer to get William out of his ink-stained school uniform and into a presentable suit. Helen was grateful that she was not responsible for looking after William's presentability. A nanny saw to that.

The young governess ended the lesson with a few general remarks on the importance of grammar, to which the two boys listened only halfheartedly. Immediately afterward, William leaped up excitedly, without giving his schoolwork a backward glance.

"I have to show Mummy, real quick, what I've made!" he declared, successfully foisting the work of cleaning up on Helen. She couldn't risk having him flee in tears to his mother, telling her about some outrageous injustice on the part of his teacher. George cast a glance at William's poorly executed drawing, which his mother would no doubt praise with cries of delight. Then he quickly packed his things. Helen noticed that he cast an almost sympathetic look her way as he left. She caught herself thinking about George's comment from earlier that, if she never found a husband, she would have to wrestle with hopeless cases like Willy the rest of her days.

Helen reached for the church leaflet. She had meant to throw it away but then thought better of it. She snuck it into her bag and took it with her to her room.

Robert Greenwood did not have much time for his family, but dinnertime with his wife and children was sacred to him. The presence of the young governess did not bother him a bit. On the contrary, he often found it stimulating to include Helen Davenport in conversation and learn her views on current events, literature, and music. She clearly had a better understanding of these matters than his spouse, whose classical education was somewhat lacking in this regard. Lucinda's interests were limited to keeping house, idolizing her younger son, and working on the ladies' committees of various charitable organizations.

So on this particular evening, Robert Greenwood smiled amiably as Helen entered, and pulled out a chair for her after formally greeting the young instructor. Helen returned the smile, taking care, however, to include Lucinda Greenwood. Under no circumstances did she want to arouse the suspicion that she was flirting with her employer, even if Robert Greenwood was an undeniably attractive man. Tall and slim, he had a thin, intelligent face and inquisitive brown eyes. His brown three-piece suit and gold watch chain suited him admirably, and his manners were second to none—even those of the gentlemen from the noble families in whose social circles the Greenwoods moved. Nevertheless, they were not entirely recognized in these circles and were still regarded as parvenus. Robert Greenwood's father had built his flourishing company from practically nothing, and his son worked hard to increase their prosperity and social standing. Which explained his marriage to Lucinda Raiford, who came from an impoverished noble family. The Raifords' poverty could be easily traced to Lucinda's father's penchant for gambling and horses, or so the rumors went. Lucinda had only grudgingly accepted her bourgeois status and tended a bit toward showing off. Thus the Greenwoods' receptions and garden parties were always a touch more opulent than those of other London society notables. Though the other ladies enjoyed them, they criticized them nevertheless.

Even this evening, Lucinda had once again over-primped for a simple dinner with her family. She wore an elegant dress of lilac-colored silk, and her maid must have been busy for hours with her hair. Lucinda chatted on about a meeting of the ladies' committee for the local orphanage that she'd attended that afternoon, but she did not get much of a response; neither Helen nor Robert Greenwood were especially interested.

"And what have you all done with this lovely day?" Lucinda Greenwood asked, finally turning her attention to her family. "I don't need to ask you, Robert; presumably, it was work, work, work." She showered her husband with a gaze that was no doubt meant to convey loving indulgence.

Lucinda Greenwood was of the opinion that her spouse paid too little attention to her and her social obligations. Now he grimaced unintentionally. Robert likely had an unkind response on the tip of his tongue, for his work not only provided for the family but also made Lucinda's involvement in the various ladies' committees possible in the first place. Helen doubted that Lucinda Greenwood's organizational abilities had secured her election—it was more likely a result of her spouse's charitable nature.

"I had a very interesting conversation with a wool producer from New Zealand, and..." Robert began, glancing at his eldest son. But Lucinda simply carried on speaking, now turning her indulgent smile on William.

"And you, my dear children? Surely you played in the garden, didn't you? Did you beat George and Miss Davenport at croquet again, William dearest?"

Helen stared fixedly at her plate. Out of the corner of her eye, she saw George blinking heavenward in his usual manner, as though calling out to an understanding angel for succor. In reality, William had succeeded in winning more points than his older brother in only one instance, and George had had a nasty cold at the time. Although Helen hit the ball more skillfully through the hoops than William, she often let him win. Lucinda approved, but her husband admonished her whenever he observed the ruse.

"The boy must get used to the fact that the world plays rough with fools," he said sternly. "He has to learn to lose. That's the only way he will ever win!"

Helen doubted that William would ever win, in any field at all. But her flash of sympathy for the unfortunate child was immediately eclipsed by his next comment.

"Oh, Mummy, Miss Davenport didn't let us play at all," William said with a pout. "We sat inside the whole day and studied, studied, studied."

Lucinda shot Helen a disapproving look. "Is this true, Miss Davenport? You know, of course, that the children need fresh air. At this age they can't simply sit with their noses in books all day!"

Helen seethed within, but she could not accuse William of lying. To her relief, George stepped in.

"That's simply not true. Just like every day, William took a walk after lunch. But then it started to rain, and he didn't want to go out. The nanny dragged him around the park once, and there wasn't any time left for croquet before our lesson."

"William painted instead," Helen said, in an effort to redirect the conversation. Maybe Lucinda Greenwood would start praising William's museum-worthy sketch and forget about William's lack of fresh air. But it didn't turn out as she'd hoped.

"Even so, Miss Davenport, when the weather at noon doesn't cooperate, you simply must take a break in the afternoon. In the circles in which William will someday move, physical fitness is almost as important as intellectual ability."

William seemed to enjoy the reprimand for his teacher, and Helen thought once more of the aforementioned advertisement.

George seemed to read Helen's thoughts. Ignoring the discussion with William and his mother, he took up the conversation where his father had left off. Helen had noticed this trick between father and son several times before and was generally astounded at the elegant transition. This time, however, George's comment made her blush.

"Miss Davenport is interested in New Zealand, Father."

Helen swallowed convulsively as all eyes turned to her.

"Oh, really?" Robert Greenwood asked calmly. "Are you considering emigrating?" he smiled. "New Zealand is a good choice. No excessive heat and no malaria-infested swamps like in India. No bloodthirsty natives like America. No offspring of criminal settlers like Australia…"

"Really?" Helen asked, happy to have the conversation brought back around to neutral ground. "Was New Zealand not also settled by convicts?"

Robert Greenwood shook his head. "Not at all. The communities there were almost entirely founded by good Christian Brits, and so it remains today. I don't mean to say that there aren't dubious subjects there. Some crooks might have come ashore, especially in the whaling camps on the west coast, and sheep shearing colonies aren't likely to consist entirely of good, respectable men. But New Zealand is most assuredly not a catch pit of social scum. The colony there is still quite young. It won't be able to support itself for a few years yet."

"But the natives are dangerous!" George interjected. Clearly he now wanted to shine with his knowledge too. He had an affinity for military confrontations, Helen knew from lessons, and an outstanding memory. "There was fighting not long ago, right, Dad? Didn't you tell us about how one of your business partners had all his wool burned up?"

Robert Greenwood nodded at his son, pleased. "That's right, George. But that's in the past—over ten years ago now. Even if skirmishes do occasionally still flare up, they aren't due to the presence of the colonists. The natives have always been tractable. No, it was the sale of land that was the issue, and, who can say, it's entirely possible that our people cheated this or that tribal chieftain. But since the queen sent our good Captain Hobson over there as lieutenant general, those conflicts have let up. The man is an ingenious strategist. In 1849 he had forty-six chieftains sign a treaty in which they declared themselves subjects of the queen. The Crown has had right of preemption for land sales ever since. Unfortunately, not everyone has played along, and not all the colonists maintain the peace. That's why there are still occasional disturbances. But in general the country is safe—so no need to fear, Miss Davenport." Robert Greenwood winked at Helen.

Lucinda Greenwood knit her brow. "You're not really considering leaving England, Miss Davenport?" she asked sullenly. "You can't seriously be thinking of answering that unspeakable notice our pastor published in the parish leaflet? Against the express recommendation of our ladies' committee, I might add!"

Helen fought not to blush again.

"What sort of notice?" inquired Robert, turning to Helen, who merely hemmed and hawed.

"I...I don't know exactly what it was about. There was just a notice..."

"A community in New Zealand is seeking girls willing to marry," George apprised his father. "It seems that this South Sea paradise suffers from a lack of women."

"George!" his mother chided, horrified.

Robert Greenwood laughed. "South Sea paradise? Well, the climate is rather like that of England," he corrected his son. "But it's certainly no secret that there are more men than women in the colonies. With the exception of Australia, perhaps, where the female dregs of society have washed ashore: cheats, thieves, whor...ahem, women of easy virtue. But when it comes to voluntarily emigrating, our ladies are less adventurous than our lords of creation. Either they go with their husbands or not at all. A typical trait of the weaker sex."

"Indeed!" Lucinda Greenwood agreed with her husband, while Helen bit her tongue. She was far from convinced of male superiority. She merely had to look at William or think of the endlessly dragging studies of her brothers. Well hidden in her room, Helen even kept a copy of a book by women's rights advocate Mary Wollstonecraft, but she knew she had best keep that to herself. Lucinda Greenwood would have let her go immediately. "It is against the female nature to board dirty, foreign-bound ships without male protection, take up quarters in hostile lands, and possibly perform tasks God has reserved for men. And sending Christian women overseas to marry them off there borders on white slavery!"

"Now, now, they don't send the women off unprepared," Helen interrupted. "The advertisement clearly envisions previous correspondence. And it expressly mentioned highly esteemed, well-positioned men."

"I thought you hadn't even noticed the advertisement," Robert teased, though his indulgent smile softened the sharpness of his words.

Helen blushed anew. "I...ahem, it might be that I briefly skimmed it..."

George smirked.

His mother did not seem to have caught the brief exchange. She had already moved on to a different aspect of the New Zealand problem.

"The servant issue in the colonies strikes me as much more problematic than any lack of women," she explained. "We debated the issue thoroughly at the orphanage committee today. Apparently, the better families in...what's the name of that town again? Christchurch? At any rate, they can't find any good domestics there. Maids are almost impossible to come by."

"Which could be entirely the result of a general lack of women," Robert Greenwood remarked. Helen stifled a smile.

"In any case, our committee will be sending over a few of our orphan girls," Lucinda continued. "We have four or five good little ones who are around twelve years old, old enough to earn their living themselves. In this country we'd be hard-pressed to find a position for them. People here prefer somewhat older girls. But over there they should be smacking their lips."

"Now *that* sounds more to me like white slavery than marriage brokering," objected her husband.

Lucinda shot him a poisonous glance.

"We only have the best interests of the girls in mind," she maintained, folding her napkin together primly.

Helen had her doubts. It was unlikely that anyone had made any effort to prepare the girls for the kind of polished manners expected of maids in good houses. They could always be used as kitchen help, but even there the cooks would naturally prefer strong farm girls over poorly nourished twelve-year-olds from the poorhouse.

"In Christchurch the girls stand a chance of finding a good placement. And, naturally, we'll only send them to well-reputed families."

"Naturally," Robert remarked derisively. "I'm sure you'll carry out at least as extensive a correspondence with the girls' future employers as these young girls who want to marry will with their future spouses."

Lucinda Greenwood knit her brow, indignant. "You're not taking me seriously, Robert," she reproved her husband.

"Of course I am taking you seriously, my love." He smiled. "How could I ascribe anything but the best and most laudable intentions to the honorable orphanage committee? Besides, I'm sure you don't plan to send your little wards overseas without supervision. Maybe among those ladies looking to marry there's a trustworthy person who could look after the girls during the journey for a pittance from the committee..."

Lucinda did not respond, and Helen looked involuntarily down at her plate. She had hardly touched the delicious roast, which the cook had probably spent half the day preparing. But Helen had noticed Robert Greenwood's searching, amused side-glance when he made his last remark. Her mind bubbled with questions. Helen had never really considered that a trip overseas had to be paid for. Could a person in good conscience ask her future spouse to take care of that? Or did that give him rights that he should really only be entitled to when the "*I do*s" were said face-to-face?

No, the whole New Zealand idea was mad. Helen had to put it out of mind. She wasn't meant to have her own family. But what if?

No, she mustn't think any more of it.

Yet over the following days, Helen Davenport thought of nothing else.

2

"Would you like to see the flock straightaway, or shall we have a drink first?"

Lord Terence Silkham greeted his guests with a powerful handshake, which Gerald Warden returned equally firmly. Terence Silkham had not been sure how to picture this man from overseas, who was referred to by the breeders association in Cardiff as the "sheep baron." What he saw pleased him a good deal. The man was suitably dressed for the weather in Wales but was also entirely fashionable. His breeches were elegantly cut and made of good material, and his raincoat was of English manufacture. Clear blue eyes looked out from a broad, somewhat angular face partially covered by a wide-brimmed hat typical of those worn in the region. A full, brown head of hair shot out beneath it, neither shorter nor longer than was customary in England. In short, nothing in Gerald Warden's appearance reminded him in the least of the "cowboys" in the penny dreadfuls that a few of his lordship's servants—and to his wife's horror, even his unfilial daughter Gwyneira—occasionally perused. Depicting bloody battles between American settlers and hate-filled natives, that literary rubbish was full of clumsy drawings of youths with long, untamed heads of hair, wide-brimmed hats, chaps, and strangely shaped boots to which were affixed long, showy spurs. To top it off, the drovers always had their weapons ready at hand—"Colts," as they were called—which they wore in holsters on loose belts.

Terence Silkham's guest that day carried no weapon on his belt, but rather a flask of whiskey, which he now opened and offered to his host.

"I daresay this here'll suffice to fortify a man," Gerald Warden said in a deep, pleasant voice accustomed to giving commands. "We'll raise a few more glasses to our dealings after I've seen the sheep. Let's be on our way quickly before it starts raining again. Here, help yourself."

Terence Silkham nodded and took a healthy swig from the flask. First-class scotch. Not cheap rotgut. That further secured his visitor's favor in the eyes of the tall, red-haired lord. He nodded at Gerald, reached for his hat and riding whip, and let out a soft whistle. As if they had been waiting for that sound, three lively black and mixed brown and white sheepdogs hurried over from the end of the stable where they had sought shelter from the fickle weather. Clearly they were burning with desire to join the riders.

"Not used to the rain?" inquired Terence Silkham as he mounted his horse. A hand had brought his powerful horse, Hunter, out to him while he greeted Gerald Warden. Gerald's horse still appeared fresh despite having already ridden the long stretch from Cardiff to Powys that morning. Surely a rented horse, but undoubtedly from one of the best stables in the city. It was another hint as to where the moniker "sheep baron" came from. Although Gerald Warden wasn't of noble birth, he certainly appeared to be rich.

Gerald laughed as he slid into the saddle of his elegant bay. "On the contrary, Silkham, on the contrary."

The lord swallowed but then decided not to hold Warden's disrespectful form of address against him. Wherever the man came from, "my lord" and "my lady" were clearly unknown species.

"We have around three hundred rainy days a year. The weather in the Canterbury Plains is quite similar to here, at least in the summer. The winters are milder, but it's sufficient for first-class quality wool. And the grass is good for fattening the sheep. We have an abundance of grass, Silkham. Acres and acres. The plains are a paradise for grazers."

At that time of year one could not complain about a shortage of grass in Wales either. The hills were covered in a lush green velvet carpet as far as the mountains. Even the wild ponies could enjoy it without having to come down into the valleys to feed on Terence Silkham's land. His sheep, not yet shorn, ate until they were round as balls. In fine spirits, the men observed a flock of ewes, which were housed near the manor for birthing.

"Splendid animals!" Gerald Warden praised the sheep. "More robust than Romneys or Cheviots. They should provide wool of at least as high quality."

Terence Silkham nodded. "Welsh Mountain sheep. In the winter they run free in the mountains sometimes. They're a hardy breed. So, tell me, where is this ruminant paradise of yours? You must forgive me, but Lord Bayliff only mentioned 'overseas.'"

Lord Bayliff was the president of the sheep breeders association and had facilitated the meeting between Gerald Warden and Terence Silkham. The sheep baron, as it said in his letter, was considering acquiring a few studbook sheep in order to refine his own breed overseas.

Gerald let out a booming laugh. "And that's a broad term. Let me guess...you were probably imagining your sheep struck through with Indian arrows somewhere in the Wild West. No need to worry about any of that. The animals will remain safe and sound on British imperial soil. My property lies in New Zealand on the Canterbury Plains of the South Island. Grassland as far as the eye can see. Looks a lot like it does here, only bigger, Silkham, so much bigger!"

"This is hardly a peasant's farm," the lord chimed in indignantly. Who did this fellow think he was, treating his farm like a cliché? "I have nearly seventy-five acres of pastures."

Gerald Warden grinned again. "Kiward Station has nearly four hundred," he crowed. "Though not everything's been cleared yet. We still have our work cut out for us. Nevertheless it's a glorious estate. Add to that a stock of the best sheep studs, and it should prove a gold mine one of these days. Romneys and Cheviots crossed with Welsh Mountain sheep—that's the future, believe me!"

Terence did not want to contradict him. He was considered one of the best sheep breeders in Wales, if not all of Britain. The animals he bred would improve any population. As he was thinking this, he caught sight of the first sheep in the flock he intended for Gerald. They were all young ewes that had not yet given birth. In addition, there would be two young rams of the highest pedigree.

Terence whistled to the dogs, who immediately set about herding the scattered sheep who were grazing across the huge meadow. They encircled the animals from a distance, managing almost imperceptibly to make the sheep move toward the men. They never gave the flock cause to run; as soon as they were moving in the right direction, the dogs lowered themselves down onto the grass in a sort of stalking posture, ready to leap into action in case any sheep fell out of line.

Gerald Warden watched, fascinated by how independently the dogs operated.

"Unbelievable. What sort of breed are they? English sheepdogs?"

Terence nodded. "Border collies. They have herding in their blood and hardly require any instruction. And that was nothing. You must see Cleo in action—an amazing dog. She's won one award after another." Terence looked around searchingly. "Where is she hiding anyway? Actually, I wanted to take her along. I promised my lady I would. So that Gwyneira doesn't once more…oh no!" The lord had been looking about, searching for the dog, but now his gaze rested on a horse and its rider, approaching quickly from the living quarters. They did not bother to use the paths between the sheep paddocks or to open the gates and ride through. Instead, without hesitation, the powerful brown horse cleared all of the fences and walls that bordered the paddocks. A dog accompanied them, leaping over obstacles, hopping up and over walls like they were steps, and ducking beneath fences. The energetic, tail-wagging creature was finally ahead of the rider in the sheep paddock, in the lead of the trio. The sheep seemed almost able to read the dog's thoughts. As though responding to a single command from the bitch, they formed a tight group and stopped obediently in front of the men, without getting worked up for even a moment. Unperturbed, the sheep's heads sank once more into the grass, attended by Terence's three sheepdogs. The new arrival approached Terence at his command and seemed to beam at him from her whole friendly collie face. However, the dog did not look at the men directly. Her gaze was focused on the brown horse's rider, who slowed the horse to a trot and then came to a complete stop behind the men.

"Good morning, Father!" a bright voice said. "I wanted to bring Cleo to you. I thought you might need her."

Gerald Warden looked over at the boy, about to say a few words of praise about his elegant full-speed ride. He stopped short when he noticed the lady's saddle, the worn, dark-gray riding dress, and the rider's mass of fiery red hair carelessly tied at the nape. It was possible that the girl had pinned her locks up primly as was customary, but she couldn't have spent much time on it. Then again, during that wild ride almost any sort of braid would have come undone.

Terence Silkham looked on, less impressed. Then he remembered to introduce the girl to his guest.

"Mr. Warden—my daughter, Lady Gwyneira. And her dog, Cleopatra, the excuse she has given me for her presence here. What are you doing here, Gwyneira? If I recall correctly, your mother spoke of a French lesson this afternoon."

Usually Terence did not have his daughter's schedule committed to memory, but Madame Fabian, Gwyneira's French tutor, suffered from a severe dog allergy. Lady Silkham therefore always reminded her spouse to keep Cleo away from his daughter before her lessons, not an easy task. The dog stuck to her mistress like glue and could be lured away only by particularly interesting herding tasks.

Gwyneira shrugged charmingly. She sat impeccably straight, but loose and confident on her horse as she held her small, powerful mare serenely by the reins.

"Yes, that was the original plan. But poor Madame Fabian had a bad asthma attack. We had to put her to bed; she couldn't say a word. Where could it have come from? Mother is so careful that no animal comes near her."

Gwyneira tried to look indifferent and feign remorse, but her expressive face couldn't help but reveal a certain triumph. Warden now had a chance to observe the girl more closely: she had a very light complexion that tended to freckle and a heart-shaped face that would have appeared sweet and innocent if it weren't for her somewhat large mouth, which lent a certain sensuality to Gwyneira's appearance.

More than anything else, though, her face was defined by her large, unusually blue eyes. Indigo blue, Gerald Warden thought. That's what that color was called in the paint box that his son frittered away much of his time with.

"And Cleo did not, by chance, have another walk through the salon after the maid had removed every dog hair one by one, so that Madame Fabian might dare to step out of her room?" Terence asked sternly.

"Oh, I don't believe so," Gwyneira said with a soft smile that lent a warmth to her blue eyes. "I brought her to the stable personally and made sure she knew that she was to wait for you there. She was sitting in front of Igraine's stall when I went back. Maybe she sensed something? Dogs can be so perceptive."

The lord remembered the navy-blue velvet dress that Gwyneira had worn to lunch. If she had taken Cleo to the stables in that and crouched down to give her commands, plenty of dog hair might have stuck to it, enough to put the poor woman out of commission for three weeks.

"We'll discuss this later," Terence remarked, hoping that his wife would take on the role of judge and prosecutor. He didn't want to cross-examine Gwyneira further in front of his visitor. "How do you like the sheep, Warden? Are they everything you imagined they'd be?"

Gerald Warden knew that he should, at least as a matter of form, go from animal to animal and confirm the quality of their wool, build, and feeding. However, he entertained no doubts about the first-class quality of the ewes. All of them were large and appeared healthy and well fed, and it appeared that their wool grew right back after being shorn. Above all, he knew that Terence Silkham's sense of honor would not allow him under any circumstances to betray an overseas buyer. He would rather offer him his best sheep to secure his name as a top breeder, even in New Zealand. For that reason, Gerald's gaze remained fixed on Terence Silkham's extraordinary daughter. She was far more interesting to him than the breeding animals.

Gwyneira had by then slid from her saddle without any assistance. A spirited rider like her could probably also climb into the saddle without any help. Gerald wondered why she had even chosen a sidesaddle; likely she preferred to ride in the male position. But he guessed that might be too much for her father—the proverbial straw that broke the camel's back. He appeared unenthusiastic about seeing the girl, and her behavior toward the French governess seemed anything but ladylike.

Gerald, however, liked the girl. He observed Gwyneira's figure with pleasure, noting that it was petite but filled out in all the right places. Although she was quite young, surely no older than seventeen, the girl looked to be fully grown. However, she still seemed rather childlike; grown women generally did not display such an interest in horses and dogs. In any case, Gwyneira's rapport with the animals was a far cry from mere feminine sentimentality. Laughing, she pushed the horse away, which had just been attempting to nuzzle her shoulder expressively with its head. The mare was markedly smaller than Terence Silkham's horse, Hunter, and extremely stocky, but still elegant. Her rounded throat and short back reminded Gerald of the Spanish and Neapolitan horses that he had occasionally been offered on his travels through the continent. He had found most of the horses he'd ridden on his travels altogether too big and maybe even too sensitive for Kiward Station. He wouldn't even have trusted them to make the Bridle Path from the docks to Christchurch. This horse, on the other hand...

"You have a lovely pony, my lady," Gerald Warden remarked. "I caught myself admiring his jumping form. Do you take that horse hunting as well?"

Gwyneira nodded. At the mention of her mare, her eyes beamed just as they had when the dog was the topic of discussion.

"This is Igraine," she offered. "She's a cob. The breed typical of this region, very sure-footed and just as good for a coach as to ride. They grow up wild in the mountains." Gwyneira pointed to the jagged mountains rising up beyond the pastures, a tough landscape that no doubt required a robust nature.

"But not exactly a typical lady's horse, am I right?" Gerald asked, chuckling. He had already seen other women riding in England and knew that most of them preferred light thoroughbreds.

"That depends on whether the lady can ride," Gwyneira answered him. "I can't complain...Cleo, now keep away from my feet!" she called down to the little dog after she almost tripped over the animal. "Yes, you've been a good girl. All the sheep are there. But that wasn't a hard job, now was it?" She turned to her father. "Should Cleo fetch the rams, Father? She's getting bored."

The lord had wanted to show off the ewes first. Gerald now forced himself to take a closer look at the animals while Gwyneira let her horse graze and scratched her dog. Finally her father nodded to her.

"All right then, Gwyneira, show Mr. Warden what your dog can do since you're so keen to show off. Come along, Warden, we must ride a stretch. The young rams are up in the hills."

As Gerald had predicted, Terence made no move to help his daughter into the saddle. Gwyneira accomplished the difficult feat on her own, first putting her left foot in the stirrup and then swinging her right leg elegantly over the saddle horn, graceful and self-assured, while her horse stood there as still as a statue. As Gwyneira spurred the horse into motion, Gerald watched her grand, elegant movements. He liked the girl and horse equally, and even the small, three-colored dog fascinated him. During the ride over to the rams, he learned that Gwyneira had trained the dog herself and that they had already won several herding contests together.

"The shepherds can't stand me anymore," Gwyneira explained with an innocent smile. "And the women's association raised the question of whether it was even decent to let a girl present a dog. But what's indecent about it? I just stand around and maybe open a door now and again."

A few hand motions and a whispered command sufficed to send out the lord's well-trained dogs. Gerald Warden did not see any sheep at first as he gazed across the large plot. This time Gwyneira opened the gate to the pasture casually from atop her horse, instead of simply leaping over it. The smaller horse showed its worth in this case, as it would have been difficult for either man to lean that far down from astride their larger horses.

Cleo and the other dogs required only a few minutes to collect the flock, although the young rams were much more recalcitrant than the peaceful ewes. A few tried to get away while they were being herded and even acted aggressively toward the dogs, which did not fluster the sheepdogs one bit. Cleo wagged her tail excitedly as she returned to her mistress in answer to a terse call. All the rams now stood close by. Terence indicated two of them to Gwyneira, which Cleo separated from the others with breathtaking speed.

"These are the ones I picked out for you," the lord explained to his visitor. "The best animals for your stud book, first-class pedigree. Afterward I can show you their fathers if you want. I would have put them to stud myself and won a great many prizes. But this way...I think you might mention my name in the colonies as their breeder. And that's more important to me than another award in Cardiff."

Gerald nodded earnestly. "You can count on that. Marvelous animals! I can hardly wait for their offspring with my Cheviots. But we should talk about these dogs too. Not that we don't have sheep-dogs in New Zealand. But a dog like this one and a male to go with it would be worth some money to me."

Gwyneira, who had been stroking her dog in praise, heard his comment. She turned toward him angrily and glowered at the New Zealander. "If you're looking to buy my dog, you'd do better to deal with me, Mr. Warden. But I'll tell you right away: you won't get Cleo no matter how much you offer. She belongs to me. She won't go anywhere without me. Besides, you couldn't command her anyway because she won't listen to just anyone."

Her father shook his head disapprovingly. "Gwyneira, is this any way to behave?" he asked firmly. "Of course we can sell Mr. Warden a few dogs. It doesn't have to be your favorite." He looked at Gerald. "I'd recommend a few pups to you from the last litter, Mr. Warden. Cleo isn't the only dog we have that wins competitions."

But she's the best of them, thought Gerald. And for Kiward Station only the best was good enough. In the stables as well as in the house. If only blue-blooded girls were as easy to woo as studbook sheep.

As the three rode back to the house, Gerald Warden was already working on a plan.

Gwyneira picked out her clothes for dinner with great care. After everything that had transpired with Madame Fabian that day, she wanted to be as unobtrusive as possible. Her mother had already given her hell. By now, she knew those lectures by heart: she would never find a husband if she kept behaving so wildly and spent more time in the stables and on horseback than in her lessons. It was no secret that Gwyneira's French left something to be desired. That was true of her housewifery skills as well. Gwyneira's handwork never resulted in anything that you would want to decorate your home with—in fact, before each church bazaar, the pastor pushed her projects quietly aside instead of putting them up for sale. The girl also didn't have much of a knack for planning large dinners or having detailed discussions with the cook on questions like "salmon or pike perch?" Gwyneira ate whatever was on her plate; though she knew which fork and which spoon to use for each dish, she thought it was utter nonsense. Why spend hours decorating the table when everything would be eaten in a few minutes? And then there was the matter of flower arranging. For the past few months, decorating the salon and dining room with flowers had been among Gwyneira's duties. Unfortunately, however, her taste rarely passed muster. When she had picked wildflowers and distributed them among the vases to her liking, she had thought the effect quite charming, but her mother had almost swooned at the sight. And then all over again when she discovered a spider that had been carried in unintentionally. Ever since, Gwyneira cut the flowers from the rose garden under the gardener's supervision and arranged them with Madame Fabian's help. At least she had managed to avoid the annoying task that day. The Silkhams were having not only Gerald Warden but Gwyneira's oldest sister, Diana, and her husband to dinner as well. Diana loved flowers and had busied herself almost exclusively with the cultivation of the most eccentric and best-tended garden in all England since her wedding. Earlier that day, she had brought over a selection of her garden's most beautiful flowers for her mother and had immediately distributed them skillfully in vases and baskets. Gwyneira sighed. She would never be able to do that so well. Should men really be looking for those skills when choosing a wife, she would surely die an old spinster. Gwyneira sensed, however, that both her father and Diana's husband, Jeffrey, were completely indifferent toward the floral decorations. No man—aside from the less than enthusiastic pastor—had ever even bothered to look at her stitching. So why couldn't she impress the young men with her real talents? She could inspire no end of astonishment on a hunt, for example, since Gwyneira could usually chase the fox faster and more successfully than the rest of the hunting party. That, however, seemed to do as little to win the men over as her skillful handling of the sheepdogs. Sure, the young chaps expressed their admiration, but their gaze was often a little deprecatory, and on ball nights she usually found herself dancing with other girls. But that might also have had to do with Gwyneira's paltry dowry. She had no illusions about that—as the last of three daughters, she knew that she couldn't expect much. In addition, her brother was still leeching off her father. John Henry "studied" in London. Gwyneira wondered what subject. For as long as he lived at Silkham Manor, he didn't get any more out of the sciences than his little sister, and the bills he sent back from London were far too high to have only been for the purchase of books. Her father always paid without question, only occasionally mumbling something about "sowing wild oats," but Gwyneira was well aware that the money was coming out of her dowry.

Despite all this, she did not worry much about her future. For the present, things were going well, and at some point, her imperturbable mother would scare up a husband for her too. Already her parents' invitations to dine consisted almost solely of married friends who just happened to have marriageable sons. Sometimes they brought the young men with them, but more often the parents would come alone, and even more often the mothers would come to tea alone. Gwyneira hated that ritual in particular, because then all of the talents that girls supposedly needed to maintain a noble household's preeminence came under scrutiny. It was expected that Gwyneira would serve the tea artfully, though she had once unfortunately scalded Lady Bronsworth. And she had been shocked during this difficult transaction to hear her mother announce that Gwyneira had made the tea biscuits herself—a big fat lie.

After tea, they reached for their embroidery tambours. Lady Silkham often snuck Gwyneira her own, on which a work of art in petit point was almost finished, while they discussed the latest book by Mr. Bulwer-Lytton. Those books were like a sedative to Gwyneira; she had yet to make it through even one of those tomes. She nevertheless knew a few terms like "edifying" and "sublime power of expression," which one could make use of again and again in this context. Beyond that, the women naturally discussed Gwyneira's sisters and their wonderful husbands, at which point her mother would express her hope that Gwyneira too would soon be blessed with a similarly good match. Gwyneira didn't know herself if she hoped for that. She found her brothers-in-law boring, and Diana's husband was almost old enough to be her father. There was a rumor that that was why the couple had yet to be blessed with children, though the connection wasn't entirely clear to Gwyneira. True, one did stop using old studs too... She giggled when she pictured Diana's stiff husband Jeffrey with Cesar the ram, which her father had just removed from stud duty against his will.

And then there was Larissa's husband, Julius. Although he came from one of the best noble families, he was dreadfully colorless. Gwyneira remembered how her father had furtively murmured something about "incest" after their first meeting. At least Julius and Larissa already had a son, but he looked like a ghost. No, those were not the sorts of men Gwyneira dreamed of. Were the offerings overseas any better? This Gerald Warden made a lively impression, though he was too old for her, of course. But he knew his way around a horse, and he hadn't offered to help her into the saddle. Did women in New Zealand ride like men without reprimand? Gwyneira caught herself dreaming from time to time over the servants' novellas. What might it really be like to race horses with one of those dashing American cowboys? To watch him in a pistol duel, heart pounding? And the pioneer women over there in the West even reached for guns themselves! Gwyneira would have chosen a fort surrounded by Indians to Diana's rose garden any day.

She finally forced herself into her corset, which she tied more tightly than the old thing she wore when riding. She hated this torture, but when she looked at herself in the mirror she did like her extremely thin waist. Neither of her sisters was as petite as she was. And her sky-blue velvet dress suited her quite brilliantly. It made her eyes look more radiant and emphasized the luminous red of her hair. What a shame that she had to pin it up. And how troublesome for the maid, who stood waiting nearby with comb and barrettes. Gwyneira's hair was naturally curly; when there was moisture in the air—as there almost always was in Wales—it frizzed and proved especially difficult to tame. Often she had to sit still for hours before her maid had completely subdued it. And for Gwyneira, sitting still was harder than anything.

Sighing, Gwyneira sat down at her dressing chair and steeled herself for a dull half hour. Then a nondescript paperback lying on the dressing table caught her eye. *In the Hands of the Redskins* read the lurid title.

"I thought my lady might wish for a little diversion," commented the young maid and smiled at Gwyneira in the mirror. "But it's really very scary. Sophie and me couldn't sleep the whole night after we'd read it to each other!"

Gwyneira had already reached for the paperback. She wasn't so easily scared.

Meanwhile, Gerald Warden was bored in the salon, where the gentlemen were having a drink before dinner. Terence Silkham had introduced Gerald to his son-in-law, Jeffrey Riddleworth. Lord Riddleworth, Terence Silkham explained, had served in the Indian Crown Colony and had returned to England highly decorated for his services there just two years before. Diana Silkham was his second wife, the first having died in India. Gerald did not dare ask what of, but he was nearly certain that the lady had died of neither malaria nor a snakebite—that is, unless she had possessed a great deal more vim and vigor than her spouse. Jeffrey Riddleworth, in any event, seemed never to have left regimental quarters during his entire posting in India. He couldn't say anything about the country beyond the fact that it was loud and dirty outside of the English sanctuaries. He thought the natives were all beggars, the maharajahs above all, and everything beyond city limits was infested with snakes and tigers.

"Once we even had a keelback in our quarters," Jeffrey Riddleworth explained with disgust, twirling his well-groomed mustache. "I shot the beast straightaway, of course, although some coolie said it wasn't poisonous. But, I ask you, can you trust these people? What's it like where you are, Warden? Do your servants have these repugnant people under control?"

Gerald thought with amusement that Jeffrey Riddleworth's shooting in a building had likely caused more damage than even a tiger could have wrought. Besides, he didn't actually believe that the small, well-fed colonel could hit a snake's head on the first shot. Regardless, the man had chosen the wrong country to make a name for himself.

"Our servants take...ahem, a little getting used to," Gerald said. "We mostly employ natives to whom the English lifestyle is rather foreign. But we don't have to worry about snakes and tigers. There aren't any snakes in all of New Zealand. Originally there were hardly any mammals either. It was the missionaries who first brought work animals, dogs and horses and the like, to the island."

"No wild animals?" Jeffrey asked, wrinkling his brow. "Come now, Warden, you don't mean to tell us that before the settlers came it looked like it did on the fourth day of creation."

"There were birds," Gerald Warden reported. "Big, small, fat, thin, flying, walking...oh yes, and a few bats. Besides that, insects of course, but they're not very dangerous either. You'd have to work hard if you wanted to be killed on New Zealand, sir. Unless you resort to dealing with bipedal robbers with firearms."

"Presumably those with machetes, daggers, and krises too, eh?" Riddleworth asked with a chuckle. "Well, it's a puzzle to me how one could volunteer to live in such a wilderness. I was happy to leave the colonies."

"Our Maori are mostly peaceful," Warden said calmly. "A strange people...at once fatalistic and easy to please. They sing, dance, carve wood, and don't know how to make any weapons worthy of mention. No, sir, I'm sure you would have been rather more bored than afraid."

Jeffrey Riddleworth wanted to correct him that he hadn't lost a single drop of sweat to fear during his entire time in India. But the gentlemen were interrupted by Gwyneira's arrival. The girl entered the salon—and looked around, clearly confused, when she saw that her mother and sister were not among those present.

"Am I early?" Gwyneira asked, instead of first properly greeting her brother-in-law.

Jeffrey looked suitably offended, but Gerald Warden could not take his eyes off her. The girl had struck him as pretty earlier, but now, in formal attire, he recognized her as a true beauty. Her blue velvet dress highlighted her pale skin and her vibrant red hair. Her more chaste hairstyle emphasized the noble cut of her face. Completing the effect were her bold lips and luminous blue eyes, which sparkled with a lively, almost provocative expression. Gerald was enraptured.

It was clear that this girl didn't fit here. He couldn't possibly picture her at the side of a man like Jeffrey Riddleworth. Gwyneira was more likely to wear a snake around her neck and tame tigers.

"No, no, dear, you are punctual," her father said, glancing at the clock. "Your mother and sister are late. Likely they were once more too long in the garden."

"Were you not in the garden, then?" Gerald Warden asked, turning to Gwyneira. Really he would have expected her to be out in the fresh air more than her mother, whom he had met earlier and considered rather dull and prim.

Gwyneira shrugged. "I don't know much about roses," she admitted, though in doing so she incurred Jeffrey's displeasure once more and surely that of her father as well. "Now, if there were vegetables or something else that didn't prick..."

Gerald Warden laughed, ignoring the other men's acerbic countenances. The sheep baron found the girl enchanting. Of course, she wasn't the first girl he'd eyed surreptitiously on his trip through the old homeland, but so far none of the other young English ladies had opened themselves up so naturally and willingly.

"Now, now, my lady," he teased her. "Do you really mean to confront me with the dark side of the English rose? Does the milk-white skin and copper hair hide only thorns?"

The term "English rose" for the light-skinned, red-haired girls common to the British Isles was also known in New Zealand.

Normally Gwyneira would have blushed, but she only smiled. "It's safer to wear gloves," she remarked, seeing her mother gasping for air out of the corner of her eye.

Lady Silkham and her oldest daughter, Lady Riddleworth, had just entered and overheard Gerald and Gwyneira's short exchange. They didn't know whether they were more shocked by their guest's lack of shame or Gwyneira's quick-witted riposte.

"Mr. Warden, my daughter Diana, Lady Riddleworth." Lady Silkham decided in the end to ignore the matter entirely. The man obviously did not possess any social grace, but he had agreed to pay her husband a small fortune for a flock of sheep and a litter of puppies. That would ensure Gwyneira's dowry—and give Lady Silkham just enough leverage to marry the girl off quickly, before word of her sharp tongue got out.

Diana greeted the overseas visitor grandly. She had been assigned to Gerald Warden as a dining partner, for which she was soon sorry. Dinner with the Riddleworths dragged on, and was beyond dull. While Gerald expressed pleasantries and pretended to listen to Diana's explanations about growing roses and garden exhibitions, he kept an eye on Gwyneira. Aside from her loose manner of speech, her behavior was impeccable. She knew how to behave in society and chatted with her dining partner, Jeffrey, politely, even if she was obviously bored. She dutifully answered her sister's questions about her progress in French conversation and dear Madame Fabian's health, who deeply regretted having to miss the evening meal due to illness. Otherwise, she would have all too gladly spoken with her favorite former pupil, Diana.

Only when dessert was being served did Jeffrey Riddleworth return to his question from earlier. Apparently, the table talk had even gotten on his nerves. Diana and her mother had transitioned to chattering about shared acquaintances, discussing which ones they found completely "charming" and which had "well-off" sons, whom they evidently considered potential matches for Gwyneira.

"You've yet to tell us how the winds blew you ashore overseas, Mr. Warden. Did you go on business of the Crown? Or perhaps in pursuit of the legendary Captain Hobson?"

Gerald Warden shook his head, smiling, and let the servant refill his wineglass. Until that moment, he had only drunk a modest quantity of the excellent vintage. He knew that later there would be plenty of his host's excellent scotch, and if he wanted to have even the slightest chance of pulling off his plan, he needed a clear head. An empty glass, however, would raise suspicion. So he nodded to the servant, but reached for his water glass.

"I sailed out a full twenty years before Hobson," he answered. "At a time when things were still a bit rougher on the islands. Especially in the whaling stations and with the seal hunters."

"But aren't you a sheep grazier?" Gwyneira chimed in keenly. Finally an interesting topic! "You didn't really hunt whales, did you?"

Gerald laughed grimly. "Did I ever hunt whales, my lady. Three years on the *Molly Malone*..."

He did not want to say more, but Terence Silkham now knit his brow.

"Oh, come now, Warden, you know too much about sheep for me to buy these pirate stories. You certainly didn't learn all that on a whaling ship!"

"Of course not," Gerald answered calmly. The flattery did not faze him. "In fact, I come from the Yorkshire Dales; my father was a shepherd."

"But you sought adventure!" That was Gwyneira. Her eyes flashed with excitement. "You set out on a dark and stormy night, leaving land behind and..."

Gerald was amused and inspired at once. This girl was without a doubt the one, even if she was spoiled and had a completely unrealistic understanding of the world.

"I was, you see, the tenth of eleven children," he explained. "And I didn't like the idea of earning my living watching other people's sheep. My father wanted me to take up the trade at thirteen. But I hired on a ship instead. Saw half the world. The coasts of Africa, America, the Cape...we sailed as far as the Arctic. And finally to New Zealand. And I liked it there best. No tigers, no snakes..." He winked at Jeffrey Riddleworth. "The land still unexplored to a large extent and a climate like the homeland. In the end one just seeks out his roots."

"And then you hunted whales and seals?" Gwyneira asked again, incredulously. "You didn't start right off with sheep?"

"Sheep don't come free, little lady," Gerald Warden said, smiling. "As I got to learn anew today. In order to purchase your father's flock, you'd have to kill more than just one whale. And though the land was cheap, the Maori chiefs don't exactly give it away for free."

"The Maori are the natives, right?" Gwyneira asked with evident curiosity.

Gerald Warden nodded. "It means something like 'moa hunter.' The moas were giant birds, but apparently the hunters were too zealous and the beasts have all died out. Incidentally, we immigrants are also named after birds. We call ourselves 'kiwis,' which is a curious, stubborn, and vivacious bird. You can't escape a kiwi. They're everywhere in New Zealand. Don't ask me who came up with the idea to label us kiwis, of all things."

Only a few members of the dining party laughed, mostly Terence Silkham and Gwyneira. Lady Silkham and the Riddleworths were indignant that they were dining with a former shepherd boy and whaler, even if he had since acquired the title of sheep baron.

Lady Silkham soon brought the meal to a close and retired to the salon with her daughters. Gwyneira only reluctantly quit the gentlemen's circle. Finally the conversation had turned to more interesting subjects than Diana's unspeakably boring roses and endlessly dull society. She longed to return to her room, where *In the Hands of the Redskins* awaited her, half-read. The Indians had just abducted the daughter of a cavalry officer. However, Gwyneira still had at least two cups of tea in her female family's company ahead of her. Sighing, she resigned herself to her fate.

Meanwhile, Terence Silkham offered cigars to the men in the study. Gerald Warden's connoisseurship in selecting the best variety of Cubans impressed him. Jeffrey Riddleworth simply reached into the case and picked one at random. Then they spent an endless half hour discussing the queen's latest decision regarding British agriculture. Both Terence and Jeffrey thought it regrettable that the queen clearly sided with industrialization and trade over strengthening traditional industry. Gerald Warden said little on the topic. He didn't know much about it, and he didn't really care. However, the New Zealander perked back up when Riddleworth cast a regretful glance at the chessboard that waited, set up, on a little table nearby.

"It's a shame that we won't get to our game today, but we wouldn't want to bore our guest," he remarked.

Gerald Warden caught the undertones. If he were a true gentleman, Jeffrey wanted to imply, he would make up some reason to retire to his rooms. But Gerald was no gentleman. He had played that role well enough until now; it was now time to get down to his real business.

"Why don't we play a little card game instead?" he suggested with an innocent smile. "One plays blackjack even in the salons in the colonies, eh Riddleworth? Or would you prefer a different game? Poker, perhaps?"

Jeffrey Riddleworth looked at him with disgust. "I beg your pardon! Blackjack...poker...one might play such games in port town pubs but certainly not among gentlemen."

"Well, I'll gladly play a hand," Terence declared, glancing eagerly at the card table. He did not seem to be taking up Gerald's offer simply to be polite. "During my time in the military, I played often, but here we hardly ever do anything on social occasions other than talk shop about sheep and horses. Hop to it, Jeffrey! You can deal first. And don't be stingy. I know you make a fine salary. Let's see if I can't win back some of Diana's dowry."

Terence Silkham spoke bluntly. During dinner he had partaken heavily of the wine, and upon entering the salon had tossed back his first scotch quickly. Now he gestured eagerly for the other men to take their places. Gerald Warden sat down happily, while Jeffrey did so reluctantly. He reached for the cards against his will and shuffled clumsily.

Gerald set his glass aside. He had to be alert now. He noted with pleasure that the tipsy Terence opened with a high ante. Gerald readily let him win. A half hour later, a small fortune in coins and notes lay before Terence and Jeffrey. The latter had thawed somewhat, even if he still did not appear entirely enthusiastic. Silkham helped himself to more whiskey.

"Don't lose the money for my sheep," he warned Gerald. "You've already played away another litter of pups."

Gerald Warden smiled. "Who doesn't dare, doesn't win," he said and upped the ante again. "How is it, Riddleworth, going to call?"

The colonel was no longer sober either, but he was mistrustful by nature. Gerald Warden knew that he'd have to get rid of him—while losing as little money as possible in the process. When Jeffrey went all in, Gerald struck.

"Blackjack, my friend," he said almost regretfully as he laid his ace on the table. "My unlucky streak had to end sometime. Another hand! Come, Riddleworth, win your money back double."

Jeffrey stood up peevishly. "No, deal me out. I should have quit sooner. Oh well, easy come, easy go. I'm not putting any more money in your pockets tonight. And you should quit too, Father. Then you'll at least come out ahead."

"You sound like my wife," Terence remarked, though his voice sounded a little unsure. "And what do you mean 'come out ahead'? I didn't call last time. I still have all my money. And my luck's holding! Today's my lucky day anyway, eh, Warden? Today I'm really lucky."

"Then I hope you keep having fun," Jeffrey said icily.

Gerald Warden breathed a sigh of relief as Jeffrey left the room. Now the coast was clear.

"Then let's double your winnings, Silkham," he encouraged the lord. "How much is that now? Fifteen thousand altogether? Lord almighty, so far you've lightened my wallet by more than ten thousand pounds. Double that and you'll have as much as you got for the sheep!"

"But...but if I lose, then it's all gone." The lord was now having misgivings.

Gerald Warden shrugged. "That's the risk. But we can keep it small. Look, I'll deal you a card and myself one as well. Peek at it. I'll uncover mine—and then you can decide. If you want to play, all the better. I can, of course, also decline after I've seen my first card." He smiled.

The lord received the card doubtfully. Didn't this peek go against the rules? A gentleman should never look for loopholes or shy away from risks. Nevertheless, he stole a look at his card.

A ten! Except for an ace, it couldn't have been better.

Gerald, who kept the pot, revealed his card. A queen. That counted for ten points. Not a bad start. Still the New Zealander wrinkled his brow and seemed doubtful.

"My luck doesn't seem to be holding," he sighed. "And how about you? Shall we play, or leave it be?"

The lord was suddenly very eager to continue.

"I'd gladly take another card," he declared.

Gerald Warden looked at his queen with resignation. He seemed to be wrestling with himself, but dealt another card anyway.

The eight of spades. Eighteen points total. Would that be enough? Silkham broke out in a sweat. But if he took another card, he was in danger of going bust. Better to bluff. The lord attempted a poker face.

"Ready when you are," he declared curtly.

Gerald revealed another card. A two. So far twelve points. The New Zealander reached for the cards again.

Terence Silkham prayed for an ace. Then Gerald would go bust. But still, his own chances weren't bad. Only an eight or a ten could save the sheep baron.

Gerald drew—a three.

He let his breath out sharply.

"If only I were clairvoyant..." he sighed. "But, no matter, I don't imagine you have any less than fifteen. So I'll risk it."

The lord trembled as Gerald drew his fourth card. The danger of going bust was huge. But it was the four of hearts.

"Nineteen," Gerald counted. "And I'll stay. Cards on the table, my lord!"

Terence revealed his bluff. He had lost by one point. And he had been so close!

Gerald Warden seemed to see it the same way. "By a hair, my lord, by a hair. That cries for revenge. I know I sound crazy, but we can't let that stand. Another hand."

Terence shook his head. "I don't have any more money. That wasn't just my winnings, that was everything I had to bet. If I lose any more, I'll be in serious trouble. It's out of the question; I'm out."

"But I beg you, my lord!" Gerald shuffled the cards. "It just starts getting fun with high stakes. As for a bet...wait, let's play for the sheep. Yes, the sheep you wanted to sell me. That way, even if things go badly, you won't lose anything. After all, if I hadn't suddenly shown up to purchase the sheep, you wouldn't have had the money in the first place." Gerald Warden flashed his winning smile and let the cards pass nimbly between his hands.

The lord emptied his glass and prepared to stand. He swayed a little as he did so, but he still articulated his words clearly: "That would suit you, Warden! Twenty of this island's best breeding sheep for a few card tricks? No, I'm done. I've lost enough. Maybe such games are common in the wilderness you come from, but here we keep a cool head."

Gerald Warden raised the whiskey bottle and filled the glasses once more.

"I would have taken you for a braver man," he said regretfully. "Or better said, for a more daring one. But maybe that's typical of us kiwis—in New Zealand, you are only considered a man if you dare to take a few risks."

Terence Silkham frowned. "You can hardly accuse the Silkhams of cowardice. We have always fought bravely, served the Crown, and..." The lord found it visibly difficult to find the right words and stand at the same time. He let himself sink down once more into his chair. But he wasn't drunk yet. He could still ante up to this rogue.

Gerald Warden laughed. "In New Zealand we serve the Crown too. The colony is developing into an important economic engine. In the long run we'll pay England back everything the Crown has invested in us. The queen is braver than you on that count, my lord. She's playing her game, and she's winning. Come, Silkham! You don't want to give up now, do you? A few good cards, and you'll have been paid twice for the sheep."

With those words he threw two cards facedown on the table. The lord could not have said why he reached for them. The risk was too great, but the prize was tempting. If he won, not only was Gwyneira's dowry secure, but it would also be large enough to please even the best families in the region. As he slowly picked up the cards, he saw his daughter as a baroness...who knew, maybe even a lady-in-waiting to the queen...

A ten of diamonds. That was good. Now if the other one... Silkham's heart began to beat loudly when he uncovered a ten of spades. Twenty points. That was hard to beat.

He looked at Gerald triumphantly.

Gerald Warden took his first card from the deck. Ace of spades. Terence groaned. But it didn't mean anything. The next card could be a two or three, and then the chances were good that Gerald would bust.

"You can still back out," Gerald offered.

Terence laughed. "Oh no, my friend, that wasn't the bet. Now play your card! A Silkham keeps his word."

Gerald took another card.

Terence suddenly wished he'd shuffled the deck himself. On the other hand...he'd watched Gerald shuffle; he hadn't tried anything. Whatever happened next, he couldn't accuse Warden of cheating.

Gerald Warden turned the next card over.

"I'm sorry, my lord."

The lord stared at the ten of hearts lying in front of him on the table as though hypnotized. The ace counted for eleven; the ten made an even twenty-one.

"Then I can only congratulate you," he said stiffly. There was still whiskey in his glass, and he threw it back quickly. When Gerald moved to refill it, he covered the glass with his hand.

"I've already had too much, thank you. It's time that I stop... drinking and playing before I not only cheat my daughter out of her dowry but my son out of house and home as well." His voice sounded choked. He attempted to stand up again.

"I thought that might be the case," Gerald remarked in a conversational tone, filling his own glass. "The girl is your youngest, is that right?"

Terence nodded bitterly. "Yes. I've already married off two other daughters. Do you have any idea what that costs? This last wedding will ruin me. Especially now that I've lost half my capital at the gambling table."

Lord Silkham wanted to go, but Gerald shook his head and raised the whiskey bottle. Slowly the golden temptation flowed into Terence Silkham's glass.

"No, my lord," said Gerald, "we can't leave things like this. It wasn't my intention to ruin you, nor to rob poor Gwyneira of her dowry. Let's play a final hand, my lord. I'll bet the sheep again. If you win this time, then everything will be as it was."

Terence laughed derisively. "And what would I bet against that? The rest of my flock? Forget it!"

"How about...how about your daughter's hand?"

Gerald Warden spoke softly and calmly, but Terence reeled as though Warden had struck him.

"You're out of your mind! You don't seriously mean to woo Gwyneira? The girl could be your daughter."

"I would wish for just that with all my heart." Gerald tried to imbue his voice and gaze with as much sincerity and warmth as he could muster. "Because my proposal is not for myself, naturally, but for my son, Lucas. He is twenty-two years old, my only heir, well bred, full grown, and clever. I could easily picture Gwyneira at his side."

"But not I," Terence retorted rudely, stumbling and seeking support from his chair. "Gwyneira belongs to the high nobility. She could marry a baron!"

Gerald Warden laughed. "With almost no dowry? And don't fool yourself; I've seen the girl. She's not exactly what the mothers of baronets dream of."

Terence Silkham was incensed. "Gwyneira is a beauty!"

"That's true," Gerald reassured him. "And no doubt she's the jewel of every fox hunt. I wonder if she'd shine as brightly in a palace though. She's a wild young thing, my lord. It'll cost you twice as much to fetch the girl a husband."

"I should challenge you to a duel!" Terence Silkham exclaimed in a rage.

"I've already challenged you to one." Gerald Warden raised the cards. "Let's play. You shuffle this time."

The host reached for his glass. His thoughts were racing. This was entirely contrary to custom. He couldn't bet his daughter in a card game. This Warden had lost his mind. On the other hand...such a transaction wouldn't hold up. Gaming debts were honorable debts, but a girl was not an acceptable wager. If Gwyneira said no, no one could force her aboard a ship bound for faraway shores. Then again, it wouldn't even have to come to that. He would win this time. His luck had to turn sometime.

Terence shuffled the cards—not ponderously as usual, but fast, as though he wanted to put this debasing game behind him as quickly as possible.

Almost in a rage he dealt Gerald a card. He gripped the rest of the deck with trembling hands.

The New Zealander turned over his card without showing any reaction. The ace of hearts.

"That's..." Terence didn't say another word. Instead, he drew a card himself. Ten of spades. Not bad at all. The lord attempted to deal with a steady hand but shook so much that the card fell onto the table in front of Gerald before he could reach for it.

Gerald Warden did not even make an attempt to keep the card hidden from view. He serenely laid the jack of hearts next to his ace.

"Blackjack," he said calmly. "Will you keep your word, my lord?"

3

Though this was not her first time here, Helen's heart raced as she stood before the office of St. Clement's parish priest. She usually felt quite comfortable inside these walls, so like those of her father's parish. Reverend Thorne was, moreover, an old friend of the late Reverend Davenport. A year earlier, he had helped Helen secure the position at the Greenwoods' and had even taken her brothers in for a few weeks before Simon first, and then John, found rooms through their student fraternity. Though the boys had been happy to move out, Helen had been less pleased about it. Thorne and his wife not only let her brothers live with them for free but even helped out a little, while room and board in the fraternity house cost money and offered the students distractions not necessarily conducive to their academic progress. Helen often aired her grievances to the reverend over that. In fact, she spent many of her free afternoons in the Thornes' house.

However, she didn't expect to enjoy a relaxing cup of tea with the reverend and his family on her visit that day, and the booming, joyful "Enter with God!" with which he usually greeted his flock did not sound from his rectory either. Instead, Helen could hear a woman's voice, one that sounded accustomed to giving commands, coming from inside the office after Helen finally worked up the nerve to knock. This afternoon in the reverend's rooms Lady Juliana Brennan awaited her. The wife of a pensioned lieutenant from William Hobson's staff, she was formerly a founding member of the Anglican parish in Christchurch and more recently a patron of the London congregation once again. Lady Brennan had answered Helen's letter and arranged this meeting in the parish rectory. She was eager to see in person the "decent women, well-versed in housekeeping and child rearing" who had answered her advertisement before she introduced them to the "highly esteemed, well-situated members" of the Christchurch community. Fortunately she was flexible and able to meet them at their convenience. Helen had only one afternoon free every two weeks, and she was loath to ask Lucinda Greenwood for additional time off. Lady Brennan had agreed immediately to Helen's suggestion that they meet that Friday afternoon.

When she called the young woman into the room, she observed with pleasure that Helen curtsied respectfully upon entering.

"Leave that, girl, I'm not the queen," she remarked coolly, causing Helen to blush.

She was struck by the similarities between the austere Queen Victoria and the equally round and darkly clad Lady Brennan. Both smiled rarely and seemed to view life above all as a God-given burden that one was to suffer through as publicly as possible. Helen made an effort to look just as austere and expressionless. She had checked in the mirror to make sure that not a single hair had fallen from her tightly wound bun in the London streets. The better part of her prim hairstyle was covered by her plain dark blue hat anyway, which Helen had worn as necessary protection from the rain and which was now completely soaked through. She had at least been able to deposit her equally wet coat in the antechamber. She wore a blue skirt and a carefully starched, light-colored quilled shirt. Helen wanted more than anything to make as good and distinguished an impression as possible. Lady Brennan could under no circumstances take her for a flighty thrill-seeker.

"So you want to emigrate?" Lady Brennan asked straightaway. "A pastor's daughter, moreover with a good job, I see. What calls you overseas?"

Helen considered her answer carefully. "It's not adventure that calls me, my lady," she stated. "I'm happy with my job, and my employers treat me well. But every day I see their family's happiness, and my heart burns with longing to someday stand in the center of such a loving body."

Hopefully Lady Brennan didn't think that overstated. Helen herself had almost laughed as she put that sentence together. After all, the Greenwoods weren't exactly the model of harmony—and the absolute last thing Helen wanted was progeny like William.

Lady Brennan, however, did not seem put off by Helen's response. "And you don't see any possibility of that here at home?" she inquired. "You don't think you will find a husband here who will meet your expectations?"

Helen wanted to ask a few questions about the "highly esteemed, well-situated members" of the Christchurch community, but that would clearly have to wait. "I don't know if my expectations are too high," she said carefully, "but my dowry isn't large. I can save very little, my lady. I've been supporting my brothers during their studies, so there's nothing left over. And I'm twenty-seven. There's just not much time left for me to find a husband."

"And your brothers no longer need your support?" Lady Brennan wanted to know. Clearly she was implying that Helen wanted to escape her familial obligations by emigrating. She wasn't entirely wrong either. Helen had had more than enough of financing her brothers.

"My brothers have almost finished their studies," she said. That wasn't even a lie: if Simon failed one more class, he would be expelled from the university, and John wasn't in much better shape. "But I don't think it likely that they will be able to come up with my dowry afterward. Neither legal nor medical assistants make much money."

Lady Brennan nodded. "Won't you miss your family?" she inquired acerbically.

"My family will consist of my husband and—God willing—our children," Helen explained firmly. "I will stand by my husband in making a home overseas. There won't be much time left over to mourn my lost homeland."

"You sound very determined," the lady remarked.

"I hope God will lead me," Helen said humbly, bowing her head. Questions about the men would have to wait. The main thing was to get this dragon in black on her side. And if the gentlemen in Christchurch were put through their paces like the women here, nothing could possibly go wrong. Lady Brennan now became more gracious. She even let slip some details about the Christchurch community: "a budding colony, founded by settlers handpicked by the Church of England. The city will be made a bishopric in the foreseeable future. The construction of a cathedral is planned, as is a university. You won't miss anything, child. The streets were even named after the English diocese."

"And the river that runs through the city is called the Avon, like the one in Shakespeare's hometown," Helen added. She had been busy the last few days tracking down all the literature she could get her hands on. In doing so, she had aroused Lucinda Greenwood's anger, as William had been bored to death in the London Library while Helen explained to the boy how to navigate the massive stacks. George must have guessed that the reason for their visit to the library was only a pretense, but he hadn't given Helen away and had even offered to return her books for her.

"Quite right," Lady Brennan confirmed, satisfied. "You should see the Avon on a summer night sometime, child, when the people are standing on the banks watching the rowing regattas. You feel as though you're back in good old England."

These images reassured Helen. Indeed, she was quite determined to undertake the adventure, which is not to say that some true pioneer spirit stirred within her. She simply hoped for a peaceful, urban home and the chance to cultivate a circle of friends. Everything would be a bit smaller and less ostentatious than life at the Greenwoods', but intimate nevertheless. Perhaps her "highly esteemed" man would even be an official of the Crown or a small-business owner. Helen was ready to give anyone a chance.

However, when she left the office with a letter and address of a certain Howard O'Keefe, a farmer in Haldon, Canterbury, Christchurch, she was a little unsure. She had never lived in the country; her experience outside the city was limited to a vacation stop with the Greenwoods in Cornwall. They had visited friends there, and everything had proceeded very civilly. However, no one at Mr. Mortimer's country home had spoken of a "farmyard," and Mr. Mortimer had not called himself a "farmer" but instead a...

"Gentleman farmer," it finally occurred to Helen, at which she immediately felt better. Yes, that was how the Greenwoods' acquaintance had spoken of himself. And that would surely fit Howard O'Keefe as well. Helen could hardly imagine a simple farmer being a "well-situated" member of society in Christchurch.

Helen would have much preferred to read Howard O'Keefe's letter on the spot, but she forced herself to be patient. There was no way she could rip open the missive in the reverend's antechamber, and it had turned wet out on the street. So she bore her unopened treasure back home and merely cheered herself with the sharp, clear penmanship on the envelope. No, surely no uneducated farmer wrote like that. Helen briefly considered taking a cab back to the Greenwoods', but she did not find any and in the end told herself it was not worth it. It was late by the time she got back, and she had just enough time to put her hat and coat away before dinner was served. With the precious letter in her pocket, she hurried to the table, attempting to ignore George's curious glances. The boy could certainly put two and two together. No doubt he suspected where Helen had spent her afternoon.

Lucinda Greenwood, on the other hand, nursed no such suspicions and inquired further when Helen reported her visit to the pastor's.

"Oh yes, I need to track the reverend down in the coming weeks as well," Lucinda said in a distracted manner. "Regarding the orphans for Christchurch. Our committee has selected six girls, but the reverend believes half of them are too young to send on such a journey alone. I don't mean to question the reverend, but sometimes he's a bit naïve. He doesn't consider what the children cost here when they could be happy over there."

Helen let her carry on without interruption, and Robert Greenwood seemed disinclined to fight that evening as well. He was probably enjoying the pleasant atmosphere at the table, which could be traced to William's state of exhaustion. Since the school lessons had been called off and the nanny had found other tasks to excuse herself with, the youngest servant girl had been tasked with playing with him in the garden. The quick little thing had worked him up into a proper sweat playing ball, astutely letting him win in the end. Consequently, he was now calm and content.

Helen excused herself right after dinner. Out of politeness, she usually spent an additional half hour with the Greenwoods, working on whatever sewing she had while Lucinda reported on her endless committee meetings. Tonight, though, she left immediately, fumbling in her pocket for the letter on her way to her room. Finally she took a seat triumphantly in her rocking chair, the only piece of furniture she had brought with her to London from her father's house, and opened the missive.

As soon as she'd read the first words, Helen's heart warmed.

Dearest Lady,

I hardly dare send you word, so unimaginable is it to me that I should attract your precious attention. The path I've chosen is no doubt unconventional, but I live in a still young land in which we do revere the old customs but must find new and extraordinary solutions to problems that pull at our hearts. In my case it is a profound loneliness and longing that often keeps me up at night. True, I live in a cozy house, but what it's missing is the warmth that only a woman's touch can bring. The country around me is endlessly expansive and beautiful, but all this splendor seems to lack that center that would bring light and love into my life. Short and sweet, I dream of a girl who would like to share in all that I am, who would share in my success as my farm grows, and who is prepared to help me endure any setbacks. Indeed, I yearn for a woman who would be prepared to tie her fate to mine. Could you be this woman? I pray to God for a loving woman, whose heart my words can soften. But she would, of course, want more from me than a mere glimpse into my thoughts and longings. Well then, my name is Howard O'Keefe, and as my name suggests, I have Irish roots. But that was long ago. I can hardly count the years now that I've toiled in this often unfriendly world. I am no longer an inexperienced youth, my dear. I have lived and suffered much. But now, here on the Canterbury Plains, in the foothills of New Zealand's Alps, I have found a home. My farm is small, but this country's breed of sheep has a future, and I am sure that I can support a family. I'd wish for the woman at my side to be practical and sincere, skilled in all household matters, and willing to raise our children according to Christian principles. I would support her in that to the best of my abilities with all the strength of a loving spouse.

Could it be, my dear reader, that you share but a part of these wishes and desires? Then write me! I will lap up each word of yours like water in the desert, and already, for the courtesy of reading my words, you've received a permanent place in my heart.

Your most obedient servant,

Howard O'Keefe

After finishing the letter, Helen had tears in her eyes. How wonderfully this man could write! How precisely he expressed those feelings that stirred so often in Helen. She too felt the lack of a center in her life. She too wanted to feel at home somewhere, to have her own family, and a home that she not only governed for someone else but that was part of who she was. True, she hadn't exactly been picturing a farm, more like a house in town. But life was full of little compromises, especially when undertaking such adventures. And in the Mortimers' country house, she had felt completely at home. It had been especially pleasant when Mrs. Mortimer had come smiling into the salon in the morning with a basket of fresh eggs in one hand and a bouquet of bright flowers from the garden in the other. Helen, who usually got up early, had helped her set the breakfast table and had relished the fresh butter and creamy milk from the Mortimers' own cows. Mr. Mortimer had made a good impression too when he returned from his morning ride across the fields, fresh and hungry from the cool air, bronzed by the sun. Helen imagined her Howard to be just as vibrant and attractive. Her Howard. The sound of it! The feel of it! Helen almost danced across her little room. Would she be able to take the rocking chair with her to her new homeland? It would be exciting to someday tell her children about this moment when their father's words had first found her and immediately touched the innermost parts of her.

Dearest Mr. O'Keefe,

I read the lines you wrote today with a warm and joyful heart. I too set out only haltingly on this path to our acquaintance, but only God knows why He leads two people who live worlds apart to each other. Upon reading your letter, however, I felt that the miles that separate us seemed to melt away. Can it be that we've already met before innumerable times in our dreams? Or is it merely common experience and longing that make us seem so much closer? I am no longer a young girl either. I was forced quite early on, by my mother's death, to take on responsibility. Hence I know the ins and outs of managing a large household. I raised my siblings myself and now have a position in a London manor as governess. That keeps me busy most of the day, but at night I feel that emptiness in my heart. Though I live in a busy house in a loud and populous city, I nevertheless felt myself condemned to a lifetime of loneliness, until your call to cross the seas caught my eye. Still I am unsure whether I should dare to follow it. I would like to know more about the country and your farm, but even more about you, Howard O'Keefe! I would be happy if we could continue our correspondence. That is, if you too feel you recognize a kindred spirit in me. I can only hope that in reading these lines of mine you might feel the sense of warmth and home that I wish to give—to a loving husband and, if God wills it, a house full of wonderful children in your young country! For now, I remain confidently

Yours,

Helen Davenport

Helen had put her letter in the post first thing the next morning, and despite knowing better, her heart beat more quickly for days afterward whenever she saw the postman in front of the house. During this period, she could hardly wait to end the morning lessons so that she could hurry into the salon where the housekeeper laid out the mail for the family and for Helen.

"You needn't get so worked up. He can't have written back yet," George remarked one morning three weeks later, when Helen blushed and once again closed the books in a flustered state, having just discerned the letter carrier from the classroom window. "A ship to New Zealand can take up to three months to get there. For letters that means three months there, three months back. That's if the addressee answers right away and the ship sails back directly. So you see, it could be half a year before you hear from him."

Six months? Helen could have worked that out herself, but she was nonetheless surprised. How long would it take with these interruptions before she and Mr. O'Keefe came to some agreement? And how did George know?

"What makes you talk of New Zealand, George? And who is '*he*'?" she asked primly. "You're so impertinent sometimes. As punishment, I'll give you work enough to keep you busy all day."

George laughed mischievously. "Maybe I can read your thoughts," he said cheekily. "At least that's what I'm working on. But something remains concealed. Oh, what I wouldn't give to know who '*he*' is. An officer of Her Majesty's in Wellington's division? Or a sheep baron from the South Island? The best would be a merchant in Christchurch or Dunedin. Then my father could keep his eye on you, and I'd always know how you were doing, miss. Though, of course, I shouldn't be curious, certainly not about romantic things like this. So just go ahead and give me my punishment. I will accept it with all humility and crack the whip so that William keeps writing as well. Then you'll have time to go out and check the mail."

Helen had turned beet red. But she had to remain calm.

"You have an overexcited imagination," she said. "I'm just waiting on a letter from Liverpool. An aunt of mine is sick."

George smirked. "Please give her my best wishes for a speedy recovery," he said stiffly.

Howard O'Keefe's reply did indeed take nearly three months, and Helen was about to give up hope. Instead of a letter, however, she received a message from Reverend Thorne. He asked Helen to tea on her next free afternoon. He had, as he let it be known, important things to discuss with her.

Helen did not anticipate good news. In all likelihood, it had something to do with John or Simon. Who knew what they had done this time? Perhaps the deacon's patience had worn thin. Helen wondered what would become of her brothers if they were expelled from university. Neither one of them had ever performed any kind of manual labor. So it could only be a question of finding them clerk's positions, where they would start out as office errand boys. They would no doubt view that as beneath them. Once more Helen wished that she were far away. Why didn't this Howard write back? And why were ships so slow when they were using steam power and no longer had to rely on advantageous winds?

The reverend and his wife received Helen warmly, as always. It was a glorious spring day, and Mrs. Thorne had set the tea table in the garden. Helen breathed in the scent of flowers and enjoyed the quiet. The Greenwoods' park was, it's true, much larger and more stylishly arranged than the reverend's tiny garden, but she hardly had a moment's peace there.

With the Thornes, she did not even have to speak. The three of them serenely enjoyed their tea, Mrs. Thorne's cucumber sandwiches, and homemade cake. Then, however, the reverend came to the point.

"Helen, I'd like to be forthright. I hope you won't think ill of me. Naturally, everything that takes place here is strictly confidential, especially the talks between Lady Brennan and her young...visitors. But, of course, Linda and I know what they're about. And we would have had to be blind to let your visit to Lady Brennan escape our attention."

Helen's face flushed and paled by turns. So that's what the reverend wanted to talk about. He must be thinking that she would bring shame to her father's memory if she left her family and gave up her life here to take up an adventure with an unknown person.

"I..."

"Helen, we're not your conscience's keepers," Mrs. Thorne said, laying a friendly hand soothingly on her arm. "I can even understand what might push a young woman to take this step, and we in no way disparage Lady Brennan's work. The reverend would hardly let her use his rectory otherwise."

Helen got a hold of herself a little. So no dressing down? But what did the Thornes want, then?

Almost reluctantly, the reverend spoke up. "I know that my next question borders on the indiscreet, and I hardly dare ask it. Now, Helen, has anything come of your...ahem, application with Lady Brennan?"

Helen bit her lip. Why, for heaven's sake, did the reverend want to know that? Did he know anything about Howard O'Keefe that she needed to know? Had she been—Lord help her—taken in by a swindler? She would never get over a shame like that.

"I've answered a letter," she said properly. "Otherwise, nothing has happened."

The reverend briefly calculated the time that had passed since the advertisement appeared. "Of course not, Helen, that would be as good as impossible. For one, it would have taken more than a good tailwind on the way over. For another, the young man would practically have to have been waiting for the ship at the pier and would have had to give his letter straight to the next captain. The usual post route takes a lot longer, believe me. I exchange letters regularly with a fellow pastor in Dunedin."

"But...but if you know that, what do you want from me?" Helen blurted out. "If something develops between Mr. O'Keefe and myself, it could take a year or longer. For now..."

"We thought we might speed things up a bit," Mrs. Thorne explained. The considerably more practical-minded half of the couple, she got straight to the point. "What the reverend really wanted to ask was...did this Mr. O'Keefe's letter touch your heart? Could you really see yourself making such a trip for the sake of this man and burning all the bridges behind you?"

Helen shrugged. "The letter was so lovely," she confessed and could not stop a smile from playing on her lips. "I read it again and again, every night. And, yes, I could see myself starting a new life overseas. It's my only chance for a family. And I pray that God will lead me… that He was the one who had me read this notice…that He was the one who had me receive this letter and not another."

Mrs. Thorne nodded. "Perhaps God really is directing things just as you think, child," she said softly. "To wit, my husband has a suggestion for you."

When Helen struck out for the Greenwoods' from the Thornes' home an hour later, she did not know whether she should dance for joy or square her shoulders against her own audacity. Her stomach fluttered with butterflies because everything was now set: there was no going back. In approximately eight weeks her ship would leave for New Zealand.

"It's about the orphan girls whom Mrs. Greenwood and her committee are bent on sending overseas." Helen could still hear every word of Reverend Thorne's explanation. "Half of them are children—the oldest is thirteen, the youngest just turned eleven. The girls are already scared half to death by the prospect of taking a position here in London. And now they're to be shipped all the way to New Zealand, to work for total strangers! Of course, it doesn't help that the boys in the orphanage don't have anything better to do than tease the girls. They talk all day about sinking ships and pirates who kidnap children. The littlest is utterly convinced she'll end up in some cannibal's stomach, and the oldest has some crazy notion that she might be sold as some oriental sultan's playmate."

Helen laughed, but the Thornes remained straight-faced.

"We find it funny too, but the girls believe it," said Mrs. Thorne with a sigh. "Even disregarding the dangers of such a voyage, the route to New Zealand is traveled from beginning to end exclusively by sailing ships since it's too far a stretch for steam ships. So you're dependent on good wind. There might be mutinies, fires, epidemics… I can entirely understand why the children are afraid. They become more hysterical as each passing day brings them closer to departure. The oldest has already asked for her last rites before setting sail. The ladies on the committee don't understand any of this, of course. They have no idea what they're doing to the children. I, on the other hand, do know, and it weighs on my conscience."

The reverend nodded. "No less on mine. That's why I gave the ladies an ultimatum. The home belongs *de facto* to the parish, that is, nominally at least, I'm in charge. The ladies, therefore, need my agreement in order to send the children off. I have made my agreement contingent on their sending a guardian along. And that's where you enter, Helen. I've suggested to the ladies that we let one of the young women the Christchurch parish sent for as brides-to-be travel along at the parish's expense. In exchange, the young woman would take responsibility for the girls. A corresponding donation has already been taken up, so the necessary amount is assured."

Mrs. Thorne and the reverend looked at Helen, silently begging for approval. Helen thought of Robert Greenwood, who'd had a similar idea only the week before, and wondered from whom this donation had come. But ultimately it didn't matter. There were more pressing questions.

"And I should act as guardian?" she asked unsurely. "But I...like I said, I haven't heard back from Mr. O'Keefe..."

"It's no different for the other women, Helen," Mrs. Thorne remarked. "Besides, most of them are still green behind the ears, hardly older than the charges themselves. Only one of them, who supposedly worked as a nanny, has any experience with children. Which makes me wonder what good family employs someone who is barely twenty as a nanny! In general, many of these girls seem to me to be of...well, rather doubtful reputation. Lady Brennan has not yet decided whether she will give all of the applicants her blessing. You, on the other hand, are entirely dependable. I have no reservations about entrusting the children to you. And the risk is small. Even if you don't end up coming to a marriage agreement, a young woman with your qualifications will find a new position right away."

"You'll be taken in by my colleague in Christchurch when you arrive," Reverend Thorne explained. "I'm sure he can help you find employment in a good house in case Mr. O'Keefe turns out not to be such the…er, man of honor he claims to be. You just need to decide for yourself, Helen. Do you really want to leave England, or was the idea of emigrating just a product of your imagination? If you agree now, you'll leave from London on the eighteenth of July for Christchurch on the *Dublin*. If not…well, then this conversation never took place."

Helen breathed in deeply.

"Yes," she said.

4

Gwyneira did not react half as badly to Gerald Warden's unusual proposal as her father had feared. After her mother and sister had responded with fits of hysteria to the mere suggestion of marrying the girl off in New Zealand—they seemed unsure whether the poor alliance with the bourgeois Lucas or the exile to the wilderness represented the worse fate—Terence Silkham had anticipated tears and lamentations from his youngest daughter. But, if anything, the girl had seemed rather entertained when Lord Terence revealed the outcome of the fateful card game.

"Of course, you don't have to go," he said, in an effort to lessen the magnitude of his news. "Something like this is not the least bit customary. But I promised Mr. Warden to at least weigh his offer."

"Well, well, Father," Gwyneira chided, threatening him with her finger while she smiled at him. "Gambling debts are honor debts. You can't get out of it that easily. At the very least, you'd have to offer him my value in gold—or a few extra sheep. He'd probably prefer that. Give that a try!"

"Gwyneira, you need to take this seriously!" her father exhorted her. "Do you really think I haven't already tried to talk the man out of it?"

"Oh?" Gwyneira asked, curious. "How much did you offer?"

Lord Terence ground his teeth. It was a nasty habit, he knew, but Gwyneira always drove him to desperation.

"Of course I didn't offer him anything. I appealed to his reason and sense of honor. However, these qualities don't seem to hold much weight for him." Terence turned away, visibly ashamed.

"So you don't have any scruples about marrying me off to a sharper's son?" Gwyneira concluded with amusement. "But in all seriousness, Father, what do you think I should do? Refuse the proposal? Or accept it reluctantly? Should I act dignified or dejected? Cry or wail? Maybe I could run away. That would be the most honorable solution. If I disappeared into the night, you'd be free of the whole affair!" Gwyneira's eyes flashed at the thought of such an adventure. However, rather than running away, she'd prefer to be kidnapped...

He balled his hands into fists. "Gwyneira, I don't know either. Of course, it would be embarrassing for me if you refused. But it would be just as embarrassing to me if you felt bound to it. And I would never forgive myself if you were unhappy over there. That's why I'm asking you...well, perhaps you could hear the proposal, how should I put this...graciously?"

Gwyneira shrugged. "Very well. Then let's hear it. But for that I must go fetch my prospective father-in-law, don't you think? And Mother as well, I suppose...then again, no, her nerves couldn't handle it. We'll tell Mother after the fact. So, where is Mr. Warden?"

Gerald Warden had been waiting in the next room. He found the events playing out that day in the Silkham house quite entertaining. Gwyneira's sisters had called for the smelling salts six times already; they had also complained alternately of nervous agitation and weakness. The maids had hardly had a moment's rest. For the moment, Lady Silkham was resting in the salon with a bag of ice to her forehead while Diana implored her husband to effect Gwyneira's rescue somehow, even if it meant challenging Warden to a duel. Understandably, the colonel demonstrated little inclination to do any such thing. He merely punished the New Zealander with his contempt and seemed to wish with all his heart for nothing more than to leave his in-laws' house as quickly as possible.

Gwyneira appeared to be taking the whole thing in stride. The lord had refused to call Gerald in immediately to converse with her, but it would have been hard not to hear such a spirited girl having a temper tantrum, even from the next room. Afterward, when Warden was called into the study, he found that Gwyneira was not crying, but rather, that her cheeks were glowing. He'd been hoping for just such a reaction; his proposal had no doubt come as a surprise to Gwyneira, but she did not appear to be averse to it. She turned her enchanting blue eyes intently upon the man who had just won her hand in such an unusual way.

"Is there perhaps a picture or something?" Gwyneira did not bother with small talk but came straight to the point. Warden found her just as charming as she had been the day before. Her simple blue skirt highlighted her slim figure, and her quilled blouse made her look more mature, though she had not bothered pinning up her luscious red mane this time. Her maids had merely tied two strands together behind her head with a blue velvet ribbon to keep her hair out of her face. Otherwise, it fell curly and free far down Gwyneira's back.

"A picture?" Gerald Warden asked, taken aback. "Well...floor plans...I have a sketch of the house somewhere around here because I wanted to discuss it with an English architect first..."

Gwyneira burst out laughing. She did not seem a bit shaken or afraid. "Not of your house, Mr. Warden! Of your son. Of...uh, Lucas. Don't you have a daguerreotype or photograph?"

Gerald Warden shook his head. "Regrettably not, my lady. But you'll like Lucas. My wife, may she rest in peace, was a beauty, and everyone says Lucas was cut from the same cloth. And he's tall, taller than I am, but of a thinner build. He's tow-headed, has gray eyes...and was very well brought up, Lady Gwyneira. Which cost me a fortune, one private tutor from England after another...Sometimes I think, we...ahem, overdid it. Lucas is...well, society is charmed by him at any rate. And you'll like Kiward Station just as much. The house is built after English models. It's not one of the usual wood huts, but rather, a manor house built from gray sandstone. Nothing but the best! And I had the furniture sent from London, made by the best joiners. I even entrusted a decorator with the selection so as not to do anything wrong. You won't miss a thing, my lady. Naturally, the help is not as well trained as your maids here, but our Maori are willing and ready to learn. We could add a rose garden on quite easily, if you want..."

He stopped short when Gwyneira made a face. The rose garden seemed to scare her off.

"Could I bring Cleo along?" the girl asked. The little dog had been lying under the table but raised her head when she heard her name. With that adoring collie gaze that Gerald was by now familiar with, she looked up at Gwyneira.

"And Igraine too?"

Gerald Warden had to think a moment before he realized Gwyneira was talking about her mare.

"Gwyneira, not the horse too," her father interrupted moodily. "You're acting like a child. Here we're talking about your future, and you can only think of your toys!"

"You think my pets are toys?" Gwyneira snapped, visibly hurt by her father's remark. "A sheepdog that wins every competition and the best hunting horse in Powys?"

Gerald Warden saw his chance. "My lady, you can bring along anything you want," he said, appeasing her by taking her side. "Your mare will be the jewel of my stables. We need only think about acquiring a suitable stallion. And the dog…well, you know I already expressed my interest in her yesterday."

Gwyneira still seemed angry at her father's comment, but she steeled herself and even managed a joke.

"So that's what you're up to," she said with a mischievous grin, but rather cold eyes. "This whole proposal is really only aimed at wrangling away my father's prize-winning sheepdog. Now I get it. But I will nevertheless consider your offer in a positive light. I'm probably worth more to you than to my father. At the very least, Mr. Warden, you seem able to tell a riding horse from a toy. Now allow me please to withdraw. And I must ask that you excuse me likewise, Father. I must give this all some thought. We'll see each other at tea, I think."

Gwyneira swept out of the room, still filled with a vague but glowing rage. Her eyes filled with tears, but she would not let anyone see that.

As always, when she was angry and hatching schemes of revenge, she sent her maids away and curled up in the farthest corner of her canopy bed, pulling the curtains closed. Cleo made sure that the servants had really gone. Then she slipped through a fold and snuggled up to her mistress consolingly.

"Now at least we know what my father thinks of us," Gwyneira said, scratching Cleo's soft fur. "You're just a toy, and I'm a blackjack bet."

Before, when her father had admitted what had transpired over cards, she hadn't thought the bet was all that bad. It was even amusing that her father had gone wild like that, and surely the proposal wasn't something to be taken seriously. On the other hand, it wouldn't have been a good thing for Terence Silkham's honor if Gwyneira had refused outright to consider Warden's suggestion. Then there was the fact that her father had gamed away her future; after all, Warden had won the sheep with or without Gwyneira. And the revenue from the flock was supposed to have been her dowry. Now Gwyneira didn't have a shot at a marriage. Then again, she was fond of Silkham Manor and would have liked best to take over the farm one day. She would undoubtedly handle it better than her brother, who, when it came to country living, was interested only in hunting and the occasional race. As a child, Gwyneira had painted herself a brightly colored future: she would live on the farm with her brother and take care of everything while John Henry pursued his pleasures. At the time, both children had thought it a good plan.

"I'll be a jockey!" John Henry had declared. "And breed horses!"

"And I'll take care of the sheep and ponies!" Gwyneira had revealed to their father.

As long as the children were little, their father had laughed and called his daughter "my little forewoman." But as the children grew older and the farmhands spoke more respectfully of Gwyneira, and Cleo often beat John Henry's dog in competitions, Terence Silkham became increasingly displeased to see his daughter in the stables.

Today he had even admitted he viewed her work as mere child's play. Gwyneira squeezed her pillow with rage. But then she began to think it through more carefully. Had her father really meant it that way? Wasn't it, in fact, that he saw Gwyneira as competition for his son and heir? At least as a hindrance and obstacle to her brother's training as a future manorial lord? If that was the case, then she certainly had no future at Silkham Manor. With or without a dowry, her father would marry her off, at the very latest before her brother finished college the following year. Her mother was pushing for that already; she couldn't wait to exile her wild child to the hearth and embroidery tambour. And given her financial situation, Gwyneira knew she couldn't make any demands. There would most certainly not be a young lord with an estate comparable to Silkham Manor. She would have to be happy if a man like Colonel Riddleworth condescended to her. She would likely end up being forced to live in a house in the city, married to some second or third son of a noble family who was slogging it out as a doctor or barrister in Cardiff. Gwyneira imagined the daily tea parties, the charity committee meetings...and shivered.

But then there was still Gerald Warden's proposal.

Thus far she had viewed the journey to New Zealand only as a hypothetical question. Very attractive, but wholly impossible. Just the thought of tying the knot with someone on the other side of the world—a man whose own father could come up with only twenty words to describe him—struck her as absurd. But now she found her thoughts turning seriously to Kiward Station: a farm, of which she would be the mistress, a pioneer wife, just like in the penny novels! No doubt Warden was exaggerating in his description of his salon and the grandeur of his manor house. He likely just wanted to make a good impression on her parents. The farming operation must still be in development. It had to be, or Warden wouldn't be buying any sheep. Gwyneira would work hand in hand with her husband. She could help with herding the sheep and till a garden in which she would grow real vegetables instead of boring roses. She could picture herself sweating behind a plow pulled by a strong cob across land made arable for the first time.

And Lucas...well, he was young at least and supposedly good looking. She couldn't ask for much more. Even in England love would hardly have been a consideration in her choice of a husband.

"What do you think of New Zealand?" she asked her dog, scratching her belly. Cleo looked at her, rapt, and gave her a collie smile.

Gwyneira smiled back.

"Well all right. Agreement duly noted!" She giggled. "That means...we still have to ask Igraine. But what'll you bet she says yes when I tell her about the stallion?"

The selection of Gwyneira's trousseau turned into a long, hard struggle between Gwyneira and her mother. After Lady Silkham recovered from her many fainting spells following Gwyneira's decision, she set about making wedding preparations with her usual fervor. She lamented endlessly and verbosely that the event wouldn't be taking place at Silkham Manor this time but instead somewhere out "in the wilderness." Gerald Warden's grand descriptions of his manor house on the Canterbury Plains always found considerably more approbation with her than with her daughter. It likewise contributed to Lady Silkham's relief that Gerald took a healthy interest in all matters relating to her daughter's trousseau.

"But, of course, your daughter needs a splendid wedding dress," he declared, for example, after Gwyneira had rejected her mother's vision of white quilling and a yard-long train, saying she would surely have to ride to the wedding and those would just get in the way.

"We will either celebrate the big day in the Christchurch chapel or—what I would personally prefer—in a ceremony at home on the farm. In the former case, the wedding itself would, of course, be more festive, but it would be difficult to rent out the necessary space and personnel for the reception afterward. So I hope I can talk Reverend Baldwin into a visit to Kiward Station. Then I can host the guests in greater style. Illustrious guests, you understand. The lieutenant general will attend, leading representatives of business and the Crown...all the better society of Canterbury. For that reason, Gwyneira's dress can't be costly enough. You'll look marvelous, my child!"

Gerald patted Gwyneira lightly on the shoulder and then went off to discuss the shipment of the horses and sheep with her father. Both men had come to a mutually agreeable understanding never to mention the fateful card game again. The lord sent the flock of sheep and the dogs as Gwyneira's dowry overseas while Lady Silkham framed the engagement with Lucas Warden as an entirely suitable alliance with one of New Zealand's oldest families. And, in fact, that was true: Lucas's mother's parents had been among the very first settlers to the South Island. If people still whispered about it in the salons anyway, it did not reach the lady's or her daughters' ears.

Gwyneira would not have cared anyway. She only reluctantly dragged herself to the many tea parties where her supposed "friends" duplicitously celebrated her "exciting" departure, only then to swoon over their own future spouses in Powys or the city. If she had a moment free from visiting, Gwyn's mother insisted that she give her opinion on cloth samples and then stand for hours modeling for the dressmaker. Lady Silkham had her measured for holiday and afternoon dresses, fussed over elegant traveling clothes, and could hardly believe that Gwyneira would need more light summer dresses than winter apparel. Yet on the other side of the globe, as Gerald tirelessly reminded her, the seasons were indeed reversed.

Additionally, he always had to arbitrate when the "another afternoon dress or third riding dress" fight escalated anew.

"There's no way," Gwyneira said, becoming agitated, "that in New Zealand I'll be passed from one tea party to another like in Cardiff. You said it was a new country, Mr. Warden. Parts of it still unexplored! I won't need any silk dresses there."

Gerald Warden smiled at both adversaries. "Lady Gwyneira. At Kiward Station you'll find the same social structure as you have here, so don't worry," he began, although he knew, of course, that it was really Lady Silkham who had reservations. "However, the distances are much greater. The closest neighbor we call on lives forty miles away. So you don't drop in for afternoon tea. Besides, road construction there is still in its infancy. For that reason we prefer to ride to visit our neighbors rather than taking a coach. That doesn't mean, however, that we approach our social contacts in any less civilized a fashion. You merely need to accustom yourself to multiple-day visits since short ones aren't worthwhile, and clearly you'll need a corresponding wardrobe.

"By the way, I've booked our ship passage. We'll be leaving for Christchurch from London aboard the *Dublin* on the eighteenth of July. Part of the cargo hold will be prepared for the animals. Would you like to ride out this afternoon to see the stallion, my lady? It seems to me you've hardly been out of the dressing room all week."

Madame Fabian, Gwyneira's French governess, was worried above all about the dearth of culture in the colonies. She lamented in all the languages available to her that Gwyneira wouldn't be able to continue her musical education, even though playing the piano was the only skill recognized by society for which the girl demonstrated the least bit of talent. However, Gerald could calm these waters too: naturally, there was a piano in his house; his late wife had played beautifully and had even taught their son how to play. Apparently, Lucas was an exceptional pianist.

Astoundingly, it was Madame Fabian of all people who was able to draw more information out of the New Zealander about Gwyneira's future spouse. The artistically inclined teacher simply asked the right questions—whenever concerts, books, theaters, and galleries in Christchurch were mentioned, Lucas's name came up. It appeared that Gwyneira's fiancé was extremely cultivated and artistically gifted. He painted, played music, and maintained an exhaustive correspondence with British scientists, mostly concerning the ongoing research of New Zealand's unusual animal kingdom. Gwyneira hoped to share this interest with him, since the depiction of the rest of Lucas's proclivities seemed almost uncanny. She had expected fewer highbrow activities from the heir to a sheep farm. The cowboys in the penny novels would never have mixed with knights, guaranteed. But perhaps

Gerald Warden was exaggerating. No doubt the sheep baron wanted to depict his home and family in the best light. The reality would be wilder and more exciting! In any case, Gwyneira managed to forget her sheet music when the time finally came to pack her trousseau in chests and suitcases.

Lucinda Greenwood took Helen's announcement with astounding calm. George, who would be attending college after the summer anyway, no longer needed a tutor, and William…

"As for William, perhaps I'll look about for somewhat more indulgent help," she said. "He is still such a child, and one has to take that into account."

Helen checked herself and forced herself to agree, already thinking about her new little charges on the *Dublin*. Lucinda Greenwood had generously allowed her to extend her Sunday outing to church to meet with the girls in Sunday school. As expected, they were frail, undernourished, and browbeaten. All of them wore clean, gray, oft-patched button-up dresses, but even the oldest, Dorothy, still showed no hint of a woman's figure beneath her dress. The girl had just turned thirteen and had spent ten years of her short life in the almshouse with her mother. Early on, Dorothy's mother had had a job, but the girl could no longer remember those days so long ago. She knew only that her mother had eventually gotten sick and then died. She'd been living in the orphanage ever since then. She was scared to death of the journey to New Zealand, but was nevertheless prepared to do anything she could to please her future masters. Dorothy had only first learned to read and write in the orphanage but was trying with all her might to make up for lost time. Helen silently decided to continue teaching her on the ship. She felt sympathy for the delicate, dark-haired girl, who would doubtless grow to be a beauty if she were properly fed and no longer forced to bow and scrape, back bent and cowering like a beaten dog before everyone. Daphne, the next oldest, appeared somewhat braver. She had managed to live alone on the street for a long time; that she hadn't been caught stealing but rather found sick and exhausted under a bridge was surely thanks to luck and not innocence. She had been treated strictly in the orphanage. The headmistress seemed to have taken her flaming red hair for an unmistakable sign of a lust for life, even a hunger for life, and punished her for every wanton side-glance. Daphne was the only one of the six girls who had volunteered for the journey overseas. For Laurie and Mary, ten-year-old (at most) twins from Chelsea, that certainly was not the case. Neither was especially bright, though they were well behaved and somewhat skillful, when they could figure out what was being asked of them. Laurie and Mary believed every word the malicious little boys in the orphanage had told them about the dangers of the sea voyage, and they could hardly believe that Helen was making the journey without serious reservations. Elizabeth, on the other hand, a dreamy twelve-year-old with long, blonde hair, thought it romantic to set out on a journey to an unknown husband.

"Oh, Miss Davenport, it'll be like in the fairy tales!" she whispered. Elizabeth lisped slightly and was constantly teased for it, so she rarely spoke up. "A prince waiting for you! He must be pining away and dreaming of you every night."

Helen laughed and attempted to extricate herself from the grip of her youngest charge, Rosemary. Rosie was supposedly eleven years old, but Helen put the distraught child at no more than nine. Whoever thought this timid creature was ready to make her own way in the world was beyond comprehension. Until Helen arrived, Rosemary had clung to Dorothy. Now that a friendlier grown-up was present, she switched seamlessly to Helen. She was touched by the feel of Rosie's tiny hand in her own, but knew she couldn't encourage the girl's clinginess; employers had already been found for the children in Christchurch, so she knew she mustn't feed Rosie's hope to remain with her after the journey.

Besides, Helen's own fate was just as uncertain. She still hadn't heard a word from Howard O'Keefe.

Regardless, Helen prepared a sort of trousseau for herself. She invested what little there was of her savings in two new dresses and underwear and purchased some linens for her new home. For a small charge, she was allowed to take her beloved rocking chair on the ship, and Helen spent several hours packing it up with care. In order to contain her excitement, she began her preparations for the trip early and was already more or less finished four weeks before the ship was scheduled to depart. She put off the unpleasant task of informing her family of her departure until just before she was to leave. Finally, she could not delay any longer. Their reactions were as she'd expected: Helen's sister was shocked, her brothers furious. If Helen could no longer provide for their room and board, they would have to seek refuge with Reverend Thorne again. Helen thought that would only do them good and told them so in as many words.

As for her sister, Helen didn't take her emotional tirade seriously for a second. Susan went on for pages about how much she would miss her sister, and some of the letter's pages even had tearstains, but Helen knew that these could be traced to John's and Simon's student expenses being thrust on her shoulders now.

When Susan and her husband finally came to London "just to talk things over one last time," Helen didn't even respond to Susan's show of grief when they said their farewells. Instead, she pointed out that her move would hardly change anything about their relationship. "We haven't written to each other much more than twice a year even up to now," Helen said coldly. "You are busy with your family, and it surely won't be any different for me."

If only there was something concrete to make her believe that.

She had received no further word from Howard. However, a week before Helen's departure, after she'd long since given up lying in wait for the letter carrier every morning, George brought her an envelope covered in many bright stamps.

"Here, Miss Davenport!" he said excitedly. "You can open it immediately. I promise I won't tattle, and I won't look over your shoulder. I'll be playing with William, OK?"

Helen was in the garden with her charges; she had just ended their lessons for the day. William was alone, busy hitting the ball intermittently through the croquet hoops.

"George, you mustn't say 'OK,'" Helen chided him out of habit, while reaching with unseemly haste for the letter. "Where did you even learn that word? From those smutty novels the help reads? For heaven's sake do not leave them lying around. If William..."

"William can't read," George interrupted her. "We both know that, Miss Davenport, whatever Mother likes to believe. And I won't say 'OK' again; I promise. Are you going to read your letter now?" The expression on George's narrow face was unexpectedly serious. Helen had rather expected his usual insinuating smirk.

But what was that supposed to mean? Even if he did inform his mother that she, Helen, was reading private letters during work, in a week she would be at sea, unless...

Helen ripped the letter open with trembling hands. If Mr. O'Keefe no longer showed an interest in her now...

My dearest Miss Davenport,

Words cannot express how much your lines touched my soul. I have not put your letter down since I received it a few days ago. It accompanies me everywhere, when working on the farm, during my rare trips to the city—whenever I reach for it, I find comfort and an effervescent joy in knowing that somewhere far away a heart beats for me. And I must admit that in the darkest hours of my loneliness I occasionally bring it to my lips. This paper that you have touched, over which your breath has passed, is as sacred to me as the few reminders of my family, which I guard like treasures.

But how shall we continue? Dearest Miss Davenport, I would like nothing more now than to tell you to come! Let us leave our loneliness behind us. Let us brush away the scurf of despair and darkness. Let us start anew, together!

Here we can hardly wait for the first whiffs of spring to blossom. The grass is beginning to turn green; the trees are beginning to bud. How gladly I would share this sight with you! For that to happen, however, there are more tedious considerations than the flight of burgeoning affection. I would gladly send you the money for the journey, my dear Miss Davenport—oh why not, my dearest Helen! But that will have to wait until my sheep have lambed and the farm's earnings this year can be estimated. After all, I do not want to burden our life together with debt right from the beginning.

Can you, my dear Helen, have patience for these concerns? Can you, will you, wait until my call can finally go out to you? There is nothing on earth I wish so earnestly.

I remain your ever devoted,

Howard O'Keefe

Helen's heart was beating so quickly that she thought she might need the smelling salts for the first time in her life. Howard wanted her; he loved her! And now she could give him the nicest surprise. Instead of sending a letter, she'd come herself. She was eternally grateful to the Reverend Thorne. She was eternally grateful to Lady Brennan. Yes, even to George who had just brought her this missive.

"Are...are you done reading, Miss Davenport?"

Absorbed as she was, Helen had not noticed that the boy was still standing next to her.

"Is it good news?"

George did not look like he wanted to share in her happiness. On the contrary, he seemed despondent.

Helen looked at him with concern but could not contain her happiness.

"The best news one could ask for!" she said ecstatically.

George did not return her smile.

"So...he really wants to marry you? He...he didn't say you should stay where you are, miss?" he asked in a monotone.

"Now George! Why should he say that?" In her blissful state, Helen completely forgot that up until that very moment, she had repeatedly denied having replied to the advertisement in question. "We fit together wonderfully. A very cultivated young man, who..."

"More cultivated than me, Miss Davenport?" George blurted out. "Are you sure he's better than I am? Smarter? Better read?

Because…if it's only about love…I…well, he can't love you more than I do…"

George turned away, shocked by his own courage. Helen had to grab him by the shoulder and turn him around to look him in the eye. He seemed to shiver at her touch.

"Now George, what are you saying? What do you know about love? You're only sixteen! You're my student!" Helen exclaimed, astonished—but knew even as she spoke that she was talking nonsense. Why couldn't you feel deeply at sixteen?

"Now look, George, I've never ever compared you and Howard," she continued. "Or even seen you as rivals. After all, I didn't know that you…"

"And you couldn't have known!" Something almost like hope now glimmered in George's clever brown eyes. "I had…just had to tell you. Even before all this about New Zealand. But I didn't think you…"

"That was the right thing and completely normal, George," she said in a conciliatory tone. "You yourself knew that you're far too young for such things, and normally you wouldn't have put your feelings into words. Why don't we forget it now…"

"I'm ten years younger than you, Miss Davenport," George interrupted her. "And I'm your student, of course, but I'm not a child anymore. I'm starting my studies, and in a few years I'll be a respected merchant. Then, no one will care about my age or my wife's."

"But I will," Helen said softly. "I want a man my own age who is right for me. I'm sorry, George…"

"And how do you know the man in the letter will live up to that?" the boy asked in despair. "Why do you love him? You have only just received a letter from him for the first time. Did he give his age? Do you know whether he can keep you suitably fed and clothed? Will you even have anything to talk about? You've always enjoyed speaking with my father and me. So if you'll wait for me…just a few years, Miss Davenport, until I've finished my studies. Please, Miss Davenport! Please give me a chance!"

George reached uncontrollably for her hand.

Helen pulled away.

"I'm sorry, George. It's not that I wouldn't like you; quite the opposite. But I'm your teacher, and you're my student. Nothing more can come of that…besides, you'll think about things in a whole new light in a few years."

Helen wondered whether Richard Greenwood had guessed something of his son's blind lovesickness. Perhaps that was why she had him to thank for the generously donated ship's passage—and perhaps he also wanted to make the hopelessness of his son's feelings plain to him.

"I'll never feel differently," George said passionately. "As soon as I'm of age, as soon as I can support a family, I'll be there for you! If only you'll wait, Miss Davenport."

Helen shook her head. She had to end this conversation now. "George, even if I did love you, I cannot wait. If I want to have a family, I have to seize the opportunity now. Howard is that opportunity. And I will be a true and loving wife to him."

George looked at her in desperation. His narrow face reflected all the torment of love spurned, and Helen thought she could almost discern, behind the still unripe features of the boy's face, the countenance of the man George would one day be. A lovable, worldly man who would not commit himself overly hastily—and who would keep his promises. Helen would have liked to comfort the boy in her arms, but of course that was out of the question.

She waited silently for George to turn away. Helen imagined that childish tears were building in his eyes, but George returned her gaze calmly and firmly.

"I will always love you," he stated. "Always. No matter where you are and what you're doing. No matter where I am and what I'm doing. I love you, only you. Don't ever forget that, Miss Davenport."

5

The *Dublin* was an imposing ship even before it was under full sail. To Helen and the orphan girls it seemed as big as a house, and in reality the *Dublin* would shelter considerably more people over the next three months than a common tenement house. Helen hoped it wasn't as prone to fire and collapse, but the ships bound for New Zealand were inspected for seaworthiness before departure. The ship owners had to demonstrate to the Crown inspectors that the cabins received enough air and that they had sufficient provisions on board. This last consideration was still being fulfilled that day, and Helen sensed what awaited her as she watched the barrels of salted meat, the sacks of flour and potatoes, and the packets of hardtack being loaded on board from the pier. She had already heard that the cuisine on board lacked variety—at least for the passengers in steerage. The first-class guests in cabins were served very differently. It was rumored that they even had their own cook on board.

A gruff ship's officer and a doctor oversaw the boarding of the "common people." The latter looked Helen and the girls over briefly, felt the children's foreheads, most likely to check for febrile illnesses, and had them stick out their tongues. When he did not find anything questionable, he nodded to the officer, who then checked their names off a list.

"Cabin one in the rear," he said and waved Helen and the girls on quickly. The seven of them felt their way through the tight, dark corridors in the hold of the ship, which were all but blocked by excited passengers and their belongings. Helen did not have much baggage, but even her small travel bag became increasingly heavy. The girls carried even less; they only had little bundles with their night things and one change of dress apiece.

When they finally reached their cabin, the girls tumbled in, gasping. Helen was anything but excited by the tiny chamber that would serve as their living quarters for the next three months. The furnishings in the dark, low-ceilinged room consisted of a table, a chair, and six berths—bunk beds—Helen confirmed with horror, and one too few to boot. Luckily, Mary and Laurie were accustomed to sharing a bed. They took possession of one of the middle berths and snuggled in close together. They were already terrified about the journey to come, and the crowds and noise on board only scared them further.

Helen, on the other hand, was more bothered by the permeating stench of sheep, horses, and other animals wafting up to them from belowdecks. Someone had erected provisional pens for sheep and swine, as well as a cow and two horses next to and below Helen's billet, of all places. Helen found all this unconscionable and decided to complain. She ordered her girls to wait in the cabin and set out for the deck. Fortunately, there was a shorter way up to the fresh air than the way they had come through steerage: directly in front of Helen's cabin was a set of stairs that led upward, on which provisional ramps had been set up for the loading of the animals. None of the crew could be seen from the aft of the ship, however; unlike the entrance on the other end, this one wasn't being watched. However, it swarmed with people too; emigrating families were hauling their baggage aboard and embracing their loved ones with tears and lamentations. The crowds and noise were unbearable.

Then, suddenly, the crowd parted along the gangways over which the cargo and livestock were being brought. The reason for that was easy to see: just then two horses were being loaded, and one of them had been spooked. A wiry little man with blue tattoos on his arms that identified him as a member of the crew had his hands full trying to calm the animal down. Helen wondered whether the man was being forced to take on this un-seamanlike task as part of some punishment. He clearly had no experience with horses since he was handling the powerful black stallion with no skill whatsoever.

"Now come on, you black devil, I don't have all the time in the world!" he bellowed at the animal, who remained uncooperative. In fact, the black horse dragged him forcefully backward, angrily flattening its ears as it did. He seemed determined not to set a single hoof on the dangerously wobbling ramp.

The second horse, which Helen could only vaguely make out behind him, seemed calmer, and its guide appeared far more in control. To her surprise, Helen saw that she was a petite girl in elegant traveling clothes. She waited impatiently with the stock brown mare's lead in her hand. Since the stallion still did not show any signs of moving forward, the girl intervened.

"That's not going to do anything; give him here!"

Helen observed in amazement as the young lady handed her mare over to one of the waiting émigrés and took the stallion from the sailor. Helen expected the horse to tear itself away; after all, the man could hardly hold on to it. Instead, the black horse calmed down immediately when the girl shortened its lead and started speaking gently to it.

"So, we'll do it step by step, Madoc. I'll go ahead; you follow me. And don't you dare run me over!"

Helen held her breath as the stallion followed the young girl—tensely, but behaving impeccably. The girl complimented and petted him when he finally stood safely on board. The stallion drooled on her navy-blue velvet travel dress, though the girl didn't seem to notice.

"What are you doing down there with the mare?" she called to the sailor below. "Igraine, don't cause him trouble. Just come forward!"

Although she pranced a bit, the brown mare proved calmer than the young stallion. The sailor held her lead from its far end, making a face as though he were balancing a stick of dynamite. Regardless, he brought the horse on board, and Helen could now make her complaint. As the girl and the man led the animals directly past her cabin on their way belowdecks, she turned to the sailor.

"Though it's probably not your fault, still someone must do something. We cannot possible stay here next to the stables. The stench is unbearable. And what if the animals break loose? Then our lives would be in danger!"

The sailor shrugged. "I can't do anything about it, madam. Order of the cap'n. The critters're coming with. And the cabin arrangement's always the same: men traveling alone up front, families in the middle, women traveling alone in the back. Since you're the only women traveling alone, you can't trade with anyone. You'll just have to get over it, madam." The man hastened behind the mare, who appeared eager to follow the stallion and the young lady. The girl maneuvered first the black horse and then the brown into two neighboring stalls and tied them in tightly. When she emerged again, her blue velvet skirt was covered with straw.

"Stupid dress!" the girl cursed as she attempted to shake the dress clean. Then she gave up and turned to Helen.

"I'm sorry if the animals bother you, madam. But they can't break free; the ramps are being taken down...which isn't without its dangers. If the ship should sink, I'll never get Igraine out of here! But the captain insists on it. The stalls should be cleaned every day. And the sheep won't smell so strongly as soon as they've dried. Besides, you get used to—"

"I will never get used to living in a stall," Helen remarked regally.

The girl laughed. "But where's your pioneer spirit? You are emigrating, aren't you? Really, I'd gladly trade with you, madam. But I sleep all the way up top. Mr. Warden booked the salon cabin. Are these all *your* children?"

She cast an eye over the girls, who had at first followed Helen's orders to remain in their cabin, but who now poked their heads out cautiously but curiously when they heard Helen's voice. Daphne, in particular, eyed the horses with interest, as well as the young lady's elegant clothing.

"Of course not," Helen said. "I'm only taking care of them during the passage. They're orphans. Are those all *your* animals?"

The girl laughed. "No, just the horses...one of the horses, to be precise. The stallion belongs to Mr. Warden. The sheep too. I don't know whom the other animals belong to, but maybe we could even milk the cow! Then we'd have fresh milk for the children. They look like they could use it."

Helen nodded sadly. "Yes, they're severely undernourished. Hopefully they'll survive the long journey; one hears so much about disease and child mortality. But at least we have a doctor on board. I can only hope he knows his business. Oh, by the way, my name is Helen Davenport."

"Gwyneira Silkham," answered the girl. "And those two are Madoc and Igraine," she said, introducing the horses as matter-of-factly as if they were guests at the same tea party. "And Cleo...where's she hiding now? Ah, there she is. She's making friends again."

Helen followed Gwyneira's gaze and saw a furry little creature that seemed to be giving her a friendly smile. However, in doing so, it also revealed its imposingly large teeth, which sent a shiver through Helen. She startled when she saw Rosie next to the animal. The little girl snuggled as trustfully into the dog's fur as she did into the folds of Helen's skirt.

"Rosemary!" Helen called in alarm. The girl shrank back and let go of the dog, which turned back to her and raised an imploring paw.

Gwyneira laughed and made her own placating hand motion. "Don't worry about letting the little one play with her," she told Helen calmly. "Cleo loves children. She won't harm her. I'm afraid I must be going. Mr. Warden will be waiting. And I really shouldn't even be here, as I should be spending some time with my family. After all, that's why my parents and siblings came all the way to London. It's just more nonsense though. I've seen my family every day for seventeen years now. Everything's been said. But my mother has been crying the whole time and my sister bawls alongside her in accompaniment. My father's wallowing in self-pity for sending me to New Zealand, and my brother is so jealous he'd like nothing better than to strangle me. I can't wait for us to push off. What about you? Did no one come for you?" Gwyneira looked around. Everywhere else in steerage, people were weeping and wailing. Parting gifts were exchanged, final well wishes relayed. Many of these families would be forever separated by this departure.

Helen shook her head. She had set out from the Greenwoods' home in a cab alone. The rocking chair, her only cumbersome piece of luggage, had been picked up the day before.

"I'm traveling to meet my husband in Christchurch," she explained, as if that would explain the absence of her loved ones. But she didn't want under any circumstances to be pitied by this rich and obviously privileged young woman.

"Oh? Then is your family already in New Zealand?" Gwyneira asked excitedly. "You must tell me about it sometime; that is, I've never been...but now I really must be going. I'll see you tomorrow, children. Don't get seasick! Come, Cleo." Gwyneira turned to go, but little Dorothy stopped her, tugging bashfully on her skirt.

"Miss, pardon me, miss, but your dress is dirty. Your mother is going to yell."

Gwyneira laughed, but then looked down at herself, concerned. "You're right. She'll have a fit! I'm impossible. I can't even behave during good-byes."

"I can brush it off for you, miss. I know velvet." Dorothy looked solicitously up at Gwyneira, then motioned her to the chair in the cabin.

Gwyneira sat down. "Where did you learn that, little one?" she asked, surprised, as Dorothy went to work skillfully with Helen's clothes brush; apparently, the girl had observed earlier when Helen had laid her things in the tiny wardrobe that was part of each berth.

Helen sighed. When she'd bought that expensive brush, she had not planned for it to be used for the removal of muck.

"We get clothing donations all the time at the orphanage. But we don't keep them; the clothes are sold. Before that, though, we have to clean them of course, and I always help with that. Look, miss, it's all pretty again." Dorothy smiled shyly.

Gwyneira hunted in her pockets for a gold piece with which to reward the girl, but didn't find anything. The outfit was too new.

"I'll bring you all a thank-you gift tomorrow; I promise!" she told Dorothy as she turned to go. "And you'll make a good housewife someday. Or a maid to very fine people. I'll be seeing you!" Gwyneira waved to Helen and the girls and ran lightly up the plank.

"She doesn't even believe that herself," Daphne stated, spitting behind her. "People like that always make promises, but then you never see them again. You always have to see that they pay up right away, Dot. Otherwise, you'll never get anything."

Helen lifted her eyes to heaven. What was that about "select, well-behaved girls, raised to serve meekly"? She needed to clamp down on them.

"Daphne, you will clean that up immediately! Lady Silkham doesn't owe you a thing. Dorothy offered to be of service. That was politeness, not business. And young ladies do not spit." Helen looked for a cleaning bucket.

"But *we're* not ladies!" Laurie and Mary snickered.

Helen glared at them. "By the time we get to New Zealand, you will be," she promised. "At the very least, you will behave like you are."

She decided to get their education under way that very moment.

Gwyneira heaved a sigh of relief when the last gangways between the dock and the *Dublin* were hauled in. The hours of good-byes had been exhausting; her mother's tears alone had soaked through three handkerchiefs. Added to that were her sisters' wailing and her father's composed but funereal manner, better suited to a hanging than a wedding. Finally, there was her brother, whose obvious envy got on her nerves. He would have traded his inheritance in Wales for such an adventure. Gwyn suppressed a hysterical giggle. What a shame John Henry couldn't marry Lucas.

Now, however, the *Dublin* was finally ready to embark on its journey. A rustling as loud as a squall let it be known that the sails were set. The ship still had to clear the Channel and sail for the Atlantic this evening. Gwyneira would have liked to be with her horse, but naturally, that wouldn't have been proper. So she remained dutifully on deck and waved down to her family with her largest scarf until the shore had almost disappeared from view. Gerald Warden noticed that she did not shed any tears.

Helen's charges wept bitterly, though, the atmosphere in steerage being more fraught than among the rich travelers. For the poorer immigrants, the trip almost certainly meant a permanent farewell; in addition, most of them were sailing into a much less certain future than Gwyneira and her traveling companions above deck. Helen felt in her bag for Howard's letters while she consoled the girls. At least someone was expecting them...

She nevertheless slept poorly the first night on board. The sheep were not yet dry, and the stench of manure and wet wool continued drifting into Helen's sensitive nose. It was an eternity before the children fell asleep, and even then they would start at every noise. When Rosie crept into Helen's bed for the third time, she no longer had the heart or the energy to turn her out. Laurie and Mary clung to each other too, and the next morning Helen found Dorothy and Elizabeth snuggled up against each other in a corner of Dorothy's berth. Only Daphne had slept soundly; if she was dreaming, they must have been good dreams because the girl was smiling in her sleep when Helen finally woke her up.

The first morning at sea proved unexpectedly calm. Robert Greenwood had warned Helen that the first few weeks might be stormy since there were mostly rough seas between the English Channel and the Bay of Biscay. That day, though, the weather extended the émigrés' grace period. The sun was pale after the rain the day before, and the sea shimmered a steely gray in the wan light. The *Dublin* moved sedately across the smooth surface of the water.

"I don't see the shore at all anymore," Dorothy whispered, afraid. "If we sink now, no one will find us! Then we'll all drown!"

"You would have drowned if the ship had sunk in the harbor in London," Daphne observed. "You can't swim, you know, and you would have long since drowned before they finished rescuing everyone from the upper deck."

"You can't swim either," Dorothy retorted. "You would be just as drowned as me."

Daphne laughed. "I would not! I fell into the Thames once when I was little but doggy-paddled out. Scum floats on the surface, my old man said."

Helen decided to interrupt the conversation for more than simple pedagogical reasons.

"Your *father* said, Daphne," she corrected. "Even if he did not quite express himself in such a genteel manner. Now stop scaring the others or they won't have any appetite for breakfast. Which we can go get now. So, who's going to the galley? Dorothy and Elizabeth? Very good. Laurie and Mary will take care of the water for washing...oh, that's right, my ladies, we will wash up. Even when traveling, a lady insists on cleanliness."

When Gwyneira walked through steerage an hour later to check on her horses, she came upon a strange sight. The corridor outside the cabins was almost empty, most of the passengers being occupied either with breakfast or homesickness. However, Helen and her girls had brought out their table and chair. Helen sat enthroned, proud and upright, every ounce a lady. In front of her, on the table, was an improvised place setting, consisting of a tin plate, a bent spoon, a fork, and a dull knife. Dorothy was in the midst of presenting Helen with imaginary serving platters of food while Elizabeth handled an old bottle as though she were graciously serving a fine wine.

"What *are* you doing?" Gwyneira asked, dumbfounded.

Dorothy curtsied carefully. "We're practicing what to do when serving at table, Lady Silk...Silk..."

"Gwyneira Silkham. But you may call me *miss*. And, could you tell me again now—you're practicing *what*?" Gwyneira eyed Helen suspiciously. Yesterday the young governess had seemed completely normal, but perhaps she was a little odd.

Helen blushed slightly under Gwyneira's gaze, but composed herself quickly.

"This morning I discovered that the girls' table manners leave something to be desired," she said. "In the orphanage, they must have approached meals as though they were caged carnivores. The children eat with their fingers and stuff themselves full as if it were their last meal on earth!"

Ashamed, Dorothy and Elizabeth stared at the ground. The reproach had less of an effect on Daphne.

"Perhaps they wouldn't have gotten anything to eat otherwise," Gwyneira speculated. "When I see how thin the girls are...but what is that supposed to be?" Once again she pointed to the table. Helen corrected the placement of the knife.

"I'm showing the girls how a lady carries herself at table and in the process teaching them how to serve skillfully," she replied. "I don't think it likely that they'll be taken in by larger households where they would specialize in being a lady's maid, a cook, or a cleaning maid. The personnel situation in New Zealand is supposed to be extremely bad. So I am going to give the children as comprehensive an education as I can on the way over so that they can be useful to their employers in as many different capacities as possible."

Helen gave Elizabeth a friendly nod; the girl had just poured water into her coffee cup with perfect form, catching any spilled drops with her napkin.

Gwyneira remained skeptical. "Useful?" she asked. "These children? I wanted to ask yesterday why they were being sent overseas, but now it's becoming clear to me...am I right in guessing that the orphanage wanted to get rid of them, but no one in London wanted little half-starved serving girls?"

Helen nodded. "They're pinching pennies. Housing, feeding, clothing, and sending a child to school costs three pounds a year in the orphanage. This passage costs four, but then the children are gone for good. Otherwise, they would have to keep Rosemary and the twins on at least two more years."

"But the half-price fare is only for children twelve and under," Gwyneira objected, which astonished Helen. Had this rich girl really inquired about steerage prices? "And the girls could only first take a position at thirteen."

Helen rolled her eyes. "In practice, at twelve, though I'd swear that Rosie cannot be more than eight. But you are right: Dorothy and Daphne should really have had to pay full price. However, the honorable ladies of the orphanage committee probably made them out to be somewhat younger for the journey."

"And we'll have hardly arrived when the little ones age miraculously in order to take positions as thirteen-year-olds!" Gwyneira laughed and searched through the pockets of her white housedress, over which she'd thrown a light shawl. "The world is no good. Here, girls, have something proper to munch on. It's nice to play at serving, but you won't put any meat on your bones that way. Here you go!"

The young woman happily pulled out muffins and sweet rolls by the handful. The girls forgot their newly acquired table manners for a moment and pounced on the treats.

Helen attempted to restore order and distribute the sweets properly. Gwyneira beamed.

"That was a good idea, wasn't it?" she asked Helen, as the six children sat on the side of a lifeboat, taking small bites as they had been taught and not sticking the whole things in their mouths at once. "On the upper deck they serve food as though it were the Grand Hotel, and I couldn't help thinking of your scrawny little mice. So I polished off the table a bit. I wasn't out of line, was I?"

Helen shook her head. "They won't put on any weight from the offerings down here. The portions are not generous, and we have to get the food from the galley ourselves. So the older girls siphon off half of it on the way—and that's ignoring the few naughty rascals that belong to the midship immigrant families. They're still too shaken, but watch out—in two or three days they'll start ambushing the girls and demanding tribute to pass! But we'll survive these few weeks. And I'm doing my best to teach the children something. That's more than anyone's done for them until now."

While the children were eating and playing with Cleo, the young women chatted and strolled back and forth on deck. Gwyneira wanted to know as much as possible about her new acquaintance. Eventually, Helen told her about her family and her position at the Greenwoods'.

"So then you haven't lived in New Zealand before?" Gwyn asked, a little disappointed. "Didn't you say yesterday that your husband is waiting for you there?"

Helen blushed. "Well...my husband to be. I...you'll certainly think it absurd, but I'm crossing the sea to marry over there. A man whom thus far I know only from letters..." Ashamed, she lowered her eyes. She only ever became fully conscious of the monstrousness of her adventure when she told other people about it.

"You're doing the same thing I am," Gwyneira said breezily. "And mine hasn't even ever written me."

"You too?" Helen marveled. "You're also answering an unknown man's marriage advertisement?"

Gwyneira shrugged. "Oh, he's not really unknown. His name is Lucas Warden, and his father asked for my hand on his behalf." She bit her lip. "In a mostly conventional manner," she amended. "From that perspective, everything is in order. But as for Lucas...I hope he at least wants to marry. His father didn't tell me whether he'd asked beforehand or not."

Helen laughed, but Gwyneira was serious. She had learned over the past few weeks that Gerald Warden was a man who asked few questions. The sheep baron made his decisions quickly and on his own, and he could react gruffly to others' opinions. That was how he had succeeded in accomplishing so much work during his weeks in Europe. From purchasing sheep to negotiating agreements with wool importers to discussing matters with architects and well construction specialists—even wooing a wife for his son—he managed everything coolly and with breathtaking speed. Gwyneira liked his decisive approach, but sometimes it scared her a little. When it came to commitments, he had an explosive streak, and he sometimes demonstrated a wiliness in business transactions that Terence Silkham disliked. As he saw it, the New Zealander had bamboozled the stallion's breeder using every trick in the book—and whether the card game for Gwyneira's hand had been honestly played remained in question. Gwyneira sometimes wondered what Lucas thought of it all. Was he as energetic as his father? Was he running the farm at that moment just as efficiently and without compromise? Or did Gerald's occasionally overly hasty dealing aim at shortening Lucas's solo rule of Kiward Station as much as possible?

In any event, she now told Helen a slightly tempered version of Gerald's business relationship with her family, which had ultimately led to her wooing. "I know that I'm marrying into a flourishing farm of close to a thousand acres and a fold of five thousand sheep that should continue to grow," she concluded. "I know that my father-in-law maintains social and business ties to the best families in New Zealand. He is obviously rich; otherwise, he couldn't afford this journey and the whole lot. But I know nothing about my future spouse."

Helen listened attentively, but it was hard for her to feel sorry for Gwyneira. In fact, Helen was painfully aware that her new friend was markedly better informed about her future than she was. Howard had said nothing about the size of his farm, his animal count, or his social contacts. As for his financial circumstances, she knew only that, though he was debt free, he could not afford larger expenditures like a trip to Europe—even in steerage—without due consideration. Still, he wrote such beautiful letters. Blushing once again, Helen rustled the letters, already worn from repeated reading, out of her pocket and thrust them at Gwyneira, both women having sat down on the edge of the lifeboat in the meantime. Gwyneira read greedily.

"Yeeeeah, he can write..." she said with restraint, folding the letters back together.

"Do you think there's something strange about them?" Helen inquired anxiously. "Do you not like the letters?"

Gwyneira shrugged. "I don't have to like them. If you want my honest opinion, I find them a bit bombastic. But..."

"But?" Helen pressed.

"Well, what I find strange is...I would never have thought a farmer could write such lovely letters." Gwyneira turned away. She found the letters more than just strange. Naturally, Howard O'Keefe might be well educated. Her own father was also both a gentleman and a farmer; in provincial England and Wales that wasn't uncommon. But even with all his schooling, her father would never have used such turgid formulations as this Howard did. Moreover, among the nobility, especially when it came to marriage negotiations, people usually put all their cards on the table. Future partners had a right to know what to expect, and Gwyneira couldn't find any indications of Howard's business situation. She also found it strange that he didn't ask for a dowry or at least expressly reject one.

Now, of course, the man had not counted on Helen rushing to his arms on the next ship. Maybe this flattery only served to break the ice. But she nevertheless found it unnerving.

"He is really very passionate," Helen said, taking up her fiancé's defense. "He writes just like I dreamed he would." She smiled happily, lost in her thoughts.

Gwyneira smiled back. "Then all's well," she declared, resolving, however, to ask her future father-in-law about Howard O'Keefe at the next opportunity. He bred sheep too, after all. It was likely the men knew each other.

She did not get to ask right away, though, because the meals that usually created the perfect circumstances for such pressing inquiries were often canceled due to rough seas. The first day's lovely weather proved deceptive. They had hardly reached the Atlantic when the wind whipped around and the *Dublin* fought its way through storms and rain. Many of the passengers became seasick and opted to pass on meals or simply take them in their cabins. True, neither Gerald Warden nor Gwyneira had sensitive stomachs, but when no official dinner was prepared, they usually ate at different times. Gwyneira did so intentionally; after all, her future father-in-law certainly would not have consented to her ordering large quantities of food only to let Helen's charges have them. Gwyneira would have liked to supply all the other steerage passengers with food. The children in particular needed every bite they could get just to keep themselves halfway warm. Yes, it was the middle of summer and it was not particularly cold outside, even with the rain. But when the seas were rough, water seeped into the steerage cabins, and everything became so damp as a result that there was hardly a dry place to sit. Helen and the girls shivered in their clammy dresses, but Helen nevertheless insisted on continuing with her charges' daily lessons. The other children on the ship were not getting any schooling during this time. The ship doctor who was responsible for their lessons was himself sick and self-medicated with plenty of gin from the ship pharmacy.

Conditions in steerage were far from pleasant even on the best days. In the family and men's areas, the bathrooms overflowed during storms, and most of the passengers washed seldom, if ever. Given the cold, Helen herself felt little enthusiasm for washing but insisted that her girls use a portion of their daily water ration for personal hygiene.

"I would like to wash our clothes, but they just don't dry, so it's a lost cause," she complained to Gwyneira, who promised to at least help Helen out with a spare dress. Her own cabin was heated and perfectly insulated. Even in the roughest seas no water seeped in that might ruin the soft carpet or the elegantly upholstered furniture. Gwyneira felt guilty, but she simply couldn't ask Helen to move into her room with the children. Gerald would never allow it. At most, she brought Dorothy or Daphne up with her, under the pretense of needing her clothes mended in some way.

"Why don't you hold your lessons down with the animals?" she finally asked after once again finding Helen shivering on the deck while the girls took turns reading aloud from *Oliver Twist*. It was cold out, but at least it was dry, and the fresh air was more pleasant than the damp vapor in steerage. "Even if the sailors complain, they still clean it every day. Mr. Warden checks up on whether the sheep and horses are being well cared for. And the purser is fussy about the animals intended for slaughter. After all, he didn't bring them along to get sick and die so that he has to throw the meat overboard."

It had become clear that the swine and fowl served as living provisions for the first-class passengers, and the cow was indeed milked every day. Those traveling in steerage, however, did not receive so much as a glimpse of these good things—until Daphne caught a boy milking the cow secretly at night. She squealed on him without the slightest qualm, but not before watching him so that she could imitate the milking motions. Since then the girls had had fresh milk. Helen pretended not to notice.

Daphne agreed with Gwyneira's suggestion. She had long since noticed while milking and stealing eggs how much warmer it was in the improvised stalls belowdecks. The cows' and horses' big bodies gave off a comforting warmth, and the straw was soft and often drier than the mattresses in their berths. At first Helen rejected the idea, but she finally relented. She held lessons in a stall for a full three weeks before the purser caught them and threw them out, cursing and suspecting them of stealing food. By this time, the *Dublin* had reached the Bay of Biscay. The sea became calmer, the weather warmer. With a sigh of relief, the passengers from steerage brought their damp clothes and bed linens up to dry out in the sun. They praised God for the warmth, but the crew warned them: soon they would reach the Indian Ocean and curse the scorching heat.

6

Now that the first arduous leg of the journey was over, social life aboard the *Dublin* began to stir.

The ship doctor finally took up his work as teacher so that the emigrant children had something to occupy them other than pestering each other, their parents, and above all, Helen's girls. The girls shone in class, and Helen was proud of them. She had hoped the school lessons would give her some time to herself, but she ended up observing her charges during their lessons instead. This was because already on the second day the little gossips Mary and Laurie returned from class with troubling news.

"Daphne kissed Jamie O'Hara!" Mary reported, out of breath.

"And Tommy Sheridan wanted to feel Elizabeth up, but she said she was waiting for a prince, and then everyone laughed," Laurie appended.

First Helen dealt with Daphne, who showed no sign of remorse. "Jamie gave me a good piece of sausage for it," she admitted. "They brought it with them from home. And it went real fast anyway; he can't kiss right at all."

Helen was appalled by Daphne's apparently considerable knowledge in these matters. She admonished her strongly but knew it did no good. Daphne's sense of morality and decorum could possibly be deepened over time. For now, only self-control would help. So Helen sat in on lessons with the girls and took on more responsibilities in the school and in preparations for the Sunday service. The ship doctor was grateful to her, as he was not much of a teacher or a preacher.

There was now music almost every evening in steerage. The people had made peace with the loss of the old homeland—or at least found solace in singing old English, Irish, and Scottish tunes. A few had brought instruments with them on board; one could hear fiddles, flutes, and harmonicas. Fridays and Saturday nights there was dancing, and here again Helen had to keep Daphne in check. She was happy to let the older girls listen to the music and watch the dancing for an hour before bed. Dorothy was always demurely ready to turn in for the night, but Daphne found excuses or even tried to sneak out later when she falsely believed Helen was sleeping.

On the upper deck the social activities unfolded in a more cultivated fashion. Concerts and deck games were held, and the evening meals were now celebrated festively in the dining room. Gerald Warden and Gwyneira shared a table with a London couple whose younger son was stationed in a garrison in Christchurch and who was now playing with the idea of settling there permanently. He had asked his father to grant him an advance on his inheritance. In response, Mr. and Mrs. Brewster—spry, resolute people in their fifties—had promptly booked their trip to New Zealand. Before he emptied his pockets, Mr. Brewster explained, he wanted to take a look at the area and—even more than that—his future daughter-in-law.

"She's half Maori, Peter writes," Mrs. Brewster said uncertainly. "And she's supposed to be as beautiful as one of those South Sea girls whose picture you sometimes see. But I don't know, a native..."

"That can be very helpful for the acquisition of land," Gerald remarked. "An acquaintance of mine once received a chief's daughter as a present—and twenty-five acres of the best pastureland to boot. My friend fell in love at once." Gerald winked meaningfully.

Mr. Brewster boomed with laughter while Gwyneira and Mrs. Brewster smiled reluctantly.

"Might even be his daughter, your son's lady friend," Gerald considered further. "She would have to be about fifteen now, a suitable marrying age for the natives. And many of the mixed children are stunning. The pureblooded Maori, on the other hand...well, they're not to my taste. Too short, too stocky, and there are the tattoos...but to each his own. There's no accounting for taste."

From the Brewsters' questions and Gerald's answers, Gwyneira began to learn more about her future homeland. Up until then, the sheep baron had primarily spoken of the economic opportunities of breeding and pastureland in the Canterbury Plains, but now, for the first time, she learned that New Zealand consisted of two big islands and that Christchurch and the Canterbury Plains were situated on the South Island. She heard about mountains and fjords but also about a jungle-like rainforest, whaling stations, and gold rushes. Gwyneira remembered that Lucas was supposed to be researching the country's flora and fauna and replaced her daydreams of plowing and sowing at her husband's side with an even more exciting fantasy of expeditions into the islands' unexplored reaches.

At some point the Brewsters' curiosity was satisfied and Gerald had exhausted his cache of stories. Warden clearly knew New Zealand well, but animals and landscapes interested him only as economic ciphers. It seemed that this was also the case for the Brewster family. They cared only that the area was safe and that a possible business venture would pay off. As they discussed these questions, various merchants and farmers were mentioned. Gwyneira took the opportunity to put the plan she'd long nourished into effect and asked innocuously about a "gentleman farmer" by the name of O'Keefe.

"Maybe you know him, then. He's supposed to live somewhere in the Canterbury Plains."

Gerald Warden's reaction surprised her. Her future father-in-law turned red, and his eyes seemed to leap out of their sockets in agitation.

"O'Keefe? Gentleman farmer?" Gerald skewered each word and snorted, flaring his nostrils. "I know a scoundrel and cutthroat by the name of O'Keefe," he rumbled on. "Scum that should be sent back to Ireland as quickly as possible. Or to Australia, to the penal colonies; that's where he comes from, you know. Gentleman farmer! That's not even funny. Out with it, Gwyneira, where did you hear that name?"

Gwyneira raised a supplicating hand, and Mr. Brewster hurried to refill Gerald's glass with whiskey. He clearly hoped it would have a calming effect, as Mrs. Brewster had cringed when Warden exploded with rage.

"I'm sure I have a different O'Keefe in mind," Gwyneira said quickly. "A young woman in steerage, a governess, is engaged to him. She said he belonged to the notables of Christchurch."

"Oh?" Gerald asked leerily. "Strange that he should have escaped my notice. A gentleman farmer from the Christchurch area who shares a name with this damned son of a bitch...oh, forgive me, ladies... who has the misfortune of sharing a name with this dubious fellow O'Keefe should really be known to me."

"O'Keefe is a very common name," Mr. Brewster said in an effort to appease him. "It's entirely possible that there are two O'Keefes in Christchurch."

"And Helen's Mr. O'Keefe writes such lovely letters," Gwyneira added. "He must be well educated."

Gerald laughed loudly. "Well, then it's definitely someone else. Old Howie can hardly put his name to paper without making a mistake! But it doesn't suit me, Gwyn, that you're running around in steerage. Keep your distance from those people down there, even from this so-called governess. Her story sounds suspect to me, so don't talk to her anymore."

Gwyneira frowned. Angry, she did not say a word the rest of the night. Later, in her cabin, she let her anger out properly.

Who did Gerald Warden think he was? The transition from "my lady" to "Lady Gwyneira" and now plain "Gwyn" had been awfully quick, and now he spoke so cavalierly and informally, ordering her around. Like hell she'd break off contact with Helen! Helen was the only person she could speak frankly with. Despite their different social pedigrees and interests, the two were becoming better and better friends.

Besides, Gwyneira had taken a liking to the six girls. She had warmed to serious little Dorothy in particular, but daydreaming Elizabeth too, tiny Rosie, and even the occasionally shady but doubtlessly clever Daphne, hungry for life. She would have liked best to take them all to Kiward Station straightaway, and had planned on speaking with Gerald about taking on at least one new serving girl. It didn't look that promising, true, but the journey was still long, and Warden would no doubt calm down. The things she had learned about Howard O'Keefe caused Gwyneira much more of a headache. Sure, the name was common, and two O'Keefes in a region was not unheard of. But two Howard O'Keefes?

What exactly did Gerald have against Helen's future spouse?

Gwyneira would gladly have shared her thoughts with Helen, but then thought it best to keep them to herself. What good would it do to ruin Helen's happiness and give her things to worry about? All speculation was ultimately useless.

In the meantime it had become warm, almost hot, on board the *Dublin*. The sun now scorched the ship mercilessly from the sky. The immigrants had enjoyed the heat at first, but after almost eight weeks on board, the mood was shifting. While the cold of the first few weeks had made everyone listless, the heat and stifling air in the cabins put them increasingly on edge.

In steerage, people grated on each other's nerves and got annoyed at even the flies on the walls. The men were the first to come to blows, passengers and crew members alike, when someone felt swindled at the food or water distribution. The ship's doctor used a lot of gin to clean wounds and calm tempers. In addition, almost every family was fighting; the forced indolence got on everyone's nerves. Helen alone enforced peace and quiet in her cabin. She kept the children busy from dawn until dusk with their never-ending lessons on working in a grand house. Gwyneira's own head spun whenever she listened in.

"Goodness, I'm lucky to have escaped all that." She thanked her good fortune, laughing. "I would never have been suited to managing such a house. I would constantly have forgotten half of it. And it would never have dawned on me to have the servants polish the silver every day. It's such superfluous work. And why do you have to fold the napkins in such a complicated manner? They get used every day as well."

"It's a question of beauty and decorum," Helen informed her strictly. "Besides, you will still have to see to all of that. According to what I've heard, you're expected at Kiward Station, a manor house. You said yourself that Mr. Warden is supposed to have modeled his home's architecture after English country manors and had the rooms decorated by a London designer. Do you think he scrimped on the silverware, lamps, trays, and fruit bowls? You even have table linen packed in your trousseau."

Gwyneira sighed. "I should have married my way to Texas. But seriously, I believe...I hope...Mr. Warden exaggerates. True, he wants to be a gentleman, but under all that genteel affectation hides a rather rough character. Yesterday he beat Mr. Brewster at blackjack. What am I saying—'beat'—he cooked his goose! The other gentlemen accused him of cheating, and he wanted to challenge Lord Barrington to a duel over it. They might as well have been in any common harbor gin shack! Finally the captain himself had to ask the men to calm down. In reality, Kiward Station is probably a blockhouse, and I'll have to milk the cows myself."

"That would suit you!" Helen laughed, having gotten to know her friend well during their trip. "But don't fool yourself. You are and will remain a lady, in a cow stall if it comes to it—and that goes for you too, Daphne. Don't sit about looking slatternly, with your legs spread, just because I'm not looking. You can do Miss Silkham's hair instead. You can tell by that alone that she misses her maids. Seriously, Gwyn, your hair curls as if someone had taken a curling iron to it. Do you ever comb it?"

Under Helen's guidance and with some supplementary advice from Gwyneira on the latest fashions, Dorothy and even Daphne had grown into rather skilled chambermaids. Both were polite and had learned to help a lady dress and do her hair. Sometimes Helen had reservations about sending Daphne up to Gwyneira's room alone because she didn't trust the girl. She thought it entirely possible that Daphne would take advantage of any opportunity for theft. But Gwyneira reassured her.

"I don't know if she's honest, but she's certainly not dumb. If she steals here, we'd find out. Who else could it be, and where would she hide the stolen goods? As long as she's here on the ship, I'm quite certain she'll behave."

The third-oldest girl, Elizabeth, proved just as ready to help and was irreproachably honest and loveable. She did not, however, demonstrate an abundance of skill. She preferred reading and writing to working with her hands. As a result, she was a source of anxiety to Helen.

"She should go back to school and perhaps then to a teaching college," she remarked to Gwyneira. "She would like that too. She likes children and has a lot of patience. But who would pay for it? And is there even something like that in New Zealand? She's a hopeless case as a housemaid. When she's supposed to scrub a floor, she floods half of it and forgets the rest."

"Maybe she'd be a good nanny," Gwyneira considered, ever practical. "I will probably need one soon."

Helen reddened at this observation. With regard to her coming nuptials, she only thought reluctantly about childbearing, especially conception. It was one thing to marvel at Howard's polished writing style and bask in his admiration, but the thought of letting a complete stranger touch her...Helen had only a vague inkling of what transpired between men and women at night, but she anticipated more pain than joy. And here was Gwyneira talking so matter-of-factly about having children. Did she want to talk about it? And did she maybe know more about it than Helen herself did? Helen wondered how she could broach the topic without violating propriety from the very first word. Of course, this was a conversation that could take place only if none of the girls were nearby. Breathing a sigh of relief, she established that Rosie was playing with Cleo beside them.

In any case, Gwyneira could not have answered Helen's pressing question. Though she spoke openly about having children, she had not given a thought to the nights with Lucas. She had no idea what to expect from them—her mother had only shamefully hinted that it was just part of a woman's fate to endure these things submissively. In return for which she would, God willing, be rewarded with a child. Gwyneira sometimes wondered whether a screaming, red-faced baby could truly be a reward, but she was not under any illusions. Gerald Warden expected her to bear him a grandchild as soon as possible. She wouldn't refuse him that—not once she knew how one went about it.

The sea journey dragged on. In first class, people battled with boredom; all the pleasantries had been exchanged, all the stories told. Meanwhile, the passengers in steerage wrestled with the increasing difficulty of daily life. The paltry, monotonous diet led to sickness and symptoms of deficiency, while the narrowness of the cabins and the now constant warm weather created a perfect breeding ground for vermin. Dolphins had begun accompanying the ship, and big fish, even sharks, could be seen. The men in steerage tried to get their hands on them by means of fishing or harpooning but were rarely successful. The women yearned for even a modicum of hygiene and had resorted to collecting rainwater to wash their children and clothing. Helen found the results unsatisfying, however.

"In that broth the clothes only get dirtier," she complained, eyeing the water that had collected in the bottom of one of the lifeboats.

Gwyneira shrugged. "At least you don't have to drink it. And we're in luck with regard to water, says the captain. Although we've been making our way slowly through the...the calm belt, thus far there have been no lulls. The wind doesn't always blow here as it should, and sometimes ships run out of water."

Helen nodded. "The sailors say this place is also called the 'horse latitudes' because people used to have to slaughter the horses on board to keep from starving."

Gwyneira snorted. "I'll eat the sailors before I slaughter Igraine," she declared. "But like I said, we seem to have been lucky."

Unfortunately, the *Dublin*'s luck soon ran out. Although the wind continued to blow, a pernicious malady suddenly threatened the lives of the passengers. At first, only one sailor complained of fever, but the ship's doctor recognized the danger when several children were brought to him with fevers and breakouts. The disease spread like wildfire throughout steerage.

At first Helen hoped her girls would remain unscathed since they had little contact with the other children outside of the daily school lessons. Thanks to Gwyneira's generosity and Daphne's regular forays into the cow stalls and chicken coops, they were also in considerably better health than the other immigrant children. Then, however, Elizabeth broke out in a fever. Laurie and Rosemary followed suit shortly thereafter, and Daphne and Dorothy became mildly ill. Surprisingly, Mary did not catch it at all, despite the fact that she shared the berth with her twin the whole time, her arms tight around Laurie, mourning her ahead of time. Laurie's fever passed without doing much harm, but Elizabeth and Rosemary hung between life and death for several days. The ship's doctor treated them with the same medicine as he did every other illness—gin—and the parents of the affected children could not make up their minds whether it was to be taken internally or applied externally. Helen decided on baths and compresses, and actually managed to cool her patients somewhat. For most of the families, however, the booze ended up in the patriarch's belly, and the already tense atmosphere became even more explosive.

In the end, twelve children died of the contagion, and weeping and moaning once more dominated in steerage. The captain held a very moving funeral service on the main deck, which all passengers attended. Gwyneira played the piano, tears streaming down her face, her good intentions clearly greater than her talent. Without sheet music, she was helpless. Finally, Helen took over, and a few of the passengers in steerage fetched their instruments too. The music and wailing of the people sounded far over the ocean, and for the first time, rich and poor came together as one. They mourned together, and for days after the service, the mood was somber and peaceful. The captain, a quiet man wise in the ways of the world, held the remaining Sunday services for all the passengers on the main deck. The weather no longer presented any obstacle; if anything, it was too hot rather than too cold and rainy. Only when they rounded the Cape of Good Hope did the seas become stormy again; after that the journey continued without incident.

Meanwhile Helen rehearsed church songs with her schoolchildren. When the choir's singing one Sunday morning had been particularly successful, the Brewsters drew her into their conversation with Gerald and Gwyneira. They praised the young woman at length on her students, and Gwyneira used this opportunity to formally introduce her friend to her future father-in-law.

She only hoped that Gerald wouldn't blow up again. However, he did not lose his temper this time and instead proved rather charming. He calmly exchanged the usual pleasantries with the young woman, even commending her for the children's singing.

"So you want to marry, then," he continued when there was nothing left to say.

Helen nodded enthusiastically. "Yes, sir, God willing. I'm trusting the Lord to show me the way to a happy marriage...perhaps you even know my fiancé? Howard O'Keefe out of Haldon, Canterbury. He's a gentleman farmer."

Gwyneira held her breath. Maybe she should have told Helen about Gerald's outburst, after all. Yet her concern proved unfounded. Gerald remained perfectly composed.

"I hope you retain that faith," he remarked with a lopsided smirk. "The man plays the strangest jokes on those innocent sheep of his. But as for your question...no. I do not know of any 'gentleman' by the name of Howard O'Keefe."

The *Dublin* was now sailing across the Indian Ocean, the penultimate, longest, and most dangerous leg of the journey. Though the waters were rarely rough, the route led them far across the deep sea. The passengers had not seen land for weeks, and according to Gerald Warden, the next shores were hundreds of miles away.

Life on board had settled down once again, and thanks to the tropical weather, everyone spent more time on deck instead of in their claustrophobic cabins. This led to a further unraveling of the strict division between first class and steerage. In addition to Sunday service, communal concerts and dances now took place as well. The men in steerage improved their fishing skills and became more successful. They harpooned sharks and barracudas and caught albatrosses by dragging a fishhook baited with fish from the aft of the ship. The scent of fish and fowl being grilled wafted over the whole deck, and the mouths of the families not participating watered. Helen received some of the bounty as a gift. As a teacher, she was highly regarded among the passengers, and now that she had taken charge of lessons, almost all the children in steerage could read and write better than their parents. Daphne could almost always sweet-talk her way into a bit of fish or bird meat as well. If Helen did not watch her like a hawk, she would sneak over to the men while they were fishing, marvel at their artistry, and attract their attention by fluttering her eyelashes and pouting. The young men especially courted her favor and let themselves get carried away with sometimes dangerous tests of courage. Daphne applauded, apparently captivated when they would lay their shirts, shoes, and socks aside and let themselves be lowered into the water by the hollering crew. However, neither Helen nor Gwyneira got the impression that Daphne cared much for the boys.

"She's hoping that a shark gets him," Gwyneira remarked as a young Scot bravely sprang headfirst into the water and let himself be pulled along by the *Dublin* like bait on a hook. "What would you bet that she wouldn't have any reservations about gobbling up the beast even if?"

"It's about time for this journey to end," Helen sighed. "Otherwise, I'm going to go from teacher to prison guard. These sunsets, for example...yes, they're beautiful and romantic, but the boys and girls find them so as well. Elizabeth is swooning over Jamie O'Hara, whom Daphne turned down long ago when all the sausage had been eaten up. And Dorothy is pressed by three lads a day to come view the phosphorescent sea with them at night."

Gwyneira laughed and played with her sun hat. "Daphne, on the other hand, isn't looking for her Prince Charming in steerage. Yesterday she asked me whether she couldn't watch the sunset from the upper deck, since the view would be so much better. During which she eyed the young Viscount Barrington like a shark does fish."

Helen rolled her eyes. "We should marry her off soon. Oh, Gwyn, I'm scared to death when I think that in just two or three weeks I have to hand the girls over to total strangers, maybe never to see them again!"

"You just said you wanted to get rid of them!" Gwyneira cried, laughing. "And anyway, they can read and write. You can all exchange letters. And we can too. If I only knew how far apart Haldon and Kiward Station were from each other. Both are in the Canterbury Plains, but where are those? I just don't want to lose you, Helen. Wouldn't it be lovely if we could visit one another?"

"We can most certainly do that," Helen said confidently. "Howard must live close to Christchurch; otherwise, he wouldn't belong to that parish. And Mr. Warden must have a lot to do in the city. We'll definitely see each other, Gwyn!"

7

The journey was finally drawing to a close. As the *Dublin* sailed through the Tasmanian Sea between Australia and New Zealand, the passengers tried to outdo one another with rumors about how close they were to their new country. Many were already camping out on deck every morning before the sun rose to be the first to catch sight of their new homeland.

Elizabeth was torn when Jamie O'Hara woke her for that purpose once, but Helen ordered her sternly to remain in bed. She knew from Gwyneira that it would still be two or three days before land came into view, and then the captain would inform them right away.

It finally happened, though, in the bright light of late morning: the captain had the ship's sirens wail, and within seconds all the passengers had assembled on the main deck. Gwyneira and Gerald stood in the front row, of course, unable to see anything but clouds at first. A long, drawn-out white layer of cotton obscured the land. If the crew had not assured the passengers that the South Island was hiding behind it, they would not have paid any attention to that particular cloud.

Only as they neared the shore did mountains begin to emerge from the fog, jagged contours of rock behind which were more clouds. It looked so strange, as though the mountains were floating on a sea of luminous, cottony white clouds.

"Is it always so foggy?" Gwyneira asked, sounding unenthused. As lovely as the view was, she could well imagine the damp and chilly ride through the pass that separated Christchurch from where the deep-sea ship would be landing. The harbor, Gerald had explained to her, was called Lyttelton. The area was still under construction, and there was a laborious climb to even the first houses. To reach Christchurch proper, people would have to walk or ride. The path was at times so steep and difficult that horses familiar with the path had to be led by the bridle. Hence the path's name: the Bridle Path.

Gerald shook his head. "No. It's rather unusual for travelers to be offered such a view. And it's surely a lucky sign." He smiled, obviously happy to see his home again. "That is to say that the land revealed itself to the first travelers, who came by canoe from Polynesia to New Zealand, in the same way. That explains New Zealand's Maori name—Aotearoa, 'Land of the Long White Cloud.'"

Helen and her girls gazed, awestruck, at nature's theater.

Daphne, however, seemed concerned. "There aren't any houses," she said, puzzled. "Where are the docks and the harbor buildings? Where are the church steeples? I only see clouds and mountains. It's nothing like London."

Helen attempted to laugh encouragingly, although at heart she shared Daphne's fears. She too was a city girl, and this abundance of nature seemed eerie to her. Still, she had at least seen a variety of English landscapes, whereas the girls knew only the streets of the capital.

"Of course it's not London, Daphne," she explained. "The cities here are much smaller. But Christchurch has its steeples too, and it will be getting its own great cathedral, just like Westminster Abbey! You can't see the houses yet because we're not landing right in the city. We must...well, we must still walk a bit to—"

"Walk a bit?" Gerald Warden had overheard Helen and laughed thunderously. "I can only hope, Miss Davenport, that your wonderful fiancé sends you a mule. Otherwise, you'll wear out the soles of your city shoes before the day is out. The Bridle Path is a narrow, mountainous path, slippery and wet from fog. And after the fog lifts, it gets pretty darn warm. But, Gwyneira, look there, that's Lyttelton Harbor!"

The rest of the passengers shared Gerald's excitement as the lifting fog now exposed a pear-shaped bay to view. According to Gerald, this natural harbor had volcanic origins. The bay was surrounded by mountains, and a few houses and landings were becoming visible.

"Don't worry," the ship's doctor reassured Helen. "Nowadays a shuttle service operates daily between Lyttelton and Christchurch. You can rent a mule when we arrive. You won't have to hike the whole way like the first settlers."

Helen was hesitant. Maybe she could rent a mule, but what was she going to do with the girls?

"How...how far is it exactly?" she asked unsurely as the *Dublin* rapidly approached the coast. "And do we have to bring all our luggage with us?"

"As you like," Gerald remarked. "You can also have it ferried by boat, up the Avon River. But that costs money, of course. Most New Zealanders haul their things over the Bridle Path. It's twelve miles."

Helen decided only to have her beloved rocking chair ferried. She would carry the rest of her luggage just like the others. She could walk twelve miles—of course she could. Although it was true she had never tried such a thing before.

Meanwhile, the main deck had emptied; the passengers had rushed to their cabins to pack their bags. Now that they had almost reached their destination, they wanted to get off the boat as quickly as possible. A tumult similar to that of their first day on board reigned in steerage.

In first class, people went about things more coolly. Luggage was by and large picked up; the gentry would be taking advantage of the transportation company that carried people and their baggage to the interior on mules. Mrs. Brewster and Lady Barrington already trembled at the prospect of the ride over the pass. Neither one was accustomed to being transported by horse or mule, and both had heard horror stories about the dangers of the route. Gwyneira, however, could hardly wait to mount Igraine—and for that reason ended up in a serious dispute with Gerald.

"Stay here another night?" she said, amazed, when he indicated they would be taking advantage of the humble but newly opened guesthouse in Lyttelton. "But why do that?"

"Because we'll hardly be able to unload the animals before late afternoon," Gerald explained. "And because I have to requisition herders to bring the sheep over the pass."

Gwyneira shook her head, uncomprehending. "Why do you need help for that? I can drive the sheep on my own. And we have two horses. We don't need to wait for the mules."

Gerald boomed with laughter, and Lord Barrington joined him.

"You want to drive the sheep over the pass, little lady? On horseback, like an American cowboy?" The lord found this the best joke he had heard in a long time.

Gwyneira rolled her eyes. "Of course I wouldn't drive the sheep myself," she remarked. "That's what Cleo and the other dogs are for, the ones that Mr. Warden bought from my father. The pups are still little and haven't been fully trained, but there are only thirty sheep, after all. Cleo could do that all by herself if need be."

The little dog had heard her name and immediately emerged from her corner. Wagging her tail and with bright eyes shining with eagerness and devotion, she stopped in front of her mistress. Gwyneira petted her and informed her that their boredom on the ship would come to an end that day.

"Gwyneira," Gerald said, annoyed, "I didn't buy these sheep and dogs and have them shipped halfway around the world just to have them fall off the next cliff." He hated it when a member of his family sounded ridiculous. And it infuriated him further when someone ignored or even questioned his directions. "You don't know the Bridle Path. It's a treacherous and dangerous trail. No dog can drive sheep over it alone, and it's not as easy to ride over it as you seem to think. I've had pens prepared for the sheep tonight. Tomorrow I'll have the horses ferried over, and you'll take a mule."

Gwyneira tossed her head back imperiously. She hated it when people underestimated her or her animals' abilities.

"Igraine can cross any path and is as sure-footed as any mule," she assured them with a steady voice. "Cleo has never lost a sheep, and she won't now. Just wait, by this evening we'll be in Christchurch!"

The men kept laughing, but Gwyneira was determined. Why did she have the best sheepdog in Powys, if not in all Wales? And why had people been breeding cobs for nimbleness and sure-footedness? Gwyneira burned with impatience to show the men what she was capable of. This was a new world! She wouldn't let herself be bound by the role of the well-bred little woman who followed men's orders without protest.

Helen felt extremely light-headed when she finally set foot on New Zealand around three o'clock that afternoon. The bobbing landing platform did not seem much steadier than the planks of the *Dublin*, but she stepped across it courageously and stood at long last on solid land. She was so relieved that she would have liked nothing better than to kneel down and kiss the ground, just as Mrs. O'Hara and a few other settlers had unabashedly done. Helen's girls and the other children from steerage danced and frolicked about and were subdued only with great effort in order to join the other survivors in saying a prayer of thanksgiving. Only Daphne still seemed disappointed. The few houses hemming the Bay of Lyttelton did not meet her expectations for a town.

Helen had already commissioned the transportation of the rocking chair by ferry. Now, her travel bag in one hand and her parasol over her shoulder, she sauntered up the wide access path leading up to the first houses. The girls followed her obediently with their bundles. Thus far they found the climb demanding, but not dangerous or unreasonably difficult. If it did not get any worse, they could still conquer the road to Christchurch. For the time being, however, they found themselves in the center of the Lyttelton settlement. There was a pub, a general store, and a questionable-looking hotel. But that was there only for the benefit of the rich. The steerage passengers who did not want to leave straight for Christchurch could spend the night here in primitive barracks or tents, and many of the new settlers chose this option. A few of them had relatives in Christchurch and had arranged for them to send mules as soon as the *Dublin* had arrived.

Helen entertained a quiet hope when she saw the transport company's mules waiting in front of the pub. True, Howard did not yet know of her arrival, but the vicar of Christchurch, Reverend Baldwin, had been informed that the six orphan girls would arrive on the *Dublin*. Perhaps he had arranged transportation for the rest of their journey. Helen asked the mule drivers, but they had not received any instructions to that effect. Though they were supposed to pick up supplies for Reverend Baldwin, and they had been notified of the Brewsters' arrival, the pastor had not mentioned the girls.

"All right, girls, there's nothing left for us but to walk," Helen said, finally accepting her fate. "And we'd better get started so we can put it behind us."

The tents and barracks that were their only alternative struck Helen as rather shady. Naturally, men and women slept separately, but there were no locks on the doors, and there was no doubt an equal dearth of women in Lyttelton as in Christchurch. Who knew what would get into men's heads when seven women and girls without a chaperone served themselves up on a silver platter?

So Helen set out with a number of the other immigrant families who likewise wanted to continue on to Christchurch without delay. The O'Haras were among them, and Jamie gallantly offered to shoulder Elizabeth's things as well as his own. His mother, however, strictly forbade this, as the O'Haras were transporting all of their household supplies over the mountains, and everyone already had more than enough to carry. As the practical woman saw it, in such cases courtesy was a luxury they could not afford.

After the first few miles, Jamie might have come to the same conclusion himself. The fog had lifted, as Gerald had predicted, and now the Bridle Path basked in the warm spring sunshine. The immigrants still found the heat incomprehensible. Back home in England, they would have been facing the first autumn storms, while here in New Zealand the grass was just beginning to sprout and the sun to climb higher. Though the temperature was quite pleasant, the travelers soon broke into a sweat on the long ascent, especially since many of them wore several layers of clothing in order to have less to carry. Even the men were soon out of breath. Three indolent months at sea had robbed even the strongest laborer of his strength. Yet the path grew not only steeper but more treacherous. The girls cried in fear as they clambered along a crater's lip. Mary and Laurie clung so tightly to one another that they actually put themselves in greater danger of falling. Rosemary held onto the edge of Helen's skirt and buried her head in the folds of her traveling outfit when the trail was too frightening. Helen had long since closed her parasol. She needed it as a walking stick, and she no longer had the energy to carry it properly over her shoulder. She couldn't have cared less about looking after her pale skin that day.

After an hour, the travelers were tired and thirsty and had put only two miles behind them.

"Up there on the mountain, they sell refreshments," Jamie comforted the girls. "At least that's what they said in Lyttelton. And there's supposed to be hostels that offer a nice sit-down along the way. We just have to get up there, then the worst will be over." With that, he bravely set off on the next leg of the trail. The girls followed him over the rocky terrain.

During the climb, Helen had little time to study the landscape, but what she did see was demoralizing. The mountains looked bare and gray, with only sparse vegetation.

"Volcanic rock," explained Mr. O'Hara, who had worked in mining. But Helen could only think of the "Mountains of Hell" from a ballad her sister used to sing. When she had pictured what eternal damnation might look like—barren, wan, and infinite—it had been just like this.

Gerald Warden did indeed have to wait until all the other passengers had disembarked to unload his animals. The men from the transport company only just had the mules ready then.

"We'll make it before dark," they said reassuringly as they heaved the anxious women onto the mules. "It takes about four hours. We'll arrive in Christchurch around eight in the evening. Just in time for dinner at the hotel."

"Did you hear that?" Gwyneira asked Gerald. "We could join them. Although we'd be faster alone, of course. Igraine won't like trotting behind the mules."

To Gerald's annoyance, Gwyneira had already saddled the horses while he was monitoring the unloading of the sheep. Gerald restrained himself from expressing his anger. Regardless, he was in a bad mood. Nobody here knew what to do with the sheep; the pens had not been prepared, and the flock was spreading itself out over the hills of Lyttelton like in a painting. The animals were enjoying their freedom after their long spell in the belly of the ship and were frolicking like young lambs on the sparse grass outside the settlement. Gerald cursed two of the sailors who had helped him with the unloading and gave them strict orders to herd the sheep together and watch them until he had organized the construction of a provisional pen. The men, however, saw their job as done. After insolently remarking that they were sailors, not shepherds, they hurried to the just-opened pub. After the long drought on board, they were thirsty. Gerald's sheep did not concern them.

Suddenly a shrill whistle sounded that not only made Lady Barrington and Mrs. Brewster flinch in fright, but Gerald and the mule drivers as well. Moreover, the sound had not come from some street urchin but rather from a blue-blooded young lady they had considered until that moment to be ladylike and well bred. Another Gwyneira was making herself known. The girl had recognized Gerald's dilemma with the sheep and immediately sought help. She whistled piercingly for her dog, and Cleo followed enthusiastically. Like a little black bolt of lightning, the dog dashed up and down the hills and rounded up the sheep into a tight flock. As though guided by an invisible hand, the animals turned to Gwyneira, who was waiting calmly. Gerald's puppies, waiting in a kennel nearby and set to be delivered to Christchurch, went so wild at the sight of the sheep that the wooden box split open. The six little collies tumbled out and shot immediately toward the flock. But before the sheep could catch fright, the dogs lay down in the grass as though by command. Panting excitedly, their clever collie faces directed tensely at the flock, they lay there, ready to spring into action if a sheep should wander out of place.

"Well, all right," Gwyneira said with composure. "The whelps really know their stuff. The big one there, we'll start a breed with him that'll make people back in England wish they had one. Shall we be going, Mr. Warden?"

Without waiting for his reply, she climbed up on her mare. Igraine pranced excitedly. She too was eager to be able to move again. The sailor who had been holding the young stallion handed the nervous animal over to Gerald with a sigh of relief.

Gerald vacillated between rage and amazement. Gwyneira's performance had been impressive, but that did not give her the right to defy his commands. However, Gerald could hardly put a halt to things without losing face in front of the Brewsters and Barringtons.

He grudgingly took the small stallion's reins. He had conquered the Bridle Path more than once and knew its dangers. Taking the path in the late afternoon was always risky. Even when you didn't have shepherds with you and were sitting on a well-trained mule instead of on an unbacked stallion.

On the other hand, he didn't know what to do about the sheep here in Lyttelton. His incompetent son had once again failed to make arrangements for their accommodation at the harbor, and now there was guaranteed to be no one available to set up a pen before nightfall. Gerald's fingers clamped around the reins in rage. When would Lucas finally learn to think beyond the walls of his study?

Angrily, Gerald put a foot in the stirrup. He had naturally learned over the course of his eventful life to handle a horse reasonably well, but it was still not his favorite mode of transport. To take the Bridle Path on a young stallion felt like a test of courage to Gerald—and he nearly hated Gwyneira for forcing him into it. Her rebellious spirit, which had so pleased Gerald when it was directed against her father, was becoming a source of frustration that was hard to ignore.

Sitting on her mare, pleased with herself and entirely at ease, Gwyneira had no inkling of Gerald's thinking. No, she was simply delighted that her future father-in-law had not said anything about the man's saddle she had put on Igraine. Her father would certainly have thrown a fit if she had dared to ride astride a horse with her legs apart in society. Gerald, however, did not seem to notice how unbecoming it looked, with the skirt of her riding dress riding up, exposing her ankles. Gwyneira attempted to pull the skirt down, but then forgot all about it. She had enough to do with Igraine, who would have liked to overtake the mules and take the pass at a gallop. The dogs, thankfully, did not require any attention. Cleo knew what to do and drove the sheep deftly toward the pass even when the path narrowed. The pups followed her in order from biggest to littlest, causing Mrs. Brewster to joke, "Looks a bit like Miss Davenport and her orphan girls."

Two hours after setting out, Helen was at the end of her strength when she heard the sound of hooves behind her. The path still led upward, and now, just as before, there was nothing to see but barren, inhospitable mountains. However, one of the other immigrants had spoken a few encouraging words to them. He had spent some years at sea and had been present in 1836 for one of the first expeditions to this area. With a group belonging to Captain Rhodes, one of the first settlers, he had climbed up the Port Hills and fallen so in love with the view of the Canterbury Plains that he had now returned with his wife and child to settle here. He now told his exhausted family that after just a few more curves in the road, they would reach the top.

Still the path remained narrow and steep, and the riding mules could not overtake the hikers. Grumbling, the riders fell in line behind them. Helen wondered whether Gwyneira was among them. She had heard the altercation between Gerald and Gwyneira and was anxious to see who had won the dispute. Her sensitive nose told her that Gwyneira must have won the day. The air suddenly smelled distinctly of sheep, and she could hear *baa*s of protest behind her.

At long last, they reached the pass's highest point. Merchants awaited the hikers on a sort of platform, on which they had built stands and now offered refreshments. This was where people traditionally rested—if only to enjoy the first vista of their new country in peace. But for the moment Helen had no interest in the view. She could only drag herself to one of the stands, where she purchased a large tankard of ginger beer. Only after she'd drunk it did she make her way to the overlook, where many of the others had already paused as though in prayer.

"It's so pretty," whispered Gwyneira, enraptured. Sitting on her horse, she could see out over the others. Helen had to make do with a limited view from the third row. That was enough, however, to put a damper on her enthusiasm. Far below them, the mountainous landscape gave way to tender green grassland through which wound a small river. On the opposite bank lay the Christchurch settlement, which was anything but the burgeoning city Helen had expected. True, one could make out a tiny church steeple, but hadn't there been talk of a cathedral? Wasn't it supposed to become a bishopric? Helen had at least expected a construction site, but no such thing was visible. Christchurch was nothing more than a cluster of brightly colored houses, mostly made of wood; only a few were built from the sandstone Mr. Warden had spoken of. It reminded her very much of Lyttelton, the port town they had just left behind. And it likely had little more to offer in social life and amenities.

Gwyneira hardly gave the town a second glance. It was tiny, yes, but she was used to that from the villages in Wales. What fascinated her was the hinterland: sheer endless grassland basking in the late afternoon sun, and beyond the plains rose majestic mountains, some of which were capped with snow. They were surely many miles away, but the air was so clear that it looked like you could touch them. A few children even stretched out their hands.

The vista was reminiscent of Wales or other parts of Great Britain where grasslands bordered on hilly regions; for that reason this landscape felt familiar to Gwyneira and many of the other settlers.

But everything was clearer, larger, and more expansive. No pens or walls divided the landscape, and only the occasional house could be seen. Gwyneira experienced a sensation of freedom. She would be able to ride endlessly here, and the sheep could spread themselves out over a gigantic area. Never again would she have to discuss whether there was enough grass or if the herd needed to be thinned. Here there seemed to be an infinite amount of land.

Gerald's anger at Gwyneira dissolved when he saw her beaming face. It reflected the joy he felt anew each time he looked out over his homeland. Gwyneira would feel at home here. She might not love Lucas, but she would definitely love the land.

Helen resolved to have a positive attitude. This was not what she'd pictured, but to be fair, she'd been assured on all sides that Christchurch was a blossoming community. The town would grow. Eventually there would be schools and libraries—perhaps she could even take part in building it up. Howard seemed to be a man interested in culture; no doubt he would support her. And moreover, she didn't have to love the land but rather her husband. With renewed determination, she swallowed her disappointment and turned to the girls.

"On your feet, children. You've had your refreshment; now we have to get going. But it won't be as bad going downhill. Come, let's have the little ones race. Whoever makes it to the next inn first gets an extra lemonade!"

The next inn was not far. The first houses were already visible in the foothills of the mountains. The path widened, and the riders could pass those who were on foot. Cleo drove the sheep ably past the settlers, and Gwyneira followed on the still-prancing Igraine. Earlier, on the more precarious narrow paths, the cobs had remained remarkably calm. Even little Madoc had scrambled nimbly over the stony paths, and Gerald had soon felt quite safe. He had decided to put the upsetting interlude with Gwyneira behind him. Fine, the girl had prevailed against his will, but he wouldn't let that happen again. This wild little Welsh princess needed to be reined in. Gerald was optimistic in that regard: Lucas would demand impeccable behavior of his wife, and Gwyneira had been raised to live at a gentleman's side. She might like hunting and training dogs better, but in the long run, she would acquiesce to fate.

The travelers reached the Avon River as daylight was fading, and the riders were ferried across the river. There was even enough time to load the sheep onto the ferry before the hikers arrived, so Helen's companions could only curse about a ferry soiled with sheep dung, but not about delays.

The London girls stared enchanted into the river's crystal clear water; until that moment, they had only ever known the dirty, foul-smelling Thames. Helen didn't care about anything anymore; she longed only for a bed. She hoped the reverend would take her in like a proper host. And he must have prepared something for the girls; he couldn't possibly be sending them off to their respective homes that day.

Exhausted, Helen stood in front of the hotel and the stable with stalls for rent and asked for directions to the parsonage. She saw Gwyneira and Mr. Warden as they were emerging from the stables. They had left the animals in good hands and were now looking forward to a banquet. Helen felt a profound pang of envy for her friend. How she would have liked to freshen up in a clean hotel room and sit at a set table. But she still had to march through the streets of Christchurch and make arrangements with the pastor. The girls behind her muttered quietly among themselves, and the little ones wept from exhaustion.

Fortunately, it was not far to the church; in those days nothing was far in all of Christchurch. Helen had only to lead her girls around three street corners before they were standing in front of the parsonage. Compared to Helen's father's home and the Thornes' house, the yellow-painted building made a meager impression, and the church next door hardly made a better one. Nevertheless, the house door was adorned with a beautiful brass door-knocker in the shape of a lion's head. Daphne boldly made use of it.

At first nothing happened. Then a grumpy, broad-faced girl appeared in the doorframe.

"What do you all want, then?" she asked inhospitably.

All the girls except Daphne stepped back in fear. Helen stepped forward.

"First, miss, we would like to wish you a good evening," Helen declared resolutely. "And then I would like to speak with Reverend Baldwin. My name is Helen Davenport. Lady Brennan must have mentioned me in a letter. And these are the girls the reverend wrote to London for in order to find them positions here."

The young woman nodded and assumed a somewhat friendlier expression. Still she could not bring herself greet the group properly, and instead cast deprecatory glances at the orphans. "I believe my mother did not expect you until tomorrow. I'll tell her you're here."

The young girl turned to go, but Helen called her back.

"Miss Baldwin, the children and I have just made a journey of eighteen thousand miles. Do you not think that common courtesy requires that you ask us to come in and offer us a place to sit?"

The girl made a face. "You can come in, if you want," she said. "But not them brats. Who knows what sort of vermin they'll bring in after their passage in steerage. My mother definitely won't want that in her house."

Helen boiled with rage, but restrained herself.

"Then I'll wait out here as well. I shared a cabin with these girls, so if they have vermin, so have I."

"Suit yourself," the girl said, unconcerned, as she shuffled back into her house and shut the door behind her.

"A proper lady!" Daphne said with a smirk. "I must not have quite understood what you were trying to teach us, Miss Davenport."

Helen should have reprimanded her, but she lacked the energy. Besides, if the mother acted in as un-Christian a manner as her daughter, she would still need to have a little fight left in her.

Mrs. Baldwin appeared very quickly and made an effort to be friendly. She was shorter and less plump than her daughter and lacked her frying-pan face. Her features were instead rather hawkish; she had small, narrowly spaced eyes and a mouth that had to force itself to smile.

"This is quite a surprise, Miss Davenport. But Mrs. Brennan did indeed mention you—and very positively, if I may say so. Please come right in. Belinda is preparing the guest room for you as we speak. Now, we'll have to put up the girls for a night too, although..." She deliberated briefly, apparently going through a list of names in her mind. "The Lavenders and Mrs. Godewind live nearby. I can send someone there straightaway. Perhaps you would like to take your girls to be received tonight. The remaining children can sleep in the stables. But first come in, Miss Davenport, come in. It's getting cold out here."

Helen sighed. She would have loved to accept the invitation, but of course that wouldn't be right.

"Mrs. Baldwin, the girls are cold too. They've come twelve miles on foot and require a bed and a warm meal. And until I hand them over to their employers, I am responsible for them. That is what I agreed to with the director of the orphanage, and that is what I was paid for. So please show me where the girls will be staying first, and then I will gladly accept your hospitality."

Mrs. Baldwin made a face but said nothing more. Instead, she dug a key out of a pocket on the wide apron she wore over an expansive housedress and led Helen and the girls around to the side of the house. Here there was a stall for a horse and a cow. A pungent-smelling haystack next to it had a few blankets thrown over it to make it more comfortable. Helen gave in to the inevitable.

"You heard her, girls. Tonight you'll be sleeping here," she instructed the girls. "Spread out your bedsheets—nice and carefully; otherwise, your clothes will be covered in hay. There will no doubt be water for washing up in the kitchen. I will see to it that it is available for you to use. I will come back later to make sure you have done your bedtime chores like proper Christian girls. First wash and then go to bed." Helen wanted to sound strict, but tonight she could not quite manage it. She wouldn't have wanted to strip down and wash with cold water in this stall. For that reason, she already knew that her inspection tonight would not be all that thorough. The girls did not seem to take her instructions to heart. Instead of acknowledging her with a proper "Yes, Miss Davenport," they inundated their teacher with questions.

"Are we not going to get anything to eat?"

"I can't sleep on the straw, Miss Davenport, I'll be sick!"

"There are bound to be fleas!"

"Can't we come with you, Miss Davenport? And what about these people that might come tonight? Do they want to take us, Miss Davenport?"

Helen sighed. She had tried throughout the trip to prepare the girls for their impending separation when they arrived, but it didn't seem like a good idea to tear the group apart that night. However, she also didn't want to prejudice Mrs. Baldwin against the girls and herself any more than she already had. So she answered evasively.

"Clean yourselves up first, and settle down, girls. Everything will work out, so don't worry." She stroked Laurie's and Mary's blonde hair. The children were visibly exhausted. Dorothy even made Rosemary's bed since she was already almost asleep. Helen nodded with approval.

"I will check up on you again later," she declared. "I promise!"

8

"The girls seem rather spoiled," Mrs. Baldwin remarked with a forbearing expression. "I hope they will actually be of some use to their future employers."

"They are children." Helen sighed. Hadn't she already had this conversation with Lucinda Greenwood, who was on the London orphanage committee? "To be honest, only two of them are even old enough to take a position. But they are all well behaved and skilled. I do not think anyone will have complaints."

Mrs. Baldwin seemed provisionally placated upon hearing that. She led Helen to the guest room, and for the first time that day, the young woman was pleasantly surprised. The room was bright and clean, with floral wallpaper and gardenias arranged invitingly in country-home style, and the bed looked big and comfortable. Helen breathed a sigh of relief. She may have been stranded in the backwoods, but here was evidence of civilization. Just then, the heavyset girl appeared with a large pot of warm water, which she emptied into Helen's washbasin.

"Freshen yourself up a bit, Miss Davenport," Mrs. Baldwin told her. "After that we'll expect you at dinner. It won't be anything special; we weren't prepared for guests, after all. But if you like chicken and mashed potatoes..."

Helen smiled. "I'm so hungry that I would eat the chicken and the potatoes raw. And the girls..."

Mrs. Baldwin seemed ready to lose her patience. "The girls will be taken care of," she declared abrasively. "I'll see you in a moment, then, Miss Davenport."

Helen took her time washing herself thoroughly, letting her hair down, and then pinning it back up. She contemplated whether it was worth changing her clothes. Helen owned only a few dresses, two of which were dirty through and through. She had been saving her best outfit for meeting Howard. On the other hand, she couldn't appear at dinner with the Baldwins in a ragged and sweaty dress. In the end, she decided on the navy-blue velvet dress. Something festive was in order for her first evening in her new homeland.

The food was already being served when Helen finally stepped into the Baldwins' dining room. Here too the furnishings trumped her expectations. The sideboard, table, and chairs were made of heavy teak and decorated with artistic carvings. Either the Baldwins had brought the furniture from England, or Christchurch could boast excellent joiners. This last thought comforted Helen. If worse came to worst, she could get used to a wooden house if its interior was comfortably furnished.

Her tardiness caused her some unease, but with the exception of the Baldwins' daughter, who seemed rather spoiled, everyone stood up at once to welcome her. In addition to Mrs. Baldwin and Belinda, there were the reverend and a young vicar. Reverend Baldwin was a tall, gaunt man with a serious demeanor. He was formally dressed—his dark brown three-piece tweed suit appeared almost too elegant for the domestic table—and he did not smile when he held out his hand to Helen. Instead, he seemed to be sizing her up.

"Are you the daughter of a fellow clergyman?" he inquired in a sonorous voice that she could easily imagine filling a chapel.

Helen nodded and told him about Liverpool. "I know that the circumstances of my visit to your home are somewhat unusual," she admitted, blushing. "But we all follow the way of the Lord, and he does not always lead us along the beaten path."

Reverend Baldwin nodded. "That is indeed true, Miss Davenport," he replied gravely. "No one knows that better than we do. I too had not expected that my church would take me to the ends of the earth. But this is a very promising place. With God's help we'll turn it into a thriving city imbued with Christianity. You probably know that Christchurch is supposed to become a bishopric..."

Helen nodded enthusiastically. She likewise gathered why Reverend Baldwin had not turned down the call to New Zealand despite his apparent loyalty to England. The man seemed to have ambitions—though perhaps not the connections one doubtless needed to receive a bishop's appointment in England. Here, on the other hand...Baldwin undoubtedly had high hopes. But was he as able a minister as he was a strategist of church politics?

Regardless, Helen thought the young vicar at Baldwin's side considerably kinder. He smiled graciously as Baldwin introduced him as William Chester, and his handshake was warm and friendly. Thin and pale, with a bony, nondescript face, Chester had delicate features, a too-long nose, and a too-wide mouth. But his lively and clever brown eyes made up for all that.

"Mr. O'Keefe has already been raving about you to me," he explained enthusiastically after he had taken his seat at Helen's side and shoveled generous amounts of chicken and mashed potatoes onto her plate. "He was so happy to receive your letter...I'd bet he'll come running here in the next few days, as soon as he hears about the arrival of the *Dublin*. He's hoping for another letter. How surprised he'll be to find you here already, miss!" Vicar Chester was so enthusiastic it was as though he'd introduced the young couple himself.

"In the next few days?" Helen asked, taken aback. She had expected to meet Howard the following day. Surely a messenger could be sent to his house.

"Well, yes, news doesn't travel all that quickly to Haldon," Chester said. "You should allow at least a week. But it could go more quickly. Didn't Gerald Warden arrive with the *Dublin* as well? His son mentioned he was en route. Once he's back, word will get around fast. No need to fret!"

"And until your fiancé arrives, you are most welcome here," Mrs. Baldwin assured her, even if her face suggested otherwise.

Helen nevertheless felt uncertain. Was Haldon not a suburb of Christchurch? Just how much farther would she have to go before she reached her final destination?

She was just about to ask when the door was flung open. Without so much as a hello or by-your-leave, Daphne and Rosemary stormed in. Both had already let their hair down for sleep, and hay stalks were caught in Rosie's brown locks. Daphne's unruly red tresses framed her face as though it were swathed in flames. Her eyes too threw out sparks as she took in the reverend's heavily laden table. Helen was instantly wracked with guilt. Judging by Daphne's expression, no one had given the girls anything to eat yet.

But for the moment, the two girls appeared to have other concerns. Rosemary ran to Helen and pulled on her skirt. "Miss Davenport, Miss Davenport, they're taking Laurie away! Please, you have to do something. Mary's screaming and crying and Laurie is too."

"And they want to take Elizabeth too!" cried Daphne.

"Please, Miss Davenport, do something!"

Helen leaped to her feet. If Daphne, who was usually so unflappable, was this alarmed, something terrible must have happened.

She looked around suspiciously.

"What is going on here?" she demanded.

Mrs. Baldwin rolled her eyes. "Nothing, Miss Davenport. As I already told you, we could hand two of the orphans over to their employers tonight. They are here to pick up the girls." She took a list from her pocket. "Here: Laurie Alliston goes to the Lavenders and Elizabeth Beans to Mrs. Godewind. Everything is in order. I do not understand why such a fuss is being made about it." She looked at Daphne and Rosemary coldly. The little one started to cry. Daphne, however, returned her gaze with eyes ablaze.

"Laurie and Mary are twins," Helen explained. She was furious, but forced herself to remain calm. "They have never been separated before. I do not understand how they could have been placed with different families. There must be some mistake. And Elizabeth surely does not want to leave without saying good-bye. Please, Reverend, you must come along and clear this up." Helen decided to no longer bother with the coldhearted Mrs. Baldwin. The children fell within the reverend's purview, and it was high time he did something for them.

The pastor got to his feet, though clearly against his will.

"No one told us they were twins," he explained as he walked thoughtfully to the stables beside Helen. "Naturally, it seemed likely that the girls were sisters, but placing them in the same household is out of the question. There are hardly any English servants here. There's a waiting list for these girls. We can't give one family two girls."

"But they'll be useless to anyone alone; the children cling to each other like ivy," Helen explained.

"They will have to be separated," the reverend responded curtly.

In front of the stables were two vehicles, one of them a delivery wagon to which two bored bays were hitched. A spirited pony that could hardly stand still pulled an elegant black chaise beside the wagon. A tall, haggard man held it with a light hand on the reins, mumbling a few soothing words to it now and then. He looked upset. Shaking his head, he kept looking to the stables, where the girls' crying and wailing had not abated. Helen thought she recognized a sympathetic look in his gaze.

Seated among the cushions of the chaise was a frail older woman. She was dressed in black, and her snow-white hair, pinned up beneath her hat, was a striking contrast. Her skin tone was very light, smooth as porcelain and creased by only a few wrinkles, like old silk. Elizabeth stood before her and curtsied beautifully. The old lady seemed to have a friendly and gracious manner. Every now and then, though, she and her driver glanced with irritation and sympathy in the direction of the stables.

"Jones," the woman finally said to her driver as Helen and the reverend passed by. "Couldn't you go in and put a stop to that howling? It does bother us so. Those children are going to cry their eyes out! Please do find out what the matter is and resolve the problem."

The driver tied the reins to the post and stood up. He did not seem especially enthusiastic about the task before him. Comforting children did not likely count among his usual chores.

In the meantime, the old lady had noticed Reverend Baldwin and greeted him in a friendly manner.

"Good evening, Reverend! Good to see you. But I don't want to keep you since your presence seems to be required in there."

She indicated the stables, at which her driver lowered himself back down into his seat with a sigh of relief. If the reverend was seeing to it, then his services were no longer necessary.

Baldwin seemed to be considering whether he should introduce Helen and the lady to each other before he entered the stables. However, he abandoned the idea and headed straight into the uproar.

Mary and Laurie were sobbing and holding each other tightly while a powerful woman attempted to pry them from each other. A broad-shouldered but passive man stood helplessly to the side. Even Dorothy seemed unsure whether to take action or pray and flee.

"Why don't you just take both of them?" she asked desperately. "Please, you can see it won't work this way."

The man seemed to agree. With a forceful tone in his voice, he turned to his wife. "Yes, Anna, we should ask the reverend to give us both girls. The girl is still too young and tender. She won't be able to do the hard work alone. But if the two work together..."

"If the two remain together, they'll just gossip and not get anything done!" the woman replied angrily. Helen looked into the woman's cold blue eyes, which belonged to a bright, self-satisfied face. "We only asked for one—and we're only taking one with us."

"Then just take me!" Dorothy offered. "I'm bigger and stronger and..."

Anna Lavender seemed rather taken with this solution. Pleased, she eyed Dorothy's considerably stronger build.

But Helen shook her head. "That is very Christian of you, Dorothy," she declared with a side-glance at the Lavenders and the reverend. "But it does not solve the problem, it only delays it another day. Your new employers will come tomorrow, and then Laurie would have to go with them. No, Reverend, Mr. Lavender, we must find some way to keep the twins together. Are there no neighboring families looking for maids? Then the two could at least see each other during their free time."

"And whine for each other the rest of the day!" Mrs. Lavender interjected. "It's not an option. I'll take this girl, or another. But only one."

Helen looked imploringly at the reverend. However, he made no move to support her.

"I can only agree with Mrs. Lavender," he said. "The sooner the girls are separated, the better. So listen, Laurie and Mary. God brought you to this country together, which was gracious of Him—He could have chosen only one of you and left the other back in England. But now He's leading you down different paths. This doesn't mean forever; you'll surely see each other at Sunday service or at least at the high holidays. God has not forsaken you, and He knows what He is doing. We have been charged with following His commands. You will be a good maid for the Lavenders, Laurie. And Mary will go with the Willards tomorrow. Both are good Christian families. You will get enough to eat, clothes to wear, and they will ensure you lead a Christian life. There is nothing to fear, Laurie, if you go with the Lavenders now, like a good girl. If there's no other way, Mr. Lavender will have to take the rod to you."

Mr. Lavender did not look at all like the kind of man who would beat little girls. On the contrary, he gazed with evident sympathy at Mary and Laurie.

"Now look, children, we live here in Christchurch," he said, in an effort to comfort the distraught children. "And all the families in the area come here every so often to shop and attend service. I don't know the Willards, but we could certainly contact them. Then, whenever they come here, we'll let you off, and you can spend the whole day with your sister. Does that make you feel better?"

Laurie nodded, but Helen wondered whether she really understood. Who knew where these Willards lived—it wasn't a good sign that Mr. Lavender did not even know them. And would they be as understanding with their little maid as he was? Would they even bring Mary along when they made their occasional shopping trips to town?

Laurie now seemed overcome by grief and exhaustion. She allowed herself to be pulled away from her sister. Dorothy handed Mr. Lavender Laurie's bundle. Helen kissed her good-bye on the forehead.

"We'll all write you!" she promised.

Laurie nodded listlessly while Mary continued to cry.

It broke Helen's heart when the Lavenders led the little girl out. She then heard Daphne speaking to Dorothy in a low voice.

"I told you! Miss Davenport can't do anything about it," the girl whispered. "She's nice, but she's in the same boat we are. Tomorrow her man's coming to take her away, and she has to go with this Mr. O'Keefe, same as Laurie with the Lavenders."

Anger bubbled up in Helen, but it quickly gave way to a burning feeling of disquiet. After all, Daphne wasn't wrong. What would she do if Howard didn't want to marry her? What would happen if he didn't like her? She couldn't return to England. But were there even positions for governesses or teachers here?

Helen did not want to think about it any longer. She would have liked to crawl into some corner and cry, just as she had done as a little girl. But that had not been an option after her mother died. From that point on, she'd had to be strong. And right at this moment, that meant patiently letting herself be introduced to the old woman who had come for Elizabeth.

The reverend braced himself, but there appeared to be no drama this time. On the contrary, Elizabeth seemed elated.

"Miss Davenport, this is Mrs. Godewind," she said, introducing them before the reverend could even say anything. "She's from Sweden! That's way in the north, even farther away from here than England. There's snow there the whole winter—the whole winter! Her husband was captain of a big ship, and he would sometimes take her with him on his trips. She's been to India! And America! And Australia!"

Mrs. Godewind laughed at Elizabeth's excitement. She had a kind face that hardly showed her age.

She held out a friendly hand to Helen. "Hilda Godewind. So you're Elizabeth's teacher. She raves about you; did you know that? And about a certain Jamie O'Hara." She winked.

Helen returned the smile and the wink, and introduced herself by her full name. "Do I understand correctly? You'll be taking Elizabeth into your service?" she inquired.

Mrs. Godewind nodded. "If Elizabeth likes. I do not by any means want to tear her from here like those people just did with that little girl. That was reprehensible! I had somehow thought that the girls would be older."

Helen nodded. Now on the verge of tears, she would have loved to pour out her heart to this woman. Mrs. Godewind sized her up.

"I can already tell that you're not happy with this arrangement," she remarked. "And you're just as exhausted as the girls—did you come over the Bridle Path on foot? That is unacceptable! You should have had mules sent for you. And I, of course, should not have come until tomorrow. The girls would no doubt have preferred to stay together another night. But when I heard that they would be sleeping in the stables..."

"I'm happy to come with you, Mrs. Godewind." Elizabeth beamed. "And I can read *Oliver Twist* to you first thing tomorrow. Can you imagine, Miss Davenport, Mrs. Godewind doesn't know *Oliver Twist*! I told her that we read it together on the trip."

Mrs. Godewind nodded amiably. "Then gather your things, child, and say good-bye to your friends. You like her too, don't you, Jones?" She turned to her driver, who naturally nodded obligingly.

Shortly thereafter, as Elizabeth made herself comfortable with her bundle next to Mrs. Godewind and the two fell once again into excited conversation, the driver took Helen aside.

"Miss Davenport, the girl makes a good impression, but is she trustworthy? It would break my heart if Mrs. Godewind were disappointed. She's been so looking forward to having a little English girl."

Helen assured him that they would not find a more clever or pleasant child anywhere.

"So does she want the girl for company? I mean...one usually engages older and better-educated young women for that," she said.

The servant nodded. "True, but first you have to find them. And Mrs. Godewind can't afford all that much; she only has a small pension. My wife and I take care of her household, but my wife is Maori, you know...she can do Mrs. Godewind's hair, cook for her, and care for her, but she can't read to her or tell her stories. That's why we thought of an English girl. She'll live with me and my wife and help around the house a bit, but most importantly, she'll offer Mrs. Godewind company. You can rest assured; she won't lack for anything."

Helen nodded, comforted. At least Elizabeth would be well taken care of. It was a little ray of light at the end of an awful day.

"Do come the day after tomorrow for tea," Mrs. Godewind said to Helen before the chaise rode away.

Elizabeth waved happily.

Helen no longer had the strength to return the stables to comfort Mary, nor did she manage to make further conversation at Reverend Baldwin's table. She was still hungry, but she comforted herself with the thought that her uneaten leftovers would, with any luck, do the girls some good. She excused herself politely and then collapsed into bed. Tomorrow could hardly be any worse.

The next morning the sun rose beaming over Christchurch and bathed everything in warm and gentle light. The window in Helen's room offered a breathtaking view of the mountain chain that overlooked the Canterbury Plains, and the streets of the little town looked clean and inviting. The scent of fresh bread and tea drifted up from the Baldwins' breakfast room. Helen's mouth watered. She hoped this promising start to the day could be taken as a good omen. Surely she had only imagined yesterday that Mrs. Baldwin was unfriendly and coldhearted, her daughter mean and ill mannered, and Reverend Baldwin bigoted and wholly uninterested in the happiness of his parishioners. In the light of this new morning, she planned to judge the pastor and his family more favorably. First, however, she needed to check on the girls.

In the stables, she found Vicar Chester trying to console Mary, who was still in tears, to no avail. The little girl cried, asking for her sister between sobs. She did not even take the pastry that the young pastor held out to her, as though a little sugar could alleviate all the suffering in the world. The child looked totally exhausted; she had clearly not gotten a wink of sleep. Helen could not bring herself to think about handing the girl over to total strangers.

"If Laurie is crying like this and not eating like this, the Lavenders will definitely send her back," Dorothy speculated hopefully.

Daphne rolled her eyes. "You don't even believe that yourself. The old lady'll beat her first, or lock her in the cleaning cupboard. And if she doesn't eat, she'll be happy she's saved on a meal. She's cold as a dog's nose, the piece of shit...oh, good morning, Miss Davenport. I hope you slept well at least." Daphne glowered disrespectfully at her teacher and made no attempt to apologize for her unsuitable language.

"As you yourself noted yesterday," Helen replied icily, "there was nothing I could do for Laurie. However, I will try to reestablish contact with the family. Yes, I slept very well, as I'm sure you did. No doubt that was the first time you let yourself be moved by your feelings for others."

Daphne lowered her head. "I'm sorry, Miss Davenport."

Helen was astonished. Had she really achieved such an improvement in the girl's behavior?

Later that morning, little Rosemary's future employers appeared. Helen had been apprehensive about this handoff, but was pleasantly surprised. The McLarens, a short rotund man with a soft, chubby face and his no less well-fed wife, who looked like a doll with her apple-red cheeks and round blue eyes, arrived on foot around eleven o'clock. As it turned out, they owned the Christchurch bakery—the fresh rolls and pastries whose aroma had woken Helen that morning were their doing. Because Mr. McLaren began work before the sun came up and went to bed correspondingly early, Mrs. Baldwin had not wanted to bother the family the day before, informing them instead first thing that morning of the girl's arrival. They'd closed the shop to come pick Rosemary up.

"God, she's still just a child!" Mrs. McLaren marveled when Rosemary curtsied anxiously before her. "And we've got to fatten you up, you little bean pole. What's your name, dear?"

Mrs. McLaren then turned accusingly to Mrs. Baldwin, who received these complaints without comment. As she began talking to Rosemary, she hunched over amiably and smiled at her.

"Rosie," the little girl whispered.

Mrs. McLaren ruffled her hair. "Now what a pretty name. Rosie, we thought you might like to come live with us and help out a little in the house and kitchen. In the bakery too, of course. Do you like baking cakes, Rosemary?"

Rosie considered. "I like to eat cake," she said.

The McLarens laughed, making a chortling sound while Rosemary responded with a happy twittering.

"That's the best place to start!" Mr. McLaren explained seriously. "Only someone who likes to eat can bake well. What do you think, Rosie, will you come with us?"

Helen breathed a sigh of relief when Rosemary nodded gravely. The McLarens did not seem at all surprised to be welcoming more of a foster child than a servant into their home.

"I once got to know a youth from an orphanage in London," Mr. McLaren said, chatting with Helen while his wife helped Rosie pack her things. "My master had asked for a fourteen-year-old who would catch on immediately, and they sent a tot who looked like he was ten. Still, he was an industrious boy. The master's wife fed him well, and since then he's become a well-regarded journeyman baker. If our Rosie takes to it like that, we won't have reason to complain about the costs of bringing her up." He laughed and placed a little bag of baked goods he had brought along for the girls into Helen's hand.

"But distribute them properly, girl," he exhorted her. "I knew there would certainly be more children, and our Madam Pastor is not exactly known for her generosity."

At that, Daphne stuck her hand out hungrily for the pastries. She had clearly not eaten breakfast, at least not a sufficient one. Mary, on the other hand, remained inconsolable and only sobbed more loudly when Rosemary left too.

Helen decided to try to distract them and informed the girls that she would be holding lessons that day just as she had on the ship. Until the girls were with their families, it was better for them to be learning than sitting around doing nothing. In consideration of the fact that they were in a pastor's house, Helen reached for the Bible for lessons.

Daphne began to read the story of the wedding at Cana, clearly bored, and closed the book gladly when Mrs. Baldwin appeared a short time later. She was accompanied by a tall, squarely built man.

"It's very commendable of you, Miss Davenport, to dedicate yourself to the girls' edification," the pastor's wife declared. "But instead you really could have been working on quieting this child."

She looked antagonistically over at the still-weeping Mary. "It doesn't matter now though. This is Mr. Willard, who will be taking Mary Alliston with him to his farm."

"She's to live alone with a farmer?" Helen was incensed.

Mrs. Baldwin raised her eyes to heaven. "For goodness' sake, of course not! That would be against all propriety. No, no, Mr. Willard, naturally, has a wife, and seven children."

Mr. Willard nodded proudly. He seemed kind. His face, thoroughly creased by laugh lines, wore the traces of hard work in the open air in all weather. His hands were calloused paws, and his muscular figure was visible beneath his clothes.

"The older boys are already working hard with me in the fields," the farmer explained. "But my wife needs help with the little ones. In the house, and in the stables too, of course. And she doesn't like the Maori women. She says her children should only be raised by good, Christian folk. So which is our girl? She should be strong, if possible; the work is hard!"

Mr. Willard looked just as appalled as Helen when Mrs. Baldwin introduced Mary to him. "That little thing? This must be a joke, madam! That would just make eight kids in the house."

Mrs. Baldwin looked at him sternly. "If you don't spoil the girl, she is definitely capable of hard work. In London they assured us that every girl had turned at least thirteen and was fit for any kind of work. So, do you want the girl or not?"

Mr. Willard seemed to waver. "My wife really needs the help," he said almost by way of excuse in Helen's direction. "The next child's coming into the world around Christmas, so someone's got to help her out. Well, come on then, little one, we'll make this work. Come on, up, what're you waiting on? And why are you crying? Lord above, I really don't need any more problems." Without giving Mary another look, Mr. Willard left the stables. Mrs. Baldwin shoved the little girl's bundle into her hand.

"Go with him. And be an obedient maid," she told the child. Mary obeyed without protest, crying all the while.

"Let's hope the wife shows the girl a little sympathy," sighed Vicar Chester. He had watched the scene as helplessly as Helen.

Daphne snorted. "You try showing sympathy with eight tykes hanging on your apron," she said, "and every year your husband making you another. But there's no money and he drinks the last bit away. Your sympathy'll get caught in your throat. Then you just try not hurting anyone."

Vicar Chester looked at the girl in shock. He was obviously asking himself how this girl was going to work out as a demure servant to one of Christchurch's notables. Daphne's eruptions no longer surprised Helen, however—and she found herself increasingly sympathetic toward them.

"Now, now, Daphne. Mr. Willard does not give the impression of drinking his money away," she said, in an effort to placate the girl. She couldn't fault Daphne; she was undoubtedly right. Mrs. Willard would not spare Mary. She had too many children of her own to be able to worry about her too. The little girl would not be anything more to her than cheap labor. The vicar had to see that too. In any event, he did not say a word regarding Daphne's insolence, and instead only made a small gesture of blessing toward the girls before leaving the stables. No doubt he had already left his duties unattended long enough to have earned the reverend's censure.

Though Helen felt she should open the Bible again, neither she nor her pupils had the heart for edifying texts.

"I'm anxious to see what happens to us next," Daphne said, saying aloud what all the remaining girls were thinking. "These people must live far away if they haven't appeared yet to pick up their slaves.

Start practicing milking cows, Dorothy." She motioned to the pastor's cow, which they had relieved of a few liters of milk the night before. Which is to say that Mrs. Baldwin had not let the children partake of the leftovers from dinner, and had instead sent some thin soup and old bread out to the stables. The girls certainly would not miss the reverend's cheerful house.

9

"How long does it take to ride from Kiward Station to Christchurch?" Gwyneira inquired. She sat with Gerald Warden and the Brewsters at a heavily laden breakfast table in the White Hart hotel. Though not especially elegant, it was clean, and after the stress of the day before, she had slept like the dead in her comfortable bed.

"Well now, that depends on the man and the horse," Gerald remarked moodily. "It's about fifty miles. With the sheep, we'll need about two days. But a mail rider who's in a hurry and changes horses a few times could make it in a few hours. The way isn't paved, but it's mostly flat. A good rider can gallop the whole way."

Gwyneira wondered if Lucas Warden was such a rider—and why the devil he hadn't leaped on his horse yesterday to come and see his bride. Naturally, he might not have heard anything about the *Dublin*'s arrival yet. But his father had already informed him of the ship's departure date, and it was well known that ships needed between 75 and 130 days to make the crossing. The *Dublin* had been underway for 104 days. So why wasn't Lucas waiting here for her? Was he indispensable at Kiward Station? Or was he just not that eager to meet his future wife? Gwyneira would have liked to set out that day to see her new home and finally stand across from the man to whom she had blindly engaged herself. Lucas had to feel the same way.

Gerald laughed when she made a comment to this effect.

"My Lucas has patience," he replied. "And a sense of style. He likes grand entrances. He probably couldn't in his wildest dreams imagine meeting you for the first time in sweaty riding clothes. In that respect he's all gentleman."

"But I wouldn't think anything of it!" Gwyneira objected. "And wouldn't he be staying in this hotel? He would have been able to change clothes beforehand if he thought I cared so much about formalities."

"I think this hotel isn't up to his standards," murmured Gerald. "Just be patient, Gwyneira, you'll like him."

Mrs. Brewster smiled and primly laid her silverware aside. "It really is very nice when a young man affects a certain restraint," she remarked. "After all, we're not among savages. In England you wouldn't have met your fiancé in a hotel either, but rather at tea or at his home."

Gwyneira had to concede that she was right, but she couldn't bring herself to give up all her dreams of a ready-for-anything pioneer husband, a farmer and gentleman tied to the earth, driven by a need to explore. Lucas simply had to be different from all those bloodless viscounts and baronets back home.

Suddenly she felt renewed hope. Maybe this shyness of his didn't have anything to do with Lucas and was merely the result of his overly proper upbringing. No doubt he believed Gwyneira would be just as stiff and difficult as his governesses and tutors once were. In addition to which, she was of noble rank. Surely Lucas was simply afraid of making the smallest mistake in her presence. Maybe he was even afraid of her.

Gwyneira tried to comfort herself with these thoughts, but she did not entirely succeed. For her, curiosity would have triumphed over fear. But maybe Lucas really was shy and just needed a little time to warm up. Gwyneira thought about her experiences with dogs and horses: the shiest and most reserved animals were often the best once you found the right way to approach them. Why should it be any different with men? When Gwyneira finally got to know Lucas, he would certainly come out of his shell.

In the meantime, Gwyneira's patience was further put to the test. Gerald Warden had no intention of setting off for Kiward Station that day. He still had a few things to accomplish in Christchurch and had to organize the transport of the many pieces of furniture and other household items he had brought in from Europe. All of that, he disclosed to a disappointed Gwyneira, would take a day or two. She should rest up in the meantime; surely the long journey had worn her out.

The journey had bored her more than worn her out. The last thing she wanted was more inactivity. So, she decided she'd go for a ride that morning—and instantly found herself in a disagreement with Gerald over that. At first Gerald didn't say a word when she announced that she was going to have Igraine saddled. It was only when Mrs. Brewster observed with horror that one couldn't possibly let a lady go out on horseback without accompaniment that the sheep baron made an about-face. Under no circumstances would he allow his future daughter-in-law to do anything considered unbecoming in the best circles. Unfortunately, there were no stable boys and, naturally, not yet any ladies' maids who could accompany the girl on her ride. The request itself seemed foreign to the hotelier: in Christchurch, as he made absolutely clear to Mrs. Brewster, people did not ride for pleasure, only to get from one place to another. The man could certainly understand Gwyneira's reasoning that she wanted to get her horse moving after the long period of immobility on the ship, but he was neither willing nor able to provide her with an escort. In the end, Lady Barrington suggested her son, who immediately declared that he was prepared to ride along on Madoc. The fourteen-year-old viscount was not the ideal chaperone, but Gerald did not seem to notice, and Mrs. Brewster held her tongue so as not to offend Lady Barrington. Gwyneira had thought young Charles rather dull on the trip, but he proved to be a spirited rider—and sufficiently discreet. Thus he did not reveal to his horrified mother that Gwyneira's ladies' saddle had long since arrived but instead confirmed that only men's saddles were available. Then he pretended that he could not control Madoc and let the stallion storm off from the hotel's yard, which gave Gwyneira the opportunity to follow him without any further discussion about propriety. They both laughed as they left Christchurch behind at a brisk trot.

"Whoever makes it to that house over there first!" Charles called, spurring Madoc to a gallop. He did not have eyes for Gwyneira's high-riding skirts. A horse race over endless grasslands was still more intoxicating to him than a woman's figure.

Around noon the pair of riders returned, having amused themselves terrifically. The horses snorted contentedly, Cleo seemed once more to be smiling from ear to ear, and Gwyneira even managed to adjust her skirts before they rode into town.

"In the long run I'm going to have to think of something," she murmured, draping the right side of her skirt modestly over her ankle—at which her dress naturally rose higher on the left side. "Maybe I'll just cut a slit into the back."

"That would only work as long as there wasn't any wind." Her young chaperone grinned. "And as long as you don't gallop. Otherwise, your skirt will fly up and people will be able to see your...ahem...well, whatever you have on underneath. My mother would probably faint!"

Gwyneira giggled. "That's true. Ah, I wish I could just wear pants. You men don't know just how good you have it."

That afternoon, at teatime, Gwyneira ventured out to find Helen. Of course, in doing so, she risked crossing paths with Howard O'Keefe, which Gerald would not appreciate. But she was burning with curiosity, and Gerald really couldn't dispute her presenting herself to the parish pastor. After all, this was the man who was supposed to preside at her wedding, so this was less a courtesy call than an obligation.

Gwyneira found the parsonage right away and was cheerfully shown in. Indeed, Mrs. Baldwin treated her guest as obsequiously as she would a member of the royal family. Gwyneira did not believe that this was due to her noble lineage—the Baldwins weren't fawning over the Silkhams—to them, Gerald Warden was the social giant. Likewise, they seemed to know Lucas. And though they had thus far been rather reticent about Howard O'Keefe, they could not praise Gwyneira's fiancé highly enough.

"An extremely cultivated young man," Mrs. Baldwin lauded.

"Impeccably raised and highly educated. A very mature and serious man," the reverend added.

"Very interested in art!" Vicar Chester declared with beaming eyes. "Well-read and intelligent. The last time he was here, we passed the whole night in such exciting conversation that I almost missed service in the morning."

Gwyneira became increasingly nauseated at these descriptions. Where was her farmer, her cowboy? Her hero out of the penny romances? Although there weren't any women here who needed to be rescued from the hands of the redskins, would an adventurous six-shooter hero have stayed up half the night talking with a pastor?

Helen, too, was quiet. She wondered why Chester did not express similar praise for Howard; besides, she could not get Laurie and Mary's crying out of her head. She was worried about the remaining girls, who were still awaiting their employers in the stables. It didn't even help that she had already seen Rosemary again. The little girl had appeared giggling at the parsonage in the afternoon, feeling extremely important with a basketful of pastries. This commission was her first assignment from Mrs. McLaren, and she was extremely proud to carry it out to everyone's satisfaction.

"Rosie sounds happy," Gwyneira said happily, having heard about the girl's visit.

"If only the others had been so well placed."

Under the pretext of needing some fresh air, Helen accompanied her friend outside after tea. The two women went for a stroll through the town's relatively wide streets and were finally able to talk openly. Helen almost lost her composure when, with tears in her eyes, she told Gwyneira about Mary and Laurie.

"And I don't get the feeling that they'll get over it," she finished. "True, time is supposed to heal all wounds, but in this case...I think it will kill them, Gwyn! They're just so young. And I can't stand to look at those bigoted Baldwins anymore. The reverend could certainly have done something for the girls. They keep a waiting list of families looking for servants. Surely they could have found two houses next to each other. Instead, they've sent Mary to this Willard family where the little thing is certain to be overwhelmed. Seven children, Gwyneira! And an eighth on the way. Mary's even supposed to help as a midwife."

Gwyneira sighed. "If only I'd been there. Perhaps Mr. Warden could do something. Kiward Station no doubt needs servants. And I need a chambermaid. Just look at my hair—that's what happens when I put it up myself."

Gwyneira did look a little wild.

Helen smiled through her tears, steering them back toward the Baldwins' house. "Come along," she invited Gwyneira. "Daphne can put your hair in order. And if no one else turns up for her or Dorothy, maybe you should speak with Mr. Warden. What will you bet the Baldwins will comply if he asks for Daphne or Dorothy?"

Gwyneira nodded. "And you could take the other," she suggested. "A proper household needs a maid; your Howard should see that. We just need to decide between ourselves who gets Dorothy and who has to put up with Daphne's cheeky mouth."

Before she could propose settling this question with a game of blackjack, they reached the parsonage, in front of which stood a coach. Helen realized her lovely plan could hardly become a reality. In the yard, Mrs. Baldwin was already chatting with an elderly couple while Daphne waited quietly off to the side. The girl looked like a paragon of virtue. Her dress was spotless and Helen had rarely seen her hair so primly and properly pinned up. Daphne must have done herself up especially for her meeting with her employers; apparently, she had asked about the people ahead of time. Her appearance seemed to particularly impress the woman, who was simply and neatly dressed herself. From beneath her small, unobtrusive hat decorated with a tiny veil, calm brown eyes in a bright face looked out. Her smile seemed open and friendly, and she obviously could not believe how perfectly chance had brought her and her new maid together. "We just came from Haldon the day before yesterday, and we wanted to set off again yesterday already. But then my tailor still had a few alterations to make to my order, and I said to Richard: let's stay and spoil ourselves with a dinner at the hotel. Richard was very excited when he heard from all the interesting people who had just arrived on the *Dublin*, and we had a very stimulating evening. And how lucky that Richard had the idea to ask straightaway about our girl here!" As the lady spoke, her features lit up, and she occasionally used her hands to emphasize a point. Helen thought her very nice. Richard, her husband, appeared more sedate, but just as friendly and good-tempered.

"Miss Davenport, Lady Silkham—Mr. and Mrs. Candler." Mrs. Baldwin introduced them, interrupting Mrs. Candler's endless monologue. "Miss Davenport accompanied the girls during the passage. She can tell you more about Daphne than I can. So I'll simply leave her now to your care and go look for the necessary papers for you. After that you can take the girl with you."

Mrs. Candler turned to Helen, just as chatty as she had been with the pastor's wife before. Helen did not have to do much to gather information about Daphne's future employment. In fact, the two of them gave a lengthy synopsis of their life thus far in New Zealand. Mr. Candler told Helen crankily about their first years in Lyttelton, which was still called Port Cooper at the time. Gwyneira, Helen, and the girls listened, raptly, to his stories of whale and seal hunting. Mr. Candler had not, however, braved the seas himself.

"No, no, that's for crazies who have nothing to lose. And back then I already had Olivia and the boys—so I wasn't about to slug it out with giant fish that would have just wanted to get me by the throat! It makes me a little sorry for the critters. The seals especially, they look at you so trustingly."

Instead, Mr. Candler had run a general store that was so successful that later, when the first settlers in the Canterbury Plains were beginning to build, he was able to afford a nice piece of farmland.

"But I realized quickly that I'm completely lost when it comes to sheep," he admitted freely. "Animal breeding is just not for me, or my Olivia either." He cast a loving gaze over his wife. "So we sold everything again and opened a store in Haldon. That's what we like—that's a life; there's enough to eat, and the area is growing. It's the best prospect for our boys."

The "boys"—the Candlers' three sons—ranged in age from sixteen to twenty-three. Helen noticed how Daphne's eyes lit up when Mr. Candler mentioned them. As long as the girl was clever about it and let her charms work, her allure couldn't fail to attract one of them. And though Helen could never picture her willful charge as a maid, she would be right where she belonged as a well-esteemed merchant, no doubt adored by the male clientele.

Helen's heart was beginning to brim with happiness for Daphne when Mrs. Baldwin returned to the yard from the stables, accompanied this time by a tall, broad-shouldered man with an angular face and inquisitive bright blue eyes. Those eyes took in the scene in the yard quick as a fox, glancing at the Candlers, during which his gaze remained markedly longer on Mrs. Candler than on her husband; then it passed over Gwyneira, Helen, and the girls. It was clear to Helen that she could not hold his attention. He seemed to find Gwyneira, Daphne, and Dorothy far more captivating. Nevertheless, his passing glance was enough to make Helen flush with embarrassment. Maybe it was because he did not look her in the face like a gentleman but rather seemed to be conducting an examination of her figure. But that could be a delusion or just her imagination...Helen sized up the man suspiciously, but could not accuse him of anything else. He even smiled disarmingly, even if it looked a bit masklike.

Helen, however, was not the only one who seemed ill at ease. Out of the corner of her eye, she saw Gwyneira instinctively retreat before the man, and Mrs. Candler's distaste was written all over her face. Her husband put his arm around her as though he wanted to clearly establish his right of ownership. The man leered when he noticed the gesture.

As Helen turned to the girls, she saw that Daphne looked alarmed and Dorothy appeared fearful. Mrs. Baldwin alone seemed not to sense that anything was amiss.

"And here we have Mr. Morrison," she said, introducing him placidly. "The future employer of Dorothy Carter. Say hello, Dorothy. Mr. Morrison will be taking you along right away."

Dorothy did not budge. She seemed to be paralyzed with fear. Her face turned pale, and her pupils widened.

"I..." the girl choked when she began to speak, but Mr. Morrison interrupted her with a booming laugh.

"Not so fast, Mrs. Baldwin, I want to look the little minx over first. After all, I can't bring just any girl home to my wife. So you're Dorothy."

The man approached the girl, who still did not budge—not even when he brushed a strand of hair from her face, stroking the tender flesh on her neck as if by accident in the process.

"A pretty little thing. My wife will be delighted. Tell me, are you good with your hands, little Dorothy?" The question seemed harmless enough, but even to Helen, who was completely ignorant in all things sexual, it was clear that she was being asked about more than her domestic skills. Gwyneira, who had read the word "lust" at least once before, caught the hungry expression in Morrison's eyes.

"Show me your hands now, Dorothy."

The man opened Dorothy's tightly closed fingers and gently ran his fingers over her right hand. It was more of a caress than an examination of her calluses. He held the hand tightly, definitely for longer than was socially acceptable. At some point Dorothy broke out of her frozen state. She withdrew her hand abruptly and took a step backward.

"No!" she said. "No, I...I won't go with you...I don't like you!" Terrified by her own audacity, she lowered her gaze.

"Now, now, Dorothy. You don't even know me." Mr. Morrison moved closer to the girl, who shrank under his penetrating gaze—or rather at Mrs. Baldwin's subsequent admonition:

"What sort of way to behave is that, Dorothy? You will apologize immediately!"

Dorothy shook her head forcefully. She would rather die than go with this man; she could not express in words the images that sprang to mind when his lustful eyes looked at her. Images from the poorhouse, of her mother in the arms of a man she was supposed to call "uncle." She vaguely recalled the hard, sinewy hands that reached for her one day, sliding under her skirt...Dorothy had cried and tried to defend herself. But the man had continued, stroking her and feeling his way to that unspeakable part of her body that you didn't even completely uncover when you washed. Dorothy had thought she would die of shame—but her mother had returned just in time, before the pain and fear became unbearable. She pushed the man away and came to her daughter's defense. Later she had held Dorothy in her arms, rocking, comforting, and warning her.

"You can never let that happen, Dottie! Don't let anyone touch you, whatever they promise beforehand. Don't even let them look at you like they'd do that. But that was my fault. I should have seen how he was looking at you. Never let the men here catch you alone, Dottie. Never! Will you promise me?"

Dorothy had promised and stayed true to her promise until her mother died shortly thereafter. Afterward she had been taken to the orphanage where she was safe. But now this man was staring at her—even more lustfully than her "uncle" had before. And she couldn't say no. She wasn't allowed. She belonged to him; the reverend himself would beat her if she refused. In a moment she would have to leave with this Morrison. On his horse, to his house...

Dorothy swallowed. "No! No, I'm not going. Miss Davenport! Please, Miss Davenport, you have to help me! Don't send me with him. Mrs. Baldwin, please...please!"

The girl sought refuge, leaning on Helen, then fled to Mrs. Baldwin when Mr. Morrison approached her, laughing.

"What's wrong with her?" he asked, appearing genuinely astonished when the pastor's wife rudely rebuffed him. "Is she perhaps sick? We'll put her straight to bed."

Dorothy looked with an almost mad gaze around the circle.

"He's the devil! Doesn't anyone else see it? Miss Silkham, please, Miss Silkham! Take me with you. You need a chambermaid. Please, I'll do anything! I don't want any money, I..."

In her desperation the girl fell to her knees in front of Gwyneira.

"Dorothy, calm yourself," Gwyneira said uncertainly. "Of course I'll ask Mr. Warden..."

Morrison seemed annoyed. "Can we put an end to this now?" he asked brusquely. Helen and Gwyneira ignored him, so he turned instead to Mrs. Baldwin. "The girl is out of her mind! But my wife needs the help, so I'll take her anyway. Don't try and pawn a different one off on me. I rode here well out of my way from the plains."

"You rode here?" Helen asked. "Then how did you expect to take the girl with you?"

"Behind me on my horse, of course. It'll be fun for her. You just have to hold on tight, little one."

"I…I won't do it," Dorothy stammered. "Please, please, don't ask me to." She knelt down before Mrs. Baldwin while Helen and Gwyneira looked on appalled and Mr. and Mrs. Candler looked disgusted.

"That's horrible," Mr. Candler said finally. "Say something, Mrs. Baldwin! If the girl won't go, you must find her a different placement. We'd be happy to take her along. In Haldon there are two or three families who could certainly use the help."

His wife nodded energetically.

Mr. Morrison inhaled sharply. "You don't want to indulge this little girl's whims, do you?" he asked Mrs. Baldwin with an incredulous expression on his face.

Dorothy whimpered.

Daphne had thus far observed the scene with an almost indifferent mien. She knew exactly what lay ahead for Dorothy, for she had lived—and survived—on the street long enough to comprehend Morrison's gaze better than Helen or Gwyneira. Men like him couldn't afford a maid in London. But there were enough children for them on the banks of the Thames who would do anything for a piece of bread. Children like Daphne. She knew precisely how you buried the fear, the pain, and the shame, how you separated your body from your mind when a shithead like that wanted "to play" again. She was strong. But it would crush Dorothy.

Daphne looked at Helen Davenport, who was just learning—plenty late, in Daphne's opinion—that you couldn't change the ways of the world, no matter how much you behaved like a lady. Then she looked at Gwyneira Silkham, who obviously still had to learn that as well.

But Gwyneira Silkham was strong. Under different circumstances, for example as the wife of a powerful sheep baron, she could have done something. But she hadn't come that far yet.

And then there were the Candlers: charming, kind people who would give her, little Daphne from the gutter, a once-in-a-lifetime chance. If she just played her cards right, she'd marry one of their heirs, lead a respectable life, have children, and become one of the region's "notables." Daphne could have laughed. Lady Daphne Candler—that sounded like something from one of Elizabeth's stories. Too beautiful to be real.

Daphne ended her reverie abruptly and turned to her friend.

"Get up, Dorothy! Don't howl like that," she snapped at the girl. "It's unbearable how you get so worked up. For my part, I don't care if we trade. You go with the Candlers. I'll go with him." Daphne indicated Mr. Morrison.

Helen and Gwyneira held their breath, and Mrs. Candler gasped. Dorothy raised her head slowly, revealing her face, which was red and swollen from crying. Mr. Morrison frowned.

"Is this a game? Red Rover, Red Rover? Who says I'm just going to trade our girl away?" he asked angrily. "This one was promised to me." He reached for Dorothy, who screamed in terror.

Daphne looked at him, the hint of a smile appearing on her lovely face. As though inadvertently, she ran her hand over her prim hairdo, freeing a few strands of glowing red hair.

"It won't be any loss to you," she breathed as the locks fell down over her shoulder.

Dorothy fled into Helen's arms.

Morrison grinned, and this time there was no disguising his pleasure. "Well, if it's like that..." he said and pretended to help Daphne fix her hair. "A red minx. My wife will be delighted. And you will surely be a good maid to her." His voice sounded like silk, but Helen felt as though she were being sullied by the sound of his voice alone. The other women seemed to feel the same way. Only Mrs. Baldwin was immune to feelings, regardless of what kind. She wrinkled her brow disapprovingly and appeared to seriously consider whether she should allow the girls to follow through with their exchange. Then she graciously handed the papers she'd prepared for Daphne to Mr. Morrison.

The girl looked up only once briefly before following the man out.

"Well, Miss Davenport?" Daphne asked. "Did I behave…like a lady?"

"I love you and will pray for you," she whispered as she watched the girl go.

Daphne laughed. "I thank you for your love. But you can save your prayers," she said bitterly. "First wait until you see what card your God pulls out of his sleeve for you!"

Helen cried herself to sleep that night after excusing herself from dinner with the Baldwins under the flimsiest of pretexts. She would have liked to leave the parsonage and curl up in the blanket Daphne had forgotten in the stall. She could have screamed at the very sight of Mrs. Baldwin, and the reverend's prayers made a mockery of the God her father had served. She had to get out. If only she could afford the hotel. If only it would have been even halfway decent for her to meet her fiancé without a go-between and chaperone. But it couldn't last much longer. Dorothy and the Candlers were on their way to Haldon. Tomorrow Howard would learn about her arrival.

Something Like Love

Canterbury Plains—West Coast

1852–1854

1

Gerald Warden and his baggage did little more than creep forward, though Cleo and the young flock kept a brisk pace. Gerald had needed to rent three wagons to transport his European purchases to Kiward Station, as well as Gwyneira's comprehensive dowry of occasional furniture, silver, and fine linen. Lady Silkham had not scrimped in that regard, going so far as to reach into the contents of her own trousseau. It first struck Gwyneira when they were unpacking how many useless extravagances her mother had packed in her chests and baskets—items that no one at Silkham Manor had needed for thirty years. What Gwyneira was supposed to do with them here at the edge of the world was a mystery, though Gerald seemed to hold the bric-a-brac in high regard and wanted to bring it all to Kiward Station straightaway. So three teams of sturdy horses and mules lurched across the Canterbury Plains. The rains had made the trails muddy in places, which dragged the trip out considerably. The spirited riding horses did not like the slow pace, and Igraine had been pulling at her reins all morning. Yet, to her own surprise, Gwyneira wasn't at all bored: she was enthralled by the endless landscape through which they rode, the silky carpet of grass on which the sheep would gladly have paused, and the view of the towering and majestic mountains in the background. After the past few days of rain, it was as clear as the day after they had arrived, and the mountains appeared once more to be close enough to touch. Near Christchurch, the land had been mostly flat, but it was becoming noticeably hillier. It consisted primarily of grassland, stretching as far as the eye could see, and was broken only occasionally by hedges or boulders that protruded so sharply from the green that it was as though a giant child had thrown them into the landscape. Now and then they crossed streams and rivers whose currents were so mild that they could be waded through without danger. Now and then they rounded inconspicuous hills—suddenly to be rewarded with the sight of a small, crystal-clear lake in whose water the sky or the rock formations above were reflected. The majority of these lakes, Warden revealed, had volcanic origins, although there were no longer active volcanoes in the area.

Not far from the lakes and rivers stood the occasional humble farmhouse with sheep grazing in the meadows beside it. When the settlers noticed the riders, they came out from their farmhouses, hoping for a chat. Gerald spoke only briefly with them, however, and took none of them up on their offers of rest and refreshment.

"If we start accepting their invitations, we won't reach Kiward Station for another two days," he explained when Gwyneira found fault with his gruffness. She would have liked to have a look inside one of these sweet little houses because she assumed that her own future home would look similar. But Gerald allowed only short rests on riverbanks or at hedges, and otherwise insisted on maintaining a rapid pace. Only in the evening of the first day did he accept accommodations at a farm, which appeared considerably larger and neater than the houses of the roadside settlers.

"The Beasleys are wealthy. For a while, Lucas and their eldest son shared a tutor, and we invite them over every now and then," Gerald explained to Gwyneira. "Beasley spent many years at sea as a first mate. An exceptional seaman. Just doesn't have a knack for sheep breeding, or they'd have even more. But his wife wouldn't settle for anything but a farm. She comes from rural England. And that's why Beasley's having a go at agriculture. A gentleman farmer." Coming from Gerald's mouth it sounded a bit derogatory. But then he smiled. "With an emphasis on the 'gentleman.' But they can afford it, so what's the harm? And they provide a little culture and social life. Last year they even put together a fox hunt."

Gwyneira wrinkled her brow. "Didn't you say that there weren't any foxes here?"

Gerald smirked. "The whole thing suffered a little because of that. But his sons are prodigious runners. They provided the bait."

Gwyneira had to laugh. This Mr. Beasley sounded quite original, and he appeared to have a good eye for horses. The thoroughbreds resting in the paddock in front of his house were definitely imported from England, and the composition of the garden along the approach struck her as classically English. Indeed, Beasley turned out to be a pleasant, red-faced gentleman who reminded Gwyneira vaguely of her father. He too resided on the land rather than working the soil with his own hands, yet he lacked the landed gentry's aptitude, cultivated over many generations, of running the farm effectively, even from the salon. The path leading up to his farm might have been elegant, but the horse pastures' fences could have used a fresh coat of paint. Gwyneira also noticed that the meadows were overgrazed and the water troughs were dirty.

Beasley seemed sincerely pleased by Gerald's visit. He uncorked his best bottle of whiskey straightaway and fell all over himself with compliments—alternating between Gwyneira's beauty, the skill of the sheepdogs, and the Welsh Mountain sheep. His wife, a well-groomed middle-aged woman, welcomed Gwyneira heartily.

"You must tell me about the latest English fashions! But first I'll show you my garden. My goal is to grow the prettiest roses in the plains. But I won't be upset if you outdo me, my lady. No doubt you've brought the prettiest examples from your mother's garden and spent the whole trip taking care of them."

Gwyneira swallowed. Not even Lady Silkham had thought to give her daughter some of her roses to bring along. But now she felt obliged to marvel at the flowers that so perfectly mirrored her mother's and sister's blossoms. Mrs. Beasley almost fainted when Gwyneira casually mentioned this, dropping the name "Diana Riddleworth" in the process. Apparently, it was the crowning achievement of Mrs. Beasley's life as a rose gardener to be compared to Gwyneira's famous sister. Gwyneira let her enjoy the moment. She certainly had no plans to outdo Mrs. Beasley. Not especially captivated by the roses, she found herself instead much more interested in the native plants that grew all around the manicured garden.

"Oh, those are cabbage trees," Mrs. Beasley explained, disinterested, when Gwyneira pointed to a palmlike plant. "It looks like a palm, but supposedly belongs to the lily family. They shoot up like weeds. Be careful you don't get too many of those in your garden, child. Or those over there."

She pointed to a blooming bush that Gwyneira actually liked more than Mrs. Beasley's roses. Its blossoms glowed a fiery red, in handsome contrast to its lush green leaves, which were unfolding beautifully after the rain.

"A rata," Mrs. Beasley explained. "They grow wild across the whole island. Can't get rid of them. I always have to take care that they don't sneak in with the roses. And my gardener is no great help. He doesn't understand why you care for some plants and weed out others."

As it turned out, the Beasleys' entire staff was Maori. They had hired only a few white adventurers who claimed to know what they were doing to look after the sheep. Gwyneira saw a pureblooded native for the first time here and was initially a bit frightened. Mrs. Beasley's gardener was short and stocky. His hair was dark and curly and his skin light brown; his face was marred by tattoos—or at least that's how Gwyneira saw it. The man must have liked the whirls and zigzags himself, however, since he'd agreed to have them scratched painfully into his skin. Once Gwyneira had gotten used to his appearance, she found she liked his grin. He was very polite too, greeting her with a deep bow and holding the garden gate open for the ladies. His uniform was no different from that of white servants, though Gwyneira assumed that the Beasleys had ordered it. Before the whites had appeared, the Maori had no doubt dressed differently.

"Thank you, George," Mrs. Beasley said to him kindly as he shut the door behind her.

Gwyneira was surprised.

"His name is George?" she asked, taken aback. "I would have thought...but your help are no doubt baptized and have taken English names, is that right?"

Mrs. Beasley shrugged. "To be honest, I don't even know," she admitted. "We don't go to church regularly. That would mean a day's journey to Christchurch every time. So on Sunday I just hold a little devotional here for us and the help. But if they come because they're Christian or because I demand it...I don't know."

"But if his name is George..." Gwyneira insisted.

"Oh, child, I gave him that name. I'll never learn the language of these people. Their names alone are unpronounceable. And he doesn't seem to care either way, do you George?"

The man nodded and smiled.

"Proper name Tonganui!" he then added, pointing at himself when Gwyneira still looked dismayed. "Means 'Son of Sea God.'"

It didn't sound very Christian, but Gwyneira didn't find it unpronounceable either. She determined not to rename her own servants.

"Where exactly did the Maori learn English?" she asked Gerald as they continued their journey the next day. The Beasleys had protested when they left, but understood that after his long absence Gerald wanted to make sure everything was in order at Kiward Station. They didn't have much to say about Lucas—other than the usual praise. It appeared he had not left the farm during Gerald's absence. At least he hadn't honored the Beasleys with a visit.

Gerald seemed to be in a bad mood that morning. The two men had stayed up and partaken generously of the whiskey, while Gwyneira, mentioning the long ride that lay behind and ahead, had said good night early. Mrs. Beasley's monologue about roses had bored her, and she had known since they arrived in Christchurch that Lucas was a cultivated man and gifted composer who, what's more, always had the latest works of Mr. Bulwer-Lytton and similarly great authors to lend.

"Oh, the Maori..." Gerald took up the question unenthusiastically. "You never know what they understand and what they don't. They always pick some up from their employers, and the women pass it on to their children. They want to be like us. Which is helpful."

"But they don't go to school?" Gwyneira inquired.

Gerald laughed.

"Who do you think would teach them? Most of the colonist mothers are happy when they can manage to teach their own brood a little civilization. To be sure, there are a few missions, and the Bible has been translated into Maori. But if you feel moved to teach a few black brats the Queen's English—I won't stand in your way."

Gwyneira did not really feel so moved, but maybe that would provide Helen with a new field to work in. She smiled at the thought of her friend, who was even now still sitting on her hands at the Baldwins' home in Christchurch. Howard O'Keefe had not shown any sign of appearing, but Vicar Chester had assured her every day that this was nothing to worry about. There was no way of being certain that news of Helen's arrival had even reached him yet, and then of course he would have to be free to come and get her.

"What do you mean by 'free to come'?" Helen had asked. "Does he not have any farmhands?"

The vicar had not responded to the question. Gwyneira hoped there wasn't an unpleasant surprise awaiting her friend.

Gwyneira had been quite happy with her new homeland from the start. Now, as they approached the mountains, the landscape became hillier and more varied but it remained just as lovely and well suited to sheep. Around noon Gerald happily revealed that they had crossed the property line of Kiward Station and that from now on they would be moving across his own land. To Gwyneira the landscape was a garden of Eden: an abundance of grass; good, clean drinking water for the animals; and a tree or even a shady copse here and there.

"As I said, it hasn't all been cleared yet," Gerald Warden explained as he let his gaze wander over the landscape. "But we could leave part of the forest. Some of it is rare wood, and it would be such a shame to burn it all. It could even be worth something someday. We might be able to use the river as a flume. In the meantime, though, we'll leave the trees alone. Look, there are the first sheep! I wonder what the critters are doing here though. They should have long since been driven up into the hills."

Gerald frowned. Gwyneira knew him well enough by now to realize that he was contemplating how to punish whomever was responsible. Normally he had no compunctions about expressing his thoughts to his listeners at length, but today he kept it to himself. Could it be because Lucas was the one responsible? Did Gerald not want to disparage his son in front of his fiancée—right before their first meeting?

All the while, Gwyneira could barely contain her excitement. She wanted to see the house, of course, but more than anything she wanted to meet her future husband. During the last few miles, she pictured him coming out to greet her, laughing, from a stately farmhouse like the Beasleys'. Meanwhile, they were already passing some of Kiward Station's outbuildings. Gerald had had shelters and shearing stations for his sheep set up all over his property. Gwyneira found that very prudent of him but was astounded by the scope of the grounds. In Wales, her father's stock of some four hundred sheep had been considered large. But here they counted by the thousands.

"So, Gwyneira, I'm curious what you think."

It was late afternoon and Gerald's whole face shone as he guided his horse alongside Igraine. The mare had just stepped from the usual muddy path onto a paved trail that led from a little lake around a hill. A few more steps revealed the farm's main house.

"Here we are, Lady Gwyneira," Gerald said proudly. "Welcome to Kiward Station!"

Gwyneira should have been prepared, but she almost fell from her horse in surprise. In front of her, in the sun, in the middle of an endless grassland, with the mountains rising up in the background, was an English manor house. Not as large as Silkham Manor and with fewer turrets and side buildings, but otherwise comparable in every way. Kiward Station was even more beautiful in some ways, having been perfectly planned by a single architect instead of being rebuilt and added onto like most English manors. The house was constructed of gray sandstone as Gerald had mentioned. It had oriels and large windows, which were partially adorned with small balconies; an ample path led up to it with flower beds that had not yet been planted. Gwyneira decided to sow rata bushes. That would highlight the facade and, moreover, they were easy to take care of.

Everything seemed as though it were out of a dream. Surely she would wake up anytime now and realize that peculiar game of blackjack had never happened. Instead, her father had married her off with a dowry from the sale of the sheep to some Welsh nobleman and now she was to take possession of some manor house near Cardiff.

Only the help, who were lined up before the front door to receive their master just as in England, didn't fit the picture. Though the male servants were wearing livery and the housemaids wore aprons and little bonnets, their skin was dark, and many of their faces were emblazoned with tattoos.

"Welcome home, Mr. Warden!" A short, compact man greeted his master, smiling across his broad face, which made the perfect canvas for his tattoo designs. He gestured to the sky, which remained blue despite the hour, and the sunny landscape. "And welcome, miss! As you see—the *rangi*, the sky, beams with joy at your arrival, and *papa*, the earth, smiles because you wander over it."

Gwyneira was touched by his hearty welcome. She impulsively extended her hand to the short man.

"This is Witi, our butler," Gerald said. "And that's our gardener, Hoturapa, and the housemaid and cook, Moana and Kiri."

"Miss...Sil...ha..." Moana wanted to greet Gwyneira properly as she curtsied, but apparently, she found the British name unpronounceable.

"Miss," Gwyneira shortened it. "Just call me *miss*."

She herself did not find it difficult to note the Maori's names, and she decided to learn a few polite phrases in their language as soon as possible.

So that was the staff. It struck Gwyneira as rather small for such a big house. And where was Lucas? Why wasn't he standing here to greet her and make her feel welcome?

"Now, where is..." Gwyneira launched into the pressing question of her fiancé's whereabouts, but Gerald beat her to it. He seemed just as vexed by his son's absence as Gwyneira.

"Where is that son of mine, Witi? He ought to be dragging his hide out here to meet his fiancée...ahem, I mean to say...Lady Silkham is naturally awaiting his appearance with great anticipation."

The butler smiled. "Young master rode out, checking on pastures. Mr. James say, someone from house must authorize buying material for horse pen. As it is now, horses not staying in. Mr. James very angry. That why young master rode away."

"Instead of receiving his father and bride? Now what a great way to start things!" roared Gerald.

Gwyneira, however, found it excusable. She would not have had a moment's peace if Igraine had been put in a stall that wasn't secure. And a ride to check up on the pastures was more fitting for her dream man than reading or playing the piano.

"Well, Gwyneira, it looks like there's nothing to do but have patience," Gerald said, finally calming down himself. "But maybe it's not as bad as all that. In England you wouldn't have met your fiancé for the first time in riding clothes and with your hair down."

He thought that Gwyneira, with her hair only half up and her face slightly pink from riding in the sun, looked ravishing himself, but Lucas might not see it that way.

"Kiri will show you your room now and help you freshen up and do your hair. In an hour we'll all meet for tea. My son should be back by five—he doesn't generally prolong his rides. Then your first encounter will go as properly as anyone could ask for."

Gwyneira could indeed have asked for something else, but she gave in to the inevitable.

"Can someone take my bag?" she asked, looking at the help. "Oh, no, that is too heavy for you Moana. Thank you, Hotaropa... Hoturapa? Pardon, but I'll remember it now. Now how do you say 'thank you' in Maori, Kiri?"

Helen had settled in at the Baldwins' against her will. As abhorrent as the family was to her, there was no alternative until Howard arrived. So she did her best to be friendly. She asked Reverend Baldwin to write down the texts for the church newsletters and then took them to the printer. She ran errands for Mrs. Baldwin and tried to make herself useful around the house, taking on small sewing projects and checking Belinda's homework. This last task soon made her the most hated person in the house. The girl did not like having her work checked and complained to her mother at every opportunity. This was how it became clear to Helen how weak the teachers in the newly opened school in Christchurch must be. She considered applying for a position there if things did not work out with Howard. Vicar Chester persisted in his encouragement: it could still be a while before O'Keefe learned of her arrival.

"After all, the Candlers were hardly going to send a messenger to his farm. They were probably waiting for him to come shopping in Haldon, and that could take a few days. But when he hears that you're here, he'll come. I'm sure of it."

For Helen that was further cause for concern. She had gotten over the fact that Howard did not live right next to Christchurch. Haldon was obviously not a suburb but its own independent and growing town. Helen could get used to that too. But now the vicar was telling her that Howard's farm lay outside of Haldon. Where exactly was she going to be living? She would have loved to talk it over with Gwyneira; perhaps Gwyneira could even have unobtrusively sounded Gerald out on the subject. But Gwyneira had left for Kiward Station the day before, and Helen had no idea when or even if she would see her friend again.

At least she had something pleasant planned for the afternoon. Mrs. Godewind had formally reissued her invitation, and right at teatime her chaise arrived to pick Helen up, with Jones, her driver, on the coach box. Jones beamed at her and helped her into the coach with perfect form. He even complimented her on her smart appearance in her new lilac-colored afternoon dress. Then he sang Elizabeth's praises the entire way.

"Our missus is a whole other person, Miss Davenport; you won't believe it. She seems to be getting younger every day, laughing and joking with the girl. And Elizabeth is such a charming child, constantly looking to help out my wife and always in a good mood. And can the girl ever read! My word, if I can find any, I always find some work in the house whenever the girl reads to Mrs. Godewind. She does it with such a sweet voice and emphasis—you'd think you were right there in the story."

Nor had Elizabeth forgotten Helen's lessons on serving and behaving at the table. She poured the tea and passed the pastries around skillfully and with care; moreover, she looked adorable in her new blue dress and neat white bonnet.

She cried, however, when she heard about Laurie and Mary and also seemed to better grasp Helen's watered-down version of Daphne and Dorothy's story than Helen had supposed she would. True, Elizabeth was a dreamer, but she had been found as a London street urchin. She shed hot tears for Daphne and demonstrated great faith in her new mistress, to whom she immediately turned for help.

"Couldn't we send Mr. Jones and take Daphne away? And the twins? Please, Mrs. Godewind, we'll surely find work for them here. There has to be something we can do."

Mrs. Godewind shook her head. "I'm afraid not, child. These people have signed work contracts with the orphanage, just as I did. The girls cannot simply walk away from those. And we'd be in hot water if we then gave them jobs ourselves! I'm sorry, love, but the girls have to find their own way to survive. Though after everything you've told me," Mrs. Godewind turned to Helen, "I wouldn't worry too much about little Daphne. She'll slog her way through. But the twins...oh, it's so sad. Pour us another cup of tea, Elizabeth. Then let's say a prayer for them; perhaps God will take up their cause."

But God was shuffling the cards for Helen as she sat in Mrs. Godewind's cozy salon, enjoying cookies from Mr. and Mrs. McLaren's bakery. Vicar Chester was waiting for her with great anticipation in front of the Baldwins' house when Jones held the door open for Helen to get out.

"Now where were you, Miss Davenport? I had almost given up hope of being able to introduce you today. You look beautiful—as if you'd sensed it! Now come in quickly. Mr. O'Keefe is waiting for you in the salon."

The front door of Kiward Station led into a spacious entrance hall where guests could set down their things and ladies could fix their hair. Gwyneira was amused when she noticed a mirrored cabinet with the requisite silver tray for calling cards. Who announced their presence here so formally? No guests would ever come here without notice, and certainly no strangers. And if a stranger did happen to wander in here, did Lucas and his father really wait until the housemaid had told Witi, who would then inform the masters of the house? Gwyneira thought of the farming families who had rushed out of their homes just to watch strangers ride past and the Beasleys' obvious excitement at their visit. Nobody had asked for their cards there. The exchange of calling cards might even have been unknown to the Maori. Gwyneira wondered how Gerald had explained it to Witi.

Beyond the entrance hall was a still sparsely furnished parlor—this too had without question been modeled after British manor houses. Guests could wait here in comfort until the lord of the manor found time for them. A fireplace and a buffet with a covered tea set were at hand; Gerald had suitable chairs and sofas among his luggage. It would look lovely, but what purpose it would serve remained a mystery to Gwyneira.

The Maori girl, Kiri, led her rapidly through to the salon, which was already amply furnished with old, heavy English furniture. Were it not for the Dutch door that led to a large terrace, it would have looked almost gloomy. It was not modeled on the latest fashion; the furnishings and carpets in here were antiques. Perhaps part of Lucas's mother's trousseau? If so, her family must have had a fortune. But that stood to reason too. Gerald might be a successful sheep breeder now, but before that he was just a swashbuckling sailor and the canniest card player ever to come out of the whale hunting colonies. But to build a house like Kiward Station in the middle of the wilderness, you needed more money than what could be earned from whales or sheep. Mrs. Warden's inheritance had undoubtedly contributed.

"Are you coming, miss?" Kiri asked amiably, but somewhat concerned. "I should you help but make tea too and serve. Moana no good with tea. Is better, we done before drops she cup."

Gwyneira laughed. She couldn't hold that against Moana.

"I'll be pouring the tea today," she explained to the astonished girl. "It's an old English custom. I've been practicing for years. It's one of the skills that's absolutely necessary to find a husband."

Kiri looked at her frowning. "You ready for husband when make tea? For us is important first bleeding."

Gwyneira reddened at once. How could Kiri talk so openly about something so unspeakable? Then again, Gwyneira was thankful for any information she could get. The monthly bleeding was a precondition for a marriage—it was no different in her culture. Gwyneira still remembered distinctly how her mother had sighed when it had happened to her. "Oh, dearie," she had said, "now the curse has struck you too. We'll have to start looking for a husband for you."

No one had ever explained to the girl how it was all connected. Gwyneira suppressed the urge to giggle when she thought of the face her mother would make at such a question. When Gwyneira had brought up possible parallels to dogs in heat, Lady Silkham had asked for her smelling salts and retired to her room for the rest of the day.

Gwyneira looked around for Cleo, who naturally had been following her. Kiri seemed to find that strange but said nothing.

A wide, winding staircase led up to the family's living quarters. To Gwyneira's surprise, her rooms were already completely furnished.

"Room supposed to be for wife of Mr. Warden," Kiri enlightened her. "But then died. Room always empty. But now young master make ready for you!"

"Lucas prepared these rooms for me?" Gwyneira asked, amazed.

Kiri nodded. "Yes. Picked out furniture from storage and sent for...how you say? Linen for window...?"

"Drapes, Kiri," Gwyneira helped her, unable to shake her astonishment. The late Mrs. Warden's furniture was made of light-colored wood, and the rugs had retained their colors of old rose, beige, and blue. To go with them, Lucas or someone else had chosen old rose silk curtains with a blue-beige border and tastefully hung them in front of her windows and around her bed. The bedsheets were made of snow-white linen, and a blue bedspread made the bed look cozy. Next to the bedroom were a dressing room and a small salon; this too had been tastefully furnished with small chairs, a tea table, and a small sewing cabinet. The usual little silver frames, candleholders, and bowls adorned the mantelpiece. A daguerreotype of a thin, light-haired woman had been placed in one of the frames. Gwyneira took the picture in her hands and looked at it more closely. Gerald hadn't been exaggerating. His late wife had been a perfect beauty.

"You change now, miss?" Kiri pressed.

Gwyneira nodded and set about unpacking her suitcase with the Maori girl. Kiri took out Gwyneira's holiday and afternoon dresses, full of reverence for the fine material.

"So beautiful, miss! So smooth and soft. But you thin, miss. Not good for having babies!"

Kiri didn't mince words. Gwyneira explained to her with a smile that she wasn't really so thin but owed her appearance to her corset. For the silk dress that she picked out, the corset would have to be tied even more tightly. Kiri worked diligently as Gwyneira showed her the grips but was clearly afraid of hurting her new mistress.

"Don't worry about that, Kiri, I'm used to it," Gwyn groaned. "My mother liked to say: you have to suffer for beauty."

Kiri seemed to understand for the first time. With a bashful laugh, she touched her tattooed face. "I see. Is like *moku*, yes? But every day again!"

Gwyneira nodded. In principle, she was right. Her wasp waist was just as painful and unnatural as Kiri's permanent face art. Here in New Zealand Gwyneira meant to relax the custom a bit. One of the girls would have to learn to let her clothing out, but then she wouldn't need to punish herself by tightening the cords so much to get into them. And after she was pregnant...

Kiri was an able help in getting her into her dress but had some difficulties with her hair. Untangling Gwyneira's curls was a difficult task and putting them up even more so. Kiri had obviously never done it before. Gwyneira ended up lending an energetic hand, and while the result didn't exactly meet the art of the coiffure's strict standards and Helen would no doubt have found it horrifying, Gwyneira thought it charming. They had managed to tie up most of her red-golden tresses; the few strands that escaped on their own despite their efforts played around her face, making her features appear softer and more girlish. Gwyneira's skin shone after the ride in the sun, and her eyes flashed with anticipation.

"Has Lucas returned?" she asked Kiri.

The girl shrugged. How should she know? After all, she had been with Gwyneira the whole time.

"So what is Lucas like, Kiri?" Gwyneira knew her mother would have upbraided her sharply for this question: one didn't ask the help to gossip about their employers. But Gwyneira couldn't help herself.

Kiri raised her shoulders and eyebrows, which looked humorous.

"The young master? Don't know. Is *pakeha*. For me all the same." The Maori girl had apparently never considered her employers' defining characteristics. She thought about it a little harder when she noticed Gwyneira's disappointed expression. "The young master...is nice. Never scream, never angry. Nice. Only little thin."

2

Helen hardly grasped what was going on, but she couldn't put off her first meeting with Howard O'Keefe any longer. Nervously she smoothed her dress and ran a hand over her hair. Should she take off her little hat or keep it on? There was a mirror in Mrs. Baldwin's parlor, and Helen cast an uncertain glance at her reflection before looking at the man on the sofa. He had his back turned to her, since Mrs. Baldwin's furniture set was turned toward the fireplace. So Helen had a chance to steal a peek at his figure before making her presence known. Howard O'Keefe looked bulky and tense. Clearly self-conscious, he balanced a thin-rimmed cup from Mrs. Baldwin's tea set in his large, calloused hands.

Helen was about to clear her throat to make herself known to the pastor's wife and her visitor. But just then Mrs. Baldwin caught a glimpse of her. The pastor's wife smiled coolly as always but feigned warmth.

"Oh there she is now, Mr. O'Keefe! You see, I knew she wouldn't stay out long. Come in, Miss Davenport. I'd like to introduce you to someone." Mrs. Baldwin's tone was almost whimsical.

Helen stepped nearer. The man stood up from the couch so quickly that he almost knocked the tea service from the table.

"Miss…ahem, Helen?"

Helen raised her gaze to look her future husband in the eye. Howard O'Keefe was tall and heavy—not fat but built with a sturdy bone structure. The cast of his face was earthy, but not unattractive. His bronzed, leathery skin spoke of long years of hard work in the open air. It was marked by deep lines that indicated a rich range of expressions; at the moment, however, he could only manage a look of astonishment—even awe. There was recognition in his steely blue eyes—Helen seemed to please him. His hair caught her attention above all else: it was dark, full, and neatly cut—she assumed he had squeezed in a visit to the barber's before this first meeting with his fiancée. However, his hair was already graying at the temples. Howard was considerably older than Helen had pictured him.

"Mr.…Mr. O'Keefe…" she said tonelessly and could have hit herself. After all, he had called her "Helen," so she could have called him "Howard."

"I…eh, well, you're here now!" Howard remarked, in a sort of non sequitur. "That…eh, was something of a surprise."

Helen wondered if that was meant as censure. She blushed.

"Yes. The…ahem, circumstances. But I…I'm happy to finally meet you."

She held her hand out to Howard. He took it and gave it a firm handshake.

"I'm happy too. I'm only sorry you had to wait."

Ah, that's what he meant. Helen smiled, relieved.

"Nothing to be sorry for, Howard. I was told it might take some time before you heard of my arrival. But now you're here."

"Now I'm here."

Howard smiled too, which softened his features and made him more appealing. On account of his polished writing style, Helen had at least expected a more intellectual conversation. But what did it matter? Maybe he was shy. Helen took over steering the conversation.

"Where exactly did you come here from, Howard? I had thought Haldon lay closer to Christchurch. But it turns out it's its own city. And your farm lies somewhere outside of it?"

"Haldon lies on Lake Benmore," Howard explained, as though that meant anything to Helen. "Don't know if you could call it a 'city.' But it has a few stores. You can buy the important things there. The things you need, at least."

"And how far is it from here?" Helen inquired, feeling dumb. Here she was sitting with the man she was likely to marry and they were gabbing about distances and town shops.

"Just about two days with the team," said Howard after brief contemplation. Helen would have preferred a clarification in miles but didn't want to nitpick. Instead, she said nothing, which created an awkward silence. Howard cleared his throat.

"And...did you have a safe journey?"

Helen sighed with relief. Finally a question with a story she could tell. She described her passage with the girls.

Howard nodded. "Hm. A long journey..."

Helen hoped he would tell of his own immigration, but he remained quiet.

Fortunately, Vicar Chester now joined them. As he greeted Howard, Helen finally found the time to catch her breath and take a closer look at her future husband. The farmer's clothing was simple but clean. He wore leather breeches that had clearly seen many rides, and a waxed jacket over a white shirt. A splendidly decorated brass belt buckle was the only valuable piece of his wardrobe—other than a silver necklace around his neck, from which hung a green stone. His bearing had initially been stiff and unsure, but now that he was loosening up, she saw that he carried himself erectly and in a self-assured manner. His movements were limber, almost graceful.

"Now tell Miss Davenport a bit about your farm," the vicar encouraged him. "Maybe about the animals or the house..."

Howard O'Keefe shrugged. "It's a lovely house, Helen. Very sturdy, built it myself. And the animals...well, we have a mule, a horse, a cow, and a few chickens. And sheep, of course. Thousands of them."

"That...that's a great many," Helen remarked, wishing fervently she had listened more closely to Gwyneira's endless stories about sheep breeding. How many sheep had she said Mr. Warden had?

"That's not many, but there'll be more. And there's plenty of land; it'll work out. So how...eh, how do we proceed?"

Helen wrinkled her brow. "How do we proceed with what?" she asked, feeling for a few strands of hair that had fallen from her chaste hairdo.

"Well, uh..." Howard played awkwardly with his second cup of tea. "With the wedding..."

With Gwyneira's permission, Kiri finally scampered off in the direction of the kitchen to come to Moana's aid. Gwyneira spent the last few minutes before teatime conducting a more thorough inspection of her rooms. Everything was impeccably arranged, down to the lovingly arrayed toiletries in the dressing room. Gwyneira marveled at the ivory combs and matching brushes. The soap smelled of roses and thyme—surely not a creation of the indigenous Maori tribe; the soap must have been bought in Christchurch or imported from England. A pleasant aroma wafted from a little dish of dried flower petals in her salon. There was no doubt about it—even a perfect housewife in her mother's or sister Diana's vein could not have arranged her rooms any more invitingly than...Lucas Warden? Gwyneira simply could not imagine how a man could be responsible for this display.

She could barely contain her curiosity. She told herself that she didn't really have to wait for teatime; Gerald and Lucas might already be in the salon. Gwyneira walked over to the stairs, across halls laid out with expensive rugs—and heard raised voices coming from the salon that echoed through half the house.

"Can you tell me why today of all days you absolutely had to check on the pastures?" Gerald thundered. "Couldn't it have waited until tomorrow? The girl will think she doesn't mean anything to you!"

"Forgive me, Father." The voice sounded calm and cultivated. "But Mr. McKenzie simply wouldn't let up. And it was urgent. The horses had already broken out three times."

"The horses had *what*?" Gerald bellowed. "Broken out three times? That means that for three days I've been paying the men to catch their nags all over again? Why didn't you step in earlier? McKenzie wanted to make the repairs right away, didn't he? And while we're on the subject of pens—why was nothing prepared for the sheep in Lyttelton? If it weren't for your soon-to-be wife and her dogs, I'd have had to spend the whole night watching the beasts myself!"

"I had a lot to do, Father. Mother's portrait for the salon had to be finished. And I had to take care of Lady Gwyneira's rooms."

"Lucas, when will you finally learn that oil paintings don't run away, unlike horses? And as for Gwyneira's rooms...*you* arranged her rooms?" Gerald seemed just as unable to comprehend that as Gwyneira herself.

"Who would have done it otherwise? One of the Maori girls? She would have found palm mats and a fire pit!" Now Lucas sounded a bit heated. Only as much, however, as a gentleman ever allowed himself to become in company.

Gerald sighed. "All right, fine, let's hope she knows how to appreciate it. Let's not fight now; she'll be coming down any minute."

Gwyneira decided to take that as her cue. With even steps, her shoulders squared, and her head raised high, she came down the stairs. She had practiced such entrances for days before her first debutante ball. Now it was finally paying off.

As expected, her entrance left the men in the salon speechless. Before the background of the dark staircase, Gwyneira's delicate figure clad in pale blue silk seemed to have stepped out of an oil painting. Her face shone brightly, and the loose strands of hair framing it looked like spun gold and copper in the light of the salon's candles. Gwyneira's mouth hinted at a shy smile. She lowered her eyelids, but that did not stop her from being able to peek out from her long red lashes. She had to catch a glimpse of Lucas before she was formally introduced to him.

What she saw, however, made it hard for her to preserve her dignified poise. She came close to losing her composure, opening her eyes and mouth, to stare without impediment at this perfect example of the male species.

Gerald had not exaggerated in his description of Lucas. His son was the very definition of a gentleman and, what's more, blessed with all the attributes of masculine beauty. The young man was tall, considerably taller than Gerald, and thin, but muscular. He had none of the lankiness of a young Barrington or the meek tenderness of a Vicar Chester. Lucas Warden no doubt played sports, but not so excessively as to assume the muscle-packed physique of an athlete. Symmetrical and noble, his narrow face had an intellectual look to it. Gwyneira found herself reminded of the statues of Greek gods that lined the path to Diana's rose garden. Lucas's lips were finely carved, neither too wide and sensual nor too thin and tight. His clear eyes were a shade of intense gray that Gwyneira had never seen before. Usually gray eyes had a hint of blue, but Lucas's eyes looked as though only black and white tones had been introduced into the mix. He wore his bright blond, lightly curled hair short, as was fashionable in London salons. Lucas was formally dressed; for this meeting, he had chosen a gray three-piece suit of the best cloth and wore shiny black shoes.

As Gwyneira approached him, she smiled. In response, his face became all the more attractive. His eyes, however, remained expressionless.

Finally he bent forward and took Gwyneira's hand in his long, svelte fingers, intimating a kiss on the hand in perfect form.

"My lady...enchantée."

Howard O'Keefe looked at Helen in astonishment. Obviously he did not understand why his question had rendered her speechless.

"What...what about the wedding?" she stammered finally. "I...I thought..." Helen tugged at her strands of hair.

"And I thought you had come to marry me," Howard said, looking a little peevish. "Was there a misunderstanding?"

Helen shook her head. "No, of course not. But it's all happening so fast. We...we don't know anything about each other. U...usually the man courts his wi...wife-to-be first, and then..."

"Helen, it's a two-day ride from here to my farm," Howard said sternly. "You can't really expect me to make that trip several times just to bring you flowers. As for me, I need a wife. Now I've seen you, and I like what I see."

"Thank you," Helen murmured, blushing.

Howard did not respond to that. "Everything is clear as far as I'm concerned. Mrs. Baldwin tells me that you're very maternal and domestic, and I like that. I don't need to know anything more. If you still have questions about me—please, I'd be happy to answer them. But then we should talk about the...eh, particulars. Reverend Baldwin would be the one to marry us, is that right?" At this last question, Vicar Chester nodded vigorously.

Helen searched feverishly for questions to ask. What did you need to know about someone you were going to marry? Finally she settled on family.

"You come from Ireland originally; is that right?"

O'Keefe nodded. "That's right, miss. Connemara."

"And your family...?"

"Richard and Bridie O'Keefe were my parents, and I had five siblings—or maybe more, I left home early on."

"Because...the land couldn't feed so many mouths?" Helen asked cautiously.

"You could say that. It wasn't really up to me."

"Oh, I'm so sorry, Howard!" Helen suppressed the impulse to lay her hand consolingly on his arm. Naturally, that was the "heavy fate" he had written about in his letter.

"And then you came straightaway to New Zealand?"

"No, I've...eh, traveled around a bit."

"I could see that," Helen responded, although she did not really have the faintest idea where an adolescent kicked out of his house could go. "But in all that time...in all that time, did you never consider marriage?" She reddened.

Howard shrugged. "The places I wandered, there weren't many women, miss. Among whaling stations, seal hunters. There *was* once..." Then the look on his face retreated.

"Yes, Howard? Forgive me if I'm being pushy, but I..." Helen was desperate for some emotion from this man that would make it a little easier for her to size up this Howard O'Keefe.

The farmer grinned widely. "That's all right, Helen. You want to get to know me. Well, there's not much to say. She married another... which might be the reason I want to wrap this business up quickly. This business with us, I mean."

Helen was touched. So it wasn't a lack of feeling on his part but rather an understandable fear that she might run off just like the first girl he had loved back then. She still could not understand how this taciturn, hard-seeming man could write such beautiful letters, but she thought she understood him better now. Howard O'Keefe was a still water.

But did she want to dive in blindly? Helen feverishly considered her options. She could not live with the Baldwins any longer; they would never understand why she had deferred her marriage. And Howard himself would take any delay as a rejection and perhaps withdraw entirely. And then what? Would she take a position at the school here—which was by no means guaranteed? Would she spend the rest of her life teaching children like Belinda Baldwin and slowly becoming an old spinster? She couldn't take that risk. Perhaps Howard was not exactly what she had in mind, but he was honest and direct, was offering her a house and a home, wanted a family, and worked hard to grow his farm. She couldn't ask for more.

"All right, Howard. But you will need to give me a day or two to prepare. A wedding like this..."

"Of course we'll throw a little party," Mrs. Baldwin declared, sweet as sugar. "No doubt you'll want to have Elizabeth and the other girls who are still in Christchurch at your side. Your friend Lady Silkham has already left, though."

Howard frowned. "Silkham? As in the noblewoman? Gwenevere Silkham who's supposed to marry old Warden's son?"

"Gwyneira," Helen corrected him. "That's right. We became friends during the voyage here."

O'Keefe turned to her, and his previously amiable face contorted with rage.

"Just so we're clear, Helen—you will never receive a Warden in my house! Not as long as I live. Keep far away from that clan. The old man is a crook and the son is a dandy! And the girl can't be any better or she wouldn't have let herself be bought. The whole brood ought to be weeded out. Don't you dare invite them onto my farm. Sure, I don't have the old man's money, but my gun shoots just as straight!"

Gwyneira had been making conversation for two hours now, which was more of a strain than if she had spent all that time in the saddle or at a dog show. Lucas Warden covered every topic, one after another, that she had been trained to discuss in her mother's salon, but his expectations were markedly higher than Lady Silkham's.

Yet things had begun well. Gwyneira had managed to pour the tea impeccably—even though her hands shook the whole time. The first sight of Lucas had simply been too much for her. Now, however, her heart no longer raced out of control, as the young gentleman gave her no cause for further excitement. He made no move to undress her with his eyes, to brush her fingers as though by accident as the two both reached—purely by coincidence—for the sugar, or to look her in the eye for a heartbeat too long. Instead, Lucas's neutral gaze appeared to rest on her left earlobe while they conversed, his eyes lighting up only when he asked a question that particularly interested him.

"I heard that you play piano, Lady Silkham. What's the latest thing you've been working on?"

"Oh, my mastery of the piano is incomplete at best. I only play for fun, Mr. Warden. I…I'm afraid I'm terribly untalented." She looked bashfully down, then up, and made a slight frown. Most men would have said something complimentary and let the subject drop. Not Lucas.

"I can't imagine that, my lady. Not if you enjoy it. Everything we do with joy we'll succeed at; I'm convinced of it. Do you know Bach's 'Notebook'? Minuets and dances—it would suit you!" Lucas smiled.

Gwyneira tried to remember who had composed the etudes that Madame Fabian had tortured her with. She had heard the name "Bach" somewhere. Had he composed the church music?

"I make you think of chorales?" she asked playfully. Maybe she could bring the conversation down to the level of a light exchange of compliments and banter after all. That would have suited her much better than this discussion of art and culture. Lucas, however, did not take the bait.

"Why not, my lady? Chorales should mimic the exultation of the choirs of angels as they praise God. And who wouldn't want to praise God for such a beautiful creature as you? What especially fascinates me about Bach is the almost mathematical clarity of his compositions, united with his undoubtedly deeply felt faith. Naturally, the music can only come to life in its proper element. What I wouldn't give to listen just once to one of his organ concertos in one of Europe's great cathedrals! That would be..."

"Illuminating," Gwyneira remarked.

Lucas nodded enthusiastically.

After discussing music, he moved on eagerly to contemporary literature, the works of Bulwer-Lytton above all—"Edifying," Gwyneira commented—and then it was time to exchange ideas on his favorite topic: painting. He was most inspired by the mythological motifs of the renaissance artists—"Sublime," Gwyneira responded—as well as the light and shadow play in the works of Velasquez and Goya. "Refreshing," Gwyneira improvised, who had never heard the first thing about them before.

After two hours, Lucas seemed enthusiastic about her, Gerald was battling with exhaustion, and Gwyneira just wanted to get out. Finally she lightly touched her temples and looked at the men apologetically.

"I'm afraid I'm getting a headache after the long ride and now the warmth from the fire. I think I need a little fresh air."

As she prepared to stand, Lucas sprang to his feet. "But of course, you'll want to relax before dinner. It was my fault! We've stretched our teatime out too long with our stimulating conversation."

"Really I'd rather take a short stroll," Gwyneira said. "Not far, just to the stables to look in on my horse."

Cleo was already dancing around her with excitement. Even the dog had been bored. Her happy barking roused Gerald's spirits.

"You should accompany her, Lucas," he prompted his son. "Show Lady Silkham the stables and make certain the farmhands don't drool over her."

Lucas blinked, indignant. "Please, don't speak like that in the presence of a lady."

Gwyneira attempted to blush, but deep down she was looking for an excuse to refuse Lucas's company.

Fortunately, Lucas also had his reservations. "I think perhaps that such an outing may overstep the boundaries of decency, Father," he said. "It would be inappropriate for me to linger alone in the horse stables with Lady Silkham."

Gerald snorted. "The horse stables are probably as busy as a pub right now. When the weather's like this, the shepherds hang around where it's warm and play cards." Rain had set in late that afternoon.

"Just so, Father. Tomorrow they would be flapping their mouths about how their masters retreat to the stables to perform indecent acts." Lucas seemed unpleasantly struck by the mere thought of becoming the target of such a rumor.

"Oh, I'll be all right alone," Gwyneira said. She wasn't afraid of the hands. After all, she'd earned the respect of her father's shepherds. And the shepherds' crude speech was much more appealing to her at the moment than any further edifying conversation with a gentleman. On the way to the stalls he was likely to examine her knowledge of architecture too. "I should have no trouble finding the stall myself."

She would have liked to grab a coat, but it was better to leave before Gerald came up with any objections.

"It was exceedingly in…vigorating chatting with you, Mr. Warden," she informed her fiancé with a smile. "Shall we see each other at dinner?"

Lucas nodded and squared himself for another bow. "But of course, my lady. In just about an hour, dinner will be served in the dining room."

Gwyneira ran through the rain. She dared not think about what the moisture was doing to her silk dress. The weather had been so lovely earlier. Oh well, no rain, no grass. The moist climate of her new homeland was ideal for raising sheep, and of course she was used to such weather in Wales. It was just that she wouldn't have been traipsing through the mud in such elegant clothing there, since the paths leading between the farm buildings had been paved. On Kiward Station, in contrast, this had so far been neglected; only the approach was paved. If it had been up to Gwyneira, she would have paved the area in front of the stalls rather than the splendid but rarely used path to the front door. But Gerald probably had other priorities—and Lucas most definitely did. No doubt he was already planning a rose garden too. Gwyneira was happy to see bright light shining from the stalls, as she wouldn't have known where to find a stable lantern. Voices now issued from the sheds and stalls as well. Obviously the shepherds had indeed gathered here.

"Blackjack, James!" someone called with a laugh. "Drop your pants, my friend! I'm taking your pay today."

As long as the men don't place other people as bets, Gwyneira thought, catching her breath and opening the stable door. The path before her led left to the horse stalls; to the right it widened into a depot where the men were sitting around a fire. Gwyneira counted five in all, rough-looking fellows who did not appear to have washed yet that day. Some had beards, while others looked like they'd gone three days without their razors. Three of the young sheepdogs had curled up next to a tall, thin man with an angular, darkly bronzed face that was deeply creased by laugh lines.

Another man handed him a bottle of whiskey.

"Here, as consolation."

So that was the "James" who had lost the hand.

A blond giant who was shuffling the cards looked up by chance and caught sight of Gwyneira.

"Hey, boys, are there ghosts around here? Normally I don't see such pretty ladies till after the second bottle of whiskey."

The men laughed.

"What radiance in our humble abode," said the man who had just handed the whiskey bottle around, with a voice that was failing him. "A...an angel!"

Renewed laughter.

Gwyneira did not know how to respond.

"Now be quiet, boys, you're embarrassing the poor girl." The oldest among them now spoke up. He was apparently still sober and was stuffing his pipe at the moment. "That's neither an angel nor a ghost, just the young mistress. The one Mr. Warden brought back for Lucas to…well, you know already."

Embarrassed tittering.

Gwyneira decided to take the initiative.

"Gwyneira Silkham," she said, introducing herself. She would have extended her hand to the men but so far none of them had made the effort to stand up. "I wanted to check on my horse."

Cleo, meanwhile, had toured the stalls, greeted the sheepdog pups, and waggled from one man to the next. She paused by James, who petted her with adept hands.

"And what's this little lady's name? A beautiful animal. I've already heard about her, and just as much about her mistress's wondrous skill at driving sheep. By your leave, James McKenzie." The young man stood up and stretched out his hand to Gwyneira, looking at her steadily with brown eyes. His hair was likewise brown, plentiful, and unkempt as though he'd been fussing with it nervously during the card game.

"Hey, James! Don't get too worked up," one of the others teased him. "She's the boss's; didn't you hear?"

McKenzie rolled his eyes. "Don't listen to the scoundrels; they don't have any class. But they were baptized at any rate: Andy McAran, Dave O'Toole, Hardy Kennon, and Poker Livingston. He's pretty lucky at blackjack too."

Poker was the blond, Dave the man with the bottle, and Andy the dark-haired, somewhat older giant. Hardy seemed to be the youngest of the lot and had already partaken a bit too much of the bottle to show any signs of life.

"I'm sorry that we're all already a bit tipsy," McKenzie said frankly. "But if Mr. Warden's gonna send over a bottle to celebrate his return…"

Gwyneira smiled benevolently. "It's all right. But be sure to put the fire out properly afterward. Not that you would set my stables on fire."

While they were talking, Cleo leaped up at McKenzie, who immediately set about scratching her. Gwyn remembered that McKenzie had asked for the dog's name.

"That is Cleopatra Silkham. And the little ones are Daisy Silkham, Dorit Silkham, Dinah Silkham, Daddy, Daimon, and Dancer."

"Whoa, they're all noble," Poker said, alarmed. "Do we have to bow whenever we see them?" He pointed in a friendly way to Dancer, who was just then trying to gnaw on his cards.

"You should have already when you received my horse," Gwyneira returned nonchalantly. "She has a longer family tree than any of us."

James McKenzie laughed, and his eyes gleamed. "But I don't always have to address the critter by her full name, right?"

Gwyneira's eyes twinkled with mischief. "You'll have to decide on that among yourselves with Igraine," she explained. "But the dog doesn't put on airs at all. She answers to the name Cleo."

"And what do you answer to?" McKenzie asked, passing his gaze appreciatively, but not lasciviously, over Gwyneira's figure. She shivered. After that run through the rain, she was beginning to freeze. McKenzie saw that at once. "Wait a moment, miss, I'll grab you a shawl. It's getting to be summer, but it's still pretty miserable outside."

He reached for a waxed coat.

"Here you go, Miss..."

"'Miss' will do," Gwyneira said. "Thank you. Now, where's my horse?"

Igraine and Madoc were well put up in clean stalls, but her mare stamped with impatience when Gwyneira came up to her. The slow ride that morning had not tired her, and she was burning for more action.

"Mr. McKenzie," Gwyneira said, "I would like to go for a ride tomorrow morning, but Mr. Warden thinks it would be improper for me to go alone. I would not like to burden anyone, but would it be possible for me to accompany you and your men on some job? Inspecting the pastures, for example? I would be happy to show you how to train the dogs. They have naturally good instincts when it comes to sheep, but there are a few tricks to further improve what they can do."

McKenzie shook his head regretfully. "In principle, we'd be happy to take you up on your offer, miss. But for tomorrow we've already been charged with saddling two horses for your ride. Mr. Lucas will accompany you and show you the farm." McKenzie grinned. "Surely that sounds a whole lot better than a survey ride with a few unwashed shepherds, eh?"

Gwyn didn't know how to reply to that—even worse, she didn't know what she thought. Finally she pulled herself together.

"Wonderful," she said.

3

Lucas Warden was a good rider, even if he lacked passion. The young gentleman sat properly and at ease in his saddle, managed the reins with confidence, and knew how to keep his horse calmly beside that of his companion in order to chat with her occasionally. To Gwyneira's astonishment, he did not own a horse of his own, nor did he show any inclination to test the new stallion, something Gwyneira had been dying to do ever since Warden had bought the horse. So far she had been denied a ride on Madoc based on the argument that a stallion was not a lady's horse—even though that horse was of a considerably calmer temperament than her own stubborn Igraine, if not as used to the ladies' saddle, of course. However, Gwyneira was optimistic. The shepherds, who, due to the lack of grooms, also served as stable hands, had no concept of propriety. Hence Lucas had specifically had to ask a confused McKenzie to fit Gwyneira's mare with the sidesaddle. For himself, he had ordered one of the farm horses, which were bigger but lighter than the cobs. Most of them seemed quite lively, but Lucas chose the calmest among them.

"That way I can intercede if my lady has difficulties without also having to grapple with my own horse," he explained to the bewildered McKenzie.

Gwyneira rolled her eyes. If she really were to have difficulties, she and Igraine would already be on the horizon before Lucas's placid gray horse had even taken a step. However, she recognized the argument from the etiquette books and so pretended to appreciate Lucas's circumspection. The ride across Kiward Station passed rather harmoniously. Lucas chatted with Gwyneira about fox hunts and expressed his astonishment at her participation in dog competitions.

"That seems to me a rather...ahem, unconventional occupation for a young lady," he admonished her mildly.

Gwyneira bit her lip slightly. Was Lucas already starting to tell her what to do? If so, she had better nip it in the bud.

"I'm afraid you'll have to get past that," she said coolly. "Besides, it is also rather unconventional to pursue a marriage proposal in New Zealand. Especially when you don't even know your future spouse."

"Touché." Lucas smiled, but then became serious. "I have to admit that I did not approve of my father's conduct at first. However, it's difficult to arrange a suitable match here. Please don't misunderstand me; New Zealand was not settled by crooks as Australia was but by thoroughly honest men. But most of the settlers...simply lack class, education, culture. For that reason, I am more than happy to have agreed to this unconventional marriage proposal, which has brought me such a charmingly unconventional bride. Might I hope that I too meet your expectations, Gwyneira?"

Gwyneira nodded, though she had to force herself to smile. "I was pleasantly surprised to find such a perfect gentleman as yourself here," she said. "Even in Britain I could not have found a more cultured and better-educated husband."

That was no doubt true. In the circles of landed Welsh gentry in which Gwyneira had moved, everyone had a basic education, but the talk in the salons centered more on horse races than Bach cantatas.

"Naturally, we should get to know each other better before we decide on the wedding day," Lucas said. "Anything else would be improper. I told Father that as well. He would have liked to fix the date for the day after tomorrow."

Gwyneira herself thought that enough words had been exchanged and that they knew each other well enough already, but she agreed, of course, and acted charmed when Lucas invited her to visit him in his studio that afternoon.

"Naturally, I'm just an unknown painter, but I hope to continue to improve," he explained to her as they rode along at a welcome gallop. "Right now I'm working on a portrait of my mother. It'll have a home in the salon. Unfortunately, I have to work from daguerreotypes since I can hardly remember her. She died when I was still young. However, as I work, more memories come to me, and I feel that I'm becoming closer to her. It's a very interesting experience. I would love to paint you too sometime, Lady Gwyneira!"

Gwyneira agreed only halfheartedly. Before her departure, her father had commissioned a portrait of her, and she had almost died of boredom sitting as a model.

"I'm anxious to hear your opinion of my work. Surely you've visited many galleries in England and are far better informed about the latest developments than those of us here at the ends of the earth."

Gwyneira could only hope that a few impressive words would come to mind for that purpose. She had depleted her reserve of appropriate remarks the day before, but hoped that perhaps the pictures would give her some fresh ideas. In truth, she had never been inside a gallery, and she was completely indifferent to the latest developments in art. Her ancestors—and those of her neighbors and friends—had over the course of many generations amassed countless paintings, which decorated their walls. The pictures primarily depicted forebears and horses, and their quality was judged only on the criterion of likeness. Terms like "play of light" and "perspective," which Lucas ranted about endlessly, were entirely new to Gwyneira.

Still, the landscapes through which they were riding enchanted her. That morning it had been foggy; however, the sun was burning off the fog, and as it cleared, Kiward Station was revealed as though nature were making Gwyneira a special present of it. Lucas did not lead her far out to the mountains' foothills where the sheep grazed free, but even the land right next to the farm was beautiful. The lake reflected the sky's cloud formations, and the rocks in the meadows looked as though they had just punctured the carpet of grass like powerful teeth, or like an army of giants that could spring to life at any moment.

"Isn't there a story where the hero sows rocks and soldiers for his army then grow from them?" Gwyneira asked.

Lucas seemed excited at her knowledge. "They weren't stones, but dragon's teeth that Jason puts in the earth in Greek mythology," he corrected her. "And the army of iron that grew out of them rose up against him. Oh, it is wonderful to be able to talk with classically educated people on the same level, don't you think?"

Gwyneira had been thinking instead of the stone circles in her homeland about which her nanny used to tell her adventure stories. If she remembered correctly, priestesses had burned Roman soldiers there, or something like that. But that story wouldn't be classical enough for Lucas.

A flock of Gerald's sheep grazed among the stones, including ewes who had just lambed. Gwyneira was taken with the unquestionably beautiful lambs. Gerald had been right, though: a drop of Welsh Mountain sheep blood would improve their wool quality.

Lucas frowned as Gwyneira told him to have the sheep mate with the rams from Wales right away.

"Is it usual in England for young ladies to talk about sexual things so...so unabashedly?" he asked cautiously.

"How else should I say it?" Gwyneira had never made a connection between proper decorum and sheep breeding. She didn't have any idea how a woman got pregnant, but she had watched sheep mate more than once without anyone finding it problematic.

Lucas blushed slightly. "Well, this...ahem, this whole realm of conversation is off-limits to ladies, isn't it?"

Gwyneira shrugged. "My sister Larissa raises Highland terriers, my other sister roses. They talk about it all day. Where would you draw the line?"

"Gwyneira!" Lucas turned beet red. "Oh, let's drop this subject. God knows, it is not proper in our particular situation. Why don't we just watch the lambs play a bit? Are they not adorable?"

Gwyneira had been assessing them more from the standpoint of wool yield, but like all newborn lambs, they were indeed cute. She agreed with Lucas and made no objections when he suggested they bring their ride to a close.

"I think you've seen enough to get around Kiward Station on your own," he said as he helped Gwyneira off her horse in front of the stables—a comment that made up for all of his stodginess. Apparently, he had nothing against his fiancée riding out alone. At least he had not mentioned a chaperone—whether because he'd skipped that chapter in the etiquette book or because he simply couldn't imagine a girl might wish to ride alone she didn't know—and didn't care.

Gwyneira seized the opportunity straightaway. Lucas had hardly turned away before she said to the older shepherd who took her horse, "Mr. McAran, I'd like to ride out alone early tomorrow. Please make the new stallion available for me at ten o'clock—with Mr. Warden's saddle."

Helen's marriage to Howard O'Keefe was not as spartan as the young woman had feared it would be. In order to avoid performing the ceremony in an empty church, Reverend Baldwin held it alongside the Sunday service. As a result, there ended up being a long line of well-wishers who paraded past Helen and Howard and congratulated them. Mr. and Mrs. McLaren had done their part to make the service festive, and Mrs. Godewind had contributed flowers to decorate the church, which they had tied into splendid arrangements. Mr. and Mrs. McLaren had outfitted Rosemary in a pink Sunday dress, which she wore as she strewed flower petals, herself looking like a little rosebud. Mr. McLaren gave the bride away, and Belinda Baldwin and Elizabeth acted as Helen's bridesmaids. Helen had hoped to see the other girls at Sunday service, but none of the families living out of town showed up. Even Laurie's employers did not let her come. Helen was unsettled but didn't want that to ruin her big day. She had by now gotten over the precipitous nature of the marriage and had firmly decided to make the best of it. Moreover, she had been able to observe Howard closely over the last few days since he was staying in town and had joined the Baldwins for almost every meal. Though it was true that his violent reaction to the Wardens had alienated Helen at first, scared her even, he otherwise appeared to be quite collected. He used his stay in the city to stock up on a great many things for the farm, so he didn't seem to be doing all that bad financially. He looked very dapper in the gray tweed Sunday suit he had picked out for the wedding, though it didn't fit the season and he was perspiring as a result.

Helen wore a spring-green summer dress that she had been measured for in London with her wedding in mind. Naturally, she would have liked to wear a white lace dress, but she had dismissed that as an unnecessary waste of money. After all, she would never have an occasion to wear such a dream in silk again. Helen's luminous hair fell freely down her back—a hairstyle that Mrs. Baldwin eyed distrustfully but that Mrs. McLaren and Mrs. Godewind had approved. They had simply pulled Helen's mane of hair out of her face with a bandeau decorated with flowers. Helen thought that she had never looked so lovely, and even taciturn Howard managed a rare compliment: "You look...uh, very pretty, Helen."

Helen fondled the letters he'd sent, which she always kept with her. When would her husband finally open up enough to repeat those beautiful words to her face?

The wedding itself was very festive. Reverend Baldwin proved to be an excellent speaker who knew how to captivate his parish. As he spoke of love "in good times and bad," every last woman in the church was in tears and even the men were sniffling. The choice of maid of honor was the only bitter note for Helen. She had wanted to ask Mrs. Godewind, but Mrs. Baldwin had forced herself on Helen, and it would have been impolite to refuse her. Besides, she was very happy with the best man, Vicar Chester.

Howard surprised her when he spoke his vows freely and with a steady voice, looking at Helen almost lovingly as he did. Helen did not manage it quite so perfectly herself—she cried as she spoke.

But then the organ sounded, the parish sang, and Helen felt overjoyed as she strode from the church on her husband's arm. Outside, the well-wishers were already waiting.

Helen kissed Elizabeth and let herself be embraced by a sobbing Mrs. McLaren. To her surprise, Mrs. Beasley and the whole O'Hara family had appeared, although the latter did not belong to the Anglican Church. Helen shook hands and laughed and cried until in the end only one young woman remained whom Helen had never seen before. She looked over at Howard—maybe the woman had come for him—but Howard was talking with the pastor and seemed to have missed this last well-wisher.

Helen smiled at her. "I don't mean to be rude, but may I ask where I know you from? There have been so many new things over the last few days that..."

The woman gave her a friendly nod. She was petite, with a plain, childlike face and thin blonde hair that she had pinned up primly under a hat. She wore the simple clothing typical of a Christchurch housewife going to church. "There's no need to apologize; you don't know me," she said. "I wanted to introduce myself because... we have a few things in common. My name is Christine Lorimer. I was the first."

Helen looked at her, confused. "The first what? Come, let's step into the shade. Mrs. Baldwin has prepared some refreshments in the house."

"I don't want to impose," Mrs. Lorimer said quickly. "But you could say I'm your predecessor. The first who came from England to be married here."

"That is interesting indeed," Helen said, surprised. "I thought I was the first. They said the other women had yet to receive any replies to their letters, and I came without any explicit agreement."

The young woman nodded. "Me too, more or less. I didn't answer an advertisement though. I was twenty-five and had no prospects for a husband. And how would I, without a dowry? I lived with my brother and his family, which he supported more poorly than properly. I tried to earn enough as a seamstress to help out, but I'm not much use. I have bad eyes; they didn't want me in the factory. Then my brother and his wife had the idea to emigrate. But what would have become of me? We stumbled on the idea of writing a letter to the pastor here. Was there perchance a proper Christian man in Canterbury looking for a bride? We received an answer from a Mrs. Brennan. It was very stern, and she wanted to know everything about me. She must have enjoyed it. At any rate, I received a letter from Mr. Thomas Lorimer. And what can I say—I fell in love at once!"

"Seriously?" Helen asked, not wanting to admit that she had felt no differently. "After one letter?"

Mrs. Lorimer giggled. "Of course. He wrote so beautifully. I can still repeat his words by heart: 'I yearn for a woman who would be prepared to tie her fate to mine. I pray to God for a loving woman, whose heart my words can soften.'"

Helen's eyes widened. "But...but that's in my letter!" she exclaimed, becoming agitated. "Howard wrote exactly those same words to me. I can't believe what you're telling me, Mrs. Lorimer. Is this some kind of joke?"

The woman looked shocked. "Oh no, Mrs. O'Keefe! I didn't mean to hurt you. I had no way of knowing they'd done it again."

"What do you mean, 'done it again'?" Helen asked, although she was beginning to put the pieces together.

"Well, what they did with the letters," Christine Lorimer explained. "My Thomas is a good-hearted man. Really, I couldn't wish for a better husband. But he is a joiner; he doesn't make big speeches, nor does he write romantic letters. He told me, he had tried again and again, but he didn't like any of the letters he wrote me enough to send them. After all, he wanted to touch my heart, you know. So, he just turned to Vicar Chester."

"Vicar Chester wrote the letters?" asked Helen, who didn't know whether to laugh or cry. Yet a few things suddenly made sense: the lovely fine handwriting typical of a cleric; the well-selected choice of words; the lack of practical information that Gwyneira had observed. And, of course, the vicar's obvious interest in the success of the romance.

"I wouldn't have thought they'd dare do it again," Mrs. Lorimer said. "Especially since I gave both of them a thorough dressing down when I learned of the whole thing. Oh, I'm so sorry, Mrs. O'Keefe. Your Howard should have had the chance to tell you himself. But I'm going to deal with this Vicar Chester. I've certainly got a few things to say to him!"

Christine Lorimer leaped resolutely into action, while Helen remained behind, contemplative. Who was the man she had just married? Had Chester really only helped him put his feelings into words, or had Howard not really cared how he lured his future bride to the ends of the earth?

She would soon find out, though she wasn't entirely certain that she wanted to know the truth.

The wagon had been bouncing over muddy paths for more than eight hours. Helen felt the journey would never end. Moreover, the infinite expanse of the landscape depressed her. They hadn't passed a house for more than an hour. Besides, the vehicle in which Howard transported his young wife, her worldly goods, and his own purchases was without a doubt the most uncomfortable form of transportation that Helen had ever traveled in. Her back hurt from the uncushioned seat, and the constant misting rain gave her headaches. Howard didn't do anything to make the trip any easier on her. He hadn't said a word to her for at least a half hour, at most muttering a command to the brown horse and gray mule that pulled the wagon.

Helen, therefore, had all the time in the world to dwell on her thoughts, which were not exactly joyful. The debacle over the letter was the least of her troubles. Howard and the vicar had begged for forgiveness for their little ruse the day before, admitting that it had been a venial sin. However, they had brought the matter to a successful conclusion: Howard had his wife and Helen her husband. What was infinitely more troubling was the news that Helen had heard from Elizabeth the night before. Mrs. Baldwin had said nothing—perhaps because she was ashamed or because she didn't want to unsettle Helen—but Belinda Baldwin had not been able to hold her tongue and had revealed to Elizabeth that little Laurie had run away from the Lavenders on her second day with them. She had been found quickly and sharply rebuked, but she had tried it again the next evening. After the second time, she had been beaten. After her third attempt, she had been locked in the broom closet.

"Only getting bread and water!" Belinda declared dramatically.

Helen had spoken to the reverend about it that morning before their departure; naturally, he had told her he would see that right was done by Laurie. But would he keep his word when Helen was not there to exhort him to do his duty?

Then there had been the departure with Howard. Helen had spent her last night chastely in her bed at the Baldwins'. To bring her man into the parsonage was out of the question, and Howard couldn't or wouldn't pay for a night in the hotel.

"We have our whole lives together," he had declared, kissing Helen awkwardly on the cheek. "Not everything needs to happen tonight."

Helen had been relieved but also a little disappointed. She would have preferred the amenities of a hotel room to the blanket bed in the covered wagon that likely awaited her during this trip. She had laid her good nightshirt at the top of her travel bag, but where she was supposed to dress and undress decently was a mystery to her. In addition to all that, the mist had made her clothing—and doubtless the blankets, too—cold and damp. Whatever awaited her that night, these conditions certainly would not contribute to its success.

However, Helen was spared an improvised camp in the covered wagon. Shortly before dark, when she was completely exhausted and just wished the clattering of the carriage would finally cease, Howard stopped before a humble farmhouse.

"We can stay here with this family tonight," he told Helen, helping her down from the box in a gentlemanly manner. "I know Wilbur from Port Cooper. He's married and settled down now too."

A dog began barking inside the house, and Wilbur and his wife came out, curious about their visitors.

When the short, wiry man recognized Howard, he let out a shout and embraced him roughly. They clapped each other on the shoulder and began reminding each other of their great former exploits—and probably would have liked to uncork their first bottle right there in the rain.

Helen looked imploringly at Wilbur's wife. To her relief, the woman smiled openly and warmly.

"You must be the new Mrs. O'Keefe! We could hardly believe it when we heard that Howard was ready to marry. But come in out of the rain, you're no doubt chilled to the bone. And the rattling of these wagons—you come from London, isn't that so? No doubt you're used to fine carriages!" The woman smiled as though she hadn't meant her last comment seriously. "I'm Margaret."

Helen introduced herself. Apparently, people didn't stand on ceremony here. Margaret was thin and a little taller than her husband and looked a bit haggard. She wore a simple gray dress that had been patched many times. The house into which she led Helen was rather primitive: the tables and chairs of were made of unfinished wood, and an open fireplace was also used for cooking. But the food simmering in a large caldron smelled good.

"You're in luck; I just slaughtered a chicken," Margaret explained. "Not exactly the youngest of the lot, but she'll make a proper soup. Sit down by the fire, Helen, and dry off a bit. Here's some coffee, and I'll find a swig of whiskey around here too."

Helen looked at her, bewildered. She had never drunk whiskey in her life, but Margaret didn't seem to think twice about it. She filled Helen's enamel cup with coffee as bitter as gall, which she had been keeping warm near the fire for what must have been an eternity. Helen hadn't dared ask for sugar or even milk, but Margaret set both out readily in front of her on the table. "Take plenty of sugar; it gets your spirits up. And a slug of whiskey!"

The liquor really did enhance the taste of the coffee, and the mixture was perfectly drinkable with milk and sugar. Alcohol was supposed to chase away sorrows and relax strained muscles. So Helen justified it as medicine and didn't refuse when Margaret topped off her cup a second time.

By the time the chicken soup was ready, Helen was viewing everything as though through a light fog. She was finally warm again, and the firelit room had a welcoming atmosphere. If she should experience the "unspeakable" here for the first time—what of it?

The excellent soup did its part to raise her spirits, but it made her tired. Helen would have liked to go straight to bed, though Margaret obviously enjoyed chatting with her.

But even Howard seemed to want to bring the evening to a conclusion. He had emptied several glasses with Wilbur and laughed loudly when his friend suggested a card game.

"Nah, m'friend, no more tonight. Tonight I got something else in mind that has a lot to do with that enchanting woman who fled from the old country to me."

He bowed gallantly to Helen, who reddened.

"So, where can we retire to? This is...so to speak...our wedding night!"

"Oh, then we still need to throw some rice!" Margaret squealed. "I didn't know you tied the knot so recently. Unfortunately, I can't offer you a proper bed. But there's plenty of fresh hay; it'll be warm and soft for you. Wait a moment, I'll give you sheets and blankets; yours'll be clammy from the drive through the rain. And a lantern, so you can see something...though the first time, people usually prefer doing it in the dark."

She giggled.

Helen was appalled. She was supposed to spend her wedding night in a stall?

The cow mooed hospitably as Helen and Howard entered the shed—she with an armful of blankets, he with the stall lantern. It was relatively warm. In addition to Howard's team, the stall sheltered the cow, two horses, and a mule. The animals warmed the room up but also filled it with permeating smells. Helen spread their blankets on the hay. Had it really only been three months since she had been so upset by the presence of a sheep pen? Gwyneira would certainly have found this amusing. Helen, however...if she were honest, she was just afraid.

"Where...can I undress here?" she asked shyly. She couldn't possibly undress in front of Howard in the middle of the stall.

Howard frowned. "Are you crazy, woman? I'll do all I can to keep you warm, but this is no place for lace shirts. It'll cool down tonight, and what's more there are bound to be fleas in the hay. Leave your dress on."

"But...but when we..." Helen turned a burning red.

Howard laughed, pleased. "You let me worry about that!"

He calmly loosened his belt buckle. "Now get under the covers, so you don't catch cold. Do you need my help to loosen your corset?"

Howard obviously wasn't doing this for the first time, and he didn't seem nervous. On the contrary, his face shone with anticipation. Helen bashfully declined his help. She could loosen the ties herself. But to do so, she had to unbutton her dress, which wasn't easy since the buttons were in the back. She shrank when she felt Howard's fingers. He ably undid one button after the other.

"Better?" he asked with a sort of smile.

Helen nodded. She just hoped that this night would pass quickly as she lay down in the hay with desperate determination. She just wanted to put it behind her, whatever "it" was. Silently she lay on her back and closed her eyes. Her hands clamped down on the sheets after she'd pulled the covers over her. Howard slipped in next to her and undid his fly. Helen felt his lips on her face. Her husband kissed her cheeks and her mouth. Well all right, she had let him do that already. But then he attempted to insert his tongue between her lips. Helen stiffened immediately, feeling relieved when he noticed her reaction and backed off. Instead, he kissed her neck, pulling down the neckline of her dress and corset and beginning awkwardly to fondle her breasts.

Helen hardly dared breathe, while Howard breathed faster and faster until he was panting. Helen wondered if that was normal—and was scared to death when he reached under her dress.

Perhaps it would have been less painful in a more comfortable setting. On the other hand, more inviting surroundings might have made the whole interlude worse. As it was, it all simply felt unreal. It was pitch black, and the covers as well as Helen's voluminous skirts, now pushed up to her hips, blocked her view of what Howard was doing to her. But it was horrible enough just to feel it. Her husband stuck something between her legs, something hard, pulsing, alive. It was terrifying and disgusting and painful. Helen screamed as something seemed to rip within her. She noticed she was bleeding, which did not stop Howard from tormenting her further. It was like he was possessed, moaning and moving himself rhythmically on top of and inside of her, almost seeming to enjoy it. Helen had to clench her teeth to keep from crying out in pain. Finally, she felt a gush of warm fluid, and a moment later, Howard collapsed on top of her. It was over. Her husband fell away. He was still breathing quickly, but he soon calmed down. Helen wept quietly as she fixed her skirts.

"Next time it won't hurt like that," Howard said in an effort to console her and kissed her cheek awkwardly. He seemed to be pleased with her. Helen forced herself not to shrink from him. Howard had a right to do what he'd done to her. He was her husband, after all.

4

The second day of the journey was even more arduous than the first. Helen's lower body hurt so much that she could hardly stay seated. Beyond that, she was so ashamed she did not want to look at Howard. Even breakfast in their hosts' house had been torture. Margaret and Wilbur would not hold off on the teasing and innuendos, which Howard only moodily returned. Only at the end of the meal did Margaret notice Helen's pallor and lack of appetite.

"It gets better, child," she turned to her confidingly as the men went outside to hitch the team. "The man just has to open you up for it at first. That hurts, and you bleed a bit. But then it goes in easy, and it doesn't hurt anymore. It can even be fun; believe me."

Helen would never take pleasure in this act; she was sure of that. But if men liked it, you had to let them do it to keep them in a good mood.

"And otherwise, there'd be no children," Margaret said.

Helen could hardly imagine that children came into being from this indecent business full of pain and fear, but then she remembered the stories in ancient mythology. In those stories too, women were sometimes defiled and bore children as a result. Maybe it was totally normal, then. And it wasn't indecent; they were married, after all.

Forcing herself to speak in a calm voice, Helen asked Howard about his land and his animals. She didn't really listen to his answers, but she didn't want him to think she was upset with him. Howard did not seem worried about that, however. In fact, it was clear that he was not the least bit ashamed about the night before.

Late that afternoon they crossed the boundary onto Howard's farm, which was marked by a muddy stream. The wagon promptly became stuck in it, and Helen and Howard were forced to get out and push. When they finally climbed back onto the coach box, they were wet, and the hem of Helen's skirt was weighted down with mud. But then the farmhouse came into view and Helen promptly forgot all her concerns about her dress, her pain, and even her fear of the coming night.

"This'd be us," Howard said, stopping the team in front of a hut. If feeling generous, one might also call it a blockhouse. It was made of unfinished logs that had been bound together. "Go on in, I'll take care of things in the stable."

Helen stood as though paralyzed. This was supposed to be her house? Even the stalls in Christchurch were more comfortable—not to mention London.

"Well, get going. It's not locked. There're no thieves here."

It wasn't like there was anything to steal either. When Helen, still speechless, pushed open the door, she entered a room that made even Margaret's kitchen seem livable. The house consisted of two rooms—the first was a combination kitchen and living room, sparsely furnished with four chairs and a chest. The kitchen was somewhat better supplied; unlike in Margaret's home, there was a proper stove. At least Helen wouldn't have to cook over an open fire.

Nervously she opened the door to the neighboring room—Howard's bedroom. No, their bedroom, she corrected herself. She would simply have to make it more comfortable.

It held only a timber-frame bed, which was sloppily made with dirty linen. Helen thanked heaven for her purchases in London. With new bed linens, it would immediately look better. As soon as Howard brought her bag in, she would change the sheets.

Howard entered with a basket of firewood under his arm. A few eggs were balanced on the logs.

"Lazy rats, these no good Maori!" he cursed. "They milked the cow yesterday all right, but not today. She's standing there with bursting udders, the poor animal, moaning her heart out. Can you go on and milk her? That'll be your job from now on anyway, so go on now and figure it out."

Helen looked at him, confused. "You want me to…milk? Now?"

"Well, wait till tomorrow and she'll kick it," Howard said. "But you can put on some dry clothes first; I'll bring your things right in. You'll catch your death of cold in this room as it is now. Here's some firewood."

This last comment sounded like an order. But Helen wanted to resolve the matter of the cow first.

"Howard, I can't milk a cow," she admitted. "I've never done that before."

Howard frowned.

"What do you mean, you've never milked a cow before?" he asked. "Aren't there any cows in England? You wrote that you were responsible for your father's household for years!"

"Yes, but we lived in Liverpool. In the middle of the city, next to the church. We didn't have any livestock!"

Howard looked at her coldly. "Then see that you learn how. I'll do it today. You clean the floor in the meantime. The wind's blowing all this dust around. Then get the stove going. I've already brought the wood in, so you just need to light it. Mind that you stack the wood carefully; otherwise, it'll smoke us out of the cabin. But surely you can do that. Or do they not have stoves in Liverpool?"

Howard's contemptuous expression made Helen drop any further objections. It would just anger him further if she told him that in Liverpool they'd had a maid for the heavy housework. Helen's tasks had been limited to raising her younger siblings, helping in the rectory, and leading the Bible circle. What would he think if she described the manor in London? The Greenwoods kept a cook, a servant who lit the stove, maids who anticipated their every wish, and Helen as governess. Though she was certainly not considered one of the masters of the house, no one would have expected her to so much as touch a piece of firewood.

Helen didn't know how she was supposed to manage everything. But she didn't see a way out either.

Gerald Warden could not hide his delight that Gwyneira and Lucas had arrived at an agreement so quickly. He fixed the wedding day for the second weekend of Advent. That was the height of summer, and part of the reception could take place in the garden, which still needed to be fixed up, of course. Hoturapa and two other Maori who had been hired especially for the purpose worked hard to plant the seeds and seedlings that Gerald had brought back from England. A few native plants also found a place in Lucas's carefully planned garden design. Since it would take too long for maple or chestnut trees to grow big enough, southern beeches, nikau, and cabbage trees were planted so that Gerald's guests could take a stroll in the shade in the foreseeable future. That didn't bother Gwyneira, who found the native flora and fauna interesting. It was finally an area where her proclivities and those of her future husband overlapped, though Lucas's research focused primarily on ferns and insects. The former were found primarily in the rainy western region of South Island. Gwyneira could only wonder at their diverse and filigreed shapes from Lucas's own well-executed drawings and in his textbooks. However, when she saw a living example of one of the native insects for the first time, even hard-bitten Gwyneira let out a scream. Lucas, ever the most attentive of gentlemen, rushed immediately to her side. However, the sight seemed to fill him with more joy than horror.

"It's a weta!" he said, getting excited, and poked at the six-legged creature that Hoturapa had just dug up with a twig. "They are perhaps the largest insects in the world. It's not uncommon to see specimens that are eight centimeters long or more."

Gwyneira could not share in her fiancé's joy. If the bug had only looked more like a butterfly or a bee or a hornet...but the weta most closely resembled a fat, wet, glistening grasshopper.

"They belong to the same family," Lucas lectured. "More precisely to the ensifera suborder. Except for the cave weta, which belongs to the rhaphidophoridae."

Lucas knew the Latin designation for several weta subfamilies. Gwyneira, however, found the Maori name for the bugs more appropriate. Kiri and her people called them *wetapunga*, which meant "god of ugly things."

"Do they sting?" Gwyneira asked. The bug didn't seem particularly lively and only moved forward sluggishly when Lucas poked it. However, it had an imposing stinger on its abdomen and Gwyneira kept her distance.

"No, no, they're generally harmless. At most they sometimes bite. And it's no worse than a wasp sting," Lucas explained. "The stinger is...it...well, it indicates that this is a female, and..." Lucas turned away, as always, when it had to do with anything "sexual."

"It's for laying eggs, miss," Hoturapa clarified casually. "This one big and fat, soon lay eggs. Much eggs, hundred, two hundred...better not to take in house, Mr. Warden. Not that egg laying in house."

"For heaven's sake!" Just the thought of sharing her living quarters with two hundred of this unattractive bug's offspring sent chills up Gwyneira's back. "Just leave her here. If she runs away..."

"Not walking quickly, miss. Jumping. Whoops and you have *wetapunga* in lap!" Hoturapa explained.

Gwyneira took another step back, just to be sure.

"Then I'll draw it right here on the spot," Lucas gave in reluctantly. "I would have preferred to take it into my study and compared it directly with the images in the field guide. But I guess my drawings will have to do. You'd also like to know, no doubt, Gwyneira, whether we have a ground weta or a tree weta here."

Gwyneira had rarely cared so little about anything.

"Why can't he be interested in sheep like his father?" she asked her patient audience, consisting of Cleo and Igraine, afterward. Gwyneira had retreated to the stables and was grooming her mare while Lucas sketched the weta. The horse had worked up a sweat during the ride that morning, and the girl did not want to pass up the chance to smooth her coat, which had since dried. "Or birds! Though they probably don't hold still long enough to let themselves be sketched."

Gwyneira found the native birds considerably more interesting than Lucas's creepy crawlies. The farmworkers had shown and told her about a few types of birds since her arrival. Most of them knew quite a lot about their new homeland; the frequent nights out under the open sky had made them familiar with the nocturnal birds. James McKenzie, for example, told her about the European settlers' name-sake: the kiwi bird was short and plump, and Gwyneira found them quite exotic with their brown feathers that almost looked like fur and their much-too-long beaks, which they often used as a "third leg."

"They have something else in common with your dog," McKenzie explained cleverly. "They can smell. Which is rare for birds."

McKenzie had accompanied Gwyneira several times on her over-land rides the last few days. As expected, she had quickly earned the respect of the shepherds. Her first demonstration of Cleo's shepherding abilities had inspired the men from the first.

"That dog does the work of two shepherds," Poker marveled and stooped to pat Cleo's head in recognition. "Will the little ones grow up like that?"

Gerald Warden had made each of the men responsible for train-ing one of the new sheepdogs. In theory, it made sense to have each dog learning from the man with whom it was supposed to shepherd. In practice, however, McKenzie undertook the work with the pups almost alone, supported occasionally by Andy McAran and young Hardy. The other men found it dull to go through the commands over and over again; they also thought it gratuitous to have to fetch the sheep just to practice with the dogs.

McKenzie, on the other hand, showed an interest and a marked talent for handling animals. Under his guidance, little Daimon soon approached Cleo's skill level. Gwyneira supervised the exercises, despite the fact that it displeased Lucas. Gerald, by contrast, let her do as she pleased. He knew that the dogs were accruing value and use for the farm.

"Maybe you could put on a little show after the wedding, McKenzie," Gerald said, satisfied, after having watched Cleo and Daimon in action once again. "Most of the visitors would be interested in seeing that...I say, the other farmers will turn green with envy!"

"I won't be able to lead the dogs properly in a wedding dress," Gwyneira said, laughing. She savored the praise, as she always felt so hopelessly inept in the house. She was still technically a guest, but it was already clear that as mistress of Kiward Station she would have the same things demanded of her that she had hated at Silkham Manor: the direction of a large, noble manor with servants and the management of the whole charade. To make it even more difficult, none of the employees here were even educated. In England one could overcome a lack of organization by hiring capable butlers and matrons, by not scrimping when it came to personnel and hiring only people with first-class credentials. Then the household would practically run itself. Here, however, Gwyneira was expected to show her Maori servants the ropes, and she lacked the enthusiasm and conviction for that.

"Why clean silver every day?" Moana asked, for example, which struck Gwyneira as a perfectly logical question.

"Because, otherwise, it tarnishes," Gwyneira answered. She at least knew that much.

"But why take iron that changes color?" Moana asked, turning the silver over unhappily in her hands. "Take wood. Is simple, wash off, clean!" The girl looked at Gwyneira, expecting praise.

"Wood isn't...for every taste." Gwyn recalled one of her mother's answers. "And it becomes unsightly after it's been used a few times."

Moana shrugged. "Then just cut new ones. Is easy, I can show, miss."

The New Zealand natives were great masters in the art of carving. A few days earlier, Gwyneira had seen the Maori village that was part of Kiward Station. It was not far but lay hidden behind rocks and a copse of trees on the other side of the lake. Gwyneira would probably never have found it had she not noticed the women doing their laundry and the horde of almost-naked children bathing in the lake. At the sight of Gwyneira, the little brown children retreated shyly, but on her next ride she distributed sweets to them, thus winning their trust. The women invited her with big gestures into their camp, and Gwyneira marveled at their houses and grill pits. She was most impressed with their meetinghouse, which was adorned with plentiful carvings.

Slowly she began to understand her first bits of Maori.

Kia ora meant hello. *Tana* was man, *wahine* woman. She learned that you did not say "thank you" but showed your gratitude through actions and that the Maori did not shake hands in greeting but rubbed noses instead. This ritual was called *hongi*, and Gwyneira practiced it with the giggling children. Lucas was appalled when she told him about it, and Gerald reproved her: "We should under no circumstances get too close to them. These people are primitive; they need to learn their boundaries."

"I think it's always good when people can understand each other better," Gwyneira disagreed. "Why should it be the primitives who learn the civilized language? It must be much easier the other way around."

Helen crouched next to the cow and attempted to cajole her. The animal seemed friendly, which wasn't a given, if she had correctly understood Daphne on the ship. Apparently, you had to be careful with some dairy cows that they did not attack you while you milked them. Yet even a willing cow could not effect the milking herself. Helen was necessary—but could not make it happen. No matter how much she tugged and kneaded the udders, she never released more than one or two drops. It had looked so easy when Howard did it. But he had shown her only once; he was still in a bad mood after last night's disaster. When he had returned from milking, the stove had turned the room into a smoky hell. Helen squatted before the iron monstrosity in tears, and, of course, she hadn't managed to sweep yet either. In sullen silence, Howard had lit the stove and fireplace, cracked a few eggs in a skillet, and set the food on the table for Helen.

"Starting tomorrow, you cook!" he declared as he did so, sounding as though he would accept no further excuses. Helen wondered what she should cook. There wasn't anything in the house but milk and eggs the next day either. "And you have to bake bread. There's grain in the cupboard there. Besides that, there's beans, salt...you'll figure something out. I know you're tired, Helen, but you're no good to me otherwise."

That night Helen repeated the experience of the night before. This time she wore her prettiest nightgown and lay between clean sheets, none of which made it any more bearable. Helen was sore and horribly ashamed, and Howard's face, reflecting naked lust, made her fearful. But this time she at least knew that it would be over quickly. Afterward Howard fell right asleep.

That morning he had gone out to inspect the flocks. He let Helen know he would not be back before evening. When he returned, he expected a warm house, a good meal, and a clean room.

Helen could not even manage the milking. But now, as she once more tugged desperately on the udder, a furtive giggle sounded from the direction of the stable door. Then somebody whispered something. Helen would have been afraid of the voices had they not sounded so high-pitched and childlike. As it was, she simply stood up.

"Come out; I see you," she said.

Fresh chuckling.

Helen went to the door but saw only two little dark figures disappear quick as lightning through the half-open door.

Well, they wouldn't go far; they were much too curious for that.

"I won't hurt you!" Helen called. "What did you want, to steal some eggs?"

"We not stealing, missy!" A wounded voice. Helen must have piqued someone's honor. A small, chestnut-brown figure emerged from around the corner of the stable, dressed only in a short skirt. "We milk when Mr. O'Keefe away."

Aha! Helen had them to blame for the scene the day before.

"But you didn't milk her yesterday," she said sternly. "Mr. O'Keefe was very angry."

"Yesterday *waiata-a-ringa...*"

"Dance," the second child elaborated, a boy dressed in a loincloth. "All people dancing. No time for cow."

Helen refrained from giving them a lesson on the need to milk cows daily without regard to festivals, seeing as she hadn't known that until the day before herself.

"But today you can help me," she said instead. "You can show me how to do it."

"How to do what?" the girl asked.

"How to milk. What you do with the cow," Helen sighed.

"You not know how to milk?" Fresh giggling.

"What you then doing here?" inquired the young boy, grinning. "Stealing eggs?"

Helen had to laugh. The kid was sly. But she couldn't be upset with him. Helen thought both children were sweet.

"I'm the new Mrs. O'Keefe," she introduced herself. "Mr. O'Keefe and I got married in Christchurch."

"Mr. O'Keefe marry *wahine* who no can milk?"

"Well, I have other qualities," Helen said, laughing. "For example, I can bake sweets." And she could; it had always been her last resort when she needed to convince her brothers to do something. And Howard had syrup in the house. She would have to improvise with the other ingredients, but first she had to get the two children into the cow's stall. "But only for good children, of course."

The term "good" did not seem to mean much to the Maori children, but they knew the word "sweets" and the deal was quickly finalized. Helen then learned that the children were named Rongo Rongo and Reti and lived in a Maori village farther down the river. They milked the cow with lightning speed, found eggs in places Helen had not even thought to look, and then followed her curiously into the house. Since cooking the syrup for candy would have taken hours, Helen decided to just serve them pancakes with syrup. The two observed, fascinated, how she stirred the batter and turned the cakes over in the pan.

"Like *takakau*, flat bread!" Rongo Rongo exclaimed.

Helen saw her chance. "Can you make that, Rongo? Flat bread, I mean? Can you show me how?"

It turned out it was rather easy. She needed little beyond water and grain. Helen hoped it would meet with Howard's approval, but at least it was something to eat. To her amazement, there were also things to eat in the neglected garden behind the house. On first inspection, she had not been able to find anything that fit her idea of a vegetable, but after Rongo Rongo and Reti dug around for a few minutes, they proudly held out a few mysterious roots to her. Helen made a stew from them that tasted astoundingly good.

That afternoon she cleaned the room while Rongo and Reti inspected her trousseau. Her books especially piqued their interest.

"That's a magic thingy!" Reti said weightily. "Don't touch it, Rongo, or you'll be eaten!"

Helen laughed. "What makes you say that, Reti? Those are just books; there are stories in them. They are not dangerous. When we're finished here, I can read to you from them."

"But stories are in head of *kuia*," Rongo said. "Of storyteller."

"Well, when someone can write, the stories flow out of their heads through their arms and hands and into a book," Helen said, "and anyone can read it, not just the person the *kuia* tells his stories to."

"Magic!" concluded Reti.

Helen shook her head. "No, no. Look, that's how you write your name." She took a piece of letter paper and set down first Reti's and then Rongo Rongo's name on paper. The children followed her hand with gaping mouths.

"See, now you can read your names. And you can write down anything else, as well. Anything you can say."

"But then you have power," declared Reti seriously. "Storyteller has power."

Helen laughed. "Yes. Do you know what? I'll teach you two to read. In exchange you'll show me how to milk the cow and teach me what grows in the garden. I'll ask Mr. O'Keefe if there are books in your language. I'll learn Maori, and you'll learn better English."

5

It looked like Gerald would be proved right. Gwyneira's wedding was the most glamorous social event the Canterbury Plains had ever seen. Guests began arriving days before from remote farms and even from the barracks in Dunedin. Half of Christchurch was on hand as well. Kiward Station's guest rooms were soon completely full, but Gerald had had tents erected all around the house so that everyone had a comfortable place to sleep. He engaged the cook from the hotel in Christchurch so that he could offer his guests a meal that would be both familiar and exquisite. Meanwhile, Gwyneira was supposed to be schooling the Maori girls in how to be perfect servers; however, she was in a bit over her head. Then it occurred to her that in Dorothy, Elizabeth, and Daphne, there was a well-trained staff to be had in the area. Mrs. Godewind was happy to lend her Elizabeth, and the Candlers, Dorothy's employers, had been invited anyway and could just bring her along. Daphne, however, could not be found. Gerald had no idea where Morrison's farm was, so there was no hope of making contact with the girl directly. Mrs. Baldwin maintained that she had attempted to contact them but had received no answer from Mr. Morrison. Gwyneira thought sadly once again about Helen. Maybe she knew something about her lost pupil. But she had yet to hear anything from her friend, nor had she found the time or opportunity to make inquiries.

Dorothy and Elizabeth looked happy, at least. In their blue serving dresses with white lace aprons and bonnets that had been tailored for the wedding, they looked very tidy and sweet, and they had not forgotten any of their training. However, in the excitement, Elizabeth dropped two of the most expensive porcelain plates, but Gerald did not notice, the Maori girl did not care, and Gwyneira ignored it. She was more worried about Cleo, who only partially responded to James McKenzie. Hopefully everything would go well during the sheepdogs' show.

The weather was exceptional and the wedding took place under a richly ornamented canopy specially erected in the lush and blooming garden. Gwyneira recognized most of the plants from England. The fertile land seemed receptive to all the new plants and animals that the immigrants brought with them.

Gwyneira's English wedding dress garnered many admiring looks and comments. Elizabeth, in particular, was beside herself.

"I'd like to have one like that when I get married," she sighed longingly, no longer swooning over Jamie O'Hara, but Vicar Chester now.

"You can borrow it, then," Gwyneira said generously. "And you too, of course, Dot!"

Dorothy was pinning Gwyneira's hair up at that moment, which she did much more adeptly than Kiri or Moana, if not as capably as Daphne. Dorothy did not respond to Gwyneira's gracious offer, though Gwyneira had seen how she looked after the youngest of the Candlers' sons with interest. They were a good fit age-wise—perhaps something would develop in a few years.

Gwyneira made a beautiful bride, and in his black-tie wedding suit, Lucas did not look bad either. While Gwyneira twice stumbled over her words, Lucas spoke his vows confidently and with a steady voice before placing an expensive ring on his wife's finger and kissing her modestly on the lips when Reverend Baldwin encouraged him to. Gwyneira felt strangely disappointed but quickly pulled herself together. What exactly had she expected? That Lucas would take her in his arms and kiss her passionately like the cowboys in the penny dreadfuls did with the lucky heroines they'd just saved?

Gerald was hardly able to contain his pride. Rivers of champagne and whiskey flowed. The multicourse meal was delicious, the guests excited and full of wonder. Gerald shone with happiness, while Lucas remained astoundingly even-keeled—which annoyed Gwyneira a little. He could at least have pretended he was in love with her.

But that couldn't really be expected of him. Gwyneira was attempting to put her unrealistic romantic ideals behind her, but Lucas's casual aloofness made her nervous. Then again, she seemed to be the only one who noticed her husband's strange behavior. The guests expressed only admiration for the lovely couple and gushed about how well the bride and groom suited each other. Perhaps she just expected too much.

Finally Gerald announced the sheepdog demonstration, and the guests followed him to the stables behind the house.

Gwyneira looked despondently over to Igraine, who stood with Madoc in a paddock. She had not been able to ride for the last few days, and it looked unlikely to happen for the next few days as well. As was customary, some of the guests planned to stay a few days longer, and they would have to be catered to and entertained.

The shepherds had fetched a herd of sheep for the demonstration, and James McKenzie prepared to release the dogs. Cleo and Daimon were first supposed to circle around the sheep grazing freely in the field beside the house. As a result, they desired a starting position directly across from the sheep. Cleo executed this task perfectly but then noticed Gwyneira and lay down far too far to the right of McKenzie. Gwyneira measured the distance with a look, catching the eye of her dog in the process: Cleo looked at her imploringly—and made no move to react to McKenzie. She awaited Gwyneira's command.

That didn't have to be a problem, however. Gwyneira stood in the front row of spectators not far from McKenzie. He was now giving the dogs the command to assume control of the flock—generally the critical point of such a demonstration. Cleo managed to form up her group quite capably, and Daimon assisted wonderfully. McKenzie cast a glance toward Gwyneira, begging for approval, and she returned his gaze with a smile. Gerald's foreman had done an exceptional job with Daimon's training. Gwyneira couldn't have done it better herself.

Cleo expertly herded her flock over to the shepherd—there being no issue yet regarding the fact that she was focused on Gwyneira instead of James. She had to pass through a gate on her way to them, and the sheep had to enter first. Cleo kept them moving at an even tempo, and

Daimon watched for any stragglers. Everything was going perfectly until the gate was supposed to be passed through and the sheep herded behind the shepherd, because Cleo took Gwyneira for the shepherd in question. Cleo steered the sheep toward Gwyneira and was vexed. Was she really supposed to herd the sheep into this crowd of people that had taken position behind her mistress? Gwyneira recognized Cleo's confusion and knew that she had to act. She calmly bunched her skirts, left the wedding guests, and moved toward James.

"Come, Cleo!"

The dog herded the sheep rapidly through the gate set up to James's left. Here the dogs were supposed to separate a designated sheep from the flock.

"You first!" Gwyneira whispered to James.

He had looked almost as vexed as the dog, but he smiled when Gwyneira walked up to him. He whistled for Daimon and pointed a sheep out to him. A well-behaved Cleo remained lying down while the pup singled the sheep out. Daimon did his job well, but it took him three tries.

"My turn!" Gwyneira cried in the heat of competition. "Shedding, Cleo!"

Cleo leaped up and separated her sheep from the rest on the first try.

The audience applauded.

"The winner!" Gwyneira cried, laughing.

James McKenzie looked at her beaming face. Her cheeks were red, her eyes shone triumphantly, and her smile was radiant. Earlier, standing at the wedding altar, she had not looked half as happy.

Gwyneira noticed the twinkle in McKenzie's eyes and was confused. What was it? Pride? Amazement? Or perhaps that which had been missing all day from her husband's gaze?

But now the dogs had a final task to accomplish. At James's whistle, they herded the sheep into a pen, at which point McKenzie was supposed to shut the gate behind them to signify that the job was done.

"I'll be going, then," Gwyneira said sadly as he strode toward the gate.

McKenzie shook his head. "No, it falls to the winner."

He stepped aside for Gwyneira, who hadn't noticed that the hem of her dress was trailing over the dirt. She shut the gate triumphantly. Cleo, who had been dutifully watching the sheep until the job was over, jumped up on her, begging for recognition. Gwyneira praised her, registering with some guilt as she did so that this meant the end of her white dress.

"That was a bit unconventional," Lucas remarked sourly when Gwyneira finally returned to his side. The guests had apparently had the time of their lives and showered her with compliments, but her husband appeared less enthused.

"It would be nice if you would play the lady a little more next time."

Meanwhile, the air had cooled in the garden, and it was time to move inside to start the dancing. In the salon a string quartet was playing; Lucas, of course, remarked on the frequent mistakes in their performance. Gwyneira did not notice a thing. Dorothy and Kiri had done their best to clean her dress, and now she let Lucas lead her in a waltz. As expected, the young Warden was a superb dancer. Then she danced with her father-in-law, who moved very smoothly across the floor, then with Lord Barrington, and finally with Mr. Brewster. The Brewsters had brought along their son and his young wife, and the young Maori was just as enchanting as he had described her.

Gwyneira danced with Lucas between the others—and at some point her feet began to ache from dancing. She finally let Lucas escort her onto the veranda for some fresh air. She sipped a glass of champagne and thought about the night that lay ahead. She could no longer repress the thought. Tonight it would happen—that which would make a woman of her, as her mother had said.

Music could be heard coming from the stables in the distance. The farmworkers were celebrating, though not with a string quartet—the fiddle, harmonica, and tin whistle were playing cheerful folk dances. Gwyneira wondered whether James was playing one of the instruments. And whether he was being good to Cleo, who was not allowed inside tonight. Lucas had not been enthusiastic about the prospect of the little dog following his fiancée everywhere she went. He might have allowed Gwyneira a lapdog, but he believed that sheepdogs belonged in the stables. Gwyneira was willing to indulge him this evening, but planned to reshuffle the cards the next day. And James would take good care of Cleo...Gwyneira thought about his strong brown hands scratching her dog's fur. The dog loved him...and she had other things to worry about at the moment.

The wedding festivities were still in full swing when Lucas suggested to his wife that they retire.

"Later the men will be drunk and will probably insist on escorting us to the bridal chamber," he said. "I'd rather spare us the dirty jokes."

It was all right with Gwyneira. She'd had enough dancing and wanted to put this night behind her. She vacillated between fear and curiosity. According to her mother's demure remarks, it would be painful, but in the penny novels, the woman always sank wholly smitten into the cowboy's arms. Gwyneira would let herself be surprised.

The wedding guests saw the couple off with much ado, but without any embarrassing ribaldry, and Kiri was right at her side to help her out of her wedding dress. Lucas kissed her discreetly in front of the bridal chamber.

"Take your time preparing, my love. I'll come to you."

Kiri and Dorothy helped Gwyneira out of her dress and undid her hair. Kiri giggled and made jokes the whole time, while Dorothy whimpered. The Maori girl seemed to be honestly happy for Gwyneira and Lucas and was only surprised that the married couple had retired from the party so soon. Among the Maori it was considered a symbol of the marriage's consummation to lie together before the whole family. When Dorothy heard that, she began to cry harder.

"What exactly is so sad, Dot?" Gwyneira asked, piqued. "You're acting like this is a funeral."

"I don't know, miss, but my mum always cried at weddings. Maybe it brings good luck."

"Doesn't bring good luck crying, brings good luck laughing!" Kiri said. "There, you done, miss. Miss very beautiful! Very beautiful. We going now to knock on door of young master. Handsome man, young master. Very nice. Just a little thin." She giggled as she pulled Dorothy out the door.

Gwyneira looked down at herself. Her nightgown was of the finest lace; she knew she looked good in it. But what was she supposed to do now? She couldn't receive Lucas here at her dressing table. And if she had understood her mother correctly, the whole thing played out in the bed.

Gwyneira lay down and pulled the silk sheets over her. It was unfortunate that her nightgown was no longer visible. But maybe Lucas would uncover her?

She held her breath when she heard the doorknob. Lucas entered, a lamp in his hand. He seemed confused that Gwyneira had not yet turned out the light.

"Dearest, I think we...it would be more proper to extinguish the light."

Gwyneira nodded. In any case, Lucas was not a particularly impressive sight in his long nightshirt. She had always pictured masculine nightclothes to be...well, more masculine.

Lucas slid next to her under the sheets. "I'll try not to hurt you," he whispered and kissed her softly. Gwyneira held still as he caressed and covered her shoulders, her neck, and her breasts with kisses. Then he pushed up her nightgown. His breath quickened and Gwyneira noticed how she was seized by a growing excitement as Lucas's fingers felt for her body's most intimate regions, regions she had never explored herself. Her mother had always instructed her to wear a shirt even when bathing, and she had hardly dared examine her nether regions—the curly red hair, even curlier than the hair on her head. Lucas touched her softly, and Gwyneira felt a pleasant, arousing tingling. Finally he removed his hand and lay on top of her. Gwyneira felt something between her legs that bulged, became harder, and thrust deeply into those unknown regions of her body. Suddenly Lucas seemed to encounter some resistance and softened.

"I'm sorry, dearest, it's been a long day," he excused himself.

"It was really very lovely," Gwyneira said carefully and kissed his cheek.

"Maybe we could try it again tomorrow."

"If you like," Gwyn said, confused and a little relieved. As far as marriage duties went, her mother had exaggerated greatly. This was really no reason to feel sorry for anyone.

"Then I'll say good-bye," said Lucas stiffly. "I think you'll sleep better alone."

"If you like," said Gwyneira. "But don't husband and wife usually spend their wedding night together?"

Lucas nodded. "You're right. I'll stay here. The bed is spacious enough."

"Yes." Gwyneira happily made room, rolling over to the left side of the bed. Lucas lay fixed and rigid on the right.

"Then I wish you good night, dearest."

"Good night, Lucas."

The next morning Lucas was already up when Gwyneira awoke. Witi had laid out a light-colored morning suit for him in Gwyneira's dressing room, and he was already dressed to go down to breakfast.

"I'd be happy to wait for you, my love," he said, straining to look past Gwyneira, who had sat up in bed in her lace nightshirt. "But perhaps it's preferable that I be the recipient of our guests' ribald remarks."

Gwyneira wasn't afraid of seeing even the most ardent reveler from last night so early in the morning, but nodded in agreement.

"Please send Kiri and Dorothy, if possible, to help me dress and do my hair. We'll no doubt have to dress up, so someone will have to help me with my corset," she said in a friendly tone.

Lucas seemed to be once more embarrassed by the subject of corsets. However, Kiri was already waiting by the door. Only Dorothy had to be fetched.

"And, mistress? Was it lovely?"

"Please, continue calling me *miss*, you and the others," Gwyneira said. "I like it much better."

"Gladly, miss. But now tell. How it was? First time not always so lovely. But gets better, miss," Kiri said as she straightened Gwyneira's dress.

"Well…lovely…" Gwyneira muttered. In this regard too people overrated the thing. What Lucas had done to her the night before she considered neither lovely nor terrible. It seemed practical as long as the man did not weigh too much. She giggled at the thought of Kiri, who preferred plumper men.

Kiri had already helped Gwyneira into a white summer dress decorated with bright little flowers when Dorothy appeared. The girl took over doing her hair while Kiri changed the sheets. Gwyneira thought it unnecessary; after all, she hadn't done much more than sleep between the sheets. But she said nothing. Maybe it was a Maori custom. Dorothy was no longer crying but she was quiet and couldn't look Gwyneira in the eye.

"Are you all right, miss?" she asked, concerned.

Gwyneira nodded. "Of course, why wouldn't I be? That looks really nice with the barrette, Dorothy. You should take note, Kiri."

Kiri was otherwise occupied at the moment. She was contemplating the bedding with a concerned air. It first occurred to Gwyneira after she had sent Dorothy from the room with a breakfast order.

"What is it, Kiri? Are you looking for something in the bed? Did Mr. Warden lose something?" Gwyneira though that perhaps she was looking for a piece of jewelry, maybe Lucas's wedding ring, which had sat rather loosely on his slender finger.

Kiri shook her head. "No, no, miss. Is only…is no blood on sheets." Bewildered and ashamed, she looked up at Gwyneira.

"Why should there be blood?" Gwyneira asked.

"After first night, always blood. It hurts a little at first, then blood, and then gets lovely."

It dawned on Gwyneira that she had missed out on something. "Mr. Warden is very…tender," she said vaguely.

Kiri nodded. "And surely tired too after party. Not be sad, so first thing blood tomorrow!"

Gwyneira decided not to worry about it until it came up again. In the meantime, she went down to breakfast, where Lucas was entertaining the guests in the most genial fashion. He joked with the ladies, took the gentlemen's jibes in good humor, and proved as attentive as ever when Gwyneira joined him. The next few hours passed with the usual chitchat, and with the exception of the hopelessly sentimental Mrs. Brewster—who told her, "You're so brave, child. So cheerful! But Mr. Warden is such a considerate man," no one made any reference to the previous night.

At noon, when most of the guests were resting, Gwyneira finally found time to go to the stables to visit her horse and see her dog.

The shepherds bellowed their greetings to her.

"Oh, Mrs. Warden! Congrats. Did you have a good night?" Poker Livingston inquired.

"Obviously a better one than you, Mr. Livingston," Gwyneira returned. The men all looked rather hungover. "But I'm pleased that you drank so copiously to my health."

James McKenzie eyed her more reprovingly than pruriently. There even seemed to be a look of regret in his gaze—but it was difficult for Gwyneira to read the expression in his deep brown eyes, because it seemed to change constantly. A smile returned to his face as he observed Cleo greeting her mistress.

"Did you get an earful?" James asked.

Gwyneira shook her head. "Why would I? Because of the presentation? Not at all. A girl can step out of line on her wedding day." She winked at him. "Starting tomorrow my husband will lay down the law, and our guests are keeping me on a short leash. Someone is constantly wanting something from me. So I won't get around to riding today either."

James looked surprised that she wanted to ride but said nothing; his penetrating gaze once more flashed a carefree spark.

"Then you'll have to find some way of slipping past them! How about I saddle your horse tomorrow around this time? Most of the ladies will be napping then."

Gwyneira nodded enthusiastically. "Good idea. But not around this time; I'll have work to do in the kitchen managing the cleaning up after lunch and the preparations for tea. The cook insists—heaven knows why. But early in the morning would work. If you could have Igraine ready for me at six o'clock, I can have a ride before the first guests are up."

James looked vexed. "But what will Mr. Warden say if you... pardon me. That's naturally none of my business."

"Nor Mr. Warden's," Gwyneira replied, unconcerned. "As long as I don't neglect my duties as hostess, I can certainly ride whenever I want."

It has less to do with your duties as a hostess, thought James, but he kept this observation to himself. He did not want to offend Gwyneira in any way, but it did not appear that her wedding night had been particularly passionate.

That evening Lucas visited Gwyneira again. Now that she knew what awaited her, she even enjoyed his soft caresses. She shivered when he kissed her breasts, and his touch on the tender skin below her pubic hair was even more thrilling than the first time. She even snuck a peek at his member, which was large and hard—but it once again softened quickly just as before. Gwyneira felt strangely unfulfilled in a way that she couldn't quite account for. But perhaps that was normal. She would find out soon enough.

The next morning Gwyneira stuck herself lightly in the finger with a sewing needle, squeezed out some blood, and rubbed it on her sheets. Kiri wasn't to think she and Lucas might be doing something wrong.

6

Helen began to acclimate somewhat to life with Howard. What took place at night in their marriage bed was still rather mortifying, but she now saw it as separate from the rest of her daily life and behaved in a completely normal manner with Howard during the day.

But it was not always easy. Howard expected certain things from his wife, and his temper flared quickly when Helen did not meet those expectations. He fell into a rage whenever she voiced wishes and requests, whether for more furniture or better cookware, his pots and pans being old and so caked with leftovers that no amount of scouring could remove them.

"The next time we go to Haldon," he said by way of consolation every time. Apparently, the town was too far away to be worth driving to for a few kitchen items, spices, and sugar. At this revelation Helen yearned desperately for some contact with civilization. Their life in the wilds still scared her, no matter how often Howard assured her that there were no dangerous animals in the Canterbury Plains. She simply missed the diversions and intellectual conversation of city life. She couldn't speak with Howard about anything other than the work on the farm. He wasn't even willing to share details of his earlier life in Ireland or in the whale hunting stations. The subject was off-limits—Helen knew all she needed to know, and Howard was not interested in discussing it further.

The only bright spot in her cheerless existence was the Maori children. Reti and Rongo appeared almost every day, and after Reti had shown off his new reading skills in the village—both children learned quickly and could already recite the entire alphabet in addition to reading and writing their names—new children came along.

"We also study magic," one youth said seriously, and Helen wrote out further sheets with strange first names like Ngapini and Wiramu. Sometimes she was sorry to use her expensive letter paper, but she rarely had any other need of it. Though she wrote letters avidly to her relatives as well as to the Thornes in England and the girls right there in New Zealand, it wouldn't be possible to post them until they went to Haldon. In Haldon she also wanted to order a Maori-language edition of the Bible. Howard had told her that the Scriptures had already been translated and she wanted to study it. If she learned a little Maori, maybe she could get to know the children's mothers. Rongo had already taken her to the village once and everyone there had been very friendly. But only the men who worked with Howard or who hired themselves out to other farms to herd the sheep up and down to pasture spoke any English. The children had learned it from their fathers and from a missionary couple who had made a brief appearance.

"They not nice though," Reti explained. "All the time wagging finger and saying 'hey, hey, sins, sins!' What's a sin, miss?"

After that Helen expanded the curriculum and began to read the Bible aloud in English. This raised a few problems for her. The creation story, for example, profoundly confused the children.

"No, no, that different!" declared Rongo, whose grandmother was a well-esteemed storyteller. "First there was *papatuanuku*, the earth, and *ranginui*, the sky. And they loved each other so much they not want to separate. Understand?" Rongo then made a gesture whose obscenity made Helen's blood run cold. The child, however, was completely innocent. "But children of theirs wanted world with birds and fish and clouds and moon and everything. That's why they pull apart. And *papa* cries and cries and from there come river and sea and lake. But stopped sometime. *Rangi* still cries, almost every day."

Rangi's tears, Rongo had mentioned that before, fell from the sky as rain.

"That's a very beautiful story," murmured Helen. "But you know, of course, that *pakeha* come from big foreign countries where people study and know everything. And the God of Israel told the prophets this story in the Bible, and that's the truth."

"Really, miss? God told it? No God ever talks to us!" Reti was fascinated.

"There you have it," declared Helen, with a pang of conscience. After all, her prayers too were rarely answered.

The trip to Haldon, by way of example, had yet to materialize.

The wedding guests finally departed, and life at Kiward Station returned to normal. Gwyneira hoped to return to the relative freedom she had enjoyed when she had first arrived at the farm. And to a certain extent she did: Lucas did not forbid her anything. He did not find fault with Cleo once again sleeping in Gwyneira's chambers, even when he visited his wife. The little dog had been an annoyance the first few nights, though, protesting his presence with loud barking. She'd had to be scolded and sent back to her bed. Lucas had accepted it all without a peep. Gwyneira wondered why, unable to shake the feeling that Lucas felt guilty toward her for some reason. She still had never felt pain or shed blood during their time together. On the contrary—as time went on she came to enjoy the caresses and occasionally caught herself caressing herself after Lucas left, enjoying the feeling of rubbing and tickling herself and becoming appreciably wet. Only no blood appeared. Over time she became braver and probed further with her fingers, which made the feeling even more intense. Surely it would be just as nice when Lucas inserted his member—which he was obviously trying to do, but it never stayed hard long enough. Gwyneira wondered why he didn't use his hand to help as well.

At first Lucas visited her every evening after they went to bed, but he gradually appeared less and less. He always prefaced his visits with the polite question: "And do we want to try it again tonight, my love?" and never protested when Gwyneira occasionally declined. So far Gwyneira had no problems with married life.

That said, Gerald made her life difficult. He insisted seriously that she take over the duties of a housewife—Kiward Station should be run like the households of Europe's highest nobility. Witi was to be transformed into a discreet butler, Moana into a perfect cook, and Kiri into the very model of a housemaid. The Maori employees were entirely willing and earnest and loved their new mistress, and they worked hard to anticipate her every wish. However, Gwyneira thought everything should remain as it had been before, even if a few things took some getting used to. For example, the girls refused to wear shoes in the house, as their feet felt cramped in them. Kiri showed Gwyneira the calluses and blisters she had developed on her feet after a long workday in leather shoes she was not accustomed to. They found the uniforms impractical as well, and again Gwyneira could only agree with them. In the summer their clothing was too warm; she herself was perspiring in her voluminous skirts. But she was used to suffering for propriety's sake. The Maori girls could not accept it, however. It was hardest when Gerald expressed specific wishes, usually having to do with the cooking, which so far had proved unimpressive, as Gwyneira herself agreed. Maori cuisine was not especially varied. Moana either cooked sweet potatoes and other vegetables in the oven or roasted meat or fish with exotic spices. Occasionally it did taste unusual but was thoroughly enjoyable. Gwyneira, who couldn't cook herself, ate whatever was served without complaint. Gerald, however, wanted an expanded menu.

"Gwyneira, I'd like you to pay more attention to the cooking in the future," he said one morning at breakfast. "I'm tired of this Maori food and would love to have some Irish stew again. Could you please tell the cook?"

Gwyneira nodded, her thoughts already on herding the sheep, which she had planned for that day with James and the young dogs. A few lambs had wandered from the pastures in the highland and were roaming in the pastures closer to the yard, where the young rams were upsetting the flocks. Gerald had ordered the shepherds to collect the animals and herd them back, which had been a laborious business in the past. With the new sheepdogs, however, it should be possible to accomplish the task in a day, and Gwyneira wanted to watch the first attempts herself. A short talk with Moana about the lunch menu shouldn't hold her up.

"Irish stew is with cabbage and mutton, right?" she asked.

"What else?" grumbled Gerald.

Gwyneira had the vague impression that you layered them one atop the other and then cooked them.

"Mutton we have, and cabbage...is there cabbage in the garden, Lucas?" she asked uncertainly.

"What do you think the big green leaves are in the shape of a head?" Gerald grilled her.

"I, uh..." Gwyneira had long since discovered that she was no better at gardening edible plants. She simply did not have the patience to wait until the seeds turned into cabbage heads or cucumbers or to spend endless hours in between pulling weeds. She only rarely paid the vegetable garden any attention—Hoturapa would see to it.

Moana looked confused when Gwyn gave her the task of cooking the cabbage and mutton together.

"I made never," she explained. Cabbage was completely new to the girl. "How it should taste?"

"Like...well, just like Irish stew. Just cook it, and you'll see," Gwyneira said and happily fled to the stables, where James had already saddled Madoc for her. Gwyneira now alternated between the two cobs.

The pups performed superbly, and even Gerald was full of praise when half of the shepherds returned with Gwyneira that afternoon. The sheep had been gathered successfully, and Livingston and Kennon were herding them back into the highland with the dogs' help. Cleo loped happily alongside her mistress and Daimon trotted next to James. Now and then the riders smiled at each other. They enjoyed their work together, and sometimes Gwyneira felt she could communicate as wordlessly and naturally with the brown-haired farmworker as she otherwise only could with Cleo. James always knew exactly which sheep she had her eye on, whether for separating or bringing back into the fold. He seemed to anticipate her every move and often whistled for Daimon at the very moment she was about to request help.

Now he took the stallion from her in front of the stables.

"Get going, miss, or you won't manage to change before lunch. Which Mr. Warden is so looking forward to...he ordered a dish from the old country, isn't that right?"

Gwyneira nodded, though she started to feel a bit sick. Was Gerald really so obsessed with this Irish stew that he was telling the farmhands about it? She hoped he would like it.

Gwyneira would have liked to check on the stew beforehand, but she was running late and only just managed to swap her riding clothes for a house dress before the family gathered for dinner. In principle, Gwyneira considered all this changing of clothes wholly unnecessary. Gerald always wore the same clothes to lunch that he wore when supervising the work in the stables and pastures. Lucas, however, preferred a stylish atmosphere at mealtime, and Gwyneira did not wish to fight. Today, she wore a lovely bright blue dress with a gold border on the skirt and sleeves. She had halfway straightened her hair and put it up with a comb into some sort of decent hairstyle.

"You look charming today as always, my love," Lucas remarked. Gwyneira smiled at him.

Gerald eyed her hair, pleased. "Like the purest turtledove!" he said happily. "So, we'll soon be looking forward to some little ones, eh, Gwyneira?"

Gwyneira did not know how to respond to that. They wouldn't fail for lack of effort. If what they did in her room at night was how you became pregnant, then all should be well.

Lucas, however, blushed. "We've only been married a month, Father."

"Well, one shot's enough, isn't it?" Gerald said, booming with laughter. Lucas seemed embarrassed, and once again Gwyneira did not understand what was going on. What did shooting have to do with pregnancy?

Kiri now appeared with the serving bowls, putting an end to the embarrassing conversation. As Gwyneira had taught her, the girl placed herself properly to the right of Mr. Warden's plate and served the master of the house first, then Lucas and Gwyneira. She performed capably; Gwyneira found nothing to criticize and returned Kiri's imploring smile when the girl finally took up her position dutifully next to the table, ready if called.

Gerald cast a disbelieving eye over the thin yellowy-red soup, in which were floating cabbage and hunks of meat, before exploding: "What the devil, Gwyn? That was first-class cabbage and the best mutton on this side of the globe! It cannot be so damned hard to make a decent stew out of that. But no—you leave everything to this Maori brat, and she makes the same thing out of it that we have to gulp down every day. Teach her how to do it, if you please, Gwyneira."

Kiri looked hurt, Gwyneira insulted. She thought the soup tasted quite good—if, admittedly, a bit exotic. What spices Moana had used to achieve that flavor were a complete mystery to her. As was the original recipe for mutton cabbage stew that Gerald so obviously cherished.

Lucas shrugged. "You should have looked for an Irish cook instead of a Welsh princess, Father," Lucas said mockingly. "It's obvious that Gwyneira did not grow up in a kitchen."

The young man coolly took another spoonful of stew, whose flavor did not seem to bother him either, but Lucas was not much of an eater anyway. He only looked truly happy when he could return to his books or his studio after meals.

Gwyneira tried the dish again and attempted to remember the taste of Irish stew. Her cook at home had rarely made it.

"I believe it's made without sweet potatoes," she told Kiri.

The Maori girl frowned. Apparently, she could not imagine any dish without sweet potatoes.

Gerald roared irritably. "Of course it's made without sweet potatoes. And you don't bury it to cook it or wrap it in leaves or whatever else these tribal women do to poison their masters. Make that clear, if you don't mind, Gwyn! There must be a cookbook around here somewhere. Maybe someone could translate that. They were pretty quick about doing it for the Bible."

Gwyneira sighed. She had heard that Maori women on the North Island used underground or volcanic sources of heat to cook their food. But Kiward Station had nothing of the sort, nor had she ever observed

Moana or the other Maori women digging cooking pits either. But the cookbook translation was a good idea.

Gwyneira spent the afternoon in the kitchen with the Maori Bible, the English Bible, and Gerald's late wife's cookbook. Yet her comparative studies met with limited success. In the end she gave up and fled to the stables.

"Now I know what 'sin' and 'divine justice' are in the Maori language," she told the men, thumbing through the Bible. Hardy Kennon and Poker Livingston had just returned from the mountain pastures and were waiting on their horses, and James McKenzie and Andy McAran were cleaning their saddles. "But the word for 'thyme' is nowhere to be found."

"Maybe it would still taste good with frankincense and myrrh," James remarked.

The men laughed.

"Just tell Mr. Warden that gluttony is a sin," Andy McAran advised. "But do it in Maori just in case. If you say it in English, he may bite your head off."

Sighing, Gwyneira saddled her mare. She needed some fresh air. The weather was far too lovely to be wasted poring over books.

"You lot aren't any help to me either," she chided the men, who were still kidding around as she led Igraine out of the stables. "If my father-in-law asks, tell him I'm gathering herbs for his stew."

At first Gwyneira had her horse go at a walking pace. As always, she savored the panoramic vista of the land, which extended in all directions before the breathtaking backdrop of the mountains. Once again the mountains seemed so near, as though they could be reached in an hour's ride, and Gwyneira enjoyed trotting toward them, with one of the peaks as a goal. After not getting perceptibly closer after two hours, she turned around. This was what she liked in life. But what in the world was she going to do about the Maori cook? Gwyneira without question needed female support. But the next white woman lived twenty miles away.

Was it even socially proper to pay a visit to Mrs. Beasley only a month after getting married? But maybe a trip to Haldon would suffice. Gwyneira had yet to visit the small town, but it was about time. She had letters to post, wanted to buy a few things, and above all was eager to see some new faces that did not belong to her family, the Maori servants, or the shepherds. They had all gotten to be a bit much—with the exception of James McKenzie. He could accompany her to Haldon. Hadn't he just said the day before that he had to pick up the goods he'd ordered from the Candlers? Gwyneira's spirits lifted at the thought of the excursion. And Mrs. Candler would certainly know how to make Irish stew.

Igraine was happy to gallop homeward. After the long ride, she was looking forward to the feeding trough. Gwyneira was hungry herself when she finally led the horse back into the stables. The aromatic scent of meat and spices emanated from the workers' quarters. Gwyneira could not help herself. She knocked, full of hope.

It seemed that she was expected. The men again sat around an open fire, and a bottle made the rounds. An aromatic stew was simmering over the flame. Wasn't that…?

The men were all beaming as though they were celebrating Christmas, and Dave O'Toole, the Irishman, held out a dish of Irish stew to her. "Here, miss. Give this to the Maori girl. These people are very good at copying. Maybe she'll manage to figure it out from this."

Gwyneira thanked him gratefully. Doubtless this was just the dish Gerald had hoped for. It smelled so good that Gwyneira would have liked to ask for a spoon and empty the bowl herself. But she got a hold of herself. She would not touch the delicious stew until she had given Kiri and Moana a chance to sample it.

She set it down safely on a hay bale while she waited on Igraine and then carried it carefully out of the stables. She almost ran into James, who was waiting for her at the stable doors with a bouquet of leaves, which he handed over to Gwyneira as ceremoniously as though they were flowers.

"*Tàima*," he said with a half grin, winking at her. "Instead of frankincense and myrrh."

Gwyneira took the strands of thyme and smiled at him. She did not know why her heart beat so frantically as she did so.

Helen was delighted when Howard finally announced that they would go to Haldon on Friday. The horse needed to be reshod, which was apparently always the reason for trips to town. She realized that it must have been during a visit to the blacksmith that Howard had learned of her arrival.

"How often does a horse need to be shod?" she asked carefully.

Howard shrugged. "It depends, but usually every six to ten weeks. But the bay's hooves grow slowly; sometimes a shoe lasts him twelve weeks." He patted his horse approvingly.

Helen would have preferred a horse whose hooves grew more quickly and could not stifle a remark. "I'd like to be around people more often."

"You could take the mule," he said generously. "It's five miles to Haldon, so you'd be there in two hours. If you set out right after milking, you could easily be back by evening to cook dinner."

Helen knew Howard well enough by now to know that he would not go without a warm meal under any circumstances. Still, he was easy to please: he gobbled down flat bread as readily as pancakes, scrambled eggs, and stew. It did not seem to bother him that Helen could hardly make any other dishes, but Helen still planned to ask Mrs. Candler for a few new recipes in Haldon. The meal rotation was becoming a little monotonous even for her.

"You could slaughter a chicken sometime," Howard suggested when Helen mentioned it. She was horrified—just as she had been at the idea of having to ride to Haldon alone on the mule.

"Now you can look at it that way," Howard said calmly. "Or you can hitch up the mule."

Neither Gerald nor Lucas had anything against Gwyneira joining James on the trip to Haldon. Lucas could hardly fathom why she wanted to go.

"You'll be disappointed, my love. It's a dirty little town, just a store and a pub. No culture, not even a church."

"What about a doctor?" Gwyneira inquired. "I mean, in case I sometime really..."

Lucas reddened. Gerald, however, was excited.

"Is it time already, Gwyneira? Are you showing the first signs? If that really is the case, of course we'll send for a doctor from Christchurch. We don't want to take a chance on the midwife from Haldon."

"Father, the baby would have long since been born before the doctor arrived from Christchurch," Lucas chided.

Gerald looked at him coldly. "I'll have the doctor come ahead of time. He should stay here until it's time, regardless of the cost."

"And his other patients?" Lucas asked. "Do you think he'll just leave them in the lurch?"

Gerald snorted. "That's simply a question of the sum, my son. And the Wardens' heir is worth any sum!"

Gwyneira stayed out of it. She would not even have recognized the signs of pregnancy—how should she know how it felt? Besides, she was just happy to be going to Haldon.

James McKenzie picked her up right after breakfast. He had hitched two horses to a long, heavy wagon. "If you rode, you'd get there faster," he offered, but Gwyneira did not mind the idea of sitting at James's side on the box and enjoying the landscape. Once she knew the way, she could ride to Haldon more often; today, though, she was content to ride on the wagon. Besides, James was a genial conversation partner. He told her the names of the mountains on the horizon, as well as of those of the rivers and creeks they crossed. He often knew the Maori name as well as the English.

"You speak Maori well, don't you?" Gwyneira asked, impressed.

James shook his head. "I don't think anyone speaks Maori well. The natives make it too easy on us. They're so happy about every new English word they learn. So who wants to bother with words like *taumatawhatatangihangakoauauotamateaturipukakapikimaungahoroukupokaiwhenu-akitanatahu*?"

"*What?*" Gwyneira laughed.

"It's a mountain on the North Island. The Maori also use it as a tongue twister. But it gets easier with every glass of whiskey, believe me." James winked at her and smiled his rakish smile.

"So you learned it by the campfire?" Gwyneira asked.

James nodded. "I've moved around quite a bit, hiring myself out to sheep farms. In between, I've often stayed in Maori villages—they're very hospitable."

"Why haven't you worked in whale fishing?" Gwyneira wanted to know. "There's supposed to be more money in it. Mr. Warden..."

James grinned. "Mr. Warden can also play a good hand at cards," he remarked.

Gwyneira blushed. Could it be that the story of the card game between Gerald Warden and her father had made the rounds here?

"Most people don't earn a fortune whale hunting," McKenzie continued. "And for me it was a simple choice. Don't get me wrong: I'm not squeamish, but all that wading through blood and fat...no thanks. But I make a good shepherd; I learned how in Australia."

"Don't only convicts live in Australia?" Gwyneira inquired.

"Not entirely. There are the convicts' offspring and other immigrants too. And the convicts aren't all felons. Plenty of poor fellows have ended up there for stealing a loaf of bread for their kids. And there are all the Irish who wouldn't swear loyalty to the Crown. A lot of them were very upstanding guys. There are scoundrels everywhere, and for my part, I didn't meet any more in Australia than in any other part of the world."

"Where else have you been?" Gwyneira asked eagerly. She found James fascinating.

He grinned. "Scotland. That's where I come from. A true Highlander. But I'm no lord or chieftain; my clan were always common folk. Knew sheep better than long swords."

Gwyneira found that a bit of a shame. A Scottish warrior would have been almost as captivating as an American cowboy.

"And you, miss? Did you really grow up in a castle, like they say?" James turned again to look at her. But he appeared not to be interested in gossip. Gwyneira sensed that he was honestly curious about her.

"I grew up in a manor house," she informed him. "My father is a lord—not one of those who sit on the royal council, however." She smiled. "In a way we have something in common: the Silkhams also prefer sheep to swords."

"And for you is it...forgive my asking, but I always thought... aren't ladies supposed to marry lords?"

That was indeed a rather indiscreet question, but Gwyneira decided not to hold it against him.

"Ladies are supposed to marry gentlemen," she replied uncertainly. Then her temper got the better of her. "And naturally, there was a lot of idle chatter in England about my husband being only a 'sheep baron' without real patents of nobility. But like they say, it's nice when you have the title to a thoroughbred of your own. But you don't ride on paper."

James laughed so heartily that he almost fell from the box. "Don't ever say that in society, miss! You'd be compromised for all time. But I'm beginning to get the impression that it was difficult for you to find a gentleman in England."

"I had plenty of suitors!" Gwyneira lied, insulted. "And Lucas has yet to complain."

"Then he must be dumb and blind too," James burst out, but before he could elaborate on his comment, Gwyneira noticed a settlement on a plain below the ridge they were passing over.

"Is that Haldon?" she asked.

James nodded.

Haldon seemed to perfectly mirror the pioneer towns described in Gwyneira's penny novels; just like in those books, it had a general store, a barber, a smith, a hotel, and a bar, which was called a "pub" here and not a "saloon." All the merchants were located in colorfully painted two-story buildings.

James stopped the wagon in front of the Candlers' store.

"Take your time shopping," he said. "I'm loading the wood first, then going to the barber, and for a beer at the pub after that. So there's no hurry. If you'd like, you could have tea with Mrs. Candler."

Gwyneira smiled at him conspiratorially. "Maybe she'll even teach me a few recipes. Mr. Warden has been asking for Yorkshire pudding. Do you know how to make that?"

James shook his head. "I'm afraid not even O'Toole knows how to do that. Anyway, see you soon, miss."

He held out his hand to help her from the box. Gwyneira wondered why the same feeling shot through her at this contact that she otherwise only felt when she touched herself in secret.

7

Gwyneira crossed the dusty town street, which no doubt turned into a sea of mud when it rained, and entered the Candlers' general store. Mrs. Candler was sorting colorful candies into tall glass jars, but seemed more than willing to take a break. She greeted Gwyneira enthusiastically.

"Mrs. Warden, what a surprise! And what luck. Do you have time for a cup of tea? Dorothy's making some right now. She's in the back with Mrs. O'Keefe."

"With whom?" Gwyneira asked, her heart leaping. "You don't mean Helen O'Keefe?" She could hardly believe it.

Mrs. Candler nodded, delighted. "Oh, that's right, you knew her as Miss Davenport. Well, my husband and I were the ones who got to inform her fiancé of her arrival. And as I heard it, he was in Christchurch quick as lightning and brought her right back with him. Just go on back, Mrs. Warden. I'll be right along, as soon as Richard gets back."

"Go on back," meant to the Candlers' living quarters, which were attached to the spacious store. Yet it did not seem at all temporary and was tastefully furnished with expensive-looking furniture made from native woods. Large windows allowed plenty of light in and offered a view of the wood store behind the house, where James was just receiving his order. Mr. Candler was helping him load it.

And Helen really was there in the lounge! She was sitting on a chaise lounge upholstered in green velvet, chatting with Dorothy, and sprang up when she noticed Gwyneira. Her face reflected a mixture of disbelief and joy.

"Gwyn! Or are you a ghost? I'm seeing more people today than in the last twelve weeks. So I'm beginning to think I'm seeing ghosts."

"We could each pinch the other," Gwyn said, laughing.

The friends fell into each other's arms.

"When did you get here?" Gwyneira inquired, after she had pulled away from Helen. "I would have come long before now if I'd known I'd meet you here."

"I married just over three months ago," Helen said stiffly. "But this is my first time in Haldon. We live…rather far away."

She didn't sound especially enthusiastic. But now she needed to say hello to Dorothy. The girl had just returned with a teapot and was setting another place for Gwyneira. As she went about it, Gwyneira had the opportunity to take a closer look at her friend. Indeed, Helen did not give the impression of being happy. She was thinner, and the pallor that she had so carefully preserved after disembarking had given way to the sunbaked brown she so disapproved of. Her hands too were coarser and her fingernails shorter than before. Even her clothing had suffered. True, her dress was scrupulously clean and starched, but the hem was muddy.

"Our stream," Helen said by way of apology when she noticed Gwyneira's gaze. "Howard wanted to take the heavy wagon because he had fencing material to pick up. The horses can make it through the stream only if we push."

"Why don't you build a bridge?" Gwyneira wanted to know. She had already crossed several new bridges on Kiward Station.

Helen shrugged. "Howard probably doesn't have the money. Or the people. You can't build a bridge alone, after all." She reached for her teacup. Her hand trembled slightly.

"You don't have any servants?" Gwyneira asked, uncomprehending. "Not even Maori? How do you keep the farm running? Who takes care of the garden and milks the cows?"

Helen looked at her. In her beautiful gray eyes was a mixture of pride and desperation.

"Well, who do you think?"

"You?" Gwyneira was alarmed. "But you can't be serious. Wasn't he supposed to be a gentleman farmer?"

"Strike the gentleman...by which I don't mean to say that Howard isn't a man of honor. He treats me well and works hard. But he's a farmer, no more and no less. In that regard your Mr. Warden was right. Howard hates him as much as he hates Howard. Something must have once happened between those two." Helen would have liked to change topics; she did not feel comfortable speaking disparagingly of her husband. And yet...if she did not at least drop a few hints, she would never receive any help.

But Gwyneira did not press her further on that matter. She did not care about the feud between Howard O'Keefe and Gerald Warden. She cared about Helen.

"Do you at least have neighbors who can help you out sometimes or whom you can ask for advice? You can't do everything alone!" Gwyneira said, returning to the subject of the farm work.

"I'm a quick learner, you know," Helen murmured. "As for neighbors...well, there are a few Maori, yes. The children come to me every day for lessons; they're adorable. But...but otherwise, you're the first white people I've seen...since I arrived on the farm." Helen attempted to maintain her poise but was fighting to hold back her tears.

Dorothy curled up consolingly to Helen. Gwyneira, however, was already making plans to help her friend.

"How far is the farm from here anyway? Can't I come visit sometime?"

"Five miles," Helen informed her. "But of course, I don't know in which direction."

"But that's something you should learn, Mrs. O'Keefe. If you can't get your bearings out here, you're lost!" Mrs. Candler said as she came in, bringing pastries from the store with her. A woman in town baked them and sold them there. "From here, your farm is to the east—yours too, of course, Mrs. Warden. Though not in a straight line. You have to veer off the main road. But I can explain that to you. And your husband surely knows it as well."

Gwyneira wanted to hint that it was best not to ask a Warden the way to an O'Keefe, but Helen used the opportunity to change the subject.

"How is he anyway, your Lucas? Is he really the gentleman he was said to be?"

Gwyneira looked out the window, momentarily distracted. James had just finished loading up the wood and was pulling the wagon out of the yard. Helen noticed that Gwyneira's eyes brightened as she watched the man on the driver's box.

"Is that him? The sharp-looking fellow on the wagon?" Helen asked with a smile.

Gwyneira hardly seemed able to tear her gaze away, but then she collected herself. "What's that? Sorry, I was checking on our loading. The man on the reins is Mr. McKenzie, our shepherd foreman. Lucas is...Lucas would...well, even the idea of his driving a team over these paths and loading wood without help..."

Helen looked hurt. Naturally, Howard would be loading his fencing materials alone.

Gwyneira amended her words when she noticed Helen's expression. "Oh, Helen, it's not as though there's anything wrong with that... I'm sure Gerald Warden would take care of it himself. But Lucas is something of an aesthete; do you know what I mean? He writes, he paints, he plays piano. You hardly ever catch him out on the farm."

Helen frowned. "And when he inherits it?"

Gwyneira was astonished. The Helen she had gotten to know two months before would never have asked such a question.

"I believe that Gerald is hoping for another heir," she sighed.

Mrs. Candler looked searchingly at Gwyneira. "So far nothing's visible," she said, laughing. "But of course you've only been married a couple of weeks. He has to let you have a little time. Oh the two of them made such a pretty picture at the wedding!"

With that, Mrs. Candler launched into a long panegyric praising Gwyneira's wedding celebration. Helen listened in silence, though Gwyneira would have liked to ask her about her own wedding. There was so much that she urgently needed to talk to her friend about. Tête-à-tête, if possible. Mrs. Candler was very nice, but she was doubtless the town's gossip hub.

Nevertheless, she showed herself more than willing to help the two young women with recipes and advice for housekeeping: "Without leavening, you can't bake bread," Mrs. Candler told Helen. "Here, I'll give you some to take home. And I have something that will clean your dress. You have to let the hem steep; otherwise, it will be ruined. And you, Mrs. Warden, need muffin trays; otherwise, there will be no getting Mr. Warden his proper English tea cakes."

Helen purchased a Maori Bible as well. Mrs. Candler had a few copies in stock; the missionaries had ordered the Bibles some time before, but the Maori had shown little interest.

"Most of them can't read," Mrs. Candler said. "Besides, they have their own gods."

While Howard was loading up, Gwyneira and Helen managed to find a few moments to talk privately.

"I think Mr. O'Keefe is good looking," Gwyneira remarked. She had watched him speaking with Helen from inside the store. This man fit her image of the hardworking pioneer more than the genteel Lucas. "Do you like being married?"

Helen blushed. "I don't think it's a matter of liking it. But it's... tolerable. Oh, Gwyn, we won't see each other for months. Who knows if you'll come to Haldon on the same day as I will and..."

"Can't you come alone?" Gwyneira asked.

"Without Howard?"

"It's easy for me. On Igraine I could be here in less than two hours."

Helen sighed and told Gwyneira about her mule. "If I could ride it..."

Gwyneira lit up. "Of course you can ride it! I'll teach you how. I'll visit you as soon as I can, Helen. I'll figure out a way."

Helen wanted to tell her that Howard did not want any Wardens in the house, but she held back. If Howard and Gwyneira ran into each other, she would have to think of something. But he usually spent the whole day taking care of the sheep and often rode into the mountains looking for strays and working on his fence. He usually didn't come home until it was getting dark.

"I'll wait for you," Helen said, full of hope.

The friends kissed each other on both cheeks before Helen ran outside.

"Ah, the small farmers' wives don't have it easy," Mrs. Candler said sadly. "Hard work and lots of children. Mrs. O'Keefe is lucky that her husband is a little older. He won't be giving her eight or nine little ones. She's no spring chicken herself. I just hope it all works out well. No midwife goes out to those isolated farms."

James McKenzie appeared a short while later to pick up Gwyneira. Appearing pleased, he loaded her purchases into the wagon and helped her onto the coach box.

"Did you have a nice day, miss? Mr. Candler said you ran into an old friend."

To Gwyneira's delight, James knew the way to Helen's farm. He whistled through his teeth though when she asked about it.

"You want to go to O'Keefe's? Into the lion's den? Just don't tell Mr. Warden. He'd shoot me if he found out I told you how to get there."

"I could have asked elsewhere for directions," Gwyneira said coolly. "But what is it with those two? To Gerald, Mr. O'Keefe is nothing short of the devil, and Mr. O'Keefe seems to feel likewise about Gerald."

James laughed. "No one knows exactly. Rumor has it that they used to be partners. But then they went their separate ways. Some say because of money, others because of a woman. Their lands border each other, but Mr. Warden got the lion's share. It's very mountainous around O'Keefe's property. And he's no born shepherd, though he's supposedly from Australia. Everything is very murky. Only those two know the details, but could anyone ever get them to talk? Ah, here's the fork."

James stopped the team at a path that led to the left into the mountains. "Here you ride straight. You can orient yourself by the rocks. And then just follow the path; there's only one. But sometimes it's hard to find, especially in the summer when you can't see the wagon marks as easily. There are also a few streams to cross, one of which is almost a river. Once you've oriented yourself, there are no doubt more direct paths between the farms. But at first it'd be better to take this one so that you don't get lost."

Gwyneira did not get lost easily. Besides, Cleo and Igraine would have found their way back to Kiward Station under any circumstances. She was therefore optimistic when she set out three days later to visit her friend. Lucas did not have anything against her riding to Haldon; he had other problems just then anyway.

Gerald Warden had not only decided that Gwyneira should take her duties as a housewife more seriously, but was also of the opinion that Lucas finally needed to assume a bigger role in looking after the farm. So he gave his son tasks to perform with their employees every day—frequently choosing activities that made the aesthete's cheeks flush with embarrassment—or provoked even worse reactions. The castration of the young rams, for example, made the young Mr. Warden so nauseated that he was indisposed for the rest of the day, Hardy Kennon revealed with a snort while sitting around the shepherds' fire. Gwyneira heard about the episode by chance and could hardly keep from laughing, though she had no idea whether she might have reacted similarly—there were jobs that had remained off-limits to the curious young lady even at the Silkhams'.

That day Lucas was to head out with James to drive the wethers into the mountain pastures, where the animals would remain for the summer before being slaughtered. Lucas was terrified at the prospect of having to oversee that task as well.

Gwyneira would gladly have ridden along, but some feeling kept her from doing so. Lucas did not need to see how naturally she worked alongside the shepherds—she had learned to avoid competitive situations like that with her brother at all costs. Besides, she had no desire to spend the day riding in a sidesaddle. She was no longer used to sitting that way, and after a few hours her back would no doubt start to hurt.

Igraine moved briskly forward, and after an hour or so Gwyneira reached the fork that led to Helen's farm. From here it should be only two more miles, which were certain to be rough, however. The road was in miserable condition. The idea of leading a team along it horrified Gwyneira—let alone a wagon as heavy as the one Howard O'Keefe had been pulling. No wonder poor Helen had looked exhausted.

Igraine was not concerned about the road. The strong mare was used to a rocky landscape, and the frequent stream crossings were fun and refreshing for her. It was a hot day by New Zealand standards, making the mare sweat. Cleo, however, always tried to keep her paws as dry as possible while crossing the water. Gwyneira laughed every time the little dog fell into the cool water after an ill-fated leap, which caused the dog to look up at her mistress, hurt.

The house finally came into view, though at first Gwyneira could hardly believe that the log cabin ahead was really Howard O'Keefe's farm. But it had to be; the mule was grazing in the pen in front of it. When it saw Igraine, it let out a strange sound that started out like a neigh but degenerated into a lowing. Gwyneira shook her head. Peculiar animals. She did not understand why some people preferred them to horses.

She tied the mare to the fence and set out to look for Helen. She found only a cow in the stall. But then she heard a shrill cry come from the house. It was obviously Helen; she screamed with such horror that Gwyneira's blood ran cold. Terrified, she looked for a weapon with which to defend her friend, then decided to use her riding crop, and rushed to Helen's aide.

There was no assailant to be seen. Helen looked as though she had been quietly sweeping the room—until some fearful sight made her freeze.

"Helen!" Gwyneira yelled. "What is it?"

Helen did not greet her, or even turn to look at her. She just stared in terror at the corner.

"There...there...over there! What in heaven's name is that? Help, it's jumping!" Helen fled backward in panic and almost tripped over a stool in the process. Gwyneira caught her and likewise retreated before the fat, gleaming hopper, which was now hopping away from them. The bug was a splendid specimen—at least four inches long.

"That's a weta," Gwyneira explained calmly. "Probably a ground weta, but it could also be a tree weta that's gotten lost. In any case it's a giant weta, which is to say it can't jump high."

Helen looked at her as though she'd escaped from an asylum.

"And it's a male. Just in case you want to give him a name." Gwyneira giggled. "Don't make such a face, Helen. They're gross, but they won't hurt you. Let the critter out and..."

"Ca...can't we squ...ash it?" Helen asked, trembling.

Gwyneira shook her head. "All but impossible. They're hard to kill. Supposedly even when you cook them...which I haven't tried, however. Lucas can discourse on them for hours. They're his favorite insect. Do you have a glass or something?" Gwyneira had watched before when Lucas caught a weta and now she capably brought an empty marmalade glass down over the insect. "Got you," she rejoiced. "If we can get the lid screwed on, I can take it back to Lucas as a gift."

"Don't joke like that, Gwyn! I thought he was a gentleman." Helen slowly collected herself, but kept staring in fascination and horror at the giant captured bug.

"That doesn't mean he can't have an interest in crawly things, you know," Gwyneira remarked. "Men have strange predilections."

"You can say that again." Helen was thinking of Howard's nightly pleasures. He'd have pursued them nearly every night if Helen didn't have her periods. Which had, however, ceased after a short time—the only positive aspect of her married life.

"Shall I make tea?" Helen asked. "Howard prefers coffee, but I bought tea for myself. Darjeeling, from London." Her voice took on a note of longing.

Gwyneira looked around the humbly furnished room. The two rickety chairs, the clean-scoured but worn-out tabletop on which lay the Maori Bible. The stew simmering on the shabby stove. It wasn't exactly the ideal setting for teatime. She thought of Mrs. Candler's cozy home. Then she shook her head decisively. "We'll make tea afterward. First thing, you need to saddle that mule. I'll give you…well, let's say three riding lessons. After that we'll start meeting in Haldon."

The mule proved less cooperative. When Helen tried to put reins on it, it bit at her and ran away. She heaved a sigh when Reti, Rongo, and two other children appeared. Helen's flushed face, her cursing, and the hopelessness of her attempt at putting the reins on the mule all gave the Maori children a new reason to titter, but Reti had the halter on the mule within seconds. He then showed Helen how to saddle the mule while Rongo fed the animal sweet potatoes. But beyond that, they could do nothing to help her. Helen had to mount it on her own.

Gwyneira perched on the paddock fence while Helen tried to make the animal move. The children nudged each other and giggled when the mule refused to move even a single step. Only after Helen gave it a spirited kick in the flanks did it make a sort of moaning sound and take a step forward. But Gwyneira was not satisfied.

"That won't do. If you kick it, it won't go forward, it'll just get angry." Gwyneira squatted on the fence beam like a shepherd boy and emphasized her words with her riding crop as though it were a conductor's baton. In her only concession to propriety, she lifted her feet off the ground and hid them primly under her riding skirt, which made her a bit unsteady. Helen thought the balancing act was probably unnecessary, as the smirking children would probably not have given Gwyneira's legs a second look even if they hadn't been fully absorbed in the goings-on in the paddock. After all, didn't their mothers constantly walk around barefoot, with half-length skirts, and even half-naked?

But Helen didn't have time to give the matter any further thought. She had to give her full attention to directing the stubborn mule around the paddock. She was surprised to discover that staying on was not difficult; Howard's old saddle offered sufficient support. Unfortunately, though, her mount wanted to stop before every clump of grass.

"If I don't kick it, it doesn't move at all," she complained, digging her heels into the mule's ribs again. "Maybe...if you gave me that stick of yours, then I could hit it!"

Gwyneira rolled her eyes. "Who hired you as an instructor? Hitting, kicking...you don't treat your children that way!" She cast a glance at the smirking little Maori, who were visibly enjoying the battle between their teacher and the mule. "You have to love the mule, Helen. Make it like working for you. Say something nice to it."

Helen sighed, thought about it, and then leaned forward grudgingly. "What beautiful, soft ears you have," she cooed, attempting to stroke the mule's strong, bag-like ears. The animal returned her advances with an angry snapping in the direction of her legs. Helen nearly fell off the mule with fear, while Gwyneira nearly toppled off the fence from laughing.

"Love!" Helen snorted. "It hates me."

One of the older Maori children made a comment that was met with giggles from the others and made Helen blush.

"What did he say?" Gwyneira asked.

Helen bit her lip. "Just something from the Bible," she murmured.

Gwyneira nodded in amazement. "Well, if you can get these snot-nosed brats to quote the Bible on their own, you shouldn't have any trouble getting a mule to move. That mule is your only ticket to Haldon. What's its name anyway?" Gwyneira wagged her crop, but obviously had no intention of assisting her friend in driving the mule forward.

Helen realized that she would have to give the mule a name.

They did finally have their tea after the riding lesson, during which time Helen talked about her little students.

"Reti, the oldest boy, is very sharp but cheeky. And Rongo Rongo is charming. Overall, they're nice children. In fact, the whole tribe is friendly."

"You can already speak Maori pretty well, can't you?" Gwyn asked admiringly. "Sadly, I can still only manage a few words. I just never have time to study the language. There's too much to do."

Helen shrugged but was grateful for the praise. "I've studied other languages before, which makes it a little easier. Otherwise, I don't have anyone else to talk to. If I don't want to be totally alone, I have to learn it."

"Don't you talk to Howard?" Gwyneira asked.

Helen nodded. "Yes, but...but we...we don't have all that much in common."

Gwyneira suddenly felt guilty. Helen would so enjoy the long discussions with Lucas about art and culture—not to mention his piano playing and painting. She knew she should feel grateful for her cultivated husband. Most of the time, however, she just felt bored.

"The women in the village are very outgoing," Helen continued. "I've been wondering whether one of them is a midwife..."

"Midwife?" cried Gwyneira. "Helen! Don't tell me that you...I don't believe it. Helen, you're pregnant?"

Helen looked up, agonized. "I don't know for certain. But yesterday Mrs. Candler looked at me strangely and made a few comments. Besides, sometimes I feel...strange." She blushed.

Gwyneira pressed her for more details. "Does Howard...I mean, with his...does he..."

"I think so," whispered Helen. "He does it every night. I don't know if I'll ever get used to it."

Gwyneira chewed on her lip. "Why not? I mean...does it hurt?"

Helen looked at her as though she'd lost her mind. "Of course it does, Gwyn. Didn't your mother tell you it would? But we women simply have to bear it. Why do you ask? Doesn't it hurt for you too?"

Gwyneira tried unsuccessfully to formulate a reply until Helen, ashamed, let the subject drop. But her reaction had confirmed Gwyneira's suspicions. Something was not going right between Lucas and her. For the first time, she asked herself whether perhaps there was something wrong with her.

Helen named the mule Nepumuk and spoiled it with carrots and sweet potatoes. After just a few days, a deafening greeting call filled the air every time she stepped out the door, and in the paddock the mule pushed to have her put a halter on it—after all, it knew there would be a treat both before and after. By the third riding lesson, Gwyneira was quite satisfied, and soon thereafter Helen found the courage to saddle Nepumuk and head into Haldon. She felt that she'd crossed no less than an ocean by the time she guided the mule onto the town street. It moved purposefully toward the smith since it expected to be rewarded there with some oats and hay. The smith proved friendly and promised to put the mule up while Helen visited Mrs. Candler. Mrs. Candler and Dorothy praised her endlessly, and Helen basked in her new freedom.

That evening she spoiled Nepumuk with an extra portion of hay and corn. He snorted happily, and suddenly Helen did not find it so difficult to think of him as a pleasant animal.

8

Summer was coming to a close, and they could look back on a successful breeding season at Kiward Station. All the ewes were pregnant; the new stallion had covered three mares, and little Daimon had all the farm's female dogs in heat—as well as several from other farms. Even Cleo's belly was swelling. Gwyneira was excited for puppies. As for her own attempts to get pregnant, there had been no change—especially since Lucas attempted to sleep with her only once a week. And it was always the same: Lucas was polite and attentive and apologized whenever he believed himself to be going too far in any respect, but nothing hurt and nothing bled. Gerald's jibes slowly began to get on her nerves. After a few months of marriage, her father-in-law said, you could count on a healthy young woman conceiving. This only reinforced Gwyneira's fear that something was wrong with her. In the end, she confided in Helen.

"I wouldn't care myself, but Mr. Warden is horrible. He talks about it in front of the help, even in front of the shepherds. I should spend less time in the stables and more time caring for my husband, he says. Then there would be a baby. But I won't get pregnant just watching Lucas paint!"

"But he...doesn't he visit you regularly?" Helen asked carefully. Though no one had confirmed that she was pregnant, she was now rather sure that something was different about her.

Gwyneira nodded and tugged at her earlobe. "Yes, Lucas puts in the effort. It's up to me. If I only knew whom I could ask..."

An idea came to Helen. She had to go to the Maori settlement soon, and there...she did not know why, but she was less ashamed to talk to the native women about her possible pregnancy than with

Mrs. Candler or another woman in town. Why shouldn't she take the opportunity to talk about Gwyneira's problem at the same time?

"You know what? I'll ask the Maori witch doctor, or whatever she is," she asserted. "Little Rongo's grandmother. She's very friendly. The last time I visited, she gave me a piece of jade as a token of thanks for teaching the children. The Maori look at her as a *tohunga*, or wise woman. Maybe she knows something about female troubles. She can't do more than turn me away."

Gwyneira was skeptical. "I don't really believe in magic," she said, "but it's worth a try."

Matahorua, the Maori *tohunga*, received Helen in front of the *wharenui*, the meeting hall that was so richly decorated with carvings. Rongo had explained to Helen that the airy building's form was modeled after a living creature. The ridge of the roof formed the backbone, the roof battens the ribs. In front of the hall was a covered grill, the *kauta*, where food was cooked for everyone, as the Maori were a close community. They slept together in huge sleeping houses that were not divided into individual rooms and had almost no furniture.

Matahorua motioned for Helen to sit on one of the stones that jutted from the grass next to the house.

"How can help?" she said without introduction.

Helen ran through her Maori vocabulary, which mainly consisted of Biblical terms and papal dogma. "What do when no conception?" she inquired, hoping she had left out the "immaculate."

The old woman laughed and showered her with a torrent of unintelligible words.

Helen made a gesture of incomprehension.

"Why not baby?" Matahorua then attempted in English. "You do receive baby! In winter when very cold. I coming help, when you want. Beautiful baby, healthy baby."

Helen could not comprehend it. So it was true—she would be having a baby!

"I coming help, when wanting," Matahorua reiterated her friendly offer.

"I…thank, you are…welcome to," Helen formulated with difficulty.

The witch doctor laughed.

But now Helen had to return to her original question. She tried again in Maori.

"I conception," she explained and pointed to her stomach, hardly blushing this time. "But friend not conception. What can do?"

The old woman shrugged and again repeated her comprehensive explanations in her mother tongue. Finally she waved to Rongo Rongo, who was playing nearby with other children.

The little girl approached and appeared more than happy to offer her services as an interpreter. Helen turned red with shame at the thought of discussing such things in front of a child, but Matahorua seemed untroubled by it.

"She cannot easily say," explained Rongo after the *tohunga* had repeated her words again. "Can be many reasons. With the man or woman or both…she must see the woman, or better man and woman. She can only advise then. And advising no good."

Matahorua gave Helen another piece of jade for her friend.

"Friends of Miss O'Keefe always welcome!" Rongo remarked.

Helen took a few seed potatoes from her bag as thanks. Howard would throw a fit at her giving the precious seeds away, but the old Maori woman was visibly pleased. With a few words she instructed Rongo to grab a few herbs, which she handed to Helen.

"Here, against sickness in morning. Put in water, drink before getting up."

That evening Helen revealed to her husband that he would be a father. Howard gave a contented hum. He was obviously pleased, though Helen would have liked a few more words of recognition. The one good consequence of announcing the news was that from then on Howard left his wife in peace. He did not touch her anymore, instead sleeping next to her like a brother, which was a huge relief to her. It moved her to tears when, the next morning, Howard came to her in bed with a cup of tea.

"Here. The witch said you should drink this, right? And the Maori women know something about these things. They litter children like cats."

Gwyneira was likewise happy for her friend, but at first resisted going with Helen to visit Matahorua.

"Nothing will come of it if Lucas won't be there. Maybe she'll cast a love spell or something like that. For now I'll take the jade stone—maybe I can hang it in a little bag around my neck. It brought you luck, after all."

Gwyneira gestured meaningfully at Helen's stomach, looking so hopeful that Helen did not want to break it to her that the Maori did not believe in magic or good-luck charms either. The jade stone was just supposed to be viewed as a token of thanks, as a sign of recognition and friendship.

Nor did the magic work when Gwyneira could not bring herself to place the jade stone anywhere clearly visible or even in her bed. She did not want Lucas to tease her for being superstitious or to become upset with her. In recent days, he had tried doggedly to bring his sexual efforts to a successful conclusion. With little tenderness, he attempted to force his way immediately into Gwyneira. Sometimes it hurt, but Gwyneira still felt that she wasn't doing it right.

Spring arrived, and the new settlers had to acclimate to the idea that March heralded the onset of winter in the Southern Hemisphere. Lucas rode with James McKenzie and his men into the mountains to herd the sheep together. He did so under protest, but Gerald insisted. For Gwyneira, it represented the unexpected opportunity to take part in herding the sheep into the low pastures. She took charge of the refreshment cart with Witi and Kiri.

"Get your Irish stew!" she announced to the men, pleased, when they returned to camp the first evening. After that first time, the Maori knew the recipe inside and out, and Gwyneira could now all but cook it by herself. However, she had not spent the day peeling potatoes and cooking cabbage. Instead, she had ridden out with Igraine and Cleo to look for a few sheep who had gone astray in the mountains. James McKenzie had asked her to do so, pledging secrecy.

"I know that Mr. Warden doesn't look on it fondly, miss, and I'd do it myself or get one of the boys to. But we need every man for herding; we're hopelessly shorthanded. The last few years we always got some help from the Maori camp. But since the young Mr. Warden is riding with us this time..."

Gwyneira knew what he meant, and likewise understood what went unsaid. Gerald had saved on expenditures for additional hands and was overjoyed about it. She had heard that much at the family dinner table. Lucas, however, could not replace the experienced Maori shepherds. He wasn't suited to farm work, and he wasn't tough enough. He had already grumbled to Gwyneira while they were pitching camp that every part of him down to his bones ached—and the herding had just begun. Of course, the men did not complain openly about the their junior boss's lack of skill, but when Gwyneira heard comments like, "It would have gone much quicker if the sheep hadn't broken out three times," she could piece the rest together. If Lucas were lost in the observation of a cloud formation or an insect, he wouldn't let himself get distracted by a few sheep trotting by.

As a result, James McKenzie had him work only with other shepherds, which left them at least one man short. Of course, Gwyneira enjoyed helping out. As the men returned to camp, Cleo was herding an additional fifteen sheep that Gwyneira had found in the highlands. She was a little concerned what Lucas would say, but he didn't appear to even notice. He ate his stew in silence, then retired to his tent.

"I'll help clean up," Gwyneira announced, as though there were a five-course meal's worth of dishes to clean. In reality she left the few dishes for the Maori and joined the men, who were telling stories about their adventures. Naturally, a bottle was making the rounds, and with every round the tales became more dramatic and dangerous.

"By God, if I hadn't been there, the ram would have run a horn through him!" Young Dave chuckled. "Anyway, he's running toward him, and I call, 'Mr. Warden!' but he still doesn't see the animal. So I whistle for the dog, and he dashes between man and beast, driving the ram away...but do you think the fellow is thankful? As if! He rails at me! He was looking at a kea, he says, and the dog drove the bird away. The ram nearly had him, I'm telling you! If I hadn't been there, he'd have even less in his pants than he already does."

The other men bawled with laughter. Only James McKenzie looked uncomfortable. Gwyneira saw that she had better retire if she did not want to hear any more embarrassing stories about her husband. James followed her when she stood up.

"I'm sorry, miss," he said as she stepped into the shadows beyond the campfire. The night was not dark: the moon was full, and the stars were shining. Tomorrow would be clear too—a gift for the shepherds, who often had to slog through rain and fog otherwise.

Gwyneira shrugged. "You don't have to be sorry. Or did you almost let yourself be skewered?"

James stifled a laugh. "I wish the men would be a bit more discreet."

Gwyneira smiled. "Then you would need to explain to them what discretion means. No, no, Mr. McKenzie. I can picture only too well what happened up there, and I understand why the men are disgruntled. The young Mr. Warden was...well, he wasn't made for these things. He plays the piano marvelously and paints beautifully, but riding and sheep herding..."

"Do you even love him?" The words had hardly slipped out before James wanted to slap himself. He hadn't wanted to ask that. Never—it wasn't his business. But he'd been drinking; he too had had a long day, and he had cursed Lucas Warden more than once over the course of it.

Gwyneira knew what her good breeding demanded. "I respect and honor my husband," she said by way of an answer. "I married of my own free will, and he treats me well." She should also have added that it was none of James McKenzie's business anyway, but she didn't manage it. Something told her he had a right to ask her.

"Does that answer your question, Mr. McKenzie?" she inquired softly instead.

James McKenzie nodded. "Sorry, miss. Good night."

He did not know why he held out his hand to her. It was not customary and certainly not proper to take leave of someone so formally after a few hours around the campfire. After all, they'd see each other again in the morning at breakfast. Still, Gwyneira took his hand as though it were the most natural thing in the world. Her small, slender hand, hardened from riding and working with the animals, rested lightly in his. James could hardly overcome the impulse to raise it to his lips.

Gwyneira kept her gaze downcast. It felt good to have his hand wrapped around hers, and it gave her a reassuring sense of security. Warmth spread throughout her body—even there, where it was anything but proper. She slowly raised her gaze and saw an echo of her joy in James McKenzie's dark, searching eyes. Suddenly, they both smiled.

"Good night, James," Gwyneira said softly.

They managed to complete the herding in three days, faster than ever before. Kiward Station had lost only a few animals; most of the remaining animals were in excellent condition, and the mutton fetched a good price. A few days after the return to the farm, Cleo had her pups. Gwyneira watched the tiny puppies in their basket with fascination.

Gerald, however, seemed to be in a bad mood.

"Seems that everyone can—except you two," he grumbled, casting an evil look at his son. Lucas walked out without a word. Things had been tense between father and son for weeks. Gerald could not forgive Lucas his ineptitude at farm work, and Lucas was angry with Gerald for making him ride with the men. Gwyneira often felt that she was standing between two fronts, and she increasingly sensed that Gerald was angry with her.

In winter there was less work in the pastures and little that Gwyneira could help with. Cleo was indisposed for a few weeks anyway. Gwyneira, therefore, directed her mare more often in the direction of the O'Keefes' farm. During the herding, she had found a considerably shorter way between the two farms and she now visited Helen several times a week. Helen was grateful. The farm work was becoming more difficult as her pregnancy advanced, as was riding her mule. She hardly ever went to Haldon to drink tea with Mrs. Candler anymore, preferring instead to spend her days studying the Maori Bible and sewing baby clothes.

She continued teaching the Maori children, who took over many of her chores. However, she still spent most of her day alone. Howard had taken to riding to Haldon for a beer in the evening and did not return until late. Gwyneira was concerned.

"How are you going to let Matahorua know when the birthing begins?" she inquired. "You can't possibly go yourself."

"Mrs. Candler wants to send Dorothy here. But I don't like the idea...the house is so small that she would have to sleep in the stables. From what I understand, children are always born at night. That means Howard will be there."

"Are you sure?" Gwyneira asked, confused. "My sister gave birth to her child around midday."

"But the pains would have set in at night," Helen explained with conviction. She had learned the basics of pregnancy and birthing. After Rongo Rongo had told her several wild delivery stories in broken English, Helen had mustered her courage and asked Mrs. Candler for enlightenment. She had a very technical mastery of the subject. After all, she had given birth to three sons and not under the most civilized conditions either. Helen now knew how a birth announced itself and what needed to be done to prepare for it.

"If you say so," Gwyneira said, unconvinced. "But you should really consider having Dorothy come to stay. She'll survive a few nights in the stables, but if you have to birth the child all on your own, you could die."

As the birth approached, Helen became more inclined to take Mrs. Candler up on her offer. Howard was at home less and less. Her condition seemed to embarrass him, and it was clear that he no longer liked sharing the bed with her. When he returned from Haldon at night, he stank of beer and whiskey and often stumbled around so much getting ready for bed that Helen doubted he would even be able to find the Maori village. So Dorothy moved in with them in early August. Mrs. Candler refused, however, to let the girl sleep in the stables.

"Though I wish it would, Mrs. O'Keefe, that won't do. I see in what condition Mr. O'Keefe rides away from here at night. And you are…I mean, he has…he might miss sharing a bed with a woman, if you understand my meaning. If he arrives in the stables and comes across a half-grown girl…"

"Howard is a man of honor!" Helen declared in defense of her husband.

"A man of honor is still a man," Mrs. Candler replied drily. "And one drunk man is as dangerous as the rest. Dorothy will sleep in the house. I'll talk to Mr. O'Keefe."

Helen worried about this discussion, but her concerns proved unfounded. After he had picked up Dorothy, Howard simply carried his bedding into the stables and made his camp there.

"It doesn't matter to me," he said gallantly. "I've slept worse places before. And the girl's virtue has to be guarded; Mrs. Candler's right there. There can't be any talk."

Helen admired Mrs. Candler's sense of diplomacy. Apparently, she had argued that Dorothy needed a chaperone and would not be able to look after Helen and the baby with Howard in the house.

So in the days leading up to the birth, Helen shared her home with Dorothy, during which she spent a great deal of time trying to keep the girl calm. Dorothy was deathly afraid of the delivery—so much so that Helen suspected that her mother had not died of some mysterious disease but rather while giving birth to a sibling.

Gwyneira, by contrast, was quite cheerful—even on a foggy day at the end of August when Helen felt especially sick and depressed. Howard had driven to Haldon that morning; he wanted to build a new shed, and the wood for it had finally arrived. He would surely not drive straight back after loading the building materials in his wagon, but instead stop at the pub for a beer and a game of cards. Dorothy milked the cow while Gwyneira kept Helen company. Her clothes were damp after the ride through the fog, and she was freezing. All the more reason to be happily settled in front of Helen's fireplace with a cup of tea.

"Matahorua will take care of it," she said when Helen told her of Dorothy's fears. "Oh, I wish I could be there. I know you're feeling miserable right now, but you should see what it's like for me these days. Gerald hints at it every day, and he's not the only one. Even the ladies in Haldon look at me so...so probingly, as if I were a mare in a breeding show. And Lucas likewise seems to be angry with me. If I only knew what I was doing wrong!" Gwyneira played with the cup. She was close to tears.

Helen frowned. "Gwyn, there's no way a woman can do it wrong. You don't turn him away, do you? You let him do it?"

Gwyneira rolled her eyes. "What do you think? I know that I'm supposed to lie there still. On my back. And I'm kind and hold him and everything...what else am I supposed to do?"

"That's more than I've done," Helen remarked. "Maybe you just need more time. You're much younger than me, after all."

"Which should make it that much easier," Gwyneira said, sighing. "That's what my mother said anyway. Maybe it has something to do with Lucas after all? What exactly does 'limp dick' mean?"

"Gwyn, how could you!" Helen was scandalized to hear such an expression come from her friend's mouth. "That's not something you say!"

"The men say it when they're talking about Lucas. Only when he's not listening, of course. If I knew what it meant..."

"Gwyneira!" Helen stood up to reach for the teakettle on the stove. But then she screamed and seized her stomach. "Oh no!"

A puddle spread beneath Helen's feet. "Mrs. Candler says this is how it begins!" she exclaimed. "But it's not even eleven in the morning. This is so embarrassing...can you wipe that up, Gwyn?" She lurched into a chair.

"Your water broke," Gwyneira said. "Don't act like that. There's nothing to be embarrassed about. I'll help you to bed, and then I'll send Dorothy to fetch Matahorua."

Helen clenched her fists with pain. "It hurts, Gwyn, it hurts!"

"It'll pass soon," Gwyn reassured her, taking Helen's arm energetically and leading her into the bedroom. She undressed Helen, helped her into her nightgown, calmed her again, then ran into the stables to send Dorothy to the Maori village. The girl burst into tears and ran blindly out of the stables. Hopefully in the right direction. Gwyneira considered whether it might have been better for her to ride there herself, but it had taken her sister hours to bring her baby into the world. In all likelihood, it would be the same for Helen. And Gwyneira was certain to be more reassuring to Helen than the wailing Dorothy.

So Gwyneira wiped down the kitchen and made a new pot of tea, which she brought to Helen in bed. She was now having regular pains. Every few minutes, she screamed and tensed up. Gwyneira took her hand and spoke to her in comforting tones. An hour passed. Where was Dorothy with Matahorua?

Helen did not seem to notice that time was passing, but Gwyneira became increasingly nervous. What if Dorothy really had gotten lost? After more than two hours, she heard someone at the door. Gwyneira was initially terrified, but it was only Dorothy, who was still crying. She had not brought Matahorua as planned, but Rongo Rongo.

"She can't come!" Dorothy sobbed. "Not yet. She…"

"Another baby comes," Rongo explained placidly. "And is hard. Is early, mama sick. She has to stay. She say, Miss O'Keefe strong, baby healthy. I should help."

"You?" Gwyneira asked. Rongo was no more than eleven years old.

"Yes. I already seen and helped *kuia*. In my family many children," Rongo said proudly.

To Gwyneira, she was not the optimal midwife, but she had more experience than any other available girl or woman.

"All right, fine. What do we do now, Rongo?" she inquired.

"Nothing," the little one answered. "Wait. Lasts hours. Matahorua says, when ready, comes."

"That's a real help," sighed Gwyneira. "But all right, we'll wait it out." She didn't know what else to suggest.

Rongo was right. It took hours. Sometimes it was bad, and Helen screamed with pain; then she would calm down, seemingly able to sleep for a few minutes. Starting in the evening, however, her pains became stronger and came at shorter intervals.

"That normal," remarked Rongo. "Can I make syrup pancakes?"

Dorothy was horrified that the little one could only think of food, but Gwyneira didn't think it was a bad idea. She was hungry too, and maybe she could even convince Helen to have a bite.

"Go help her, Dorothy," she commanded.

Helen looked at her desperately. "What will happen to the baby if I die?" she whispered.

Gwyneira wiped the sweat from her brow. "You're not going to die. And the baby has to be here first, before we can worry about what to do with it. But where's that Mr. O'Keefe of yours? Shouldn't he be back by now? Then he could ride to Kiward Station and say that I'll be coming back later. Otherwise, they'll worry about me."

Helen almost laughed despite her pain. "Howard? Easter and Christmas will have to take place on the same day before he'll ride to Kiward Station. Maybe Reti…or one of the other children…"

"I wouldn't let her on Igraine. And that donkey doesn't know the way any better than the children."

"He's a mule," Helen corrected her, then moaned. "Don't call him a donkey or he'll hold it against you."

"I knew you'd love him. Listen, Helen. I'm going to lift up your nightgown and look underneath. Maybe the little one is already sticking his head out."

Helen shook her head. "I would have felt that. But…but now…"

Helen buckled under a new pain. She remembered Mrs. Candler saying something about pushing, so she tried and groaned with pain.

"It might be that now…" The next pain came before she had a chance to finish. Helen bent her knees.

"Goes better when you kneel down, misses," Rongo remarked with a full mouth. She was just entering with a plate of pancakes. "And walking around helps. Because baby has to come down, you see?"

Gwyneira helped a moaning, protesting Helen onto her feet. She only managed a few steps before she collapsed from the pain. Gwyneira lifted Helen's nightgown while she knelt and saw something dark between her legs.

"It's coming, Helen, it's coming! What should I do now, Rongo? If it falls out now, it'll fall onto the floor."

"Won't fall out so quickly," Rongo said, stuffing another pancake in her mouth. "Mmmm. Tastes good. Mrs. O'Keefe can eat as soon as baby here."

"I want to get back in bed," Helen wailed.

Gwyneira helped her back into bed, though she did not think it very smart. It had clearly gone more quickly when Helen was standing upright.

But then there was no more time for reflection. Helen let out another shrill cry, and the little dark crown that Gwyneira had seen became a baby's head pushing out into the open air. Gwyneira recalled the many lamb births that the shepherds had helped with as she watched in secret. That experience might be helpful here too. Taking heart, she reached for the little head, tugging while Helen wheezed and screamed in pain. This drove the little head all the way out. Gwyneira pulled when she saw the shoulders—and suddenly the baby was there, and Gwyneira was staring into its wrinkly little face.

"Cut now," Rongo said calmly. "Cut cord off. Beautiful baby, Mrs. O'Keefe. Boy!"

"A little boy?" Helen moaned, attempting to sit up. "Really?"

"Looks that way," said Gwyneira.

Rongo reached for the knife she had laid out earlier and cut through the umbilical cord. "Now must breathe!"

The baby did not just breathe; it started bawling right away.

Gwyneira beamed. "Looks like he's healthy!"

"Surely healthy...I said, healthy..." The voice came from the door. Matahorua, the Maori *tohunga*, entered the room. As protection against the cold and wet, she had wound a blanket around her body, securing it with a belt. Her many tattoos were more clearly visible than usual, as the old woman was pale from the cold, maybe from weariness too.

"Me sorry, but other baby..."

"Is the other baby healthy too?" Helen asked languidly.

"No. Dead. But mama live. You beautiful son!"

Matahorua now took charge in the nursery. She cleaned off the little one and charged Dorothy with heating water for a bath. Before doing anything else, though, she laid the baby in Helen's arms.

"My little son," whispered Helen. "How tiny he is...I'll name him Ruben, after my father."

"Doesn't Mr. O'Keefe have a say in that as well?" Gwyneira asked. In her circles, it was customary for the father to at least agree to the name of a male child.

"Where is Howard?" Helen asked scornfully. "He knew the baby would be born any day now, but instead of being here for me, he's bent over the bar in some pub, drinking away the money he earned with his mutton. He has no right to give my son a name!"

Matahorua nodded. "Right. Is your son."

Gwyneira, Rongo, and Dorothy gave the baby a bath. Dorothy had finally stopped weeping and now could not tear her gaze from the infant.

"He's so sweet, miss. Look, he's already laughing!"

Gwyneira was thinking less about the baby's facial expressions than about the business of his birth. Aside from the fact that it took longer, it hadn't been all that different from the birth of a foal or a lamb, not even in the discharge of the afterbirth. Matahorua advised Helen to bury this in a particularly beautiful place and to plant a tree there.

"*Whenua* to *whenua*—soil," said Matahorua.

Helen promised to honor the tradition while Gwyneira continued her musings.

If the birth of a human child was like that of an animal, then in all likelihood conception was too. Gwyneira blushed as it all became clear to her, but now she had a pretty good idea what wasn't working with Lucas.

Finally Helen lay happily in a freshly made bed, her sleeping baby in her arms. He had already eaten—Matahorua had insisted on placing the baby on Helen's breast, though the business of nursing was embarrassing to her. She would have preferred to have the baby grow up on cow's milk.

"Is good for baby. Cow milk good for cows," Matahorua declared decisively.

Again, the parallel to animals. Gwyneira had learned a great deal that night.

Meanwhile, Helen found time to think of others. Gwyneira had been wonderful. What would she ever have done without her support? Now she had the opportunity to repay her.

"Matahorua," she turned to the *tohunga*. "This is the friend we recently spoke about. With the…the…"

"Who thinks she not have baby?" asked Matahorua, casting a searching gaze over Gwyneira, her breasts, and her nether regions. What she saw seemed to please her. "Yes, yes," she announced finally. "Beautiful woman. Very healthy. Can have many babies, good babies."

"But she's been trying so long now," Helen said doubtfully.

Matahorua shrugged.

"Try with other man," she advised placidly.

Gwyneira wondered whether she should ride home at this hour. It had long since turned dark, cold, and foggy. On the other hand, Lucas and the others would be worried to death if she didn't return. And what would Howard O'Keefe say when he arrived home, most likely drunk, to find a Warden in his house?

The answer to the latter question seemed about to present itself. Someone appeared to be busy in the stables—though Howard O'Keefe would hardly have knocked at the door of his own house. This visitor was apparently intent on announcing himself politely.

"Open the door, Dorothy," Helen ordered, bewildered.

Gwyneira was already at the door. Had Lucas come to find her? She had told him about Helen, and he had reacted kindly, even expressing a wish to meet her friend. The feud between the Wardens and the O'Keefes seemed to mean nothing to him.

But it was James McKenzie, not Lucas, standing in front of the door.

His eyes lit up when he saw Gwyneira, though he must have already seen in the stables that she was there. After all, Igraine was waiting there.

"Mrs. Warden! Thank God I found you."

"Mr. McKenzie…do come in. How kind of you to come pick me up."

"How kind to come pick you up?" he asked angrily. "Are we talking about a tea party here? What were you thinking, being gone the whole day? Mr. Warden is crazy with worry and conducted excruciating interrogations of us all. I told him about a friend in Haldon that you might be visiting. And then I rode here before he could send someone to Mrs. Candler's and learn…"

"You're an angel, Mr. McKenzie," Gwyneira beamed, oblivious to his admonishing tone. "Not to mention if he knew I had just helped deliver his archenemy's son. Come in! Come meet Ruben O'Keefe."

Helen looked a touch embarrassed when Gwyneira led the strange man into the room, but James McKenzie behaved impeccably, greeting her politely and expressing his delight at little Ruben. Gwyneira had already seen this light in his eyes many times before. James McKenzie always seemed overjoyed when he helped bring a lamb or a foal into the world.

"You managed that on your own?" he asked, impressed.

"Helen also made a negligible contribution," Gwyneira said, laughing.

"Either way, you pulled it off wonderfully!" James beamed. "Both of you. Nevertheless, I would gladly accompany you home now, miss. That would no doubt be best for you as well, madam," he said, turning to Helen. "Your husband…"

"Would certainly not be pleased that a Warden had delivered his son." Helen nodded. "A thousand thanks, Gwyn!"

"Oh, you're welcome. Maybe you'll be able to repay the favor sometime." Gwyneira winked at her. She didn't know why she was suddenly so much more optimistic about being pregnant soon, but all the new information had given her wings. Now that she knew where the problem lay, she was certain she could find a solution.

"I've already saddled your horse, miss," James said. "We should really be going."

Gwyneira smiled. "Let's hurry, then, so my father-in-law calms down," she said, realizing only afterward that James had yet to say a word about Lucas. Wasn't her husband worried at all?

Matahorua followed her with her eyes as Gwyneira left with James McKenzie.

"With that man good baby," she remarked.

9

"How wonderful of Mr. Warden to think of throwing this garden party," said Mrs. Candler. Gwyneira had just brought her invitation to the New Year's party. Since the new year fell in the middle of summer in New Zealand, the party would take place in the garden—with fireworks at midnight for the climax.

Helen shrugged. As always, she and her husband had received no invitation, though Gerald had probably not honored any of the other small farmers with one either. Nor did Gwyneira give the impression that she shared Mrs. Candler's excitement. She still felt overwhelmed by the job of running Kiward Station's manor, and a party would demand still new feats of organizational prowess. Besides, at that moment she was occupied with trying to get little Ruben to laugh by making faces and tickling him. Helen's son was now four months old, and Nepumuk the mule shuttled mother and child on occasional excursions into town. In the weeks following his birth, she had not risked the journey and had found herself once again isolated, but with the baby, her loneliness had not been as acute. Early on, little Ruben had kept her busy all hours of the day, and she was still delighted by every aspect of him. The infant had not proved troublesome. Already at four months he generally slept through the night—at least when he was allowed to stay in bed with his mother. However, that didn't suit Howard, who would have liked to resume his nightly "pleasures" with Helen. Whenever he approached her, though, Ruben began to cry loudly. It broke Helen's heart, but she lay there obediently until Howard was finished. Only then did she worry about the baby. Howard disliked both the background noise and Helen's obvious tension and impatience. As a result, he usually retreated when Ruben began to cry, and when he came home late at night and saw the baby in Helen's arms, he went straight to bed in the stables. Helen felt guilty about it but was thankful to Ruben all the same.

During the day the baby almost never cried but lay quietly in his cradle while Helen taught the Maori children. He didn't sleep but watched the teacher seriously and attentively, as though he already understood what was going on.

"He's going to be a professor," Gwyneira said, laughing. "He takes entirely after you, Helen."

At least in terms of appearance, she was not far off the mark. Ruben's eyes, which had started out blue, had turned gray like Helen's, and his hair seemed to be turning dark like Howard's. But it was straight, not curly.

"He takes after my father," confirmed Helen. "He is named after him, you know. But Howard is determined that he'll become a farmer and not a reverend."

Gwyneira giggled. "Others have made that mistake before. Just think of Mr. Warden and Lucas."

Gwyneira was reminded of that conversation as she handed out invitations in Haldon. Strictly speaking, the New Year's party had not been Gerald's idea but Lucas's—born from a desire to keep Gerald happy and busy. The mood at home was palpably tense, and with every month that Gwyneira did not get pregnant, the tension only heightened. Gerald now responded to the lack of offspring with naked aggression, even though he didn't know which one in the couple he should hold accountable. Gwyneira now kept more to herself, having gradually gotten accustomed to her household duties and, therefore, providing Gerald with few avenues of attack. Besides, she had a fine sense for his moods. When he criticized the muffins first thing in the morning—washing them down with whiskey instead of tea, which happened more and more often—she disappeared straightaway to the stables, preferring to spend the day with the dogs and the sheep rather than playing lightning rod for Gerald's low spirits. Lucas, on the other hand, faced the full force of his father's wrath, almost always unexpectedly. Gerald frequently ripped his son away from whatever task he was immersed in without compunction and pushed the boy to make himself useful around the farm. He even went so far as to tear up a book Lucas was reading when he caught Lucas with it in his room while he should have been overseeing the sheep shearing.

"You don't need to do anything more than count, damn it!" Gerald raged. "Otherwise, the shearers charge too much! In warehouse three, two of the boys just got into a fight because both laid claim to the pay for shearing a hundred sheep, and no one can arbitrate because no one was comparing their counts. You were assigned to warehouse three, Lucas! Now go see you put things in order."

Gwyneira would have been glad to take over warehouse three, but as housewife, the food, and not the oversight of the migrant workers who had been hired on to shear the sheep, fell to her. For that reason, outstanding care was taken of the men: Gwyneira appeared again and again with refreshments because she could not get enough of seeing the shearers at work. At home in Silkham sheep shearing had been a rather leisurely affair; the few hundred sheep were sheared by the shepherds themselves over the course of a few days. Here, however, they had thousands of sheep to shear, which first had to be fetched from the extensive pastures and then penned together. The shearing itself was the work of specialists. The best work groups managed eight hundred animals a day. On big operations like Kiward Station there was always a competition—and this year James McKenzie was well on his way to winning it. He was neck and neck with a top shearer from warehouse one, even though he was also responsible for supervising the other shearers in warehouse two. Whenever Gwyneira came by, she took over the supervision for him, lightening his load. Her presence seemed to redouble his energy; his shears moved so quickly and smoothly over the sheep's bodies that the animals hardly had time to bleat in protest at their rude treatment.

Lucas found the handling of the sheep barbaric. He felt for them when the animals were seized, thrown on their backs, and shorn, often getting cuts on their skin if the shearer was inexperienced or the sheep fidgeted excessively. Lucas also couldn't stand the overwhelming odor of lanolin that pervaded the shearing warehouses. As a result, he was constantly letting sheep escape instead of pushing them through a bath after the shearing, which was supposed to clean out any cuts and kill off parasites.

"The dogs don't listen to me," he said, defending himself against a new fit of anger from his father. "They answer to McKenzie, but when I call—"

"You don't call these dogs, Lucas! You whistle for them," Gerald exploded. "There are only three or four whistles, all of which you should have learned long ago. You think so highly of your musical abilities!"

Lucas recoiled, insulted. "Father, a gentleman—"

"Don't tell me a gentleman doesn't whistle. These sheep finance your painting, piano playing, and so-called studies."

Gwyneira, who caught this conversation by chance, fled into the nearest warehouse. She hated it when Gerald took her husband to task in front of her—and it was even worse when James McKenzie or the other farmworkers witnessed the confrontations. They not only embarrassed Gwyneira, but moreover, they seemed to have a negative effect on her and Lucas's nightly "attempts," which went awry with increasing frequency. Gwyneira had taken to viewing their efforts together only as the first stage of reproduction, since ultimately it was no different from what took place between a stallion and mare. Yet she harbored no illusions: luck would have to be very much on her side. She gradually began thinking of alternatives, though the image of her father's old ram—one that he had had to retire due to a lack of success in mating—came back to her time and again.

"Try with other man," Matahorua had said. Every time Gwyneira recalled those words, she felt a pang of guilt. It was inconceivable for a Silkham to cheat on her husband.

Then came the garden party. Lucas devoted himself energetically to the preparations. Planning the fireworks show alone required days, which he spent poring over the catalogs before placing the order in

Christchurch. He took on the landscaping of the garden, as well as the arrangements of the tables and chairs. Instead of a grand banquet, lamb and mutton were going to be roasted over the fire; vegetables, poultry, and mussels would be prepared on cooking stones, according to Maori tradition. Salads and other dishes rested on long tables and were to be presented to guests on request. Kiri and Moana had mastered this task and were once again to wear the uniforms that had been made for them for the wedding. Gwyneira made them promise to wear shoes.

Otherwise, they kept out of the preparations; between father and son, it required great tact and diplomacy to get any decisions made. Lucas enjoyed the preparations and longed for recognition. Gerald, however, felt that his son's efforts were "unmanly" and would have preferred to leave everything to Gwyneira. Nor did the workers approve of Lucas's domestic occupations, which did not go unnoticed by Gerald or Gwyneira.

"Limp dick's folding napkins," Poker Livingston replied when James McKenzie asked him where Lucas was hiding this time.

Gwyneira pretended not to understand. She had developed a rather precise idea of what the term "limp dick" meant but could not fathom how the men in the stables were drawing their conclusions about Lucas's failures in bed.

The day before the party, Kiward Station's garden shone in full splendor. Lucas had had lampions brought out, and the Maori set up torches. As the guests were being received, there was still enough light for them to marvel at the rose borders, the cleanly cut hedges, and the twisting paths and lawns, laid out according to the classic model of an English garden. Gerald had also arranged a new dog demonstration—this time not only to show off the now legendary talents of his dogs but also as a sort of promotion. Daimon and Dancer's first offspring were available for sale, and the local sheep breeders would pay handsomely for purebred border collies. Even the mixed breeds with

Gerald's old sheepdogs were in high demand. Gerald's employees no longer needed Gwyneira's and Cleo's help to stage a perfect show. At James McKenzie's whistle, the young dogs herded the sheep through the obstacle course without incident. Gwyneira's elegant party dress, a dream in sky-blue silk with gold-colored eyelet appliqué, remained clean, and Cleo too merely followed the show from the sidelines, whimpering as though insulted. Her whelps had finally been weaned, and the little dog was looking for new tasks. Today, however, she had been exiled to the stables again. Lucas did not want any dogs capering about, and Gwyneira was occupied with entertaining the guests—though her strolls among the guests and chats with the ladies of Christchurch increasingly resembled a gauntlet. She felt people's eyes on her as the guests observed her still slender figure with a mixture of curiosity and sympathy. Early on she heard only a few comments, but then the gentlemen—Gerald above all—started knocking back the whiskey, which rapidly loosened their tongues.

"Well, my lady, you've been married almost a year now," intoned Lord Barrington. "How long until there are little ones?"

Gwyneira did not know how to reply. She blushed as deeply as the viscount, whose father's behavior embarrassed him too. He changed the subject, asking Gwyneira about Igraine and Madoc, whom he still remembered fondly. He had yet to find comparable horses in this new homeland of theirs. Gwyneira came alive at once. The breeding of the horses had been successful, and she would be happy to sell young Barrington a foal. She seized the opportunity to escape Lord Barrington by leading the viscount over to the pasture. A month before, Igraine had given birth to a black colt as pretty as a picture, and Gerald had put the horses' pen close enough to the house for the guests to marvel at them.

Next to the paddock where the mare and foal were grazing, James McKenzie was overseeing the preparations for the help's party. The employees of Kiward Station still had work to do, but when the meal was over and the dancing had started, they could then have their fun. Gerald had been happy to provide two sheep and plenty of beer and whiskey for their party, and the fire for cooking the meat was just being lit.

James greeted Gwyneira and the viscount, and she used the opportunity to congratulate him on his successful presentation.

"I believe Mr. Warden sold five dogs today," she said in recognition.

James returned her smile. "Still not to be compared to the show with your Cleo, miss. But naturally, I miss the charms of the dog's mistress too."

Gwyneira turned her gaze away. His eyes once again sparkled in that way that she found simultaneously so delightful and unsettling. And why was he paying her compliments in front of the viscount? She entertained an apprehension that it wasn't very proper.

"Try wearing a wedding dress next time," Gwyneira said to draw out the humor in the situation.

The viscount chuckled. "Why, he's in love with you, my lady." He giggled, with all the insolence of his fifteen years. "Watch out that your husband doesn't challenge him to a duel."

Gwyneira cast a chastising look at the boy. "Don't say such nonsense, viscount! You yourself know how quickly gossip spreads here. If a rumor like that were to come out..."

"Not to worry, your secret is safe with me!" The rascal laughed. "By the way, did you ever cut a slit into your riding dress?"

Gwyneira was happy when the dancing finally began, releasing her from the obligations of conversation. Perfectly led as always, she floated with Lucas across the dance floor that had been specially set up in the garden. The musicians, hired by Lucas this time, were a good deal better than those who had played at their wedding. The dance selection was more conventional. Gwyneira was almost a bit envious when she heard the happy ditties wafting over from the employees' party. Someone was fiddling over there—not always perfectly, it was true, but with no lack of spirit.

Gwyneira danced with the most important guests, one after the other. She was spared Gerald, at least, who had long since drunk too much to hold himself upright for a waltz. The party was a complete success, but Gwyneira nevertheless hoped it would soon be over. It had been a long day, and the guests would have to be entertained again from morning until at least noon the following day. Many of them planned to stay beyond that, until the day after next. Still, Gwyneira had to stay through the fireworks before she could retire. Lucas had excused himself an hour earlier in order to review the setup one last time. Young Hardy Kennon was to help him with it if he wasn't too drunk already. Gwyneira went to check on the champagne stores. She found Witi just taking a bottle from the ice bucket where they were being kept cool.

"Hopefully not shoot someone," he said with concern. The pop of the cork when the champagne bottles were opened still made the Maori servant nervous.

"It's totally harmless, Witi," Gwyneira said in an effort to calm him. "When you've done it a few more times..."

"Yes, whe...when...there was mo...more often a reason!" That was Gerald, who had just tottered back up to the bar to uncork a new bottle of whiskey. "But you don't give us an...any reason to celebrate, my Wel...Welsh princess! Thought you weren't so prudish, loo...look like you got fire enough for ten and could even get Lu...Lucas hot, that limp...that block of ice!" Gerald slurred, catching himself before he said something even more inappropriate as he stared at the champagne. "But now...a year, Gwyn...Gwyneira, and still no grand..."

Gwyneira breathed a sigh of relief when Gerald was interrupted by a fireworks rocket climbing into the sky with a hiss—a test shot for the later spectacle. Witi popped the corks, squeezing his eyes shut anxiously as he did so. Gwyneira thought about the horses in a searing flash. Igraine and the other mares had never experienced fireworks before, and the paddock was relatively small. What if the animals panicked?

Gwyneira cast a glance at the big clock, which had been specially brought into the garden and placed in a highly visible spot.

Maybe there was still enough time to bring the horses into the stables. She could have kicked herself for not having given James McKenzie the directions to do so earlier. Muttering apologies, Gwyneira made her way through the mass of guests and ran to the stables. But the pen was already empty, except for one mare, which McKenzie was just then leading out. Gwyneira's heart leaped. Had he read her thoughts?

"I thought the animals were looking unsettled, so I thought I'd bring them in," James said when Gwyneira opened the stable door for him and the mare. Cleo jumped up on her mistress as she did so.

Gwyneira laughed. "That's funny. I was thinking the same thing."

McKenzie gave her a rakish look, between flirtation and mischief. "We should think about why that happens," he said. "Maybe we're soul mates? In India they believe in the transmigration of souls. Who knows, maybe in a past life we were..." He pretended to think hard.

"As good Christians, we shouldn't give it a thought," Gwyneira said, interrupting him sternly, but James just laughed. In perfect harmony, they filled the horses' hayracks, and Gwyneira tossed a few carrots in the stall for Igraine. After all that, her dress no longer looked quite so clean. Gwyneira looked down at herself ruefully. Oh well, no one would notice in the lantern light.

"Are you done here? I should wish the help a happy New Year while I'm here."

James smiled. "Maybe you even have time for a dance? When does the big fireworks show start?"

Gwyneira shrugged. "As soon as it strikes twelve and cheering has died down." She smiled. "Or, better yet, as soon as everyone has wished everyone else all the happiness in the world, even if he doesn't mean it."

"Now, now, miss. So cynical today? It's such a wonderful party!" James looked at her probingly. Gwyneira knew this look too—and it set her on edge.

"Spiced with a good dose of schadenfreude," she sighed. "Over the next few days, everyone's mouths will be flapping, and Mr. Warden only makes it worse—with the way he talks."

"What do you mean 'schadenfreude'?" James asked. "Kiward Station is in tip-top shape. With the profit Mr. Warden is going to make from the wool, he could throw a party like this every month. How can he be unhappy?"

"Oh, let's not talk about it," Gwyneira muttered. "Let's start the year with something more cheerful. Did you say something about a dance? As long as it's not a waltz."

Andy McAran fiddled a rollicking Irish jig. Two Maori servants beat the drum in accompaniment, which did not quite fit but was great fun nevertheless. Poker Livingston and Dave O'Toole swung the Maori girls around. Moana and Kiri let themselves be led in the foreign dance. The other dancers included the servants of the more genteel guests, who either hardly knew Gwyneira or didn't know her at all. Lady Barrington's English maid looked over disapprovingly as Kiward Station's staff greeted Gwyneira with hoots and hollers. James held his hand out to lead her into the dancing area. Gwyneira took it, once again feeling that soft shock that sent waves of arousal through her. It always seemed to happen when she touched James. He laughed, catching her as she stumbled a bit. Then he bowed to her—but that was all this dance had in common with a waltz, which she had been dancing all night.

"She is handsome, she is pretty, she is the queen of Belfast City!" Poker and a few other men sang the melody happily while James spun Gwyneira around so many times she felt dizzy. And every time she flew back into his arms after being energetically spun, she saw that glint in his eye, the admiration, and...well, what? Desire?

In the middle of the dance, the rocket heralding the new year soared into the sky—and then the whole glorious fireworks display fired off. The men around Andy McAran broke off the jig and Poker started "Auld Lang Syne." All the other immigrants joined in, and the Maori hummed along, enthusiastically if not entirely in tune. Only James and Gwyneira had neither ears for the song nor eyes for the fireworks. Though the music had stopped, they still held each other's hands, now frozen in midair. Neither wanted to let the other go. They seemed to be standing on an island, far from the tears and laughter. There was only him. There was only her.

Finally Gwyneira pulled herself free. She did not want to break up the moment, but she knew that their feelings could not be consummated here.

"We should...check on the horses," she said without inflection.

James took her hand on the way to the stables.

Just before the entrance he stopped her. "Look, miss," he whispered. "I've never seen such a thing. Like it's raining stars!"

Lucas's fireworks made for a spectacular effect. But Gwyneira saw only the stars in James's eyes. What she was doing was stupid, forbidden, and entirely improper. But she leaned on his shoulder nevertheless.

James tenderly brushed away the hair that had fallen into her face during their wild dance. His fingers wandered light as a feather over her cheeks and along her lips.

Gwyneira made a decision. It was New Year's. So you could kiss someone. She raised herself carefully on tiptoe and kissed James on the cheek.

"Happy New Year, Mr. McKenzie," she said softly.

McKenzie drew her into his arms, very slowly, very softly—Gwyneira could have freed herself at any time, but she didn't. Not even when his lips found hers. Gwyneira instinctively and passionately opened herself up to the kiss. She felt like she was coming home—a home where a world of wonder and surprise awaited her.

It was as though a spell had been cast on her when he finally let go.

"And a happy New Year to you, Gwyneira," said James.

The guests' reactions at the party, not least of all Gerald's breakdown, confirmed Gwyneira's decision to effect a pregnancy with or without Lucas's assistance. It had nothing to do with James and their kiss at midnight, of course—that had been a mistake, and the next day Gwyneira didn't even know herself what had come over her. Fortunately, James McKenzie behaved just as he always had.

She would see to the business of getting pregnant without interference from her emotions. It was just like breeding, after all. At this thought, she suppressed an absurd, hysterical giggle. Being absurd was not appropriate. The situation called for sober consideration of who would make a good candidate for the father of the child. This was in part a matter of discretion, but above all, one of inheritance. The Wardens, Gerald especially, could not be allowed to entertain any doubts that their heir was of their blood. As for Lucas, that was a bit more complicated, but if he was sensible, he would hold his peace. Gwyneira was not too worried. Her husband was overly cautious, stiff, and not very good under pressure, true, but he had never proved irrational. Besides, it was in his own best interest that the innuendo and teasing by others at his and her expense be stopped.

Gwyneira began to seriously consider what her and Lucas's child might look like. Her mother and all her sisters were redheads, so that seemed to be hereditary. Lucas was towheaded, but James had brown hair...however, Gerald also had brown hair. And he had brown eyes. So if the child took after James, one could claim he looked like his grandfather.

Eye color: blue and gray...and brown if she took Gerald into account. Build...that worked. James and Lucas were roughly the same height, Gerald considerably shorter and stockier. She too was markedly shorter. But it just had to be a boy and he would no doubt take after his father. Now she just needed to convince James...but why James specifically? Gwyneira decided to put off the decision a bit longer. After all, maybe tomorrow her heart wouldn't beat quite so quickly when she thought of James McKenzie.

The next day she came to the conclusion that there was no one other than James who could serve as the father of her child. But then again, maybe she should consider a stranger? She thought about the "lonesome cowboys" in the penny dreadfuls. They came and went and would never learn about the child if they were just passing through...maybe one of the shearers? No, she couldn't bring herself to do that. Besides, the sheep shearers came back every year. Not to mention what would happen if the man talked, gloating that he had slept with the lady of Kiward Station. No, that was out of the question. She needed a man she trusted, one who was understanding and discreet and, moreover, who only had good traits to pass on to the child.

Gwyneira reviewed all the candidates carefully in her mind. Feelings, she convinced herself, did not play a role in this.

She chose James.

10

"All right, to begin with…I'm not in love with you!"

Gwyneira wasn't sure that that was the best way to broach the subject, but it burst out of her when she next found herself alone with James McKenzie. A week had passed since the party. The last guests had left the day before, and Gwyneira could finally get back on her horse. Lucas had begun work on a new painting. The brightly lit garden had inspired him, and he was working on a party scene. Gerald had done little other than drink all week and was now sleeping off his hangover. And McKenzie planned to return the sheep that had been used for the demonstration back into the highlands. The dogs had demonstrated their skills several times over the last week, and five guests had purchased a total of eight pups. Cleo's puppies were not among them, however; they were to remain at Kiward Station as breeding stock and now accompanied their mother during sheep herding. Though they occasionally tripped over their own legs, their talent was unmistakable.

James had been pleased when Gwyneira joined him for the sheep herding. However, he had become wary as she rode next to him in silence. Finally, she took a deep breath to begin the conversation. He seemed to find her remark funny.

"Of course you're not in love with me, miss. Where would I ever have gotten that idea?" he said, fighting a smile.

"Don't mock me, Mr. McKenzie. I have something very serious to discuss with you."

James looked at her, shocked. "Did I hurt you? I didn't mean to. I thought it was what you wanted too…the kiss, I mean. But if you want me to go…"

"Forget the kiss," Gwyneira said. "This is regarding something very different, Mr. McKenzie…ahem, James. I…wanted to ask you for some help."

James stopped his horse. "Whatever you want, miss. I would never deny you anything."

He looked her straight in the eye, which made it difficult for her to continue.

"But it's rather…it's not proper."

James smiled. "I'm not all that concerned with what's proper. I'm not a gentleman, miss. I believe we've talked about that before."

"That's a shame, Mr. McKenzie, namely because…what I wanted to ask you…it requires the discretion of a gentleman."

Gwyneira was turning red. What would become of her once she stated what she had in mind?

"Perhaps a man of honor's enough," ventured James. "Someone who keeps his word."

Gwyneira considered that for a moment. She nodded.

"Then you must promise to tell no one whether you…we…go through with it or not."

"Your wish is my command. I'll do whatever you ask me to." Once again James had that glint in his eye. Today, however, it was not playful, but more like a supplication.

"That's not very wise," Gwyneira chided him. "You don't even know what I want. Imagine if I wanted you to murder someone."

James had to laugh. "Now, out with it, Gwyn! What do you want? Shall I kill your husband? That's worth a thought. Then afterward I'd have you all to myself."

Gwyneira looked at him, horrified. "Don't say such things! That's terrible."

"The thought of killing your husband or of belonging to me?"

"Neither…both…oh, now you've got me all mixed up!" Gwyneira was almost ready to give up.

James whistled for the dogs and got off his horse. Then he helped Gwyneira out of the saddle. She let him. It was exciting but also comforting to feel his arms on her.

"All right, Gwyn. Now let's sit down here, and you can tell me nice and easy what's on your mind. And then I can say yes or no. And I won't laugh; I promise."

McKenzie removed a blanket from his saddle, spread it out, and motioned for Gwyneira to sit.

"All right, good," she said softly. "I need to have a baby."

James smiled. "No one can force you to."

"I *want* to have a baby," Gwyneira corrected herself. "And I need a father for it."

James frowned. "I don't understand…you're already married."

Gwyneira felt his proximity and the warmth of the ground beneath her. It was so pleasant sitting here in the sun, and it was so good to finally get it off her chest. Yet she couldn't help but burst into tears.

"Lucas…he can't manage it. He is a…no, I can't say it. Anyway…I've never bled and it's never hurt."

McKenzie smiled and took her gently into his arms. He kissed her lightly on the temple. "I can't guarantee that it'll hurt, Gwyn. I'd rather you enjoyed it."

"The main thing is that you do it right, so that I have a baby," Gwyneira whispered.

James kissed her again. "You can trust me."

"So you've done it before?" Gwyneira asked seriously.

James choked back a laugh. "A time or two, Gwyn. Like I said, I'm not a gentleman."

"Good. You see, it has to happen quickly. Otherwise, there's too much of a risk that we'll be found out. When should we do it? And where?"

James stroked her hair, kissed her forehead, and tickled her upper lip with his tongue.

"It doesn't have to happen quickly, Gwyneira. And you also can't be sure that it takes the first time. Even if we do everything right."

Gwyneira looked suspicious. "Why not?"

James sighed. "Look, Gwyn, you know about animals…what's it like with mares and stallions?"

She nodded. "When the time is right, one go is enough."

"When the time's right. That's just it."

"The stallion senses it…does that mean that you don't sense it?"

James didn't know if he should laugh or feel insulted. "No, Gwyneira. People are different in that respect. We always want to make love, not just on the days when a woman can become pregnant. So it might be that we have to try it a few times."

James looked around. Their location was quite good, pretty far in the highlands. There was no danger of anyone riding by. The flock had scattered to graze, the dogs were keeping an eye on them, and he had tied the horses to a tree that could offer them shade.

James stood up and offered Gwyneira his hand. As she got up, bewildered, he spread the blanket out in the semishade. He embraced Gwyneira, picked her up, and laid her down on the blanket. He carefully opened her blouse and kissed her. His kisses set her on fire, and when he touched her most intimate parts, he set off sensations like Gwyneira had never felt before, spiriting her away to a state of bliss. When he finally pushed into her, she felt a brief flash of pain that then dissolved in a delirium of sensation. It was as though she'd always been seeking someone and had now finally found him—as though they were indeed the "soul mates" he had recently teased her about. Afterward, they lay next to each other, half-naked and exhausted, but infinitely happy.

"So would you be against it if we had to do it several times?" James asked.

Gwyneira beamed at him. "I'd say," she replied, striving for a properly serious tone, "we should do it just as much as necessary."

They did it whenever they found an opportunity. Gwyneira especially lived in fear of being caught and preferred abstention to taking even the slightest risk. Finding credible excuses to disappear together were hard to come by, so it took several weeks before Gwyneira was pregnant. They were the happiest weeks of her life.

When it rained, James made love to her in the shearing warehouses that had been abandoned since the shearing was done. They held each other in their arms and listened to the raindrops on the roof, snuggling close and telling each other stories. James laughed at the Maori legend of *rangi* and *papa* and suggested that they make love again to comfort the gods.

When the sun shone, they made love in the silky golden tussocks of grass in the hills, to the accompaniment of the steady chewing of the horses who grazed nearby. They kissed in the shadows of the mighty stones on the plains, and Gwyneira talked about the enchanted soldiers while James maintained that the stone circles in Wales were part of a love spell.

"Do you know the story of Tristan and Isolde? They loved each other, but her husband couldn't know about it, and so the elves made a circle of stone around their bed in the fields to remove them from the world's gaze."

They made love on the shores of ice-cold crystal clear mountain lakes, and one time James even convinced Gwyneira to take off all her clothes and get into the water with him. Gwyneira reddened all over. She couldn't remember having been fully naked since childhood. Yet James told her she was so beautiful that *rangi* would become jealous if she continued standing on *papa*'s solid ground, and pulled her into the water, where she clamped onto him, screeching.

"Can't you swim?" he inquired, disbelieving.

Gwyneira spat out water. "Where was I supposed to learn how? In the bathtub at Silkham Manor?"

"You traveled halfway around the world on a ship and couldn't swim?" James shook his head but now held her tightly. "Weren't you afraid?"

"I would have been more afraid if I'd had to swim. Now stop talking and teach me how! It can't be that hard; even Cleo can do it."

Gwyneira learned in no time how to keep herself above water, then lay exhausted and frozen on the lakeshore while James caught fish, then grilled them over an open fire. Gwyneira always loved it when he found something edible in the wild and served it to her then and there. She called it their "wilderness survival" game, and James knew how to play superbly. The wild seemed to be a cafeteria for him. He shot birds and rabbits, caught fish, and collected roots and strange fruits. In that sense, he mirrored the pioneer of Gwyneira's dreams. Sometimes she thought about what it would be like to be married to him and run a small farm like Helen and Howard. James wouldn't leave her alone all day; they would instead share all the work together. She dreamed of plowing with a horse, of working side by side in the garden, and of watching James teaching a young red-haired boy how to fish.

She had woefully neglected Helen during this time, but Helen did not even mention it when Gwyneira appeared at her place with a happy demeanor but a grass-stained dress, after James had ridden on into the highlands. "I have to ride to Haldon, but help me brush off my dress first, please. It's somehow gotten dirty."

Gwyneira was supposedly riding to Haldon three to four times a week. She claimed to have joined a housewives club. Gerald was ecstatic about it, and Gwyneira did indeed return home every week with new recipes that she had had Mrs. Candler dash off for her. Lucas seemed to find it rather strange, but he didn't have any objections either; he was happiest when people left him alone.

Gwyneira gave a sewing circle as an excuse, James missing sheep. They thought up names for their favorite meeting places in the wild, and awaited one another there, making love against the backdrop of the mountains on clear days or under a provisional tent consisting of James's waxed coat when the fog rolled in. Gwyneira once pretended to quake with shame under the curious gaze of a couple of keas who arrived to pilfer the remains of their picnic, and James took off half-naked after two kiwis that tried to make off with the belt he had dropped in the dirt.

"Thieving as magpies!" he called out, laughing. "No wonder people named the immigrants after them."

Gwyneira looked at him, confused. "Most of the immigrants I know are very respectable people," she objected.

James nodded grimly. "Toward other immigrants. But look how they behave toward the Maori. Do you believe the land for Kiward Station was bought at a fair price?"

"Since the treaty of Waitangi, doesn't all land belong to the Crown?" Gwyneira inquired. "The queen certainly wouldn't let herself be fleeced."

James laughed. "That would be unlikely. According to what I've heard, she's got a good head for business. But for that reason the land still belongs to the Maori. The Crown only has the right of preemption. Which naturally guarantees people a certain baseline price. But for one thing, that's not how the world works, and for another, even now not all of the chiefs have signed the treaty. The Kai Tahu, for example, haven't as far as I know."

"The Kai Tahu are our people?" Gwyneira asked.

"You've got it," James replied. "Of course they're not really 'our people.' They merely carelessly sold the land on which their village rests to Mr. Warden because they let themselves be tricked. That in itself shows how unfairly the Maori have been treated."

"But they seem perfectly happy," Gwyneira objected. "They're always very nice to me. And they're often not even there." Whole Maori tribes occasionally took long treks to other hunting grounds and fishing areas.

"They still haven't figured out how much money they've been swindled out of," James said. "But the whole thing is a powder keg. If the Maori ever have a chief who learns to read and write, there will be trouble. But forget all that for now, my sweet. Shall we try again?"

Gwyneira laughed at his words. It was the same way Lucas prefaced their efforts in the marriage bed. But what a difference between Lucas and James!

Gwyneira increasingly enjoyed the physical act of love the more time she spent with James. At first he was tender and gentle, but when he recognized the passion that was awakening within Gwyneira, he loved to play with the tigress within her. Gwyneira had always liked wild games and she loved it when James moved inside her quickly, bringing their intimate dance to a passionate crescendo. With every new tryst, she cast more of her reservations about propriety aside.

"Does it work if I lie on top of you instead of the other way around?" she asked at one point. "You're kind of heavy, you know."

"You were born to ride," James said, laughing. "I always knew that. Try it sitting down, then you'll have more freedom to move."

"Now how do you know all that?" Gwyneira asked suspiciously, when, intoxicated with happiness, she later snuggled her head onto his shoulder, the commotion inside her slowly ebbing away.

"You don't want to know that," he dodged.

"I do. Have you already loved a girl? I mean, properly, from your heart...so much that you would have died for her, like in books?" Gwyneira sighed.

"No, not until now. Though one rarely learns these things with the love of one's life. Rather, it's an education you have to pay for."

"Men can be instructed in this sort of thing?" Gwyneira asked, astonished. Those must have been the only lessons that Lucas ever skipped. "And girls just get thrown into the deep end? Seriously, James, no one tells us what to expect."

James laughed. "Oh, Gwyn, you're so innocent, but you've got an instinct for the most important things. I can imagine those teaching positions would be highly sought after." Over the next quarter of an hour, he imparted a lesson on how love could be bought. Gwyn vacillated between disgust and fascination.

"At least the girls make their own money," she said in the end. "But I would insist that the fellows washed up first!"

When, during the third month of their affair, she didn't get her period, Gwyneira could hardly believe it. Of course she had already noticed signs—her swollen breasts and intense cravings if there wasn't a specific cabbage dish on the table. Now that she was completely sure, her first feeling was one of joy. But a bitter feeling of imminent loss followed.

She was pregnant, so there was no longer a reason to continue cheating on her spouse. The idea that she would never again touch James, never again lie naked beside him, kiss him, feel him inside her, or scream with lust at the climax cut her like a knife to the heart.

Gwyneira could not bring herself to reveal the news to James right away. For two days she kept it to herself and saved up every one of James's stolen, tender glances like a treasure. Never again would he wink at her secretively as he muttered, "Good day, miss" or "But of course, miss," in passing when they met each other in company.

Never again would he steal a quick kiss from her when no one was looking, and never again would she chide him for taking such a risk.

She continued to postpone the moment of truth longer and longer.

But it couldn't go on like that. Gwyneira had just returned from riding when James waved to her, pulling her into an empty horse stall with a smile. He wanted to kiss her, but Gwyneira extricated herself from his embrace.

"Not here, James..."

"But tomorrow, in the ring of stone warriors. I'm herding the ewes out. If you want, you can come along. I've already mentioned to Mr. Warden that I could really use Cleo." He winked at her meaningfully. "That wasn't even a lie. We'll leave the sheep to her and Daimon, and the two of us will play a little game of 'survival in the wilderness.'"

"Sorry, James." Gwyneira did not know how to break the news. "But we can't do it anymore."

James frowned. "What can't we do anymore? Are you busy tomorrow? Is there another visitor coming? Mr. Warden didn't mention anything."

Gerald Warden seemed to have been increasingly lonely the last few months. He had been inviting more guests to stay at Kiward Station, usually wool merchants or newly well-off settlers to whom he could show off his exemplary farm by day and with whom he could get soused at night.

Gwyneira shook her head. "No, James, it's just...I'm pregnant." There. The truth was out.

"You're pregnant? That's wonderful!" On impulse James took her in his arms and swung her around. "Oh yes, you've already gotten heavier," he teased her. "Soon I won't even be able to lift the two of you."

When he saw that she wasn't smiling, he promptly became serious. "What is it, Gwyn? Aren't you happy?"

"Of course I'm happy," Gwyneira said, blushing. "But I'm also a little sorry. It...it's been fun with you."

James laughed. "Well, there's no reason to stop right away." He tried to kiss her, but she pushed him away.

"It's not about desire!" she said sternly. "It's about morality. We can't anymore." She looked at him. In her gaze was sorrow, but also determination.

"Gwyn, am I hearing you right?" James asked, shocked. "You want to call it quits, to throw away everything that we had together? I thought you loved me."

"It doesn't have anything to do with love," Gwyneira said quietly. "I'm married, James. I'm not allowed to love another man. And we agreed from the start that you were only helping me to...to bless my marriage with a child." She hated that she sounded so pathetic, but she didn't know how else to express it. And she didn't want to cry under any circumstances.

"Gwyneira, I've loved you since the first time I saw you. It just... happened, like rain or sunshine. You can't change something like that."

"When it rains, you can seek shelter," Gwyneira said softly. "And when the sun's out, find shade. I can't stop the rain or heat, but I don't have to get wet or sunburned."

James pulled her to him. "Gwyneira, I know you love me too. Come with me. We'll leave here and start from scratch somewhere else."

"And where will we go, James?" she asked, mocking him in order not to sound desperate. "What sheep farm will you work on when it becomes known that you abducted Lucas Warden's wife? The whole South Island knows the Wardens. Do you think Gerald will let you get away with that?"

"Are you married to Gerald or Lucas? And regardless which of the two—neither one stands a chance against me!" James balled his fists.

"Is that so? And how do you intend to compete with them? Fisticuffs or pistols? And then are we supposed to flee into the wilderness to live off nuts and berries?" Gwyneira hated fighting with him. She had hoped to bring everything to a peaceful conclusion with a kiss—bittersweet and heavy as fate, like in a Bulwer-Lytton novel.

"But you like life in the wilderness. Or were you lying? Are you really better suited to the luxury here on Kiward Station? Is it important to you to be the wife of a sheep baron, to throw big parties, to be rich?" James was trying to sound angry, but his words spoke of bitterness instead.

Gwyneira suddenly felt tired. "James, let's not fight. You know none of that is important to me. But I gave my word. I *am* a sheep baron's wife. I'd keep it just the same if I were a beggar's wife."

"You broke your word when you shared a bed with me!" James flared up. "You've already cheated on your husband."

Gwyneira took a step back. "I never shared a bed with you, James McKenzie," she said. "You know that very well. I would never have brought you into the house. That…that would've…it was different."

"And what was it? Gwyneira! Please don't tell me that you were only using me like an animal for breeding."

Gwyneira just wanted to bring this conversation to an end. She could no longer bear his imploring gaze.

"I asked you, James," she said softly. "You agreed. To all the conditions. It's not about what I want. It's about what's right. I'm a Silkham, James. I can't walk away from my obligations. Whether you understand or not. In any event it can't be changed. From now on…"

"Gwyneira? What's going on? Weren't you supposed to meet me fifteen minutes ago?"

Gwyneira and James hurriedly separated as Lucas entered the stables. He rarely came around there of his own free will, but the day before Gwyneira had promised him that she would finally start sitting for an oil painting the next day. She only agreed because she felt sorry for him—Gerald had once again torn him apart, and Gwyneira knew that she could end all this torture with a word. But she had not been able to bring herself to talk about her pregnancy before breaking the news to James. So she had thought of sitting for the painting to comfort Lucas. What's more, she would have plenty of time and leisure to sit still on a stool in the months ahead.

"I'm coming, Lucas. I had...a small problem, and Mr. McKenzie helped me fix it. Thank you very much, Mr. McKenzie." Gwyneira managed to speak calmly and smile benignly at James, but hoped that she didn't look too distraught. If only James had been able to keep his feelings under control. His desperate, wounded expression broke her heart.

Fortunately, Lucas did not notice. He only saw the picture he would be sketching of Gwyneira.

That evening Gwyneira told Lucas and Gerald that she was pregnant.

Gerald was overjoyed. Lucas performed his duty as a gentleman, assuring Gwyneira that he was very happy and kissing her formally on the cheek. A few days later a costly pearl necklace arrived from Christchurch. Lucas presented it to Gwyneira as a token of gratitude and appreciation. Gerald rode to Haldon to celebrate that he would finally be a grandfather and paid for drinks for everyone in the pub for that night—with the exception of Howard O'Keefe, who was fortunately sober enough to clear the area as quickly as possible. When Helen learned from Howard that Gerald had made a public announcement about Gwyneira's pregnancy, she was mortified.

"You don't think it's embarrassing to me?" Gwyneira asked when she visited Helen two days later and learned that her friend had already heard the news. "But that's just how he is. The exact opposite of Lucas. You wouldn't think those two were even related." She bit her lip almost as soon as she said it.

Helen smiled. "As long as they're both convinced of it." she said equivocally.

Gwyneira smiled. "Anyway, it's finally here. You must tell me what I need to do in the next few months, so I don't do anything wrong. And I'll need to crochet some baby clothes. Do you think someone can learn to do that in nine months?"

11

Gwyneira's pregnancy passed without incident. Even the infamous morning sickness of the first three months had been hardly noticeable. And so neither did she take seriously those warnings that her mother had been heaping on her practically since her marriage had been decided for heaven's sake to finally quit riding. Instead, Gwyneira took advantage of almost every pretty day to visit Helen or Mrs. Candler, thereby avoiding James. At first it was painful every time she looked at him, and they did their best not to see each other at all. When they did run into each other, they both looked away, embarrassed, trying not to see the pain and sorrow in the other's eyes.

So Gwyneira spent a great deal of time with Helen and little Ruben, learning to change him and sing lullabies while Helen knit baby clothes for Gwyneira.

"Just no pink," said Gwyneira, horrified when Helen started a bright onesie to use up leftover wool. "It'll be a boy!"

"Now how do you know that?" Helen replied. "A girl would be lovely too."

Gwyneira dreaded the possibility of not being able to provide the desired male offspring. She had never given much thought to children before. Only now that she was helping look after Ruben—and experiencing on a daily basis that the little thing already had rather strict ideas about what he wanted and what he didn't and what he liked and what he didn't—was it becoming clear to her that she not only carried the heir to Kiward Station within her; what was growing inside her was a small being with its own individual personality, and it was just as likely to be female as male. Either way, she had already condemned it to live a lie. When Gwyneira thought about it too much, she felt pangs of guilt for the baby, who would never know its real father. It was better not to brood on it, so Gwyneira threw herself into helping Helen with her endless housework. Gwyneira could milk, and the Maori children's school had continued to grow. Helen now taught two classes, and to her surprise, Gwyneira saw three of the half-naked children who normally splashed around in Kiward Station's lake.

"The sons of the chieftain and his brother," explained Helen. "Their fathers wanted them to learn something, so they sent the children to relatives in the village here. It's quite an extravagance. It's rather demanding for the children. Whenever they get homesick, they go home on foot. And the little one is constantly homesick!"

She indicated a handsome youth with curly black hair.

Gwyneira recalled James's remarks about the Maori and that children who were too well educated could be dangerous to whites.

Helen shrugged when Gwyneira told her about it. "If I don't teach them, someone else will. And if this generation doesn't learn, then the next one will. Besides, it's impossible to deny people an education."

"Now don't get excited," Gwyneira said, holding up her hand in a placating gesture. "I'd be the last person to try to stop you. But war wouldn't be a good thing."

"Oh, the Maori are peaceful," Helen said, waving the notion away. "They want to learn from us. I think they've recognized that civilization makes life easier. Besides, it's different here from in the other colonies. The Maori aren't indigenous. They're immigrants themselves."

"Seriously?" Gwyneira was astounded. She hadn't heard that before.

"Yes. Of course, they've still been here much, much longer than we have," Helen said. "But not since time immemorial. They arrived in the early fourteenth century, in seven double canoes. They still remember it. Every family can trace its lineage back to the crew of one of those canoes."

Helen had learned to speak Maori quite well and had been listening to Matahorua's stories with increasing comprehension.

"So the land doesn't belong to them either?" Gwyneira asked hopefully.

Helen rolled her eyes. "When the time comes, both sides will probably claim the right of discovery. Let's just hope that they get along peacefully. I plan teach them math—whether that suits my husband and Mr. Warden or not."

With the exception of the hostility between Gwyneira and James, the mood on Kiward Station was joyful. The prospect of a grandchild had lightened Gerald's step. He once again paid more attention to his farm and sold several stud rams to other breeders, making good money in the process. James took the opportunity to herd the animals over to their new owners, which enabled him to be away from Kiward Station for a few days. Gerald had ordered for more land to be cleared for pastureland. When it came time to calculate which rivers could be used as a flume and which wood was valuable, Lucas's mathematical skills proved useful. Though he complained about the loss of the forests, he did not protest with much vehemence—after all, he was just happy that Gerald's derision had ceased. He never asked where the child could have come from. Perhaps he hoped it was an accident, or it was possible he simply didn't want to know. In any case, they were not together often enough for such an embarrassing conversation to take place. Lucas abandoned his nightly visits immediately after Gwyneira announced her pregnancy; after all, his "attempts" had not been much fun for him. However, he enjoyed painting his beautiful wife. Gwyneira sat demurely for an oil portrait, and Gerald did not once snicker at this endeavor. As the mother of the next generation, Gwyneira's portrait deserved a place of honor next to that of his late wife, Barbara. All agreed that the finished oil painting was very successful. Only Lucas was not entirely satisfied. He felt that he had not perfectly captured Gwyneira's "mysterious expression," and the play of light did not strike him as optimal. But every visitor praised the picture effusively. Lord Barrington even asked Lucas to paint a portrait of his wife. Gwyneira learned that good money could be earned in England for such work, but Lucas would have taken it as an insult to his honor to ask for so much as a penny from his neighbors and friends.

Gwyneira did not see how the sale of a picture was any different from that of a sheep or horse, but she did not argue and noted with relief that Gerald did not upbraid his son for his lack of business sense either. On the contrary, for the first time, he almost seemed proud of Lucas. Sunshine and harmony reigned in the house.

As the birth approached, Gerald searched in vain for a doctor for Gwyneira since to have one brought from Christchurch would have meant leaving the city without a doctor for several weeks. Gwyneira didn't think it would be problematic to have to do without a doctor. After having seen Matahorua at work, she was prepared to put herself in the hands of a Maori midwife. Gerald, however, declared this unacceptable, and Lucas took this position decisively as well.

"It would be unacceptable to entrust you to some savage. You're a lady and are to be treated with corresponding care. It's simply too much of a risk. You should deliver in Christchurch."

That brought Gerald back onto the barricades. He declared that the heir of Kiward Station would be born on the farm and nowhere else.

In the end, Gwyneira confided to Mrs. Candler about the problem, though she was afraid that Mrs. Candler would then offer her Dorothy. The merchant's wife did just that, but then suggested a much better solution.

"The midwife here in Haldon has a daughter who often goes to help her. As far as I know, she's also taken on deliveries by herself. Go ahead and ask her if she'd be willing to come to Kiward Station for a few days."

Francine Hayward, the midwife's daughter, proved to be a bright, optimistic twenty-year-old young woman. She had blonde hair and a round, happy face with a snub nose and attractive light green eyes. She got along beautifully with Gwyneira from the very first. After all, the two of them were almost the same age. After the first two cups of tea, Francine revealed to Gwyneira her secret love for the Candlers' oldest son, while Gwyneira told her how as a girl she'd dreamed of cowboys and Indians.

"In one novel there's a woman who has her baby while the redskins have the house surrounded! And she's all alone with her husband and daughter too."

"Well, I don't find that all too romantic," said Francine. "On the contrary, that would be my worst nightmare. Just imagine your husband running back and forth between shooting and swaddling, alternating between yelling "Push, dear!" and "I've got you, you damned redskin!"

Gwyneira giggled. "My husband would never say such a thing in the presence of a lady. He would probably say: 'Pardon me a moment, my love. I just have to quickly eliminate one of these savages.'"

Francine gave a snort.

Since her mother was likewise in agreement with the arrangement, Francine rode out behind Gwyneira that same evening to Kiward Station. She sat relaxed and fearless on Igraine's bare back, dismissing Lucas's admonishment—"What a risk to take, riding two to a horse! We could have picked up the young lady." Awestruck, she moved into one of the lavish guest rooms. Over the next few days, she enjoyed the luxury of not having anything to do other than keep Gwyneira company until the birth of the "crown prince." To that end she enthusiastically went to work decorating the knitted and crocheted pieces by sewing golden crowns onto everything.

"You are a member of the nobility," she explained when Gwyneira declared how embarrassing she found that. "The baby must be somewhere on the list of heirs to the British throne."

Gwyneira hoped Gerald wasn't listening. She wouldn't have put assassination attempts on the queen and her heirs past the proud grandfather if it meant seeing his grandson on the throne. For the time being, however, Gerald limited himself to adding a small crown to Kiward Station's branding mark. He had bought a few cows recently and now needed to register a mark. Lucas sketched a coat of arms according to Gerald's specifications, combining Gwyneira's little crown with a shield, a symbol of the Warden name.

Francine was witty and always in good spirits. Her companionship was good for Gwyneira, and she did not allow any fear of the coming birth to set in. Gwyneira felt a pang of jealousy, for Francine had forgotten the young Candler boy and could not stop swooning over James McKenzie.

"He's interested in me, no doubt about it," she said excitedly. "Every time he sees me, he asks me a lot of questions. About my work and after that how you're doing. He's so sweet! And it's so obvious that he's trying to find things to talk about that interest me. Why else would he inquire when you're supposed to have the baby?"

Several reasons occurred to Gwyneira, and she thought it reckless of James to show such a visible interest. Above all, though, she longed for him and his comforting presence. She would have liked to feel his hand on her stomach and to have him share her breathless joy at the baby's movements in her womb. Whenever the little thing was "boxing" inside her, she thought of how happy he had looked when he first saw newborn Ruben. She also recalled a scene in the horse stables when Igraine was near the end of her gestation.

"Do you feel the foal, miss?" he had asked, beaming. "It's moving. You should talk to him now, miss! Then it will already recognize your voice when it's born."

Now she spoke with the baby, whose nest was already so perfectly prepared. His cradle sat next to her bed, a marvel of blue and golden-yellow silk built by Kiri according to Lucas's instructions. His name had already been decided: Paul Gerald Terence Warden—Paul after Gerald's father.

"We can name the next son after your grandfather, Gwyneira," Gerald declared generously. "But first I'd like to establish a certain tradition."

Gwyneira didn't really care about the name. The baby was becoming heavier every day; it was time for him to be born. She caught herself counting the days and comparing them with her adventures the year before. "If it comes today, it was conceived at the lake...if it waits until next week, then it's a fog baby...a little warrior come to being in the stone circle..." Gwyneira remembered every nuance of James's tenderness, and sometimes she cried longingly in her sleep.

The pains set in on a day in late November when the weather resembled a June day in faraway England. After several weeks of rain, the sun came up shining; the roses in the garden were blooming, and all the colorful flowers that Gwyneira actually preferred unfurled in all their splendor.

"How lovely that is," gushed Francine, who was setting the breakfast table by the bay window in Gwyneira's room. "I'll have to convince my mother to plant some flowers. Only vegetables grow in our garden. Though there are always rata bushes coming up."

Gwyneira was about to reply that she had fallen instantly in love with the rata bushes' abundance of red flowers upon her arrival, when she felt the pains. Right then her water broke.

Gwyneira did not have an easy delivery. Because she was so healthy, her lower body muscles were very well developed. While her mother had thought that so much riding would lead to a miscarriage, it instead made the baby's passage through the pelvis more difficult. Francine assured her frequently that everything was going well and that the baby was perfectly positioned, but that did not stop Gwyneira from screaming—or cursing. Lucas did not hear any of it though. At least she was lucky that no one was crying by her bedside—Gwyneira didn't know whether she would have been able to handle Dorothy's weeping. Kiri, who was assisting Francine, remained calm.

"Baby healthy. Said Matahorua. Always right."

Before the birth, however, all hell broke loose. At first Gerald was tense, then concerned, and by the end of the day, he flew into a rage at anyone who approached him as he drank himself into oblivion. He slept through the last few hours of the delivery in his armchair in the salon. Lucas worried and drank in moderation, as was his custom. Even he fell asleep in the end, though it was only a light slumber. Anytime something stirred in Gwyneira's chamber he raised his head, and he asked Kiri for news several times throughout the night.

"Mr. Lucas so thoughtful," she informed Gwyneira.

James McKenzie did not sleep at all. He spent the day in a state of obvious suspense and skulked that night into the garden outside Gwyneira's window. He was the only one who heard her cries. Helpless, with balled fists and tears in his eyes, he waited. No one told him whether it was going well, and he feared for Gwyneira's life with every cry. Finally something furry and soft brushed up against him, someone else who had been forgotten. Francine had mercilessly cast Cleo out of Gwyneira's room, and neither Lucas nor Gerald had paid any attention to her. She whined when she heard Gwyneira's screams.

"Sorry, Gwyn, I'm so sorry," James whispered into Cleo's silky hair.

He was still embracing the dog when he suddenly heard another cry, this time softer, but stronger and rather higher than Gwyneira's. The baby greeted the new morning's first ray of light. And Gwyneira accompanied it with a final painful scream.

James cried with relief into Cleo's soft fur.

Lucas awoke right away when Kiri stepped onto the landing holding the baby in her arms. She stood there like an actor, fully aware of the importance of her role. Lucas wondered briefly why Francine wasn't presenting the child to him herself, but Kiri was beaming from ear to ear, so he assumed that mother and child were both fine.

"Is everything...all right?" he nevertheless asked dutifully, standing up to approach the young woman.

Gerald stumbled to his feet as well. "Is he here?" he asked. "And healthy?"

"Yes, Mr. Warden!" Kiri rejoiced. "A beautiful baby. Beautiful. Has red hair like mother!"

"A little firebrand!" said Gerald, laughing. "He's the first red-haired Warden."

"I think, not called 'he,'" Kiri corrected him, "called 'she.' Is girl, Mr. Warden. Beautiful girl!"

Francine suggested naming the baby "Paulette," but Gerald resisted. "Paul" was to be reserved for the male heir. Lucas, ever the gentleman, appeared at Gwyneira's bedside with a red rose an hour after the birth, assuring her in measured tones that he found the child adorable. Gwyneira only nodded. How else would anyone have described this perfect little creation that she now held proudly in her arms? She couldn't get enough of the individual fingers, the button nose, or the long red eyelashes around the big blue eyes. The baby already had quite a lot of hair. She was an unequivocal redhead like her mother. As Gwyneira stroked her baby, the little thing reached for her finger. She was already astoundingly strong. She would have sure control of the reins...Gwyneira would start teaching her to ride early.

Lucas suggested "Rose" as a name and had a giant bouquet of red and white roses brought into Gwyneira's room, which immediately filled the air with their enchanting fragrance.

"I've rarely seen the roses bloom as enchantingly as today, my love. It is as though the garden blossomed especially for the birth of our daughter." Francine had laid the baby in his arms; he held her ineptly, as though he did not know what to make of her. Still, he spoke the words "our daughter" naturally. He did not seem to entertain any doubts.

Gwyneira, who was thinking of Diana's rose garden, responded: "She's much more beautiful than any rose, Lucas. She's the most beautiful thing in the world!"

She took the baby back from him. It was crazy, but she felt a prick of jealousy.

"Then you'll have to think of a name yourself, my love," Lucas said mildly. "I'm sure you'll find something fitting. But now I must leave you two to take care of Father. He can't get over the fact that she's not a boy."

A few hours passed before Gerald could pull himself together sufficiently to visit Gwyneira and her daughter. He congratulated the mother halfheartedly and looked the baby over. Only after she wrapped her tiny hand possessively around his finger while blinking did she wring a smile from his lips.

"Oh well, at least everything is there," he grumbled reluctantly. "The next will have to be boy. Now that you two know what you're doing."

As Warden closed the door behind him, Cleo slipped in. Happy to have finally succeeded, she trotted over to Gwyneira's bed, set her front paws on the covers, and gave her best collie smile.

"Where have you been hiding?" Gwyneira asked, delighted, stroking her dog. "Look here; I want to introduce you to someone!"

To Francine's horror, she let the dog sniff the baby. Which is when she noticed a bouquet of spring flowers that someone had secured in Cleo's collar.

"How original!" remarked Francine as Gwyneira carefully freed the little bouquet. "Who do you think it was? One of the men?"

Gwyneira knew exactly who it was. Though she said nothing, her heart ran over with happiness. So he knew about their daughter—and of course he had picked colorful wildflowers instead of cutting roses.

The baby sneezed when the flowers brushed her nose. Gwyneira smiled.

"I'm going to name her Fleurette."

Something Like Hate

CANTERBURY PLAINS—WEST COAST

1858–1860

1

After his ascent up the Bridle Path, George Greenwood was lightly out of breath. He slowly drank the ginger beer sold at the highest point between Lyttelton and Christchurch, savoring the view of the town and the Canterbury Plains below.

So this was Helen's new homeland. This is what she left England for...George had to admit it was a beautiful country. Christchurch, the town near which he assumed her farm must be located, was supposed to be a burgeoning community. As the first settlement in New Zealand, it had received its charter last year and was now a bishopric too.

George recalled Helen's last letter, in which she reported with schadenfreude that the aspirations of the unkind Reverend Baldwin had not been fulfilled. The archbishop of Canterbury had instead called a pastor by the name of Henry Chitty Harper to the bishop's chair, who had traveled from the homeland with his family expressly for that purpose. He seemed to have been beloved in his earlier parish, though Helen did not report anything else about his character, which rather surprised George. After all, he imagined that she must have long since gotten to know him from all the church activities that she was always writing about. Helen O'Keefe participated in ladies' Bible circles and worked with native children. George hoped that she hadn't become as bigoted and self-righteous as his mother through these activities. He couldn't picture Helen in silk dresses at committee meetings, but her letters made it sound as though she spent most of her time with the children and their mothers.

Could he still picture Helen? So many years had passed, and he'd had an endless stream of experiences since then. College, his travels through Europe, to India and Australia—those should have been enough to erase the image of a much older woman with gleaming brown hair and clear gray eyes from his memory. Yet George could still see her before him as though she had left only the day before: her narrow face, her prim hairstyle, her erect gait—even when he knew she was tired. George remembered her well-concealed anger and her strenuously contained impatience when dealing with his mother and his brother, William, but also her secret smile whenever he succeeded in breaking through her armor of self-restraint with some impertinence. Back then he had read every emotion lurking within her—hidden behind the calm, equanimous expression she exhibited to the world. That fire, burning under still waters, which had flared up over some crazy advertisement from the other end of the world. Did she really love this Howard O'Keefe fellow? In her letters she spoke with great respect of her husband, who worked hard to make a comfortable life for her and to make the farm profitable. Yet George read between the lines that her husband didn't always succeed. George Greenwood had been active enough in his father's business to know that New Zealand's first settlers had almost all become wealthy. Whether they focused on fishing, trade, or animal breeding, business was booming. Anyone who didn't make an inept start of things turned a profit. Gerald Warden, the largest wool producer on the South Island, was a perfect example. Visiting him at Kiward Station was at the top of the list of activities that had brought Robert Greenwood's son to Christchurch. The Greenwoods were considering opening a branch of their international trading firm here. There was growing interest in New Zealand's wool trade, and steamships would soon be trafficking between England and the islands. George himself had already traveled on a ship driven by a steam engine in addition to traditional sails. No longer dependent on the capricious winds in the calm belt, the ship could now make the trip in just eight weeks.

Even the Bridle Path had become less treacherous than what Helen had described to George in her first letter. It had been expanded and could now be crossed with wagons. George could easily have spared himself the arduous trip on foot, but after the long trip aboard the ship, he was yearning for movement. Besides, it was exciting for him to retrace Helen's experiences on her arrival. George had been obsessed with New Zealand during his studies. Even when he received no letters from Helen for long periods, he devoured all the available information on the country in order to feel closer to her.

Now refreshed, he began the descent. Maybe he would even see Helen the next day. If he could rent a horse and the farm lay as near to the city as Helen's letters implied, there was nothing to stop him making a little courtesy visit. In any case, he would soon be headed to Kiward Station, which had to be near Helen. After all, she and the farm's mistress, Gwyneira Warden, were friends. So the two estates could hardly be more than a short coach ride apart.

After taking the ferry across the Avon River, George walked the last few miles into Christchurch and took a room at the local hotel. It was simple but clean—and unsurprisingly, the manager knew the Wardens.

"Naturally. Gerald and Lucas Warden always stay here when they have business in Christchurch. Very cultivated gentlemen, especially the younger Warden and his lovely wife. Mrs. Warden has her clothes tailored in Christchurch, so we see her two or three times a year."

However, the hotelier had not heard of Howard and Helen O'Keefe. Neither one of them had ever stayed there, nor did he know them to be members of the church community.

"But they wouldn't be part of our community, if they're the Wardens' neighbors," the hotelier explained. "They must belong to the Haldon congregation, which recently got its own church. It's much too far to ride here every Sunday."

George absorbed this news with astonishment and inquired about a rental stable. First thing the next day he planned to pay a visit to the Union Bank of Australia, the first bank office in Christchurch.

The bank director was exceedingly polite and happy about the Greenwoods' plans in Christchurch.

"You should talk to Peter Brewster," he advised. "Up until now he's been handling the local wool trade. But from what I hear, he's moving to Queenstown—the gold rush, you know. Brewster surely won't be doing any digging himself, but likely has the gold trade in mind."

George frowned. "Do you think that will be much more lucrative than wool?"

The banker shrugged. "If you ask me, wool is growing every year. But how much gold is lying in the earth over there in Otago, no one knows. Brewster is young and entrepreneurial though. Besides, he has family reasons. His wife's family comes from there. They're Maori, and she's inherited some land. He shouldn't be upset if you take over his clients here. That would certainly make founding your business much easier."

George could only agree with him and thanked him for the tip. He also used the opportunity to make inquiries about the Wardens and the O'Keefes. The director was naturally full of praise when it came to the Wardens.

"The elder Warden is an old warhorse, but he knows a thing or two about sheep breeding! The younger is more of an aesthete and isn't much for farm work. That's why the old man was hoping for a grandchild who would make more of a go of it, but so far without any luck. Still, his young wife is pretty as a picture. A crying shame that she has trouble having children. So far just one girl in almost six years of marriage. Oh well, they're young; there's still hope. As for the O'Keefes..." The bank director was clearly searching for words. "What can I say? It's a bank secret, you understand."

George understood. Howard O'Keefe was evidently not a well-loved client. He probably had debts. The farms lay a two-day ride from Christchurch, so Helen had lied in her letters about life in town—or at least exaggerated it. Haldon, the closest large settlement to Kiward Station, was hardly more than a village. What else might she have kept secret and why? Was she embarrassed about the way she lived? Was it possible she wouldn't be pleased to see him? But he had to see her. By God, he had traveled eighteen thousand miles to see her!

Peter Brewster proved to be quite affable and immediately invited George to lunch for the following day. George had to push his plans back, but it would have been unsociable to refuse. The meeting went very harmoniously. Brewster's ravishing wife served a traditional Maori meal of fresh fish from the Avon and artfully prepared sweet potatoes. His children barraged their visitor with questions about good old England, and naturally, Peter knew the Wardens as well as the O'Keefes.

"Just don't talk to one about the other," he warned, laughing. "They're like cats and dogs, and to think they used to be partners. Kiward Station once belonged to both of them, hence the name: 'Kee' and 'Ward.' But they were also both gamblers, and Howard O'Keefe lost his share. No one knows anything more, but the both of them still take the whole thing hard."

"Understandable on the part of O'Keefe," George remarked. "But the winner certainly shouldn't have any reason to brood on it."

"Like I said, I don't know the specifics. And in the end, Howard still kept enough for a farm. But he doesn't have the know-how. This year he lost practically all of his lambs—herded them up too soon, before the last storms. A few always freeze to death, even when there isn't a late winter storm. But herding up to the highlands at the beginning of October? God help you!"

George recalled that October here was the equivalent of March, when it was also appreciably cold in the Welsh highlands.

"Why would he do that?" he asked, uncomprehending. Though what really bothered him was why Helen let her husband go through with such nonsense. It was true that she had never taken an interest in agricultural work, but if her economic survival depended on it, she would certainly have gotten involved.

"Oh that's a vicious circle," Brewster sighed, offering a cigar. "The farm is too small or the land too poor for the large number of animals. But keeping fewer animals wouldn't bring in enough to live on, so you have to rely on luck. In good years there's enough grass; in bad, you run out of fodder for winter. Then you have to buy more—and then you don't have enough money again. Or you herd the animals into the highlands and hope it doesn't snow anymore. But let's talk about more pleasant things. You were interested in taking over my clients. Very well, I would be glad to introduce you to all of them. We'll no doubt come to an agreement on a transfer fee. Could I possibly interest you in our offices? Bureaus and storehouses in Christchurch and Lyttelton? I could rent the buildings to you and guarantee right to buy…or we could form a partnership, and I would maintain part of the business as a silent partner. That would provide me with some insurance in case the gold rush dries up."

The men spent the afternoon visiting the properties, and George was very taken with Brewster's operation. They agreed to negotiate the terms of the takeover after George's excursion to the Canterbury Plains. George left his business partner in good spirits and wrote a letter straightaway to his father. Greenwood Enterprises had yet to acquire a branch in a new country with such speed and so little hassle. Now there only remained the question of a capable manager. Brewster himself would have been ideal, but of course he planned to leave.

George set these considerations aside for the time being. Now he could set out for Haldon the following day without any worries. He would soon be seeing Helen again.

"More guests so soon?" Gwyneira asked reluctantly. She had been planning to use the gorgeous spring day for a visit to Helen. Fleurette had been whining for days about wanting to play with Ruben; besides, mother and child were running out of reading material. Fleurette was crazy for stories. She loved it when Helen read aloud to her, and was already making her own first attempts at copying letters when she sat in on Helen's lessons.

"Just like her father," said the people in Haldon whenever Gwyneira ordered new books to read aloud to her little one. Mrs. Candler continually found physical similarities to Lucas. The girl was gracile and red-haired like Gwyneira, but the original blue of her irises had given way to a light brown flecked with amber. In their own way, Fleur's eyes were just as captivating as Gwyneira's. The amber in them seemed to spark whenever she got excited and flared up properly when the little girl grew upset—which happened easily, as even her loving mother had to admit. Fleurette was not a calm, easily satisfied child like Ruben. She was whiny, made difficult demands, and resorted to anger when things did not go her way. Then she would rant and rave, turning red and even spitting in extreme cases. The almost four-year-old Fleurette Warden was most definitely not a lady.

Nevertheless, she had a good relationship with her father. Lucas was not put off by her temper and gave in to her moods far too often. He rarely made any effort to correct her behavior and seemed content to classify his daughter in the category of "highly interesting object of research." As a result, Kiward Station now had two residents who passionately collected, drew, and observed wetas. Fleur, however, was interested in seeing how far the bugs could jump and thought it a good idea to paint them with bright colors. Gwyneira developed an extraordinary talent for getting the giant bugs back into their collection jars.

Now she wondered how she would be able to explain to the child that the ride she had promised would not take place.

"Yes, another guest," growled Gerald. "By my lady's leave. A merchant from London. He spent the night at the Beasleys' and will arrive here this evening. Reginald Beasley was kind enough to send a messenger so that we can receive the gentleman properly. Of course, only if it pleases my lady!"

Gerald raised himself unsteadily. It wasn't quite midday, but he did not appear to have sobered up since the evening before. The more he drank, the crueler his comments to Gwyneira. In recent months, she had become his favorite object of ridicule—which no doubt had to do with the fact that it was winter. In winter, Gerald made more allowances for his son's holing up in his study rather than seeing to the farm, and he ran more often into Gwyneira, whom the rainy weather kept in the house. In the summer, when the sheep shearing, lambing, and other farm work lay ahead, Gerald once again focused his attention on Lucas, while Gwyneira took off on officially sanctioned rides—in reality fleeing to see Helen. Gwyneira and Lucas were familiar with this cycle from the last few years, but that didn't make it any easier. There was only one possibility of breaking the cycle: Gwyneira would have to provide Gerald with his desired heir. But Lucas's energy in this regard seemed to have faded over time. Gwyneira simply didn't arouse him; there could be no contemplating the conception of another child. And Lucas's increasing inability at marital coitus made it impossible for Gwyneira to repeat the pretense of Fleur's conception. Gwyneira did not have any illusions about this being a possibility anyway. James McKenzie would never agree to such an arrangement a second time. And she knew that she would not be able to break it off afterward a second time. It had taken months after Fleurette's birth before Gwyneira was no longer seized by the pain of longing and desperation that crippled her whenever she touched or even saw James. The former was not always avoidable—it would have looked strange if James had suddenly stopped holding out his hand to her to help her from the wagon, or if he had no longer taken the saddle from her after she had led Igraine into the stables. If their fingers touched in the process, it was like an explosion of love and recognition, dissipated by a constant refrain of "never again, never again" that almost made Gwyneira's head burst. At some point it had gotten more bearable, thank God. Gwyneira learned greater self-control, and the memories faded. But to go through it all again was unthinkable. And with another man? No, she wouldn't put herself through that. Before James, it hadn't mattered to her; one man seemed to her more or less like the next. But now? It was hopeless. Short of a miracle, Gerald would have to get over the fact that Fleur would be his only grandchild.

Gwyneira had no problem with that. She loved Fleurette and recognized herself in her as well as everything she had loved about James McKenzie. Fleur was adventurous and smart, bullheaded and clever. Thanks to her Maori playmates, she had a fluent command of the Maori language. More than anyone else though, she loved Helen's son, Ruben. Older by a solid year, he was her hero and idol. When she was with him, she even managed to sit in Helen's lessons and not utter a word the entire time.

Well, that wouldn't be the case today. Sighing, Gwyneira called for Kiri to have her clean the breakfast table. Kiri probably would not have thought of it on her own. She had recently married and could think of nothing but her husband. Gwyneira was just waiting for her to announce her own pregnancy—and for Gerald to explode about it.

Afterward, Gwyneira had to persuade Kiri to polish the silver, and then she would have to discuss dinner with Moana. Something with lamb. And Yorkshire pudding wouldn't be bad either. But first Fleur...

Fleurette had not been idle while her parents had breakfast. She wanted to get going, which meant saddling or harnessing the horse. Gwyneira usually took her daughter on Igraine with Fleurette sitting in front, but Lucas preferred that his "ladies" rode in a carriage. He'd had a dogcart specially sent for Gwyneira, which she commanded excellently. The light, two-wheeled vehicle was extremely good for travel over rough terrain, and Igraine pulled it effortlessly over the difficult paths. However, it could not go off road, nor could you jump in it. That meant the shortcut through the bush to Helen's was ruled out. Unsurprisingly, Gwyneira and Fleur preferred to ride, and that's what Fleurette decided on that day.

"Can you saddle up Igraine, Mr. McKenzie?" she asked James.

"With the sidesaddle or a different one, little miss?" James asked seriously. "You know what your father said."

Lucas was seriously considering having a pony sent from England for Fleurette, so that she would learn to ride properly in a sidesaddle. Gwyneira declared, however, that she would be too big for the pony by the time it arrived. Gwyneira started out teaching her daughter to ride astride Madoc. The stallion was very well behaved. The problem lay in keeping it secret.

"With a saddle for grown-ups!" Fleur declared.

James had to laugh. "A real saddle, you got it, my lady. Do you plan to ride alone today?"

"No, Mummy's coming. But she still has to play 'walking target' for Grandfather. She told Daddy. Is he really going to shoot at her, Mr. McKenzie?"

Not if I can help it, James thought grimly. It wasn't a secret to anyone on the farm that Gerald tormented his daughter-in-law. In contrast to Lucas, against whom the workers all harbored a certain resentment, Gwyneira had their sympathy. Sometimes the boys came dangerously close to the truth when they made jokes about their employer's manhood. "If the miss only had a real man," went the standard comment, "then the old man'd already be a grandfather ten times over."

Often enough, the fellows would then offer themselves in jest as the "stud" and try to outdo each other with their ideas of how they could make their lovely mistress and her father-in-law happy at the same time.

James tried to put an end to these dirty jokes, but it wasn't always easy. If only Lucas would make some effort to be useful on the farm. But he never learned anything about it and had become increasingly stubborn and recalcitrant when Gerald forced him into the stables or the fields.

While James put the saddle on Igraine, he chatted with Fleur. He hid it well, but he loved his daughter and couldn't bring himself to view her as a Warden. This red-haired whirlwind was his child—and he didn't care in the least that she was "just" a girl. He waited patiently until she had climbed on top of a crate, from which she could brush Igraine's tail.

Gwyneira entered the stables just as James was cinching the saddle, and as always, she reacted involuntarily to his gaze. Her eyes lit up, her cheeks flushed…then the iron control clamped down again.

"Oh, Mr. McKenzie, have you already saddled the horse?" asked Gwyneira sadly. "I'm afraid I can't go out for a ride with Fleur; we're expecting a visitor."

James nodded. "Ah, right, that English merchant. I should have remembered that you would be tied up today." He made a move to unsaddle the mare.

"We're not riding to school?" Fleur asked, hurt. "But then I'll stay dumb, Mummy!"

That was her latest argument to justify making the ride to Helen's whenever possible. Helen had used it on a Maori child who liked to skip class, and the remark had made an impression on Fleur.

James and Gwyneira had to laugh.

"Well, we couldn't take that risk," said James with mock seriousness. "With your permission, miss, I'll take her to school."

Gwyneira looked at him, astonished. "Do you really have time?" she asked. "I thought you were going to check on the pens for the ewes."

"Well, that's on the way," James explained, winking at her. The pens did not lie on the main road to Haldon, but alongside Gwyneira's secret shortcut through the wild. "Naturally, we'll have to ride. I'll waste time if I hook up the carriage."

"Please, Mummy," Fleur entreated, preparing herself for a tantrum should Gwyneira dare to refuse her.

Fortunately, her mother was not difficult to convince. Without the disappointed, grouchy child at her side, the work, which she didn't care for under the best of circumstances, would go much more smoothly. "Very well," she said. "Have fun. I wish I could come along."

Gwyneira watched enviously as James led his gelding out and lifted Fleur in front of the saddle. She sat lovely and upright on the horse, and her red locks bounced in time with the horse's steps. James took his place in the saddle just as easily. Gwyneira was almost a little worried when the pair rode away.

Was she the only one who noticed the resemblance between man and girl?

Lucas Warden, painter and trained observer, watched the riders from his window. Noticing Gwyneira's lonely figure in the yard, he believed he could read her thoughts.

He was happy in his own world, but sometimes...sometimes he would have liked to love that woman.

2

George Greenwood received a friendly welcome in the Canterbury Plains. Peter Brewster's name quickly opened the farmers' doors to him, but they probably would have welcomed him even without a reference. He was familiar with the phenomenon from the farms he'd visited in Australia and Africa—anyone who lived in such isolation was generally happy for a visit from the outside world. For that reason, he listened patiently to Mrs. Beasley's complaints about the help, admired her roses, and rode out across the pastures with her husband to admire the sheep as well. The Beasleys had gone to great lengths to turn their farm into a little piece of England, and George had to smile when Mrs. Beasley told him about her efforts to permanently ban sweet potatoes from her kitchen.

Kiward Station, he quickly realized, was very different. House and garden presented a unique combination: though someone here had clearly made every effort to recreate the life of the English country gentry, there was evidence of Maori culture here as well. In the garden, for example, rata and roses bloomed peacefully next to each other; beneath the cabbage trees were benches adorned with typical Maori carvings; and the tool shed was covered in nikau leaves, following Maori tradition. The housemaid who opened the door for George wore a demure servant's uniform, but no shoes, and the butler greeted him with a friendly *haere mai*, the Maori phrase for "welcome."

George recalled what he had heard about the Wardens. The young woman descended from an English noble family—and judging from the furnishings, she evidently had good taste. It appeared that she was pushing for Anglicization with even more perseverance than Mrs. Beasley; after all, how often did a visitor leave his calling card on the silver tray resting on the dainty little table in the front hall? George took the trouble to do so, which brought a radiant smile to the face of the young redheaded woman who was just entering. She wore an elegant beige tea gown embroidered with a bright indigo that matched the color of her eyes. Yet her skin tone did not match the fashionable pallor of the ladies in London. Her face was lightly bronzed, and she clearly made no effort to whiten her freckles. Nor was her elaborate hairstyle especially proper, given that a few tresses had already come loose.

"We'll keep that there forever," she declared, looking at the calling card. "It will make my father-in-law so happy. Good day and welcome to Kiward Station. I'm Gwyneira Warden. Come in and make yourself comfortable. My father-in-law will be back shortly. Or would you like to freshen up first and change for dinner? It looks to be quite a meal."

Gwyneira knew she was crossing the boundaries of good decorum by dropping such a big hint. But this young man simply did not look like he was expecting a multicourse dinner during his visit to the bush for which his hosts planned to squeeze into evening wear. If he appeared in the breeches and leather jacket he was wearing at the moment, Lucas would be consternated and Gerald quite possibly insulted.

"George Greenwood," George introduced himself with a smile. Fortunately, he did not seem angry. "Thank you for the hint. I would love a chance to wash up first. You have a beautiful home, Mrs. Warden." He followed Gwyneira into the salon and stood amazed before the grand furniture and the large fireplace.

Gwyneira nodded. "Personally, I find it a bit big, but my father-in-law had it designed by the most famous architects. All the furniture comes from England. Cleo, get off the silk rug. Don't even think about having your litter there!"

Gwyneira was speaking to a rotund collie that had lain down in front of the fireplace on an exquisite oriental rug. Insulted, she rose and tottered over to another rug that was surely no less valuable.

"She feels very important when she's pregnant," remarked Gwyneira, petting the dog. "But she's got a right to. She litters the best sheepdogs in the area. The Canterbury Plains are now teeming with little Cleos. Mostly grandchildren, though, since I only rarely let her breed. I don't want her getting fat!"

George was astounded. After hearing the stories of the bank director and Peter Brewster, he had pictured the all but childless mistress of Kiward Station as prudish and highly proper. But here was Gwyneira speaking quite naturally to him about dog breeding, and she not only let her sheepdog in the house but let her lie on the silk rugs! And she had not said so much as a word about the maid in bare feet.

Chatting amiably, the young woman led her visitor to his guest room and instructed the butler to fetch his saddlebags.

"And please tell Kiri she should put her shoes on. Lucas will have a fit if she serves like that."

"Mummy, why do I have to put on shoes? Kiri isn't wearing any."

George met Gwyneira and her daughter in the corridor outside his room just as he was about to go down to dinner. He had done his best as far as evening wear went. Though slightly wrinkled, his light brown suit was handsomely tailored and much more becoming than the comfortable leather pants and waxed jacket he had acquired in Australia.

Gwyneira and the captivating little red-haired girl who was squabbling so loudly were likewise elegantly attired.

Though not in the latest fashion. Gwyneira was wearing a turquoise evening gown of such breathtaking refinement that, even in the best London salons, it would have created a stir—especially with a woman as beautiful as Gwyneira modeling it. The little girl wore a pale green shift that was almost entirely concealed by her abundant red-gold locks. When Fleur's hair hung down loose, it frizzed a bit, like that of a gold tinsel angel. Her delicate green shoes matched the adorable little dress, but the little one obviously preferred to carry them in her hands than wear them on her feet.

"They pinch!" she complained.

"Fleur, they don't pinch," her mother declared. "We just bought them four weeks ago, and they were on the verge of being too big then. Not even you grow that fast. And even if they do pinch, a lady bears a small degree of pain without complaining."

"Like the Indians? Ruben says that in America they take stakes and hurt themselves for fun to see who's the bravest. His daddy told him. But Ruben thinks that's dumb, and so do I."

"That's her opinion on the subject of being 'ladylike,'" Gwyneira remarked, looking to George for help. "Come, Fleurette. This is a gentleman. He's from England, like Ruben's mummy and me. If you behave properly, maybe he'll greet you by kissing your hand and call you 'my lady.' But only if you wear shoes."

"Mr. McKenzie always calls me 'my lady' even if I walk around barefoot."

"He must not come from England, then," George said, playing along. "And he certainly hasn't been introduced to the queen." This honor had been conferred on the Greenwoods the year before, and George's mother would probably chatter on about it for the rest of her life. It did not seem to impress Gwyneira all that much—but it worked wonders with her daughter.

"Really? The queen? Did you see a princess?"

"All the princesses," averred George. "And they all had shoes on."

Fleurette sighed. "Very well," she said, slipping into her shoes.

"Thank you," said Gwyneira, winking at George. "You've been a great help. At the moment, Fleurette isn't sure whether she's going to be an Indian queen in the Wild West or would prefer to marry a prince and breed ponies in his palace. Beyond that, she finds Robin Hood very appealing and is considering the life of an outlaw. I'm most afraid she will decide on the latter. She loves to eat with her fingers, and she's already practicing archery." Ruben had recently carved bows for himself and his little friend.

George shrugged. "Well, you know, Maid Marian surely ate with fork and knife. And you won't get far without shoes in Sherwood Forest."

"Now there's an argument!" Gwyneira said, laughing. "Do come, Mr. Greenwood, my father-in-law will be waiting."

The threesome descended the stairs side by side in perfect harmony.

James McKenzie had accompanied Gerald Warden into the salon. This occurred only rarely, but today there were a few bills to be signed that James had brought back from Haldon. Gerald wanted to get it out of the way quickly—the Candlers needed their money, and James would be setting out at the crack of dawn to pick up the next shipment. Kiward Station was, as always, under construction; at the moment, a cowshed was being built. Cattle farming had been flourishing since the gold rush in Otago—all the gold miners wanted to be fed, and there was nothing they valued more than a good steak. The Canterbury farmers drove whole herds of cattle to Queenstown every few months. At the moment, though, the old man was sitting next to the fireplace studying the bills. James glanced around the expensively fashioned room and wondered idly what it would be like to live there—with all the gleaming furniture and the soft carpets...and a fireplace that filled the room with comforting warmth, which you didn't have to light as soon as you came home. After all, what were servants for? James found it all very enticing, but foreign too. He didn't need it and certainly didn't long for it. But perhaps Gwyneira did. Well, if he ever managed to win her for himself, he would have a house like this built and squeeze into suits just as Lucas and Gerald Warden did.

Voices could be heard on the stairs. James looked up anxiously. Seeing Gwyneira in her evening dress enchanted him and caused his heart to beat faster—as did the sight of their daughter, whom he rarely saw in formal attire. At first he thought he recognized the man with them as Lucas—upright bearing, an elegant brown suit—but then he saw that it was someone else. He realized that he should have known that at once, as he had never seen Gwyneira laughing and so at ease in Lucas's presence. This man seemed to amuse her though. Gwyneira was teasing him or their daughter or both, and he was just as quick to riposte. Who the devil was that man? What gave him the right to joke around with his Gwyneira?

The stranger was certainly handsome. He had a thin, well-shaped face and clever brown eyes with a hint of mockery in them. His body was lanky, but he was tall and strong and moved lithely. His whole demeanor conveyed self-assurance and confidence.

And Gwyneira? James noticed the usual flash in her eyes when she spotted him in the salon. But was it the spark of their old love flaring up from the ashes at every encounter, or merely surprise in Gwyneira's gaze? James's sense of distrust blazed. Gwyneira gave no sign acknowledging his peevish demeanor.

"Mr. Greenwood!" Gerald too had noticed the threesome on the steps. "Please pardon me for not being home on your arrival. But it looks like Gwyneira's already shown you around the house." Gerald held out his hand to the visitor.

Oh, right, that had to be the merchant from England whose arrival had thrown off Gwyneira's plans for the day. She no longer appeared upset about it, though, and gestured for George to take a seat.

James, however, was left standing. His jealousy turned into anger.

"The bills, Mr. Warden," he remarked.

"Yes, right, the bills. Everything is in order, McKenzie; I'll sign off on them right away. A whiskey, Mr. Greenwood? You must give us an update on good old England!"

Gerald scribbled a signature at the bottom of the papers, then turned his attention to his visitor—and the whiskey bottle. The small flask he always carried must have been empty by afternoon—and Gerald was in correspondingly bad spirits. Andy McAran had informed James of an ugly altercation between Gerald and Lucas in the cow barn. It was about a calving cow who had experienced complications during her delivery. Lucas had once again not proved up to the challenge; he simply couldn't bear the sight of blood. For that reason, it hadn't been the older Warden's best idea to make cattle breeding Lucas's primary responsibility. In James's opinion, the management of the fields would have suited Lucas a great deal more. Obviously Lucas was better with his head than with his hands, and when it came to calculating returns, fertilizer allocation, and cost-benefit analyses regarding farm machine purchases, he thought in purely profit-oriented terms.

Lowing animals giving birth, however, robbed Lucas of his composure, and the situation must have come to a head once again that afternoon. Still, it was lucky for Gwyneira. When Gerald unloaded his wrath on Lucas, she was spared. But she was evidently becoming quite good at her role. The guest seemed to be enjoying himself tremendously.

"Is there something else, McKenzie?" Gerald asked, pouring himself some whiskey.

"Did you see?" Fleurette asked. "I have shoes on like a princess."

James laughed, immediately at ease. "They are very sweet, my lady. But of course you're always an enchanting sight, regardless of what sort of shoes you're wearing."

Fleurette frowned. "You only say that because you're not a gentleman," she declared. "Gentlemen only have respect for a lady when she wears shoes. Mr. Greenwood says."

Normally this remark would have amused James, but now his anger surged once again. Who did this fellow think he was, turning his daughter against him? James could hardly control himself.

"Well, my lady, then takest thou better care to associate with real men instead of bloodless men with big names wearing suits. Since if their respect is tied to shoes, then it's sure to run out quickly." He directed his words at the frightened child, but they struck Gwyneira, who was watching her daughter.

She looked at him, vexed, but James only glowered at her before withdrawing to the stables. Tonight he would help himself to a big slug of whiskey too. She could go ahead and drink wine with her rich fop.

The meal's main course consisted of lamb and a sweet potato casserole, which confirmed what George had already observed. Though the maid was now wearing shoes and served flawlessly, honoring tradition was clearly not of the utmost importance to Gwyneira. The maid showed so much respect to the lord of the manor, Gerald Warden, that it almost bordered on fear. The old gentleman clearly had a lively temper; he spoke excitedly, if a little drunkenly, of God and the world and had an opinion on every topic. The young master, Lucas Warden, seemed quiet by comparison, almost as though he were in pain. Whenever his father voiced opinions that he found too radical, it seemed to afflict him physically. Otherwise, Gwyneira's husband struck him as pleasant and well-bred, the perfect gentleman in every way. Kindly but precisely, he corrected his daughter's table posture—in fact, he seemed to have a talent for dealing with the child. Fleur did not quarrel with him as she did with her mother. At dinner, Fleur simply spread her napkin properly over her knees and transported the lamb to her mouth with her fork rather than picking it up with her fingers like the merry men in Sherwood Forest. But perhaps this too was the result of Gerald's presence. In fact, no voices were raised while the old man was present.

Despite the quiet, George enjoyed himself considerably that evening. Gerald knew how to talk charmingly about farm life, and George confirmed the people's opinions of him in Christchurch. Old Man Warden certainly knew a great deal about the sheep and wool industry, had caught the right wind with regard to acquiring cattle, and kept his farm in excellent shape. George would have liked to continue chatting with Gwyneira, though, and Lucas did not seem half the bore Peter Brewster and Reginald Beasley had made him out to be. Gwyneira had revealed earlier that her husband had painted the portraits in the salon himself. She made the announcement uncertainly and with a hint of mockery in her voice, but George looked on the paintings with nothing but respect. He would not have identified himself as an art connoisseur but was frequently invited to private viewings and art auctions in London. An artist like Lucas Warden would certainly have found a following there; with a spot of luck, he might even have arrived at fame and fortune. George considered whether it might pay off for him to take a few pieces back to London with him. He was certain he could sell the pictures there. On the other hand, he might run the risk of spoiling his relationship with Gerald Warden. The old man clearly wanted nothing less than to have an artist in the family.

The conversation that evening did not turn to art. Gerald monopolized the visitor from England the entire time, drinking a whole bottle of whiskey in the process, and seemed not to notice that Lucas had left early. Gwyneira had also fled at the earliest possible moment after the meal to tuck the child in. They did not employ a nanny, which George found strange. After all, Gerald Warden's son had obviously had a proper English upbringing. Why would Gerald not do the same for his granddaughter? Did he not like the results it had produced before? Or did it have to do with Fleurette being "just" a girl?

The next morning offered the opportunity for a much more thorough conversation with the young couple. Gerald did not come down for breakfast—at least not at the usual time. Bacchus demanded his tribute from the night before. Gwyneira and Lucas appeared much more relaxed. Lucas inquired about the cultural scene in London and was obviously overjoyed that George had more to say about it than "sublime" and "edifying." Confronted with praise for his portraits, he seemed to swell with pride and invited their guest into his studio.

"You're welcome to come if you like. I know you're taking a look at the farm this morning, but this afternoon…"

George nodded uncertainly. Gerald had promised him a ride through the farm, and George was very interested in doing that. Ultimately all other business on the South Island would be measured against Kiward Station. But Gerald was nowhere in sight.

"Oh, I can ride with you," Gwyneira offered spontaneously after George made a cautious remark to this effect. "Lucas too, of course… but I didn't make it out of the house at all yesterday. So if my presence would be acceptable to you…"

"To whom would your presence *not* be acceptable?" George asked gallantly, though he did not expect much from a ride with the lady. He had been counting on informative commentary and a peek into the breeding and pasture management. He was therefore all the more astounded when he met Gwyneira in the stables a short while later.

"Please saddle Morgaine for me, Mr. McKenzie," she instructed the foreman. "She desperately needs training, but when Fleur's around, I don't like to take her. She's too impetuous."

"Do you think the young man from London can handle your impetuosity, miss?" inquired the shepherd sarcastically.

Gwyneira frowned. George wondered why she did not give the brazen churl a dressing down.

"I hope so," was all she said. "Otherwise, he'll have to ride in back. He's not going to fall off. Can I leave Cleo here with you? She won't like it, but it will no doubt be a long ride, and she's already pretty heavy." The little dog that followed Gwyneira everywhere seemed to have understood her and tucked its tail between its legs.

"These will be your last pups, Cleo, I promise," Gwyneira comforted her. "I'm going to ride with Mr. Greenwood as far as the stone warriors. We'll see if we catch sight of a few rams. Can I take care of anything on the way?"

The young man seemed to make a pained face in response to one of her remarks. Or was he mocking her? Was that how he reacted to her offer to make herself useful with the farm work?

Though the young man did not answer, another farmworker answered her question as he was passing by.

"Oh yeah, miss, one of the little rams, the little charmer Mr. Warden promised to Mr. Beasley, keeps going off on his own. Runs around by the ewes and drives the whole flock crazy. Could you possibly herd him back? Or just bring along the two meant for Beasley; then we'll have order up there. Does that sound good, James?"

The foreman nodded. "They need to be gone by next week anyway. Do you want Daimon, miss?"

When the word "Daimon" left his lips, a big black dog rose up.

Gwyneira shook her head. "No, I'll take Cassandra and Catriona. We'll see how they do. We've certainly trained them long enough."

Both dogs looked like Cleo. Gwyneira introduced them to George as her daughters. Even her rather lively mare was the product of two horses she had brought from Great Britain. George noticed Gwyneira exchange looks with the foreman when he brought the mare out to her.

"I could have ridden with a sidesaddle," Gwyneira remarked. She would have been willing to uphold decorum for their visitor from London.

Although George did not hear the man's response, he did see that Gwyneira flushed with anger.

"Now come, too many people had too much to drink last night on this farm!" she burst out and urged her mare into a trot. George followed her, confused.

James McKenzie remained in the stables. He could have kicked himself. How could he have lost control like that? The impertinent comment he had just made played over again and again in his mind—"Forgive me. Your daughter said yesterday that she preferred a saddle for 'grown-ups.' But if my lady would like to play the little girl today and ride in a sidesaddle..."

It was unforgivable. If Gwyneira hadn't figured out for herself what a catch this English fop might be, he had now most certainly shown her.

Once she had calmed down and reined in her mare so that his rental horse could keep pace with her, George was surprised by the amount of technical information Gwyneira gave him during their tour. Gwyneira obviously knew the breeding operation on Kiward Station forward and backward, and was able to supply him with detailed information regarding the pedigree of each animal and commentary on the successes and failures of breeding.

"We're still breeding purebred Welsh Mountains and crossing them with Cheviots—that creates the perfect combination. Both are a down type. With Welsh Mountains, you can get thirty-six to forty-eight strands per pound of raw wool; with Cheviots it's in the range of forty-eight to fifty-six. They complement one another, and the wool quality is consistent. It's actually not ideal to work with Merinos. That's what we always tell people who want purebred Welsh Mountain sheep, but most of them think they're smarter than we are. Merinos produce 'fine wool,' which means about sixty to seventy strands per pound. Very nice, but you can't breed purebreds here; they're not robust enough for it. And when combined with other breeds, there's no telling what you'll get."

George understood only half of what she was saying but was impressed by the scope of her knowledge—and became even more so when they successfully reached the highlands where the young rams grazed freely. Gwyneira's young sheepdogs first herded the flock together, then separated out the two animals that had been sold—which Gwyneira recognized straightaway—and started to steer them placidly back down to the valley. Gwyneira slowed her mare to ride in tempo with the sheep. George took the opportunity to finally move on from the subject of sheep and ask a question that lay much nearer and dearer to his heart.

"In Christchurch I was told that you know Helen O'Keefe," he began carefully. In no time, he had a second rendezvous scheduled with the lady of Kiward Station. He would tell Gerald that he wanted to ride to Haldon the next day, and Gwyneira would offer to accompany him part of the way to take Fleur to Helen's school. In reality, he would follow her all the way to the O'Keefe farm.

George's heart beat in his throat. He would finally see her tomorrow!

3

If Helen had to describe her life over the last few years—honestly and without the pretty words she used to comfort herself and hopefully impress the recipients of her letters to England—she would have chosen the word "survival."

While Howard's farm had seemed a promising undertaking upon her arrival, it had only gone downhill since Ruben's birth. While the number of sheep for breeding increased, the quality of the wool only seemed to be getting worse; the losses early in the year had been crushing. After seeing Gerald's successful attempts with cattle, Howard had also tried his hand at raising a herd.

"Madness!" Gwyneira said to Helen. "Cattle need much more grass and fodder in winter than sheep," she explained. "That's not a problem on Kiward Station. Even counting only the land that's already been cleared, we could sustain twice the number of sheep. But your land is meager and lies much higher up. Not as much grows up here; you barely have enough to feed the sheep you already have. And cattle on top of that! It's hopeless. You could try goats. But the best thing would be to get rid of all the livestock you have running around and start again with a few good sheep. It's about quality, not quantity."

Helen, for whom a sheep had always just been a sheep, had initially been bored as she listened to these speeches on breeds and crosses, but she finally began to pay closer attention to Gwyneira's lectures. If her friend was to be believed, Howard had fallen in with some dubious livestock dealers when he bought his sheep—or he had simply not wanted to spend the money for good quality animals. In any case, his animals were wild mixed breeds from which a consistent wool quality could never be achieved, no matter how carefully one chose their food or managed their pastures.

"You can even see it in their color, Helen," Gwyneira explained. "They all look different. With ours, on the other hand, you can't tell one apart from another. It has to be that way if you want to sell large batches of good quality wool and receive a good price."

Helen could see that and even attempted to broach the subject with Howard. He did not prove very open-minded about her suggestions, though, rebuking her curtly whenever she brought it up. He could not handle any criticism—which did not make him any friends among livestock dealers or wool buyers. He had fallen out with almost all of them by now—with the exception of the long-suffering Peter Brewster, who did not offer him top price for his third-rate wool, it was true, but took it off his hands all the same. Helen did not dare to think what would happen if the Brewsters moved to Otago. Then they would be dependent on his successor, and there could be no relying on diplomacy from Howard. Would the new buyer show any understanding or simply pass the farm over on future buying trips?

The family already lived hand to mouth. Without the help of the Maori, who were always sending food from the hunt, fish, or vegetables with the schoolchildren to pay for their lessons, Helen wouldn't have known what to do. Hiring extra help for the stables and the household was out of the question—in fact, Helen was now required to do more of the farm work because Howard could not even afford a Maori assistant. But Helen generally failed woefully at her farm chores. Howard admonished her sternly when she blushed for the umpteenth time during lambing instead of rolling up her sleeves, or when she burst out in tears during the slaughter.

"Don't act like that!" he would yell, forcing her to grab hold of the emerging lamb. Helen tried to swallow her disgust and fear to do what was asked of her. She could not bear it, however, when he treated their son that way, which happened more and more frequently. Howard could hardly expect him to grow up and make himself "useful" when it was already obvious that Ruben would not be any better suited to farm work than she was. Though the child shared a few physical similarities with Howard—he was tall, with full, dark locks, and would no doubt grow up to be strong—he had his mother's dreamy gray eyes, and Ruben's nature did not fit the harshness of farm life. The boy was Helen's pride and joy; he was friendly, polite, and pleasant to be around, and what's more, very intelligent. At five years old, the boy could already read fluently and devoured tomes like *Robin Hood* and *Ivanhoe* on his own. He was astoundingly clever in school, solving the math problems assigned to the twelve- and thirteen-year-olds, and already spoke fluent Maori. Handiwork, however, was not his strong suit; even little Fleur was more adept at making and firing the arrows from the bows they had just carved for their Robin Hood game.

But Ruben was more than willing to learn. Whenever Helen asked him to do something, he always made every effort to master it. Howard's gruff tone, however, scared him, and the lurid stories his father told him to toughen him up terrified him. As a result, Ruben's relationship with his father grew worse with each passing year. Helen could already predict a disaster similar to the one between Gerald and Lucas on Kiward Station—alas, without the fortune that enabled Lucas to hire a capable manager.

When Helen thought about all this, it sometimes made her sorry that their marriage had not produced any more children. Sometime after Ruben's birth, Howard had resumed his visits to her, but they never managed to conceive again. It may have had to do with Helen's age or with the fact that Howard never slept with her again as regularly as he had in their first year of marriage. Helen's obvious unwillingness, their child's presence in the bedroom, and Howard's increased drinking did not exactly set the proper mood. Howard now more often sought his pleasures at the gambling table in the Haldon pub than in bed with his wife. If there were women there too—and maybe some of his winnings went into a whore's purse—Helen did not want to know.

Still, today was a good day. Howard had remained sober the day before and had ridden out into the mountains before dawn to check on the ewes. Helen had milked the cows, Ruben had collected the eggs, and the Maori children would be arriving for school shortly. Helen was also hoping for a visit from Gwyneira. Fleurette would throw a fit if she wasn't allowed to come to school again—though she was still much too little, she was eager to learn to read so as not to have to rely on her mother's failing patience to read aloud. Her father was certainly more patient in that regard, but Fleur did not like his books. She didn't like hearing about good little girls who fell into bad luck and poverty only to make it through thanks to luck or chance. She would have been more likely to burn down the horrible stepmothers', foster parents', or witches' houses than light their fireplaces. She preferred reading about Robin Hood and his merry men or going with Gulliver on his travels. Helen smiled at the thought of the little whirlwind. It was hard to believe that quiet Lucas Warden was her father.

George Greenwood had a pain in his side from the rapid trotting. This time Gwyneira had given in to the demands of propriety and had her horse hitched to the carriage. The elegant mare, Igraine, pulled the two-seater with élan; she could easily have won any coach race. George's rental horse could only keep up with great effort and by occasionally galloping, which jangled George to the bone in the process. However, Gwyneira was in a chatty mood and revealed a great deal about Howard and Helen O'Keefe that was of serious interest to George—which was why he tried to keep up despite the fact that it hurt to do so.

Shortly before reaching the farm, Gwyneira reined in her horse. She didn't want to run over one of the Maori children on their way to school. Nor could anyone pass by the little highwayman who was waiting for them just beyond the ford in the stream. Gwyneira seemed to have expected something like this, but George was properly surprised when a small, dark-haired boy, his face painted green, leaped from the underbrush with a bow and arrow in his hands.

"Halt! What are you doing in my woods? State your names and purpose!"

Gwyneira laughed. "But you know me, don't you, Master Robin?" she exclaimed. "Look at me. Am I not the lady-in-waiting to Lady Fleurette, the lady of your heart?"

"That's not right at all! I'm Little John!" crowed Fleur. "And this is a messenger of the queen." She indicated George. "He's come from London!"

"Did our good King Richard send you? Or do you come from John, the usurper?" Ruben inquired suspiciously. "Perhaps from Queen Eleanor with the treasure for the king's deliverance?"

"Precisely," said George seriously. The boy was adorable, with his bandit's outfit and serious diction. "And I must continue on today to the Holy Land. So, wilt thou let us pass now? Sir..."

"Ruben!" declared the little boy. "Ruben Hood, at your service."

Fleur leaped from the carriage.

"He doesn't have any treasure," she snitched. "He just wants to visit your mummy. But he really did come from London!"

Gwyneira drove on. The children could find their own way back to the farm. "That was Ruben," she explained to George. "Helen's son. Quite a bright boy, don't you think?"

George nodded. *She's done well in that respect*, he thought. He once again recalled that endlessly dull afternoon with his hopeless brother, William; the one when Helen made up her mind. Before he could say anything, though, the O'Keefes' farm came into view. George was just as horrified at the sight of it as Helen had been six years before. What's more, the hut wasn't even new anymore as it had been then, and now showed the first signs of dilapidation.

"This isn't how she pictured it," he said softly.

Gwyneira stopped her dogcart in front of the cabin and unhitched the mare. George had a chance while she did so to look around, taking in the small stables sparsely strewn with hay, the thin cow, and the mule whose best years were far behind him. He saw the well in the yard—apparently, Helen still had to carry her water into the house by bucket—and the chopping block for the firewood. Did the master of the house see to the supply himself? Or did Helen have to reach for the ax herself if she wanted to keep warm?

"Come, the school is on the other side," Gwyneira said, tearing George from his thoughts and already moving behind the blockhouse. "We have to go through the bush a ways. The Maori built a few huts in the copse between Helen's house and their own village. But you can't see them from the house—Howard doesn't like to have the children too close by. He doesn't like the idea of the school to begin with; he'd prefer to have more help around the farm. But in the end it's better this way. If Howard needs somebody desperately, Helen sends one of the older boys. They much prefer that sort of work."

George could picture that. He could even manage to picture Helen doing housework. But Helen castrating lambs or helping with a cow's birth? Not in this lifetime.

The path to the grove was well worn, but even here George could see signs of the farm's lamentable condition. A few of the rams and ewes stood in pens, but the animals were in terrible shape—thin, their wool patchy and dirty. The fences looked worn down, the wire was poorly laid, and the gates were at sharp angles. There was no comparison with the Beasleys' farm or Kiward Station. Taken all together, it was beyond bleak.

Still, children's laughter could be heard from the grove. The tone there seemed to be happy.

"In the beginning," a high voice read in a funny accent, "God created the heavens and the earth, *rangi* and *papa*."

Gwyneira smiled at George. "Helen is wrestling with the Maori version of the creation story again," she remarked. "It's rather colorful, but now the children always present it this way so that Helen no longer blushes."

While one student talked explicitly and with obvious pleasure about the love-hungry Maori gods, George peered through the brush at the open huts covered with palm branches. The children sat on the ground, listening to the little girl read aloud about the first days of creation. Then it was the next child's turn. And then George saw Helen. She sat, upright and slender, at an improvised lectern at the edge of the scene, just as he remembered her. Her dress was threadbare but clean and high necked—at least from this angle she was every inch the proper, self-assured governess he remembered. His heart beat wildly as she now called another student to the front, turning her face in George's direction as she did so. Helen...to George she was still beautiful, and she always would be, regardless of how she changed or how much older she looked. This last notion frightened him though. Helen Davenport O'Keefe had aged markedly in the last few years. The sun that had bronzed her once carefully maintained white skin had not been kind, and her once slender face now looked sharper, almost haggard. Her hair, however, remained the same shining chestnut color as before. She wore it in a long, thick braid that fell down her back. A few strands had freed themselves, and Helen brushed them carelessly out of her face as she joked with the students—more than she had with William and himself, George noted jealously. Helen appeared overall more flexible than before, and the interaction with the Maori children seemed to delight her. And her little Master Ruben was obviously good for her as well. Ruben and Fleurette were just sneaking in. They arrived late to class, hoping that Helen wouldn't notice. Of course she did. Helen interrupted class after the third day of creation.

"Fleurette Warden. So lovely to see you. But don't you think a lady should say a polite hello when she takes her seat at a gathering? And you, Ruben O'Keefe—are you feeling ill? If not, why is your face so green? Run to the well quickly and wash up so you look like a gentleman. Where is your mother, Fleur? Or did you come with Mr. McKenzie again?"

Fleur attempted to shake her head and nod gravely at the same time. "Mummy is at the farm with Mr....something Wood," she let slip. "But I ran here fast because I thought you were reading more of the story. Our story, not the stuff and nonsense with *rangi* and *papa*."

Helen rolled her eyes. "Fleur, you should listen to the creation story at every opportunity. We do have a few children here who do not know it, at least not the Christian version. Sit down now and listen. We'll see what we do afterward." Helen wanted to call on the next child, but Fleur had just espied her mother.

"There they are, Mummy and Mr...."

Helen peered through the brush—and froze when she recognized George Greenwood. She grew pale for a moment and then blushed. Was it joy? Horror? Shame? George hoped that joy won out. He smiled. Helen closed her books nervously. "Rongo..." Her gaze wandered over the assembled children and stopped on one of the older girls, who until that moment had not been following the lesson very attentively. She must have been one of the children for whom the creation story was no longer new. The girl would have liked to be browsing the new book, which Fleur also appeared to find much more interesting. "Rongo, I need to leave the class alone for a few minutes, as I have a visitor. Would you please take over the lesson? Please be sure that the children read properly and don't just tell stories—and that they do not leave out a single word."

Rongo Rongo nodded and stood up. Full of her own importance as assistant teacher, she sat down at the lectern and called a girl up.

As the girl began struggling through the story of the fourth day after creation, Helen walked over to Gwyneira and George. Just as he had been in the past, George was awed by her bearing. Any other woman would have quickly tried to fix her hair, or smooth her dress, or whatever else she could to spruce herself up. Helen did nothing of the sort. Calm and poised, she stepped up to her visitor and held out her hand to him.

"George Greenwood! I'm so happy to see you."

George's whole face shone and looked as hopeful and earnest as it had when he was sixteen.

"You were able to recognize me, miss!" he said joyfully. "You haven't forgotten it."

Helen blushed lightly. It didn't escape her notice that he had said "it" and not "me." He was referring to his promise, to his silly declaration of love and his desperate attempt to stop her at the outset of what was to be her new life.

"How could I forget you, Mr. Greenwood?" she said amiably. "You were one of my most promising students, and now you have made good on your dream to travel the world."

"Not quite the whole world, miss...or should I say Mrs. O'Keefe?" George looked at her with the old mischievous look in his eyes.

Helen shrugged. "They all call me *miss.*"

"Mr. Greenwood is here to set up a branch office for his company," Gwyneira explained. "He'll be taking over Peter Brewster's wool trading business when the Brewsters move to Otago."

Helen smiled bitterly. She was not sure whether that would be to Howard's benefit or not.

"That's...nice," she said hesitantly. "And now you're here to get to know your clients? Howard won't be back until this evening."

George smiled at her. "More than anything, I'm here to see you again, miss. Mr. O'Keefe can wait. I told you that before, but you didn't want to listen."

"George, you should...I mean, really!" The old governess voice. George waited for a "You are so impertinent!" to follow, but Helen held back. Instead, she seemed shocked that she had accidentally called him "George" instead of "Mr. Greenwood." George wondered if that had to do with Gwyneira's introduction. Was Helen apprehensive about the new wool buyer? She seemed to have a reason to be, based on what he'd heard.

"How is your family, Mr. Greenwood?" Helen said, attempting to redirect the conversation. "I'd love to chat at greater length, but the children walked three miles to come to school, and I cannot disappoint them. Do you have time to wait?"

George nodded, smiling. "You know I can wait, miss." Another allusion. "And I always did enjoy your lessons. Might I take part?"

Helen seemed to relax. "Education has yet to do anyone harm," she said. "Please, join us."

Amazed, the Maori children made room as George took his seat with them on the ground. Helen explained in English and Maori that he was a former student of hers from faraway England and as such he had come the farthest way of all to school. The children laughed and George once again noted how Helen's tone as a teacher had changed. She'd had much less fun before.

The children greeted their new classmate in their language, and George learned his first few Maori words. By the end of the lesson, he could even read the first section of the creation story, though the children were constantly laughing and correcting him. Later the older students were allowed to ask him questions, and George told stories from his own school days—first with Helen in his London home, then at college in Oxford.

"Which did you like better?" one of the oldest boys asked cheekily. Helen called him Reti, and he spoke English very well.

George laughed. "Lessons with Miss O'Keefe, of course. When the weather was nice, we sat outside, just like this. And my mother insisted that Miss O'Keefe play croquet with us, but she was never very good and always lost." He winked at Helen.

Reti did not seem surprised. "When she first got here, she couldn't milk a cow either," he revealed. "What is croquet, Mr. Greenwood? Do you have to be able to play it to work in Christchurch? You see, I want to work with the Englishmen one day and become rich."

George registered this remark and made a mental note of it. He would have to speak to Helen about this promising young man. A perfectly bilingual Maori could be of great use to Greenwood Enterprises. "If you're considered a gentleman and want to get to know a lady, you should at least be good enough at croquet to lose with dignity," he replied.

Helen rolled her eyes. Gwyneira noticed how young she suddenly seemed.

"Can you teach it to us?" Rongo Rongo asked. "As a lady one surely also has to be able to play."

"Certainly," George said seriously. "But I don't know if I have enough time. I..."

"*I* can teach you how to play," Gwyneira interjected. The game was an unexpected chance to pull Helen away from her lesson. "What would you think if we left the reading and arithmetic for today and instead made mallets and hoops? I'll show you all how, and Miss O'Keefe will have time to see to her visitor. No doubt she wants to show him the farm."

Helen and George shot her grateful looks. Helen rather doubted that Gwyneira was all that excited about such a slow-paced game, but she was likely better at it than Helen and George together.

"So, we need a ball…no, not such a big ball, Ruben, a little one… yes, we could also use that rock. And little hoops…good idea, braiding them, Tani."

As the children launched into their task, Helen and George moved away. Helen led him back to the house the same way that he had just come with Gwyneira.

She seemed to be ashamed of the condition of the farm.

"My husband hasn't had time to fix the pens after this past winter," she said apologetically as they passed the paddocks. "We have a lot of livestock in the highlands, spread across the pastures, and now that it's spring, the lambs are being born."

George did not comment, though he knew how mild the New Zealand winters were. Howard should have had no trouble repairing the pens even during the coldest months of the year.

Naturally, Helen knew that too. She was silent for a moment, then turned to him suddenly.

"Oh, George, I'm so ashamed! What must you think of me after you've seen all this, compared with my letters."

The expression on her face pained his heart.

"I don't know what you mean, miss," he said softly. "I see a farmhouse…not big, not luxurious, but well-built and lovingly furnished. True, the livestock won't be winning any prizes, but they've been fed and the cows milked." He winked. "And that mule really seems to love you."

Nepumuk let out his customary piercing neigh as Helen passed his pen.

"Of course I'll also come to know your husband as a gentleman who makes every effort to support his family well and work his farm in an exemplary manner. You can rest assured, miss."

Helen looked at him incredulously. Then she smiled. "You're wearing rose-colored glasses, George."

He shrugged. "You make me happy, miss. Wherever you are I can only see goodness and beauty."

Helen turned a burning red. "George, please. You should really have put that behind you."

George grinned at her. Had he put it behind him? To an extent, yes; he couldn't deny that. His heart had raced when he had laid eyes on Helen again; he rejoiced at the sight of her, at her voice, at her ongoing balancing act between decorum and authenticity. But he no longer struggled with longing to know what it would be like to kiss her and make love to her. That was in the past. He felt only a vague tenderness for the woman now standing before him. Would he have felt the same way if she hadn't refused him then? Would his passion have given way to friendship and a sense of responsibility? Likely even before he had completed his studies and been able to seal the bond of marriage with her? And would he really have married her then, or would he simply have hoped that he would someday feel such a burning love for another woman?

George was unable to answer any of these questions with certainty—except for the last. "When I say forever, I mean just that. But I won't importune you with that anymore. You're not going to run away with me anyway, are you now?" The old, impertinent grin.

Helen shook her head and held a carrot out to Nepumuk. "I could never leave the mule," she joked, with tears in her eyes. George was so sweet and still so innocent. How happy he would make the first girl to take his promises seriously.

"Now come in and tell me about your family."

The interior of the hut was what George had expected: simple furniture, made cozy by the tireless hand of a tidy and busy housewife. A bright cloth and a pitcher full of flowers decorated a table, and the chairs were made more comfortable by homemade pillows.

A spinning wheel stood in front of the fireplace alongside Helen's old rocking chair, and her books were neatly organized on a shelf. There were even a few new ones. Were they presents from Howard, or on loan from Gwyneira, he wondered. Though George could hardly picture Gerald reading, Kiward Station had a comprehensive library.

George reported on London while Helen prepared tea. She worked with her back to him, surely not wanting him to see her hands. Raw and worn down, they were no longer the soft, manicured hands of his old governess.

"Mother still oversees her charitable committees—only she left the orphanage committee after the scandal back then. She still holds that against you, Helen. The ladies are convinced you spoiled the girls on the passage over."

"I did what?" Helen asked, dumbfounded.

"Your, I'm quoting here, 'emancipated style' led the girls to forget humility and devotion toward their employers. That's the only way this scandal could have come about. Of course, no mention was made of the fact that it was you, in fact, who revealed everything to Pastor Thorne. Mrs. Baldwin never said a thing."

"George, those were young girls in distress! They delivered one up to a pervert and sold another into slavery. A family with eight children, George, for whom a girl of ten—at most—was supposed to manage the household. And serve as a midwife too. No wonder the child ran away. And Laurie's so-called employers weren't much better. I can still hear that impossible Mrs. Lavender: 'No, if we take two they'll only talk the livelong day instead of working.' And the little one bawling her eyes out the whole time."

"Have you heard anything more about the girls?" George inquired. "You never wrote anything more about them."

It sounded like the young man knew each of Helen's letters by heart.

Helen shook her head. "All anyone knows is that Mary and Laurie disappeared on the same day. Exactly a week after they were separated. It's suspected that they arranged it ahead of time. I don't believe that though. Mary and Laurie never needed to arrange anything. The one always knew what the other was thinking—it was almost eerie.

No one heard another word from them after that day. I fear they're dead. Two little girls alone in the wilderness...it's not as though they lived two miles down the road from one another and could easily have met each other. These...these *Christians*," she spat the word out, "they sent Mary to a farm behind Haldon, and Laurie stayed in Christchurch. There are almost fifty miles of wilderness in between the two. I dare not think about what those children endured."

Helen poured the tea and sat down next to George at the table.

"And the third one?" he asked. "What happened to her?"

"Daphne? Oh we found out about that scandal a few weeks later. She ran away. But before that she threw a pot of boiling water at her employer, this Morrison fellow—full in the face. At first they said he wouldn't survive it. He managed to after all, but he's blind and his face is deformed by scars. Dorothy says that now Morrison looks like the monster he's always been. She's seen him once or twice since the Morrisons come shopping in Haldon. The wife really blossomed after her husband had his...accident. They're still searching for Daphne, but unless she walks straight through Christchurch and into the police station, she won't be found. If you ask me, she had good reasons for doing what she did. I just don't know what sort of a future she'll have now."

George shrugged. "Probably the same future that would have awaited her in London. Poor child. But the orphanage committee got what was coming to it; Reverend Thorne saw to that. And this Baldwin..."

Helen smiled almost triumphantly. "He had Harper paraded right in front of him. So much for his dream of being bishop of Canterbury. I take a very un-Christian joy in that. But go on! Your father..."

"...holds his position in Greenwood Enterprises, same as always. The company is growing and thriving. The queen supports our foreign trade, and we're making a fortune in the colonies, though often at the expense of the natives. I've witnessed it...your Maori should consider themselves lucky that the white colonists, as well as they themselves, are peacefully inclined. But my father and I can't change the way things are—and we profit from the exploitation of these countries. In England, industrialization is booming, though with consequences that I like as little as the oppression I've seen overseas. The conditions in some factories are appalling. When I think about it, I've liked nowhere else as much as New Zealand. But I digress."

As George attempted to return to the subject, he realized that he hadn't just made this last remark to flatter Helen. He really did like this country: the upstanding but peaceful people, the broad landscape with the majestic mountains, the large farms with their well-fed sheep and cattle grazing on ample pastures—and Christchurch, which was in the process of turning itself into a typical English bishop's seat and university town on the other end of the world.

"What is William doing?" Helen inquired.

George sighed with a telling look at the ceiling. "William did not end up going to college, but you hadn't really counted on that happening, had you?"

Helen shook her head.

"He had a series of tutors who were regularly let go—at first by my mother because she thought they were too strict with William and then by my father because they didn't teach him anything. He's been working in the company for the last year, if you can call it work. Basically he's just killing time, and he never lacks for company, male or female. After the pubs, he discovered women. Alas, predominantly those from the street. He doesn't distinguish between them. On the contrary, ladies scare him, while easy women amaze him. It sickens my father, and my mother still hasn't realized it. But how it's going to turn out when..."

He did not continue, but Helen knew exactly what he was thinking: when his father died someday, both brothers would inherit the company. George would then either have to buy out his brother—which would destroy a business like the Greenwoods'—or continue to endure him. Helen did not think it likely that George would be able to maintain the latter situation for long.

As they lapsed into silence, thoughtfully drinking their tea, the front door flew open, and Fleur and Ruben stormed in.

"We won!" Fleurette beamed, swinging an improvised croquet mallet. "Ruben and I are the winners!"

"You cheated," Gwyneira chided, appearing behind the children. She looked flushed and a little dirty, but seemed to have enjoyed herself immensely. "I very clearly saw you secretly push Ruben's ball through the last hoop."

Helen frowned. "Is that true, Ruben? And you didn't say anything?"

"With the funny mallets, it doesn't work pre…pre…what's that word again, Ruben?" Fleur asked, defending her friend.

"Precisely," Ruben finished her thought. "But the direction was right."

George smiled. "When I get back to England, I'll send you proper mallets," he promised. "But then there can't be any more cheating."

"Really?" Fleur asked.

Other thoughts were going through Ruben's mind. With his clever brown eyes, he looked at Helen and her visitor, who were obviously close.

"You're from England. Are you my real father?"

Gwyneira gasped for air and Helen reddened.

"Ruben! Don't say such nonsense. You know very well that you only have one father." Apologizing, she turned to George. "I hope you don't get the wrong idea. It's only that Ruben…he doesn't have the best relationship with his father, and recently he's gotten it stuck in his head that Howard…well, that perhaps he has another father somewhere in England. I imagine it has to do with my talking so much about his grandfather. Ruben is very much like him, you know. And he takes that the wrong way. Now apologize immediately, Ruben!"

George smiled. "He doesn't have to apologize. On the contrary, I'm flattered. Who wouldn't gladly be related to Ruben Hood, brave yeoman and masterful croquet player? What do you think, Ruben, could I be your uncle? One can have more than one uncle."

Ruben considered.

"Ruben! He's going to send us croquet mallets. An uncle like that is good. You can be *my* uncle, Mr. Greenwood." Fleur was unfailingly practical.

Gwyneira rolled her eyes. "If she stays so open-minded with regard to financial considerations, she'll be an easy one to marry off."

"I'm marrying Ruben," Fleur explained. "And Ruben's marrying me too, right?" She waved the croquet mallet about. Ruben had better not turn down her request.

Helen and Gwyneira looked at each other helplessly. Then they laughed, and George joined in.

"When can I meet the groom's father?" he asked finally, glancing at the sun's position in the sky. "I promised Mr. Warden I'd be back for dinner, and I'd like to keep my word. It looks like the discussion with Mr. O'Keefe will have to wait until tomorrow. Is there a possibility that he'll meet me in the morning, miss?"

Helen bit her lip. "I'll gladly give him the message, but sometimes Howard is…well, stubborn. If he gets the idea that you want to impose a time on him…" It was visibly difficult for her to talk about Howard's stubbornness and bravado, and she couldn't even admit how often his moods and decisions were guided by caprice or whiskey.

As always, she spoke with calm and restraint, but George could read her eyes—just as he'd done at the Greenwoods' dinner table. He saw anger and revulsion, desperation and disdain. Back then these feelings had been directed toward his superficial mother—now they were reserved for the husband Helen had once believed she could love.

"Don't worry, miss. You don't have to tell him I'm coming from Kiward Station. Simply tell him I'm stopping by on the way to Haldon—and I would like to see the farm and make a few business suggestions."

Helen nodded. "I'll try."

Gwyneira and the children had already gone outside to hitch up her horse. Helen heard the children fighting over the currycomb and brush. George did not seem to be in much of a hurry. He looked around the hut before he made a move to say good-bye. Helen struggled inside herself. Should she speak to him frankly, or would he misunderstand her request? Finally she decided to broach the topic of Howard one last time. When George took over the local wool trade, her entire welfare would depend on him. And Howard would probably snub the visitor from England.

"George..." she began hesitantly. "When you talk to Howard tomorrow, please be indulgent. He is very proud and is quick to take offense. Life dealt him bad cards, and it's hard for him to control himself. He is...he's..."

"Not a gentleman," she wanted to say, but could not get the words out.

George shook his head and laughed. In his usually teasing eyes, she saw a gentleness and an echo of his old love. "No need to say a thing, miss! I'm sure that I'll come to a mutually satisfactory agreement with your husband. I did attend the best school for diplomacy, after all." He winked at her.

Helen smiled, faint of heart. "Then, I'll see you tomorrow, George."

"I'll see you tomorrow, Helen." George wanted to shake her hand, but then had another thought. Once, just this once, he would kiss her. He put his arm around her and brushed her cheek with his lips. Helen let him—and then gave in and leaned for a few seconds on his shoulder. Perhaps someday, someone aside from herself could be strong. Perhaps someday someone would keep his word.

4

"Now, look, Mr. O'Keefe, I've visited several farms in this area," George said. He sat with Howard O'Keefe on the veranda of Helen's hut, and Howard had just poured himself some whiskey. Helen found that reassuring: her husband only drank with men he liked. So the tour of the farm earlier must have gone well. "And I have to admit," George continued in a measured tone, "that I'm a little concerned."

"Concerned?" grumbled Howard. "How do you mean? There's plenty of wool here for your business. You certainly don't need to worry about that. And if you don't like what I've got...just as well, you don't need to pretend with me. Then I'll just look for another buyer." He emptied his glass in one go and poured himself another.

George arched his eyebrows in confusion. "Why should I reject your product, Mr. O'Keefe? On the contrary, I'm very interested in working together. Precisely because of my concern. You see, I've visited several farms now, and it seems to me that a few sheep breeders are striving for a monopoly, Gerald Warden of Kiward Station first and foremost."

"You can say that again!" O'Keefe replied, working himself up and taking another slug. "Those fellows want the whole market for themselves...only the best price for the best wool...even what they call themselves: sheep barons! Delusions of grandeur, that lot."

Howard reached for the whiskey.

George nodded and sipped from his glass. "I would put it more mildly, but in principle, you're not wrong. And it's very astute of you to mention prices—Warden and the other top producers are driving them high. Of course, they're also raising the expectations of quality, but as far as I'm concerned...well, my negotiating position would naturally be stronger if there were more variety."

"So you'll be buying more from smaller breeders?" Howard asked hungrily. His eyes shone with interest but also with suspicion. What trader would knowingly buy lower-quality wool?

"I would like to, Mr. O'Keefe. But the quality has likewise to match. If you ask me, the little farms are stuck in a vicious circle that must be broken. You know it yourself—you don't have much land, and you have too many rather low-quality animals; the yields are quantitatively acceptable but qualitatively poor. So there's not enough revenue left over to buy better livestock and increase the quality of the results long term."

O'Keefe nodded avidly. "You're completely right there. That's what I've been trying to make these bankers in Christchurch understand for years. I would need a loan."

George shook his head. "You need first-class breeding material. And it's not just you, but other small farms as well. An injection of money can help, but it's not always the answer. Imagine you buy a prize-winning ram and the next winter he dies on you."

George's real fear was that a loan for Howard would more likely be gambled away in the pub than invested in a ram, but he had thought over his arguments at some length.

"Well, that's exactly the ri...risk," said Howard, who was gradually losing full command of his tongue.

"A risk you cannot afford, O'Keefe. You have a family. You can't risk someone chasing you out of house and home. No, my proposal looks a little different. I'm considering having my company, Greenwood Enterprises, acquire a stock of first-class sheep and then offering them to the breeders on loan. As for reimbursement, we can work out an agreement. You would care for the animals, and return them in good health a year later—a year during which a ram mates with all the ewes in your flock or a purebred ewe delivers two lambs to you, which provide the foundation for a new flock. Would you be interested in such an arrangement?"

Howard grinned. "And Warden will start to look shabby when he suddenly finds farmers all around him with purebreds." He raised his glass as though to toast George.

George nodded at him seriously. "Well, Mr. Warden won't starve as a result. But you and I will have better business opportunities ahead. Agreed?" He held out his hand to Helen's husband.

Helen saw from the window that Howard took it. She had not heard what they said, but Howard had rarely looked so pleased. And George had that old clever-as-a-fox look on his face, winking in her direction no less. Yesterday she had reproached herself, but now she wished she had kissed him.

George was very pleased with himself when he left Kiward Station the next day to ride back to Christchurch. Not even the dirty looks of that impertinent stable boy James McKenzie could spoil his mood. The fellow had neglected to saddle his horse for him, and that after there had nearly been an incident the day before when George had set off for Helen's farm with Gwyneira. James had led Gwyneira's mare out equipped with a sidesaddle after Gwyneira had asked him to prepare her mare for another ride with her visitor. Mrs. Warden had made an angry remark, to which he had offered a barbed reply, the only word of which George heard was "ladylike." At that, Gwyneira had reached for little Fleur in a rage, whom McKenzie had been lifting up to set behind her on Igraine, and forced the girl to ride in front of George.

"Would you please let Fleur ride with you?" she asked sweet as sugar, casting an almost triumphant look at the shepherd. "I can't have her with me on the sidesaddle."

James McKenzie had stared at George with near murderous rage when he wrapped his arm around the little girl so that she would be secure. There was something brewing between that man and the lady of Kiward Station...but he had no doubt that Gwyneira could take care of herself if she felt put upon. George decided not to get involved and moreover not to say anything to Gerald or Lucas Warden. It didn't concern him—and besides, he needed to keep Gerald in the best possible spirits. After an ample farewell meal and three glasses of whiskey, George made his offer for a flock of purebred Welsh Mountain sheep. An hour later, he was a small fortune poorer, but Helen's farm would soon be populated with the best breeding stock New Zealand had to offer. Now George only needed to find a few other small farms in need of start-up help to keep Howard from becoming suspicious. But that wouldn't be difficult; Peter Brewster could give him a few names.

This new business venture—since that's how George would have to explain this foray into sheep breeding—meant that George had to prolong his stay on the South Island. The sheep needed to be distributed and the breeders involved in the project observed. The latter was perhaps not necessary since Brewster could probably have recommended partners who knew their work and had come into debts through no fault of their own. But if Helen was to be helped over the long term, Howard O'Keefe would require constant guidance and supervision—diplomatically packaged as help and advice against his archenemy Warden—since O'Keefe was unlikely to follow simple directions. Least of all if they came from the mouth of a manager employed by the Greenwoods. So George would have to stay—a thought that pleased him more and more as he rode through the clear air of the Canterbury Plains. The many hours in the saddle gave him time to think over his situation in England as well. After just a single year of working together, his brother, William, had driven him to despair. While his father deliberately looked the other way, even during George's rare visits to London he could see his brother's mistakes and the sometimes horrendous losses the company had to contend with as a result. The pleasure George derived from traveling could in part be traced back to his inability to watch passively. He'd hardly set foot on English soil before chief clerks and managers had come to the junior executive with concerns: "You have to do something, Mr. Greenwood!"—"I'm afraid of being charged with breach of trust, Mr. Greenwood, if things continue like this, but what am I supposed to do?"—"Mr. Greenwood, I gave Mr. William the balance sheets, but I almost get the impression he can't read them."—"Please speak to your father, Mr. Greenwood!"

Naturally, George had tried to do just that, but it was hopeless. Their father attempted again and again to successfully employ William in the company. Instead of limiting his son's influence, he tried to give him ever more responsibility, hoping that it would guide him onto the right path. But George had had enough of that and, what's more, feared having to clean up the mess when his father retired.

This New Zealand branch, however, offered an alternative—if he could only convince his father to leave the Christchurch business entirely in his hands, as an advance of sorts on his inheritance, then he could build up something here that would be safe from William's escapades. He would have to live more humbly than in England at first, since manor houses like Kiward Station seemed out of place in this newly developed land. Besides, George had no need for luxury. He would be fine with a comfortable townhouse, a good horse for his trips around the area, and a nice pub where could find relaxation and stimulating conversation in the evening—all of which could no doubt be found in Christchurch. Naturally, a family would be even better. Until that moment, George had never thought about starting a family—at least not since Helen had turned him down so long ago. But now, having seen his first love again and left his romantic ideals behind, he could think of little else. A marriage in New Zealand—a "love story" that could touch his mother's heart and encourage her to support his plans...above all, though, it was a good excuse to remain here. George decided to look around Christchurch in the coming days and perhaps ask the Brewsters and the bank director for some advice as well. They might even know of a suitable girl. But first he needed a place to live. The White Hart was a passable hotel, but unsuitable as a permanent residence in his new homeland.

George employed the services of the local real estate office the next day. He had spent a restless night at the White Hart. A band had been playing dances in the room below, and the men had fought over the girls—which gave George the impression that looking for a wife in New Zealand did not come without peril. He suddenly found himself thinking of the advertisement that Helen had responded to in a whole new light. Even the search for a home did not prove easy. Those who moved here did not generally buy houses, but built them. Finished houses were rarely up for sale and were correspondingly valuable. Even the Brewsters had long since rented out their home before George arrived. They didn't want to sell it, as their future in Otago remained uncertain.

Though George toured the few addresses that people had mentioned to him at the bank, the White Hart, and in the pubs, the majority were shabby. A few families and older ladies living alone were seeking subletters. This was no doubt an appropriate and reasonable alternative to the hotel for colonists who were getting their feet on the ground in their new country, but there was nothing suitable for George, accustomed as he was to more upscale accommodations.

Frustrated, he ended up strolling through the new parks along the Avon's banks. In the summer, boat regattas took place here, and there were viewpoints and scenic picnic spots. For the time being, though, it being spring, they were quite empty. The still-fickle spring weather only allowed for a short spell on the riverfront benches, and only the main paths had people on them. Yet a stroll here gave George the impression that he could almost be in Oxford or Cambridge. Nannies led their charges on walks, children played ball on the grass, and a few couples modestly sought the shade of trees. Though it did not pull him entirely out of his reverie, the scene had a calming effect on George. He had just looked at the last building for rent on his list, a shack that it took a good deal of imagination to call a house and which would gobble up at least as much time and money in renovations as building a new house. Moreover it was not well situated. Short of a miracle, George would have to begin looking for land plots the next day and consider building a new house after all. How he was supposed to explain such a thing to his parents was beyond him.

Tired and in low spirits, he continued to stroll aimlessly, watching the ducks and swans on the river. Suddenly he became aware of a young woman who was watching two children nearby. The little girl might have been seven or eight years old, a little plump, with thick, almost black locks. She was chatting happily with her nanny while tossing old bread to the ducks from a pier. The little boy, a blond cherub, was, in contrast, a real menace. He had left the pier and was playing in the mud on the bank.

The nanny expressed her concern. "Robert, don't go so near the river! How often do I have to tell you? Nancy, look out for your brother!"

The young woman—George placed her at no more than eighteen years old—stood seemingly helpless at the edge of the muddy strip of bank. She wore neat black lace-up shoes polished to a shine and a simple navy-blue shift. She would doubtlessly ruin both if she followed the little boy into the brackish water. The little girl in front of her was no different. She was clean and neatly dressed and had surely received instructions not to get dirty.

"He won't listen to me, missy!" the little girl said dutifully.

The boy had already smeared mud on his sailor suit from top to bottom.

"I'll come back when you make me a little boat!" he now called back naughtily to his nanny. "Then we'll go to the lake and watch them float."

The "lake" was no more than a large pool that remained from the high water in winter. It did not look very clean, but at least there was no dangerous current.

The young woman looked undecided. No doubt she knew that it was wrong to negotiate with him, but she clearly did not want to wade through the muck to retrieve the little boy forcibly. She resorted to a counteroffer.

"But first let's practice your equations. I don't want you not to know anything when your father asks you questions."

George shook his head. Helen would never have given in to George in a similar situation. But this governess was considerably younger and obviously much less experienced than Helen had been when she worked for the Greenwoods. She seemed practically desperate; the child was obviously too much for her. Despite her cross demeanor, she was attractive: she had a delicate heart-shaped face with pale skin, clear blue eyes, and bright pink lips. Her hair was fine and blonde, tied up in a loose knot at the nape of her neck, and was not holding well. Either her hair was too soft to stay pinned up, or the girl was not very good with hair. On her head sat a prim bonnet that suited her dress. Although her attire was simple, it was not a servant's uniform. George revised his first impression. The girl must be a tutor, not a nanny.

"I'll solve a problem, then I get the boat!" Robert called out confidently. He had discovered a rather decrepit jetty that led farther out into the river, and was balancing on it, clearly pleased. George was alarmed. Up to this point, the little boy had only been defiant, but now he was in real danger. The current was very strong.

The tutor saw it too but did not want to give up without a fight.

"You'll solve three problems," she announced. Her voice sounded strained.

"Two!" The boy, who might have been six years old, rocked back and forth on a board.

That was enough for George. He was wearing heavy riding boots in which he could easily cross the mud. In three strides he was on the jetty, where he swept up the unhappy boy and carried him back to his tutor.

"Here, I believe this one got away from you." George laughed.

The young woman hesitated at first—unsure of the appropriate response in this situation. Relief won out, and she smiled. Besides, it was funny to watch Robert, tucked under this stranger's arm, pedaling in the air like an unruly puppy. His sister giggled with delight.

"Three problems, young man, and I'll let you loose," said George.

Robert wailed in acquiescence, at which point George set him down. The tutor took him immediately by the collar and pushed him onto the next available park bench.

"Thank you," she said, with demurely lowered eyes. "I was worried. He is often so badly behaved."

George nodded his head and wanted to continue on his way, but something held him back. So he sought a bench not far from the tutor, who was now working to calm her charge. Holding him on the bench, she tried to elicit, if not the answer, then at least some response to a math question.

"Two plus three—how many is that, Robert? We did it with building blocks; do you remember?"

"Don't know. Can we make the boat now?" Robert fidgeted.

"After arithmetic. Look, Robert, here are three leaves. And here are two more. How many are there?"

The boy only had to count. But he was recalcitrant and uninterested. George saw William once more in front of him.

The young tutor remained patient. "Just count, Robert."

The boy counted against his will. "One, two, three, four...four, missy."

The tutor sighed, as did little Nancy.

"Count again, Robert."

The child was not only unwilling but dumb. George's sympathy for the tutor grew as she inched arduously closer to each answer. It could not have been easy to remain kind, but the young woman only laughed stoically when Robert yelled, "Make the boat, make the boat!" again and again. She gave in when the boy finally correctly solved the third and easiest problem. However, she showed neither patience nor skill when it came to folding paper boats. The model that Robert finally accepted did not look very seaworthy. In no time, the little boy was back again, interrupting the arithmetic lesson with Nancy that had followed his own. His sister reacted indignantly to the interruption. The little girl was good with numbers, and unlike her tutor, she seemed aware of their audience. Whenever she gave an answer, as though firing it off from a pistol, she cast a triumphant look in George's direction. George, however, was focusing his attention on the young teacher. She asked her questions in a soft, high-pitched voice, pronouncing her Ss with some affectation—like an aspiring member of the British aristocracy or a girl who had lisped as a child but now consciously controlled her speech. George found it charming;

he could have listened to her all day. But here was Robert interrupting her and his sister's peace and quiet once again. George knew exactly how the little girl felt. And he saw the same strained patience that Helen had so often expressed in the tutor's eyes.

"It sank, missy! Make a new one," Robert ordered, tossing his wet boat into his teacher's lap.

George decided to step in once more.

"Come here; I know how to do it," Robert offered. "I'll show you how to fold one, and then you can do it yourself."

"But you really don't need to..." the young woman began, giving him a helpless look. "Robert, you're bothering the gentleman," she said sternly.

"Not at all," George said with a dismissive hand gesture. "On the contrary. I love making paper boats, and I haven't done it in nearly ten years. It's about time I tried it again before I forget how to do it."

While the young woman continued to work on math equations with Nancy—occasionally stealing glances at George—he quickly folded the paper into a little boat. He tried to explain to Robert how to do it himself, but the boy was only interested in the finished product.

"Come along, let's make it sail," he invited George. "In the river."

"Not in the river!" The tutor leaped up. Although it would undoubtedly mean upsetting Nancy, she was ready to accompany Robert to the "lake" as long as he did not put himself in harm's way again. George walked beside her, marveling at her easy, gracious movements. This girl was no country girl like those who had been dancing at the White Hart the night before. She was obviously a young lady.

"The boy is difficult, isn't he?" George said sympathetically.

She nodded. "But Nancy is sweet. And perhaps Robert will grow out of it," she said hopefully.

"Do you think?" George asked. "Do you have experience with that?"

The girl shrugged. "No. This is my first job."

"After your teaching seminar?" George was curious. She seemed incredibly young for an educated teacher.

The girl shook her head, embarrassed. "No, I never took a seminar. There aren't any to take in New Zealand—at least not here on the South Island. But I know how to read and write, and I know a little French and quite a bit of Maori. I've read the classics, though not in Latin. Besides, the children won't be going to college for a long time."

"And?" George asked. "Do you enjoy it?"

The young woman looked at him and frowned. George motioned toward a space on a bench near the "lake" and was pleased when she sat down.

"Enjoy it? Teaching? Well, not always. But what sort of job earns you money and is always enjoyable?"

George sat down beside her and decided to act boldly.

"Since we're already chatting, allow me to introduce myself: George Greenwood of Greenwood Enterprises—London, Sydney, and recently Christchurch."

If she was impressed, she didn't let him see it. Instead, she just calmly and proudly told him her name: "Elizabeth Godewind."

"Godewind? That sounds Danish. But you don't have a Scandinavian accent."

Elizabeth shook her head. "No, I'm from London. But my foster mother was Swedish. She adopted me."

"Just a mother? No father?" George berated himself for his curiosity.

"Mrs. Godewind was already quite old when I came to her. To provide her with some company, so to speak. Later she wanted to leave me the house, and the simplest way for her to do that was to adopt me. Mrs. Godewind was the best thing to ever happen to me." The young woman fought back tears. George looked away so as not to embarrass her, and kept an eye on the children. Nancy was picking flowers, and Robert was doing his best to sink the second ship.

Elizabeth found her handkerchief and regained her composure.

"Please pardon me. But it's only been nine months since her death, and it still upsets me."

"But if you're well off, then why did you take a position as a tutor?" George asked. It was improper to press so much, but the girl fascinated him.

Elizabeth shrugged. "Mrs. Godewind received a pension and we lived off that. After her death, we still had the house. At first we tried renting it out, but that didn't work out. I lack the necessary sense of authority, as does Jones, the butler. The people who took the place didn't pay rent, were rude, made a mess of the rooms, and bossed around Jones and his wife. It was unbearable. It no longer felt like our home. So I sought out this teaching position. I like looking after the children a great deal more. Also, I only spend the day with them; I can go home at night."

So her evenings were free. George wondered if he could dare to ask her to meet again. Dinner in the White Hart, perhaps, or a walk. But no—she would turn that down. She was clearly a well-bred girl; already this conversation in the park was pushing the boundaries of propriety. An invitation without a go-between from a friendly family or a chaperone, without the proper framework, was completely out of the question. But, damn it, this wasn't London. They were on the other end of the world, and he didn't want to lose sight of her. He had to take a chance. She would have to dare…what the hell, even Helen had risked it.

George turned to the girl and gazed at her with all the charm and poise he could muster.

"Miss Godewind," he said deliberately. "The question I would like to put to you oversteps all convention. Naturally, I could stay true to form, follow you unobserved, find out the name of your employers, have myself brought to their home by some well-known member of the Christchurch community—and then wait for us to be officially introduced to one another. But by then, it's possible someone else will have married you. So, if you do not want to spend the rest of your life wrestling with children like Robert, then please listen to what I have to say: you are exactly what I'm looking for: You're a beautiful woman, charming and educated, with a house in Christchurch…"

Three months later, George Greenwood married Elizabeth Godewind. The groom's parents were not present; Robert Greenwood had to forgo the journey due to business obligations. He sent the couple his blessing and best wishes, and he signed over all the branch offices in New Zealand and Australia to George as a wedding present. His mother told all her friends that her son had married a Swedish captain's daughter and dropped hints of ties to the Swedish royal family. She was never to know that Elizabeth had been born in Queens and exiled to the New Country by her own orphanage committee. Nothing in her demeanor gave away the young bride's true heritage either. She looked ravishing in her white lace dress, whose train a well-behaved Robert and Nancy carried behind her. Helen watched the boy with eagle eyes the entire time, so George was certain he wouldn't get up to any mischief. Since George had recently made a name for himself as a wool trader and Mrs. Godewind had been regarded as a pillar of the community, the bishop insisted on marrying the couple himself. After the ceremony, the marriage was celebrated in grand style in the salon of the White Hart Hotel, where Gerald Warden and Howard O'Keefe got drunk in opposite corners of the room. Helen and Gwyneira did not let themselves get upset by this and saw to it that, despite all the bad blood, Ruben and Fleur strewed flower petals together. Observing them together, Gerald Warden seemed to realize for the first time that Howard O'Keefe's marriage had been blessed with a hale and hardy son, which only worsened his mood. So there was an heir for that ramshackle O'Keefe farm. Gwyneira, however, remained as skinny as a pole. Seeing Gerald sink deep into his whiskey bottle, Lucas was happy to retire with Gwyneira to their hotel room before his father's anger exploded at high volume. That night he attempted once again to approach Gwyneira. As always she showed herself willing and did her best to encourage him. Yet Lucas failed again.

5

It took a long time for James McKenzie and Gwyneira's relationship to return to normal after George's visit. Gwyneira was angry, and James was vexed as well. Above all, it became clear to both of them that it wasn't truly over between them. Gwyneira's heart still ached when she saw how desperately James looked at her, and James could not bear to picture Gwyneira in the arms of another. Yet a fresh start for their relationship was impossible—Gwyneira knew that she would never let go of James again if she touched him even once more.

Life on Kiward Station was gradually becoming unbearable. Gerald got drunk every day and did not give Lucas and Gwyneira a moment's peace. He did not even rein in his attacks when guests were present. Gwyneira became so distraught that she worked up the nerve to talk to Lucas about his sexual difficulties.

"Look, dearest," she said one evening in a low voice as Lucas lay beside her once again, exhausted by his efforts and sick with shame. Gwyneira shyly suggested that she try arousing him by touching his member—just about the least proper thing a lady and gentleman could do together, but Gwyneira's experiences with James gave her hope in this regard. However, Lucas was hardly aroused, even when she stoked the smooth, tender skin and massaged it gently. She had to do something. Gwyneira decided to appeal to Lucas's imagination. "If you don't like how I look…because I have red hair or because you prefer more full-bodied women…why not picture someone else? I wouldn't be upset."

Lucas kissed her gently on the cheek. "You're so sweet." He sighed. "So understanding. I don't deserve you. I'm horribly sorry about everything." He wanted to turn away, ashamed.

"Being sorry won't get me pregnant," Gwyneira said curtly. "Just picture something that excites you."

Lucas tried it. But he was so horrified by the arousing image that popped into his head that the shock sobered him up straightaway. It couldn't be! He could not be sleeping with a woman and thinking about the slender, well-cut George Greenwood.

The situation escalated one evening in December, a scorching summer day without even the smallest breeze. That was a rare thing in the Canterbury Plains, and the heat had frayed the nerves of all the residents of Kiward Station. Fleur whined, and Gerald had been insufferable all day. In the morning he had blown up at the workers because the ewes weren't in the mountains yet—and that after having already directed James to herd the flock into the highlands only after the last lamb was born. That afternoon he cursed Lucas for sitting in the garden with Fleur drawing instead of making himself useful in the stables—and thereafter fought with Gwyneira, who explained that nothing could be done with the sheep at the moment. In the afternoon heat, it was best to leave the animals in peace.

Everyone longed for rain, and there was no doubt that a storm was coming. But as the sun went down and dinner was called, there was still not a cloud in the sky. Gwyneira sighed as she entered her overheated room to change. She was not the least bit hungry; she would have preferred to sit on the veranda in the garden and wait for the evening to bring a little relief. Perhaps she would have felt the first storm winds—or conjured them herself, since the Maori believed in weather magic—and Gwyneira had walked around all day with the strange feeling of being part of heaven and earth, mistress of life and death. An exaltation always seized her when she was present for and helped with the arrival of new life. She remembered precisely that she had felt it for the first time during Ruben's birth. Today Cleo was the reason for it. The little dog had given birth to five beautiful, healthy puppies. Now she lay in her basket on the terrace suckling the puppies. No doubt she would have welcomed Gwyneira's company and admiration, but Gerald insisted on her presence at the table—three long courses in a tense atmosphere of constant uncertainty as to what Gerald would say or do. Gwyneira and Lucas had learned long ago to weigh their words carefully when dealing with Gerald; thus, Gwyneira knew that it was better not to speak of Cleo's puppies, and Lucas knew not to mention the watercolors he had sent to Christchurch the day before. George Greenwood wanted to send them to a gallery in London; he was sure that Lucas's talent would be recognized there. However, they had to have something to discuss at the table—otherwise, Gerald would select his own subjects, and those were certain to be unpleasant.

Gwyneira slipped out of her tea gown in low spirits. She was tired of always changing for dinner, and her corset pinched in the heat. But she could dispense with that for today, as she was slender enough to fit into the loose-hanging summer dress she had chosen without it. Without her fish-bone armor, she felt instantly better. She quickly fixed her hair and ran down the steps. Lucas and Gerald stood waiting in front of the fireplace, each with a glass of whiskey in his hand. The mood seemed peaceful, and Gwyneira smiled at both of them.

"Is Fleur already in bed?" Lucas inquired. "I haven't even said good night to her yet."

This was without a doubt the wrong thing to say. Gwyneira had to change the subject quickly.

"She was half-dead from exhaustion. Your painting lesson in the garden was certainly stimulating, but also taxing in the heat. And she couldn't sleep this afternoon because it was so hot. Oh, and there was the excitement over the puppies, of course."

Gwyneira bit her lip. She was making it worse. As expected, Gerald pounced at once.

"So that dog's had another litter, then?" he grumbled. "And once again without complications, right? If only her mistress could learn a thing or two from her. It always goes so quickly with the animals. In heat, mate, pregnant. What's wrong with the two of you, my little princess? Are you never in heat, or—"

"Father, it's time to eat," Lucas interrupted him in measured tones as always. "Please calm yourself and don't insult Gwyneira. There's nothing she can do about it."

"So, the problem lies with you, you...perfect gentleman!" Gerald spat the words out. "Have you completely forgotten the genteel upbringing your mother gave you, eh?"

"Gerald, not in front of the help," said Gwyneira with a side-glance at Kiri, who had just entered the room and was about to serve the first course. It was something light, a salad, and she knew that Gerald would eat little of it. She hoped that the evening would be over all the more quickly for that. She could withdraw as soon as dinner was over.

But this time the otherwise affable and reliable Kiri provoked an incident. The girl had worked herself to the bone all day and now looked tired as she served her employers. Gwyneira wanted to talk to her about it but let it go. Intimate conversations with the help were among the things that always set Gerald off. So she did not say a word about Kiri's inept serving. After all, everyone had had a bad day.

Moana, who had become a rather skillful cook by this time, knew exactly what her employers wanted. She knew Gwyneira and Lucas's preference for light summertime fare, but was also aware that Gerald insisted on at least one meat course. Lamb was served as the main course, and Kiri seemed even more exhausted and inattentive than earlier as she brought out the food. The aroma of the roast mixed with the heavy scent of the roses Lucas had cut in the garden earlier. Gwyneira found the combination obtrusive, almost nauseating, and it seemed that Kiri felt the same way. When she moved to place a slice of lamb in front of Gerald, she suddenly began to sway. Gwyneira leaped up in shock as the girl collapsed beside Gerald's chair.

Without stopping to consider whether it was appropriate to do so, she knelt beside Kiri, shaking the girl as Lucas attempted to clear the plate shards and to provisionally clean the meat juice off the carpet. Witi, who had seen the whole thing, helped his master and called Moana. The cook hurried out to cool Kiri's forehead with a rag soaked in ice water.

Gerald Warden observed the scene with a scowl. The incident further darkened his already bad mood. Damn it, Kiward Station was supposed to be a household worthy of the high nobility. Had anyone ever heard of a serving girl fainting in a London manor and then half the household, young master and mistress included, scurrying about her like domestics?

It was evidently not a grave situation, as Kiri seemed to be coming to already. She looked around, horrified, at the mess she'd made.

"I'm sorry, Mr. Warden! It won't happen again, I promise!" Fearfully, she turned toward the master of the house, who looked her over mercilessly. Witi was wiping at Gerald's sauce-splattered suit.

"That wasn't your fault, Kiri," Gwyneira said gently. "It can happen in weather such as this."

"It's not the weather, miss. Is baby," Moana explained. "Kiri having baby in winter. That why she feels bad today all day and can't smell meat. I tell her, she not to serve, but..."

"So sorry, miss," Kiri moaned.

Gwyneira thought with a silent sigh that they had just hit the lowest point of this botched evening. Did the unfortunate creature have to blurt out that news—of all things—in front of Gerald? However, there was nothing Kiri could do about feeling sick, and Gwyneira forced herself to smile reassuringly.

"But that's no reason to apologize, Kiri," she said kindly. "On the contrary, it's a reason to feel happy. But you must take it easy the next few weeks. For the moment, go home and lie down. Witi and Moana will clean up here."

Kiri curtsied at least three times before Gerald, then disappeared amid more apologies. Gwyneira hoped that would appease him, but his countenance did not change, and he made no move to reassure the girl.

Moana attempted to rescue a portion of the main course, but Gerald shooed her away impatiently.

"Leave it, girl! I've lost my appetite anyway. Get out of here, go to your friend...or get pregnant yourself. But just leave me in peace!"

The old man stood up and went to his liquor cabinet. Another whiskey double. Gwyneira could sense what awaited Lucas and herself. The servants, however, must not have realized it.

"You heard him, Moana...and you too, Witi. The master's giving you the evening off. Don't worry about the kitchen. I'll fetch the dessert myself if we'd like it later. You can clean the carpet tomorrow. Enjoy your evening."

"In village they're doing rain dance, miss," explained Witi as though to justify his departure. "That useful." As though to prove it, he opened the top half of the Dutch door that led to the terrace. Gwyneira hoped a breeze would blow through, but the hot air outside did not stir. Drumbeats and song could be heard from the direction of the Maori village.

"There you go," Gwyneira said amiably to her servant. "You will make yourself more useful in the village than here. Just go. Mr. Warden is not feeling well."

She breathed a sigh when the door closed behind the butler. Moana and Witi wouldn't waste any time, except to perhaps tidy up the kitchen. They would gather up their things and be gone within minutes.

"A sherry to calm your nerves, my love?" Lucas asked.

Gwyneira nodded. She wished, not for the first time, to be able to drink just once with the same lack of restraint as men. But Gerald did not give her a moment to enjoy her sherry. He had gulped down his whiskey and now stared at both of them with bloodshot eyes.

"So this Maori hussy is pregnant now too. And old O'Keefe has a son. Everyone around here is fertile; everywhere there's bleating and screaming and yelping. Only you two can't seem to make anything happen. Where's the problem, Miss Prude or Mister Limp Dick? Who's the problem?"

Gwyneira looked into her glass, mortified. The best thing to do was simply not to listen. The drums could still be heard outside. Gwyneira tried to concentrate on those and to forget about Gerald. Lucas, on the other hand, tried calmly to placate him.

"Father, we don't know what the problem is. It must be God's will. You know that not every marriage is blessed with many children. You and Mother only had one child, you know."

"Your mother..." Gerald reached for the bottle again. He no longer even made the effort to pour himself a glass, and instead raised the bottle directly to his lips. "Your wonderful mother thought only of you, boy, you...she gave me an earful every night; that would drive the lust right out of even the best cocksman." Gerald cast a hateful glance at the portrait of his dead wife.

Gwyneira looked on with growing fear. The old man had never let himself get this carried away. Until this moment, Lucas's mother had always been mentioned with the highest regard. Gwyneira knew that Lucas had deified her memory. She looked for an excuse, but there was nothing she could do. Gerald would not have listened to her anyway. He turned once again to Lucas.

"But I didn't fail," he said, slurring. "Because you're male if nothing else...or at least look the part. But are you really, Lucas Warden?" Gerald stood up and approached Lucas in a threatening manner. Gwyneira saw the rage blazing in his eyes.

"Father..."

"Answer, limp dick! Do you know what I'm saying? Or are you a bugger like they whisper in the stables? Oh yes, they whisper, Lucas! Little Johnny Oates claims you're making eyes at him. He can hardly keep you off him...is that true?"

Gerald raged at his son.

Lucas's face went beet red. "I don't make eyes at anyone," he whispered. At least he had not done so intentionally. Could it be that those men had caught a whiff of his most secret, sinful thoughts?

Gerald spat before turning his attention to Gwyneira.

"And you—my prude little princess. Don't you know how to get him going? But you know how to turn a fellow on. I still think often of Wales, how you would look at me...a li'l hussy, I thought, such a shame for an ol' aristocrat in England...she needs a real man. And in the stables they make eyes at you, princess. All the boys're infatuated with you. Did you know that? You encourage 'em, eh? But you're cold as ice to your genteel husband."

Gwyneira sank deeper into her chair. The burning gaze of the old man shamed her. She wished she had put on a more conservative dress. Gerald's gaze wandered from her pale face to her neckline. If he looked closely, he might notice...

"And what's this?" he intoned scornfully. "Not wearing a corset today, princess? Are you hoping that a real man'll come by when your limp dick husband is lying in his bed?"

Gwyneira leaped up as Gerald reached for her. Instinctively she backed away. Gerald followed her.

"Aha, when you see a real man, you run away. I thought as much... lady! You're making me beg. But a real man don't give up."

Gerald lunged for her bodice. Gwyneira stumbled as he pressed into her. Lucas threw himself between them.

"Father, you forget yourself!"

"Huh? I forget myself? No, my dear boy." The old man struck Lucas with a hard blow to the chest. Lucas did not dare strike back. "I was out of my mind when I bought this thoroughbred pony here for you. Such a shame for you, such a shame...shoulda took 'er straightaway for myself. Then I'd have a stable full o' heirs."

Gerald bent over Gwyneira, who had fallen back into her chair. She tried to stand up and flee, but he knocked her to the ground with one blow and was on top of her before she could sit up.

"Now I'll show you two," Gerald wheezed. He was three sheets to the wind, and his words failed him, but not his strength. Gwyneira saw the naked lust in his eyes.

In a state of panic, she tried to remember. What had happened in Wales? Had she provoked him? Had he always felt that way about her, and had she only been too blind to see it?

"Father..." Lucas seized him halfheartedly from behind, but Gerald's fist was faster. Drunk or not, his blows struck true. Lucas was knocked back and lost consciousness for several seconds. Gerald tore his pants open. Gwyneira heard Cleo barking on the terrace. The dog was scratching on the door in alarm.

"Now I'll show you how, princess…now I'll show you what it's like."

Gwyneira whimpered as he ripped apart her dress, shredded her silk underwear, and brutally thrust himself into her. She smelled whiskey, sweat, and the sauce that had been spilled on his shirt, and was overcome with disgust. She saw hate and triumph in Gerald's glowing evil eyes. With one hand he held her down; with the other he kneaded her breasts as he kissed her neck greedily. She bit him when he tried to shove his tongue down her throat. After the initial shock, she began to fight back, defending herself so desperately that he seized both her hands in order to hold her down. But still he kept thrusting into her. The pain was all but unbearable. Now she knew what Helen had meant, and she clung to her friend's words: "At least it's over quickly."

Despairing, Gwyneira held still, listening to the drumming outside and to Cleo's hysterical barking. Hopefully she wouldn't attempt to jump over the half door. Gwyneira forced herself to remain calm. It had to be over soon.

Gerald noticed her resignation and took it for consent. "Now… you like that, eh, princess?" he wheezed, thrusting harder. "Now you like it! Can't even…get enough, eh? It's different…a real man, like me, eh?"

Gwyneira did not have the strength to curse him. The pain and humiliation seemed to have no end. Seconds stretched into hours. Gerald moaned, wheezed, and spewed incomprehensible words that merged with the drumming and barking in a deafening cacophony. Gwyneira could not even have said herself whether she screamed or endured the torture in silence. She just wanted Gerald to get off her, and if that meant him…

Gwyneira felt a final wave of revulsion as he finally emptied himself into her. She felt soiled, defiled, degraded. She turned her head away in despair as he sank down on top of her, wheezing as he pressed his hot face into her neck. His heavy body pinned her to the ground. Gwyneira felt like she couldn't breathe. She tried to push him off her, but she could not manage it from beneath him. Why wasn't he moving? Did he die on top of her? She would not have been sorry if he had. If she had had a knife, she would have stabbed him in the gut.

But then Gerald stirred. He picked himself up without looking at her. What was he feeling? Satisfaction? Shame?

The old man stood there swaying, and reached for the bottle.

"Let that be a lesson to you two," he said halfheartedly. Not triumphantly, but as though he were now remorseful. He cast a side-glance at Gwyneira, who lay below him whimpering. "Too bad if it hurt. But in the end you liked it, right, princess?"

Gerald stumbled up the stairs without looking back. Gwyneira wept silently.

Finally Lucas bent over her.

"Don't look at me! Don't touch me!"

"But I'm not doing anything to you, my love." Lucas moved to help her up, but she drove him away.

"Get out of here," she said, sobbing. "It's too late now; you can't do anything now."

"But..." Lucas faltered. "What was I supposed to do?"

Gwyneira could have thought of quite a few things. He would not even have needed a knife—the fire iron right next to Lucas would have been enough to strike his father down.

Yet the idea did not seem to even have crossed Lucas's mind. Other things took precedence. "But...but you didn't like it, then?" he asked softly. "You didn't really..."

Every muscle in Gwyneira's body hurt, but her rage enabled her to sit up. "And even if, you...you limp dick?" she blew up at Lucas. She had never before felt so insulted, so betrayed. How could this idiot believe she could possibly have enjoyed this humiliation? Suddenly she wanted nothing more than to hurt Lucas. "What if someone else really could do it better? Would you go up to him and challenge him to a duel, Fleur's father? Yes? Or would you once again tuck your tail between your legs, like you just did for a fight with an old man? I'm sorry I'm such a burden to you! Like your father who's too much for you! What exactly is a 'bugger,' Lucas? Or is that something else one prefers to keep a secret from ladies?" Gwyneira saw the pain in his eyes and forgot her anger. What was she doing? Why was she taking out her anger toward Gerald on Lucas? Lucas could not help who he was.

"Fine, well and good, I don't want to know," she said. "Get out of my sight, Lucas. Disappear. I don't want to see you again. I don't want to see anyone. Get the hell out of here, Lucas Warden! Go away!"

Imprisoned by her misery and pain, she did not hear him go. She tried to concentrate on the drumming in order not to have to hear the thoughts beating in her brain. Then she remembered her dog. The barking had stopped; Cleo was now only whining. Gwyneira hauled herself to the terrace door, let Cleo in, and dragged the basket with the puppies over the threshold as the first drops fell outside. Cleo licked the tears from her face while she listened intently to the rain lashing at the tiles...*rangi* wept.

Gwyneira wept.

She managed to drag herself to her room as the storm dumped itself upon Kiward Station; the air became cooler and her head clearer. She finally fell asleep next to her dog and its litter on the fluffy pale blue carpet that Lucas had picked out for her so many years before.

She did not notice that Lucas left the house before dawn.

Kiri did not remark on what she saw when she came into Gwyneira's room the next morning. She said nothing about the untouched bed, the torn dress, or Gwyneira's dirty, blood-speckled body. Yes, this time she had bled.

"You bathe, miss. Then is better for certain," Kiri said sympathetically. "Young master surely not meant it so. Men drunk, weather god angry, bad day yesterday."

Gwyneira nodded and let herself be led to the bath. Kiri ran the water and moved to add some flower extract, but Gwyneira stopped her. The nauseating scent of roses from the evening before was still too fresh.

"I bring breakfast to room, yes?" Kiri asked. "Fresh waffles, Moana made for saying sorry to Mr. Warden. But Mr. Warden still not awake."

Gwyneira wondered how she was ever supposed to face Gerald Warden again. She felt somewhat better after she had soaped herself up several times, thoroughly washing Gerald's sweat and stench from herself. But she was still sore and it hurt to move the least bit. That would pass, she knew, but the disgrace she would feel for the rest of her life.

Finally she wrapped herself in a light bathrobe and left the bathroom. Kiri had opened the window in her room, and the tatters of her clothes had disappeared. The world outside seemed freshly washed after the rainstorm. The air was cool and clear. Gwyneira breathed deeply, trying to bring her thoughts to rest as well. Yesterday's experience had been abominable—but no worse than what happened to some women every night. If she worked at it, she would be able to forget it. She simply had to act as though nothing had occurred.

She nevertheless shrank back when she heard the door. Cleo growled, sensing Gwyneira's anxiety. But it was only Kiri and Fleurette. The little girl was in a disgruntled mood. Gwyneira couldn't blame her. Normally she woke the child herself with a kiss, and then she and Lucas had breakfast together with Fleur. This "family hour" without Gerald, who was generally still sleeping off his whiskey at that hour, was sacred to them, and all three of them seemed to enjoy it. Gwyneira had assumed that Lucas had seen to Fleur that morning, but apparently, the child had been left on her own. Her attire was correspondingly adventurous. She wore a skirt that she had pulled on over an incorrectly buttoned dress like a poncho.

"Daddy's gone," the little girl said.

Gwyneira shook her head. "No, Fleur. Daddy is not gone. Perhaps he went for a ride. He…we…we had a bit of a fight with Grandfather yesterday." She admitted it unwillingly, but Fleur had so often been a witness to her confrontations with Gerald that it couldn't possibly come as a surprise to her.

"Oh yes, maybe Daddy went for a ride," said Fleur. "With Flyer. He's gone too, I mean, Mr. McKenzie said. But why is Daddy going for a ride before breakfast?"

Gwyneira also wondered about that. Clearing the head at a gallop through the wilderness was more her style than Lucas's. He also rarely saddled the horse himself. The hands joked that when it came to farm work, he let the shepherds call his horse while he sat on top of it. And why did he take the oldest workhorse? Though Lucas wasn't an enthusiastic rider, he was a good one. Now only occasionally ridden by Fleur, Old Flyer would make for a dull ride. But maybe Fleur and James were both mistaken and Flyer's and Lucas's disappearances had nothing to do with each other. The horse might have broken out. Such things were always happening.

"Daddy will no doubt be back soon," Gwyneira said. "Have you already checked his studio? But come now, eat a waffle first."

Kiri had set the breakfast table by the window. She poured Gwyneira some coffee. Even Fleur received a spot of coffee with a lot of milk.

"In his room he isn't, miss." The housemaid turned to Gwyneira. "Looked in, Witi. Bed not touched. Surely somewhere on farm. Ashamed because of..." She looked at Gwyneira meaningfully.

Gwyneira began to be worried. Lucas had no reason to feel ashamed...or did he? Had Gerald not disgraced him just as he had her? And she herself...it was unforgivable how she had treated Lucas.

"We'll go looking for him right away, Fleur. We'll no doubt find him," Gwyneira said, uncertain whether she meant to comfort herself or the child with those words.

They did not find Lucas, either in the house or on the farm. Flyer had not reappeared either. James reported that an ancient saddle and an often repatched bridle were also missing.

"Is there something I should know?" he asked quietly, looking at Gwyneira's pale face and noting her difficulty walking.

Gwyneira shook her head, accepting that, having hurt Lucas, she was now hurting James too: "Nothing that has anything to do with you."

James, she knew for a fact, would have killed Gerald.

6

Lucas's absence stretched into weeks. A circumstance that, astoundingly, contributed to somewhat normalizing Gwyneira and Gerald's relationship—after all, they had to make arrangements for Fleur between the two of them. In the first few days after Lucas's departure, they were brought together by their mutual concern over what might have happened to him or what he might have done to himself. Attempts to track him down proved fruitless, and after a great deal of contemplation, Gwyneira did not believe he had resorted to suicide. She had looked through Lucas's things and established that a few simple articles of clothing were missing—to her astonishment, precisely those that her husband had liked the least. Lucas had packed work clothes, rain gear, underwear, and a very small amount of money. That fit with the old horse and the old saddle: he clearly did not want to take anything from Gerald; the separation should be a clean break. It hurt Gwyneira that he had left her without a word. As far as she could tell, he had not taken anything to remember her or their daughter by, with the exception of a pocketknife she had once given him as a gift. It appeared that she hadn't meant anything to him; the transient friendship that had bound the couple had not even been worth a farewell letter to him.

Gerald inquired about his son in Haldon—which naturally provided fodder for the gossip mill—as well as in Christchurch, with more discretion and the help of George Greenwood. Neither provided any answers; Lucas Warden had not been seen in either place.

"God only knows where he could be," Gwyneira said, airing her grief to Helen. "In Otago, in the gold diggers' camps, on the West Coast, maybe even on the North Island. Gerald wants to have inquiries made, but that's hopeless. If he doesn't want to be found, he won't be found."

Helen shrugged and put the inevitable teakettle on. "Maybe it's for the best. It certainly wasn't good for him to be so completely dependent on Gerald. Now he can prove himself—and Gerald will no longer pester you for not having a child. But why did he disappear so suddenly? Was there really no reason? No fight?"

Gwyneira said no, reddening as she did so. She had told no one, not even her best friend, about her rape. If she kept it to herself, she hoped, the memory would eventually fade. Then it would be as though the evening had never happened, as though it had been an ugly nightmare. Gerald seemed to look at the incident the same way. He was exceptionally polite to Gwyneira, rarely looked at her, and took pains to not even touch her. They saw one another at mealtimes, so as not to give the servants reason to gossip, and managed at those times to make small talk. Gerald still drank as before, but now generally waited until after dinner when Gwyneira had already retired. Gwyneira took Helen's favorite student, the now fifteen-year-old Rongo Rongo, for her personal lady's maid, and insisted that the girl sleep in her room to always be at hand. She hoped to hold off any new assaults by Gerald, but her concern was unfounded. Gerald's behavior remained irreproachable. In that sense, Gwyneira might have been able to forget that fateful summer night at some point. But there were, in fact, consequences. When she missed her period for the second time and Rongo Rongo smiled meaningfully when dressing her, stroking her stomach, Gwyneira was forced to admit that she was pregnant.

"I don't want to have it!" she said, sobbing after riding at full speed to Helen. She had not been able to wait for school to end to speak to her friend. Helen could tell by her horrified countenance that something terrible must have happened. She let the children go early, sent Fleur and Ruben to play outside, and took Gwyneira into her arms.

"Did they find Lucas?" she asked quietly.

Gwyneira looked at her as though she were crazy. "Lucas? What about Lucas…oh, it's much worse, Helen; I'm pregnant! And I don't want to have the baby!"

"You're a mess," Helen murmured, leading her friend into the house. "Come now, I'll make some tea, and then we'll talk about it. Why in heaven's name aren't you happy about the baby? You've been trying for years to have one after all, and now…or are you afraid that the baby might come too late? Is it not Lucas's?" Helen looked searchingly at Gwyneira. She had sometimes suspected that there was a secret behind Fleur's birth—no woman could miss the way Gwyneira's eyes lit up at the sight of James McKenzie. But she hadn't seen the two of them together for a long time. And Gwyneira would never be so stupid as to take a lover right after her husband left. Or did Lucas leave because there already was a lover? Helen could not imagine that. Gwyneira was a lady. Certainly not faultless, but faultlessly discreet.

"The baby is a Warden," Gwyneira answered firmly. "There can be no doubt about it. But I still don't want it!"

"But it's not something that requires your approval," Helen said helplessly. She could not follow Gwyneira's thoughts. "When you're pregnant, you're pregnant."

"Nonsense! There has to be some way to get rid of the baby. Miscarriages happen all the time."

"Yes, but not to healthy young women like you." Helen shook her head. "Why don't you go to Matahorua? She can surely tell you whether the baby is healthy."

"Maybe she can help me," Gwyneira said hopefully. "Maybe she knows a potion or something. Back on the ship, Daphne said something to Dorothy about 'abortives'…"

"Gwyneira, you can't even think of such a thing!" Helen had heard rumors of "abortives" in Liverpool; her father had buried some of their victims. "That's ungodly! And dangerous. You could die from that. And why, in heaven's name…"

"I'm going to Matahorua!" Gwyneira declared. "Don't try to stop me. I don't want this baby!"

Matahorua motioned Gwyneira to a row of stones behind the communal houses where the two could be alone. She too must have seen from Gwyneira's face that something serious had happened. But this time, she would have to sort it out without a translator—Gwyneira had left Rongo Rongo at home. The last thing she needed was another conspirator.

Matahorua made a noncommittal face as she offered Gwyneira a seat on one of the stones. Her expression was no doubt meant to be friendly, perhaps it was even a smile, but it looked threatening to Gwyneira. The tattoos on the face of the old witch doctor seemed to alter every facial expression, and her figure cast strange shadows in the sunlight. "Baby. I already know from Rongo Rongo. Strong baby...much power. But also much anger."

"I don't want the baby!" Gwyneira cried out without looking at the witch doctor. "Is there anything you can do?"

Matahorua sought eye contact with the young woman. "What should I do? Kill baby?"

Gwyneira winced. She had not yet dared to phrase it so explicitly. But that's what it came down to. Feelings of guilt rose up within her.

Matahorua looked her over attentively, studying both her face and her body. As always she seemed to be looking through the person and into some distant place known only to herself.

"Is important to you baby die?" she asked quietly.

Gwyneira suddenly felt anger welling up inside her. "Would I be here otherwise?" she burst out.

Matahorua shrugged. "Strong baby. If baby die, you die too. Important enough?"

Gwyneira shuddered. What made Matahorua so sure? Why did no one ever doubt her words, no matter how nonsensical they might be? Could she really see into the future? Gwyneira considered. She felt nothing for the baby in her womb, at most repugnance and hatred, just as she felt for its father. But the hatred was not so violent as to be worth dying for. Gwyneira was young and enjoyed life. Besides, she was needed. What would become of Fleurette if she lost her second parent as well? Gwyneira decided to let the matter rest. Perhaps she could give birth to this unfortunate child and then forget about it? Gerald should be the one to care for it.

Matahorua laughed. "I see you not die. You live, baby live...not happy. But live. And will someone be who want..."

Gwyneira frowned. "Who wants what?"

"There will be someone who want baby. In the end. Makes... rounds..." Matahorua outlined a circle with her finger, then rummaged around in her bag. Finally she dug out an almost round piece of jade and handed it to Gwyneira. "There, for the baby."

Gwyneira took the small stone and thanked her. She did not know why, but she felt better.

None of that stopped Gwyneira from attempting every conceivable method of inducing a miscarriage. She worked in the garden to the point of exhaustion, bent over as often as possible, ate unripe apples until the indigestion nearly killed her, and trained Igraine's newest daughter, a remarkably difficult foal. To James's astonishment, she even insisted on teaching the unruly animal to accept a sidesaddle—a last, desperate effort, since Gwyneira was naturally aware that the sidesaddle did not make her seating less secure, but more so. Accidents in the sidesaddle almost always resulted from the horse stumbling and the rider being unable to free herself from the seat and roll away. Such accidents often ended in death. But the mare, Vivian, was just as sure of foot as her mother—and Gwyneira had no intention of dying with her baby. Her last hope was the considerable jolting that came from trotting, which could not be easily avoided in a sidesaddle. After a half hour of riding at full speed, she could hardly stay on the horse for the pains it caused in her sides, but it did not seem to bother the baby a bit. It withstood the dangerous first three months without a problem, and Gwyneira wept with rage when she saw that her belly was beginning to swell. At first she tried to contain the telltale curves by pulling her laces tighter, but that would not work for long. In the end, she resigned herself to her fate and steeled herself against the inevitable torrent of best wishes. Who else could ever know how unwanted the little Warden was who was now growing within her womb?

The women in Haldon naturally recognized Gwyneira's pregnancy right away and immediately started turning the rumor mill. With Mrs. Warden pregnant and Mr. Warden absconded—wild speculation ensued. Gwyneira did not care. It horrified her, however, to think that Gerald would say something about it. But more than anything, she was afraid of James McKenzie's reaction. Soon he wouldn't be able to help noticing it or at least hearing about it. And she couldn't tell him the truth. She had been avoiding him since Lucas's disappearance because there were questions in his eyes. Now he would want answers. Gwyneira was ready for accusations and anger, but not for his honest reaction. It caught her completely off guard, when she ran into him one morning in the stables in his riding gear and raincoat—because it was drizzling again—and with his saddlebags packed. He was just tying a portmanteau to the back of his bony gray horse.

"I'm going, Gwyn," he said calmly when she looked at him questioningly. "You can imagine why."

"You're going?" Gwyneira did not understand. "Where? What..."

"I'm going away, Gwyneira. I'm leaving Kiward Station and looking for another job." James turned his back to her.

"You're leaving me?" The words burst out before she could stop herself. But the anguish had come upon her so suddenly—the shock shook her to her core. How could he leave her alone? She needed him, more than ever.

James broke out laughing, but he sounded more bitter than amused. "Does that surprise you? Did you think you had a claim to me?"

"Of course not." Gwyneira sought support from the stable door. "But I thought you..."

"You can't really be expecting declarations of love now, can you, Gwyn? Not after what you've done." James continued securing his saddle as though he were having a casual conversation.

"But I didn't do anything!" Gwyneira said, defending herself, but she knew how wrong it sounded.

"Oh no?" James turned around and looked her over with a cold gaze. "So that thing in there is a new edition of the immaculate conception." He gestured toward her stomach. "Don't tell tales, Gwyneira. I'd prefer to hear the truth. Who was the stallion? Did he come from better stables than me? With a better pedigree? Better opportunities? Perhaps a title of nobility?"

"James, I never wanted..." Gwyneira did not know what to say. She would have loved to come clean with the truth, to unburden her soul. But then he'd do Gerald in. Then there would be dead men or at least injured ones, and afterward, all the world would know where Fleurette had come from.

"It was that Greenwood, wasn't it? A real gentleman. A good-looking fellow, educated, well-mannered, and no doubt very discreet. Shame that you didn't know him back when we..."

"It wasn't George! What's gotten into you? George came because of Helen. And now he has a wife in Christchurch. There was never any reason to be jealous." Gwyneira hated the imploring tone in her voice.

"So who was it, then?" James stepped closer to her almost threateningly. Fired up, he seized her upper arm as though he wanted to shake her. "Tell me, Gwyn! Someone in Christchurch? The young Lord Barrington? You like him, don't you? Tell me, Gwyn. I have a right to know!"

Gwyneira shook her head. "I can't tell you, and you have no right to know."

"And Lucas? He figured you out, didn't he? Did he catch you, Gwyn? In bed with someone else? Did he have you watched and then give you the nod? What was between you and Lucas?"

Gwyneira looked at him desperately. "It was nothing like that. You don't understand..."

"Then explain it to me, Gwyn! Explain to me why your husband left you in the middle of the night, and not just you but the old man too, the child, and his heir. I'd like to know." James's face softened, though he still kept a tight grip on her. Gwyneira wondered why she wasn't afraid. But she had never been afraid of James McKenzie. Behind all the mistrust and anger, she still saw love in his eyes.

"I can't, James. I can't. Please accept that. Don't be angry. And please don't leave me!" Gwyneira let herself slump into his shoulder. She wanted to be near him and didn't care whether she was welcome or not.

James did not push her away, but he did not embrace her either. He just let go of her arm and nudged her softly away from him until they no longer touched.

"No matter what happened, Gwyn, I can't stay. Maybe I could if you had an explanation for all this...if you would really trust me. But as things are, I don't understand you. You're so bullheaded, so fixated on names and heirs that even now you want to stay true to the memory of your husband...and yet you're pregnant by someone else."

"Lucas isn't dead!" Gwyneira cried out.

James shrugged. "That's beside the point. Whether he's dead or alive, you would never speak frankly with me. And that's getting to be too much for me. I can't see you every day but make no claim on you. I've been trying for five years, but anytime you come into view, I want to touch you, kiss you, be with you. Instead, it's 'Miss Warden' and 'Mr. McKenzie.' You're polite and distant—although one can see the longing in you just like in me. That kills me, Gwyn. I could have borne it if you had borne it too. But now...it's too much, Gwyn. The baby is too much. At least tell me whose it is!"

Gwyneira shook her head again. It wrenched her apart inside, but she did not reveal the truth. "I'm sorry, James. I can't. If you have to go because of that, then go."

She suppressed a sob.

James put a bridle on the horse, moving to lead it outside. As always, Daimon followed him. James stroked the dog.

"Will you take him?" Gwyneira asked in a choked voice.

James said no. "He doesn't belong to me. I can't just let the best breeding dog on Kiward Station walk off."

"But he'll miss you." Gwyneira observed with an aching heart how the dog stuck to him.

"There are a great many things that I'll miss too, but we'll all learn to live with that."

The dog barked in protest as James started to leave the stables.

"I'm giving him to you." Gwyneira suddenly wanted James to have a memento of her. Of her and Fleur. Of their days in the highlands. Of the dog performance at her wedding. Of all the things they had done together, the thoughts they had shared.

"You can't give him away. He doesn't belong to you," James said softly. "Mr. Warden bought him in Wales, don't you remember?"

Certainly Gwyneira remembered. Just as she remembered the polite words she had exchanged with Gerald back then. At the time, she had thought he was a gentleman, somewhat exotic perhaps, but honorable. And how well she remembered the first days with James, when she had taught him the tricks for training the young dogs. He had taken her seriously even though she was a girl.

Gwyneira looked around her. Cleo's puppies were ready to be sold, but still followed after their mother and scurried about Gwyneira now. She bent over and picked up the biggest and most beautiful of the puppies. A young bitch, almost black, with Cleo's typical collie smile.

"But these are mine to give away. They belong to me. Take her, James. Please take her!" She thrust the puppy quickly into James's hands. The puppy immediately tried to lick his face.

James smiled and blinked, ashamed of the tears forming in his eyes. "Her name is Friday, right? Friday, Robinson's companion in his loneliness."

Gwyneira nodded. "You don't have to be lonely," she said softly.

James petted the dog. "Not anymore. Thank you, miss."

"James..." She stepped closer to him and raised her face to him. "James, I wish it were your child."

James kissed her lightly on the mouth, as softly and calmly as only Lucas had ever done before.

"I wish you luck, Gwyn. I wish you happiness."

Gwyneira wept without stopping once James had gone. She watched him from her window as he rode away over the fields, the little dog in front of him on the saddle. He turned toward the highlands. Or was he taking her shortcut to Haldon? It didn't matter to Gwyneira; she had lost him. She had lost both men. Aside from Fleur, there was only Gerald and this cursed, unwanted baby.

Gerald Warden did not broach the subject of his daughter-in-law's pregnancy, not even when it became so obvious that anyone could tell at first glance. Thus the question of delivery was not discussed. No midwife was brought to the house this time, no doctor consulted to check on the course of the pregnancy. Gwyneira herself tried to ignore her condition as much as possible. Up until the last few weeks of her pregnancy, she rode the most spirited horses and tried not to think about the birth. Maybe the baby wouldn't survive if she did not receive the help of a specialist.

Contrary to Helen's expectations, Gwyneira's feeling toward the baby had not changed over the course of her pregnancy. The first stirrings of the new life, which she had greeted so enthusiastically for Ruben and Fleur, she did not even mention. And when the baby once kicked so hard that Gwyneira cried out, no remark on the obvious health of the unborn baby followed; instead, she just said angrily, "It's bothering me again today. I just wish it were gone!"

Helen wondered what Gwyneira meant by that. The baby would not just disappear when it was born but announce its rights at the top of its lungs. Perhaps Gwyneira's maternal instincts would finally kick in then.

Kiri's time was approaching first, however. The young Maori was delighted about her baby and constantly tried to draw Gwyneira into her joy. She compared their belly sizes and teased Gwyneira that her baby may be younger but was certainly much bigger. Gwyneira's belly was indeed enormous. She tried to hide it, but sometimes, in her darkest hours, she feared that she was carrying twins.

"Impossible!" said Helen. "Matahorua would have noticed that."

Even Rongo Rongo laughed at her mistress's fears. "No, there's only one baby in there. But beautiful, strong. No easy birth, miss. But no danger. My grandmother says it will be a gorgeous baby."

When the pains set in for Kiri, Rongo Rongo disappeared. As an ardent student of Matahorua, she was, despite her youth, much sought after as a midwife and spent many nights in the Maori village. This time she came back toward morning, looking pleased. Kiri had given birth to a healthy girl.

Just three days later, she showed her baby off proudly to Gwyneira.

"I her name Marama. Beautiful name for beautiful baby. Means 'moon.' I bring her with me to work. Can play with baby from miss!"

Gerald Warden would surely have his own opinions about that, but Gwyneira did not comment on the remark. For a while now, Gwyneira had no longer found it difficult to defy her father-in-law. Gerald generally ceded ground silently. The power relations on Kiward Station had shifted without Gwyneira's really understanding why.

This time no one stood in the garden as Gwyneira lay in pain, and no one waited anxiously in the salon. Gwyneira did not know whether anyone had informed Gerald of the imminent birth and would not have cared either way. The old man was probably spending another night with a bottle in his room—and by the time it was over, he would no longer be capable of comprehending the news, regardless.

As Rongo Rongo had predicted, this birth did not go as smoothly as Fleurette's. The baby was considerably larger—and Gwyneira was unwilling. With Fleurette she had yearned for the birth, hung on the midwife's every word, and striven to be a truly shining example of motherhood. With this birth, she let everything happen to her in a stupor; at times she bore the pain stoically, at others with defiance. The entire time, she was plagued by the memory of the pain under which this child had been conceived. She thought she could feel Gerald's weight on top of her again, that she could smell his sweat. Between the pains, she vomited several times, felt weak and beaten down, and finally cried out in anger and pain. By the end she was totally drained and wanted nothing more than to die. Or even better, that this being that held tight in her womb like an evil parasite should die.

"Just come out," she moaned. "Just come out and leave me in peace."

After nearly two full days of torture—and, toward the end, of almost maniacal hatred for everyone who had done this to her—Gwyneira gave birth to a son. She felt nothing but relief.

"Such a beautiful little boy, miss!" Rongo beamed. "Like Matahorua said. Wait, I'll wash him off, and then you can hold him. We'll give him a little time before we cut the umbilical cord."

Gwyneira shook her head wildly. "No, cut it, Rongo. And take him away. I don't want to hold him. I want to sleep...have to rest..."

"But that you can do in minute. Look at baby first. Here, isn't sweet?" Rongo had expertly cleaned the baby and laid it at Gwyneira's breast. He was making his first suckling motions. Gwyneira pushed it away. Fine, it was healthy, it was complete with all its tiny fingers and toes, but she still didn't like it.

"Take it away, Rongo!" she demanded with authority.

Rongo did not understand. "But where should I take it, miss? It need its mother!"

Gwyneira shrugged. "Take it to Mr. Warden. He wanted an heir; now he has it. He should figure out what to do with it. Just leave me in peace. Will it take long, Rongo? Oh, God, no, it's starting again..." Gwyneira moaned. "It can't really take another three hours before the afterbirth comes out."

"Is now tired, miss. Is normal," Kiri said in a conciliatory tone when an anxious Rongo came into the kitchen with the baby. Kiri and Moana were busy cleaning up after the dinner that Gerald had taken by himself. Little Marama slumbered in a small basket.

"That isn't normal!" Rongo contradicted her. "Matahorua has brought thousands of children into the world, but no mother has acted like Miss Warden."

"Oh, every mother is different," maintained Kiri, thinking back to the morning when she had found Gwyneira lying on the floor in her room in a torn dress. There was a great deal to suggest that this child had been conceived that night. Gwyneira might have her reasons for not loving it.

"And what I now do with it?" Rongo asked hesitantly. "I can't take it to Mr. Warden. He can't have children around him."

Kiri laughed. "Baby needs also milk, no whiskey. Start with that soon enough. No, no, Rongo, leave it just here." Calmly she unbuttoned her servant's dress, unveiled her plump breasts, and took the child from Rongo's arms. "That now better."

The newborn began to suckle greedily at once. Kiri rocked him gently. When he finally fell asleep at her breast, she laid him next to Marama in her basket.

"Tell miss, it well looked after."

Gwyneira did not even want to know. She was already asleep and did not ask about the baby in the morning either. Only when Witi brought in a bouquet of flowers and gestured at the card hanging from them did she show any reaction at all.

"From Mr. Warden."

An expression of revulsion and hatred, but also of curiosity, crossed her face. She tore the card open.

I thank you for Paul Gerald Terence.

Gwyneira screamed, flung the flowers across the room, and ripped the card into shreds.

"Witi!" she ordered the shocked butler. "Or better, Rongo, words won't fail you! Go immediately to Mr. Warden, and tell him the baby will only be named Paul Terence, or I'll strangle it in the crib."

Witi did not understand, but Rongo looked horrified.

"I'll tell him," she promised quietly.

Three days later the Wardens' heir was baptized Paul Terence Lucas. His mother stayed far from the celebration; she was indisposed. But her servants knew better. Gwyneira had yet to even look at the child.

7

"When are you finally going to introduce Paul to me?" Helen asked impatiently. Naturally, Gwyneira was not able to ride immediately after giving birth, and even now, four weeks later, she came with Fleur in the coach. However, this was her third visit, and to all appearances she had recovered from the strain of the delivery. Helen only wondered why she did not bring the baby along. After Fleur's birth Gwyneira had not been able to wait to show off her little daughter to her friend. Yet she hardly mentioned her son. And even now, when Helen inquired about him explicitly, Gwyneira only made a dismissive gesture with her hand.

"Oh, soon. It's tiresome, carrying him around, and he cries all the time when you take him away from Kiri and Marama. He feels comfortable with them, so what's to be done?"

"Well, I would like to see him at least once," admitted Helen. "What's with you, Gwyn? Is there something wrong with him?"

Fleurette and Ruben had set off on an adventure right after Gwyneira's arrival, and the Maori children would not be coming that day because of some celebration in their village. Helen figured that this was the ideal day to press Gwyneira to tell her the truth.

She shook her head disinterestedly. "What could be wrong with him? Everything is there. He's a strong baby—and finally a boy. I've fulfilled the duty expected of me." Gwyneira played with her teacup. "And now, tell me what's new. Did the organ for the church in Haldon finally arrive? And will the reverend finally allow you to play it since he hasn't found a male organist?"

"Forget the stupid organ, Gwyn." Helen took refuge in impatient words but felt helpless. "I asked you about your baby! What is going on with you? You talk about every puppy with more excitement than you talk about Paul. And he's your son, you know...you should be over the moon with happiness. And what about the proud grandfather? In Haldon they're already whispering that something's not right with the baby because Gerald hasn't bought a single round to celebrate his grandson."

Gwyneira shrugged. "I don't know what Gerald's thinking. Can we talk about something else now?"

Determined to relax and enjoy herself, she took a tea biscuit.

Helen would have liked to shake her.

"No, we can't, Gwyn. You'll tell me right now what's going on! Something must have happened with you or the baby or Gerald. Are you angry with Lucas for leaving you?"

Gwyneira shook her head. "Oh that, that's ancient history. He must have had his reasons."

In reality she did not know how she felt about Lucas. Though she was angry because he had left her alone in this quandary, she could understand his flight. Yet Gwyneira had not felt much of anything since James's departure and Paul's birth; it was as though she were keeping her thoughts and feelings under a bell jar. If she did not feel anything, she would not be vulnerable.

"Those reasons didn't have anything to do with you? Or with the baby?" Helen drilled further. "Don't lie to me, Gwyn, you have to clear this up. Otherwise, everyone will be talking about it. In Haldon they're already whispering, and the Maori are talking too. You know they raise their children communally; the word 'mother' does not have the same meaning for them as for us, and Kiri does not find it strange to care for Paul as well. But the lack of interest you show your baby... you should ask Matahorua for advice."

Gwyneira shook her head. "What advice is she supposed to give me? Can she bring Lucas back? Can she—" She stopped short, shocked. She had nearly given away more than anyone in the world was ever allowed to know.

"Maybe she could help you get along better with the child," Helen said. "Why don't you breastfeed it? Are you not producing milk?"

"Kiri has enough milk in her for two," Gwyneira said dismissively. "And I'm a lady. It's not common for women like myself to breastfeed their children in England."

"You've gone crazy, Gwyn." Helen shook her head. She was slowly growing angry. "At least think of better excuses. No one believes all that about your being a lady. So, once again: did Lucas leave because you were pregnant?"

Gwyneira shook her head. "Lucas doesn't know anything about the baby," she said quietly.

"So you cheated on him? That's what they're saying in Haldon, and if it keeps up—"

"How many times do I have to tell you, damn it? This damned baby is a Warden!" All of Gwyneira's anger suddenly burst forth, and she began to sob. She didn't deserve any of this. She had been so discreet about Fleur's conception. No one, absolutely no one doubted her legitimacy. And now the real Warden was supposed to be the bastard?

Helen thought hard while Gwyneira wept. Lucas knew nothing of the pregnancy—and Gwyneira's problems having children up until then lay, in Matahorua's opinion, with him. So if a Warden had impregnated her with this child, then...

"Oh God, Gwyn..." Helen knew she could never speak her suspicion aloud, but now she could see it all clearly for herself. Gerald Warden must have impregnated Gwyneira—and it did not look like it had been accomplished with her friend's approval. She took her friend in her arms to comfort her. "Oh, Gwyn, I was so stupid. I should have known right away. Instead, I've been torturing you with a thousand questions. But you...you have to forget all that now. Regardless of how Paul was conceived. He's your son."

"I hate him!" Gwyneira sobbed.

Helen shook her head. "Foolish girl. You can't hate a little baby. Paul can't help whatever happened. He has a right to his mother, Gwyn. Just like Fleur and Ruben. Do you think his conception was much fun for me?"

"At least you did it of your own will!" Gwyneira erupted.

"The baby doesn't care. Please, Gwyn, at least try. Bring the little fellow along, introduce him to the women in Haldon—try to be a little bit proud of him. Then the love will come."

The crying did Gwyneira good, and she was relieved that Helen knew but didn't judge her. Her friend obviously had not thought for even a moment that Gwyneira would have slept with Gerald of her own free will—a nightmare that had plagued Gwyneira ever since she had become pregnant. Since James had left, a rumor to that effect had been making the rounds in the stables, and Gwyneira was only happy that it had escaped James McKenzie. She could not have handled James asking her about it. Gwyneira's "breeder self" could follow the thinking that had caused her employees and friends to come to this conclusion. After Lucas's failure had become common knowledge, conceiving the heir with Gerald would have been the next best thing. Gwyneira wondered why the thought had not crossed her mind when she was in search of a father for her first child—perhaps because Lucas's father acted so aggressively toward her that she feared every conversation and every moment alone with him. But Gerald might have toyed with the idea himself, and perhaps that was also a reason for his drinking and his anger: quite possibly everything had served to keep his forbidden lust—and the monstrous idea of simply siring his own "grandson"—from raising its head at all.

Gwyneira was lost in thought as she directed the carriage home. Fortunately, she did not need to keep Fleur occupied; she rode proudly and happily on her own next to the chaise. George Greenwood had presented little Paul with a pony for his christening—he must have planned it far in advance and ordered the little mare while he was still in England, just after learning of Gwyneira's pregnancy. Fleurette had naturally taken the horse for herself right away and had gotten along very well with it from the first. There was no way she would give it up when Paul got older. Gwyneira would have to think of something, but there was time for that. Before anything else, she had to address the problem of Paul being regarded as a bastard in Haldon. It wouldn't do to have the Warden heir being whispered about. Gwyneira had to defend her honor and her good name.

When she finally arrived at Kiward Station, she made straight for her rooms, looking for the baby. As expected, she found his crib empty. After looking around, she discovered Kiri in the kitchen with both infants, one on each breast.

Gwyn forced herself to smile.

"There's my boy," she remarked kindly. "When he's done, can I...can I hold him awhile, Kiri?"

If this desire struck Kiri as surprising, she did not show it. She just beamed at Gwyneira. "Of course! Will be happy to see mama."

But Paul was not happy at all and started bawling as soon as Gwyneira took him from Kiri's arms.

"He not mean it like that," Kiri murmured, embarrassed. "Is just not used."

Gwyneira rocked the baby in her arms and strove to suppress the impatience rising up within her. Helen was right; the baby couldn't do anything about it. And when she looked at him objectively, Paul was a handsome child. He had large, clear eyes, still blue and round as marbles. His hair was dark, curly, and unruly, and the noble shape of his mouth reminded Gwyneira of Lucas. It shouldn't be all that difficult to learn to love this baby...but before anything else, she needed to clean out the rumor mill.

"I'll be holding him more often, so he gets used to me," she declared to the amazed but delighted Kiri. "And I'm taking him with me tomorrow to Haldon. You can come along if you like. As his nanny."

Then at least he won't scream the whole time, Gwyneira thought, when the baby still had not calmed down after a half hour in his birth mother's arms. Only after she laid him down again in the improvised baby basket—Kiri would have loved to carry the babies around with her constantly, but Gerald did not allow that during work—did the little one calm himself. Moana sang a song for the children while she cooked. For the Maori, every female relative of the appropriate generation was considered a mother.

Mrs. Candler and Dorothy were delighted to finally have the Wardens' heir presented to them. After giving Fleur a lollipop, Mrs. Candler could not get enough of little Paul. Gwyneira understood clearly that a test of his physical health was being carried out, and so she was happy to allow her old friend to take Paul out of his blankets and weigh him in her arms. The little boy was in fine spirits. He and Marama had enjoyed the rocking of the carriage. Both children had slept sweetly during the trip, and just before arriving, Kiri had fed them again. Now both babies were awake. Paul looked at Mrs. Candler with big, attentive eyes and moved his legs energetically. The Haldon housewives' suspicions that the baby might be handicapped were thus definitively laid to rest. All that remained were the concerns about his paternity.

"The dark hair! And the long eyelashes! Just like his grandfather," cooed Mrs. Candler.

Gwyneira also pointed out the shape of Paul's lips, as well as his definite chin cleft, which both Lucas and Gerald shared.

"Has the father heard about his luck yet?" another matron butted in, having just interrupted her shopping to have a look at the baby. "Or is he still…oh, forgive me; that's really none of my business."

Gwyneira smiled sunnily. "But of course! Although his well-wishes haven't had time to make their way back to us yet. My spouse is in England, Mrs. Brennerman—without my father-in-law's approval. Hence all the secrecy, you know. Lucas received an invitation from a well-known art gallery to display his works there."

That was not even a lie. In truth, George Greenwood had been able to interest several London galleries in Lucas's work—though Gwyneira had first heard this news after Lucas had left Kiward Station. But she didn't need to tell them everything.

"Oh, that's wonderful." Mrs. Candler was delighted. "And here we thought…oh, forget it! And the proud grandfather? The men in the pub missed his celebratory merrymaking."

Gwyneira forced herself to exhibit a relaxed but slightly concerned face.

"Mr. Warden has not been feeling well lately," she explained, which was pretty close to the truth, since her father-in-law fought daily battles with the whiskey he'd enjoyed the night before. "But naturally, he's still planning a party. Perhaps another big garden party since the christening was a rather spartan affair. We'll make up for it, right, Pauly?" She took the baby from Mrs. Candler and thanked heaven it did not scream.

And that was it. She had survived it. The conversation now shifted from Kiward Station to the wedding being planned for Dorothy and the Candlers' youngest son. Two years earlier, the oldest had married Francine, the young midwife, and the middle son was off exploring the world for the first time. Mrs. Candler reported that they had just received a letter from him from Sydney.

"I think he's in love," she said with an impish smile.

Gwyneira was truly happy for the young couple, though she could vividly picture what was coming Mrs. Candler's way. The rumor, "Leon Candler is marrying a convict girl from Botany Bay," would soon eclipse the rather meager sensation, "Lucas Warden is displaying art in London."

"Just send Dorothy to me for her wedding dress," Gwyneira said as she bid them a friendly farewell. "I once promised her I'd lend her mine when the time came."

Hopefully it will at least bring her luck, thought Gwyneira as she steered Kiri and her brood back to the coach.

Well, that had been a success.

Now for Gerald…

"We're throwing a party!" Gwyneira declared, having hardly set foot in the salon. With a look of determination, she took the whiskey bottle out of Gerald's hand and locked it behind the glass in the liquor cabinet. "We're going to start planning it right away, and you'll need a clear head for that."

Gerald already seemed a little foggy. Despite his glassy eyes, he evidently could still follow Gwyneira.

"Wha...what is there to celebrate, exactly?" he inquired drunkenly.

Gwyneira glared daggers at him. "The birth of your 'grandson'!" she said. "Most people would call that a happy event, if you care to recall. And all of Haldon is waiting for you to honor it appropriately."

"Qui...quite a party...when the mo...mother is sulking and the fa...father is off somewhere else," Gerald scoffed.

"You're not exactly innocent with regard to Lucas's and my lack of enthusiasm!" Gwyneira fired back at him. "But as you see, I'm not sulking. I'll be there, I'll smile—and you will read aloud a letter from Lucas who, regretfully, is still in England. Everything is burning down, Gerald! They're walking all over us in Haldon. There are rumors that Paul...well, that he's not a Warden."

The party took place three weeks later in Kiward Station's garden. Rivers of champagne flowed once again. Gerald acted amiable and let himself be saluted. Gwyneira kept a smile glued to her face and revealed to the assembled guests that Paul was named after his great-grandfathers. She pointed out the obvious similarities to Gerald to nearly all the members of the community. Blessedly, Paul himself slumbered in the arms of his nanny. Gwyneira prudently avoided presenting him herself. He still howled when she held him, and she still reacted with anger and impatience. She understood that she had to welcome this child into the family and secure his position—but she could not feel anything deeper for the boy. Paul remained estranged from her, and what was worse—every time she looked into his eyes, she was reminded of Gerald's lustful grimace on the fateful night of his conception. When the party was finally over, Gwyneira fled into the stables and cried without restraint into Igraine's soft mane just as she had done as a child when something seemed hopeless. Gwyneira wished it had never happened. She yearned for James, even for Lucas. She still had not heard a word from her husband, and Gerald's researches had proved fruitless. The country was simply too big. Whoever wanted to stay missing, stayed missing.

8

"Just hit him, Luke! Once, with something behind it, on the back of the noggin. He won't feel a thing." Even as Roger spoke, he did in another abandoned seal pup—in accordance with the rules of the seal hunting profession, the animal died without his pelt being harmed. The hunters killed by hitting the seal on the back of the head with a club. If blood flowed at all, it flowed out the nose of the young seal. After that they got straight to work skinning it, without even bothering to make sure the animal was dead beforehand.

Lucas Warden raised his club, but he could not bring himself to harm the small animal looking at him with the trusting eyes of a child. The lamentations of the mother seals all around him didn't help. The men were only there for the pups' soft and valuable pelts. They wandered across the seal banks where the mothers raised their children, killing the pups before their mothers' eyes. The rocks of Tauranga Bay were already red with their blood—and Lucas had to fight the urge to vomit. He could not comprehend how the men could be so heartless. The suffering of the animals did not bother them in the least; they even made jokes about how benevolently and helplessly the seals awaited their hunters. Lucas had joined the party three days before but had yet to kill an animal. At first the men appeared to hardly notice that he only helped with the skinning and storing of the pelts on the wagons and flats. But now they were insisting that he take part in the slaughter too. Lucas felt hopelessly sick. Was *this* what made a man? What was so much more honest about the work of killing helpless animals than painting and writing? Lucas, however, was tired of asking himself these questions. He was here to prove himself, determined to do exactly the work that his father had done to lay the foundations of his wealth. Originally Lucas had hired himself onto a whaling ship, but that had ended in ignominious failure. Lucas did not like to admit it, but he had fled—this despite the fact that he had already signed the contract and really liked the man who had hired him.

Lucas had met Copper, a tall, dark-haired man with the angular, weathered face typical of "Coasters," in a pub in Greymouth. Right after his flight from Kiward Station, when he was still so full of anger and hatred for Gerald that he could hardly think straight. He had set out pell-mell for the West Coast, an Eldorado for "tough guys" who proudly dubbed themselves "Coasters" and earned their living with whaling and seal hunting and, more recently, the search for gold. Lucas had wanted to show everyone—to earn his own money, to prove himself a "real man" so that he might return at some point fabulously wealthy, weighed down with...with what, exactly? Gold? In that case, he probably should have taken up a shovel and gold pan and ridden into the mountains instead of signing on to a whale ship. But Lucas had not thought that far ahead. He just wanted to get away, far away, preferably out at sea—and he wanted to use his father's own weapons against him. He had reached Greymouth, a poor settlement with little to offer other than a pub and a ship landing, after an adventurous ride through the mountains. Nevertheless, there was a dry corner in the pub where Lucas could make camp. For the first time in days he had a roof over his head. His blankets were still damp and dirty from his nights beneath the open sky. Lucas would have liked to draw himself a bath, but they were not equipped for such a thing in Greymouth. Lucas was not surprised. "Real men" did not seem to bathe very often. Instead of water, plenty of beer and whiskey flowed, and after a few glasses, Lucas had told Copper about his plans. He took heart when the Coaster did not just wave him away.

"Don't look much like a whaler," he remarked, taking a long look at Lucas's thin face and soft gray eyes. "But not like a weakling neither." The man reached for Lucas's upper arm and felt his muscles.

"All right, why not. Been plenty o' men who learned to hold a harpoon." He laughed. But then his gaze became searching. "But can you handle being on your own for three or four years? Won't you miss the pretty girls in port?"

Lucas had already heard that you had to sign on for two to four years when you hired on to a whaling ship these days. The golden era of whaling, when sperm whales were easily found right off the South Island's coast—the Maori had even hunted the beasts from their canoes—were past. By now the whales just off the coast were all but extinct. One had to sail far out to sea to find them and often spent weeks, if not years, on the hunt. Lucas had few concerns about that. The company of men even seemed attractive to him, as long as he didn't stand out as he had on Kiward Station as the boss's son. He would make it through this all right—no, he would go so far as to earn respect and recognition. Lucas was determined, and Copper did not turn him away. On the contrary, he seemed to regard him with interest, slapping him on the shoulder and patting him on the arm with the paws of an experienced ship's carpenter and whaler. Lucas was somewhat ashamed of his manicured hands, his lack of calluses, and his relatively clean fingernails. On Kiward Station the men had occasionally alluded to the fact that he cleaned them regularly, but Copper didn't say a word about it.

Lucas had followed his new friend onto the ship, had himself introduced to the skipper, and signed a contract that bound him to three years on the *Pretty Peg*, a pear-shaped sailing ship that, though small, appeared just as resilient as its owner. The skipper, Robert Milford, was short but built of solid muscle. Copper spoke of him with great respect and praised his skills as the main harpooner. Milford greeted Lucas with a powerful handshake, told him what his pay would be—which struck Lucas as shockingly low—and directed Copper to show him to a berth. The *Pretty Peg* would soon be setting sail. Lucas had only two days to sell his horse, bring his things on board the whaler, and take over the pallet next to Copper's. That suited him just fine. Even if Gerald had sent out search parties, he would long since have set sail before word reached out-of-the-way Greymouth.

But life on board sobered him up quickly. On the first night, the fleas belowdecks kept him awake; what's more, he had to battle against seasickness. Lucas made every effort to pull himself together, but his stomach rebelled whenever the ship rocked in the waves. It was worse in the dark room inside the ship than on deck, which led him to finally try spending the night outside. The cold and the damp soon drove him back to his quarters, and he knew it would be impossible to sleep outside once they were at sea, when water would be washing over the deck. Once again, the men were laughing at him, though he did not mind so much this time because Copper was obviously on his side.

"He's just a polite little lord, our Luke!" he remarked good-naturedly. "He's just got to get used to it. But just wait till he's baptized in blubber. He'll be all right, believe me!"

Copper commanded great respect from the crew. He was not only a capable ship's carpenter, but was also considered a first-class whaler.

His friendship did Lucas good, and the furtive touches Copper seemed to seek on occasion were not unpleasant. Lucas might even have enjoyed them if the hygienic conditions aboard the *Pretty Peg* were not so appalling. There was limited drinking water, and no one even considered wasting it on washing. The men rarely shaved, and they did not own any changes of clothes. After a few nights, the whalers and their lodgings stank worse than the sheep stalls on Kiward Station. Lucas tried washing himself with seawater as a last resort, but it was difficult and drew laughter from the rest of the crew. Though the other men seemed to enjoy the shared company and hardly appeared to notice the stench of their unwashed bodies, Lucas was ashamed of his dirty, flea-bitten condition. He realized it wasn't necessary, given the state of the others, but he couldn't help but be bothered by it.

There was little to do. The ship could have sailed with a much smaller crew, and there would only be work for everyone once the hunt began. As a result, they spent a lot of time in close company. They told stories, exaggerating without compunction, sang dirty songs, and killed time playing cards. Lucas had always disdained poker and blackjack as being ungentlemanly, but he knew the rules, and played to avoid standing out. Unfortunately, he had not inherited his father's talent for cards. Lucas could not sell a bluff or a poker face. You could look at him and know exactly what he was thinking, which was not an asset when it came to men and gaming. In short order, he had lost what little money he had brought with him from Kiward Station and had to let his losses stand. No doubt there would have been difficulties with the men if Copper had not had his hand on him. The older man fawned over him so explicitly that Lucas was starting to wonder about it. It was not unpleasant, but it was bound to draw attention sooner or later. Lucas still thought with horror of the allusions the shepherds made on Kiward Station when he preferred to be with the younger Dave O'Toole than with the more experienced men. The comments of the whalers on board the *Pretty Peg* stayed within proper limits, however. There were close friendships between other men on the whaler as well, and sometimes at night sounds emanated from the berths that made Lucas blush with embarrassment—but they also aroused feelings of lust and envy within him. Was that what he had dreamed about on Kiward Station and what he had thought about when he tried making love to Gwyneira? Lucas knew that there was a connection, but something within him prevented him from seriously considering love in these surroundings. There was nothing exciting about embracing stinking, unwashed bodies, male or female. The only model he had for his secret yearnings—the Greek ideal of the mentor who took in a handsome boy not only to provide him with love but also to impart wisdom and life experience—had little in common with this scenario.

If Lucas were honest with himself, he loathed every minute of his stay aboard the *Pretty Peg*. It was impossible for him to imagine spending three years on board, but there was no possibility of dissolving his contract. And the ship would not be docking anywhere for months. Any thought of flight was futile. Lucas could only hope that he would eventually grow accustomed to the cramped quarters, the rough sea, and the stench. The latter proved the easiest. After only a few days, he already felt less revolted by Copper and the others—presumably because he had begun to give off the same odor himself. His seasickness ebbed, and there were days when Lucas retched only once.

But then came the first hunt, and with that everything changed.

In an unusual stroke of luck, the *Pretty Peg*'s helmsman spotted a sperm whale just two weeks after setting sail. His excited call awoke the crew, who were still lying in their berths at that early hour of the morning. The men sprang up at once and stormed onto the deck at lightning speed. They were wound up and energized by the thrill of the hunt, which was no wonder. When successful, the whalers received premiums that enhanced their meager pay. When Lucas came on deck, he saw the skipper gazing over the side, frowning at the whale, which was playing a game with the waves within sight of the New Zealand coast.

"Gorgeous specimen!" Milford rejoiced. "Huge! I hope we take him. If we do, we'll fill half the barrels today. He's fat as a pig ready for slaughter!"

The men bellowed with laughter. It was Lucas's first encounter with a whale, and he was having trouble viewing the majestic and fearless animal before them as prey.

The powerful sperm whale, almost as big as the whole *Pretty Peg*, slid elegantly through the waves, leaping out from time to time, turning and twisting in the air like a bucking, carefree horse, with a pure embodiment of the joy of life. How were they supposed to bring this gigantic animal down? And why did they want to destroy this beauty? Lucas could hardly get enough of the grace and sprightliness displayed by the whale despite its immense mass.

The other men, however, had no eyes for that. They were already separating themselves into teams and assembling around their individual boat commanders. Copper waved Lucas over to him. Apparently, he was among the select few who commanded their own boats.

"This is it, boys!" The skipper ran excitedly around the deck and gave the boats their launching orders. His core crew performed as a well-rehearsed team. The men lowered the small but sturdy rowboats skillfully into the water—six rowers took their places in each one, followed by the boat commanders and harpooners, and sometimes a boatsteerer as well. To Lucas, the harpooners looked very tiny in comparison to the animal they wanted to bring down. But Copper merely laughed when he made a comment to that effect.

"The size is what does it, boy! Sure, a single shot just tickles the beast. But six'll lay 'im low. Then we pull 'im up to the ship an' cut the fat from 'im. Hard work but worth it. And the skipper there ain't greedy. If we bag that one, we'll all be getting a couple extra dollars. So put your back in it!"

The sea was not too rough that day, and the rowboats quickly neared the whale. It did not seem to be trying to escape. On the contrary, it seemed to find the commotion of boats all around it quite diverting and made a few extra leaps, as though entertaining an audience—until the first harpoon struck home.

A harpooner from boat one rammed a spear into the animal's fin. Shocked and annoyed, the whale threw itself around and swam directly at Copper's boat.

"Careful around its tail! When he's seriously hurt, he'll flap around. Don't get too close, boys!"

Copper gave directions as he aimed for the whale's rib cage. He finally landed the second hit, which he placed much better than the first. The whale seemed to be weakening. Now an onslaught of harpoons rained down on the animal. Lucas watched with a mixture of fascination and horror as the whale reared up under the assault, now trying to flee but too late. The harpoons were attached to ropes, which was how the whale was to be hauled back to the ship. The whale was now almost deranged with pain and fear. It tore at its bonds, occasionally succeeding in pulling out one of the harpoons. But the whale bled from dozens of wounds, and the water around it foamed red. Lucas was nauseated by this theater, by the merciless slaughter of this majestic creature. The battle of the colossus against its opponents raged for hours, and the men poured all their strength into rowing, throwing, and pulling on the ropes to overcome the whale. Lucas did not notice the blisters forming and bursting on his hands. Nor did he feel any fear when Copper, determined to distinguish himself, came ever closer to the thrashing, dying whale. Lucas felt nothing but disgust and sympathy for the creature fighting valiantly until its last breath. He could hardly comprehend having a part in this unfair fight, nor could he abandon his crew. He was here now, and his life too depended on the whale being brought down. He could ponder it all later.

Finally the whale floated motionless in the water. Lucas did not know whether it was really dead or simply exhausted, but regardless, the men were able to pull it up alongside the ship. What came next was—if possible—worse. The men began to stick long knives in the body to cut out the fat, which was hauled straight up to the ship to be rendered into blubber. Lucas hoped the creature was really dead when the first chunks were ripped from its body and thrown on deck. Minutes later, they were wading through fat and blood. Someone opened up the whale's head to draw out the sought-after spermaceti. Copper had told Lucas that candles and cleaning and skincare products would be made from that. Others were looking in the bowels of the whale for the even more valuable ambergris, a basic ingredient for the perfume industry. It stank bestially, and Lucas shivered when he thought of all the eau de cologne he and Gwyneira had owned on Kiward Station. He never would have thought that any part of that was obtained from the stinking innards of a gruesomely slaughtered animal.

In the meantime, fires were being lit under giant kettles, and the stench of the whale fat being rendered filled the ship. The air was suffused with fat, which felt like it stuck to Lucas's air passages when he inhaled. Lucas bent over the guardrail but could not escape the stench of fish and blood. He would have liked to vomit, but his stomach was long since empty. He had been thirsty earlier, but now he could not imagine anything that wouldn't taste like blubber. He vaguely remembered that someone had explained the whaling process to him as a child and that he had found it ghastly. Now he was stuck in the middle of a nightmare of fat and flesh, which people were throwing into reeking kettles. The kettles of rendered blubber would then be emptied into barrels. The cask maker—responsible for the filling and sealing of the barrels—called to Lucas to help him close the containers. Lucas did so, trying not to look into the kettles, where pieces of the whale were cooking.

The other men did not exhibit the least aversion to this job. On the contrary, the stench seemed to give them an appetite; they were obviously excited about the prospect of a meal that featured fresh meat. The men regretted that they could not bring in the whale meat, but it rotted too quickly. So after removing the fat, they would leave most of the body in the sea. The cook would spend the next two days cutting meat out of the whale, having promised the men a solid meal. Lucas knew he would not touch a morsel of it.

Finally the time came to release the remains of the whale from the ship. The creature had been largely gutted. The deck was still covered in pieces of fat, and the crew waded through slime and blood. The cooking of the blubber would still last a few hours, and Lucas realized that days might tick by before the deck was cleaned. Lucas doubted it was even possible—certainly not with the simple broom and buckets of water the men usually used to swab the deck. Presumably, they would simply wait for the next heavy storm to flood the deck and wipe away all traces of the slaughter. Lucas practically longed for such a storm. As he thought over the events of that day, panic began to well up inside him. He would probably acclimate eventually to the journey's living conditions, to the cramped berths and the unwashed bodies, but never to days like this. Not to the killing and gutting of these massive but obviously peaceful creatures. Lucas had no idea how he was supposed to make it through the next three years.

The fact that the *Pretty Peg*'s first whale had entered "the net" ended up working in his favor. Captain Milford decided to land at Westport and drop off their prize before setting sail again. Their stop would ensure a good price for the fresh blubber and allow them to empty the barrels for the next stage of the journey—and it would cost the men only a few days. The men rejoiced. Ralphie, a short, blond Swede, began swooning over the girls in Westport.

"It's a little dump but it's being built up. Till now just whalers and seal hunters, but a couple of gold diggers on their way. S'pposed to be real mountain men there—someone said something about coal deposits. Anyway, there's a pub and a few ready-and-willing girls. I had a redhead there once who was well worth the jack, I tell you!"

Copper approached Lucas, who was leaning on the guardrail, exhausted and sick.

"You thinking about the next brothel too? Or would you consider celebrating the successful hunt right here?" Copper had laid his hand on Lucas's shoulder and was now running it slowly down his arm in what could almost be called a caressing gesture. Lucas could hardly miss the invitation underpinning Copper's words—but he was undecided. There was no question he owed Copper something; the older man had been good to him. And hadn't he thought about sharing a bed with a man his whole life? Hadn't images of men come to him whenever he pleasured himself and when—with God as his witness—he had lain with his wife?

But this here...Lucas had read the writings of the Greeks and Romans. Back then, the male body had been the quintessential ideal of beauty; love between men and youths was not considered objectionable as long one did not force the boys into it. Lucas had wondered at the pictures of the statues that had been created back then. How beautiful they had been! How smooth, how clean, and inviting... Lucas had stood in front of the mirror and compared himself to them, had attempted the poses those youths had assumed, had dreamed of himself in the arms of a loving mentor—who certainly looked nothing like this whaler. Though he was friendly and good-humored, he was still massive and reeking. There was no possibility of washing himself that day on the *Pretty Peg*. The men would slip between the decks, covered in sweat and filth, sullied with blood and slime...Lucas pulled away from Copper's inviting stare.

"I don't know...it was a long day...I'm tired."

Copper nodded. "Don't worry; go to your berth, boy. Relax. Maybe later I could...well, I could bring you something to eat. Good chance there's even whiskey around here."

Lucas swallowed. "Another time, Copper. Maybe in Westport. You...I...don't misunderstand me, but I need a bath."

Copper let out a booming laugh. "My little gentleman! Fine, fine, I will personally see to it that the girls draw you a bath—or even better, for the both of us. I could use one too. Would you like that?"

Lucas nodded. The important thing was that the man leave him alone for today. Full of loathing and disgust for both himself and the men whom he had joined for this adventure, he retired to his flea-ridden bunk. Perhaps the fleas would be put off by the stench of blubber and sweat. A hope that quickly proved futile. On the contrary, it seemed only to attract more bugs. After squashing dozens of them on his body, Lucas only felt dirtier. Still, as he lay awake, listening closely to the laughing and shouting on deck—the skipper had evidently offered up the whiskey—and finally to the men's drunken songs, a plan began to form in his mind. He would leave the *Pretty Peg* in Westport. He didn't care whether he would be in breach of contract or not. This life was altogether too unbearable.

His escape had actually been rather easy. The only problem was that he'd had to leave all of his belongings behind on the ship. It would have looked suspicious if he had taken his sleeping bag and his few articles of clothing along for the brief shore leave the skipper had allowed the men. He took a few things to change into—after all, Copper had promised him a bath, so he could justify them on those grounds. Copper laughed about that, but Lucas did not care. He was only looking for an opportunity to run away. This quickly presented itself when Copper consulted with an attractive red-haired girl about finding a bathtub somewhere nearby. The other men in the pub were not paying attention to Lucas; they only had whiskey on their minds or were staring at the girls' ample curves. Lucas still had not ordered a drink, and thus avoided the guilt of skipping out on his tab when he now stole out of the bar and hid himself in the stables. As it turned out, there was a rear exit. Lucas took it and slunk across a blacksmith's yard, a coffin maker's shed, and a few unfinished houses. Westport was indeed a dump—he had been right about that—but it was also true that it was being built up.

The village was situated on the bank of a river, the Buller, which was wide and calm where it emptied into the sea. Lucas made out sandbanks interrupted by a rocky bank. Most importantly, though, a fern forest began just beyond Westport, a deep green wilderness that looked, and likely was, completely unexplored. Lucas looked around, but he was alone. Apparently, no one else sought the emptiness beyond the houses. He would be able to flee without being seen. Once he'd decided on a course of action, he ran along the river's edge, seeking cover between the ferns wherever possible. He followed the river upstream for an hour before he thought he'd gone far enough to relax. The skipper would not miss him right away, as the *Pretty Peg* was not set to leave until the following morning. Naturally, Copper would look for him, but not by the river, at least not at first. Later, he might look around the riverbanks, but surely he would limit himself to the area around Westport. Lucas would have liked to head deeper into the jungle right away, but his revulsion at his own filth made him pause. He had to clean himself up. Lucas stripped down, shivering, and hid his dirty things behind a couple of rocks—he gave some brief thought to washing them and taking them with him, but shuddered at the prospect of scrubbing the blood and fat out. So he held on only to his underwear, and would have to abandon his shirt and pants. That was regrettable; if he dared to come into contact with people again, he wouldn't own anything more than what he wore on his back. But anything was better than the slaughter on board the *Pretty Peg*.

Lucas finally slid down into the ice-cold waters of the Buller River. The cold pierced him to the bone, but the clear water washed all the dirt from him. Lucas lowered himself deeply into the river and reached for a pebble, which he began to rub on his skin. He scrubbed his body until he was red as a crab and hardly felt the water's cold anymore. Then he finally left the river, put on his clean clothes, and looked for a path through the jungle. The forest was terrifying—damp and thick and full of massive, unfamiliar plants—but Lucas's interest in his homeland's flora and fauna came in handy. He had seen many of the giant ferns, whose leaves sometimes rolled up like caterpillars and seemed almost to come alive, in textbooks and overcame his fear by trying to name them. None of them were poisonous and even the largest tree weta was less likely to attack him than the fleas on board the ship. Even the various animal noises that filled the jungle did not frighten him. There was nothing here but insects and birds, mostly parrots, who filled the forest with their strange calls but were utterly harmless. That evening Lucas made a camp out of ferns and slept not only more easily but also more peacefully than during his weeks on the *Pretty Peg*. Though he had lost everything, he awoke the next morning with refreshed courage—which was surprising given that he had walked out on his employer, broken a contract, and amassed gambling debts that he had not paid back. *Still*, he thought, almost amused, *soon no one will be calling me a "gentleman"!*

Lucas would have liked to remain in the jungle, but despite the abundant fertility of this green hell, nothing could be found to eat. At least not by Lucas—a Maori tribe or a true ranger might have seen things differently. As it was, however, his growling stomach forced him to look for a human settlement. But which one? Westport was out of the question. Everyone there was guaranteed to know by now that the skipper was looking for a sailor who had jumped ship. It was possible that the *Pretty Peg* was even waiting for him.

Then he recalled that Copper had mentioned Tauranga Bay a few days earlier. Seal banks, twelve miles from Westport. The seal hunters surely knew nothing about the *Pretty Peg* and weren't likely to care. But the hunting in Tauranga was supposed to be flourishing; doubtless he could find work there. With a light heart, Lucas headed that way. Seal hunting could not be any worse than whaling.

The men in Tauranga had indeed welcomed him, and the stench of their camp was more bearable. After all, it was in the open air, and the men were not penned together. It must have been evident to the men that something was not quite right about Lucas, but they did not ask any questions about his tattered appearance, his missing equipment, or his lack of money. They dismissed Lucas's threadbare explanations with a wave.

"No worries, Luke. We get enough of your type. Just make yourself useful and bag a few pups. On the weekends we take the pelts to Westport. Then you'll have money again." Norman, the oldest hunter, sucked good-naturedly on his pipe. Lucas had a sneaking suspicion that he was not the only one here running from something.

Lucas could even have felt comfortable among these reticent, laid-back Coasters if it weren't for the hunt itself—if you could even call the slaughtering of helpless pups in front of their horrified mothers' eyes "hunting." Doubtfully, he looked at the club in his hand and the animal before him.

"Well, do it, Luke! Take the pelt. Or do you think they'll give you money in Westport on Saturday because you helped us with the skinning? We all help each other out here, but you only bring in money for your own pelts."

Lucas saw no way out. He closed his eyes and swung.

9

By the end of the week Lucas had almost thirty seal pelts—and was plagued by even more shame and self-hatred than after his stint on the *Pretty Peg*. He was determined not to return to the seal banks after the weekend in Westport. The town was a burgeoning settlement. There had to be employment there that did not cause such personal torment—even if it meant admitting that he was not a real man.

The fur buyer, a short, wiry man who also ran the general store in Westport, was quite optimistic on his behalf. As Lucas had hoped, he did not connect the new hunter from the seal banks with the whaler who had fled the *Pretty Peg*. Perhaps his thoughts did not carry him that far back—or he simply did not care. In any event, he gave Lucas a few cents for each pelt and then readily answered his questions about other work in Westport. Lucas did not admit, of course, that he found the killing unbearable. Instead, he pretended it was the loneliness and the all-male company on the seal banks that had become too much for him.

"I'd like to live in town for once," he explained. "Maybe find a wife, start a family…just not see any more dead seals and whales." Lucas laid the money for the sleeping bag and clothing he had just bought to change into on the table. The trader and Lucas's new friends bellowed with laughter.

"Well, you'll find work easy enough. But a girl? The only girls here're those in Jolanda's establishment above the pub. They'd be about the right age to marry though."

The men just took Lucas's remark for a joke and could hardly stop laughing.

"You can ask 'em yourself right now!" Norman said good-naturedly. "You're coming to the pub, aren't you?"

Lucas could not refuse. He would have preferred to save his meager pay, but a whiskey sounded good—a little liquor might help him forget the seals' eyes and the whale's desperate thrashing.

The fur trader named a few other opportunities for work in Westport. The blacksmith might be able to use a hand. Had Lucas ever worked with iron? Lucas cursed himself for never having given a thought to how James McKenzie shod the horses on Kiward Station. Those sort of skills could have made him money here, but Lucas had never laid a hand on hammer and nails. He could ride a horse—but nothing more.

The man correctly interpreted Lucas's silence. "Not a hand worker, eh? Never learned anything except how to beat seals' brains in. But construction would be a possibility. The carpenters are always looking for help. They can hardly keep up with the contracts, with all the world suddenly wantin' houses on the Buller. We're going to be a real city! But they don't pay much. No comparison with what you earn doing that." He pointed to the fur.

Lucas nodded. "I know. But I figured I'd ask anyway. I…I've always been able to see myself working with wood."

The pub was small and not particularly clean. But Lucas was just relieved that none of the patrons remembered him. They probably hadn't given the *Pretty Peg*'s sailors a second look. Only the red-haired girl who was serving again that day seemed to look at him appraisingly as she wiped down the table before putting whiskey glasses in front of Norman and Lucas.

"Sorry it looks like a pigsty in here again," the girl said. "I told Madame Jolanda the Chinese doesn't clean right." The "Chinese" was the rather exotic-looking barman. "But so long as no one complains… just the whiskey or something to eat too?"

Lucas would have liked to eat something. Anything that did not smell of the sea and seaweed and blood and was not quick-roasted over the seal hunters' fire and gobbled down half raw. The girl seemed to care about cleanliness. So perhaps the kitchen was not as filthy as he might have feared at first glance.

Norman laughed. "Something to munch on, my dear? No, we can eat in camp, but there's no sweet dessert like you there." He pinched the girl's rear.

"You know that'll cost you a cent, right, dear?" she asked. "If I tell Madame Jolanda, she'll go and put it on your tab. But I won't be like that—for that cent, you can have a grab up here too." The redhead pointed to her breasts. He groped heartily, joined by Johlen, one of the other men. Then the girl skillfully removed his hand. "There'll be more of that later when you've paid."

The men laughed as she stalked away. She was wearing tantalizingly red high-heeled shoes and a dress in various shades of green. It was old and had been patched more than once, but it was clean, and the sexy lace flounces had been carefully starched and pressed. She reminded Lucas a bit of Gwyneira. Sure, she was a lady, and this half-grown child here a whore, but she also had frizzy red hair, pale skin, and that flash in her eyes that indicated that she was not at all resigned to her fate. This was certainly not the final station for this girl.

"A real sweetheart, right?" remarked Norman, who had perceived Lucas's gaze but misinterpreted it. "Daphne. The best horse in Madame Jolanda's stable and, what's more, her right hand. Without her, nothing would run around here, I tell you. She's got everything under control. If the old lady was clever, she'd adopt the dear thing. But she only thinks of herself. One of these days that girl's going to run away and take the best attractions with her. What do you think? You want her first? Or do your tastes run to something wilder?" He looked at the others with a wink.

Lucas did not know what to say.

Fortunately, Daphne returned with a second round of whiskey.

"The girls are ready upstairs," she said as she passed the glasses around. "Drink up at your leisure—I'd be happy to bring the bottle too—and then come on up!" She smiled encouragingly. "But don't make us wait too long. You know, a little liquor provokes the desire but takes away the performance." Just as quickly as Norman had reached for her rear before, she now seized him between the legs for revenge.

Norman jumped back but then had to laugh.

"Do I get a cent for that too?"

Daphne shook her head, letting her red hair fly as she did so.

"Maybe a kiss?" she twittered and drifted away before Norman could answer. The men whistled after her.

Lucas drank his whiskey and felt dizzy. How would he get out of here without failing miserably once more? Daphne did not arouse him at all. And yet she seemed to have set her eye squarely on him. Even just now, her gaze had lingered a bit longer on his face and slender, but muscular form than on the bodies of the others. Lucas knew that women found him attractive—that was unlikely to be any different with the whores in Westport than with the matrons in Christchurch. What was he supposed to do if Norman really did expect him to join them upstairs?

Lucas contemplated escaping again, but that was out of the question. Without a horse, he had no chance of leaving Westport; he would have to remain in town for the time being. And that would not work if, first thing on the first day, he marked himself for all time by fleeing from a red-haired whore.

Most of the men were already lightly swaying when Daphne finally reappeared and invited the company upstairs. But none of them were drunk enough not to notice Lucas's absence if doubts were raised about him. And then Daphne kept resting her eyes on him.

The girl led the men into a salon decorated with plush furniture and diminutive tables that would have looked vulgar in any setting. Four girls clad in elaborate negligees were awaiting them there, as well as Madame Jolanda, of course—a short, fat woman with cold eyes who, before anything else, took a dollar from every man. "Then at least no one will run away before he's paid," she explained calmly.

Lucas paid his dollar, gnashing his teeth. Soon there would be nothing left of his week's pay.

Daphne led him to one of the red seats and pushed another glass of whiskey into his hand.

"All right, stranger, how can I make you happy?" she said breathily. She had been the only girl not wearing a negligee, but now undid her bodice as though unintentionally. "Do you like me? But I'll warn you: I glow red like fire! I've already set fire to a few." As she spoke, she brushed her long strands of hair across his face.

Lucas did not react.

"No?" whispered Daphne. "Afraid? Tsk, tsk. Well, fine, maybe the other elements are more your thing. We have something for everyone. Fire, air, water, earth..." One after the other, she gestured to three of the girls, who were busy at work on the other men at the moment. The first was a pale, almost ethereal-looking creature with straight, pale blonde hair. Her limbs were petite, she was almost skin and bones, but he could detect big breasts beneath her thin shirt. Lucas found that repulsive. He would never be able to overcome his distaste and make love to this girl. A blonde dressed in blue with topaz-colored eyes embodied the element "water." She appeared quite lively and was joking with the obviously enthusiastic Norman. "Earth" was a brown-skinned girl with black tresses, without a doubt the most exotic creature in Madame Jolanda's collection, if not exactly pretty. Her facial features made her look tough, and her body was stocky. She nevertheless appeared to be charming the man she was flirting with just then. As he so often did, Lucas marveled at the criteria other men used to select their partners. Daphne was the prettiest of the girls, and Lucas knew he should have felt flattered that she had chosen him. If only she aroused him even a tiny bit, perhaps if she...

"Tell me, don't you have anything younger to offer?" Lucas asked finally. He did not like the way that came out, but if he wanted to save face tonight, he had the best chance with a slender, boyish girl.

"Even younger than me?" Daphne asked, blown away. She was right; she was a mere child herself. Lucas guessed she was nineteen at most. Before he could answer, though, she looked him over with a careful eye.

"Now I know where I've seen you before! You're the fellow who ran away from the whaler. While the fat queer, that Copper, was ordering a bath for you and him. I could have laughed myself half to death—there's no way that guy had ever come into contact with soap before! So the love was unrequited, eh...but you do prefer boys, right?"

Lucas's blushing saved him from having to answer her half question, half assertion.

Daphne smiled—a little deviously but also with understanding. "Your fine friends don't know it, is that it? And you don't want to stand out. Pay attention, my friend, I have something for you. No, not a boy, we don't have any of those. But something special—but for looking only, the girls aren't for sale. Interested?"

"In...what?" Lucas stammered. Daphne's offer seemed to be giving him a way out. Something special, prestigious, that did not require him to sleep with anyone? Lucas's only misgiving was that the rest of his pay would likely disappear for this.

"It's a sort of...well, erotic dance. Two very young girls, barely fifteen. Twins. I promise you: you've never seen anything like it."

Lucas gave himself over to fate. "How much?" he forced himself to ask.

"Two dollars," Daphne declared quickly. "One for each of the girls. And the one you've already paid for me. I don't leave the girls alone with the men, you see."

Lucas cleared his throat. "They...ahem, they're not in any danger with me."

Daphne laughed. Lucas was amazed at how young and tinkling it sounded. "I believe you there. Fine, I'll make an exception. Don't have any money, is that right? Left everything on the *Pretty Peg*? You're a real hero! But now off you go, room one. I'll send for the girls. And I'll see to it myself that I make Uncle Norman a happy man."

She sauntered over to Norman and made the blonde-haired "water" girl look instantly shabby. Daphne was, without question, radiant—but what was more, she had something approaching style.

Lucas entered room one, which confirmed his expectations. The room was furnished like a third-rate hotel with a great deal of plush, a wide bed...was he supposed to stretch himself out on it? Or would that scare the girls? Lucas ultimately settled in a plush chair, partly because the bed did not look very trustworthy to him. After all, he had only just gotten rid of the fleas from the *Pretty Peg*.

The arrival of the twins announced itself with murmuring and admiring calls from the "salon," which the girls had to cross to reach his room. Apparently, it was considered a luxury—and no doubt a special honor—when one was allowed to order the twins. Then again, Daphne had left no doubt that the girls were under her protection.

The twins seemed to find the attention embarrassing, though an additional mantle hid their bodies from the men's prurient gazes. They slipped into the room, cleaving to one another, and lifted the giant hood beneath which they had hidden their heads until they felt they were safe. As safe as this place got.

They kept their blonde heads lowered; presumably they usually remained that way until Daphne entered to introduce them. Since that was not the case today, one of them looked up. Lucas found himself looking into a narrow face with mistrustful light-blue eyes.

"Good evening, sir. We feel honored that you've requested us," she said, obviously reciting a well-rehearsed speech. "I'm Mary."

"And I'm Laurie," the second one explained. "Daphne told us you..."

"I'll only watch you, no need to worry," Lucas said kindly. He would never have touched these children, though in one respect they certainly met his expectations: as Mary and Laurie let their mantle fall to the floor, standing there naked as God made them, he saw how boyishly slender they were.

"I hope you enjoy our presentation," Laurie said politely, taking her sister's hand. It was a reassuring gesture, more of a search for protection than the beginning of a sexual show. Lucas wondered how these girls had fallen into this line of work.

The girls moved to the bed but did not slip between the sheets. Instead, they knelt before each other and began to embrace and kiss each other. Over the next half hour, Lucas saw gestures and positions that alternatingly made him blush and made his blood run cold.

The things the girls did with each other were the height of impropriety. But Lucas did not find it revolting. It reminded him too much of his own dreams of uniting with a body that mirrored his own—a loving union of dignity and mutual respect. Lucas did not know whether the girls derived any pleasure from their obscene acts but could not imagine that they did. Yet there was undoubtedly love in the looks the sisters gave each other, and tenderness inherent in their touches. Their erotic performance had a confusing effect on the observer—as time went on, the boundaries between their bodies seemed to blur; the girls looked so similar that at one point they gave rise to the illusion they were a single dancing goddess with four arms and two heads. Lucas remembered seeing pictures of such a thing from the Crown Colony of India. Though he preferred drawing girls to making love to them, he found the sight strangely alluring. There was something almost artistic about their dance. The two of them finally froze in a tight embrace on the bed and did not release one another until Lucas applauded.

Laurie cast a searching gaze at the fly of his pants when she came out of her trance.

"Did you enjoy it?" she asked anxiously when she noticed that Lucas's fly was still done and that his face showed no sign of his having masturbated. "We...we could touch you too, but..."

The girl's expression showed that she would not be enthusiastic about it, but there must have been men who asked for their money back if they did not reach climax.

"Though Daphne usually does that," Mary added.

Lucas shook his head. "That won't be necessary, thank you. I very much enjoyed your dance. Like Daphne said—it was something very special. But how did you end up doing this? One doesn't expect to see something like that in establishments like this."

The girls sighed with relief as they wrapped themselves up in their mantle again, but they remained seated on the edge of the bed. Apparently, they no longer viewed Lucas as a threat.

"Oh it was Daphne's idea," Laurie informed him freely. The two girls had sweet, twittering voices—another sign that they had hardly grown out of adolescence.

"We had to earn money," Mary continued. "But we didn't want to...we couldn't...it is sinful to lie with a man for money, you know."

Lucas wondered if they had also learned that from Daphne. However, they did not seem to actually subscribe to this belief themselves.

"Though it is necessary sometimes," Laurie defended her colleague. "But Daphne says you have to be grown up for that. Only—Madame Jolanda didn't think so, and so..."

"So Daphne found something in one of her books. A weird book full of...dirty things. But Madame Jolanda says that where the book comes from it's not sinful if you..."

"And what we do isn't sinful anyway!" Mary said with conviction.

"You are good girls," Lucas agreed. He suddenly wanted to know more about them. "Where are you from? Daphne isn't your sister, is she?"

Laurie was about to answer, but the door opened just then and Daphne entered. She looked visibly relieved when she saw that the girls were covered and having a relaxed conversation with their strange customer.

"Were you happy with it?" she asked, likewise with the apparently unavoidable look at Lucas's fly.

Lucas nodded. "Your wards have done a fine job of entertaining me," he said. "And they were just about to tell me where they were from. You all ran away from somewhere, isn't that right? Or do your parents know what you're doing here?"

Daphne shrugged. "Depends on what you believe. If my mom and theirs are sitting on a cloud in heaven playing the harp, I suppose they should be able to see us. But if they ended up where our kind usually ends up, then they're only looking at the radishes from below."

"Your parents are all dead," Lucas said, ignoring her cynicism. "I'm sorry about that. But how exactly did you end up here?"

Daphne straightened herself up confidently before him. "Now listen, Luke, or whatever your name is. If there's one thing we don't like, it's prying questions. Understood?"

Lucas wanted to reply that he meant no harm. On the contrary, he had been considering how he might be able to help them out of the miserable situation they had landed themselves in. Laurie and Mary were not whores yet, and for a capable and obviously smart girl like Daphne, there had to be alternatives. But at the moment, he was as penniless as the three girls—perhaps more so since Daphne and the twins had earned three dollars—and he imagined that the greedy Jolanda would probably leave them no more than one.

So Lucas merely said, "Sorry. I did not mean to offend you. Listen, I...I need a place to sleep tonight. I can't stay here. As inviting as the rooms are." With a broad sweep of his hand, he indicated Madame Jolanda's hourly hotel, at which Daphne laughed her bell-like laugh and the twins giggled cautiously. "But that would be out of my price range. Is there a place in the stables or something else along those lines?"

"You don't want to return to the seal banks?" Daphne asked, surprised.

Lucas shook his head. "I'm looking for a less bloody job. Someone told me the carpenters are hiring."

Daphne cast a glance at Lucas's slender hands, which, it's true, were less manicured than the month before, but were still less callused and rough than Norman's or Copper's.

"Then just be careful you don't hit yourself too often on the finger," she said. "Hammers draw more blood from fingers than clubs from seals—your pelt just happens to be less valuable, my friend."

Lucas had to laugh. "I'll look after myself, thank you. As long as the fleas don't suck out what's left of my blood. Am I mistaken or is this place crawling with them too?" He scratched himself unabashedly on the shoulder—which, naturally, a gentleman would never do, but gentlemen also did not spend so much time grappling with insects.

Daphne shrugged. "Must be from the salon. Room one is clean since we clean it. After all, it would be distracting if the twins left their show covered in pustules. That's why we don't let any of the filthy fellows sleep here, regardless of what they pay. Your best bet would be to try the rental stables. That's where a lot of the boys who are passing through sleep. And David keeps it neat. I think you'll like him. But don't pervert him!"

With those words, Daphne left her guest and shooed the twins from the room. Lucas stayed a little longer. After all, the men outside were expecting him to have been busy with girls and he would need some time to get dressed now. When he finally reentered the salon, a few cheers issued from several drunken throats. Norman raised his glass and drank to him.

"There you have it. Our Luke! Does it with the three best girls and comes out looking like he just hatched from the egg. Did I hear some something going on in there? Pardon yourselves right quick, boys, before he steals your girls too."

10

Lucas let them cheer a little longer before leaving the pub for the rental stables. Daphne had not oversold the place. The business made a tidy impression. Naturally, it smelled of horses, but the path between the stalls had been swept clean, the horses stood in boxes generously strewn with hay, and the saddles and bridles in the tack room were old but well maintained. A single stable lantern bathed the interior in weak light—enough to orient himself by and to see to the horses at night, but not bright enough to bother the animals.

Lucas looked around for a place to sleep, but he seemed to be the only overnight guest. He was considering making camp without asking around. But then a high-pitched voice, more fearful than authoritative, sounded through the dark stables: "Who's there? State your name and what you want, stranger!"

Lucas raised his arms nervously. "Luke…uh…Denward. I have no bad intentions, I'm just looking for a place to sleep. And this girl, Miss Daphne, said…"

"We let people sleep here who have put up their horses here," the voice answered, coming closer. Its owner finally appeared. A blond boy, perhaps sixteen years old, stretched his neck over the wall of one of the stalls. "But you don't have a horse."

Lucas nodded. "That's right. But I could still pay a few cents. And I don't need a whole stall either. A corner would do."

The boy nodded. "How'd you get here without a horse, sir?" he asked curiously, stepping around to reveal himself entirely. He was tall but gangly, and his face still looked childlike. Lucas gazed into the boy's bright round eyes, whose color he could not make out in the dim light. The boy seemed open and friendly.

"I came from the seal banks," Lucas said, as though this were an explanation for how someone had crossed the mountains without a mount. But maybe the boy could figure out for himself that his guest must have arrived by ship. Lucas hoped that this did not make him think right away of the *Pretty Peg*'s deserter.

"Were you hunting seals? I tried to do that once; you earn a lot of money for it. But I couldn't do it...the way the things look at a guy..."

Lucas's heart warmed.

"That's exactly why I'm looking for another job," he explained.

The young boy nodded. "You can help the carpenters or the lumberjacks. There's certainly enough work. I'll take you along on Monday. I'm also working construction."

"I thought you were the stable boy here." Lucas was surprised. "What's your name? David?"

The boy shrugged. "That's what they call me. My name is actually Steinbjörn. Steinbjörn Sigleifson. But no one here can pronounce it. So that girl, Daphne, just started calling me David. After David Copperfield. I think he wrote a book or something."

Lucas smiled, once more astonished by Daphne. A barmaid who read Dickens?

"And where do people name their children 'Steinbjörn Sigleifson'?" Lucas inquired. David had been leading him to a shed, which he had made habitable. Straw bales served as tables and chairs, and hay had been piled into a sort of shelf. More hay lay in a corner, and David indicated to Lucas that he should use it for a bed.

"In Iceland," he replied, helping Lucas energetically. "That's where I come from. My father was a whaler. But my mother, who was Irish, always wanted to leave. She would have liked nothing more than to return to her island, but then her family immigrated to New Zealand. So she wanted to come here because she couldn't stand the weather in Iceland anymore; it's always dark, always cold...she got sick and died on the boat on the way here. On a sunny day. That was important to her, I think." David wiped his eyes furtively.

"But your father was still around?" Lucas asked amiably, spreading out his sleeping bag.

David nodded. "But not for long. When he heard that there was whaling here too, it lit a fire under him. We left Christchurch for the West Coast, and he signed on straightaway with the next whaler. He wanted to take me along as a half-deck boy, but they didn't need one. So that was that."

"He just left you alone?" Lucas was horrified. "How old were you? Fifteen?"

"Fourteen," David said calmly. "Old enough to survive on my own, thought my father, though I couldn't even speak English. But as you can see, he was right. I'm here; I'm alive—and I don't think I would have made a good whaler. I always felt ill when my father came home smelling of blubber."

While the two of them got comfortable in their sleeping bags, the boy spoke freely of his experiences among the hard men of the West Coast. Apparently, he felt just as uncomfortable around them as Lucas and had been very happy to find a job as a stable boy. In exchange for keeping the stables neat, he was allowed to sleep there. He worked construction during the day.

"I'd really like to become a carpenter and design houses," he admitted to Lucas.

He smiled. "To design houses you would have to become an architect, David. And that's not easy."

David nodded. "I know. It also costs money. And you have to go to school for a long time. But I'm not dumb; I can even read."

Lucas decided to give him the next copy of *David Copperfield* that came into his hands. He felt inexplicably happy when the two finally said good night and curled up in their sleeping bags. Lucas listened to the sound of the boy sleeping, to his even breathing, and thought about the lithe way he moved despite his gangly limbs, his bright, high-pitched voice. He could love a boy like this.

David kept his word and introduced Lucas first thing the next day to the stable owner, who was happy to clear him a place to sleep for free.

"Just help David out a bit in the stalls. The boy works too much as it is. Do you know anything about horses?"

Lucas explained that he knew how to clean, saddle, and ride them, which was true and seemed to be enough for the stable owner. David spent his Sundays cleaning the stalls thoroughly since he could not always get around to it during the week, and Lucas was happy to help him. While they worked, the boy talked the entire time, reporting on his adventures, hopes, and dreams, and Lucas was an enthusiastic audience. He swung the pitchfork with unexpected élan to boot. Never before had work been so much fun.

On Monday David took Lucas along to work construction, and the master carpenter assigned him straightaway to a lumberjack camp. The jungle had to be cleared for the new houses, and the exotic wood they felled was either stored in Westport to be used for building later or sold in other parts of the island or even in England. Wood prices were high and climbing higher; moreover, steamships now crossed back and forth between England and New Zealand, simplifying the export of even the most cumbersome goods.

The Westport carpenters, however, did not think beyond the construction of the next house. Practically none of them had studied his craft, let alone heard of architecture as a discipline. They built simple log houses for which they fashioned equally simple furniture. Lucas regretted the destruction of the exotic trees, and the work in the jungle was hard and dangerous; there were constant injuries due to sawing and falling trees. But Lucas did not complain. Navigating life seemed easier and less troubled since he had gotten to know David, and he found himself in consistently high spirits. What was more, the boy seemed to seek out his company. He talked with Lucas for hours, and quickly realized that this older man was very knowledgeable and could answer considerably more of his questions than any of the other men around him. Lucas often found it difficult not to give away too much about his origins. Outwardly, he could hardly be differentiated from the other Coasters these days. His clothing was ragged, and he had practically no money. It was a feat just to keep himself clean. To his delight, David was also very concerned with his physical hygiene and bathed regularly in the river. The youth seemed not to feel the cold. While Lucas began shivering on the approach to the river, David was already swimming to the other bank with a laugh.

"It's not that cold!" he teased Lucas. "You should try the rivers in Iceland sometime. I swam through those with our horse when ice blocks were still floating in them!"

When the boy waded ashore, wet and naked, Lucas felt like he was seeing his beloved Greek statues of boys come alive. To him, this was not Dickens's David: he was Michelangelo's David. The boy had heard as little about the Italian painter and sculptor as about the English writer. Nevertheless, Lucas could help with that. With rapid strokes, he drew sketches of the most famous sculptures on a sheet of paper.

David could hardly hold back his astonishment, though he was less interested in the marble boy than in Lucas's drawings themselves.

"I always try to draw houses," he confided to his older friend, "but they never quite look right for some reason."

Lucas's heart raced as he explained to David where his problem lay and then introduced him to the art of perspective drawing. David was a fast learner. From then on, they spent every free minute on these lessons. When the master carpenter saw them at it one day, he promptly pulled Lucas from the lumberjack group and put him on construction. Until then, Lucas had known little about structural analysis and architecture—just the basics that every true lover of art acquired by necessity if he was interested in Roman churches or Florentine palaces. That by itself was significantly more than most of the people involved in construction here knew; added to which, Lucas was a gifted mathematician. He quickly made himself useful by producing construction drawings and formulating the directions for the sawmill much more precisely than the builders had done thus far. True, he was not very adept at working with the wood, but David showed a real talent for that and was soon attempting to make furniture from Lucas's designs. The future occupants of the new house—the wood trader and his wife—could hardly contain their delight when Lucas and David presented them with the first results of their work.

Naturally, Lucas thought incessantly about approaching his young student and friend physically. He dreamed of intimate embraces and then awoke with an erection or, worse, between wet sheets. But he kept an iron grip on himself. In Ancient Greece a physical relationship between a boy and his mentor would have been completely normal; in modern Westport they would both be damned for such a thing. That said, David became closer to his friend without thinking anything of it. When he lay naked next to Lucas after swimming, drying himself in the paltry sunlight, he often brushed against an arm or a leg. When it grew warmer after the winter and even Lucas would splash around in the water, the boy encouraged him to engage in wild wrestling matches. He did not think anything of gripping Lucas with his legs or pressing his upper body into Lucas's back. Lucas was thankful that the Buller River remained cold in the summer and that his erections were therefore short-lived. Getting to sleep with David would have represented a consummation, but Lucas knew he could not be too greedy. What he was currently experiencing was already more than he had ever hoped for. To dream of anything more would be presumptuous. Lucas also knew that his good fortune could not last forever. David would eventually grow up, perhaps fall in love with a girl, and forget all about him. Lucas hoped that by then the boy would have learned enough to make a financially secure living as a master carpenter. And he would do everything he could do to make that happen. He tried to inculcate the basics of arithmetic in the boy in order to train him not only to be a good craftsman but also a shrewd businessman. Lucas loved David selflessly, devotedly, and tenderly. He was happy for every day with him and simply tried not to think about the inevitable end. David was so young that they should still have a few years together ahead of them.

David—or Steinbjörn, as he still thought of himself—did not share Lucas's happiness. The boy was clever, diligent, and hungry for success and life. Above all, he was in love, a secret he had never shared with anyone, not even Lucas, his fatherly friend. Steinbjörn's love was also the reason he had so willingly adopted his new name and why he used every free moment to fight his way through *David Copperfield.* He would be able to use it as an excuse to talk to Daphne—naturally and innocently—and no one would ever guess how he pined for the girl. Of course he knew that he had no chance with her. She would probably not take him into her room with her even if he managed to save up enough money. To Daphne, he was no more than a child, deserving of protection like the girls she took care of, but by no means a customer.

But the boy didn't want to be just another customer. He did not see Daphne as a whore, but imagined her as a respectable wife by his side. Someday he would make a lot of money, buy Jolanda's right to the girl, and convince Daphne that she had earned an honorable life. She could bring along the twins—in his dreams, David could support them with ease.

If all that was to happen, David needed money, a great deal of it, and fast. It cut him to the core to see Daphne serving in the pub and then disappearing up to the second floor with some john. She would not be doing that forever; but most importantly, she would not be staying *here* forever. Daphne cursed the yoke under which Jolanda kept her. Sooner or later, she would vanish and take a chance on a new beginning elsewhere.

Unless David came to her with a proposal beforehand.

It was clear to him that he would never earn the necessary money as a construction worker, or even as a luxury furniture maker. He had to get rich more quickly. As luck would have it, new opportunities were popping up right at that moment in that part of the South Island. Gold had been found right next to Westport, a few miles upriver on the Buller. Gold miners were beginning to overrun the town, equipping themselves with provisions, spades, and gold pans and then disappearing into the jungle or the mountains. At first no one took them seriously, but when the first of them returned, chests swollen with pride and a small fortune in gold nuggets tucked into linen bags on their belts, gold fever took hold of even the most established Coasters all around Westport.

"Why don't we try it too, Luke?" David asked one day by the river as they watched a troop of gold prospectors paddle by them in canoes.

Lucas had just been explaining a special drawing technique and looked up in surprise. "Why don't we try what? Digging for gold? Don't be silly, David; that's not for us."

"But why not?" The hungry look in David's big-as-saucer eyes made Lucas's heartbeat quicken. There was still nothing in them of the greed of the experienced gold panners, those who had already passed through several other stations before news of the new discoveries had driven them to Westport. There was no reverberation of old disappointments, unending winters in primitive camps, blazing hot summers throughout which they dug, rerouted streams, watched endless amounts of sand trickle through a sieve, hoping, hoping, hoping—until once again others found the nuggets as wide as a finger in the river or the rich gold veins in the rocks. No, David looked more like a boy at the toymaker's. He already saw himself in possession of new treasures—as long as his father, unwilling to make any purchases, did not throw a wrench into his plans. Lucas sighed. He would have been all too glad to fulfill the boy's wish, but he saw little likelihood of success.

"Davey, we don't know anything about panning for gold," he said gently. "We wouldn't even know where to look. Besides, I'm not a trapper and adventurer. How are we supposed to make it out there?"

If Lucas were honest, the few hours he had spent in the jungle after fleeing from the *Pretty Peg* had been enough for him. Though the area's unusual flora fascinated him, the possibility of getting lost made him nervous. At the time, he had still had the river to orient him. If they were to embark on a new adventure, they would have to move farther away from it. It was true that they could follow a stream, but Lucas did not share David's optimistic notion that gold would simply come pouring down on them.

"Please, Luke, we could at least try it. We don't have to give up everything right away. Just give it a weekend. Mr. Miller will definitely lend me a horse. We'll ride upriver on Friday evening, look around up there on Saturday..."

"Where is 'up there' supposed to be, Davey?" Lucas asked mildly. "Do you have some idea already?"

"Rochford found gold in Lyell Creek and Buller Gorge. Lyell Creek is forty miles upriver."

"And the gold panners will probably already be cheek by jowl up there," Lucas said skeptically.

"We don't have to look there! There's probably gold everywhere; we need our own claim anyway. Come on, Luke, don't be a spoilsport! One weekend." David resorted to begging—and Lucas felt flattered. The boy could have joined up with any gold-digging troop but wanted to be with him. Nevertheless, Lucas vacillated. The adventure struck him as too risky. The dangers of a ride through the rainforest on unfamiliar paths far from the next settlement stared him too clearly in the face. He might never have agreed, but then Norman and a few other seal hunters appeared in the rental stables. They greeted Lucas good-naturedly—taking the opportunity to refresh everyone's memory about his night with the twins at full volume. Norman clapped him on the shoulder, pleased. "Boy, and here we thought you didn't have any spunk in ya! And what're you doing now? Heard tell, you're a big man on the construction site. Good for you. But you ain't going to get rich thataway. Listen up, we're going up the Buller to find some gold. Don't you want to come? Try to strike it rich too?"

David, who had just been equipping the mules Norman had rented with saddles and saddlebags, looked at the old man with glowing eyes. "Have you done it before? I mean, panning for gold?" he inquired excitedly.

Norman shook his head. "Not me. But Joe here did somewhere over in Australia. He can show us. Shouldn't be too hard. Hold the pan in the water, and the nuggets swim on in." He laughed.

Lucas, for his part, sighed. He could already guess what was coming his way.

"You see, Luke; everyone says it's easy," David remarked predictably. "Let's try it, *please*."

Norman saw the earnest look in the boy's eyes and laughed equally at Lucas's and David's expressions. "Well, the boy's got fire! Won't be able to hold on to him much longer, Luke. So what do you think, you two going to come with us, or do you still need to think about it?"

If there was something Lucas had not been counting on, it was a gold-seeking expedition with the whole group. On the one hand, it was certainly attractive to pass off the organization to others, or at least to share them among the group. A few of the men might even have experience as foresters. But they doubtless had no knowledge of mineralogy. If they found gold, it would be by pure chance, and then infighting was guaranteed. Lucas declined.

"We can't just leave here whenever we want," he explained. "But sooner or later...I'll be seeing you, Norm!"

Norman laughed and parted with a handshake that made Lucas's fingers ache afterward for several minutes.

"I'll be seeing you, Luke. And who knows but maybe we'll both be rich by then!"

They set out before first light. Mr. Miller, the owner of the rental stables, had lent David a horse, but since there had been only one available, he just tossed the saddlebags over its bare back and mounted behind Lucas. Although it slowed them down a bit, the horse was strong, and the forest of ferns was so thick that trotting or galloping was out of the question. Lucas, who had been so reluctant at first, soon began to enjoy the ride. It had rained over the last few days, but now the sun was shining. Banks of fog descended over the jungle, hiding the mountaintops and wrapping the land in a strange, surreal light. The horse was sure-footed and calm, and Lucas enjoyed feeling David's body behind him. Forced to sit tightly pressed against him, the boy had put his arm around Lucas's waist. Lucas could feel the movement of the boy's muscles, and his breath on the back of Lucas's neck gave him pleasant goose bumps. The boy eventually dozed off, his head sinking onto Lucas's shoulder. When the fog cleared, the river shimmered in the sunlight, sometimes reflecting on the stone walls that now rose up close to the riverbanks. Ultimately, the rocks narrowed so that it was no longer possible to continue alongside it, and Lucas had to ride back a ways to find a way up and over. Finally he discovered a sort of mule path—which may have been trampled down by Maori, or by earlier gold panners—along which he could follow the river's course from above the cliffs. Thus they slowly made their way inland. Earlier expeditions had discovered gold and coal deposits in the area. Where and by what means, however, remained a riddle to Lucas. It all looked the same to him: a mountainous landscape, consisting mostly of hills overgrown with ferns. Here and there, rock walls led up to a high plateau, and they were frequently interrupted by streams, which occasionally emptied out into the Buller River as charming waterfalls, big and small. They occasionally came upon small strands of sand along the riverbanks, which invited them to dally. Lucas wondered whether the excursion would not have been better carried out with a canoe than on a horse. It was possible that even the sand in the strands held gold, but Lucas had to admit that he had no knowledge of these matters to fall back on. If only he had taken an interest in geology or mineralogy instead of plants and insects. No doubt the earth formations, the soil, and the types of rock could have indicated where they might find gold deposits. But *no*, he had simply had to draw wetas. Lucas gradually came to the conclusion that the people around him—Gwyneira most of all—had not been entirely wrong. Unprofitable arts had defined his interests; without the money his father made from Kiward Station, he was nothing, and his chances of managing the farm successfully himself had always been slim. Gerald had been right: Lucas had failed in every way.

While Lucas dwelled on his gloomy thoughts, David was waking up behind him.

"Hey, I think I fell asleep," he reported cheerfully. "Oh man, Luke, what a view! Is that Buller Gorge?"

Below the mule path, the river wound its way between the rocky cliffs. The view over the river valley and the mountains around it was breathtaking.

"I suppose so," said Lucas. "But whoever found gold here didn't put up any signs explaining how."

"Then it would be too easy," David said optimistically. "And then everything would already be gone, since it took us so long to get out here. Hey, I'm hungry! Why don't we stop for a bit?"

Lucas shrugged, though the path they were on was ill suited for a rest stop, being rocky and lacking grass for the horse. So they agreed to ride for another half hour and look for a better place.

"Doesn't look like there's gold here anyway," David said. "And when we do stop, I want to look around."

Their patience was soon rewarded. A short while later they reached a high plateau on which grew not only the omnipresent ferns but also lush grass for the horse. The Buller followed its course far below them; directly beneath their stopping place was one of the small strands of golden-yellow sand.

"Do you think anyone's ever had the idea to pan there?" David took a bite of bread, forming the same idea Lucas had earlier. "Could be that it's full up with nuggets."

"Wouldn't that be too easy?" Lucas smiled. The boy's enthusiasm cheered him up. But David refused to give up that easily.

"Exactly! That's why no one's tried it yet. What do you bet, they get green eyes when we pan a couple of nuggets out of there nice and easy?"

Lucas laughed. "Try it on a strand that's easier to reach. You'd have to be able to fly to get down to that one."

"Another reason no one's tried it. This is the spot where we find our gold, Luke! I'm sure of it. I'll climb down there."

Lucas shook his head, concerned. The boy seemed to have become possessed. "Davey, half of all the gold panners take the river. They've already been through here and have probably rested on that strand the same as we're resting up here. There's no gold, believe me."

"Now how do you know that?" David leaped up. "I, at least, believe in my luck. I'm going to climb down and have a look!"

The boy searched for a good point of departure, and Lucas watched him, horrified, over the precipice.

"David, it's at least fifty yards! And it gets steep near the bottom. You can't climb down there!"

"Of course I can!" The boy disappeared over the edge of the cliff.

"David!" Lucas had the feeling his voice sounded like a screech. "David, wait! At least let me tie a rope around you."

Lucas had no idea if the ropes they had brought along were long enough, but he pulled them out of the saddlebags, panicking.

David didn't wait. He didn't detect any danger; climbing was fun for him, and he didn't experience vertigo. However, he was not an experienced mountain climber. He could not tell whether a rock ledge was secure or likely to break, and he had not counted on the soil on that seemingly secure ledge, on which grew a patch of grass, being wet and slippery from the rain when he carelessly burdened it with his whole weight.

Lucas heard the scream before he had finished gathering all the rope. His first impulse was to run to the cliff's edge, but then he realized that David must be dead. No one could survive a fall from this height. Lucas began to shake and for several seconds leaned his forehead against the saddlebags that were draped over the patient horse. He did not know whether he could summon the courage to look down at the shattered body of his beloved.

Suddenly he heard a weak, choked voice.

"Luke...help me! Luke!"

Lucas ran. It couldn't be true; he couldn't...

Then he saw the boy on a rock protrusion maybe twenty yards below him. He was bleeding from a wound above his eye, and his leg was bent at a strange angle, but he was alive.

"Luke, I think I broke my leg! It hurts so bad."

David sounded afraid; he seemed to be fighting back tears, but he was alive. And his position was, for the moment, not especially precarious. The rock protrusion was big enough for one, maybe two people. Lucas would have to lower himself down on a rope, grab hold of the boy, and help him climb up. He considered whether he could make use of the horse, but without a saddle on whose horn the rope could be knotted, it wasn't very promising. Besides, he didn't know the animal. If it ran off while they were hanging on the rope, it could kill them both. So he'd have to tie it to one of the rocks. Lucas looped the rope around one. It wasn't long enough for a descent all the way to the canyon floor, but it easily reached David's precipice.

"I'm coming, Davey! Stay calm." Lucas slid over the rocky ledge. His heart was beating heavily, and his shirt was damp from sweat. Lucas had never been a climber—heights scared him. But lowering himself down was easier than he had thought it would be. The rock was not smooth, and Lucas kept finding handholds on ledges, which gave him courage for the climb back up. He just couldn't look down.

David had dragged himself to the edge of the protrusion and awaited Lucas with outstretched arms. But Lucas had not correctly estimated the distance. Though he was now at the same height as David, he had ended up to the left of the rock protrusion. He would have to get the rope swinging lightly so that the boy could grab hold of it. Lucas felt sick just thinking about it. Until then he had maintained at least a light grip on the rock, but in order to swing he would have to push himself away from the cliff.

He took a deep breath.

"I'm coming now, David! Reach for the rope, and pull me toward you. As soon as I have a foothold, scoot over to me, and I'll grab onto you. I'll hold onto you; don't be afraid."

David nodded. His face was pale and streaming with tears. But he seemed to be holding himself together, and he was very capable. He should have no trouble grabbing hold of the rope.

Lucas let go of the rock and kicked off forcefully in order to land close to Dave with as little pendulating as possible. On his first attempt, however, he swung in the wrong direction and ended up too far from the boy. He felt around for his foothold, then tried again.

This time he succeeded. David seized the rope while Lucas's foot cast about for a hold.

But then the rope slackened. The rock above on the cliff's edge must have moved, or Lucas's ineptly tied knot must have slipped. At first Lucas's body slid down only a few inches. He screamed—and then everything happened in a few seconds that stretched into an eternity. The rope above the cliff came completely loose. Lucas fell, and David clung to the rope. The boy tried desperately to halt his friend's fall, but from his prone position, it was hopeless. The rope slipped faster and faster through his fingers. If it slipped all the way, not only would Lucas fall to the ground, but David's last hope would be gone. With the rope, he might still be able to lower himself to the river's edge. Without, it he would die of hunger or thirst on this rock ledge. Several thoughts raced through Lucas's head as he fell. He had to make a decision—David could not support him, and if he landed below alive, he would in all likelihood be injured. Then the rope would be no good to either of them. Lucas decided for once in his life to do the right thing.

"Hold onto the rope!" he called up to David. "Whatever you do, hold tight to the rope no matter what happens!"

Pulled down by his weight, the rope slipped ever faster through David's fingers. They had to be rope-burned already; he might have to give in to the pain at any moment.

Lucas looked up at the desperate but beautiful face of the boy he loved—for whom he was prepared to die. Then he let go.

Searing pain shot like knife strokes through Lucas's back. He was not dead, but with every appalling second that passed, he wished he were. It could not be long before death took him. After falling maybe twenty yards, Lucas had crash-landed on David's "gold strand." He could not move his legs, and his left arm was broken; he could see the shattered bone that had punctured his skin. If only it could be over soon…

Lucas clenched his teeth so as not to scream and listened to David's voice above him.

"Luke! Hold on, I'm coming!"

The boy had held onto the rope and secured it somewhere on the rocky ledge. Lucas prayed that David would not fall as he had, but deep in his heart he knew that David's knots would hold.

Shaking with fear and pain, he followed the boy's descent on the rope. Despite his broken leg and his no doubt raw fingers, he shimmied adeptly down the rock surface, finally landing on the beach. He carefully shifted his weight to his good leg but then had to crawl to get to Lucas.

"I need a crutch," he said, feigning cheerfulness. "Then we can try to follow alongside the river to get back home…or ride down the river if we have to. How you doing, Luke? I'm so glad you're alive! That arm'll work again, and…"

The boy crouched next to Lucas, examining his arm.

"I…I'm dying, Davey," Lucas whispered. "It's not just my arm. But you…you make it back. Promise me you won't give up."

"I'll never give up!" David said, but he could not manage a laugh. "And you…"

"I…listen, Dave, would you…could you…hold me?" The wish burst out of Lucas; he could not hold it back. "I…I'd like…"

"You'd like to see the river?" David asked amiably. "It's beautiful and gleaming like gold. But…maybe it's better if you keep still."

"I'm dying, Dave," Lucas repeated. "Any second now…please…"

The pain was excruciating when David lifted him up, but then seemed suddenly to vanish. Lucas felt nothing except the boy's arms around him, his breath, the shoulder he was leaning on. He smelled his sweat, which was sweeter to him than Kiward Station's rose garden, and he listened to the sobbing that David could no longer suppress. Lucas let his head sink to the side and placed a surreptitious kiss on David's chest. The boy did not feel it but pulled the dying man more tightly to him.

"It will all be OK!" he whispered. "It will all be OK. You just sleep a little now, and then…"

Steinbjörn Sigleifson rocked the dying man in his arms as his mother had done to him when he was little. He found consolation in this embrace; it kept at bay the fear that he would soon be left all alone, wounded and without blankets or provisions on this stretch of sand. He pressed his face into Lucas's hair and drew him close, weeping inconsolably.

Lucas closed his eyes and gave himself over entirely to an overwhelming feeling of joy. All was well. He had what he had wished for. He was where he belonged.

11

George Greenwood led his horse into the Westport rental stables and instructed the owner to feed it well. He seemed like a man who could be trusted; the facilities gave the impression of being well maintained. He liked this small town on the mouth of the Buller River. For a long time, it had been tiny, home to barely two hundred residents, but more gold panners were moving in these days—and coal would eventually start to be extracted. George was far more interested in that particular raw material than in gold. Though the person who had discovered the coal deposits was looking for investors who would provide for the eventual construction of a mine, his first priority was to line up financing for a railroad connection, for as long as there was no way of transporting the coal efficiently, a mine would be unprofitable. George planned to use his visit to the West Coast, among other things, to get a sense of the landscape and the possibility of rail or road connections. It was always a good idea for a merchant to look around—and his growing enterprise in Christchurch allowed him for the first time to travel from one sheep farm to another without pressing business concerns.

Now, in January, after the sheep shearing and stressful period of lambing was over, he could even risk leaving Howard O'Keefe—an endless source of concern to him—on his own for a few weeks. George sighed at the thought of Helen's hopeless husband. Thanks to George's support, the valuable breeding animals, and intensive guidance, Howard O'Keefe's farm was finally turning a profit, but Howard himself remained a shaky investment. The man tended to be touchy, liked to drink, and did not like taking advice—and, if he did, only from George himself, not from his subordinates, and least of all from Reti, Helen's former student, who had slowly come to serve as George's right-hand man. Thus every conversation, every exhortation, to drive the sheep into the lowlands in April in order not to lose any animals to a possible sudden onset of winter, for example, required a ride from Christchurch to Haldon.

As much as George and Elizabeth liked spending time with Helen, the successful young businessman occasionally had other things to do besides regulating the day-to-day management of a small farm. What's more, Howard's obstinacy and his interactions with Helen and Ruben angered him. They were always incurring Howard's wrath—paradoxically because, in Howard's opinion, Helen took too much and Ruben too little interest in the affairs of the farm. Helen had long since realized that George's help was the only thing that could not only ensure their economic stability, but drastically improve their quality of life. She, unlike her husband, was in a position to understand George's suggestions and their motives. She was always pushing Howard to put her to work, which invariably set him off. It further burdened their relationship when George would then rise to her defense, and little Ruben's enthusiasm for "Uncle George" was obviously a thorn in his side. Greenwood generously supplied the boy with the books he wanted and gave him magnifying glasses and botanist's containers to encourage his scientific interests. Howard thought it was nonsense—Ruben was supposed to take over the farm, and for that a basic knowledge of reading, writing, and arithmetic sufficed. Ruben, however, was not remotely interested in farm work and had only a limited curiosity about flora and fauna. His friend Fleur had largely initiated his "research" in these fields. Ruben shared his mother's gift for the humanities. He was already reading the classics in their original languages, and his well-formed sense of right and wrong made him seem predestined for a career as a priest or perhaps the study of law. George could not see him as a farmer—a huge conflict between father and son was inevitable. Greenwood feared that even his own work with O'Keefe would eventually come to grief—and he hardly dared to think about the consequences for Helen and Ruben. But he could worry about that later. His current excursion to the West Coast was a sort of vacation for him; he wanted to finally get to know the South Island better and discover new markets. Besides, a different father-son tragedy provided his motivation: though he had not told anyone, George was looking for Lucas Warden.

More than a year had passed since the heir of Kiward Station had disappeared, and the chatter in Haldon had largely subsided. The rumors about Gwyneira's child had been silenced; it was generally accepted that her husband was spending time in London. Since the people in town had hardly ever seen Lucas Warden, they did not miss him. Besides, the regional banker was not very discreet and thus news of Lucas's immense financial success in the motherland increasingly found its way into circulation. The people of Haldon took it for granted that Lucas was earning money by painting new pictures. In reality, however, the galleries in the capital were only selling the pieces they had long had on hand. At George's request, Gwyneira had already had a third selection of watercolors and oil paintings sent to London. They obtained ever better prices, and George shared in the earnings—which was, aside from his solicitousness, another good reason to track down the lost artist.

Curiosity also played a role. In George Greenwood's opinion, Gerald had conducted far too superficial a search for his son. He wondered why old Warden had not sent messengers to look for Lucas, or even struck out to track him down himself, which he easily could have done since Gerald knew the West Coast like the back of his hand. There were simply not all that many possible hiding places. Unless Lucas had acquired forged papers somewhere—which George did not think likely—he had not left the South Island at all, seeing as the ships' passenger manifests were reliable, and Lucas's name had not appeared on any of them. He hadn't sought refuge on one of the sheep farms on the East Coast, either; word would have gotten around. As for hiding out with a Maori tribe, Lucas had simply been brought up too English. He would never have been able to adapt to the natives' lifestyle and barely spoke a word of their language. That left the West Coast—and there were only a handful of settlements there. Why hadn't Gerald taken a finer comb to them?

What had occurred to make the elder Warden so obviously happy to be rid of his son—and why had he reacted in such a delayed and disingenuous manner to the recent birth of his grandchild? George wanted to know. Westport was the third settlement he'd visited to ask about Lucas. Only whom should he ask? The stable owner? That would be a start.

Miller, the rental stables' proprietor, shook his head.

"A young gentleman with an old gelding? Not that I know of. We don't get that many gentlemen around here." He laughed. "It could be that I just didn't hear anything about it. Up until recently I had a stable boy, but he…well, it's a long story. At any rate, he was very reliable and often looked after the people who were only passing through. Best thing would be to ask in the pub. Nothing escapes little Daphne, guaranteed…at least nothing that has to do with men."

George laughed politely at the obvious joke, though he did not quite understand it, and thanked him for the tip. He wanted to go to the pub anyway. After all, they might rent rooms there. Besides, he was hungry.

The taproom was a pleasant surprise, just as the rental stables had been. This place too boasted relative order and cleanliness. Still, there seemed to be little separating the pub from the brothel. The young red-haired girl who asked George for his order was heavily made up and wore a bar wench's eye-catching clothing.

"A beer, something to eat, and a room if there are any here," George said. "And I'm looking for a girl named Daphne."

The redhead smiled. "I'll get you the beer and sandwich right away, but we only rent rooms by the hour. If you want to book me too and aren't stingy, I can let you stay here too. Who recommended me so warmly that you asked for me as soon as you popped in?"

George returned her laugh. "So you're Daphne. I hate to disappoint. You weren't recommended to me particularly for your discretion, but rather because you're supposed to know everyone around here. Does the name Lucas Warden ring a bell?"

Daphne wrinkled her brow. "Off the top of my head, no. But it does sound vaguely familiar...I'll fetch your food and think about it."

George had pulled a few coins from his pocket, which he hoped would increase Daphne's willingness to provide information. That, however, did not seem necessary; the girl did not appear to be playing coy. On the contrary, she was beaming when she emerged from the kitchen.

"There was a Warden on the ship I came from England on!" she explained excitedly. "I just knew I'd heard the name somewhere. But the man wasn't called Lucas, but Harold or something like that. And he was a bit older. Why would you want to know that?"

George was blown away. He had not counted on hearing something like that. Very well, Daphne and her family had apparently sailed to Christchurch on the *Dublin*, like Helen and Gwyneira had done. A strange coincidence, but it did not help him.

"Lucas Warden is Gerald's son," George replied. "A tall, thin man, light blond hair, gray eyes, very proper deportment. And there's reason to believe that he's on the move somewhere on the West Coast."

Daphne's open expression turned suspicious. "And you followed him here? What are you, the police?"

George shook his head.

"A friend," he explained. "A friend with very good news. I'm convinced Mr. Warden would be overjoyed to see me. In case you do know something..."

Daphne shrugged. "It wouldn't matter," she muttered. "But if you really want to know, there was a man here named Luke—I never got his last name—but the description fits. Not that it matters now, like I said. Luke is dead. But if you want, you can talk to David...if he'll talk to you. Up until now he's hardly spoken to anyone. He's pretty far gone."

George gave a start—and knew in the same moment that the girl had to be right. There were not going to be many men like Lucas Warden on the West Coast, and this girl was a keen observer. George got up. The sandwich Daphne had brought him looked good, but he had lost his appetite.

"Where can I find this David?" he asked. "If Lucas…if he really is dead, I want to know. Right away."

Daphne nodded. "I'm sorry, sir, if it really is your Lucas. He was a nice fellow. A little strange, but all right. Come along, I'll take you to David."

To George's astonishment, she did not lead him out of the bar but up the steps. The hourly hotel rooms had to be up here.

"I didn't think you rented by more than the hour," he said as the girl purposefully crossed a plush salon lined with several numbered doors.

Daphne nodded. "That's why Madame Jolanda screamed bloody murder when I had David brought up here. But where could he have gone, badly hurt as he was? We haven't got a doctor. The barber put his leg in a splint, but feverish and half dead from hunger as he was, he couldn't just be laid out in a stall. So I made my room available. I now take customers together with Mirabelle, and the old woman takes half my pay as rent. That said, the fellows are happy to pay for the double, so I'm not making any less. Oh well, the old lady is greedy as the Gates of Hell, but I'm ditching this place soon anyway. When Davey's healthy, I'm going to take my children and look for something new."

So she already had children. George sighed. The girl must have a hard life. But then George concentrated his full attention on the room that Daphne was now entering and the young man lying in the bed.

David was hardly more than a boy. He looked tiny in the plush double bed, and his splinted and heavily bandaged leg, held up by a complicated contraption of supports and ropes, exaggerated this impression. The boy lay with his eyes closed. His handsome face was pale and drawn beneath his scraggly blond hair.

"Davey?" Daphne asked cheerfully. "Here's a visitor for you. A gentleman from…"

"Christchurch," George finished her statement.

"Apparently, he knew Luke. Davey, what was Luke's last name? You know it, right?"

For George, who had been casting an eye about the room, the question was as good as answered already. On the boy's night table lay a sketchbook with drawings that were perfectly in keeping with Lucas's style.

"Denward," the boy said.

An hour later George had heard the whole story. David told him how Lucas had spent the last few months as a construction worker and draftsman, and ended by describing their ill-fated search for gold.

"It's all my fault!" he said desperately. "Luke didn't want to go at all...and then I just had to try climbing down this rock. I killed him! I'm a murderer!"

George shook his head. "You made a mistake, son, maybe more than one. But if it happened like you told me, it was an accident. If Lucas had tied the rope better, he would still be alive. You can't blame yourself forever. That doesn't do anyone any good."

Inwardly he thought that this accident seemed just like Lucas. He was an artist, hopelessly inept in practical life. But such a talent, such a waste.

"How were you saved in the end?" George asked. "I mean, if I understood correctly, you two were pretty far from here."

"We...we weren't all that far," David said. "We both miscalculated. I thought we had ridden at least forty miles, but it was no more than fifteen. I couldn't manage that on foot...with my injured leg. I was sure I was going to die. But first...first I buried Luke. Right there on the beach. Not very deep, I'm afraid, but...but there aren't any wolves here, right?"

George assured him that no wild animal on New Zealand would exhume the body.

"And then I waited...waited to die myself. Three days, I think... at some point I lost consciousness; then I had a fever. I couldn't make it to the river anymore to drink water...but during that time our horse had come home, which made Mr. Miller think that something wasn't right. He wanted to send a search party right away, but the men laughed at him. Luke...Luke was not that skilled with horses, you know. Everyone thought he had just tied the gelding up wrong, and that it had run off. But then when we didn't come back, they sent a boat up. The barber came along, and they found me right away. After only paddling two hours, they said. I was completely unconscious. When I came to, I was here."

George nodded and ran his hand over the boy's hair. David looked so young. George could not help but think about the child that Elizabeth was carrying inside her at that moment. Maybe in a few years he would have a son like this—so eager, so brave—but hopefully born under a luckier star than this young man here. What might Lucas have seen in David? The son he had wished for? Or the lover? George was no fool, and he came from a big city. Homosexual tendencies were nothing new to him, and Lucas's bearing—along with Gwyneira's years of childlessness—had given him reason to suspect early on that the younger Warden leaned more toward boys than girls. Well, that was none of his business. As for David, the loving glances he cast at Daphne left no doubt about his sexual orientation. Daphne did not, however, return these glances. Another inevitable disappointment for the boy.

George thought for a moment.

"Listen, David," he said. "Lucas Warden...Luke Denward...was not so alone in the world as you believe. He has a family, and I think his wife has a right to know how he died. When you're feeling better, there will be a horse waiting for you in the rental stables. Take it and ride to the Canterbury Plains and ask for Gwyneira Warden at Kiward Station. Will you do that...for Luke?"

David nodded seriously. "If you think that's what he would have wanted."

"He would certainly have wanted that, David," George replied. "And after that, ride to Christchurch and come to my offices. Greenwood Enterprises. You won't find any gold there, but you will find a job that pays better than being a stable boy. If you're a clever boy—and you must be or Lucas would not have taken you under his wing—you might even grow wealthy in a few years."

David nodded again, but this time reluctantly.

Daphne, though, gave George a friendly look. "You'll give him a job where he can sit, right?" she asked as she led the visitor out. "The barber says he'll always limp; the leg is bum. He can't work at the site or in the stables anymore. But if you find a place for him in an office...then he'll also change his mind, with regard to girls. It was good for him that he didn't fall for Luke, but I'm not the right bride for him."

She spoke calmly and without bitterness, and George felt a slight regret that this active, clever creature was a girl. As a man, Daphne could have made her fortune in the New Country. As a girl, she could only be what she would have been in London—a whore.

More than half a year passed before Steinbjörn Sigleifson directed his horse's steps over the approach to Kiward Station. After lying for a long while in bed, the boy slowly had to learn how to walk again. In addition to that, taking leave of Daphne and the twins had been hard for him, even though the girl had been telling him for days that it was time for him to be on his way. In the end, there had been nothing else left for him to do. Madame Jolanda expressly asked that he clear out of her room in the brothel, and though Mr. Miller allowed him to make camp in the stables again, he could no longer repay the favor. There was no work for a cripple in Westport—the hard-bitten Coasters had informed him of that without sugarcoating the matter. Even though the boy could already get around without trouble, he still had a strong limp, and he could not remain on his feet for long. So he had finally ridden away—and now stood dazed before the statues on the facade of the manor where Lucas Warden had lived. He still had no idea why his friend had left Kiward Station, but he must have had important reasons to give up such luxury. Gwyneira Warden must have been a real shrew. Steinbjörn—after leaving Daphne, he saw no reason to hold on to the name David—seriously considered turning around without accomplishing anything. Who could imagine what he would have to hear from Lucas's wife. She might even hold him responsible for Lucas's death.

"What are you doing here? State your name and your desire."

Steinbjörn started when he heard a high-pitched voice behind him. It came from the bushes below, and the young Icelander—who had grown up believing in fairies and elves who lived in stones—at first suspected a spirit.

The little girl on the pony who then appeared behind him made a suitably mundane impression on him, even if the rider and steed had a fay-like sweetness. Though the horses on his home island were not big, Steinbjörn had never seen such a small pony. But this tiny sorrel mare—whose color harmonized perfectly with the red-blonde hair of its little rider—looked like a full-grown horse in a miniature edition. The girl directed the horse purposefully toward him.

"Get moving!" she said rudely.

Steinbjörn had to laugh. "My name is Steinbjörn Sigleifson, and I'm looking for Lady Gwyneira Warden. This is Kiward Station, isn't it?"

The girl nodded seriously. "Yes, but they're shearing the sheep now, so Mummy isn't home. Yesterday she was overseeing warehouse three; today she is at number two. She's trading with the foreman. Grandfather is handling warehouse one."

Steinbjörn did not know what the girl was talking about, but assumed that the little girl must be telling the truth.

"Can you take me to her?" he inquired.

The girl frowned. "You're a visitor, right? So I have to take you into the house, and you have to put your card in the silver tray. And then comes Kiri who bids you welcome, and after that Witi, and then you go into the little salon and get tea...oh yes, and I have to entertain you is what Miss O'Keefe says. That means talking with each other, or something like that. About the weather and such. You *are* a gentleman, right?"

Steinbjörn still did not understand a thing, but he could not deny that the girl was rather entertaining.

"By the way, I'm Fleurette Warden, and this is Minty." She pointed to the pony.

Steinbjörn suddenly took more interest in the child. Fleurette Warden—she had to be Luke's daughter. So he had left this charming child behind as well...Steinbjörn understood his friend less and less.

"I don't think I'm a gentleman," he informed the girl. "At least, I don't have a card. Couldn't we just...I mean, can't you just take me to your mother?"

Fleurette did not seem to care much for polite conversation and let herself be convinced. She moved her pony so that it was in front of Steinbjörn's horse, which then had to work hard to keep up. Little Minty made short but fast strides, and Fleurette directed her with great competence. On the short ride to the shearing sheds, she revealed to her new friend that she had just come from school. She wasn't generally allowed to go by herself, but she was just then because there was no one to accompany her while the sheep were being sheared. She told him about her friend Ruben and her little brother, Paul, whom she though rather daft because he didn't talk and only screamed—most of all when Fleurette held him in her arms.

"He doesn't like any of us, only Kiri and Marama," she said. "Look, there's shed two. What do you bet that Mummy's in there?"

The shearing sheds were long buildings with space for several pens that allowed the shearers to work rain or shine. In front and behind them were more pens, where the still unshorn sheep awaited their shearing and those already shorn waited to be herded back into the pastures. Steinbjörn understood next to nothing about sheep but had seen many in his homeland—and could tell that he was looking at top-quality animals. Before being shorn, Kiward Station's sheep looked like clean, fluffy balls of wool with legs. Afterward they were run through a hygiene bath and looked well nourished and spirited, if a little peeved. Fleurette had dismounted and tied her pony in front of the warehouse with an expert knot. Steinbjörn did the same, then followed her inside, where a pervasive stench of manure, sweat, and wool grease struck him. Fleurette seemed not to notice it as she pushed her way through the orderly chaos of men and sheep. Steinbjörn observed with fascination how the shearers seized the animals quick as lightning, laid them on their backs, and unburdened them of their wool in short order. They seemed to be competing against each other in their task. They triumphantly called out new numbers to each other at regular intervals, which were evidently meant for the overseer.

Whoever was keeping the books had a hell of a job keeping up. Yet the young woman who passed among the men noting their output did not seem overly taxed. Clearly relaxed, she joked with the shearers, and it did not appear that her tallies were ever challenged. Gwyneira Warden wore a simple gray riding dress, and her long red hair was braided carelessly. Though short, she was obviously just as energetic as her daughter—and as she now turned her face in the direction of Steinbjörn, he was blown away by so much beauty. What had Luke been thinking leaving such a woman behind? Steinbjörn could hardly take in her noble features, her sensual lips, and her enchanting indigo-blue eyes. He did not realize he had been staring until her smile turned into a frown, at which point he immediately averted his eyes.

"This is Mummy. And this is Stein...Stein...something with Stein," Fleur said, attempting a formal introduction.

Steinbjörn had regained his composure and hobbled over to Gwyneira.

"Lady Warden? Steinbjörn Sigleifson. I've come from Westport. Mr. Greenwood asked me...well, I was with your late husband when..." He extended his hand to her.

Gwyneira nodded. "Mrs., not Lady, Warden," she corrected him mechanically as she shook his hand. "But welcome. George mentioned something...but we can't talk here. Wait a moment, please."

The young woman looked around, then located an older, dark-haired man among the shearers and exchanged a few words with him. Then she announced to the men in the warehouse that Andy McAran would be handling the overseeing for a while.

"And I expect that you will all maintain our lead! Right now this warehouse is well ahead of one and three. Don't let them take it from us. As you well know, the winners get a barrel of the best whiskey!" She waved cheerfully to the men, then turned to Steinbjörn. "Come with me, please; we'll go to the house. But first let's find my father-in-law. He should also hear what you have to say."

Steinbjörn followed Gwyneira and her daughter out to the horses. There Gwyneira mounted a powerful brown mare, quickly and without help. The boy also now noticed the dogs that followed her everywhere.

"Aren't you needed elsewhere, Finn, Flora? Away with you, back in the warehouse. You come along, Cleo." The young woman shooed two of the collies back to the sheep shearers; the third, an older dog who was gradually graying around the nose, joined the riders.

Warehouse one, where Gerald was working as overseer, was located west of the main house about a mile away. Gwyneira rode in silence, and Steinbjörn did not say a word either. Fleur alone provided the general entertainment by reporting excitedly about school, where there had apparently been a fight.

"Mr. O'Keefe was very angry at Ruben because he was at school and wasn't helping with the sheep since the shearers are coming in a few days. Mr. O'Keefe still has sheep in the high pastures, and Ruben was supposed to fetch them, but Ruben is horribly bad when it comes to sheep. I told him: I'll come help you tomorrow. I'll take Finn and Flora along, then it'll go quick as a flash."

Gwyneira sighed. "O'Keefe will not be particularly happy that there's a Warden with a few Silkham collies herding his sheep while his son studies Latin...watch out that he doesn't shoot at you!"

Steinbjörn found the mother's way of expressing herself as strange as that of her daughter, but Fleur seemed to understand.

"He thinks Ruben has to want to do all that because he's a boy," Fleurette remarked.

Gwyneira sighed again and halted her horse in front of a warehouse that looked just like the one they had come from. "He's not the only one. Here...come along, if you please, Mr. Sigleifson. This is where my father-in-law is working. Or wait here if you prefer, and I'll bring him right out. There's as much of a rumpus in here as there was in mine."

Steinbjörn had already dismounted, so he followed her into the warehouse. It would not have been polite to greet the older man from the saddle. Besides, he hated when people treated him differently because of his limp.

An active, noisy commotion filled warehouse one just as it had in Gwyneira's division, but the atmosphere was different here—palpably more strained, not as chummy. The men seemed less motivated, more pressed or hounded. And the powerful older man moving among the shearers criticized rather than joked with them. A half-empty bottle of whiskey and a glass stood next to the board where he noted output. He was just taking another drink when Gwyneira entered and spoke to him.

Steinbjörn saw a bloated face with bloodshot eyes; whiskey had clearly taken its toll on the man.

"What are you doing here?" he snapped at Gwyneira. "Already done with the five thousand sheep in warehouse two?"

Gwyneira shook her head. Steinbjörn noticed her simultaneously concerned and accusatory glance at the bottle.

"No, Gerald, Andy is handling it. I was called away. And I think you should come too. Gerald, this is Mr. Sigleifson. He's come to tell us about Lucas's death." She introduced Steinbjörn, but the old man's face exhibited only disdain.

"And you're leaving the warehouse in the lurch for that? To hear what your cock-sucking husband's catamite has to say?"

Gwyneira looked shocked, but to her relief her young visitor looked on uncomprehending. His Nordic accent had already caught her attention—either he had not heard or he just didn't understand what the words meant.

"Gerald, this young man was the last person to see Lucas alive." She calmly tried once more, but the old man exploded at her.

"And kissed him good-bye, eh? Spare me these stories, Gwyn. Lucas is dead. He should rest in peace, but please leave me in peace too! And I don't want to catch that boy in my house when I'm done here."

Gerald turned away. Gwyneira led Steinbjörn out with an apologetic expression on her face. "Please forgive my father-in-law; it's the whiskey talking. He never got over Lucas...well, him being what he was, or that he ended up leaving the farm...deserted it, as Gerald puts it. Lord knows he had his part in it. But that's ancient history. I'm grateful that you've come, Mr. Sigleifson. Let's go to the house; you could no doubt do with some refreshment."

Steinbjörn could hardly bring himself to set foot in the manor. He was sure he'd make one mistake after another. Luke had occasionally brought to his attention certain details of correct table posture and the rules of etiquette, and even Daphne seemed to know something of these matters. But he himself knew nothing and was terribly afraid of making a fool of himself in front of Gwyneira. She, however, led him entirely naturally in through a side door, took his jacket, and then rang, not for the maid apparently, because they met straightaway with the nanny, Kiri, in the salon. Gerald had recently lifted his prohibition on the young woman bringing the children along when she was cleaning or taking care of other housework. He had eventually realized that if he banned Kiri to the kitchen, Paul would grow up there.

Gwyneira greeted Kiri kindly and took one of the babies out of the baby basket.

"Mr. Sigleifson, my son Paul," she said, though the last words were drowned out by the baby's earsplitting scream. Paul did not seem to relish being taken from his adopted sister Marama's side.

Steinbjörn pondered a few things. Paul was still a baby. He must have been born during Luke's absence.

"I give up," sighed Gwyneira, laying the baby back in its basket. "Kiri, would you take the babies please—Fleur too; she still needs to eat, and what the two of us have to discuss is not suitable for her ears. And could you please make us some tea—or coffee, Mr. Sigleifson?"

"Steinbjörn, please," the boy said shyly. "Or David. Luke called me David."

Gwyneira's gaze passed over his features and his ruffled hair. Then she smiled. "He always was a little jealous of Michelangelo," she remarked after a pause. "Come, sit down. You had a long ride."

To his astonishment Steinbjörn did not find the conversation with Gwyneira Warden difficult at all. He had initially been worried that she didn't know about Lucas's death, but George Greenwood had obviously already said something. Gwyneira had long since overcome the first waves of sorrow and only asked sympathetically about Steinbjörn's time with her husband, how they had come to know each other and what had happened during his final months.

Finally Steinbjörn described the circumstances of his death, blaming himself anew.

But Gwyneira saw things as Greenwood had and expressed herself even more strongly. "There's nothing you could do about Lucas being unable to tie a knot. He was a good man, God knows I treasured him. And as it turns out, he was a very gifted artist. But he was hopelessly lacking in common sense. Still...I think he always wished he could be a hero just once. And he was in the end, wasn't he?"

Steinbjörn nodded. "Everyone talks about him with the greatest respect, Mrs. Warden. People are considering naming the rock after him. The rock that...that we fell from."

Gwyneira was touched. "I don't think he ever wanted more than that."

Steinbjörn was afraid she would burst into tears any moment, and he certainly had no idea how to properly comfort a lady. But then she regained her composure and continued with her questions. To his amazement, she asked a great many questions about Daphne, whom she remembered very well. After Greenwood reported having met the girl, Helen had written straightaway to Westport, but had yet to receive a response. Steinbjörn confirmed their suspicion that the red-haired Daphne in Westport was indeed Helen's charge from long ago, and he informed her about the twins as well. Gwyneira was blown away when she heard about Laurie and Mary.

"So Daphne found the girls! Now how did she manage that? And they're all doing well? Daphne's taking care of them?"

"Well, they..." Steinbjörn reddened. "They...work a bit themselves. They dance. Here...here, Luke sketched them." The boy had brought his saddlebags in with him and looked for a folder; having located it, he thumbed through it. Only as he was pulling it out did it occur to him that these drawings were hardly fit for the eyes of a lady. However, Gwyneira did not bat an eye when she laid eyes on them. In order to supply the galleries in London, she had already combed through Lucas's workroom and was therefore not nearly as innocent as she had been a few months before. Lucas had already painted nudes before—boys at first, who assumed the same pose as that of *David*, but men too in unambiguous poses. One of the images had displayed the traces of frequent use. Lucas had taken it out again and again, looked at it, and…

Gwyneira noticed that the nude sketches of the twins, but especially a study of young Daphne, contained finger indentations. Lucas? Hardly!

"You like Daphne, do you?" she asked her young visitor cautiously.

Steinbjörn blushed deeply. "Oh yes, very much! I wanted to marry her. But she doesn't want me." In the youth's voice, she discerned all the pain of a lover spurned. This young man had never been Lucas's "catamite."

"You'll marry a different girl," Gwyneira comforted him. "You… you do like girls?"

Steinbjörn's expression made it clear he thought that was the dumbest question a person could ask. Then he willingly gave her more information about his plans for the future. He planned to go looking for George Greenwood and work for him.

"I would have preferred to build houses," he said sadly. "I wanted to be an architect. Luke said I had talent. But I would have had to go to school in England for that, and I can't afford it. But here, these are for you." Steinbjörn closed Lucas's sketch portfolio and pushed it across to Gwyneira. "I brought you Luke's pictures. All his drawings…Mr. Greenwood said they might be valuable. I don't want to get rich that way. If I could maybe keep just one. The one of Daphne."

Gwyneira smiled. "Naturally, you can keep all of them. No doubt that's what Lucas would have wanted." She considered briefly, seeming to arrive at a decision. "Go ahead and put your jacket on, David. We'll ride to Haldon. There's something else there that Lucas would have wanted."

The director of the bank in Haldon seemed to think Gwyneira was crazy. He came up with a thousand reasons to refuse her request, but finally conceded when faced with her implacable determination. Reluctantly, he transferred the account into which Lucas's income from the picture sales flowed to Steinbjörn Sigleifson's name.

"You're going to regret this, Mrs. Warden. It's shaping up into a fortune. Your children..."

"My children already have a fortune. They're the heirs of Kiward Station, and my daughter does not have the slightest interest in art. We don't need the money, but this boy here was Lucas's pupil. A... soul mate, so to speak. He needs the money, he knows to cherish it, and he will have it! Here, David, you need to sign. With your full name, that's important."

Steinbjörn's breath caught when he saw the sum in the account. But Gwyneira only nodded at him kindly. "Well, go ahead and sign. I need to get back to my shearing shed to increase my children's fortune. And you'd do best to look into this gallery yourself. So that they don't swindle you when you sell the rest of the pictures. You are now more or less the manager of Lucas's artistic inheritance. So make something of it!"

Steinbjörn Sigleifson no longer hesitated but signed his name to the document.

Lucas's "David" had found his gold mine.

Arrival

Canterbury Plains—Otago

1870–1877

1

"Paul, Paul, where are you hiding this time?"

Helen called after the most rebellious of her pupils, though she knew for a fact that the boy could hardly hear her. Paul Warden was certainly not playing peacefully with the Maori children in the immediate vicinity of their makeshift schoolhouse. When he disappeared, it meant trouble in no uncertain terms—whether he was duking it out somewhere with his archenemy Tonga, the son of the chief of the Maori tribe dwelling on Kiward Station, or he was lying in wait for Ruben and Fleurette in order to play some kind of prank on them. His gags were not always funny. Ruben had gotten rather upset recently when Paul had poured an inkwell out on his newest book. That had been aggravating not only because the boy had wanted this law compendium for a long time and only just received it from England thanks to George Greenwood, but also because the book was exceptionally valuable. Although Gwyneira had reimbursed him for it, she was just as shocked by her son's deed as Helen.

"He's not all that young anymore!" she exclaimed, working herself into a state while the eleven-year-old Paul stood, unremorseful, nearby. "Paul, you knew what that book was worth! And that was no accident. Do you think money grows on trees at Kiward Station?"

"Nah, but it does on the sheep," retorted Paul, not entirely wrong. "We could afford to buy a stupid, dusty old book like that every week if we wanted." He glared spitefully at Ruben. The boy knew exactly what the economic situation in the Canterbury Plains was. True, Howard O'Keefe was doing much better under the aegis of Greenwood Enterprises, but he was still a long way from Gerald's honorary title of sheep baron. The flocks and the wealth of Kiward

Station had also grown over the past ten years, and for Paul Warden, hardly a wish went unfulfilled. He had little interest in books. Paul would rather have the fastest pony, loved toy weapons like pistols, and would surely already have had an air rifle if George Greenwood had not "forgotten" it every time he placed orders to England. Helen observed Paul's development with concern. In her opinion, no one set enough boundaries for the boy. Both Gwyneira and Gerald bought him expensive presents but otherwise hardly concerned themselves with him. By this time, Paul had largely outgrown the influence of his "adopted mother," Kiri, as well. He had long since adopted his grandfather's opinion that the white race was superior to the Maori. That was also the cause of his endless fights with Tonga. The chieftain's son was just as self-assured as the sheep baron's heir, and the boys fought bitterly over to whom the land on which both Tonga's people and the Wardens lived belonged. That too disconcerted Helen. Tonga would most likely take over as his father's successor, just as Paul would inherit from his grandfather. If their enmity lasted, then things might become difficult. And every bloody nose that one of the boys went home with deepened the rift between them.

At least there was Marama, who reassured Helen somewhat. Kiri's daughter, Paul's "adopted sister," had a sort of sixth sense for the boys' confrontations and tended to show up at every battleground to arbitrate. If she was there, innocently playing hopscotch with a few friends, then Paul and Tonga avoided trouble. Marama then gave Helen a conspiratorial smile. She was a charming child, at least by Helen's standards. Her face was narrower than that of most Maori girls, and her velvety complexion was the color of chocolate. She did not have any tattoos yet and probably never would be decorated according to custom. The Maori had increasingly abandoned the ritual and rarely even wore traditional clothing anymore. They were obviously making efforts to fit in with the *pakeha*—which delighted Helen in some ways, but which also occasionally filled her with a vague feeling of regret.

"Where's Paul, Marama?" Helen now turned directly to the girl. Paul and Marama usually came to class together from Kiward Station.

If Paul had gotten upset about something and ridden home early, she would know it.

"He rode away, miss. He's on the trail of a mystery," Marama revealed in a clear, loud voice. The little girl was a good singer, a talent treasured by her people.

Helen sighed. They had just read a few books about pirates and treasure hunts, hidden countries and secret gardens, and now all the girls were looking for enchanted rose gardens while the boys excitedly drew treasure maps. Ruben and Fleur had done the same thing at this age, but when it came to Paul, she knew that the secrets might not be so innocent. He had recently driven Fleurette into a frenzy of worry by leading her beloved horse Minette, a daughter of the mare Minty and the stud Madoc, away and hiding it in Kiward Station's rose garden. Since Lucas's death, that part of the garden was hardly kept up, and no one thought to look for the horse there. Besides, Minette had not been taken from her stall but from the O'Keefes' yard. Helen was frantic at the thought that Gerald would hold her husband responsible for the loss of his valuable animal. Minette had finally drawn attention to herself by whinnying and galloping around the yard. That did not happen, however, until hours later, after she had enjoyed her fill of the grass in the overgrown square, during which a desperate Fleurette wrongly believed her horse to be lost in the highlands or stolen by horse thieves.

Thieves and rustlers in general...this was a subject that had been disquieting farmers in the Canterbury Plains for a few years now. Although the New Zealanders had prided themselves only a decade earlier on not being the descendants of convicts like the Australians, instead building a society of virtuous colonists, criminal elements were beginning to surface here. It was nothing surprising—the abundant livestock count of farms like Kiward Station and the steadily growing fortune of their owners aroused covetousness. In addition, climbing the social ladder was no longer so simple for new immigrants. The first families were already established, land was no longer to be had for free or close to it, and the whale and seal grounds were largely exhausted. There was still the occasional spectacular gold find, so it was still possible to go from rags to riches—just not in the Canterbury Plains. But the great livestock barons' foothills, flocks, and herds had become the center of operations and the barons themselves victims of brutal thieves and rustlers. It had all begun with one man, an old acquaintance of Helen and the Wardens: James McKenzie.

At first Helen had not believed it when Howard had come home from the pub cursing Gerald's former foreman by name.

"Heaven only knows why Warden gave him the boot, but now we're all paying the price. The workers talk about him as if he were a hero. He steals only the best animals, they say, ones from the money-bags. He leaves the small farmers alone. What nonsense! How's he supposed to know the difference? But they take a devilish delight in it. Wouldn't surprise me if the fellow gathered himself a band of thieves."

"Like Robin Hood," had been Helen's first thought, but then she reproved herself for the romantic lapse. The romanticization of the rustler was nothing more than people's imagination at work.

"How is one man supposed to manage all of that?" she remarked to Gwyneira. "Herding the sheep together, culling them, taking them over the mountains...you'd need a whole gang."

"Or a dog like Cleo," Gwyneira suggested uneasily, thinking of the puppy she had given James in parting. James McKenzie was a particularly gifted dog trainer. No doubt Friday was no longer second to her mother anymore—more likely she had since lapped her. Cleo had grown very old by this time and mostly deaf. She still stuck to Gwyneira like her shadow, but she no longer served as a work dog.

It wasn't long before the odes to James McKenzie began including his brilliant sheepdog. Gwyneira's suspicions were confirmed when Friday's name was dropped for the first time.

Fortunately, Gerald made no comment on James's abilities as a shepherd or the missing pup, whose absence he must have noticed at the time. However, Gerald and Gwyneira had had other things on their minds during that fateful year. The sheep baron had probably simply forgotten about the little dog. In any event, he lost several head of livestock a year to McKenzie—as did Howard, the Beasleys, and all the other larger sheep breeders. Helen would have liked to know what Gwyneira thought about it, but her friend never mentioned James McKenzie if she could help it.

Helen had by now had enough of her senseless search for Paul. She would begin class whether he showed up or not. Chances were pretty good that he would turn up eventually. Paul respected Helen; she might have been the only person he ever listened to. Sometimes she believed that his constant attacks on Ruben, Fleurette, and Tonga might be motivated by jealousy. The bright and attentive chieftain's son was among her favorite students, and Ruben and Fleurette held a special place in her heart, of course. Paul, though certainly not stupid, was not exceptionally scholarly, preferring to play the class clown—and thus made Helen's life difficult, as well as his own.

That day, however, there was no chance that Paul would reach school during class. The boy was too far away for that; as soon as he had noticed Ruben turn conspiratorially to Paul's sister, Fleur, he had glued himself to the two older children's heels. Secrets, he knew very well, almost always involved something forbidden, and for Paul there was nothing better than catching his sister at some petty infraction. He had no compunctions about tattling, even if the results rarely proved satisfactory. Kiri never punished the adolescents, and even Paul's mother displayed lenience when she caught Fleurette telling fibs or a glass or vase broke during one of her wild games. Paul rarely experienced such mishaps. He was naturally deft, and besides, he had practically grown up among the Maori. He had adopted their fluid hunter's gait, their ability to sneak up on prey all but silently—just like his rival, Tonga. The Maori men made no distinction between the little *pakeha* and their own offspring. If there were children there, people cared for them, and it was among the hunters' duties to instruct the youths in their art, just as the women taught the girls. Paul had always been among their most gifted students, and now those skills enabled him to sneak up behind Fleurette and Ruben unnoticed. It was a shame that their whispering was probably about one of the young O'Keefe's secrets instead of some wrongdoing by his sister. No doubt Miss O'Keefe's punishment for anything her son had done would not prove harsh enough to warrant his having to listen to her harangue about tattle-telling. He would have achieved better results by telling on the boy to his father, but Paul didn't trust himself around Howard O'Keefe. He knew that Helen's husband and his grandfather did not get along, and Paul would not collaborate with Gerald's enemies; it was a question of honor. Paul only hoped his grandfather appreciated it. He made every effort to impress his grandfather, but the older Warden took little notice of him. Paul did not hold that against him. His grandfather had more important things to do than play with young boys—on Kiward Station, Gerald Warden was almost like God himself. But eventually, Paul would do something noteworthy, and then Gerald would have to notice him. The boy wanted nothing more than his grandfather's praise.

As for Ruben and Fleurette—what might they have to conceal? Paul had become suspicious when Ruben had not taken his own horse but instead settled in front of Fleurette on Minette. Minette did not have a saddle on so there was room for both riders on her back. What a strange way to ride. Ruben took the reins while Fleurette sat behind him, pressing her upper body against him with her cheek tight against his back and her eyes closed. Her curly, red-golden hair fell loosely to her shoulders—Paul remembered that one of the shepherds had said she looked good enough to eat. That must have meant that the guy wanted to do it with her—though Paul still only had a vague idea what that involved. One thing was certain: Fleurette was the last person he would ever think of for that. Paul couldn't imagine the word beauty ever being used in connection with his sister. Why was she snuggling up so to Ruben? Was she afraid of falling down? Not very likely—Fleurette was an extremely confident rider.

It did not help that Paul had to get closer to hear what the two of them were whispering. How stupid was it that his pony, Minty, made such short, quick strides. It was almost impossible to bring her into tempo with Minette so as to be less noticeable. Fleurette and Ruben, however, were oblivious. They must have been able to hear his pony's steps, but they weren't paying attention to them. Only Gracie, Fleur's sheepdog, who followed her mistress around as naturally as Cleo did their mother, cast suspicious glances into the brush. But Gracie would not attack; after all, she knew Paul.

"Do you think we'll ever find these damned sheep?" Ruben asked suddenly. His voice sounded nervous, almost fearful.

Fleurette was obviously displeased to have to lift her face from his back.

"Yes, of course," she murmured. "Don't worry. Gracie will herd them together in the blink of an eye. We...should even have time for a rest."

Paul noted with bewilderment how her hands played on Ruben's shirt and her fingers felt through his buttonholes for his naked chest.

The boy did not seem unwilling. He reached behind him briefly and stroked Fleur's neck. "Gah, I don't know...the sheep...my father will kill me if I don't bring them back."

So that was it. The sheep had gotten away from Ruben once again. Paul could even picture which ones. On the way to school the day before, he had seen the amateur repair job done to the fence holding the young rams.

"Have you at least fixed the fence?" Fleur asked. The two riders crossed a brook to an especially lovely bank covered in grass, screened by rocks and nikau palms. Fleurette removed her small brown hands from Ruben's chest and reached nimbly for the reins. She brought Minette to a halt, leaped from her back, and threw herself in the grass, where she lounged provocatively. Ruben tied the horse to a tree and lay down next to her.

"Tie her down tightly or she'll be gone in a heartbeat," Fleur told him. Her eyes were half-closed, but she had still noticed Ruben's inept knot. The girl loved her beau, but she was as distressed about his lack of practical skills as Gwyneira had once been about the man Fleur took for her father. Ruben had no artistic pretenses though, wanting instead to go to Dunedin to study law at the university being organized there. Helen supported her son's vision—erring on the side of caution, he had not yet presented his plans to Howard.

The boy got reluctantly to his feet to see to the horse. He did not hold Fleur's assertive nature against her. He knew his own weakness as well as anybody, and he was awed by Fleurette's practical capabilities.

"I'll take care of the fence tomorrow," he muttered, which made Paul shake his head uncomprehendingly. If Ruben just enclosed the rams in the same broken pen again, they would run away again by morning.

Fleurette said something to that effect. "I can help you, you know," she offered, and then they were both quiet. It annoyed Paul that he could not see anything, so he finally crept around the stone to get a better look. What he saw made him catch his breath. The kisses and caresses that Fleur and Ruben were exchanging beneath the trees looked rather like what Paul thought "doing it" was! Fleur lay in the grass, her hair spread out like a radiant web; on her face was an expression of pure delight. Ruben had opened her blouse and was stroking and kissing her breasts, which Paul also gazed upon with interest. It had been at least five years since he had seen his sister naked. Ruben too seemed happy; he was obviously taking his time and was not thrusting his body repeatedly like the Maori man Paul had once observed with a woman from afar. He also was not lying on top of Fleur but next to her—so they couldn't actually be doing it yet. But Paul was certain that Gerald Warden would be extremely interested.

Fleurette had put her arm around Ruben and was stroking his back. Then her fingers began to reach under the band of his breeches, caressing him below. Ruben moaned with pleasure and threw himself on top of her.

Oh, so they were…

"No, dearest, not now." Fleurette gently pushed Ruben off her. She did not look afraid, but rather, decisive. "We have to save something for our wedding night." Her eyes were now open and she was smiling at Ruben. The young man returned her smile. Ruben was a handsome boy who had inherited his somewhat austere, masculine features from his father, as well as his dark curly hair. Otherwise, he mostly took after Helen. His face was narrower than Howard's, his eyes gray and dreamy. He was tall, more lanky than stout, with wiry muscles. His gaze exhibited desire, but it looked more like anticipation than naked lust. Fleurette sighed happily. She felt loved.

"If there ever will be a wedding," Ruben finally said, concerned. "I don't imagine your grandfather and my father would be too happy about that."

Fleurette shrugged. "But our mothers won't object," she said optimistically. "Then the others will have to accept it. What do they even have against each other? A feud like that across the years—it's crazy!"

Ruben nodded. He had a more even-tempered nature than Fleurette, who got worked up more quickly. He couldn't rule out that Fleurette herself might be capable of bearing a lifelong grudge as well. Ruben had no trouble picturing Fleurette wielding a flaming sword. He smiled but then became serious again.

"I know what happened!" he revealed to his beloved after a moment. "Uncle George got it out of that talkative banker in Haldon and then told my mother. Do you want to hear it?" Ruben played with one of her red-gold strands of hair.

Paul pricked up his ears. It was just getting better and better. It looked as though he was not only going to learn Fleur and Ruben's secrets but also the details of the family history.

"Are you joking?" Fleurette asked. "I'm dying to know! Why haven't you told me until now?"

Ruben shrugged. "Could it be that there was always something else we could have been doing?" he asked mischievously, kissing her.

Paul sighed. No further delays, please. He would have to leave soon if he wanted to be halfway on time getting home. Kiri and Mother would ask questions if Marama came home alone—and then they would find out he'd cut class.

But Fleur too wanted to hear the story more than sweet nothings. She gingerly pushed Ruben away and sat up. She snuggled up to him while he spoke, taking a moment to rebutton her blouse. It had probably also occurred to her that it was time they went to look for the sheep.

"So, my father and your grandfather were already here in the forties when there still weren't many settlers, just whalers and seal hunters. But back then there was still a great deal of money to be made in those industries, and the two of them were very good at poker and blackjack as well. In any event, they had a fortune in their pockets when they arrived in the Canterbury Plains. My father was just passing through on his way to the Otago region, having heard some whispers about gold. But your grandfather was contemplating a sheep farm—and tried to convince my father to invest his money in livestock. And in land. Gerald established good relations with the Maori straightaway. He started haggling with them from the get-go. And the Kai Tahu were not exactly disinclined. Their tribe had sold land before, and they got along well with the buyers."

"And?" asked Fleur. "So they sold the land..."

"Not so fast. While the negotiations were dragging on and my father couldn't decide what to do, they were staying with these settlers—the Butlers, they were called. And Leonard Butler had a daughter. Barbara."

"But that was my grandmother!" said Fleur, becoming more interested.

"Right. Only really she should have been my mother," Ruben explained. "My father was in love with her, and she loved him as well. But her father was not so enthusiastic about the match. My father thought he needed more money to impress him."

"So he moved to Otago and found gold but in the meantime Barbara married Gerald? Oh, Ruben, how tragic!" Fleur sighed at the romantic tale she had envisioned.

"Not quite." Ruben shook his head. "Father wanted to make the money then and there. It came down to a card game between Father and Gerald."

"And he lost? Did Grandfather win all the money?"

"Fleurette, just let me tell the story," Ruben said sternly and waited for Fleurette to nod apologetically. She was clearly impatient to hear more.

"Father had already declared himself ready to be a partner in Gerald's sheep enterprise—they even had a name for the farm: Kiward

Station, from Ward-en and O'-Kee-fe. But then he not only lost his own money but also what Gerald had given him to pay the Maori for the land."

"Oh no!" Fleur cried, understanding at once why Gerald was so angry. "No doubt my grandfather wanted to kill him."

"It turned into quite an ugly scene," Ruben explained. "In the end, Mr. Butler lent Gerald some money—so that he would not lose face before the Maori since the land had been promised to Howard and himself. So Gerald acquired a portion of the land that now forms Kiward Station, but my father did not want to be left behind. He still harbored hopes of marrying Barbara, you see. So he put his last penny into a piece of rocky land with a few half-starved sheep on it. Our wonderful farm. But by then, Barbara had long since gotten engaged to Gerald. The money that her father had loaned your grandfather was her dowry. Later she inherited the land from old Butler. Which is why it's no wonder that Gerald rose like a meteor to become a sheep baron."

"Or that your father hated him," remarked Fleur. "Oh, what a terrible story. And poor Barbara! Did she every really love Grandfather?"

Ruben shrugged. "Uncle George didn't say anything about that. But if she had initially meant to marry my father...then she could hardly have fallen instantly in love with Gerald."

"Which Grandfather now holds against your father. Or did he hold it against him that he was then forced to marry Barbara? No, that would be too horrible!" Fleur had turned pale. Dramatic tales always struck a chord with her.

"Anyway, those are the secrets of Kiward Station," Ruben concluded. "And in spite of this legacy, we want to go before my father and your grandfather soon and tell them we want to get married. Auspicious beginning, don't you think?" He laughed bitterly.

Even less auspicious when Gerald got wind of it beforehand, thought Paul with perverse delight. This excursion into the foothills had proved more fruitful than he ever could have hoped. But for the time being, he had to plot his escape. Noiselessly he skulked back to his horse.

2

Paul reached the O'Keefes' farm as class ended. He did not dare cross Helen's path, so he waited around the first bend for the other children from Kiward Station. Marama smiled happily at him and climbed up behind him on the pony without asking any questions.

Tonga observed this with an ill-humored countenance. That Paul possessed a steed, while he had to walk the long way to school or take up residence with another tribe during the school year, was salt in his wounds. In general, he preferred doing the former because Tonga liked to be in the middle of the action and didn't want to lose his enemy from his sight for a moment. Marama's friendliness toward Paul was another thorn in his side. He felt her fondness for the boy was a betrayal—a view that few of the adults in his tribe shared. For the Maori, Paul was Marama's adopted brother whom she naturally loved. They did not view the *pakeha* as adversaries, nor did their children. Tonga, however, was beginning to see things differently. He had recently begun to covet many of the things that Paul and the other whites took for granted. He would have loved to own horses, books, and colorful toys and to live in a house like Kiward Station. His family and his tribe—Marama included—did not understand that, but Tonga felt betrayed.

"I'm telling Miss O'Keefe that you cut class!" he called to his archenemy from behind as Paul trotted away. But Paul only laughed. Tonga ground his teeth with rage. He probably wouldn't tell. It was not fitting for a chieftain's son to lower himself to tattling. The mild punishment Paul would receive was not worth it.

"So where were you?" Marama asked in her singsong voice after the riders had distanced themselves sufficiently from Tonga. "Miss O'Keefe was looking for you."

"I was learning secrets," Paul explained importantly. "You won't believe what I found out!"

"Did you find a treasure?" Marama asked quietly. It did not sound like it was going to be of much interest to her. Like most Maori, she did not make much of the things that *pakeha* viewed as valuable. If someone had held up a gold bar and a jade stone to Marama, she probably would have chosen the latter.

"No, I just said, a secret! About Ruben and Fleur. They're doing it!" Paul waited expectantly for an admiring reaction from Marama. Which did not materialize.

"Oh, I already knew they were making love. Everyone knows that," Marama replied calmly. She probably thought it completely natural that the two of them expressed their feelings physically. A rather loose sexual morality prevailed among the Maori. As long as a couple made love in private, no one paid much attention. If they set up a bed together in the meetinghouse, then a marriage was considered consummated. It all transpired without any fanfare and generally without much negotiating by the parents. A big wedding celebration was unusual.

"But they can't get married!" Paul raised the stakes. "Because of an old feud between my grandfather and Ruben's father."

Marama laughed. "But Mr. Warden and Mr. O'Keefe aren't the ones getting married, silly; Ruben and Fleur are!"

Paul snorted. "You don't understand. This is about family honor! Fleur is betraying her ancestors."

Marama wrinkled her brow. "What do the ancestors have to do with it? The ancestors watch over us; they want the best for us. You can't betray them. At least I don't think so. At least I've never heard of such a thing. Besides, there hasn't been any talk of a wedding."

"Well, there will be," Paul declared spitefully. "As soon as I tell Grandfather about Fleur and Ruben, there'll be plenty of talk of it. Believe me!"

Marama sighed. She just hoped not to be in that big house at the time because she was always a little afraid when Gerald Warden flew into one of his rages. Gwyneira liked her and Fleur did too. She did not understand what Paul had against his sister. But the master of the house...Marama decided to go straight to the village to help with the cooking there instead of lending her mother a hand at Kiward Station. Perhaps she could mollify Tonga. He had looked at her with such anger earlier, when she had mounted Paul's horse. And Marama hated it when someone did not like her.

Gwyneira waited for her son in the parlor, which she had taken to using as an office of sorts. After all, no guests dropped off calling cards, waiting for the family to notice them at tea. So she had found other uses for the room. She no longer feared her father-in-law's reactions. Gerald had given her free rein over almost all house-related decisions and only rarely raised objections to her meddling with the farm business. Gerald and Gwyneira were both born farmers and livestock breeders, and the two of them worked well together in that respect. After Gerald added cattle to his operation some years earlier, they had divided the farm responsibilities rather easily: Gerald saw to the longhorns, while Gwyneira oversaw the sheep and horse breeding. The latter was the bigger job, but Gerald was often too drunk to make complex decisions quickly—though that was never mentioned. Instead, the workers simply turned to Gwyneira when it did not seem advisable to speak to the proprietor, and from her, they received clear directions. Gwyneira had made her peace with her existence and moreover with Gerald. Particularly after she had learned his history with Howard O'Keefe, she could no longer bring herself to hate him as profoundly as she had in the first year few years after Paul's birth. She realized that he had never loved Barbara Butler. Her standards, her vision of living in a manor house and raising their son to be a gentleman, may very well have fascinated him—but in the end it disheartened him. Gerald lacked the temperament of the landed gentry; he was a gambler, a warhorse, an adventurer—and a capable farmer and businessman through and through. He never was the considerate "gentleman" with whom Barbara entered a marriage of convenience after being forced to renounce her true love—and never wanted to be either. His first encounter with Gwyneira must have opened his eyes to the kind of woman he really longed for—and doubtless it angered him that Lucas had not had the first idea what to do with her. Gwyneira had since become convinced that Gerald must have felt something like love for her when he brought her to Kiward Station. She suspected that he had not merely been venting his anger at Lucas's impotence on that terrible December night but also expressing the pent-up frustration that he had felt for years at being nothing more than a "father" to the woman he wanted.

Gwyneira also knew that Gerald regretted his behavior back then, even if no words of apology ever emerged from his mouth. His increasingly excessive drinking, his reserve and indulgence toward her—and Paul—spoke for themselves.

She raised her head from her papers about sheep breeding and watched her son storm into the room.

"Well, hello, Paul! Why are you in such a hurry?" she asked with a smile. She still found it difficult to feel genuinely happy when Paul came home. Her peace accord with Gerald was one thing, her relationship with Paul quite another. She simply could never bring herself to love the boy. Not like she loved Fleur, so naturally and unconditionally. If she wanted to feel something for Paul, she always had to engage her reason: he was handsome, with his tousled auburn hair. Gwyneira had bestowed only its color, not its consistency, and instead of curly locks, his hair had the fullness that Gerald's hair still showed. His face was reminiscent of Lucas's, though he had more determined, less soft features, and his brown eyes were clear and often hard, unlike the soft and dreamy eyes of his half brother. He was smart, but his talents lay more in the mathematical realm than in the artistic. He would surely become a good businessman, and he was quite competent. Gerald could not have asked for a better heir to the farm. Though Gwyneira felt that he sometimes lacked empathy for the animals and, more importantly, for the people on Kiward Station, she tried to shake these feelings. She wanted to see the good in Paul, wanted to love him, but when she looked at him, she did not feel any more than she felt for Tonga, for example: a nice boy, clever, and no doubt suited to what would later be expected of him. But it was not the profound, heart-wrenching love she felt for Fleurette.

She hoped that Paul did not notice this absence of love, and she always strove to be especially kind and patient with him. Even now, she was willing to forgive him for wanting to walk past her without a greeting.

"Did something happen, Paul?" she asked, concerned. "Did something upset you at school?" Gwyneira knew that Helen did not always have an easy time with Paul and was aware of his ongoing rivalry with Ruben and Tonga.

"No, nothing. I need to talk to Grandfather, Mother. Where is he?" Paul did not bother with pleasantries.

Gwyneira looked at the grandfather clock that dominated one wall of her study. It was another hour until dinner. So Gerald might already have started on his aperitif.

"Where he always is at this time," she replied. "In the salon. And you know perfectly well that it's best not to bother him at this hour. Especially not when someone hasn't washed or combed his hair, young man. If you want my advice, go change in your room before you go see him."

It was true that Gerald had not taken changing before dinner very seriously himself for a long time, and even Gwyneira only tended to change her clothes when she was coming from the stables. The tea dress that she had worn that day would be perfectly acceptable for dinner. But Gerald could be strict with the children—or rather, he was usually looking for a reason to pick a fight with someone around that time of day. The hour before the common meal was the most dangerous. By the time dinner was served, Gerald's alcohol level was usually so high that violent eruptions were no longer possible.

Paul briefly considered his options. If he went straight to Gerald with the news, his grandfather would indeed explode—but in the absence of the "victim," the effect would be limited. It would be better to tell on Fleur when she was present; then there was a better chance that he, Paul, would get to hear every detail of the ensuing confrontation. Besides, his mother was right: if Gerald was in a really bad mood, he might not even give Paul a chance to announce his news before unleashing all his fury on Paul.

So the boy decided to go to his room first. He would appear at dinner properly dressed, while Fleur would inevitably show up late—and still in her riding clothes. He would let her stammer her excuses, and then, when she was done, he would drop his bombshell. Paul went upstairs feeling smug. He lived in his father's old room, which was now crammed full with toys and fishing tackle rather than art supplies and books. The boy changed into his dinner clothes meticulously. He was eager with anticipation.

Fleurette had not promised more than she could deliver. Her dog, Gracie, had gathered together the missing sheep with lightning speed as soon as Ruben and the girl had found them. Even finding them had not proved difficult. The young rams were bound for the highlands and the pastures where the ewes were. Still, flanked by Gracie and Minette, they were content to turn back toward the farm. Gracie did not tolerate any frolicking, and quickly herded any sheep trying to break ranks back into the flock. The group was small and easy to keep track of, so Fleurette managed to shut the paddock gate behind them long before dark—and more importantly, long before Howard O'Keefe returned from the shed, where he was seeing to his last cattle. The animals were finally to be sold after Howard had endlessly clung to cattle farming as a potential second source of income against George Greenwood's advice. O'Keefe Station did not boast any land suitable for cattle; only sheep and goats could thrive here.

Fleurette looked at the position of the sun. It wasn't late yet, but if she helped Ruben fix the fence as she had promised, she wouldn't make it home for dinner. Even that wouldn't be so bad—her grandfather usually retired to his room with a last whiskey after dinner, and her mother and Kiri would no doubt save her something to eat. Still, Fleur hated to make more work for the help than was necessary. Besides, Fleur did not relish the idea of possibly running into Howard and then—horror of horrors!—bursting into the house in the middle of dinner. On the other hand, she could hardly leave Ruben alone with the fence. Then the rams would waste no time heading right back up to the highlands again the next day.

To Fleurette's relief, Ruben's mother now approached them—with her mild-mannered mule, which she had laden with tools and fencing materials.

Helen waved at her. "Go on home, Fleur, we'll take care of this," she said kindly. "It was very nice of you to help Ruben bring the sheep back. There's no reason you should be punished for your good deed with trouble at home. And that's what will happen if you're late getting home."

Fleurette nodded gratefully. "Then I'll see you at school tomorrow, Miss O'Keefe!" she exclaimed. As it was, she had more or less finished school, but it was an excuse to spend time with Ruben every day. She was good at math, could read and write, and had read many of the classics, or at least the first few pages of them, though not in their original language as Ruben had. Fleur thought that knowing Greek and Latin was unnecessary, so there was hardly anything left that Helen could teach her. However, after Lucas's death, Gwyneira had donated many of his botany and zoology books to Helen's school. Fleur browsed them with interest while Ruben dedicated himself to his books. He would have to go to Dunedin the following year if he wanted to continue his studies. Helen still had no idea how she was going to make that idea palatable to Howard. Moreover, there was no money left over for his studies; Ruben would have to rely on George Greenwood's generous help—at least until he could distinguish himself enough to earn a scholarship. But studying in Dunedin would separate Ruben and Fleurette for a time. Just as Marama had, Helen recognized that the two were obviously in love and had already spoken with Gwyneira about it. In principle, the mothers had nothing against the union, but naturally, they feared

Gerald's and Howard's reactions. They agreed that the young couple should wait a couple of years before entering into any permanent commitment. Ruben had just turned seventeen; Fleur was still not quite sixteen. Helen and Gwyneira both felt that they were still too young to tie themselves down.

Ruben helped Fleur put the saddle they had taken off to be able to ride together back on her mare. He stole a kiss before she mounted.

"I love you, until tomorrow!" he said quietly.

"Only until tomorrow?" she returned, laughing.

"No, for forever. And a few days beyond that!" Ruben's hand stroked hers softly, and Fleurette beamed at him as she rode out of the yard. Ruben watched her go until the last shimmer of her red-gold hair and her sorrel's equally luminous tail had melted into the evening light. Helen's voice shook him out of his reverie.

"Come on, Ruben, the fence isn't going to fix itself. We'd better be finished by the time your father comes home."

Fleurette spurred her horse on at a brisk pace and would almost have been punctual for dinner at Kiward Station. But there was no one in the stables to whom she could give Minette, so had to take care of her horse herself. By the time the mare had been brushed, watered, and provided with food, the first course was no doubt already on the table. Fleurette sighed. She could steal into the house and skip dinner entirely. However, she was afraid that Paul had seen her ride into the yard; she had detected movement from behind his window, and he would tell on her without question. So Fleur gave in to the inevitable. At least she would get something to eat. She was starving after her day in the highlands. She decided to approach the situation optimistically and put a beaming smile on her face when she entered the dining room.

"Good evening, Grandfather, good evening, Mummy! I'm an itty bit late today because I was an itty bit wrong about how much time it would take to...uh, to..."

Stupid that she couldn't think of an excuse off the top of her head. She could not possibly say she had spent the day herding Howard O'Keefe's sheep.

"To help your beau hunt down his sheep?" Paul asked with a sardonic expression on his face.

Gwyneira blew up. "Paul, what is that supposed to mean? Do you always have to tease your sister?"

"Did you or didn't you?" Paul asked insolently.

Fleurette blushed. "I..."

"With whom were you hunting down sheep?" Gerald inquired. He was pretty drunk. He might not have made a scene but something about what Paul said had caught his attention.

"With...um, with Ruben. A few rams had gotten away from him and Mrs. O'Keefe and..."

"From him and that nice father of his, you mean to say," Gerald scoffed. "How typical of old Howard to be too stupid or too tight-fisted to pen up his animals. And that dandy has to ask a girl to help him herd them."

The old man laughed.

Paul frowned. This wasn't going as planned.

"Fleur does it with Ruben!" burst out of him, earning a few initial seconds of stunned silence.

Gwyneira was the first to react. "Paul, where do you learn these expressions! You will excuse yourself this instant and—"

"Wai...wait a moment!" Gerald interrupted her in an unsteady but loud voice. "Wha...what is the boy saying? She's...doing it...with the O'Keefe boy?"

Gwyneira hoped that Fleurette would simply deny it, but she only needed to look at the girl to see that Paul's malicious assertion had at least some truth to it.

"It's not what you think, Grandfather!" Fleur said, trying to reassure herself. "We...well, we...uh, don't do it with each other, of course. We..."

"Oh, no? What *do* you do, then?" Gerald thundered.

"But I saw it! I saw it!" Paul sang.

Gwyneira ordered him sternly to be silent. "We...we're in love. We want to get married," Fleur explained. There. At least she had said it—even though this was hardly the ideal moment for that announcement.

Gwyneira attempted to ameliorate her daughter's position.

"Fleur, my sweet, you're not even sixteen. And Ruben's going off to university next year."

"You want to do what?" Gerald roared. "Marry? O'Keefe's brat? Have you completely lost your mind, Fleurette?"

Fleur shrugged. Whatever else may be said of her, she could not be accused of cowardice. "It's not something you choose, Grandfather. We love each other. That's how it is, and no one can change it."

"We'll just see if it can't be changed!" Gerald sprang up. "You are not to ever see that boy again. No more school—I've been wondering what that O'Keefe woman has left to teach you anyway. I'm going to ride to Haldon and settle things with O'Keefe right now. Witi! Bring my gun!"

"Gerald, you're overreacting," Gwyneira said, trying to remain calm. Perhaps she could convince Gerald to give up the crazy idea of going after Ruben—or Howard—before he did anything rash. "The girl isn't even sixteen and is in love for the first time. No one's even talking about a wedding."

"That girl is set to inherit a portion of Kiward Station, Gwyneira! *Of course* old O'Keefe's thinking of marriage. But I'll clear that up once and for all. You lock up the girl. This instant! She doesn't need anything more to eat. She should fast and think about her sins." Gerald reached for his gun, which a terrified Witi had brought, and slipped into a waxed jacket. Then he stormed out.

Fleurette moved to follow him. "I have to go warn Ruben!" she exclaimed.

Gwyneira shook her head. "Where do you expect to find a horse? All the riding horses are in the stables, and I won't let you take one of the ponies into the wild without a saddle...no, you'd break your neck and the horse's too. Gerald would overtake you anyway. Let the boys sort it out for themselves. I'm sure no one will get hurt. If he runs into Mr. O'Keefe, they'll yell at each other, maybe break each other's noses..."

"And if he runs into Ruben?" Fleur asked, turning pale.

"Then he'll kill him!" Paul rejoiced.

That was a mistake. Now mother and daughter turned on him.

"You snitching little bastard!" Fleurette yelled. "Do you have any idea what you've done, you nasty rat? If Ruben is killed, then..."

"Fleurette, calm down. Your friend will survive just fine," Gwyneira soothed her with greater conviction than she really possessed. She knew Gerald's explosive temper, and he was once more three sheets to the wind. However, Ruben's even-keeled nature gave her hope. Helen's son was not about to be provoked. "And you, Paul, go to your room this instant. I don't want to see you in the dining room again until the day after tomorrow at the soonest. You're under house arrest."

"Fleur is too, Fleur is too!" Paul would not let it go.

"That's something very different, Paul," Gwyneira said sternly, and once again she had trouble finding even a spark of sympathy for the child she had given birth to. "Grandfather is punishing Fleur because he thinks she's fallen in love with the wrong boy. But I'm punishing you because you're rotten, because you spy on people and tattle—and enjoy it too! No gentleman behaves that way, Paul Warden. Only a monster behaves that way." Gwyneira knew the moment she said it that Paul would never forgive her for that word. But she had reached her breaking point. She felt only hatred for this child who had been forced on her, who had ultimately been the cause of Lucas's death, and who was now doing his utmost to destroy Fleur's life too and to upset the very core of Helen's tenuous family harmony.

Paul looked at his mother, pale as a corpse, and saw the chasms in her eyes. This was no fit of anger like Fleurette's; Gwyneira seemed to mean what she was saying. Paul began to sob, even though he had decided more than a year before to be a man and not to cry anymore.

"What's taking you so long? Go!" Gwyneira hated herself for her words, but she could not hold them in. "Go to your room!"

Paul stormed out. Fleurette looked at her mother, stunned.

"That was harsh," she remarked soberly.

Gwyneira reached with trembling fingers for her wineglass, then had another idea, and went to the wall cupboard, where she poured herself a brandy. "You too, Fleurette? I think we both need something to calm our nerves. We can only wait. Gerald will come back eventually, of course, if he doesn't fall off his horse and break his neck somewhere along the way."

She gulped the brandy down.

"And as for Paul...I'm sorry."

Gerald Warden crossed the wilds as though possessed. His anger at young Ruben O'Keefe raged within him. Until that night, he had never seen Fleurette as a woman. She had always been a child to him, Gwyneira's little daughter, sweet but of little interest. But the little girl had blossomed; now she threw her head back just as proudly as seventeen-year-old Gwyneira had back then, and she talked back with just as much self-confidence. And Ruben, that little shit, had dared to get close to her. A Warden! His property.

Gerald calmed down somewhat when he arrived at the O'Keefes' farm and compared their shabby barns, stables, and house with his own. Howard could not possibly think that his granddaughter would ever want to marry into this.

He could see a light burning in the house's windows. Howard's horse and mule stood in the paddock in front of the house. So that bastard was at home. And his backsliding son too, for Gerald now saw three silhouettes at the table inside the hut. He carelessly threw his reins around a fence post and took his gun out of its case. A dog started barking as he approached the house, but no one inside reacted.

Gerald flung the door open. As expected, he saw Howard, Helen, and their son at the table where the evening stew had just been served. All three of them stared at the door in shock, too surprised to react. Using the advantage of surprise, Gerald stormed into the house and knocked over the table as he leaped on Ruben.

"Cards on the table, boy! What did you do to my granddaughter?"

Ruben wrenched in his grip. "Mr. Warden...can't we talk...with each other like reasonable people?"

Gerald saw red. His own unfilial son would have reacted the same way to such a charge. He punched. His left knocked Ruben halfway across the room. Helen screamed. In the same moment, Howard struck Gerald—although to lesser effect. Howard had just returned from the pub in Haldon and was no longer sober either. Gerald shrugged off Howard's blow without any trouble and turned his attention to Ruben again, who was picking himself up off the ground with a bloody nose.

"Mr. Warden, please..."

Howard put Gerald in a headlock before he could attack his son again.

"All right, fine. Let's talk like reasonable people," Howard hissed. "What's going on to make you barge in here, Warden, laying into my son?"

Gerald tried to turn around to look at him. "Your damned shit of a son seduced my granddaughter. *That's* what's going on!"

"You did *what*?" Howard released Gerald and turned to Ruben. "Tell me here and now that isn't true."

Ruben's face spoke volumes, just as Fleur's had.

"Of course I didn't seduce her," he said, which was true. "It's just..."

"Just what? You just took a bit of her virginity?" Gerald thundered.

Ruben was pale as a ghost. "I have to ask you not to talk about Fleur in that manner," he said evenly but firmly. "Mr. Warden, I love your granddaughter. I'm going to marry her."

"You're going to do what?" Howard boomed. "I can just see the little witch turning your head."

"Under no circumstances will you marry Fleurette, you little fucker!" Gerald raged.

"Mr. Warden! Perhaps we could find a way to express ourselves less crudely," Helen said in an effort to calm him.

"I will marry Fleurette no matter what, regardless of what either of you has to say about it." Ruben spoke calmly and full of conviction.

Howard seized his son and held him by his shirt just as Gerald had done. "You'll shut your mouth, boy! And you, Warden, get out of here. Now. And you keep a grip on that little whore of a granddaughter. I don't want to see her around here anymore, understand? Make that clear to her or I'll do it myself, and then she won't be seducing anyone."

"Fleurette is not—"

"Mr. Warden!" Helen positioned herself between the two men. "Please go. Howard doesn't mean it. And as for Ruben...all of us here have the greatest respect for Fleurette. The children have perhaps exchanged a few kisses, but—"

"You'll never touch Fleurette again!" Gerald moved to strike Ruben again, but the boy hung so helplessly in his father's viselike grip that he desisted.

"He won't touch her again; I promise you that. And now out! I'll sort it out with him, Warden; you can count on it."

Helen suddenly did not know whether she really wanted Gerald to go. Howard's voice sounded so threatening that she seriously feared for Ruben's safety. Howard had already been angry before Gerald appeared. He'd had to herd the young rams together again when he came home because Helen and Ruben's attempt at restoring the fence had not checked the animals' desire for freedom. Howard had been able to herd the rams back into the pen before they fled back into the highlands, but this additional task had not improved his mood. Gerald cast a murderous glance at Ruben as he left the hut.

"So you've been doing it with the little Warden girl," Howard established. "And you've got big plans, is that right? Just met Greenwood's Maori boy at the pub, and he *congratulated* me that the university in Dunedin wants to take you on. For law school! Oh, you hadn't heard? Letters like that you have sent to your dear Uncle George! But I'll beat that out of you now, my boy! Be sure to count along, Ruben O'Keefe; you've certainly learned that much. And law, that's the study of justice, right? Eye for an eye, tooth for a tooth. That's the justice we'll be studying now. This here is for the sheep!"

He struck Ruben a blow. "And this here is for the girl!" A hard right. "This is for Uncle George!" A hard left. Ruben fell to the floor.

"For law school!" Howard kicked him in the ribs. Ruben let out a moan.

"And for thinking you're better than me!" Another brutal kick, this time in the kidneys. Ruben curled up. Helen tried to pull Howard away.

"And this here is for you because you always take the little shit's side!" Howard landed his next blow on Helen's upper lip. She fell, but still tried to protect her son.

Howard seemed to be coming to his senses. The blood on Helen's face sobered him up.

"You two aren't worth it...you..." he stammered and teetered over to the cupboard in the kitchen where Helen kept the whiskey. The good kind, not the cheap stuff. She liked to keep it on hand for guests; George Greenwood often needed a drink when he was done with Howard. Howard took several long gulps before putting it back. Yet when he moved to close the cupboard, he changed his mind and took it with him.

"I'm sleeping in the stables," he announced. "I can't look at you anymore."

Helen sighed with relief when he disappeared outside.

"Ruben...is it bad? Are you..."

"Everything's OK, Mother," Ruben whispered, but his appearance indicated otherwise. He bled from cuts above his eye and lip; his nosebleed had worsened, and it was difficult for him to sit up. His left eye was swollen shut. Helen helped him up.

"Come, lie down in bed. I'll fix you up," she offered. But Ruben shook his head.

"I won't lie in his bed," he said firmly, dragging himself to the narrow pallet next to the fireplace where he liked to sleep in winter. In the summer he had taken to sleeping in the stables so as not to bother his parents.

He was shaking when Helen came to him with a bowl of water and a rag to wash his face. "It's nothing, Mother...my God, I hope nothing happens to Fleur."

Helen dabbed the blood carefully from his lip. "Nothing will happen to Fleur. But how did he find out about it? I should have kept an eye on that Paul."

"They would have figured it out eventually," Ruben said. "And then…I'm leaving here tomorrow. Prepare yourself for that. I won't stay in this house another day." He gestured in Howard's direction.

"You'll still be recovering tomorrow," Helen said. "And we shouldn't upset things. George…"

"Uncle George can't help us anymore, Mother. I'm not going to Dunedin. I'm going to Otago. There's gold there. I…I'll find some, and then I'll come back for Fleur. And you too. He…he can't be allowed to hit you anymore!"

Helen said nothing more. She rubbed her son's wounds with a cooling salve and sat by him until he fell asleep. As she sat there, she thought of all the nights she had spent by his side, when he was sick or had been frightened by a nightmare and wanted to have her nearby. Ruben had always brought her joy. But now Howard had destroyed even that. Helen did not sleep that night.

She wept.

3

Fleurette too wept that night in her sleep. She, Gwyneira, and Paul all had heard Gerald return late that evening, but no one had the courage to ask the old man what had happened. In the morning Gwyneira was the only one who came down to breakfast as usual. Gerald was sleeping off his hangover, and Paul did not dare show himself unless there was a chance of getting his grandfather on his side for the purpose of lifting his house arrest. Fleurette cowered, terrified and listless, in a corner of her bed, holding Grace tightly to her as her mother had once held Cleo, plagued by the most horrible thoughts. Gwyneira found her there after Andy McAran had informed her of an unannounced visitor in the stables. Gwyneira made certain that nothing was brewing with Gerald or Paul before she slipped into her daughter's room.

"Fleurette? Fleurette, it's nine in the morning! What are you still doing in bed?" Gwyneira shook her head in admonishment, as though it were a normal day and Fleur had merely slept past the time she needed to leave for school. "Get dressed now, and fast. There's someone waiting for you in the horse stables. And he can't wait forever."

She smiled conspiratorially at her daughter.

"Someone's there." Fleurette leaped up. "Who? Is it Ruben, Mummy? Oh if it's Ruben, if he's alive..."

"Of course he's alive, Fleurette. Your grandfather is a man quick to make wild threats and use his fists. But he's not a killer. At least not at first—if he bumps into the boy here in our barn, though, I can't make any promises." Gwyneira helped Fleur slip into a riding dress.

"And you'll make sure he doesn't come out, right? And Paul." Fleurette seemed to be almost as afraid of her little brother as her grandfather. "He's such a brat! You don't really think that we..."

"I think the boy is far too intelligent to take the risk of getting you pregnant," Gwyneira said drily. "And you are just as smart as he is, Fleurette. Ruben wants to study in Dunedin, and you must be a few years older before you can even think of a wedding. The opportunities for a young lawyer who is quite possibly going to work for George Greenwood are a lot better than for a farm boy whose father lives hand to mouth. Keep that in mind when you meet with him this morning. Although...from what Andy McAran says, he's hardly in any condition to get anyone pregnant."

Gwyneira's last comment came close to Fleur's darkest fears. Instead of looking for her waxed coat—it was pouring outside—she hastily threw a shawl over her shoulders and then hurried downstairs. She had not brushed her hair, as untangling it probably would have taken hours. Generally she liked to comb it every evening and braid it before bed, but she had not had the energy for it the night before. Now it fluttered wildly around her narrow face, but to Ruben O'Keefe, she was still the most beautiful girl he had ever seen. Fleurette, on the other hand, was horrified by the sight of her beau. The boy reclined on a bale of hay. Every movement still caused him pain. His face was swollen, one eye was shut, and the cuts still wept.

"Oh God, Ruben! Did my grandfather do that?" Fleurette wanted to embrace him, but Ruben pushed her away.

"Careful," he groaned. "My ribs...I don't know if they're broken or just bruised...either way, it hurts like hell."

Fleurette embraced him more gently. She lowered herself down beside him and laid his beaten face on her shoulder.

"The devil take him!" she cursed. "I thought he didn't kill anyone, but he almost succeeded with you."

Ruben shook his head. "It wasn't Mr. Warden. It was my father. Although they almost went at it in perfect harmony. The two of them may be archenemies, but with regard to the two of us, they couldn't agree more. I'm going away, Fleur. I can't take it anymore."

Fleurette looked at him, stunned. “You’re going? You’re leaving me?”

“Should I wait here for them to kill us both? We can’t keep meeting in secret forever—especially not with that little snitch you have in your house. It was Paul who sold us out, wasn’t it?”

Fleur nodded. “And he’d do it again too. But you…you can’t leave without me. I’m coming!” She squared herself decisively and already seemed to be packing her bags in her mind. “You, wait here; I don’t need much. We can be off within the hour.”

“Oh, Fleur, that won’t work. But I’m not leaving you either. I’ll think of you every minute, every second. I love you. But there’s no way I can take you with me to Otago.” Ruben stroked her awkwardly while Fleur thought feverishly. If she fled with him, they would have to ride at top speed, as Gerald would no doubt send a search party after them as soon as he noticed her absence. But there was no way Ruben could ride quickly in his current state…and what was he talking about Otago for?

“I think you mean Dunedin?” she inquired, kissing his forehead.

“I’ve changed my mind,” Ruben explained. “We always thought your grandfather would permit us to marry after I was an attorney. But after last night, it’s clear to me that he’ll never give us permission. If something is to come of us, I need to earn money. Not a little, but a fortune. And in Otago they’ve found gold.”

“You want to try panning for gold?” Fleur asked, surprised. “But… who’s to say whether you’ll find any?”

Deep down Ruben knew that was a good question since he didn’t have the slightest idea how to begin his quest. But, what the hell, others had managed it.

“In the area around Queenstown, everyone finds gold,” he persisted. “There are nuggets as big as your fingernails.”

“And they just litter the ground?” Fleurette asked skeptically. “Don’t you need a claim? Equipment? Do you have any money, Ruben?”

Ruben nodded. “A little. I saved some. Uncle George paid me last year for helping out in his office and for interpreting with the Maori when Reti wasn’t available. It’s not a lot, of course.”

"I don't have anything," Fleurette said, concerned. "Otherwise, I'd give it to you. But what about a horse? How do you intend to make it to Lake Wakatipu?"

"I have my mother's mule," Ruben explained.

Fleurette raised her eyes to heaven. "Nepumuk? You want to take Nepumuk over the mountains? How old is he now? Twenty-five? That's impossible, Ruben. Take one of our horses!"

"So your grandfather has me hunted down as a horse thief?" Ruben asked bitterly.

Fleurette shook her head. "Take Minette. She's little but strong. And she belongs to me. No one can stop me from lending her to you. But you have to take care of her, do you hear me? And you have to bring her back to me."

"You know I'll come back just as soon as I can." Ruben struggled to his feet and took Fleurette in his arms. She tasted his blood when he kissed her. "I'll come for you. As...as surely as the sun will rise tomorrow. I'll find gold, and then I'll come for you. You do believe me, don't you, Fleurette?"

Fleurette nodded and returned his embrace as tenderly and carefully as she could. She did not doubt his love. If only she could be as sure of his future fortune.

"I love you, and I'll wait for you," she said quietly.

Ruben kissed her again. "I'll have to be quick. There aren't many gold seekers in Queenstown yet. It's still something of a secret. So there should still be some good claims and plenty of gold and—"

"But you will come back, even if you don't find gold, right?" Fleurette said, wanting to be sure. "Then we'll think of something else."

"I'll find gold!" Ruben insisted. "Because there's no other way. But now I have to go. I've been here much too long already. If your grandfather sees me..."

"My mother's on the lookout. Stay here, Ruben, I'll saddle Minette for you. You can hardly stand up, after all. The best thing would be for you to find a place to hide so that you can recover. We could—"

"No, Fleurette. No more risks, no long good-byes. I'll make it; it's not half as bad as it looks. Just see that you get the mule back to

Mother somehow." Ruben limped over, as though he were going to lend Fleur a hand with the saddling. Just as she was about to bridle the horse, Kiri appeared in the doorway, two stuffed-full saddlebags in her hands. She smiled at Fleurette.

"Here, this is from your mother. For the boy who isn't really here." Kiri pretended not to see Ruben as she'd been instructed. "A little food for the road and some warm clothes left by your father. She thinks he'll need them."

Ruben was about to refuse them, but the Maori woman did not even acknowledge he was there as she set the bags down and then turned to go. Fleurette secured the bags on the saddle, then led Minette out.

"Take good care of him," she whispered to the mare. "And bring him back to me!"

Ruben struggled into the saddle but still managed to lean down to Fleurette to kiss her good-bye.

"How long will you love me?" he asked quietly.

She smiled. "Forever. And a few days beyond that. I'll see you soon!"

"I'll see you soon!" Ruben reaffirmed.

Fleurette watched him until he disappeared behind the curtain of rain that obscured her view of the mountains that day. It pained her heart to see Ruben hanging on to the horse, doubled over in pain. Fleeing together would never have succeeded—Ruben could only advance unencumbered.

Paul also watched as the boy rode away. He had taken up his post at his window early and was now considering whether he should wake Gerald. But by the time he managed that Ruben would be miles away—besides, his mother definitely had her eye on him. He could still vividly replay her outburst from the evening before in his mind. It had confirmed what he had always suspected: Gwyneira loved his sister much more than she loved him. He could never expect to get anything from her. But with his grandfather, there was hope. His grandfather was predictable, and if Paul could learn to handle him properly, he would take Paul under his wing. Paul decided that from this point on, there would be two opposing factions in the Warden family: his mother and Fleur, and Gerald and Paul. He just needed to convince Gerald how useful he was.

Gerald flew into a rage when he found out why the mare Minette was gone. Only with great effort did Gwyneira stop him from striking Fleurette.

"Regardless, the boy's gone now," he said, trying to assuage his own anger. "Whether to Dunedin or wherever, I couldn't care less. If he ever shows up here again, I'm going to shoot him like a rabid dog; you must understand that, Fleurette. But you won't even be here. I'm going to marry you off to the next man who's even halfway suitable."

"She's still much too young to marry," said Gwyneira. Deep down she too thanked heaven that Ruben had left the Canterbury Plains. Bound for where, Fleurette had not said, but she could imagine. The gold rush had become what whaling and seal hunting had been in Lucas's day. Anyone who wanted to make a fortune quickly and prove himself as a man made for Otago. However, she appraised Ruben's aptitude for mining as pessimistically as Fleurette.

"She was old enough to lie down with that bastard in the wilderness. So she's old enough to share a bed with an honorable man. How old is she? Sixteen? Next year she'll be seventeen. Then she can be engaged. I can still well remember a girl who came to New Zealand at seventeen."

Gerald fixed Gwyneira with a look that made her turn pale. A feeling rose in her that bordered on panic. When she had been seventeen, Gerald had fallen in love with her—and brought her across the sea for his son. Could it be that the old man was starting to see Fleur too in a different light? Until that moment, Gwyneira had never thought about how closely the girl resembled her. If one ignored that Fleurette was more delicate than her mother, her hair a little darker and her eyes a different color, one could have gotten Fleurette and the young Gwyneira confused. Had Paul's idiotic tattling made Gerald aware of that too?

Fleurette sobbed and was about to reply bravely that she would never and by no means marry a man other than Ruben O'Keefe, but Gwyneira collected herself and silenced her daughter with a shake of her head and a motion of her hand. There was no point in fighting. Besides, finding a "halfway suitable" young man might not be so easy. The Wardens were among the oldest and most respected families on the South Island; only a few others were on par with them socially and financially. Their sons could be counted on two hands—and all of them were either already engaged or much too young for Fleurette. Young Lord Barrington's son, for example, had just turned ten, and George Greenwood's oldest was only five years old. As soon as Gerald's rage had dissipated, this would become clear to him too. The danger in the house itself was much more of a concern to Gwyneira, but she was probably just seeing ghosts. In all their years together, Gerald had only touched her that one time, when he was completely drunk and caught up in the heat of the moment, and he seemed to regret it to this day. There was no reason to get worked up over nothing.

Gwyneira forced herself to calm down and urged Fleurette to relax. The whole painful incident would probably be forgotten in a few weeks.

But she was mistaken. True, nothing happened at first, but eight weeks after Ruben had ridden off, Gerald made his way to the livestock farmers' conference in Christchurch. The official reason for this "feast with boozing to follow," as Gwyneira referred to it, was the steadily increasing incidence of livestock theft in the Canterbury Plains. Over the past few months, a thousand sheep had disappeared in that region alone. As always, James McKenzie's name was being bandied about.

"Heaven knows where he disappears to with the livestock," Gerald rumbled. "But he's behind it, no doubt about it. The fellow knows the highlands like the back of his hand. We'll send out more patrols; we'll set up a proper militia!"

Gwyneira shrugged and hoped that no one noticed how heavily her heart still beat when she thought of James McKenzie. She smiled inwardly at the thought of his hit-and-run attacks and what he would say to a few more patrols in the mountains. Only parts of the foothills had been explored; the region was massive and might still be hiding entire valleys and pastures. Watching over the animals there was impossible, though the farmers sent shepherds as a formality. Those shepherds spent half the year in primitive cabins erected specifically for the purpose, mostly in pairs so that they did not go crazy with loneliness. They killed time by playing card games, hunting, and fishing, and went largely unchecked by their employers. The more responsible among them kept an eye on the sheep, but others may very well never have seen them. A man with a good sheepdog could herd away dozens of animals a day without its being immediately apparent. If James had found a still unknown refuge and, more importantly, a way to sell the stolen sheep, the sheep barons would never find him—except by chance.

Still, James McKenzie's activities always offered lively conversation material and a welcome excuse to hold livestock farmers' conventions or to undertake expeditions into the highlands together. This time too there would be a lot of talk, but little would come of it. Gwyneira was happy that she had never been asked to take part. Although she was the unofficial head of the sheep breeding operation on Kiward Station, only Gerald was taken seriously. She breathed out a sigh of relief when he rode away from the farm, surprisingly with Paul in tow. Since the incident with Ruben and Fleurette, the boy and his grandfather had grown closer. Gerald evidently finally understood that it wasn't enough simply to produce an heir. The future owner of Kiward Station had to be introduced to the business as well—and to the society of his soon-to-be peers. As Paul rode off proudly beside Gerald, Fleurette finally relaxed a bit. Gerald was still strictly prescribing where she could go and when she had to be home, and Paul spied on her and reported even the smallest infractions against his edicts. After several admonishments, Fleurette had borne her restrictions with grace, but it was irksome nevertheless. Still, the girl took real pleasure in her new horse. Gwyneira had entrusted her with Igraine's last daughter, Niniane. The four-year-old mirrored the temperament and appearance of her mother—and when Gwyneira saw her daughter riding across the meadows on Niniane's back, the uneasiness she had felt in the salon washed over her again: Gerald too must have found himself looking at a young Gwyneira. So pretty, so wild, and so completely out of her depth as only a girl could be.

His behavior in response to this revelation awoke her old fears. He was in even blacker spirits than usual, seemed to nurse an inexplicable anger for anyone who crossed his path, and consumed more whiskey than he normally did. Only Paul seemed to be able to calm him on such nights.

Gwyneira's blood would have turned to ice if she had known what the two of them discussed in the study.

It generally began with Gerald asking Paul to tell him about school and his adventures in the wilderness; it always ended with the boy talking about Fleur—whom he naturally did not describe as the enchanting, innocent wild thing Gwyneira had been in her day, but rather as spoiled, untrustworthy, and cruel. Gerald could bear his forbidden fantasies about his granddaughter when they were aimed at such a small beast—but he knew that he had to be rid of the girl as soon as possible.

An opportunity to do just that materialized in Christchurch. On their way back from the livestock farmers' conference, they were accompanied by Reginald Beasley.

Gwyneira greeted the old family friend amiably and expressed her condolences on the death of his wife. Mrs. Beasley had passed on suddenly at the end of the year before—a stroke in her beloved rose garden. Gwyneira thought that, as these things went, the old lady could not have had a more beautiful death, which did not, of course, stop her husband from missing her dreadfully. Gwyneira asked Moana to prepare a special meal and went to find a bottle of first-class wine. Reginald Beasley was known as a gourmand and a wine connoisseur, and his whole round, red face lit up when Witi uncorked the bottle at the table.

"I too just received a shipment of the best wine from Cape Town," he explained, turning to Fleurette as he spoke. "Among them are some very delicate ones; the ladies are sure to love them. What do you prefer, Miss Warden? White or red wine?"

Fleurette had never really thought about it before. She rarely drank wine, and when she did, she tasted whatever was set on the table. Helen, however, had naturally taught her how to behave like a lady.

"That depends very much on the type, Mr. Beasley," she replied politely. "Red wines are often very heavy, and white wines can be very acidic. I would rather simply leave it to you to select the right wine."

Mr. Beasley seemed to be very pleased with this response and proceeded to describe in great detail why he had come to prefer South African wines to French varietals.

"Cape Town is also much closer," Gwyneira finally said to close the subject. "And the wine is also much more reasonably priced."

Fleur smirked inwardly. This was the first argument that had come to her, but Helen had taught her that a lady under no circumstances mentioned money when speaking to a gentleman. Obviously her mother had not attended the same school of etiquette.

Reginald Beasley then explained verbosely that financial considerations did not really play a role, and segued right into describing other, considerably costlier investments that he had made lately. He had imported more sheep this, he had expanded his cattle stock that...

Fleurette wondered why the little sheep baron kept fixing his eyes on her as though she had a personal interest in the number of Cheviot heads in his flock. None of it piqued her interest until the conversation turned to horse breeding. Reginald Beasley had always been a breeder of thoroughbreds.

"Of course we could always cross them with one of your cobs, Miss Warden, if a thoroughbred would be too much for you," he explained to Fleurette eagerly. "That would certainly be an interesting approach."

Fleurette frowned. She could hardly imagine a thoroughbred more willing to run than Niniane—though they were naturally faster. But why in heaven's name was she supposed to show any interest in switching to riding thoroughbreds? In her mother's opinion they were far too sensitive for the long and arduous rides through the wilderness.

"It's often done in England," interrupted Gwyneira, who was becoming as confused as Fleurette by their guest's behavior. She was the horse breeder in the family, so why wasn't he talking to her about crossbreeding? "Some of them become very good hunting mounts. But they often have the harshness and stubbornness of cobs, paired with the explosive nature and tendency to scare of thoroughbreds. That's not something I would want for my daughter."

Reginald Beasley smiled amiably. "Oh, it was just a suggestion. Miss Warden should, of course, have a totally free hand with regard to her horse. We could also arrange another hunt. I have completely neglected that sort of thing these last few years, but...would you enjoy a hunt, Miss Warden?"

Fleurette nodded. "Certainly, why not?" she said, mildly interested.

"Although there's still a dearth of foxes," Gwyneira said, smiling. "Have you ever considered having some brought in?"

"For heaven's sake!" Gerald had worked himself into a state over the lack of game, and now turned the conversation to the scant population of native animals in New Zealand.

Fleurette contributed a bit to the subject, and dinner came to an end amid lively conversation. Fleur excused herself immediately afterward to go to her room. She had begun to spend her evenings writing long letters to Ruben; though she dropped them off in Haldon with high hopes, the postman was less optimistic. "Ruben O'Keefe, Gold Mines, Queenstown," did not strike him as sufficient for an address. But the letters had yet to be returned. At first Gwyneira went to see to the kitchen, but then she decided to join the men for a bit. She poured herself a glass of port in the salon and strolled with it toward the next room, where the men liked to smoke, drink, and occasionally play cards after dinner.

"You were right; she is enchanting!"

At the sound of Reginald Beasley's voice, Gwyneira froze in front of the half-open door.

"At first I was a bit skeptical—such a young girl, almost a child still. But now that I've seen her, I can see that she is already well developed for her age. And so well bred! A true little lady."

Gerald nodded. "I told you. She is without a doubt ready for marriage. Just between us, you must bear something in mind. You know yourself how it is with all the men here on the farms. More than one kitty has gotten carried away when in heat."

Reginald Beasley chuckled. "But she's only...I mean, don't get me wrong; I'm not hung up on it. Otherwise, I would only have been looking for a...well, perhaps for a widow, closer to my age. But if they're already having affairs at that age..."

"Reginald, please!" Gerald interrupted him sternly. "Fleur's honor is above reproach. I'm just thinking of a wedding sooner rather than later so that it remains so. The apple is ripe for the picking, if you know what I mean."

Reginald laughed again. "A true image of paradise. And what does the girl have to say? Will you convey my proposal to her, or should I...declare my intent myself?"

Gwyneira could hardly believe what she was hearing. Fleurette and Reginald Beasley? The man had to be well over fifty, or perhaps even in his sixties. Old enough to be Fleur's grandfather.

"Leave it to me; I'll take care of it. It will come as something of a surprise to her. But she'll agree; don't you worry. After all, she is a lady, as you've already said." Gerald poured another round from the whiskey bottle. "To our new ties!" he smiled. "To Fleur!"

"No, no, and again, no!"

Fleurette's voice screeched, the sound traveling from the study where Gerald had asked her to speak with him, through the salon, and into Gwyneira's office. She did not sound particularly ladylike—more like young Fleurette was having a full-blown temper tantrum before her grandfather. Gwyneira had preferred not to participate directly in this performance. If Gerald were to go too far while they were alone, she was ready to step in and mediate at any point. After all, Reginald Beasley had to be refused without being hurt. A little rebuff was not likely to do the old man much damage. How could he even consider a sixteen-year-old bride? Gwyneira had made certain that Gerald was not too drunk when he called Fleur in to him, and she had warned her daughter ahead of time.

"Remember, Fleur, he can't force you. Word may already have gotten out, in which case there might be a small scandal. But I assure you that Christchurch has gotten over other such affairs. Simply remain calm and make your stance clear."

Fleur, however, was not one for remaining calm.

"I'm supposed to submit myself?" she fired back at Gerald. "I don't need to consider it! I'll drown myself before I marry that old man. I'm serious, Grandfather; I'll throw myself in the lake!"

Gwyneira had to smile. Where had Fleur even learned such dramatic language? Presumably from Helen's books. Throwing herself in the pond near Kiward Station would hardly do her much harm. The water was flat, and thanks to her Maori friends, Fleur was an excellent swimmer.

"Or I'll take the veil!" Fleurette went on. There was not yet a convent in New Zealand, but that seemed to have escaped her at the moment. Up until then, Gwyneira had managed to see the humor in the situation. But then she heard Gerald's voice and became alarmed. There was something foul...the old man must have drunk considerably more than Gwyneira thought. While she had been preparing Fleur? Or right at that moment, while Fleur was issuing her childish threats?

"You absolutely will not take the veil, Fleurette! That is the last thing you will do. How do you even find pleasure rolling in the hay with your shitty little friend? Just wait, little one; others have been cracked before you. You need a man, Fleur, you..."

Fleurette seemed to feel the threat now too. "Mother won't allow me to marry yet anyway," she said in a markedly quieter voice, a remark that just fueled Gerald's rage.

"Your mother will do what I want. I'm going to change your tune; you can count on that!" Just as she opened the door to escape, Gerald yanked the girl back. "You will all finally do what I want!"

Gwyneira, who had been fearfully approaching the study, burst in when she heard that. She saw Fleurette being thrown into a chair, afraid and sobbing. Gerald moved to pounce on her, dropping a whiskey bottle that shattered on the floor. No great loss since the bottle was empty. It raced through Gwyneira's mind that it had been three-quarters full before.

"So the little mare is stubborn, is that it?" Gerald hissed at his granddaughter. "Still untouched by bit and bridle? Well, we'll change that now. You'll learn to submit to your rider."

Gwyneira tore him away from her. Her rage and fear for her daughter endowed her with incredible strength. She knew that light in Gerald's eyes all too well; ever since Paul's birth, it had pursued her in her darkest nightmares.

"How dare you touch her!" she railed at him. "Leave her in peace this instant!"

Gerald shook. "Get her out of my sight!" he said through his teeth. "She's under house arrest. Until she's considered her engagement to Beasley. I promised her to him. I won't break my word!"

Reginald Beasley had been waiting upstairs in his room, but the scene had naturally not escaped his attention. Deeply embarrassed, he stepped to his door and met Gwyneira and her daughter on the steps.

"Miss Warden...Mrs. Warden...please, forgive me!"

Unlike the night before, Reginald Beasley was sober now, and the look on Fleurette's distraught young face and her mother's eyes glowing with rage told him he had no chance.

"I...I couldn't have known that it would be such a...ahem, an imposition for you, to accept my proposal. You see, I am no longer young but I am not all that old, and I...I would cherish you..."

Gwyneira glared icily at him. "Mr. Beasley, my daughter does not want to be cherished. She wants first to grow up. And then she will probably want a man her own age—or at least a man who makes his own proposal instead of sending some other old goat to force her into his bed. Have I made myself clear?"

She had wanted to remain polite, but the look on Gerald's face as he loomed over Fleurette in the chair had shaken her to the core. First, she had to get rid of this geriatric suitor. But that shouldn't be difficult. Then she would have to think of what to do about Gerald. She had not even realized herself that she was living on a powder keg. But she would do whatever she must to protect Fleur.

"Mrs. Warden, I...as I said, Miss Warden, I'm sorry. Under these circumstances, I would be entirely prepared to break off the engagement."

"I'm not engaged to you!" Fleur said with a quaking voice. "I can't even, I..."

Gwyneira pulled the girl away. "Your decision pleases me and honors you," she informed Reginald Beasley with a forced smile. "Perhaps you would be so good as to share this decision with my father-in-law so that we might forget this painful incident ever happened. I have always held you in high regard and would hate to lose you as a friend of this house."

She strode regally past Reginald Beasley. Fleurette stumbled behind her. She seemed to want to say something more, but Gwyneira would not let her.

"Don't you dare tell him anything about Ruben; otherwise, you'll wound his pride," she hissed to her daughter. "Now stay in your room—preferably until he's gone. And for the love of God, don't come out of your room while your grandfather is still drunk!"

Trembling, Gwyneira shut the door behind her daughter. For the time being, disaster had been averted. Gerald would drink with Reginald that evening; there was no need to fear further outbursts. And tomorrow he would be dreadfully ashamed of his attack today. But what would come next? How long would Gerald's self-recriminations keep him away from his granddaughter? And would the safety of a door be enough to prevent him when he was drunk and had perhaps convinced himself that he needed to "break the girl in" for her future husband?

Gwyneira had made up her mind. She had to send her daughter away.

4

Putting this plan into action proved difficult. Gwyneira could find neither an excuse to send the girl away nor a suitable family to take her in. Gwyneira had been thinking she might be able to take up residence in a household with children—there was a lack of governesses in Christchurch at the moment, and an au pair as attractive and educated as Fleur should have been a welcome addition to any young family. In practice, though, only the Barringtons and Greenwoods were possibilities—and Antonia Barrington, a rather nondescript young woman, rejected the idea right away when Gwyneira carefully sounded her out. Gwyneira could not hold it against her. The young lord's first sight of Fleurette convinced her that her daughter would be stepping out of the frying pan and into the fire.

Elizabeth Greenwood would have loved to take Fleur in. George Greenwood's loyalty and affection for her were above reproach. Fleur saw him as an "uncle," and moreover in his house she would learn about bookkeeping and business management. Unfortunately, the Greenwoods were about to embark on a visit to England. George's parents wanted to finally see their grandchildren, and Elizabeth was so excited she could hardly contain herself.

"I just hope his mother doesn't recognize me," she confided to Gwyneira. "She has always thought I was from Sweden. If she were to realize that..."

Gwyneira shook her head, smiling. It was utterly impossible to see the bashful, half-starved orphan girl who had left London nearly twenty years earlier in the prim, lovely lady of today, whose impeccable manners had made her a pillar of Christchurch society.

"She'll love you," she assured the younger woman. "Don't do anything foolish like trying to fake a Swedish accent. Just say you grew up in Christchurch, which is true anyway. And there you have it: that's why you speak English."

"But they will not be able to help hearing that I speak Cockney," Elizabeth fretted.

Gwyneira laughed. "Elizabeth, compared to you, we all speak terrible English—aside from Helen, of course, from whom you get it anyway. So there's no reason to worry."

Elizabeth nodded, uncertain. "Well, George says I won't need to speak all that much anyway. Apparently, his mother prefers to carry on conversations all by herself."

Gwyneira laughed. Meeting with Elizabeth was always a breath of fresh air. She was more intelligent than the well mannered but somewhat dull Dorothy in Haldon or adorable little Rosemary, who had engaged herself to her foster father's journeyman baker. She often wondered what had become of the other three girls who had traveled with them aboard the *Dublin*. Helen had received word from Westport from a Madame Jolanda, who had explained peevishly that Daphne, along with the twins—and a whole week's earnings—had disappeared without a trace. The lady had had the nerve to demand the missing money from Helen, who had left her letter unanswered.

Gwyneira finally said a heartfelt good-bye to Elizabeth—after giving her the usual shopping list that every woman in New Zealand foisted on friends traveling back to the homeland. One could order practically anything for sale in London through George's company, but there were a few intimate items that women did not like to entrust to messengers. Elizabeth promised to clean out the London merchants on Gwyneira's behalf, and Gwyneira left in high spirits—however, still without a solution for Fleurette.

Over the course of the next few months, the situation on Kiward Station settled down. Gerald's attack on Fleur had sobered him up considerably. He avoided his granddaughter—and Gwyneira made sure that Fleurette kept it that way. In the meantime, the old man redoubled his efforts to introduce Paul to the family business. The two of them often disappeared early in the morning out to the pastures somewhere and didn't return until evening. After that, Gerald indulged in his evening whiskey, but he never reached the level of intoxication that he had before, during his all-day drinking binges. Following his grandfather's advice, Paul had begun throwing his weight around, about which Kiri and Marama expressed concern. Gwyneira overheard a conversation between her son and Marama that quite troubled her.

"Wiramu is not a bad fellow, Paul! He's hard working, a good hunter, and a good shepherd. It's not right, you firing him!"

Marama was cleaning the silver in the garden. Unlike her mother, she enjoyed this particular task; she loved the gleaming metal. Sometimes she sang while she worked, but Gerald could not stand Maori music. Gwyneira felt similarly, but only because it reminded her of the drumming on that fateful night. She liked Marama's ballads, sung in that sweet voice, and surprisingly, even Paul seemed to enjoy them. Today, however, he was eager to gloat about his excursion with Gerald the day before. The two of them had been checking on the pastures in the foothills when they had come upon the Maori boy, Wiramu. Wiramu was taking the prizes of a successful fishing trip back to his tribe on Kiward Station. That in itself was no reason to punish him, but the boy belonged to one of the shepherd patrols Gerald had recently instituted to put an end to James McKenzie's activities. Hence, Wiramu was supposed to be in the highlands, not visiting his mother in the village. Gerald had thrown a fit and given the boy a dressing down. After that he had let Paul decide on the severity of his punishment. Paul had decided to let Wiramu go, effective immediately.

"Grandfather's not paying him to fish," Paul explained gravely. "He needs to stay at his post."

Marama shook her head. "But I think the patrols move around anyway. It doesn't really matter where Wiramu is at any given moment.

And all the men fish. They have to hunt and fish. Or are you supplying them with provisions now?"

"Certainly it matters!" Paul crowed. "McKenzie isn't stealing our sheep here near the house; he's doing it up in the highlands. That's where the men need to patrol. And yes, they can hunt and fish for their own needs. But not for the whole village." The boy was adamant that he was in the right.

"That's not what they're doing!" Marama was not ready to let it go. She made a desperate effort to make her people's perspective clear to him; she could not comprehend why that should prove so difficult. After all, Paul had practically grown up with the Maori. So how was it possible that he had learned nothing except how to hunt and fish? "They just discovered the land around there. No one had ever fished there; their weirs were full. They couldn't eat all that fish right away, nor could they dry it—after all, they were supposed to be patrolling. If someone had not run to the village, the fish would have gone to waste. And that would be a shame, Paul; you know that. You don't let any food go to waste; the gods don't like it!"

The primarily Maori patrol had asked Wiramu to take the fish to the village and tell the elders about the enormous wealth of fish in the newly discovered waters. The surrounding area too should be fertile and quite rich in prey to hunt. It was possible that the tribe would soon set out to spend some time fishing and hunting there. That would have been desirable for Kiward Station, as no one would steal livestock in the area around the camp if the Maori kept their eyes on it. However, neither Gerald nor his grandson had been able or willing to think that far ahead. Instead, they had angered the Maori. Wiramu's people in the mountains would doubtless overlook any sheep thief, and the work of the patrols would slacken.

"Tonga's father says he's going to claim the new land for himself and his tribe," Marama explained further. "Wiramu will lead him there. If Mr. Warden had been nice to him, he would have shown it to you instead, and you could have had it surveyed!"

"We'll find it anyway," Paul kept on. "We don't need to be nice to this or that bastard."

Marama shook her head but refrained from pointing out that Wiramu was not a bastard but rather the chief's esteemed nephew. "Tonga says they're registering possession of the land in Christchurch," she continued. "He can read and write as well as you, and Reti will be helping him. It was dumb to let Wiramu go, Paul. It was just dumb!"

Paul stood up angrily, knocking over the tray holding the silver that Marama had already cleaned. He had clearly done it intentionally since he was not normally clumsy. "You're just a girl and a Maori. How do you know what's dumb?"

Marama laughed and picked the silver up serenely. She did not take offense easily. "You'll see who gets the land," she said calmly.

This conversation confirmed Gwyneira's fears. Paul was making unnecessary enemies. He had confused strength with harshness—which was perhaps normal at his age—but Gerald should be admonishing him for it, not encouraging him. How could he let a boy who had just turned twelve decide whether to let a worker go or not?

Fleurette resumed her old life, even paying frequent visits to Helen on O'Keefe Station—only, of course, when Gerald and Paul were definitely elsewhere and she was certain that Howard wouldn't make a sudden appearance. Gwyneira thought that was careless and, having sent Nepumuk back to Helen, preferred that the women meet in Haldon.

Fleurette continued to write long letters to Queenstown but received no answer. Nor had Helen, who also worried a great deal about Ruben.

"If only he had gone to Dunedin," she sighed. A tearoom had recently opened in Haldon where respectable women could sit and exchange their news. "He could have taken on a job as an office assistant. But panning for gold..."

Gwyneira shrugged. "He wants to get rich. And maybe he'll strike it lucky; the gold deposits there are supposed to be enormous."

Helen rolled her eyes. "Gwyn, I love my son more than anything. But the gold would have to grow on trees and fall on his head for him to find it. He takes after my father, who was only happy when he could sit in his study and lose himself in his ancient Hebrew texts. I think he would make a good attorney or judge, possibly even a businessman. George said he got along well with the clients; he can be charming. But diverting streams to pan gold out of them or digging tunnels or whatever it is they do there, that's not for him."

"He'll do it for me," Fleur said with a wistful expression on her face. "He'll do anything for me. At least he'll try!"

For the time being, the talk in Haldon concerned itself less with Ruben O'Keefe's quest for gold and more with James McKenzie's increasingly audacious livestock thefts. At the moment, a major sheep breeder by the name of John Sideblossom was suffering a great deal from McKenzie's forays.

John Sideblossom lived on the western shore of Lake Pukaki, high in the mountains. He rarely came to Haldon and practically never to Christchurch, but he held giant tracts of land in the foothills. He sold his livestock in Dunedin, so he was not among George Greenwood's clients.

Gerald seemed to know him, however. In fact, he was giddy as a schoolboy when he received the news one day that Sideblossom wanted to meet with like-minded livestock breeders in Haldon to plan another punitive expedition into the mountains against James McKenzie.

"He is convinced McKenzie is hiding out in his area," Gerald explained as he drank his obligatory whiskey before dinner. "Somewhere above the lakes there. He must have discovered new land. John writes that he must be disappearing through some pass we don't know about. And he's suggesting search actions that cover wide areas. We need to combine our manpower and smoke the fellow out once and for all."

"Does this Sideblossom know what he's talking about?" Gwyneira inquired, maintaining her poise. Over the last few years, almost all the livestock barons in the Canterbury Plains had been planning such battles from their firesides. They generally did not amount to anything, though, since not enough people gathered to comb their neighbors' land. It would take a more charismatic personality than Reginald Beasley to unite the individually minded sheep breeders.

"You bet he does!" Gerald boomed. "Johnny Sideblossom is the wildest dog you can imagine! I've known him since my whaling days. He was a little runt back then, as old as Paul is now."

Paul's ears pricked up.

"Hired on as a half-deck boy with his dad. But the old man drank like a fish, and when it came time to man the harpoon one day and the whale was flailing around like mad, the whale knocked him out of the boat—better said, it knocked over the whole boat, and everyone jumped out. Only the boy stayed behind till the last second, firing the harpoon before the tub flipped. He took the whale down, Johnny Sideblossom did! At ten years old! The whale took his old man, but he didn't let that slow him down. He became the most fearsome harpooner on the West Coast. He'd hardly heard about the gold finds near Westport before he was off. Up and down the Buller River, and always successful. Ended up buying land on Lake Pukaki. And the best livestock, some of them he even bought from me. If I remember correctly, that scoundrel McKenzie herded a flock there for me. Must be almost twenty years ago now."

Seventeen, Gwyneira thought. She remembered that James had primarily agreed to the job to avoid her. Had he explored around there back then and found the land of his dreams?

"I'll write and tell him we could hold the conference here. Yes, now there's an idea! I'll invite a few others too, and then we'll finally drive this nail home! We'll get the rat, no worries. When Johnny starts something, he means it!" Gerald would have liked to reach for pen and paper right then, but Kiri was serving dinner. Not to be deterred, he put his plan into action the very next day, and Gwyneira sighed at the thought of the feasting and drinking that would precede the great punitive expedition. Still, she was excited to meet Johnny Sideblossom. If even half of the stories that Gerald entertained them with at dinner were true, he must be an intriguing character—and perhaps even a dangerous adversary for James McKenzie.

Nearly all of the livestock farmers in the area accepted Gerald's invitation, and it sounded as though this time it would be more than just a vacation. James McKenzie had clearly taken things too far. And John Sideblossom really did appear to have the necessary strength of character to lead the men. He completely blew Gwyneira away. He rode a powerful black stallion—which was very fitting—but the horse was also well trained and easy to handle. He probably checked on his pastures and oversaw the herding with this horse. He towered over even the most powerful men by nearly a full head. His body was taut and muscular, his face angular and tan, his dark hair thick and curly. He wore it a bit long, which only emphasized his rugged appearance. And he had a dazzling, engaging personality. He immediately took charge of the men's conversation, slapping old friends on the shoulder, laughing thunderously with Gerald, and seemingly able to consume whiskey like it was water without showing it. To Gwyneira and the few other women who had accompanied their husbands, he was particularly courteous. All that said, Gwyneira did not like him, though she wasn't able to pinpoint why. From the very first she felt a certain distaste for the man. Did it have to do with the fact that his lips were thin and hard and displayed a smile that was not reflected in his eyes? Or was it the eyes themselves—so dark as to look almost black, cold as night and calculating? Gwyneira noticed that when he looked at her, his glances were unquestionably too appraising—focusing less on her face than on sizing up her still slender and feminine figure. As a young woman she would have blushed, but now she returned his looks with self-assurance. She was the mistress here; he was the visitor, and she was not interested in any association beyond that. She would likewise have liked to keep Fleurette far from Gerald's old friend and drinking buddy, but naturally, that was impossible since the girl was expected at the banquet that evening. Yet Gwyneira dismissed the idea of warning her daughter. If she said anything, Fleur would make every effort to look unattractive—and in doing so reawaken Gerald's anger. So Gwyneira merely eyed her strange visitor suspiciously when Fleur came down the stairs—as radiant and prettily dressed as Gwyneira on her first evening in Kiward Station. The girl wore a simple cream-colored dress that emphasized her light tan. It was appliquéd with gold- and brown-colored eyelet embroidery on the sleeves, neckline, and waist, which suited Fleurette's unusual light brown, almost golden eye color. She had not put her hair up, instead braiding strands of hair on either side of her head and then binding the thin braids at the back of her head. It looked very pretty, but more importantly, served the practical purpose of keeping her hair out of her face. Fleurette always did her own hair, having rejected the housemaids' help ever since she was a little girl.

Fleur's petite figure and loose hair gave her an elfin appearance. Though she looked like her mother and shared a similar temperament, Fleurette's radiance was all her own. The girl seemed more approachable and more submissive than the young Gwyneira had been, and a glow rather than a provocative spark issued from her golden-brown eyes.

The men in the room stared, enthralled, as she made her entrance. While the other men appeared enchanted, Gwyneira recognized an expression of naked desire in John Sideblossom's gaze. He held Fleurette's hand a moment too long for her taste when he greeted the girl politely.

"Is there also a Mrs. Sideblossom?" Gwyneira asked when the hosts and guests had finally sat down to dinner. Gwyneira had assigned herself to John Sideblossom as a dining partner, but the man took so little notice of her that it bordered on rudeness. He only had eyes for Fleur, who was engaged in a rather dull conversation with the elder Lord Barrington. The lord had handed over his business ventures in Christchurch to his son and retired to a farm in the Canterbury Plains, where he was raising sheep and horses with modest success.

John Sideblossom cast a glance at Gwyneira as though he had just noticed her for the first time.

"No, there's no longer a Mrs. Sideblossom," he replied. "My wife died three years ago giving birth to my son."

"I'm sorry to hear that," Gwyneira replied, having rarely meant a platitude so honestly. "For the child as well—did I understand correctly that he lived?"

The farmer nodded. "Yes, my son's now practically being raised by the Maori help. Not a particularly good solution, but while he's still little, it works. As time goes on, however, I need to look around for something else. It's not easy to find a suitable girl." As he spoke, he fixed his eyes again on Fleur, which angered and irritated Gwyneira. The man talked about girls like a pair of breeches!

"Is your daughter already engaged to someone?" he inquired drily. "She seems to be a well-bred girl."

Gwyneira was so taken aback she hardly knew what to say. The man did not waste words.

"Fleurette is still very young," she finally replied evasively.

John Sideblossom shrugged. "There's nothing wrong with that. I've always been of the opinion that you can't marry them off soon enough; otherwise, they just get stupid ideas. And birthing is easier while they're young. The midwife told me that back when Marylee died. Marylee was already twenty-five."

After these last words, he turned away from Gwyneira. Something that Gerald just said must have caught his attention, and he was soon deep in a heated conversation with several other livestock farmers.

Gwyneira appeared calm, but she was boiling with rage inside. She was accustomed to girls being wooed for dynastic or financial reasons rather than for their personalities. But this fellow had taken it too far. Even just the way he spoke of his late wife: "Marylee was already twenty-five." He made it sound as though she would have died of old age soon anyway, regardless of whether she had given her husband a child first or not.

Later, as the guests formed loose groups in the salon to finish the last of the table conversation, before the ladies retired to tea and liquor in Gwyneira's salon and the gentlemen to cigars and whiskey in Gerald's sanctuary, John Sideblossom made a beeline for Fleurette.

Gwyneira, who could not break away from her conversation with Lady Barrington, watched nervously as he spoke to Fleur. From all appearances, he was behaving courteously and turning on his charm. Fleurette smiled shyly at first but then let herself be drawn freely into conversation. Judging from the expression on Fleur's face, Gwyneira guessed that the pair were talking about dogs and horses. Otherwise, she could not imagine Fleur looking so attentive and engaged. When Gwyneira finally succeeded in tearing herself away from Lady Barrington and strolled nonchalantly in their direction, her suspicions were confirmed.

"I'd be happy to show you the mare, of course. If you like, we could go for a ride together tomorrow. I got a look at your horse; he's quite lovely!" Fleurette seemed to have taken a liking to the visitor. "Or are you leaving tomorrow?"

Most of those present would be riding back to their farms the next day. The organization of the punitive expedition had been determined, and the men proposed to raise a number of people in the area willing to take part. Several of the sheep breeders wanted to go along themselves; others promised to contribute a few armed riders.

John Sideblossom shook his head though. "No, Miss Warden, I'll be staying a few days. We agreed to assemble the men from Christchurch here and then to ride to my farm together. That will be the home base for all further activities. That being the case, I'm happy to take you up on your offer. My stallion, by the way, has some Arab blood. I was able to buy an Arab a few years ago in Dunedin and crossed our farm horses with him. The results have been very nice—sometimes a bit lightweight though."

At first Gwyneira was relieved. As long as they were discussing horse breeding, he would behave himself. And perhaps Fleur actually liked him. John Sideblossom was well respected and owned roughly as much land as Gerald Warden, although it was not as good. He was rather old for Fleur but even his age lay within the bounds of acceptability. If only she didn't have such an uneasy feeling about him. If the man didn't seem so cold and unfeeling. Then, of course, there was the situation with Ruben O'Keefe. Fleurette certainly wouldn't take leave of her love without a fight.

However, Fleur seemed to take pleasure in John Sideblossom's company over the next few days. The man was a keen rider, which Fleur liked; he told exciting stories; and he proved to be a good listener. Beyond that, he had charm and a willful manner that the girl found attractive. Fleur laughed when, while skeet shooting with Gerald, John Sideblossom did not aim for the clay pigeon, but instead shot one of the shabbiest roses in the garden from its stem.

"The rose of roses!" he said—true, it was not very original, but Fleur appeared flattered. Paul, however, looked out of sorts. He had looked up to John Sideblossom ever since hearing Gerald's stories about him, and now that he knew him in person, Paul practically worshipped him. John Sideblossom, however, hardly gave the boy a second look. Either he was drinking and talking to Gerald, or he was trying to win over Fleur. Paul considered how he could manage to reveal his sister's true face, but no opportunity to do so had presented itself yet.

John Sideblossom was a rash, impulsive man who was used to getting what he wanted. He had selected Kiward Station in order to mobilize the Canterbury Plains' sheep breeders, but once he got to know Fleurette Warden, he quickly decided to resolve another outstanding problem. He needed a new wife—and he had unexpectedly met a suitable candidate here. She was young, desirable, from a good family, and clearly well educated. At least for the first few years, he'd be able to save on a tutor for little Thomas. An alliance with the Wardens would also open more doors to high society in Christchurch and Dunedin. If he had understood correctly, Fleurette's mother even came from British nobility. The girl seemed to be a bit wild, and the mother obviously could be imperious. John Sideblossom certainly never would have allowed his wife to participate in the management of the farm, let alone direct the herding. But that was Warden's problem; he'd put Fleurette in her place soon enough. That said, she was welcome to bring along any animals she loved—that mare would bear fantastic foals, and the sheepdogs were a definite gain too. But as soon as Fleurette got pregnant, she would not be able to handle the animals. He was taking care to get on Gracie's good side—which earned him even more points with Fleurette. After three days, the farmer was convinced that Fleur would not refuse his proposal. And Gerald Warden should be happy to marry the girl off so well.

Gerald had mixed feelings about John's proposal. This time the girl did not seem disinclined—Gerald even thought his granddaughter was flirting rather shamelessly with his old friend. Yet his relief was tinged with envy. John would have what he, Gerald, could not. John would not have to take Fleur by force; she would give herself freely. Gerald drowned his forbidden thoughts in whiskey.

At least he was prepared when his friend came to him on the fourth day of his stay at Kiward Station and announced his marital intentions.

"You know I can provide for her, old friend," Sideblossom said. "Lionel Station is big. Granted, the manor house is not quite as grand as this place, but it's comfortable. We have plenty of servants. The girl will be cared for tip to toe. Of course she'll have to take care of the boy herself. But she'll have her own soon enough, I'm sure—and she can see to two as easily as one. Do you have any objections to my making a proposal?" John poured himself a whiskey.

Gerald shook his head and let John pour him one too. John was right; what he was proposing was the best solution. "I have no objections. The farm does have little in the way of liquid assets for a dowry. Would you be content with a flock of sheep? We could also discuss the possibility of two mares for breeding."

The two men spent the next hour in amiable negotiations over Fleurette's dowry. Both of them knew every trick in the book when it came to the livestock negotiations. The offers just went back and forth. Gwyneira, who was once again eavesdropping, was not unsettled; to her ears it sounded like they were injecting new blood into the flocks on Lionel Station. Fleurette's name was not mentioned once.

"I mu...must warn you, however," Gerald said after the men had finally reached an agreement and confirmed the amount of the dowry with a handshake and sealed it with a great deal more whiskey. "The gi...girl is not ea...easy. Had something for a neighbor boy...just nonsense. The boy has...sodded off in the meantime. But you kn... know how skirts are..."

"I did not get the impression that Fleur was uninterested." Sideblossom was surprised. As always, he seemed completely sober even now, although they had long since emptied the first bottle of whiskey. "Why don't we just strike while the iron is hot and ask her? Go, call for her. I'm in the mood for an engagement kiss! And the other farmers should be back by tomorrow. Then we can announce it right away."

Fleurette, who had just returned from riding and was preparing to change for dinner, was surprised by Witi's shy knock on her door.

"Miss Fleur, Mr. Warden wishes to speak with you. He...how you say? He bid you come straight in his room." The Maori servant was debating whether to add an additional comment, and ultimately decided to do so: "It best you hurry. The men much whiskey, little patience."

After the incident with Gerald the night of Reginald Beasley's proposal, Fleur was suspicious about sudden invitations to Gerald's room. Instinctively, she decided not to make herself look particularly attractive, clasping her riding dress closed again instead of putting on the dark green silk dress Kiri had laid out for her. She would have liked to bring her mother with her, but she did not know where Gwyneira was. The many visitors on top of the farm work were taking up a lot of her mother's time. At the moment, it was true, there was not all that much to do—it being January, the shearing and lambing were done, and the sheep were mostly wandering free in the highlands—but the summer had been unusually wet, so there were constant repairs to be done, and the hay harvest was becoming a game of chance. Fleur decided not to wait for Gwyneira or to waste time looking for her.

Whatever Gerald wanted, she would have to deal with him herself. There was little need to fear an assault; after all, Witi had spoken of "the men." So John Sideblossom would likewise be present and act as a mediator.

John Sideblossom was unpleasantly surprised when Fleur entered the study in her riding dress and with her hair a mess—she could have cleaned herself up a bit. However, she still looked indisputably charming. No, it would not be difficult for him to conjure up a little romance.

"Miss Warden," he said, "will you permit me to speak?" John bowed formally before the girl. "This is a matter that concerns me more than anyone else, and I am not the sort of man who sends others to do his bidding."

He looked into Fleur's shocked eyes and interpreted the nervous flickering in them as encouragement.

"It's true I first laid eyes on you three days ago, Miss Warden, but I was enthralled by you from the very first moment, by your beautiful eyes and your gentle smile. Your kindness these last few days has given me hope that my presence was not objectionable to you either. And for that reason—I am a man of bold decisions, Miss Warden, and I think you will learn to love that about me—for that reason I have decided to ask your grandfather for his permission. He joyfully agreed to an alliance between us. I may therefore, with the permission of your guardian, formally ask for your hand."

John smiled and sank down to one knee in front of Fleur. Gerald suppressed a laugh when he noticed that Fleur did not know where to look.

"I...Mr. Sideblossom, that's very nice of you, but I love someone else," she finally said. "My grandfather really should have told you, and—"

"Miss Warden," he broke in, full of confidence, "whomever you think you love, you will forget him in my arms soon enough."

Fleurette shook her head. "I won't ever forget him, sir! I promised to marry him."

"Fleur, don't talk such bloody rot!" Gerald roared. "John is the right man for you. Not too young, not too old, socially acceptable, and he's rich to boot. What more do you want?"

"I have to be able to love my husband!" Fleurette exclaimed frantically. "And I..."

"Love comes in time," John explained. "So, come now, girl. You've spent the last three days with me. I can't be all that disagreeable to you."

Impatience flickered in his eyes.

"You...you are not disagreeable to me, but...but that's why I won't...marry you. I think you're nice, sir, but...but..."

"Stop playing coy, Fleurette!" John interrupted the girl's stammering. He could not have cared less about the girl's objections. "Say yes and then we can begin discussing the formalities. I think we should have the wedding this fall—right after this unfortunate business with James McKenzie has been taken care of. Maybe you can even ride to Lionel Station straightaway...in the company of your mother, of course; we must go about this properly."

Fleurette inhaled deeply, imprisoned by anger and panic. Why the devil was no one listening to her? She resolved to say clearly and in no uncertain terms what she had to say. These men had to be capable of understanding the reality of the situation.

"Mr. Sideblossom, Grandfather," Fleurette said, raising her voice. "I've said it several times now, and I'm getting tired of repeating myself. I won't marry you, sir! I thank you for your proposal, and I appreciate your attentions, but I am already spoken for. Please excuse me from dinner, Grandfather; I'm indisposed."

Fleur forced herself not to run from the room, so she turned around in a slow and measured manner. She left the room with her head held high and without slamming the door behind her. But then she fled through the salon and up the stairs like the devil was on her heels. It was best that she shut herself in her room until John Sideblossom left.

She had not liked the flickering in his eyes. The man was no doubt unaccustomed to not getting what he wanted. And something told her that he could be dangerous when things did not go according to his plan.

5

The next day Kiward Station filled with men and horses. The sheep barons of the Canterbury Plains had not skimped on their promises: the number of participants in the punitive expedition had grown to the strength of a military company. Gwyneira did not care for the men Gerald's friends had signed up. There were few Maori shepherds and farm employees among the men. It looked as though the breeders had recruited men in the pubs and the new arrivals' barracks, and many of them looked to Gwyneira like fortune hunters, if not plain old seedy rabble. For this reason, she was happy to keep Fleurette away from the stables for the next few days. For his part, Gerald did not skimp either and ransacked his alcohol stores. The men drank and celebrated in the shearing sheds; Kiward Station's shepherds, mostly friends of James McKenzie's, stayed away, deeply uneasy.

"My God, miss," Andy McAran said to Gwyneira, summing up their thoughts. "They're going to hunt James down like a rabid wolf. They're all talking about shooting him dead! Surely he doesn't deserve to have this scum sent after his neck. All over a few sheep!"

"This scum doesn't know its way around the highlands," Gwyneira said, not knowing whether she wanted to calm the old shepherd or herself. "They'll just step on each other's toes; Mr. McKenzie will laugh himself to death over them. Just wait; they'll run out of steam. If only they'd be on their way! I don't like having these people in the yard. I've already sent Kiri and Moana and Marama away. I hope the Maori are keeping a good watch over their camp. Are you keeping an eye on our horses and saddlery? I don't want anything to go missing."

Gwyneira was in for a very unpleasant surprise. A number of the men had come on foot, and Gerald—starting out with a nasty hangover but already drunk again by midday and still incensed at Fleurette's renewed recalcitrance—had promised them horses from Kiward Station. He did not, however, let Gwyneira know right away, so she did not have time to have workhorses sent over from the summer paddocks. The men hooted as they divided up her valuable cobs that afternoon. Fleurette watched helplessly from her bedroom window as one after the other tried to ride Niniane.

"Mother, he can't just give her to them! She belongs to us," she wailed.

Gwyneira shrugged. "He's only lending them to the men; they won't be allowed to keep them. But I don't like it either. Most of these brutes can't even ride properly. That's good for us, however. You can already see how the horses are bucking them off. When they come back, though, we're going to have to break them in all over again."

"But Niniane..."

"I can't do anything to change it, dear. They want Morgaine too. Perhaps I can talk to Gerald again tomorrow, but he's taken leave of his senses today. And this Sideblossom fellow is behaving as though he owns the place: he's telling people where they can stay and ordering them around; he acts as though I weren't even here. As soon as the fool's gone, I'm going to cross myself three times. In any case, you won't be attending the banquet tonight. I've already explained that. You're sick. I don't want Sideblossom to catch sight of you again."

Secretly, Gwyneira had long since planned to take their horses to safety that night. Under no circumstances would she send her valuable broodmares into the highlands with the search party. She had arranged with Andy McAran, Poker Livingston, and her other trusted workers to drive the horses away that night. As long as they just pranced about the pastures, she would have time enough to gather them up again in the coming days. The men would fetch the workhorses and place them in the stalls. It might cause a bit of uproar in the morning, but John Sideblossom surely wouldn't delay their endeavor over different horses.

She did not tell Fleurette that, however. She was too afraid the girl might want to take part in the action.

"Niniane will be back the day after tomorrow at the latest," she comforted Fleur. "She'll throw her would-be rider and come home. She won't put up with such nonsense. But right now I need to change. Dinner with the captains of the military expedition awaits. What expense over one man!"

Gwyneira retired, and Fleurette stayed behind, brooding angrily. She was not about to acquiesce to her helplessness. Gerald was giving Niniane away out of pure spite. Fleur hatched a plan. She would lead her horse to safety while the men were getting drunk in the salon. To manage it, she would have to slip out of her room right then, since every path to the stables led through the salon, which was empty for the moment. The guests attending the banquet that night were changing, and sheer chaos reigned outside. She would not be noticed if she put her hair under a bandana and hurried. It was only a few steps from the kitchen door to the barn. If someone saw her, they'd take her for a kitchen maid.

Fleur's plan might even have succeeded if Paul had not been watching his sister. The boy was once more in low spirits; his idol, John Sideblossom, ignored him, and Gerald had gruffly turned down his request to be allowed to partake in the expedition. Since he had nothing better to do and was prowling around the stables, he was naturally very interested when he saw Fleur hide herself in the barn. Paul could piece together for himself what she had in mind. But he would make sure that Gerald caught her red-handed later.

Gwyneira needed all her patience and forbearance to get through the banquet that evening. She was the only woman present, and without exception they were all drunk by the time they sat down to dinner. Before starting to eat, they downed another couple of glasses; then wine was poured. The first one soon began to prattle. They all laughed at one another's dumb jokes, yelled dirty jibes at each other, and behaved toward Gwyneira in anything but a gentlemanlike manner.

She only began to feel truly uncomfortable when John Sideblossom suddenly approached her after the final course.

"We need to speak, Mrs. Warden," he said in his typically direct fashion, once again appearing sober among all the drunkards. However, Gwyneira had gotten to know him a bit better and knew how to recognize the signs of intoxication in him. His eyelids hung a bit lower, and his gaze was suspicious and shifty instead of cool and distant. Although Sideblossom still kept his feelings reined in, they simmered just beneath the surface.

"I think you know I asked for your daughter's hand yesterday. Fleurette turned me down."

Gwyneira shrugged. "She has the right. In the civilized world, women are asked before they're married off. And if Fleur did not like you, there's nothing I can do about it."

"You could put in a good word for me, madam," Sideblossom said.

"I'm afraid that wouldn't do any good," Gwyneira remarked, her own feelings slowly bubbling to the surface. "And I wouldn't do it of my own accord anyway. I do not know you well, Mr. Sideblossom, but I don't like what I've seen."

John Sideblossom grimaced. "Well, look-y here! The lady doesn't like me! And what do you have against me, Lady Warden?" he asked coldly.

Gwyneira sighed. She had not wanted to get into a discussion… but fine, if that's what he wanted.

"Going on the warpath against a single man," she began, "does not seem appropriate to me. And you exert a bad influence on the other farmers. Without your whispering to him, Lord Barrington would never have sunk so low as to join such a band of ruffians as the one now camped outside. Your behavior toward me is insulting, even leaving Fleurette entirely out of this. A gentleman, Mr. Sideblossom, in your position would strive to change the girl's mind. You, on the other hand, give affront to Fleurette by initiating this business with the horses. That was your idea, was it not? Gerald has been too drunk for such schemes for a long time."

Gwyneira spoke quickly and full of wrath. Everything was fraying her nerves at that moment. And there was Paul, who had joined them and avidly followed her outburst.

John Sideblossom laughed. "Touché, my dear! A little tongue-lashing. I don't like it when people don't listen to me. But just you wait. I'll get your little girl yet. I'll push my proposal when we return. Against your will if I must."

Gwyneira wanted to bring the conversation to an end. "Then I wish you luck," she said stiffly. "And you, Paul, come with me upstairs, please. I hate it when you slink behind me and eavesdrop."

The boy cringed. But what he had heard here was worth the dressing down. Perhaps Gerald was not the right audience for his information on Fleurette. It would cause her much more pain if this was the man who thwarted her "horse theft."

When Gwyneira retired to her room, Paul turned on his heels and went looking for John Sideblossom. The farmers looked increasingly bored in one another's company. No wonder—aside from him, everyone else was fall-down drunk.

"You...you want to marry my sister?" Paul spoke to him.

Sideblossom looked down at him, caught off guard.

"Well, that's my intention. You got an objection too?" he asked, sounding amused.

Paul shook his head. "As far as I'm concerned, you can have her. But you should know something about her. Fleurette acts all innocent. But she's already had a beau. Ruben O'Keefe."

Sideblossom nodded. "I know," he said, disinterested.

"But she didn't tell you everything!" Paul upped the ante. "She didn't tell you that she did it with him. But I saw it!"

Sideblossom's interest was aroused. "What did you say? Your sister's not a virgin anymore?"

Paul shrugged. The word "virgin" did not mean anything to him.

"Ask her yourself," he said. "She's in the barn."

John Sideblossom found Fleurette in Niniane's stall, where the girl was just considering what her best course of action would be. Should she simply drive Niniane outside? Then there was the danger that she would not run from the stables at all but stay close to the other horses. Maybe it would be better to ride her away and put her up in a paddock farther away. However, that seemed risky, as she would have to find her way back on foot, past all the outbuildings, which were stuffed full of the search party's drunk recruits.

Still contemplating her options, she scratched her horse under its forelock and spoke to it. The other horses suddenly got excited, and Gracie sniffed at the straw. With all that going on, it escaped Fleurette's attention that someone was quietly opening the door. By the time Gracie became aware of what was going on and started barking, it was too late. John Sideblossom was standing in the stable aisle smirking at Fleurette.

"So, little girl. At night we sneak out to the stables, eh? I'm surprised to run into you here alone."

Fleurette was frightened and moved instinctively behind her horse.

"These are our stables," she replied bravely. "I can be here whenever I want. And I'm not sneaking around; I'm visiting my horse."

"You're visiting your horse. How touching." Sideblossom stepped forward. His approach reminded Fleur of a predator slinking up to its prey, and that dangerous spark was in his eyes again. "Didn't have any other visits in mind?"

"I don't know what you mean." Fleurette hoped her voice sounded firm.

"You know very well what I mean. You play the innocent little schoolgirl who promised herself to a young buck, but in reality, you've been rolling in the hay with him already. Don't bother denying it, Fleurette. I have it from reliable sources, even if I didn't catch you *in flagrante* today. But you're in luck, sweetheart. I take used goods too. In fact, I don't care much for coy prudes. It's just troublesome to wear them down. So no worries, you can wear white at the altar. But I can have a little foretaste, can't I?"

In a single motion, he pulled Fleurette out from behind the horse. Niniane spooked and fled to a corner of the stall. Gracie began to bark.

"Leave me alone!" Fleurette yelled, kicking at her attacker, but John Sideblossom merely laughed. He pushed her against the wall of the stall with his powerful arms and smothered her face with his lips.

"You're drunk; let me go!" Fleur tried to bite him, but John's reflexes still functioned perfectly despite all the whiskey. He jerked back and slapped her in the face. Fleur fell backward out of the stall and landed on a bale of straw. Sideblossom was on top of her before she could get to her feet.

"Now let's see what you have to offer." Sideblossom ripped her blouse open and admired her still slight breasts.

"Lovely...just about a handful!" Laughing, he reached for her. Fleurette tried to kick him again, but he laid his leg over her knee, holding her down.

"Now stop romping around like an unbroken horse. Just let me..." He was looking for the fastener to her skirt, which he did not find right away on the tailored riding dress. Fleurette tried to scream, and bit him on the hand when he covered her mouth.

"I like it when a woman keeps her temper in check!" He burst out with laughter.

Fleur sobbed, and Grace barked hysterically. Then a sharp voice pierced the tumult in the stables.

"Let my daughter go before my temper gets away from me!" Gwyneira stood in the door with a rifle in her hand, which she held aimed at Sideblossom. Fleur recognized Andy McAran and Poker Livingston behind her.

"Now, now, easy, I..." John let go of Fleurette and held up his hands in a gesture of defeat.

"We're going to have a talk in a moment, Mr. Sideblossom. Fleur, did he do anything to you?" Gwyneira asked as she handed Andy the gun and took her daughter in her arms.

Fleurette shook her head. "No. He...he just grabbed me. Oh, Mummy, it was horrible!"

Gwyneira nodded. "I know, dear. But now it's over. Go into the house quickly. As far as I could tell, the party in the salon is over. But your grandfather might still be carousing with a few of them in his study, so be careful. I'll be in in a moment."

Fleurette did not need to be told twice. Trembling, she pulled the tatters of her blouse over her breasts and took flight. The men respectfully made way as she ran headlong through the barn and into the kitchen. She longed for the safety of her room—and her mother could trust her to cross the salon as fast as the wind.

"Where is Sideblossom?" Gerald Warden asked. To his mind, the evening was far from over. He was very drunk, just like the other farmers raising their glasses in the study, but that did not stop him from suggesting a card game. Reginald Beasley, who rarely drank so much, had already agreed, and Lord Barrington was also inclined to play. They needed a fourth, and John Sideblossom had for many years been his favorite buddy when it came to cleaning out his opponents in blackjack.

"He went out earlier. To bed, probably," Barrington told him. "Couldn't hold an…anymore, the yo…young buck."

"Johnny Sideblossom has yet to ever turn down a round!" Gerald defended his friend. "He always drinks everyone under the table. Has to be around here somewhere." Gerald was drunk enough to look under the table for Sideblossom. Beasley cast a glance into the salon, but only Paul was sitting there. His head was sunk in a book, but in reality he was waiting. His sister and John Sideblossom would have to return eventually. And this position offered him the opportunity to further compromise his sister.

"Are you looking for Mr. Sideblossom?" he asked politely and in such a resonant voice that it did not escape anyone in the study. "He's in the stables with my sister."

Gerald Warden stormed out of the study, filled with the kind of holy rage that only whiskey could bring about.

"The damnable little whore! First she acts as if butter wouldn't melt in her mouth, and then she disappears off to the hay with Johnny. When she knows that raises the price of the dowry. If he even takes her at all, then it'll only be because he's getting half my farm!"

Reginald Beasley followed him, hardly any less incensed. She had turned down his proposal. And now she was rolling in the hay with this Sideblossom fellow?

At first the men were uncertain whether they should head in through the main entrance or the kitchen door to catch the couple in the barn. It was silent for several seconds as they weighed the options. Before they could make a move, they heard the sound of the kitchen door opening. Fleurette shuffled into the salon—and stood shocked in front of her grandfather and his drinking buddy.

"You wicked little strumpet!" Gerald dealt her her second slap of the evening. "Where's your lover, eh? Where's Johnny? He's certainly a cad to be dragging you off practically in front of my eyes. But this isn't how someone behaves, Fleurette; it most definitely is not!" He struck her in the chest, but she remained standing. She did not manage, however, to hold tight to the tatters of her blouse. She sobbed when the thin material fell from her grasp, exposing her breasts to the view of all the men.

Gerald seemed to sober up. If he had been alone, he would no doubt have felt something other than shame, but for now the health of his business interests took precedence over his lust. After this incident, he would never be able to pawn Fleurette off on an upstanding man. John Sideblossom would have to take her, and that meant her honor had to be at least halfway preserved.

"Cover yourself and go to your room," he ordered, turning his gaze away. "We'll announce your engagement tomorrow, even if I have to force the cad to the altar with a loaded shotgun. Or you, for that matter. There'll be no more fuss." Fleurette was too shocked and exhausted to reply. She tugged her blouse closed and fled upstairs.

Gwyneira found her an hour later, weeping and trembling under her blankets. Gwyneira was trembling herself, but with rage. At herself first and foremost, for dealing with Sideblossom and taking the horses to safety instead of accompanying Fleurette back to the house. Not that it would have helped much. The two women would just have heard Gerald's outburst together instead of an hour apart, because the men had not yet gone to bed. After the tongue-lashing from Gwyneira in the stables, John Sideblossom had joined them and told them heaven only knew what. Gerald had been waiting for Gwyneira, to make more or less the same threats and accusations to her. He was not interested in the other side of the story or in witnesses. He was insistent that Fleur and John would be engaged in the morning.

"And the…the worst thing is, he's right," Fleur stammered. "No one will…will even believe me now. They…they'll tell the whole area. If I say no now, in front of the…the pastor, they'll laugh at me."

"Then let them laugh," Gwyneira said firmly. "You won't marry this Sideblossom, as sure as I'm standing here."

"But…but Grandfather is my guardian. He'll force me." Fleurette sobbed.

Gwyneira made a decision. Fleur had to leave this place. And she would only go if Gwyneira told her the truth.

"Listen, Fleur, Gerald Warden cannot force you to do anything. He is, strictly speaking, not even your guardian."

"But…"

"He's considered your guardian because he's taken for your grandfather. But he isn't. Lucas Warden was not your father."

There. She'd said it. Gwyneira bit her lip.

Fleurette's sobs caught in her throat.

"But…"

Gwyneira sat beside her and took her in her arms. "Listen, Fleur. Lucas was a good man. But he…well, he could not produce children. We tried, but it never worked. And your grandfath…and Gerald Warden made life a living hell for us because he did not have an heir for Kiward Station. And so I…so I…"

"You cheated on my fa…your husband, I should say?" There was incomprehension in Fleurette's voice.

Gwyneira shook her head. "Not with my heart, if you see what I mean. Just to have a baby. I was always true to him after that."

Fleurette frowned. Gwyneira could see right away what was going through her head.

"And where does Paul come from?" she finally asked.

Gwyneira shut her eyes. Not that too…

"Paul is a Warden," she said. "But let's not talk about Paul. Fleurette, I think it's time you left here."

Fleur did not seem to hear her.

"Who's my father?" she asked quietly.

Gwyneira thought about it for a moment. But then she resolved to tell the truth.

"Our foreman at the time. James McKenzie."

Fleurette looked at her with big eyes.

"*The* McKenzie?"

Gwyneira nodded. "None other. I'm sorry, Fleur."

At first Fleurette was speechless. But then she smiled.

"That's exciting. Truly romantic. Do you remember how Ruben and I always played Robin Hood as children? Now you could say I'm…the daughter of a bandit!"

Gwyneira rolled her eyes. "Fleurette, grow up! Life in the highlands is not romantic; it's hard and dangerous. You know what Sideblossom will do to James if he catches him."

"Did you love him?" Fleurette asked with shining eyes. "James, I mean. Did you truly love him? Were you sad when he left? Why did he leave anyway? Because of me? No, that can't be. I remember him. A tall man with brown hair, right? He let me ride with him on his horse and was always laughing."

Gwyneira nodded painfully. But she could not support Fleurette's romanticizing.

"I didn't love him. It was only a deal, a sort of…transaction between us. It was over when you were born. And his leaving had nothing to do with me."

Strictly speaking, it wasn't even a lie. It had to with Gerald, and with Paul. Gwyneira still felt the pain of his departure. But Fleurette must not know that. She couldn't know that.

"Now let's stop, Fleur, or the night will slip away. You have to leave here before they have a big engagement celebration tomorrow and make everything worse. Pack a few things. I'll get you money from my office. You can have everything that's there, but there isn't much since most of our earnings go straight to the bank. Andy will still be awake; he can fetch Niniane. And then ride like the devil so that you're far away when the boys have slept off their hangovers."

"You're not opposed to me riding to Ruben?" Fleurette asked, out of breath.

Gwyneira sighed. "I'd feel much better about it if I were sure you'd find him, but it's our only option, at least while the Greenwoods are still in England. Curses, I should have sent you with them! But now it's too late. Find Ruben, marry him, and be happy."

Fleur embraced her. "And you?" she asked quietly.

"I'll stay here," Gwyneira said. "Someone has to take care of the farm, and I like that, as you well know. As for Gerald and Paul...well, I'll just have to accept them as they are."

An hour later Fleurette was sitting astride Niniane and galloping toward the mountains. She had arranged with her mother not to ride directly to Queenstown. Gerald would be able to figure out that she would go looking for Ruben and send men after her.

"Hide in the highlands for a few days, Fleur," Gwyneira had advised her. "Then ride along the base of the mountains to Otago. Perhaps you'll run into Ruben somewhere along the way. For all I know, Queenstown isn't the only place where they've found gold."

Fleurette was skeptical. "But Sideblossom's riding into the highlands," she said fearfully. "If he comes looking for me..."

Gwyneira shook her head. "Fleur, the road to Queenstown is well-worn, but the highlands are a big area. He won't find you—you'll be a needle in a haystack. So off you go."

In the end, Fleur had accepted her mother's line of reasoning, though she was scared to death when she first pointed her horse's steps in the direction of Haldon and then toward the lakes where Sideblossom's farm lay.

And where her father was camped somewhere...the thought made her strangely happy. She would not be alone in the highlands. James McKenzie was being hunted too.

6

The land above Lakes Tekapo, Pukaki, and Ohau was beautiful. Fleurette was overcome by the beauty of the crystal-clear lakes and streams, the strange rock formations and velvety green pastures, with the mountains thrusting upward just beyond them. John Sideblossom had been right: it was entirely possible that hidden lakes and valleys were tucked away here, just waiting to be discovered. In high spirits, Fleurette directed her mare toward the mountains. Now that she had put some distance between herself and Kiward Station, she could slow down and enjoy herself. Perhaps she would find gold! Although she had no idea where to look for it. A close inspection of the ice-cold mountain streams from which she drank and in which she washed her face and hands had not revealed any nuggets. But she had caught some fish and, three days having passed, dared to make a fire to roast them. At first she had been too afraid that Sideblossom's men would appear out of nowhere, but she had since adopted her mother's view: the area was much too vast to be searched thoroughly. Her pursuers would not know where to start, and it had rained in the meantime. Even if they used bloodhounds—and there were none on Kiward Station—her trail would have long since washed out.

Fleur began to move very naturally in the highlands. She had often played with Maori children her age and visited those friends in their villages. Thus she knew how to find edible roots, how to knead and bake flour into *takakau*, how to catch fish and light fires. She left hardly a trace of her presence. She carefully covered burned-out campfires with dirt, and she buried any waste. She was certain that no one was following her. In a few days, she would turn east toward Lake Wakatipu where Queenstown lay.

If only she were not alone. After two weeks of riding, Fleur felt lonely. It was nice to snuggle with Gracie at night, but she yearned for human companionship.

She did not seem to be the only one to miss companionship of her own kind. Though she followed Fleurette's signals dutifully, Niniane sometimes neighed into space as though lost. In the end, it was Gracie who found company. The little dog had run on ahead while Niniane felt her way along a stony path. Fleurette likewise had to concentrate on the path and so did not look ahead for a few minutes. She therefore stared in sheer amazement when they passed behind a rock, where the rocky landscape again turned into grassy plain, and saw two tri-colored dogs playing with one another. At first Fleurette believed she was seeing things. But if she had suddenly started seeing double, the two Gracies would have been moving the same way. Instead, they were jumping at each other, chasing after each other, and obviously enjoying each other's company. And they looked just like each other.

Fleurette rode up to call Gracie to her. Up close she could finally discern some differences between the dogs. The new dog was a bit larger than Gracie, her nose a bit longer. But she was a purebred border collie, no doubt about it. To whom did she belong? Border collies, Fleur knew, neither roamed nor hunted. It would not have come so far into the highlands without its owner. Besides, this animal seemed to be well looked after.

"Friday!" A man's voice. "Friday, where are you? It's time to do some herding!"

Fleur looked around but could not locate the person calling for the dog. Friday turned to the west, where the plain seemed to stretch on for infinity. Fleurette should have been able to see the dog's master if he were in that direction. It was odd. Friday seemed unhappy about leaving Gracie. Then Gracie suddenly caught the scent, looked at Fleurette and her horse with gleaming eyes, and set off running with Friday, as if pulled by invisible strings.

Fleur followed them, seemingly toward nothing at first, but soon realized that she had been taken in by an optical illusion. The grassland did not reach to the horizon but descended in terraces.

Friday and Gracie raced down them. Then Fleur realized what had pulled the dogs so magically along. On the final, now clearly visible terrace, some fifty sheep were grazing, shepherded by a man leading a mule by the reins. When he saw Friday approaching with Gracie in tow, he looked just as confused as Fleur had—then looked suspiciously in the direction the dogs had come from. Fleurette let Niniane trot down the terraces. She was more curious than afraid. After all, the strange shepherd did not look dangerous, and as long as she sat on her horse, there wasn't much of anything he could do to her. His heavily laden mule would surely not get far in a chase.

In the meantime, Gracie and Friday had set about herding the sheep together. They worked as skillfully and naturally as a team that it seemed like they had never done otherwise.

The man stood as though turned to stone when he saw Fleurette bounding down on her horse.

Fleur looked into an angular, weather-beaten face with a thick brown beard and brown hair flecked with gray. The man was strong but slim, his clothing tattered, the saddle on his mule worn but in good shape and well taken care of. But the shepherd's brown eyes were looking at Fleur as though seeing a ghost.

"It can't be her," he said quietly as she stopped her horse in front of him. "That's not possible...and that can't be the dog either. She... she must be nearly twenty years old. God in heaven..." The man seemed to be struggling to comprehend. He reached for his saddle as though looking for support.

Fleur shrugged. "I don't really know who I'm not supposed to be, sir, but that's a nice dog you have."

The man seemed to regain control of himself. He breathed deeply in and out, but still looked at Fleur, disbelieving.

"I can only return the compliment," he said, now a little more fluidly. "Has...has she been trained? As a sheepdog, I mean."

Fleur did not get the feeling that the man was all that interested in Gracie; it seemed more like he wanted to gain some time while his brain worked feverishly. But Fleur nodded and looked for a suitable task with which to show off the dog's training. Then she smiled and gave Gracie a command. The little dog dashed away.

"The big ram to the right. She's going to herd him through the rocks over there." Fleurette approached the rocks. Gracie had already separated the ram and awaited further instructions. Friday lay behind her watching intently, ready at any moment to leap up beside the other dog.

But she didn't need any help. The ram trotted calmly through the rocks.

The man nodded and smiled. He seemed considerably more relaxed. Apparently, he had reached a conclusion.

"The ewe there in the back," he said, indicating a rotund animal in the back and whistling for Friday. The little dog shot out like an arrow, rounded up the flock, separated the indicated sheep, and steered it toward the rocks. But this ewe proved less submissive than Gracie's ram. Friday needed three attempts before she successfully herded it through the rocks.

Fleurette smiled, pleased.

"The winner!" she declared.

The man's eyes lit up, and Fleur thought she detected something almost like tenderness in them.

"By the way, you have lovely sheep," she added. "And I should know. I come from...a sheep farm."

The man nodded again. "You're Fleurette Warden of Kiward Station," he said. "Dear God, at first I thought I was seeing ghosts! Gwyneira, Cleo, Igraine...you're the spitting image of your mother! And you ride your horse just as elegantly. But I should have known that. I still remember how you would whine as a child until I let you ride." He smiled. "But you won't remember me. If you'll allow me to introduce myself...James McKenzie."

Fleurette was the one staring now. She finally lowered her gaze awkwardly. What did the man want from her? Should she pretend she had never heard of his fame as a rustler and thief? Not to mention the still inconceivable fact that this man was her father?

"I...listen, sir, I don't want you to think that I...that I came to arrest you or anything like that," she finally began. "I..."

James McKenzie boomed with laughter but then collected himself and answered the grown-up Fleur just as seriously as he had once upon a time answered the four-year-old girl. "I would never have expected that of you, Miss Warden. You did always have a weakness for bandits. Weren't you in the company of a certain Ruben Hood for a while?" She saw the roguish gleam in his eye and suddenly recognized him for who he was. She remembered calling him Mr. McKenzie as a child, and how he had always been her special friend.

Fleurette's reluctance fell away.

"I still am!" she replied, taking up the game. "Ruben Hood and I are promised to each other...that's one of the reasons I'm here."

"Aha," said James. "Sherwood Forest will soon be too small for the growing number in your band. Well, I can help with that, Lady Warden...however, we should move the sheep to somewhere safe first. I've got a bad feeling about this place. Would you care to accompany me, Miss Warden, and fill me in on how you and your mother are doing?"

Fleurette nodded enthusiastically. "Gladly. But...it would be best if you got out of here to somewhere really safe, sir. And perhaps just gave the sheep back. Mr. Sideblossom is on his way with a search party...half an army, my mother says. My grandfather is taking part too. They want to capture you, and me."

Fleurette looked around her warily. Until that moment, she had felt safe, but if John Sideblossom was right about his conjectures, then she was on Lionel Station, John Sideblossom's land. And perhaps he already had an idea of where McKenzie might be hiding out.

James McKenzie laughed again. "You, Miss Warden? Now what did you do to make someone send a search party after you?"

Fleur sighed. "Oh, that's a long story."

McKenzie nodded. "Well, let's put it off then, until we're safe. Just follow me, and your dog can lend Friday a hand. Then we'll be gone from here that much sooner." He whistled for Friday, who seemed to know exactly what was expected of her. She herded the sheep sideways up the terraces to the west toward the mountains.

McKenzie mounted his mule. "You needn't worry, Miss Warden. The area we'll be riding through is completely safe."

Fleurette rode beside him. "Just call me Fleur," she said. "This is all so...very strange, but it sounds even stranger when my...well, when someone like you calls me 'Miss.'"

McKenzie gave her a searching look.

The two of them rode beside each other in silence for a long time as the dogs herded the sheep over the rocky and uninviting land. There was little grass, and the path was climbing. Fleur wondered whether James McKenzie was leading her up into the mountains but could hardly believe that to be the case.

"How is it that you...I mean, how did it come about that..." she suddenly blurted out while Niniane expertly felt her way over the stony ground. The path became increasingly difficult as it wound up through a narrow streambed hemmed in by steep walls. "You were foreman on Kiward Station, weren't you, and..."

James McKenzie laughed grimly. "You mean, why did a respected and decently paid worker take to stealing livestock? That's another long story."

"But it's a long way too."

McKenzie gave her another of his almost tender glances.

"All right, Fleur. When I left Kiward Station, I actually intended to buy some land for myself and take up sheep breeding. I had saved up a bit, and a few years before, I would certainly have been successful. But these days..."

"These days?" Fleur asked.

"It's hardly possible anymore to buy pastureland at a decent price. The big farmers—Warden, Beasley, Sideblossom—are slowly claiming it all. Maori land has been considered a possession of the Crown for a few years. The Maori can't sell it without the governor's permission. And only a select group of potential buyers receive that permission. In addition to that, the boundaries are very imprecise. For example, the pastureland between the lake and the mountains belongs to Sideblossom. So far he's claimed the land up to the terraces where we met. But if someone discovers more land, he'll maintain that it belongs to him as well. And no one will protest, unless the Maori get together and claim it for themselves. But they almost never do that. After all, they have a very different understanding of land than we do. Though they come for a few weeks in the summer to fish and hunt, they rarely settle in this part of the mountains for any length of time. The breeders don't stop them—at least not if they're smart. However, the less smart ones get angry. Those are the altercations that people write off as 'the Maori Wars.'

Fleurette nodded. Helen O'Keefe had spoken of uprisings, but those had mostly occurred on the North Island.

"In any event, I didn't find any land at the time. The money would only have been enough for a tiny farm, and then I wouldn't even have been able to afford livestock. So I decided to make my way to Otago to look for gold—though what I really wanted was to come up with a new plan for my life. I'm a decent hand at panning gold since I took part in the gold rush in Australia. On the way to Otago I thought it wouldn't hurt anything to make a detour to this part of the country to have a look around...well, and then I found this."

McKenzie gestured toward the landscape with a wide, energetic sweep of his arm, and Fleurette's eyes grew large. The streambed had been widening over the last few minutes; now the vista opened up onto a high plain. She gazed out over an expanse of lush grass stretching out over the gentle hillsides. The sheep immediately spread out.

"With your permission—McKenzie Station!" James said, laughing. "So far only settled by yours truly and a Maori tribe that comes through once a year and is on as good of terms with Mr. Sideblossom as I am. That is to say, he's been fencing in large areas of pastureland and in doing so cut the Maori off from one of their holy places. But they're good friends to me. We camp together, exchange presents... they won't give me away."

"And where do you sell your sheep?" Fleur asked, curious.

James laughed. "You want to know everything, don't you? Well, fine, I know a trader in Dunedin. He doesn't ask too many questions when good animals come his way. And I only sell the ones I raised myself. If the livestock has been branded, I don't sell it; it stays here, and I sell the lambs. Come on then, this is my camp. It's rather primitive, but I don't want to build a hut. Just in case a shepherd wanders in here by accident." James led Fleurette to a tent and campfire. "You can tie your horse up there; I hang up rope between the trees. There's plenty of grass, and it should get along fine with the mule. A beautiful horse. Related to Gwyn's mare?"

Fleurette nodded. "Her daughter. And Gracie here is Cleo's daughter. Naturally, they look alike."

James laughed. "A real family reunion. Friday is also Cleo's daughter. Gwyn gave her to me as a going-away present."

Again that tender expression in his eyes when he spoke of Gwyneira.

Fleur pondered. Wasn't her conception supposed to have been strictly business? James's face suggested otherwise. And Gwyneira had given him a puppy as a good-bye—when she was otherwise always so possessive of Cleo's progeny? For Fleur, this was all very revealing.

"My mother must have liked you a great deal," she said carefully.

James shrugged. "Maybe not enough…but now tell me, Fleur, how are you? And old Warden? I heard the younger one was dead. But you have a brother?"

"I wish I didn't!" Fleurette exclaimed fiercely, becoming aware as she said it of the happy fact that Paul was only her half brother, after all.

McKenzie smiled. "So, the long story then. Would you like tea, Fleur? Or do you prefer whiskey?" He lit the fire, put on water to boil, and took a bottle out of his saddlebags. "Well, I'm going to help myself to some. To being spooked by a ghost!" He poured the whiskey in a cup and raised it to her.

Fleurette considered. "A little gulp," she said finally. "My mother says it sometimes works like medicine."

James McKenzie was a good listener. He relaxed by the fire as Fleur told the story of Ruben and Paul, of Reginald Beasley and John Sideblossom and how she wanted neither of them for a husband.

"So then you're headed to Queenstown," he concluded. "To look for Ruben. My God, if your mother had had so much pluck back then..." He bit his lip, but then went on calmly. "If you like, we can ride a ways together. All this business with Sideblossom sounds a bit dangerous. I think I'll take the sheep to Dunedin and disappear for a few months. We'll see, maybe I'll try my luck in the goldfields!"

"Oh, that would be lovely," Fleur mumbled. James seemed to know what he was talking about when it came to gold. If she could get him to work with Ruben, perhaps the adventure might meet with success.

James McKenzie held out his hand to her. "So, to a successful partnership. Though you do know, of course, what you're getting yourself into. If they catch us, the jig is up, since I'm a thief. According to the law, you have to turn me in."

Fleurette shook her head. "I don't have to turn you in," she corrected him. "Not as a family member. I'll just tell them you're... you're my father."

James McKenzie's face lit up. "So Gwyneira told you!" he said with a radiant smile. "And did she tell you about us, Fleur? Did she maybe tell you...did she finally say that she loved me?"

Fleur chewed on her lower lip. She couldn't repeat to him what Gwyneira had said—though she was now convinced that her mother hadn't told her the truth. An echo of the light she saw in James's eyes had been in her mother's too.

"She...she's worried about you," she said finally. Which was the truth. "I'm sure she would like to see you again."

Fleurette spent the night in James's tent, and he slept by the fire. They wanted to set out early the next morning, but they still took the time to fish in a stream and bake flatbread for the journey.

"I don't want to take any breaks until we've at least put the lakes behind us," James explained. "We'll ride on through the night and pass the inhabited areas during the darkest hours. It's rough, Fleur, but up until now it's never been dangerous. The big farms lie out of the way. And on the small ones, people look the other way. Sometimes as repayment, they find a good lamb among their sheep—not one that can be traced back to the big farms, but born here. The quality of the little flocks around the lakes just keeps getting better."

Fleur laughed. "Is this path through the streambed the only one out of the area?" she inquired.

McKenzie shook his head. "No. You can also ride south along the foot of the mountains. This is the easier path; the land begins descending here right away, and eventually you simply follow the course of a stream to the east. However, this path takes longer since it takes you to the fjord land rather than the Canterbury Plains. It works for an escape route, but it's not good for everyday use. So, saddle your horse. We'll want to get going before Sideblossom picks up our trail."

James McKenzie did not seem all that concerned. He herded the sheep—a good number—back the way they had come the day before. The animals reacted unwillingly to being driven from their accustomed pastures, and James McKenzie's "own" sheep bleated in protest as the dogs herded them together.

On Kiward Station, John Sideblossom did not waste any time tracking down the horses that had been swapped out. He did not care whether the men rode workhorses or livestock—all that mattered was that they got going. This became even more important to him when the men discovered Fleurette's escape.

"I'll have them both!" proclaimed John, glowing with rage. "The bastard and the girl. He can be hanged at our wedding to celebrate. All right, let's go. Warden, we ride—no, not after breakfast. I want to be after the little beast while the trail is still fresh."

That proved to be hopeless. Fleur had left no trace. The men could only hope they were on the right track when they rode in the direction of the lakes and Lionel Station. Gerald suspected, however, that Fleur had fled into the highlands. He sent a few men on fast horses to Queenstown, but he wasn't counting on their success. Niniane was not a racehorse. If Fleur wanted to outpace her pursuers, she could only do so in the mountains.

"And where exactly do you mean to look for McKenzie?" Reginald Beasley asked despondently when the company finally rode into Lionel Station. The farm lay idyllically by a lake; behind it rose a seemingly endless range of mountains. James McKenzie could be anywhere.

Sideblossom grinned. "We have a little scout!" he revealed to the men. "I think by now he'll be ready to show us the way. Before I left, he was still...how should I say...a bit uncooperative."

"A scout?" Barrington asked. "Don't speak in riddles, man."

John Sideblossom leaped from his horse. "Just before I left for the plains, I sent a Maori boy to fetch a few horses from the highlands, but he didn't find them. He said they had run away. So we tried to... well, make him more talkative, and then he said something about a pass or a riverbed, something like that. Regardless, there should be some land that's still free behind it. He'll show that to us tomorrow. Or I'll give him nothing but bread and water until the sky falls."

"You locked up the boy?" Barrington asked, shocked. "What does the tribe have to say about that? Don't stir up your Maori."

"Oh, the boy's worked for me for ages. Probably doesn't even belong to the local tribe, and even so, who cares? He'll take us to this pass tomorrow."

The boy turned out to be small, starved, and scared witless. He had spent the days that John Sideblossom was gone in a dark barn and was now a jittery bundle of nerves. Barrington tried to make John let the child go first, but the farmer only laughed.

"If I let him go now, he'll run away. He can sod off tomorrow as soon as he's shown us the way. And we're setting out early tomorrow, gentlemen, at first light. So go easy on the whiskey if you can't hold your liquor."

Comments such as these did not appeal to the farmers from the plains, and tepid representatives of the farmer barons like Barrington and Beasley had long since ceased to be enthused by their charismatic leader. Unlike previous expeditions to track down James McKenzie, this one seemed less like a relaxed hunting excursion and more like a military operation.

John Sideblossom had systematically combed the foothills above the Canterbury Plains. He now divided the men up into small companies, overseeing them scrupulously. Until that moment, men had believed this undertaking was about the search for James McKenzie. But now, since John already had a specific idea of where the thief was hiding, it occurred to them that they were actually on the trail of Fleurette Warden, which a portion of the men thought a waste of their time. Half of them were of the opinion that she would show up of her own accord soon. And if she did not want to marry John Sideblossom, well, that was her prerogative.

Regardless, they submitted, however unwillingly, to the farmer's directions, giving up on their cherished notion of finding a good dinner and first-class whiskey waiting for them before McKenzie's arrest.

"We'll celebrate," Sideblossom confirmed, "after the hunt."

The following morning, the farmer waited for the other men at the stables, the howling, dirty Maori boy at his side. John Sideblossom had the youth walk out in front, promising him that horrible punishments awaited him if he tried to escape.

That hardly seemed possible. After all, they were all riding horses, and the boy was on foot.

Still, the boy was able to walk a good distance and hopped with light feet across the stony landscape of the foothills, which proved to be difficult terrain for Barrington's and Beasley's thoroughbreds.

At one point he no longer seemed to be as sure of the way, but a few sharp words from John Sideblossom caused him to cave. The Maori boy led the search party across a stream in a dried-out riverbed that cut like a knife between stone walls.

James McKenzie and Fleur might have been able to flee if the dogs had not just herded the sheep around a bend in the riverbed in front of them, in a spot where the riverbed had just widened. The sheep were still bleating heart-wrenchingly—another advantage for the pursuers, who fanned out at the sight of the flock in the riverbed in order to cut them off.

James McKenzie's gaze fell directly on John Sideblossom, whose horse had stepped to the front of the company. The sheep thief stopped his mule and sat there, frozen.

"There he is! Wait, are there two of them?" someone in the search party suddenly yelled. The call tore James from his stupor. He looked desperately around for an escape route. He would have a head start if he turned around, as the men would first have to wade through the three-hundred-head flock of sheep crammed in the riverbed. But they had fast horses and he only had his mule, which, moreover, was laden down with everything he owned. There was no way out. Fleurette, however...

"Fleur, turn around!" James called to her. "Ride, like I told you. I'll try to hold them off."

"But you...we..."

"Ride, Fleurette!" James McKenzie reached quickly into his belt pocket, at which a few of the men opened fire—fortunately only halfheartedly and without any aim. The thief drew out a small bag and tossed it to the girl.

"Here, take it! Now ride, damn it, ride!"

In the meantime, John Sideblossom had directed his stallion through the flock and had almost reached McKenzie. In a few more seconds, he would notice Fleurette, who was still mostly hidden from view by some rocks. The girl fought back her strong desire to remain by McKenzie's side. He was right: they didn't have a chance.

Halfheartedly, but with clear instructions, she turned Niniane around while James McKenzie rode slowly toward John Sideblossom.

"Who do these sheep belong to?" the breeder spat out hatefully.

James looked at him unperturbed. "What sheep?"

Out of the corner of her eye, Fleurette could just make out John Sideblossom pulling him from the mule and striking him hard. Then she was gone. Niniane galloped at a breakneck pace into "McKenzie's Highlands." Gracie followed her, but not Friday. Fleur kicked herself for not calling the dog, but it was too late. She breathed a sigh of relief as Niniane set her hooves on grass—she had put the most dangerous of the rocky landscape behind her. She rode south as fast as the horse would take her.

No one would catch up with her again.

7

Queenstown, Otago, lay on the edge of a natural bay on the shore of Lake Wakatipu, surrounded by rugged and imposing mountains. The landscape surrounding it was overpowering, the massive lake a steel blue, the fern forests and pastures expansive and luminous, the mountain range majestic and raw and still virtually unexplored. Only the town itself was tiny. In comparison to the handful of two-story houses that had been quickly thrown up here, Haldon seemed like a big city. The only building that stood out was a three-story wooden structure whose sign read "Daphne's Hotel."

Fleurette tried not to be disappointed as she rode down dusty Main Street. She had expected a larger settlement. After all, Queenstown was supposed to be the center of the gold rush in Otago at the time. Then again, you could hardly pan for gold on the main drag. The miners probably lived on their claims out in the wilderness around the town. The small community would make it that much easier to find Ruben. Fleur stopped boldly before the hotel and tied Niniane in front. She would have expected a hotel to have its own stables, but from the first step inside, she could see that this place looked quite different from the hotel in Christchurch where she had occasionally stayed with her family. Instead of a reception desk, there was a bar. The hotel seemed to be partly a pub.

"We're not open yet!" a girl's voice called from behind the counter when Fleur stepped closer. She saw a young blonde woman, busily engaged in some task. When she got a look at Fleur, she looked up in surprise.

"Are you...a new girl?" she asked, taken aback. "I thought they were coming by coach and not until next week." The young woman had soft blue eyes and very pale, delicate skin.

Fleurette smiled at her.

"I need a room," she said, a little thrown off by the strange reception. "This is a hotel, right?"

The young woman looked Fleurette over in astonishment. "You want...now? Alone?"

Fleurette blushed. She knew it was unusual for a girl her age to be traveling alone.

"Yes, I just arrived. I'm trying to meet up with my fiancé."

The girl looked relieved. "So your...fiancé is coming soon." She said the word "fiancé" as though Fleur had not quite meant it seriously.

Fleur wondered whether her arrival was all that strange. Or was the girl not quite right in the head?

"No, my fiancé doesn't know that I'm here. And I don't know exactly where he is. That's why I need a room. I at least want to know where I'll be sleeping tonight. And I can pay for the room; I have money."

That was true. Fleurette was not only carrying her mother's money with her—but also the purse James McKenzie had thrown to her at the last minute. The bag contained a small fortune in gold dollars—apparently, everything that her father had "earned" over the last few years from his livestock theft. Fleur wasn't sure whether she was supposed to hold on to it for him or keep it for herself. But she could worry about that later. For the time being, her hotel bill would not be a problem.

"So you want to stay the whole night?" asked the girl, who clearly must have had something wrong with her. "I'll fetch Daphne for you." Obviously relieved at this thought, the blonde disappeared into the kitchen.

A few minutes later a somewhat older woman appeared. Her face was just beginning to show its first wrinkles and the traces of too much whiskey and too many long nights. But her eyes were a bright green and lively, and her voluminous hair had been pinned up saucily.

"Well look, a redhead!" she said, laughing when she caught sight of Fleur. "And golden eyes, a rare treasure. Well, if you wanted to start with me, I'd take you on at once. But Laurie says you just want a room."

Fleurette told her story once more. "I'm sure I don't know what your employee finds so strange about that," she finished, a little annoyed.

The woman laughed. "There's nothing strange about it; only Laurie isn't used to hotel guests. Look, child, I don't know where you come from, but I'd guess Christchurch or Dunedin where rich people bed down in nice hotels. Here the emphasis is on the 'bed,' if you see what I mean. People rent the rooms for an hour or two, and we provide the company to go with them."

Fleurette began to glow red. She had fallen in with whores! This was a…no, she did not want to even think the word.

Daphne observed her with a smile and grabbed her tightly when she moved to storm out. "Now, wait a minute, child! Where do you think you're going? You don't need to be afraid; no one's going to rape you here."

Fleur stopped short. It probably was absurd to flee. Daphne didn't look frightening—nor did the girl from a moment before.

"So where can I sleep? Do you also have a…a…"

"An honorable place to sleep?" Daphne asked. "I'm afraid not. The men who pass through here sleep in the rental stables next to their horses. Or they ride straight into one of the gold prospector camps. There's always a place to sleep there for a new fellow."

Fleur nodded. "Fine. Well…then I'll do that too. Maybe I'll even find my fiancé there." Pluckily she took her bag and moved to leave again.

Daphne shook her head. "I think not, dear. A child like you alone among one hundred, two hundred men who are starved to the breaking point—after all, they only earn enough to afford a girl here every six months at most. Those are not gentlemen, little miss. And your 'fiancé'—what's the boy's name? Maybe I know him."

Fleurette blushed again; this time from indignation. "Ruben would never…he would never…"

Daphne laughed. "Then he would be a rare exception among his species. Believe me, child, they all end up here. Unless they're queer. But we don't want to make that assumption in your case."

Fleur did not really know what she meant by the word, but she was certain that Ruben had never set foot in this establishment. She nevertheless gave Daphne his name. She thought about it for a long time and finally shook her head.

"Never heard of him. And I have a good memory for names. So I guess your dear heart hasn't made his fortune yet."

Fleur nodded. "If he had made his fortune, he would already have come for me by now," she said, full of conviction. "But now I need to go; it will be getting dark soon. Where did you say these camps were?"

Daphne sighed. "I can't send you there, girl, not in good conscience and certainly not at night. I guarantee that you wouldn't emerge intact. So there's nothing left for me to do but rent you a room. For the whole night."

"But I...I don't want..." Fleur did not know how she was supposed to get out of this. On the other hand, there hardly seemed to be an alternative.

"Child, the rooms have doors, and the doors have locks. You can have room one. That normally belongs to the twins, and they rarely have customers. Come along, I'll show you. The dog..." she indicated Gracie, who was lying in front of Fleur and looking up at her with her adoring collie gaze, "you can take with you," she added when Fleurette hesitated. Then they climbed the stairs.

Fleurette followed nervously, but to her relief the second floor of Daphne's Hotel more closely resembled the White Hart in Christchurch than some Sodom or Gomorrah. Another blonde woman—who looked astoundingly similar to the girl downstairs—was polishing the floor. She greeted them in surprise as Daphne led her guest past her.

Daphne smiled at her. "This is Miss...what's your name again?" she inquired. "I'm going to have to get a hold of some proper registration forms if I'm going to start renting these rooms out for more than an hour!" She winked.

Fleurette's thoughts raced. Surely it wouldn't be a good idea to use her real name. "Fleurette," she finally replied. "Fleur McKenzie."

"Related by blood or marriage to a certain James?" Daphne asked. "He's also supposed to have a dog like that."

Fleur reddened once more. "Um…not that I'm aware of…" she stammered.

"They caught him, by the way, the poor fellow. And that Sideblossom from Lionel Station wanted to hang him," Daphne explained, but then remembered her introductions. "You heard her, Mary—Fleur McKenzie. She's rented one of our rooms."

"For…the whole night?" Mary asked as well.

Daphne sighed. "The whole night, Mary. We're becoming an honest establishment. So, here's room one. Come in, girl!"

She opened the room, and Fleurette entered an astonishingly respectable little room. The furnishings were simple, roughly hewn from native wood, the bed wide and impeccably made. The establishment radiated nothing but cleanliness and order. Fleur resolved to think about nothing else.

"It's lovely!" she said and really meant it. "Thank you, miss…or mistress…?"

Daphne shook her head. "Miss. In my line of work one rarely becomes an honest woman. Though judging from all my experiences with men—and there have been many, dear—I haven't missed anything worth mentioning. Well, I'll leave you alone now, so you can freshen up. Mary or Laurie will bring you water to wash up straightaway." She was going to shut the door, but Fleur stopped her.

"Yes…no…I have to see to my horse first. Where did you say the rental stables are? And where can I perhaps find out something… about my fiancé?"

"The rental stables are around the corner," Daphne informed her. "You can ask there, but I can hardly imagine old Ron knows anything. He is not exactly the brightest fellow, never pays attention to a client, his horse maybe, at most. Maybe Ethan would know something. He's the postman. He also runs the general store and the telegraph office.

You can't miss him, just across the way. But hurry—Ethan is just about to close. He's always the first one in the pub."

Fleurette thanked Daphne again and followed her down the steps. She wanted to be done quickly too. She wanted to barricade herself in her room once business in the pub got underway.

The general store was easy to find. Ethan, a scrawny, bald, middle-aged man was just putting the display goods away in order to close.

"Yes, I know all the gold prospectors," he responded to Fleurette's initial question. "After all, I take the post to them. The address usually doesn't say anything more than 'John Smith, Queenstown.' Then they have to pick it up here, though there's a couple of boys that fight over the John Smith letters."

"My friend's name is Ruben O'Keefe," Fleur explained eagerly, though her brain was already telling her this was a dead end. If what Ethan said was true, her letters must have ended up here. And apparently, no one had picked them up.

The postman thought about it for a while. "No, miss, I'm sorry. I know the name—letters come for him all the time. They're all lying right here. But the man himself..."

"Maybe he's been using a different name!" The thought brought Fleur relief. "What about Davenport? Ruben Davenport?"

"I have three Davenports," he said casually. "But no Rubens."

Bitterly disappointed, Fleur started to leave, but then decided to give one last try. "Maybe you remember what he looks like. A tall, thin man...well, more a boy. He's eighteen. With gray eyes a bit like the sky before it rains. And dark brown hair, tousled, with a streak of chestnut red...he can never comb it right." She smiled dreamily as she described him, but the postman's expression sobered her up again.

"Don't know him. What about you, Ron? Any idea?" Ethan turned to a short, heavyset man who had just entered and now leaned expectantly on the counter.

The heavy man shrugged. "What sort of mule did he have?"

Fleurette remembered that Daphne had called the rental stables' owner Ron, and found renewed hope.

"He has a horse. A little mare, very solidly built, like mine over there." She gestured out the open window to Niniane, who was still standing in front of the hotel. "Only smaller, and a sorrel. Her name is Minette."

Ron nodded thoughtfully. "Nice horse!" he declared, though it wasn't clear whether he meant Niniane or Minette. Fleurette could hardly stand still she was so impatient.

"Sounds like little Rube Kays. The one who has that funny claim over by the Shotover River. You know Stue. He's the one—"

"The fellow who always swears my tools aren't worth anything! Oh yes, I remember that one. And the other one too, though he didn't say much. That's right; they have a horse like that." He turned to Fleur. "It's too late to ride there tonight, lady. That's at least two hours into the mountains."

"But will he be happy to see you?" Ron asked pessimistically. "It's not my place to say, but if a fellow goes to the trouble of changing his name and hiding in the farthest corner of Otago to get away from you..."

Fleurette began to glow red but was too happy about her discovery to be angry.

"He'll definitely be happy to see me," she assured him. "But it's true that it's too late for me to ride out today. Can I leave my horse with you, mister...sir?"

Fleur spent an astoundingly peaceful night in her room at Daphne's. True, she could hear someone playing the piano below, and yes, there was dancing in the pub—and there was a lively coming and going in the hall until about midnight—but she herself remained unmolested and eventually fell into a deep sleep. She woke up early, not particularly surprised that no one else seemed to be up yet. She was surprised, however, to find one of the blonde girls waiting for her downstairs.

"I'm supposed to make breakfast for you, Miss McKenzie," she said dutifully. "Daphne says you have a long ride up the Shotover ahead of you to meet your fiancé. Laurie and I think that's very romantic!"

So this was Mary. Fleur thanked her for the coffee, the toast, and the eggs and did not feel bothered when Mary sat down next to her confidingly—after she had served Gracie a little bowl of leftover meat. "Sweet dog, miss. I knew one like that once. But it was a long time ago." Mary's face looked almost wistful. The young woman did not look at all how Fleur pictured a whore.

"We used to always think we'd find a nice boy too," Mary chatted on, petting Gracie. "But the stupid fact of the matter is that a man can't marry two women. And we don't want to separate. We need to find twins."

Fleurette laughed. "I thought in your line of work, people didn't marry," she repeated Daphne's remark from the day before.

Mary looked at her very seriously with her round blue eyes. "But that isn't our line of work, miss. We're good girls; everyone knows that. We dance a bit is all. But we don't do anything dirty. Well, nothing *really* dirty. Nothing with men."

Fleurette was astonished. Could an establishment as small as Daphne's really afford to keep two girls in the kitchen?

"We also clean for Mr. Ethan and at the barber's, Mr. Fox's, to earn our keep. But always honest work; Daphne sees to that. If someone tries to touch us, she gives them trouble. Real trouble!" Mary's child's eyes took on a misty look. She really seemed to be a bit slow. Was that why Daphne took care of the girls? But now she had to be on her way.

Mary waved dismissively when she wanted to pay for the room. "You can sort that out with Daphne when you come back by. In case things don't work out with...with your friend."

Fleurette nodded gratefully and smiled to herself. Evidently, she was already the talk of Queenstown. The community did not seem very optimistic about her romantic endeavors. But Fleurette was happy as she rode south out of town along the lake and then turned westward up the broad river. She did not pass any gold-mining camps along the way. Those lay on old sheep farmland, and most of them were closer to Queenstown than Ruben's claim. The men had built up colonies of barracks there, though in Mary's eyes they were more like new renditions of Sodom and Gomorrah. The young woman had elaborated on that in vivid detail; the girl evidently knew her Bible. Fleur was happy not to have to look for Ruben among this horde of rough men. She directed Niniane along the riverbank, joyful in the clear though rather cold air. In late summer, it was still warm in the Canterbury Plains, but this region lay higher, and the trees along the way offered a foretaste of the autumnal play of colors that could be expected. In a few weeks, the lupines would bloom.

Fleur nevertheless found it strange that the region was so devoid of people. If one could set down claims here, then it really should have been crawling with prospectors.

Ethan the postman kept precise records of each individual claim's position and had given her a detailed description of Ruben and Stue's claim. It would not have been all that difficult to find anyway. The two men were camped along the river, and both Gracie and Niniane became aware of them before Fleur did. Niniane's ears stood on end and she let out a deafening whinny—which was immediately returned. Gracie then caught wind of Ruben and darted off to greet him.

Fleur saw Minette first. The mare stood tied next to a mule off to the side and looked over at her, excited. Closer to the river Fleur could make out a campfire as well as a primitive tent. Too close to the river, the thought shot through her head. If the Shotover suddenly swelled—which often happened with rivers fed by mountain streams—it would carry the camp off.

"Minnie!" Fleurette called to her mare, and Minette answered with a deep, happy neigh. Niniane hurried over to her. Fleur slipped down from her saddle in order to embrace her horse. But where was Ruben? From the sparse woods just behind the camp she heard the sound of sawing and hammer blows—which suddenly went still. Fleurette smiled. Gracie must have found Ruben.

Indeed they came running out of the woods. To Fleurette, the whole thing seemed like a dream come true. Ruben was there; she had found him! At first glance he looked good. His narrow face was tanned, and his eyes lit up like they always did when he saw her. But when she put her arms around him, she could feel his ribs; he was horribly thin. His features were marked by mental and physical exhaustion too. Ruben clearly still had no gift for manual labor.

"Fleur, Fleur! What are you doing here? How did you find me? Did you lose patience and run away? How terrible of you, Fleurette!" He laughed.

"I thought I'd take fortune-hunting into my own hands," Fleur replied, pulling out her father's purse from the pocket of her riding dress. "Look, you don't need to look for gold anymore. But that's not why I ran away…I…"

Ruben ignored the pouch, taking her hand instead. "Tell me later. First let me show you our camp. It's beautiful here, much better than the awful sheep farm where we were housed at first."

He pulled her along with him in the direction of the woods, but Fleur shook her head.

"We have to tie up the horse first, Ruben! How did you even manage not to lose Minette in all these months?"

Ruben grinned. "*She* was careful not to lose *me*. That was her assignment, remember? You told her to watch out for me!" He petted Gracie, who hung around him whining.

When Niniane finally stood reliably secured next to Minette and the mule, Fleurette followed an excited Ruben through the camp.

"This is where we sleep…nothing grand, but it's clean. You have no idea what it was like on the farm…and here's the stream. That's where the gold flows!" He pointed to a narrow but lively little stream flowing into the Shotover.

"Where do you see it?" Fleur inquired.

"You don't see it; you feel it," Ruben instructed her. "You have to pan for it. I'll show you how it works in a minute. But we're building a sluice as we speak. Here, over here, this is Stue."

Ruben's companion had left where he was working and approached the two of them. Fleurette liked him from the start. He was a muscular, light-blond giant with a wide, friendly face and laughing blue eyes.

"Stuart Peters, at your service, madam!" He held a powerful paw out to Fleurette, which her delicate hand completely disappeared into. "If I may say so, you're just as pretty as Ruben said."

"You're a flatterer, Mr. Peters!" Fleurette said, laughing, and cast a glance at the structure Stue had just been working on. It consisted of a wooden sluice box that was lowered on posts and fed by a little waterfall.

"That's a gold sluice," Ruben explained enthusiastically. "You fill it with soil, then let water flow through. It washes out the sand, and the gold gets stuck here in the gutter."

"Groove," Stuart corrected him.

Fleurette was impressed. "You know something about gold prospecting, Mr. Peters?" she asked.

"Stue. Just call me Stue. Well, really I'm a blacksmith," Stuart admitted. "But I've helped build something like this before. It's really very simple, though the old miners down there want to make a science out of it. On account of the stream's speed and all."

"But that's nonsense," Ruben agreed with him. "If something is heavier than sand, it will take longer to wash out; that's just logical. Regardless of how fast the water flows. So the gold has to remain in here."

Fleurette did not agree. Given the rapid flow of the stream, the smaller grains of gold would be flooded out. But, of course, it depended on what size nuggets the boys were after. Maybe you could manage to sieve out the larger nuggets with this. So she nodded politely and followed the two of them back to camp. Stue and Ruben quickly agreed to take a break. Shortly thereafter, coffee was brewing in a primitive contraption over the fire. Fleurette took stock of the prospectors' meager assortment of cookware. There was only a pot and two plates, and she had to share a coffee mug with Ruben. It did not look like a successful gold-mining operation.

"Well, we're just getting started," Ruben said defensively when Fleur made a cautious remark to this effect. "We just laid out the claim two weeks ago and are building our first sluice box."

"Which would be going a lot quicker if Ethan, that highway robber in Queenstown, would sell us something other than bottom-of-the-barrel tools!" Stuart cursed. "Seriously, Fleur, we've worn out three saw blades in two days. And yesterday a shovel got bent out of shape. A shovel! Those things normally last your whole life. I have to trade out the shaft every other day, and it never quite fits into the shovel head. I don't know where Ethan gets this stuff, but it's expensive and doesn't work."

"But our claim is pretty, don't you think?" Ruben asked and looked wistfully at the banks of their stream. Fleur had to agree. But she would have found it prettier if she had also seen gold.

"Who...um, advised you to make this claim?" she inquired cautiously. "I mean, it looks like you're all alone here. Was it some sort of secret tip?"

"It was intuition," Stuart declared proudly. "We saw this place and—bingo! This is our claim. We'll make our fortune here."

Fleurette frowned. "You mean...no one has found any gold in this area yet?"

"Not much," admitted Ruben. "But no one has looked either."

The two boys looked at her, expecting praise. Fleur forced a smile and decided to take matters into her own hands.

"Have you at least tried panning for gold yet?" she asked. "In the stream, I mean. Didn't you want to show me how that works?"

Ruben and Stuart nodded simultaneously. "We've found a little bit that way," they said, reaching for a gold pan.

"We'll show you how to do it and then you can pan a little while we continue working on the sluice box," Ruben suggested. "No doubt you'll bring us luck!"

Since Fleurette surely did not need two teachers and Stuart wanted to give the two of them a chance to be alone, Ruben's companion withdrew upstream. Over the next few hours, they did not hear a word from him—other than the occasional curse whenever another tool broke.

Fleurette and Ruben used their first moment of seclusion to properly greet each other. They had to reestablish how sweet their kisses tasted and how naturally their bodies responded to one another.

"Do you want to marry me now?" Fleurette finally asked drowsily. "I mean...I can't really live here with the two of you unless we're married."

Ruben nodded seriously. "True, that wouldn't work. But the money...Fleur, I have to be honest. Up until now, I haven't saved anything. The little that I earned in the Queenstown goldfields went toward our equipment here. And the little that we've eked out so far has gone to new tools. Stuart's right; that fellow Ethan only sells junk. A few of the miners still have the pans and pickaxes they brought over from Australia. But what we buy here only lasts a few days and costs a small fortune."

Fleur laughed. "Then let's just use this for something else," she said, pulling out her father's pouch for the second time that day. This time Ruben looked inside—and became ecstatic at the sight of the gold dollars.

"Fleur! That's wonderful! Where did you get it all? Don't tell me you robbed your grandfather. But, so much money! With that, we could finish the sluice box, build a cabin, maybe hire a few workers. Fleur, with that we can get all the gold there is out of this land."

Fleurette did not say anything to these plans, and instead told him the story of her flight.

"I can't believe it! James McKenzie is your father?"

Fleurette had had her suspicions that Ruben might already know. After all, their mothers kept practically no secrets from one another, and as a rule, what Helen knew trickled down to Ruben. The boy really had had no idea, though, and took it for granted that Helen had also not been told.

"I only ever thought there was a secret about Paul's birth," he said. "My mother seemed to know something about that."

As they talked, the two of them had taken up the work at the stream, and Fleur learned how to work with the gold pan. Until then, she had always thought that gold was shaken out, but really their method of extraction was simply to flush out everything but the gold. It required some skill to flick and shake the pan so that the lighter components in the soil were flushed out until only a black mass remained, the so-called "black sand." Only then did the gold finally come to light. Ruben found it difficult, but Fleur soon had the hang of it. Both Ruben and Stuart admired her for her obvious natural talent. Fleur was less enthusiastic herself because, regardless of how skillfully she panned, the tiny traces of gold only rarely stuck in the pan. By evening she had worked intensively for almost six hours, during which the men had worn out two more saw blades while working on their sluice box without making notable progress. Fleur no longer thought it mattered since she believed that getting gold from a sluice box was a hopeless endeavor. The faint traces of gold she had panned out that day would have been victims of the stream's current through a sluice box. And would it be worth the effort? Stuart valued what she had collected that day at less than a dollar.

Yet the men still raved about big gold finds while they roasted the fish that Fleurette had caught in the stream earlier. She would have earned more money selling the fish, she thought bitterly, than with all her gold panning.

"Tomorrow we need to go to Queenstown to buy new saw blades," Stuart said with a sigh when he finally retired, once more going out of his way to give the young couple some privacy. He insisted that he could sleep just as well under the trees by the horses as in the tent.

"And get married," Ruben said seriously, taking Fleurette in his arms. "Do you think it would be wrong if we celebrated the wedding night ahead of time?"

Fleur shook her head, snuggling up to him. "We just won't tell anyone."

8

It was as though the sunrise over the mountains had been made for a wedding day. The mountains glowed red-gold and mauve; the scent of forest and fresh grass filled the air, and the murmur of the brook mixed with the whooshing of the river—together they seemed like a unique form of congratulations. Fleurette felt happy and fulfilled when she woke in Ruben's arms and stuck her head out of the tent. Gracie greeted her with a wet dog-kiss.

Fleurette petted her. "Bad news, Grace, but I found someone who kisses better than you," she said, laughing. "Now go, wake Stuart, I'm making breakfast. We have a lot to do today, Gracie! Don't let the men sleep through the big day."

Stuart noticed good-naturedly that Fleurette and Ruben could hardly keep their hands off each other as they prepared for their ride. Both men found it peculiar, however, that Fleur insisted on taking half the camp along.

"We'll be back no later than tomorrow," Stuart said. "Sure, if we really go about shopping for things for the mine and such, it could take a little longer, but..."

Fleur shook her head. The night before, she had not only experienced entirely new pleasures in the realm of love, but had also considered the situation from the ground up. There was no way she was going to put her father's money into the hopeless enterprise of a mine. First, however, she had to make that clear to Ruben—as diplomatically as possible.

"Listen up, boys, there's no point in going through with the mine," she began carefully. "You said it yourselves: the material conditions are insufficient. Do you think that's going to change now that there's a little more money?"

Stuart sniffed. "Not a chance. That Ethan fellow is going to keep selling us that useless junk."

Fleur nodded. "So let's strike while the iron is hot. You're a smith. Can you tell good tools from bad tools? Not just when you're working with them, but when you're buying them?"

Stuart nodded. "That's what I mean to say! If I had my choice—"

"Good," Fleur interrupted. "So in Queenstown we'll rent a wagon or just buy one outright. We can hitch up the cobs; together they'll be able to pull a lot. And then we'll head to…what is the next big town? Dunedin? Then we'll go to Dunedin. And there we'll buy tools and other things the prospectors need here."

Ruben nodded in amazement. "Great idea. The mine won't be going anywhere. But we won't need a wagon straightaway, Fleur. We can load up the mule."

Fleurette shook her head. "We're going to buy the biggest wagon the cobs can pull and load it down with as much stuff as we possibly can. We'll haul the whole lot back to Queenstown and sell it to the miners. If it's true that they're all unhappy with Ethan's store, we should be able to make a tidy profit."

That afternoon, Queenstown's justice of the peace married Fleurette McKenzie and Ruben O'Keefe, formerly Kays, who reverted to using his real name. Fleurette wore her cream-colored dress, which was not crumpled even after her journey. Mary and Laurie had insisted on ironing it before the wedding. The two of them also eagerly decorated Fleur's hair with flowers and hung wreaths on Niniane's and Minette's bridles for the ride to the pub, where the wedding took place due to the lack of a church or other gathering place. Stuart was Ruben's witness while Daphne answered for Fleurette. Mary and Laurie were so emotional they could not stop weeping.

Ethan handed Ruben all his letters from the past year as a wedding present. Ron walked around, his chest swollen with pride, because Fleurette had told everyone the happy reunion with her husband only took place thanks to his outstanding memory for horses. Finally, Fleurette opened up her purse and invited all of Queenstown to celebrate her wedding—not entirely without ulterior motives, as it offered not only an opportunity to get to know the locals but also to sound them out. No, no one had ever found gold in the area around Ruben's claim, confirmed the barber, who had lived there since the founding of the town and who had also originally come as a prospector.

"But there's not much to be earned here anyway, Mrs. O'Keefe," he explained. "Too many people, too little gold. Sure, every once in a while someone finds a giant nugget. But then he wastes most of the money straightaway. And how much is it even worth? Two, three hundred dollars maybe, for the really lucky devils. That's not even enough for a farm and a few animals. Not to mention that the fellows all go crazy then and put all the money into more claims, more sluice boxes, and more Maori helpers. It's all gone soon enough, but there's no new money coming in. As a barber and surgeon, however...there are thousands of men in the area, and all of them need their hair cut. And everyone hits his leg with a pickax or gets in a fight or gets hurt somehow."

Fleurette took a similar view. The questions she asked the prospectors, a dozen of whom had found their way to Daphne's Hotel and were helping themselves to copious amounts of free whiskey, almost started a riot. The very mention of Ethan's tool deliveries brought their tempers to a boil. By the end, Fleur was convinced she could not only become rich by founding the hardware store she had in mind but would also be saving a life: if someone didn't do something soon, the men would end up lynching Ethan.

While Fleurette made her inquiries, Ruben spoke with the justice of the peace. The man was no lawyer, working instead as a coffin maker and undertaker.

"Someone has to do the job," he replied, shrugging at Ruben's question about his career choice. "And the boys thought I'd be interested in keeping them from killing each other. Since it saves me trouble in the end."

Fleur observed the conversation with enthusiasm. If Ruben found an excuse to study law here, then he would not push to return to the claim when they returned from Dunedin.

Fleurette and Ruben spent their second wedding night in the comfortable double bed in room one at Daphne's.

"We'll call it the honeymoon suite in the future," Daphne remarked.

"Doesn't happen often that a woman loses her virginity here!" Ron chuckled.

Stuart, who had already helped himself to plenty of the whiskey, grinned at him conspiratorially.

"That already happened," he revealed.

The friends set out for Dunedin around noon the next day. Ruben had acquired a wagon from his new friend—"Go ahead and take it, boy! I can take a few coffins to the cemetery with the pushcart!"—while Fleurette held a few more informative conversations—this time with the area's few respectable women: the wives of the justice of the peace and the barber. By the time she left, she had a second shopping list for Dunedin.

When they returned two weeks later with a fully laden wagon, all that was missing was a place to open their business. Fleurette had not planned ahead with regard to that, having counted on continued good weather. Autumn in Queenstown, however, was rainy, and in the winter a great deal of snow fell. However, few had died in Queenstown recent months, so the justice of the peace let them use his coffin warehouse for their shop. He was the only one who did not ask for new tools, though he did have Ruben explain his legal texts to him, to which a few dollars in McKenzie's fortune had gone.

The shop's brisk sales brought the money back in quickly. The prospectors stormed Ruben and Stuart's business; by the second day, all the tools were already sold out. The ladies required a little longer to make their selections—in part because the justice of the peace's wife was initially hesitant to offer her salon as a changing room for every woman in the region.

"You could, of course, use the warehouse's side room," she said with a deprecatory look at Daphne and her girls, who were burning with anticipation to try on the clothes and lingerie that Fleur had bought in Dunedin. "Where Frank usually keeps the corpses."

Daphne shrugged. "If it's not being used, it doesn't bother me. Well, and if it is—what do you bet none of these fellows ever had such a nice send-off?"

It was easy to convince Stuart and Ruben to make another trip to Dunedin, and by their second round of sales, Stuart was head over heels in love with the barber's daughter and did not want to go back to the mountains at any price. Ruben took over the little shop's bookkeeping and realized with amazement what Fleurette had known all along: every trip filled their coffers with considerably more money than a year in the goldfields would have done. It was also clear that he was much more suited to being a merchant than a prospector. By the time the last blisters and cuts on his hands had healed, after he had been wielding a pen instead of a shovel for six weeks, he was completely convinced of the merits of the business.

"We should build a shop," he said finally. "A sort of warehouse. Then we could also expand our stock."

Fleurette nodded. "Household items. The women desperately need proper pots and pans and nice dishes...now don't wave it off, Ruben. The demand for those kinds of goods will grow over time since there will be more women. Queenstown is becoming a real town!"

Six months later, the O'Keefes celebrated the grand opening of the O'Kay Warehouse in Queenstown, Otago. The name had been Fleurette's idea, and she was very proud of it. In addition to the new salesrooms, the budding enterprise had come into possession of two more wagons and six heavy cart horses. Fleurette could once more ride her cobs, and the community's dead could once more be drawn to the cemetery respectably instead of being dropped off in the handcart. Stuart Peters had cemented trade deals with Dunedin, and with that retired from his position as chief purchaser. He wanted to get married and was tiring of the constant trips to the coast. Instead, with his portion of the profits he opened a blacksmith's workshop, which proved to be a considerably more lucrative "gold mine" than any in the area. Fleurette and Ruben hired an old prospector to take his place as head of the haulage division. Leonard McDunn was easygoing, knew his way around horses, and knew how to treat people. Fleurette worried only about the deliveries for the ladies.

"I can't seriously expect him to pick out my underwear," she complained to Daphne, whom Fleurette had befriended, much to the horror of the now *three* respectable women in town. "He blushes when he just brings me the catalog. I'll have to ride along at least every second or third trip."

Daphne shrugged. "Just send the twins. They may not be the brightest—you can't trust them to handle negotiating and the like—but they have good taste. I've always valued that. They know how to dress like a lady and what we need in the 'hotel,' naturally. Besides, it'll give them a chance to get out a bit and earn their own money."

Fleurette was skeptical at first but was quickly convinced. Mary and Laurie brought back an ideal combination of modest articles of clothing and wonderfully wicked little articles that sold like hotcakes, to Fleur's surprise—and not only to the whores. Stuart's blushing bride purchased a black corset, and a few miners thought they were sure to please their wives with some colorful lingerie. Although Fleur was not sure that it was her sort of thing, business was business. And discreet changing rooms—supplied with large mirrors instead of a depressing dais for coffins—were installed.

The work in the store still left Ruben plenty of time for studying law, which he still found enjoyable, even if he had given up his dream of becoming a lawyer for good. To his delighted surprise, he soon put his studies into practice: the justice of the peace came to him for counsel with increasing regularity and began to bring him along to trials as well. Ruben proved himself authoritative and just at these proceedings, and when the next election time came, the incumbent justice created a stir. Instead of putting himself up for reelection, he proposed Ruben as his successor.

"Look at it this way, people!" the old coffin maker explained in his speech. "There was always a conflict of interest with me: if I kept the people from killing each other, no one needed a coffin. When you look at it that way, my office ruined my business. It's different for young O'Keefe, since whoever gets his head bashed in can't buy any more tools. It's in his own best interest to keep law and order. So vote for him and let me have a break!"

The citizens of Queenstown took his advice and elected Ruben as the new justice of the peace by an overwhelming majority.

Fleurette was happy for him, though she did not quite follow the former justice's line of reasoning. "You could also bash someone's head in with our tools," she whispered to Daphne. "And I very much hope Ruben doesn't prevent his customers too often from that laudable deed."

The only drop of bitterness in Fleurette and Ruben's well of happiness in the growing gold-rush town was the lack of contact with their families. Both would have liked to write to their mothers but didn't dare.

"I don't want my father to know where I am," Ruben made clear when Fleurette was getting ready to write her mother. "And it's better that you keep it hidden from your grandfather as well. Who knows what will get into their heads otherwise? You were underage when we married. They could decide to make trouble for us. Besides, I'm afraid my father would take out his anger on my mother. It wouldn't be the first time. I still try not to think about what happened after I left."

"But we have to get word to them somehow," Fleurette said. "You know what? I'll write to Dorothy. Dorothy Candler. She can tell my mother."

Ruben gripped his own head. "Are you crazy? If you write to Dorothy, Mrs. Candler will hear about it too. And then you might as well scream out the news in the marketplace in Haldon. If you have to write, write to Elizabeth Greenwood. I trust her to be more discreet."

"But Uncle George and Elizabeth are in England," Fleur objected.

Ruben shrugged. "And? They have to return home sometime. Our mothers will just have to be patient until then. And who knows, maybe your mother will have learned something from James McKenzie. I understand he's in prison somewhere in Canterbury. It's possible she's gotten in contact with him."

9

James McKenzie's trial was held in Lyttelton. Initially, there was a fuss because John Sideblossom favored having the trial in Dunedin. If the trial were held there, he argued, they would have a better chance of catching those who had accepted the stolen goods as well, thus eradicating the whole criminal enterprise.

Lord Barrington, however, spoke up vehemently against that idea. In his opinion, John Sideblossom just wanted to drag his victim to Dunedin because he knew the judge there better and saw more hope of hanging the thief in the end.

He would have liked to do that right after capturing James McKenzie. He had since taken to attributing this triumph entirely to himself; after all, he was the one who had beaten James McKenzie and taken him prisoner. The other men thought the beating in the riverbed hardly necessary. In fact, if John Sideblossom had not knocked the thief from his mule and then beat him up, the hunters could have set off after his accomplice. As it was, the second man—though some of the people in the search party believed it to have been a woman—had escaped.

Nor had the other sheep and cattle barons approved of John dragging the captive along like a slave tied to his horse. They saw no reason why the already badly beaten man should have to walk when his mule was available. At some point, levelheaded men like Lord Barrington and Reginald Beasley had stepped forward and censured John Sideblossom for his behavior. Since James had committed the majority of his crimes in Canterbury, it was the almost unanimous opinion of the group that he should answer for his crimes there. Despite John Sideblossom's protests, Barrington's men had freed the livestock thief and made him give his word not to flee, then led him only lightly bound to Lyttelton, where he would be held until the trial. John insisted, however, on keeping his dog, Friday, which seemed to hurt James more than the bruises from the beating and the shackles on his hands and feet, with which John Sideblossom had bound him at night after locking him in a barn. In a hoarse voice, he asked the men to let the dog stay with him.

But John proved inflexible. "The dog can work for me," he explained. "Somebody will be able to make it obey. A first-class sheepdog like that is worth a lot. I'll keep him as a small repayment for the damages that bastard's caused."

So Friday stayed behind, howling heartbreakingly as the men led her master away from the farm.

"John won't have much fun with it," Gerald said. "These mutts get stuck on their masters."

Gerald stood between the two factions on the subject of how James McKenzie should be handled. On the one hand, John was one of his oldest friends; on the other, he had to get along with the men from Canterbury. And like almost all the others, he felt, despite himself, a sort of respect for the ingenious thief. Naturally, he was angry about his losses, but the gambler in him knew that a person did not always take the most honorable path to making a living. And if that person made it for more than ten years without being caught even once, he deserved some respect.

James fell into a gloomy silence after losing Friday, which he did not break until the prison bars had been closed behind him in Lyttelton.

The men of Canterbury were disappointed; they would have liked to hear from the source how their captive had carried out the thefts, with whom he had worked, and who the mysterious accomplice who had escaped was. They did not have long to wait for the trial. It was set to take place in the Honorable Justice Stephen's court the following month.

Lyttelton had come into possession of its own courtroom—it had been a long time since the trials were conducted in the pub or in the open air, as was common the first few years. The room did, however, prove too small to hold all the citizens of Canterbury who wanted to lay eyes on the infamous livestock thief at the trial. Even the sheep barons who had been affected and their families had to arrive early to find good seats. For that reason, Gerald, Gwyneira, and an excited Paul had taken quarters at the White Hart in Christchurch beforehand so that they could take the Bridle Path to Lyttelton.

"Don't you mean we'll be riding there?" asked a confused Gwyneira when Gerald laid out his plans to her. "After all, it's the Bridle Path!"

Gerald laughed with pleasure. "You'll be surprised at how the path has changed," he said happily. "We'll be taking the coach, relaxed and properly attired."

On the day of the trial, he wore one of his best suits. And Paul, in his first ever three-piece, looked very grown up.

Gwyneira agonized over what was appropriate. If she were honest with herself, it had been years since she had thought so much about her clothing. But no matter how many times she told herself that it didn't matter what a middle-aged woman wore to a trial as long as it was neat and didn't draw too much attention, her heart raced at the mere thought of seeing James McKenzie again. What was worse, he would see her too, and he would recognize her, of course. But what would he feel when he saw her? Would his eyes light up again as before when she hadn't known how to appreciate it? Or would he just feel pity, because she had aged, because her first wrinkles were marking her face, because fear and worry had taken their toll on it? Perhaps he would feel only apathy; she may be only a distant, faded memory now, extinguished by ten years of wild living. What if the mysterious "accomplice" really had been a woman? His wife?

Gwyneira turned over her memories in her mind, some of them becoming girlish daydreams when she recalled her weeks with James. Could he ever forget the day on the lake? The enchanted hours in the stone circle? But then again, they had parted on bad terms. He would never forgive her for having Paul. One more thing Paul had destroyed.

In the end, Gwyneira decided on a simple navy-blue dress and a tippet, buttoned in the front, though the tortoiseshell buttons were a little precocious. Kiri put her hair up in an austere coiffure, which she offset with a bold little hat that matched the dress. Gwyneira felt as though she had spent hours in front of the mirror, pulling at this or that strand, making adjustments to her hat, and fixing the dress's sleeves so that the tortoiseshell buttons were visible. When they were finally seated in the coach, she was pale with expectation, fear, and a sort of anticipation. If it continued like this, she would have to pinch her cheeks to give herself a little color before entering the courtroom. But even more than being worried about her pallid complexion, Gwyneira hoped not to turn beet red when she saw James McKenzie again for the first time. She shivered and convinced herself that it was just the cool autumn day. She could not keep her fingers still. She tensely crumpled the curtains at the coach's window.

"What's the matter, Mother?" Paul finally asked, and Gwyneira cringed. Paul had a fine-tuned sense for human weakness. He could not, under any circumstances, get the impression there had ever been something between her and James McKenzie.

"Are you nervous for Mr. McKenzie?" he asked, already drilling her. "Grandfather says you knew him. He knew him too. He was the foreman on Kiward Station. Isn't it crazy, Mother, that he then ran away and made a living stealing sheep?"

"Yes, very crazy," Gwyneira replied. "I would never...none of us would ever have thought him capable of such a thing."

"And now he might be hanged!" Paul remarked with pleasure. "Will we go if he's hanged, Grandfather?"

Gerald snorted. "They won't hang the scoundrel. He got lucky with his judge. Stephen's not a farmer. It doesn't bother him that McKenzie brought some people to the edge of ruin."

Gwyneira almost smiled. As far as she knew, James McKenzie's thefts had been no more than pinpricks for those affected.

"But he'll spend a few years behind bars. And who knows, maybe he'll tell us a bit about the men behind the scenes today. It doesn't look like he did it all on his own." Gerald did not believe the story about there being a woman accompanying James McKenzie. He agreed that it had been a young accomplice but had only caught a glimpse of him.

"Who he was selling to would be of interest. In that respect, we would have had a better chance if they tried the fellow in Dunedin. Sideblossom was right about that. Speak of the devil! Have a look. I knew he wouldn't miss the man's trial."

John Sideblossom's black stallion galloped past the Wardens' coach, and he greeted them politely. Gwyneira sighed. She would have loved to avoid having to see the sheep baron of Otago again.

John Sideblossom had not held it against Gerald that he took sides with the men of Canterbury and went so far as to reserve seats for him and his family in the courtroom. He greeted Gerald heartily, Paul a bit dismissively, and Gwyneira with icy coldness.

"Has that charming daughter of yours reappeared?" he asked mockingly as she sat down—as far from him as possible among the four reserved seats.

Gwyneira did not answer. Paul rushed to answer in her place, assuring his idol that no one had ever heard from Fleur again.

"In Haldon they're saying she must have landed in some den of sin," Paul announced, for which Gerald rebuked him sternly. Gwyneira did not react. Over the past few weeks, she had begun responding to Paul less and less. The boy had long since outgrown her influence—if she had ever had any to begin with. These days he listened only to Gerald; he hardly even attended Helen's school lessons anymore. Gerald always talked about hiring a tutor for the boy, but Paul was of the opinion that he had attained sufficient education for a farmer and livestock breeder. When it came to the work on the farm, he soaked up the shepherds' and shearers' knowledge like a sponge. He was without a doubt the heir that Gerald had wished for—if hardly the partner of George Greenwood's dreams. The young Maori Reti, who was handling George's affairs while he was in England, complained to Gwyneira. In his opinion, Gerald was raising a second Howard O'Keefe in terms of ignorance—only one with less experience and more power.

"The boy already won't listen to anyone," Reti bemoaned. "The farmhands don't like him, and the Maori downright hate him. But Mr. Warden lets him do whatever he likes. Who's ever heard of a twelve-year-old boy overseeing a shearing shed?"

Gwyneira had already heard it all from the shearers themselves, who felt they had been treated unfairly. In his drive to make himself important and to win the traditional competition between the shearing sheds, Paul had written down considerably more shears than had actually taken place. That was good news for the shearers, who were paid by the number of sheep sheared. But later, the amount of fleece did not match up. Gerald raged and laid the blame on the shearers. The other shearers complained because the competition had been rigged and the prizes handed out to the wrong people. It was altogether a terrible mess, and in the end, Gwyneira had had to pay everyone a considerably higher wage just to ensure that the shearing gang would return the following year.

Gwyneira had had more than enough of Paul's insolent behavior. She would have liked nothing better than to send him to boarding school in England, or at least Dunedin. But Gerald would hear none of it, and so Gwyneira did what she had always done since Paul was born: she ignored him.

Now, in the courtroom, at least he held still, thank God. He listened in on the conversation between Gerald and John and noted the frosty greetings the other sheep barons gave the visitor from Otago. The room filled up quickly and Gwyneira motioned to Reti, who was one of the last to push his way into the room. There was some difficulty—a few *pakeha* did not want to make way for the Maori—but the mention of George Greenwood's name opened any door for Reti.

Finally, ten o'clock struck, and punctual to the minute, the Right Honorable Lord Justice Stephen entered his court and opened the proceedings. For most of the audience, it did not get interesting until the accused was led in. When James McKenzie appeared, the room erupted in a mixture of curses and cheers. James himself reacted to neither the one nor the other, instead keeping his head low; he seemed relieved when the judge demanded order from the crowd.

Gwyneira peeked out from behind the tall farmworker who sat in front of her—a bad choice since both Gerald and Paul had a better view. But she had wanted to sit as far from John Sideblossom as possible. She would be able to look James McKenzie over as soon as he took his place next to the unenthusiastic attorney he had been appointed. As soon as he sat down, he finally looked up.

Gwyneira had been asking herself for days what she would feel when she was once again in close proximity to James. Would she even recognize him? Would she see in him that which had once...once what? Had impressed her? Enthralled her? Whatever it had been, it lay twelve years in the past. Maybe her excitement was misplaced. Perhaps he would just be a stranger to her now, someone whom she would not even have recognized on the street.

But her very first look at the tall man on the defendant's bench told her otherwise. James McKenzie had hardly changed. At least not in Gwyneira's eyes. Based on the drawings that had appeared in the papers reporting on his capture, she had expected to see a wild, bearded fellow, but the man before her was clean shaven and wore simple but clean clothes. He was still just as slim and sensual, but the musculature beneath his somewhat tattered white shirt revealed his strength. His face was suntanned—except for the places his beard had covered. His lips seemed thin—a sign that he was worried. Gwyneira had often seen that look on his face. And his eyes...nothing, absolutely nothing had changed about their adventurous, lively expression. However, there was no mocking laughter in them now, just tension and something like fear. The lines in his face were still there, only more deeply imprinted, just as James's whole demeanor had grown harder, more mature, and more serious. Gwyneira would have recognized him at first glance. Oh yes, she would have been able to pick him out from all the men on the South Island, if not the whole world.

"James McKenzie!"

"Your Honor?"

Gwyneira would also have known his voice anywhere. That dark, warm voice that could be so tender but also stern and full of authority when calling out commands to his men or the sheepdogs.

"Mr. McKenzie, you stand accused of having carried out large-scale livestock theft in the Canterbury Plains as well as in the area around Otago. How do you plead?"

McKenzie shrugged. "There's a lot of stealing in that area. I don't know what that has to do with me."

The judge inhaled sharply. "The court has the testimony of several honorable men that you were encountered with a flock of stolen sheep above Lake Wanaka. Do you at least admit to that?"

James McKenzie repeated his shrug. "There are plenty of McKenzies. There are plenty of sheep."

Gwyneira almost laughed but then began to worry instead. This was surely the best way to bring His Honor the Lord Justice Stephen to a boil. It was useless to deny the accusation. James's face still showed signs of his fight with John Sideblossom. Sideblossom must have had a bad time of it too—Gwyneira derived a certain satisfaction from the fact that John's eye was still markedly blacker than James's.

"Can anyone in the court testify to the fact that this man is the livestock thief James McKenzie and not by chance someone else of the same name?" the judge asked with a sigh.

John Sideblossom stood up. "I can testify to that. And we have proof that should remove any doubt." He turned to the room's entrance, where he had placed an assistant. "Release the dog!"

"Friday!" A little black shadow flew like the wind through the courtroom directly to James McKenzie. He seemed to instantly forget the role he had planned to play before the court. He bent over, took up the dog in his arms, and petted her. "Friday!"

The judge rolled his eyes. "That could have been done less dramatically, but so be it. Please enter into the record that when this man was confronted with the sheepdog that herded the stolen flocks of sheep, he recognized the animal as his. Mr. McKenzie, you do not now mean to tell me this dog too has a double out there."

James smiled his old smile. "No," he said. "This dog is one of a kind." Friday panted and licked James's hands. "Your Honor, we...we can cut this trial short. I will say anything and confess everything as long as you assure me that I can keep Friday. In prison too. Just look at this dog; it clearly has hardly eaten since it was taken from me. This dog is to this...she is of no use to Mr. Sideblossom; she won't listen to anyone..."

"Mr. McKenzie, your dog is not the one on trial here," the judge said sternly. "But since you want to confess now: the thefts on Lionel Station, on Kiward Station, Beasley Farms, Barrington Station...all of these can be ascribed to you?"

McKenzie reacted with his now familiar shrug. "There're a lot of thefts. Like I said. I might have taken a sheep now and again...a dog like this needs exercise, you know." He gestured to Friday, which set off thundering laughter in the courtroom. "But a thousand sheep..."

The judge sighed again. "All right, fine. Have it your way. Let's call in the witnesses. First we have Randolph Nielson, foreman of Beasley Farms."

Nielson's appearance was the first in a chain of workers and breeders who without exception testified that hundreds of animals had been stolen from the aforementioned farms. Many had been found in McKenzie's flock. It was all very tiring, and James could have shortened the proceedings, but he proved obstinate and denied any knowledge of the stolen animals.

While the witnesses rattled off numbers and dates and McKenzie's fingers wandered over Friday's soft fur, stroking and comforting her, he let his gaze drift around the room. There were things leading up to the proceedings that concerned him more than the fear of the noose. The trial was taking place in Lyttelton—Canterbury Plains, relatively near Kiward Station. So would she be there? Would Gwyneira come? James had spent the nights leading up to the trial recollecting every moment, every incident involving Gwyneira, no matter how small—from their first encounter in the stables to their parting, when she had given him Friday. Not a day had gone by since she had cheated on him that James had not thought of it. What had happened back then? Whom had she chosen over him? And why had she looked so desperate and sad when he had pushed her to speak? Shouldn't she have been happy? After all, the business with this other fellow had turned out just as well as with him.

James saw Reginald Beasley in the first row, with the Barringtons beside him—he had suspected the young lord, but Fleurette's response to his cautious questions had assured him that he was only in limited contact with the Wardens. Would he have been so disinterested in Gwyneira if he were the father of her son? It appeared that he cared deeply for the children who sat between him and his unlikely wife on the bench. George Greenwood was not present. But according to what Fleur had said, he was hardly a candidate for Paul's father. Although it was true that he was in regular contact with all the regional farms, he had taken Helen's son, Ruben, for his protégé instead.

And there she was. In the third row, half-hidden behind a few burly shepherds who presumably planned to provide testimony as well. She was peeking at him, turning her neck a bit to keep him in view, which she managed effortlessly, slender and flexible as she was. Oh yes, she was beautiful! Just as beautiful, lively, and engaging as before. Her hair was already falling out of the austere coiffure she had tried to force it into. Her face was pale, her lips slightly open. James did not try to lock eyes. That would have been too painful. Perhaps later, when his heart was not thumping so wildly and when he no longer feared that his eyes would give away everything he still felt for her...he forced his gaze away and continued to let his eyes drift over the audience. Next to Gwyneira he expected to see Gerald, but a child sat there, a boy, maybe twelve years old. James held his breath. Naturally, that would be Paul, her son. The boy would certainly be old enough to accompany his grandfather and mother to these proceedings. James looked him over. Maybe his features would reveal who his father was...Fleurette didn't resemble him in the least, it was true, but that was hardly unusual. And this one here...

James McKenzie froze when he looked at the boy's face more clearly. It couldn't be! But it was true...the man Paul most closely resembled was sitting right next to him: Gerald Warden.

McKenzie saw that they shared the same square jaw; the alert, close-set brown eyes; the fleshy nose. Both had clear features, and the older face displayed an equally determined look as the younger one. There could be no doubt: this boy was a Warden. James's mind raced. If Paul was Lucas's son, why had he hightailed it to the West Coast back then? Or...

The realization knocked the wind out of James like a sudden punch to the stomach. Gerald's son! It couldn't be otherwise: the boy showed no resemblance at all to Gwyneira's late husband. And that might also have been the reason for Lucas's flight. He had not caught his wife committing adultery with a stranger but with his own father...but that was utterly impossible. Gwyneira would never have given herself freely to Gerald. And if she had, she would have handled it with the utmost discretion. Lucas would never have gotten wind of it. So that meant...Gerald must have forced Gwyneira into his bed.

James was struck by a pang of profound remorse and anger at himself. It was finally clear to him why Gwyneira couldn't talk about it, why she had stood before him sick with shame and helpless with fear. She could not have admitted the truth to him, or he only would have made things worse. James would have killed the old man.

Instead he, James, had abandoned Gwyneira, had made everything even worse by leaving her alone with Gerald and forcing her to raise this unfortunate child, whom Fleurette had only spoken of with abhorrence. James felt despair rising within him. Gwyneira would never be able to forgive him. He should have known or at least accepted her refusal to talk about it without question. He should have trusted her. But so...

James furtively directed his gaze once more at her narrow face—and was alarmed when she raised her head and looked at him. And then suddenly everything was extinguished. The courtroom melted away before his and Gwyneira's eyes; there had never been a Paul Warden. James and Gwyneira stood across from each other alone in a magic circle. He saw her as the young girl who had taken up her New Zealand adventure fearlessly but who was hopeless before the problem of scaring up the thyme to make English food with. He still remembered exactly how she had laughed when he handed her the bundle of herbs. And then her strange question: would he be the father of her child...the days together at the lake and in the mountains. The unbelievable feeling when he had seen Fleur in her arms for the first time.

In this moment a bond, long broken, sealed Gwyneira and James to each other, and it would never dissolve again.

"Gwyn..." James's lips formed her name inaudibly, and Gwyneira smiled faintly as though she had understood him. No, she didn't hold anything against him. She had forgiven him everything—and she was free. Now, finally, she was free for him. If only he could speak with her. They had to try again; they belonged together. If only it weren't for these unfortunate proceedings. If he were likewise free. If only they wouldn't hang him.

"Your Honor, I think we can cut this business short!" James McKenzie spoke up, just as the judge was about to call the next witness.

Judge Stephen looked up hopefully. "You want to confess?"

McKenzie nodded. Over the next hour he calmly gave an account of his thefts and how he had taken the sheep to Dunedin. "You have to understand that I can't give you the name of the man who took the animals off my hands. He never asked for my name, and I didn't ask for his."

"But you have to know who he is," the judge said, unsatisfied with this.

McKenzie shrugged again. "I know *a* name, but whether it's his...? Besides, I'm no snitch, Your Honor. The man never turned on me; he paid me properly—please don't expect me to break my word."

"And your accomplice?" someone in the court roared. "Who was the fellow who slipped through our fingers?"

James looked in the direction of the voice with a confused expression. "What accomplice? I always worked alone, Your Honor, except for my dog. I swear, so help me God."

"So then who was the man who was with you when you were captured?" the judge inquired. "Though some seem to think it was a woman."

James nodded with his head lowered. "Yes, that's right, Your Honor."

Gwyneira winced. So there was a woman. James had married or at least lived with someone else. Still…when he had just looked at her…she had thought…

"What does that mean, 'Yes, that's right'?" the Lord Justice asked, again unsatisfied with his answer. "A man, a woman, a ghost?"

"A woman, Your Honor." James kept his head lowered. "A Maori girl I lived with."

"And you gave her the horse while you sat on a mule, and then she rode away as if the devil was on her heels?" someone in the court called out, setting off laughter. "Tell it to your grandma!"

Judge Stephen called the court to order.

"I have to admit," he remarked, "your story sounds a bit far-fetched to me as well."

"The girl was very dear to me," McKenzie said calmly. "The… most precious thing that ever happened to me. I always gave her the best horse; I would do anything for her. I would give my life for her. And why shouldn't a girl know how to ride?"

Gwyneira bit her lip. So James had found a new love. And if he survived this, he would go back to his girl.

"I see," said the judge drily. "A Maori girl. Did the pretty little thing have a name and a tribe?"

James seemed to think for a moment. "She didn't belong to a tribe. She…it would be too much of a digression to explain here, but she came from the union of a man and a woman who never made their bed together in a meeting hall. Their union was blessed anyway. She was born so that she…she…" He searched for Gwyneira's eyes. "So that she could dry the tears of a god."

The judge frowned. "Well, I didn't ask for an introduction to heathen conception ceremonies. There are children in this court. So the girl was banished from her tribe and nameless."

"Not nameless. Her name is Pua…Pakupaku Pua." James looked Gwyneira in the eyes as he spoke the name, hoping that no one was looking at her just then because she turned pale then blushed. If what she believed was correct…

When the court recessed for deliberation a few minutes later, she hurried through the rows without excusing herself to Gerald or John. She needed someone who could confirm what she thought, someone who spoke better Maori than she did. She ran breathlessly into Reti.

"Reti! What luck you're here! Reti, what...what does *pua* mean? And *pakupaku*?"

The Maori laughed. "You should really know that by now, miss. *Pua* means 'flower' and *pakupaku*..."

"Means 'little'..." Gwyneira whispered. She wanted to scream, cry, dance with relief. But she merely smiled.

The girl was named Little Flower. Now Gwyneira understood what James had meant with his entreating look. He must have met Fleurette.

James McKenzie was sentenced to five years in prison in Lyttelton. Naturally, he was not allowed to keep his dog. John Sideblossom was to take care of the dog if he was so inclined. Judge Stephen could not have cared less. The court, he emphasized, was not responsible for pets.

What followed was horrible. The bailiff and court usher had to tear James away from his dog by force. The dog bit John Sideblossom as he was putting a leash on her. Afterward, Paul described with perverse delight how the thief had cried.

Gwyneira did not listen to him. She had also not been present for the reading of the sentence; she was too agitated for that. Paul would have asked questions had he seen her in that state, and she dreaded his often frightening intuition.

Instead, she waited outside under the pretense of needing fresh air and to stretch her legs. In order to escape the mass of people who were waiting in front of the building for the judgment, she strolled to the other side of the courthouse—and had a final, unexpected encounter with James McKenzie there. The condemned was twisting in the grip of two burly men, who were dragging him by force to a waiting prison-transport coach. Until that moment, he had been struggling bitterly, but at the sight of Gwyneira he calmed down.

"I'll see you again," he mouthed. "Gwyn, I'll see you again!"

10

Hardly six months had passed since James McKenzie's trial when an excited little Maori girl disturbed Gwyneira, who was in the midst of her daily work. As usual, she had had a busy morning, clouded by yet another confrontation with Paul. The boy had offended two Maori shepherds—and right before the shearing and the herding into the highlands, when they most needed every available pair of hands. Both men were irreplaceable, experienced, and reliable, and there wasn't the slightest reason to offend them simply because they had used the winter to take part in one of their tribe's traditional wanderings. That was normal: when the stores the tribe had laid up for the winter had been used up, the Maori moved on to hunt in other parts of the country. Then one day the houses on the lake were deserted, and no one came to work with the exception of a few trusted members of the help. New arrivals among the *pakeha* found it odd at first, but the more established colonists had long since gotten used to it. It wasn't that the tribes just disappeared at random; they only left when they could not find anything more to eat near their villages or had earned enough working for the *pakeha* to buy something. When it was time for sowing the fields, and there was plenty of shearing and herding work to be had, they returned—as had Gwyneira's two workers, who had no idea why Paul was rudely berating them for their absence.

"Mr. Warden has to know we come back!" one of the men said angrily. "He shared village with us so long, was like a son when little, like brother for Marama. But now...always angry. Only because angry with Tonga. He says we not listen to him, listen to Tonga. And Tonga wants us to go. But that nonsense. Tonga not yet wearing *tokipoutangata*, Ax of Chief...and young Mr. Warden not yet master of farm."

Gwyneira sighed. For the moment, Ngopini's last remark gave her a good foothold to appease the men. Just as Tonga was not yet chief, the farm still did not belong to Paul; he was not entitled to reprimand anyone, let alone let them go. After receiving ample crop seeds by way of apology, the Maori declared themselves once again prepared to work for Gwyneira. But if Paul ever took over the business, people would walk off on him. Tonga would probably uproot the whole camp when he eventually bore the chieftain's honors so as to never have to see Paul again.

Gwyneira sought out her son and reproached him, but Paul merely shrugged. "Then I'll just hire New Zealanders. They're much easier to give orders to anyway. And Tonga won't have the guts to leave this place. The Maori need the money they earn here and the land they live on. Who else will let them settle on his property? All the land now belongs to the white farmers anyway. And they don't need any troublemakers."

Though annoyed, Gwyneira had to admit that Paul was right. Tonga's tribe would not be welcome anywhere. However, the thought did little to reassure her, and instead gave her cause to fear how it would all end. Tonga was a hothead. No one could say what would happen when everything Paul had just said became clear to him.

And here was this little girl coming into the stables where Gwyneira was just saddling her horse. Another obviously shaken Maori, hopefully not with further complaints about Paul.

But the girl did not belong to the nearby tribe. Instead, Gwyneira recognized one of Helen's students. She approached Gwyneira shyly and curtsied like a well-mannered English schoolgirl.

"Miss Warden, Miss O'Keefe sent me. I'm supposed to tell you someone is waiting for you at the O'Keefe farm. And you should come quickly before it gets dark and Mr. O'Keefe comes home—in case he doesn't go to the pub tonight." The girl spoke impeccable English.

"Who could be waiting for me, Mara?" Gwyneira asked, taken aback.

"It's a secret!" she declared importantly. "And I'm not allowed to tell anyone, just you."

Gwyneira's heart raced. "Fleurette? Is it my daughter? Has Fleurette come back?" She could hardly believe it. After all, she had hoped her daughter had long since married Ruben and started a life in Otago.

Mara shook her head. "No, miss, it's a man…um, a gentleman. And I'm supposed to tell you they want you to please hurry." With these last words she curtsied again.

Gwyneira nodded. "Good job, girl. Go, quick, grab yourself something sweet from the kitchen. Moana baked some cookies earlier. I'll hitch up the chaise in the meantime. Then you can ride home with me."

The girl shook her head. "I can walk, miss. Go ahead and take your horse. Miss O'Keefe said it's very, very urgent!"

Gwyneira did not understand, but obediently continued saddling her horse. So she would be visiting Helen today instead of inspecting the shearing sheds. Who could this mysterious visitor be? She bridled Raven, one of Morgaine's energetic daughters. Raven set out at a brisk trot, quickly leaving the buildings of Kiward Station behind. The shortcut between the two farms had been so well traveled by now that Gwyneira hardly needed to hold her horse by the reins, even along the difficult stretches of the path. Raven leaped over the stream with one mighty bound. Gwyneira thought with a triumphant smile of the last hunt that Reginald Beasley had hosted. The farmer had since married again, a widow out of Christchurch closer to his own age. She managed the household splendidly and cared for the rose garden with never-ending diligence. She did not seem very passionate, however—thus Beasley continued to seek his pleasure by breeding racehorses. All the more reason it rankled him that Gwyneira and Raven had so far won every drag hunt. He planned to build a racetrack in the future. Then her cobs would no longer leave his thoroughbreds behind.

Just before arriving at Helen's farm, Gwyneira reined in her horse so that it would not run over the children coming home from school.

Tonga and a couple of other Maori from the lakeside village greeted her grumpily. Only Marama smiled, as friendly as ever.

"We're reading a new book, Miss Warden!" she declared, pleased. "One for grown-ups! By Mr. Bulwer-Lytton. He's very famous in

England. The book is about a Roman camp. The Romans are a very old tribe in England. Their camp is near a volcano, and it erupts. It's sooo sad, Miss Warden...I hope the girls survive, at least. For Glaucos to fall in love with Jone there! But the people really should have been smarter. You don't set up camp on the burning mountains. And certainly not a big one with sleeping houses and everything. What do you think: would Paul like to read it? He hasn't been reading much lately. Miss O'Keefe says that's not good for a gentleman. I'll find him later and take the book to him." Marama skipped away, and Gwyneira smiled to herself. She was still grinning when she stopped in Helen's yard.

"Your children show a lot of common sense," she teased Helen, who rushed out of the house when she heard hoofbeats. She looked relieved when she saw that it was Gwyneira. "I never knew what I didn't like about Bulwer-Lytton, but Marama put it succinctly: everything the Romans did was a mistake. If they had not built on Vesuvius, Pompeii never would have been destroyed, and Mr. Bulwer-Lytton could have saved himself five hundred pages. You should just make sure the children understand that the whole thing doesn't take place in England."

Helen's smile seemed forced. "Marama is a clever girl," she said. "But come now, Gwyn. We can't waste any time. If Howard catches him here, he'll kill him. He's still angry that Warden and Sideblossom passed him over when they were putting together the search party."

Gwyneira frowned. "What search party? And who's killing whom?"

"Well, McKenzie. James McKenzie! Oh, that's right, I didn't tell Mara his name—to be safe. But he's here, Gwyn. And he wants to speak with you urgently!"

Gwyneira's legs seemed to buckle. "But...James is in prison in Lyttelton. He can't..."

"He broke out, Gwyn! Now go; give me the horse. Mr. McKenzie is in the barn."

Gwyneira practically flew to the barn. Her thoughts tripped over each other. What should she say to him? What did he want to tell her? But James was there...he was there; he would...

James pulled Gwyneira into his arms as soon as she entered the barn. She could not pull away and did not want to either. Letting out a sigh, she burrowed into James's shoulder. It had been thirteen years, but it felt just as wonderful as it had back then. She was safe here. No matter what happened around her—when James put his arms around her, she felt protected from the world.

"Gwyn, it's been so long…I should never have left you." James whispered the words into her hair. "I should have known about Paul. Instead…"

"I should have told you," Gwyneira said. "But I would never have been able to speak the words aloud…we should stop with the apologies now. We always knew what we wanted." She smiled at him mischievously. James could not get enough of the joy in her face, still warm from her ride. He took his chance and kissed the mouth she so willingly offered.

"All right, let's get down to business," he said sternly, the old roguishness dancing in his eyes. "Before anything else, let's clear up one thing—and I want to hear the truth and nothing but the truth. Since there's no more husband for you to claim loyalty to and no baby that needs to be lied about: was it really just business back then, Gwyn? Was it really just about the baby? Or did you love me? At least a little?"

Gwyneira smiled, but then wrinkled her brow as though she was thinking hard about it. "A little? Well, yes, when I think about it, I did love you a little."

"Good." James remained serious. "And now? Now that you've thought about it and raised such a beautiful daughter? Now that you're free, Gwyneira, and no one can tell you what to do anymore? Do you still love me a little?"

Gwyneira shook her head. "I don't think so," she explained slowly. "Now I love you a great deal!"

James took her in his arms again, and she savored his kiss.

"Do you love me enough to come with me?" he asked. "Enough to run away with me? Prison is horrible, Gwyn. I had to get out."

Gwyneira shook her head. "What do you have in mind? Where do you want to go? Do you want to steal sheep again? They'll hang you if they catch you this time! And they'll put me in prison."

"It took them more than ten years to catch me," he said in his defense.

Gwyneira sighed. "Because you found that land and that pass. The ideal hiding place. They call it the McKenzie Highlands, by the way. It will probably still be called that when no one remembers who John Sideblossom or Gerald Warden ever were."

James grinned.

"But you can't seriously believe that we'll find something like that again. You have to do your five years in prison, James. When you really are free, then we can figure something out. Besides, I couldn't just up and leave here. The people here, the animals, the farm...James, it all depends on me. The whole farm. Gerald drinks more than he works, and when he does work, he just sees to the cattle a bit. But even that he's entrusting more and more to Paul."

"And the boy isn't particularly well liked," James grumbled. "Fleurette told me a bit, as did the police officer in Lyttelton. I know just about all there is to know about the Canterbury Plains. My prison guard gets bored, and I'm the only one he gets to talk to all day."

Gwyneira smiled. She knew the officer in passing from social events and knew how much he liked to chat.

"Paul is difficult, it's true," she admitted. "All the more reason people need me. At least right now. In five years everything will look different. By then Paul will almost be a legal adult and won't listen to a word I have to say anymore. I don't know that I want to live on a farm run by Paul. But maybe we could break off our own piece of land. After everything I've done for Kiward Station, I'm entitled to it."

"Not enough land to raise sheep," James said morosely.

Gwyneira shrugged. "But maybe enough to raise dogs or horses. Your Friday is famous, and my Cleo...well she's still alive, though not for much longer. The farmers would fall over themselves for a dog you trained."

"But five years, Gwyn..."

"Only four and a half!" Gwyneira curled up to him again. Five years seemed endless to her as well, but she could not picture any other solution. Under no circumstances would she flee into the highlands or live in a gold-mining camp.

McKenzie sighed. "All right, fine, Gwyn. But you'll have to leave it up to chance, then. Now that I'm free, I wouldn't even think about going back to that cell of my own free will. If they don't catch me, I'll make my way to the goldfields. And believe me, Gwyn, I'll find gold."

Gwyneira smiled. "Well, you found Fleurette. But don't pull any tricks like you did with that Maori girl story in court ever again! I thought my heart was going to stop when you started talking about your great love."

James grinned at her. "What should I have done instead? Let them know I have a daughter? They won't look for a Maori girl; they know very well they don't stand a chance. Although Sideblossom suspects she has all the money."

Gwyneira frowned. "What money, James?"

McKenzie grinned even wider. "Well, since the Wardens failed to come through in that respect, I permitted myself to give my daughter an ample dowry. All the money I made over the years with the sheep. Believe me, Gwyn, I was a rich man. I just hope Fleur will spend it wisely."

Gwyneira smiled. "That makes me feel better. I was afraid for her and Ruben. Ruben is a good fellow, but he has two left hands. Ruben as a gold prospector...that would be like you becoming a justice of the peace."

James gave her a punitive look. "Oh, I have a well-developed sense of justice, little miss! Why do you think they compared me to Robin Hood? I only stole from the moneybags, not the people who earned their living with their hands. Sure, my style is a little unconventional..."

Gwyneira laughed. "Let's just say you're not a gentleman, nor am I a lady anymore, after everything I've done with you. But do you know what? I don't care!"

They kissed once more, and James pulled Gwyneira gently down into the hay, but then Helen interrupted them.

"I hate to bother you two, but there were just people here from the police. I was terrified, but they were just asking around and didn't seem interested in searching the farm. It's just—the way it looks, it's turning into a big commotion. The farmer barons have already heard about your breakout, Mr. McKenzie, and have sent people to seize you at once. My God, couldn't you have waited a few more weeks? In the middle of sheep shearing, no one would have come after you, but right now there are plenty of workers who haven't had anything to do for months. They're eager for an adventure, but you know that already. And you, Gwyn, ride back home as fast as you can, so that your family doesn't become suspicious. This isn't a game, Mr. McKenzie. The men who were here have orders to shoot you!"

Gwyneira shook with fear when she kissed James good-bye. She would have to fear for him once more—and now, when they had finally found each other.

Naturally, Helen too advised him to return to Lyttelton, but James waved the suggestion away. He wanted to go to Otago. First to get Friday—"The height of foolishness!" Helen commented—and then to the goldfields.

"Will you at least give him some food to take along?" Gwyneira asked pitifully as Helen accompanied her out. "And thank you so much, Helen. I know what a risk you took."

Helen waved it away. "If everything went according to plan for the children, he's Ruben's father-in-law now…or do you still want to deny that Fleurette is his?"

Gwyneira smiled. "You've known all along, Helen. You sent me to Matahorua yourself and heard her advice. Didn't I pick a good man?"

James McKenzie was caught that night, though his bad luck had a silver lining. He ran right into the arms of a search party from Kiward Station, led by his old friends Andy McAran and Poker Livingston. If the two of them had been alone, they would no doubt have let him go, but they were out with two new workers and did not want to take the risk. They made no move to shoot at James, but levelheaded Andy was of the same opinion as Helen and Gwyneira. "If someone from Beasley or Barrington Station finds you, they'll put you down like a dog. Not to mention what Sideblossom would do! Warden—between you and me—is a scoundrel himself. He still has something like sympathy for you. But Barrington is deeply disappointed in you. After all, you gave him your word of honor that you wouldn't flee."

"But only on the way to Lyttelton," James said, defending his honor. "That didn't go for the five years in prison."

Andy shrugged. "Regardless, he's not happy. And Beasley is nervous he's going to lose more sheep. The two breeding stallions he ordered from England cost a fortune. The farm is up to its neck in debt. You'll receive no pardon from him. It'd be best for you to serve your sentence."

The police officer was not upset when James returned.

"It was my fault," he grumbled. "Next time I'll lock you in, McKenzie. Then it'll be your fault!"

James dutifully stayed in prison three more weeks, but when he broke out this time, certain circumstances led the officer to Gwyneira's door at Kiward Station.

Gwyneira was examining a group of ewes and their lambs one last time before they would be herded into the highlands when she saw Laurence Hanson, the chief of law enforcement in Canterbury County, riding up to the house. Laurence Hanson was approaching slowly because he was leading something small and black on a leash. The dog offered stiff resistance; it only took a few steps when it was in danger of being strangled. Then it planted all four of its feet on the ground.

Gwyneira frowned. Had one of her farm dogs run away? That never happened. And even if that were the case, surely the police chief himself was not responsible for bringing it back. She quickly excused herself from the two Maori shepherds and sent them off to the highlands with the sheep.

"I'll see you in the fall!" she said to the pair, who would be spending the summer with the animals in a hut in the pastures. "Just be careful my son doesn't see you here before fall." It was delusional to think that the Maori would spend the entire summer in the pastures without occasionally visiting their wives. But then again, perhaps their wives would move up there with them. It was difficult to say since the tribes were mobile. Gwyneira only knew that Paul would frown upon either solution.

Gwyneira went to the house to greet the sweating police officer, who was already headed her way. He knew where the stables were and obviously wanted to stable his horse. So he did not seem to be in a hurry. Gwyneira sighed. She had better things to do than spend the day chatting with the police chief. On the other hand, he might give her news of James McKenzie.

When Gwyneira arrived at the stables, Laurence Hanson was already untying the dog, whose leash he had tied to his saddle. The dog was without a doubt a collie, but it was in pitiful condition. Its fur was dull and clumpy, and it was so thin that its ribs were visible despite its long hair. When the sheriff bent over to it, the dog bared its teeth and growled. Such an unfriendly face was rare among border collies. Nevertheless, Gwyneira recognized the dog right away.

"Friday!" she said sweetly. "Allow me, Sheriff, she may remember me. She was my dog until she was five months old."

Laurence seemed skeptical that the dog would remember the woman from whom it had received its first lessons in sheepherding, but Friday reacted to Gwyneira's soft voice. He did not try to stop Gwyneira from petting the dog and undoing its leash from the cinch on the horse's saddle.

"Now where did you find her? Isn't this..."

The police chief nodded. "Yes, this is McKenzie's dog. Showed up in Lyttelton two days ago, completely exhausted. You see the shape she's in. McKenzie saw her out the window and raised a rumpus. But what was I supposed to do? I can't let her inside the prison. Where would

I be then? If one can have a dog, then another will want a pussycat, and when the cat eats a third fellow's canary, there'll be a prison riot."

"Now, now, it wouldn't be that bad," Gwyneira said, smiling. Most of the prisoners in Lyttelton did not spend nearly long enough in prison to need a pet. The majority just went there to sober up and were released the next day.

"In any event, it would be unacceptable," the sheriff said sternly. "So I took the animal home with me, but it didn't want to stay. I would hardly open the door and it would run back to the jail. This time he picked a lock and stole meat from the butcher for the mutt. Luckily it wasn't an issue. The butcher later maintained it had been a gift, so there won't be any charges...and we caught McKenzie again the next day. But of course this can't keep happening. The man's putting his own neck on the line for the mutt. And so I thought, well...because you bred the dog and your old dog just died..."

Gwyneira sniffed. Even now she couldn't think about Cleo without tearing up. She still had not picked out a new dog. The pain was too fresh. But here was Friday. And she was the spitting image of her mother.

"You thought right," she said calmly. "Friday can stay here. Please tell Mr. McKenzie that I'll look after her. Until he comes for us... ahem, her. Now come inside and have something to drink, Officer. You must be very thirsty after the long ride."

Friday lay panting in the shade. She was still on the leash, and Gwyneira knew she was taking a risk when she bent over and undid the lead.

"Come along, Friday," she said softly.

The dog followed her.

11

A year after James McKenzie's sentencing, George and Elizabeth Greenwood returned from England, and Helen and Gwyneira finally got news of their children. Elizabeth took Fleur's request for discretion very seriously and rode in her little chaise to Haldon herself to bring the letters to her friends. She hadn't even mentioned the reason for her trip to her husband when she met with Helen and Gwyneira on the O'Keefes' farm. Both women inundated her with questions about her trip, which had obviously done the young woman good. Elizabeth seemed more relaxed and at peace than before.

"London was wonderful!" she said with a wistful look. "George's mother, Mrs. Greenwood, is a little…well, takes some getting used to. But she didn't recognize me; she thought me very well-bred." Elizabeth beamed like the little girl she once was and looked to Helen for praise. "And Mr. Greenwood was charming and very nice to the children. I didn't care for George's brother. And the woman he married! How terribly common." Elizabeth rumpled her little nose smugly and folded her napkin. Gwyneira noticed that she still did so with precisely the same gestures Helen had drilled into them so many years before. "But now that I've found these letters, I'm sorry we extended the trip so long," Elizabeth apologized. "You must have been so worried, Mrs. O'Keefe and Mrs. Warden. But it looks like Fleur and Ruben are doing well."

Helen and Gwyneira were profoundly relieved, not only by the news Fleur sent, but also by her detailed description of Daphne and the twins.

"Daphne must have rounded up the girls somewhere in Lyttelton," Gwyneira read out loud from one of the letters Fleur had sent.

"Apparently, they were living on the street and eked out a living by stealing. Daphne took the girls in and looked after them lovingly. Mrs. O'Keefe can be proud of her, even though she is a—the word has to be spelled out—w-h-o-r-e." Gwyneira laughed. "So you've found all your lambs again, Helen. But what should we do with the letters now? Burn them? I would be sorry to do that, but neither Gerald nor Paul and certainly not Howard can get a hold of them under any circumstances."

"I have a hiding place," Helen said conspiratorially and went to one of her kitchen cabinets. There was a loose board in the back where a person could deposit inconspicuous little objects. Helen kept a little money she had saved and a few mementos from Ruben's childhood there. Embarrassed, she showed the other women one of his drawings and a lock of his hair.

"How sweet!" Elizabeth declared and admitted to the others that she carried a lock of George's hair in a locket around her neck.

Gwyneira would have envied this concrete proof of her love, but then she cast an eye on the little dog lying in front of the fireplace who was looking up at her adoringly. Nothing could bind her more tightly to James than Friday.

Another year later, Gerald and Paul returned angry from a breeders' conference in Christchurch.

"The governor doesn't know what he's doing," Gerald ranted, pouring himself a whiskey. After a moment of consideration, he filled a second glass for the fourteen-year-old Paul. "Banned for life! Who's going to check on that? If he doesn't like it there, he'll be back on the next ship."

"Who'll be back?" Gwyneira inquired, only moderately interested. Dinner would be served in a moment, and she had joined the men with a glass of port—to keep her eye on Gerald. It did not please her one bit that he was offering Paul something to drink. The boy would learn that soon enough. Besides, he could hardly control his temper when he was sober. He would be that much more difficult under the influence of alcohol.

"McKenzie! The damned sheep thief! The governor commuted his sentence."

Gwyneira felt the blood rising to her cheeks. James was free?

"On the condition that he leave the country as soon as possible. They're sending him to Australia on the next ship. Sounds good to me—he can't be far enough away for my liking. But he'll be a free man over there. Who's going to keep him from coming back?" Gerald blustered.

"Isn't that unwise?" Gwyneira asked flatly. If James really left for Australia forever...she was happy about his commutation, but it also meant she had lost him for herself.

"For the next three years, yes," Paul said. He sipped at his whiskey, observing his mother attentively.

Gwyneira fought to maintain her composure.

"But after that?" Paul continued. "He would have served his sentence. A few more years and it would fall under the statute of limitations. And then if he had brains enough to come back through Dunedin, for example, instead of Lyttelton...he could also change his name; after all, no one cares what it says on the passenger manifest. What's wrong, Mother? You don't look at all well."

Gwyneira clung to the thought that Paul was right. James would find some way to get back to her. She had to see him again! She had to hear it from his own mouth before she would really begin to have any hope.

Friday snuggled up to Gwyneira, who scratched her absentmindedly. Suddenly she had an idea.

The dog, of course! Gwyneira would go to Lyttelton tomorrow to take the dog back to the sheriff so that he could return her to James when he was released. She would then be able to ask the man if she could see James in order to talk to him about Friday. After all, she had taken care of the dog for almost two years now. Surely the police chief would not deny her that. He was a good-natured fellow and could not possibly suspect a relationship between herself and McKenzie.

If only that didn't also mean a separation from Friday. Gwyneira's heart bled at the thought. But there was nothing for it. Friday belonged to James.

Naturally, Gerald got upset when Gwyneira declared that she planned to take the dog back the next day. "So that fellow can start stealing again as soon as he gets to Australia?" he asked snidely. "You're crazy, Gwyn!"

Gwyneira shrugged. "Maybe, but she belongs to him. And it will be easier for him to find a decent job if he takes the dog along."

Paul snorted. "*He*'s not going to look for any decent job! Once a scoundrel, always a scoundrel."

Gerald was about to agree, but Gwyneira just smiled.

"I've heard of professional gamblers who, later, came to be very decent sheep barons," she remarked calmly.

She set out for Lyttelton at the crack of dawn the next day. The way was long, and it took even the vigorous Raven five hours before she finally trotted onto the Bridle Path. Friday, who had trotted behind them, looked completely spent.

"You can rest in the office," Gwyneira said in a friendly tone. "Who knows, maybe Hanson will even let you go straight in to your master. And I'll take a room in the White Hart. Paul and Gerald won't be able to get into much trouble in one day without me."

Laurence Hanson was just sweeping his office when Gwyneira opened the door to the police office, behind which lay the prison cells. She had never been here, but she felt tingling anticipation. She would see James in just a moment. For the first time in almost two years!

Hanson beamed when he recognized her. "Mrs. Warden! Gwyn Warden! Now isn't this a surprise. I hope I don't owe the pleasure of your visit to any unfortunate events? You don't want to report a crime, do you?" The officer winked. Apparently, he believed that to be next to impossible—a decent woman would always have sent a male member of the family. "And what a beautiful dog little Friday's become! How about it, little one, do you still want to bite me?"

He bent over to Friday, who approached him trustingly this time. "What soft fur she has. Really, Mrs. Warden, you've taken first-class care of her."

Gwyneira nodded and quickly returned his greeting. "The dog is the reason I've come, Officer," she said, coming straight to the point. "I heard that Mr. McKenzie's sentence has been commuted, and that he'll be released soon. So I wanted to bring the dog back to him."

Laurence Hanson wrinkled his brow. Gwyneira, who wanted to request to be admitted to James's cell right away, stopped cold.

"That's very laudable of you," the officer remarked. "But you've come too late. The *Reliance* pushed out to sea this morning, headed for Botany Bay. And following the governor's orders, we had to take Mr. McKenzie aboard."

Gwyneira's heart sank. "But didn't he want to wait for me? He… he surely did not want to leave without the dog."

"Are you all right, Mrs. Warden? Is something the matter? Do sit down; I'd be happy to make some tea." Concerned, Laurence pulled up a chair for her. Only then did he answer her question.

"No, naturally, he did not want to leave without the dog. He asked me if he could go get it, but of course I couldn't allow that. And then…then he predicted that you would come. I never would have thought…all this way for this rogue, and you've even grown fond of the dog! But McKenzie was certain. He asked for a delay; it would have broken your heart, but the order was clear: deportation on the next ship, and that was the *Reliance*. And he couldn't pass up this offer. Oh, but wait! He left a letter for you." The officer went to look for it straightaway. Gwyneira could have strangled him. Why hadn't he mentioned that right away?

"Here it is, Mrs. Warden. I take it he wants to thank you for looking after the dog." The police chief handed her a simple, unopened envelope and waited expectantly. Clearly he had not opened the letter earlier because he had expected her to read it in his presence. However, Gwyneira did not do him that favor.

"The...the *Reliance*, you said...are you certain that it has already set sail? Couldn't it possibly still be waiting in the harbor?" Gwyneira slid the letter, seemingly without giving it much thought, into the pocket of her riding dress. "Sometimes there are delays pushing off."

Laurence shrugged. "I didn't look. But if so, it wouldn't be waiting on the docks but anchored out in the bay somewhere. You won't be able to get out to it, except maybe in a rowboat."

Gwyneira stood up. "I'll have a look for myself, Officer. One never knows. Before that, though, thank you very much. For...Mr. McKenzie too. I think he knows all you've done for him."

Gwyneira left the office before Hanson could even register what she had said. She swung up onto Raven, who had been waiting outside, and whistled for the dog. "Come on, we'll go look for it. To the harbor!"

Gwyneira saw as soon as they reached the docks that they had missed it. No seaworthy vessel lay at anchor, and it was over a thousand nautical miles to Botany Bay. Nevertheless, she called out a few questions to one of the fishermen hanging around the harbor.

"Has the *Reliance* already sailed?"

The man cast a glance at the perspiring woman. Then he pointed out to sea.

"You can just see the back of it there, madam! It's sailing straight ahead. To Sydney, I think."

Gwyneira nodded. With burning eyes, she stared at the retreating ship. Friday nuzzled her, whining as though she knew exactly what had happened. Gwyneira petted her and pulled the letter from her pocket.

My beloved Gwyn,

I know you will come to see me before this unfortunate trip, but it will be too late. You will have to continue carrying my face in your heart. Yours comes to me whenever I think of you, and hardly an hour passes that I don't. Gwyn, for the next few years a few more miles will separate us than those between Haldon and Lyttelton, but that makes no difference to me. I promised you I'd come back, and I have always kept my promises. So wait for me; don't lose hope. I'll come back as soon as it seems safe. If you'll just believe in me, I'll come back! As long as you have Friday, she'll remind you of me. Good luck and Godspeed, my lady, and give Fleur my love as well if you hear from her.

I love you,
James

Gwyneira held the letter close to her and stared again at the ship disappearing slowly into the Tasmanian Sea in the distance. He would come back—if he survived this adventure. But she knew James would see exile as an opportunity. He would prefer freedom in Australia to boredom in a cell.

"And we didn't even have a chance to go with him," Gwyneira sighed, stroking Friday's soft fur. "All right then, come on. Let's ride home. We won't catch that ship now no matter how hard we swim!"

The years passed on Kiward and O'Keefe Stations with their usual symmetry. Gwyneira continued to like the work on the farm, just as Helen continued to loathe it. Yet more and more of the farm work fell to Helen, who only managed thanks to George Greenwood's active help.

Though he had hardly ever had a friendly word for Ruben when he was there, and though it must long ago have become clear to him that the boy was not cut out for farm work, Howard O'Keefe could not get over his son's disappearance. He was to have been the heir, and Howard had been convinced that Ruben would someday come to his senses and take over the farm. Besides, he had gloated for years over the fact that O'Keefe Station had an heir—unlike Gerald Warden's magnificent farm. But once again Gerald was coming out ahead. His grandson, Paul, was facing his takeover of Kiward Station with great pride, while Howard's heir had been missing for years. Again and again, he pressured Helen to reveal the boy's location. He was convinced that she knew something, because she no longer cried into her pillow every night as she had the first year after Ruben's flight. Instead, she seemed proud and confident. Helen never said a word, no matter how he pressed her, and he did not always go about it gently. Particularly when he came home from the pub late at night—where he might have seen Gerald and Paul leaning proudly on the bar, negotiating with some local businesspeople about something that Kiward Station needed—he was compelled to vent his rage.

If only Helen would tell him where the boy was hiding out. He would ride there and drag him back by his hair. He would rip him away from the little whore who had fled not long after him and beat the word *duty* into him. Howard balled his fists in anticipation just thinking about it.

For the time being, he did not see much sense in keeping up Ruben's inheritance. It would be the boy's job to rebuild the farm when he returned. It would serve him right if he had to re-fence the farm and repair the roofs on the shearing sheds. At the moment, Howard was looking to make money quickly. That meant selling the promising new offspring in his flock rather than continuing to breed them himself and running the risk of losing them in the highlands. It was just a shame that George Greenwood and that snotty Maori boy he thought so highly of and always wanted to shove down Howard's throat as an adviser didn't see it that way.

"Howard, the results of the last shearing were completely unsatisfactory!" George said, expressing his concerns to his problem child during one of his last visits. "Barely average wool quality, and rather dirty to boot. And we were doing so well! Where are all the first-class flocks you'd built up?" George tried to remain calm—if for no other reason than the fact that Helen was sitting next to him looking haggard and hopeless.

"We sold the three best breeding rams to Lionel Station a few months ago," Helen remarked bitterly. "To Sideblossom."

"That's right!" Howard crowed, pouring himself some whiskey. "He was determined to have them. In his opinion they were better than anything the Wardens were offering for breeding animals!" He looked over at his interlocutor, expecting praise.

George Greenwood sighed. "No doubt. Because Gwyneira Warden naturally holds on to her best rams for herself. She sells only her second tier. And what about the cattle, Howard? You've bought more. And yet hadn't we agreed that your land won't support—"

"Gerald Warden makes good money with his cattle!" Howard repeated his age-old argument truculently.

George had to force himself not to shake Howard. Howard simply did not understand: he was selling valuable breeding stock to buy additional food for his cattle. He then sold them for the same price the Wardens got, which seemed like a lot at first glance. But only Helen, who knew her farm was approaching the edge of ruin just as it had a few years before, comprehended how little profit that actually generated.

Even George Greenwood's savvier business partners, the Wardens at Kiward Station, had given him cause for concern lately. True, both the sheep and cattle breeding operations were flourishing the same as ever, but beneath the surface, tension was mounting. George first noted it when he saw that Gerald and Paul Warden no longer brought Gwyneira into their negotiations. According to Gerald, Paul had to be introduced to the business, and his mother was supposedly more of a hindrance than a help.

"Cut the apron strings, if you know what I mean," Gerald explained, pouring whiskey. "She always thinks she knows better, which gets on my nerves. How do you think Paul will feel, who's just getting started?"

In talking with the two of them, though, George quickly discovered that Gerald had long since lost track of the sheep breeding business that took place on Kiward Station. And Paul lacked understanding and farsightedness—not surprising in someone who was barely sixteen. When it came to breeding, he had fantastical theories that flew in the face of all experience. He would have liked to start breeding with Merinos again.

"Fine wool is a good thing. Qualitatively better than down-type wool. If we only crossbreed with enough Merinos we'll get a new mixed breed that will revolutionize everything!"

George could only shake his head at that, but Gerald's eyes lit up as he listened to the boy, unlike Gwyneira, who was livid when she heard about it.

"If I let the boy take over, everything will go to the dogs!" she ranted when a concerned George sought her out the next day and reported on his conversation with Gerald and Paul. "Sure, he'll inherit the farm eventually; then I won't have any more say. But until then, he has a few years to come to his senses. If Gerald would only be a little more reasonable and influence him accordingly. I don't know what's wrong with him. My God, the man once knew something about raising sheep!"

George shrugged. "Now he knows a lot more about whiskey."

Gwyneira nodded. "He's drinking his brains away. Pardon me for putting it that way, but anything else would be sugarcoating it. I desperately need support. Paul's crossbreeding notion isn't the only problem. In fact, it's the least of them. Gerald is in good health—it will be years before Paul takes over the farm. And even if a few sheep go to him, the business can compensate for it. His conflicts with the Maori are more pressing. They don't have anything like a standard age for a legal adult, or they define it differently. Regardless, they've now elected Tonga their chief."

"Tonga is the boy Helen taught; am I remembering that right?" George asked.

Gwyneira nodded. "A very bright child. And Paul's archenemy. Don't ask me why, but they have been at each other's throats since they were in the sandbox. I think it has to do with Marama. Tonga had his eye on her, but she's adored Paul since they lay next to each other in the cradle. Even now, none of the other Maori want anything to do with him, but Marama is always there. She talks with him, tries to smooth things over—Paul doesn't realize what a treasure he has there! At any rate, Tonga hates him, and I think he's planning something. The Maori have been much more secretive since Tonga started carrying the Sacred Ax. Sure, they still come to work, but they don't work as hard, aren't as…harmless. I have the feeling something is brewing—though everyone thinks I'm crazy."

George considered. "I could send Reti. Perhaps he could find out something. They're no doubt more talkative with each other. But enmity between the leader of Kiward Station and the Maori tribe by the lake could end in disaster. You need the workers!"

Gwyneira nodded. "What's more, I like them. Kiri and Moana, my housemaids, long ago became friends, but now they hardly exchange a personal word with me. Yes, miss; no, miss—I can't get anything else out of them. I hate it. I've been considering talking to Tonga myself."

George shook his head. "Let's see what Reti can do first. If you undertake any kind of negotiations behind Paul's and Gerald's backs, you won't improve matters."

George Greenwood sent out feelers, and what he found out was so alarming that he rode back to Kiward Station just a week later, accompanied by Reti this time.

This time he insisted that Gwyneira take part in the conversation with Gerald and Paul, though he would have much preferred to talk with Gerald and Gwyneira alone. Old Warden insisted, however, on calling his grandson in.

"Tonga has filed a lawsuit. In the government office in Christchurch, but it will ultimately go to Wellington. He's invoking the treaty of Waitangi. Pursuant to which the Maori were damnified upon acquisition of Kiward Station. Tonga is asking that the deed of ownership be declared null and void, or at least that a compromise be reached. That means either a return of land or compensation."

Gerald gulped his whiskey down. "Nonsense! The Kai Tahu did not even sign the treaty back then."

George nodded. "But that does not change its validity. Tonga will demonstrate that the treaty has always been invoked in the interests of the *pakeha*. Now he'll ask for that same right for the Maori. Regardless of what his grandfather decided in 1840."

"That ape!" Paul raged. "I'll—"

"You'll shut your mouth," Gwyneira said sternly. "If you had never started this childish feud, there never would have been a problem. Do the Maori stand a chance of pushing it through, George?"

George shrugged. "It's not out of the question."

"It's even rather likely," Reti joined in. "The governor is very interested in having the Maori and *pakeha* get along well. The Crown knows the value of keeping conflicts here within certain limits. They won't risk an uprising over one farm."

"Uprising is giving them too much credit! We'll grab a couple of guns and smoke the brigands out," Gerald said, working himself up. "This is the thanks you get. For years I've let them live next to the lake; they could move around freely on my land, and—"

"And have always worked for starvation wages," Reti interrupted him.

Paul looked as though he wanted to pounce on him.

"An intelligent young man like Tonga could most certainly spark an uprising; make no mistake about it," George said. "If he incites the other tribes, he'd start with the one next to O'Keefe, whose land was also acquired before 1840. And what about the Beasleys? Even not counting them: do you think people like Sideblossom pored over treaties before they pulled the Maori's land out from under them? If Tonga starts looking at the books, he'll light a fire. And then all we need is a young..." he gave Paul a look, "or an old hothead like Sideblossom to shoot Tonga from behind. Then all hell will break loose. The governor would be doing the right thing in supporting a settlement."

"Have suggestions already been made?" Gwyneira inquired. "Have you spoken with Tonga?"

"He wants the land on which the settlement lies—" Reti began, which immediately set off protests from Gerald and Paul.

"The land right next to the farm? Impossible!"

"I don't want that bastard for a neighbor! That will never come to any good."

"Otherwise, he would take money," Reti continued.

Gwyneira considered. "Well, money would be difficult. We need to make that clear to him. Better land. Perhaps we could arrange an exchange. Having two mortal enemies living next to each other is certainly not wise."

"I've heard enough!" Gerald boiled over. "You don't really believe that we'll negotiate with that brat, Gwyn. I won't hear of it. He won't get money or land. At most a bullet between the eyes!"

The conflict escalated when Paul knocked down a Maori worker the next day. The man insisted he had not done anything; he had perhaps carried out an order a little too slowly. Paul, however, declared that the worker had become insolent and had made reference to Tonga's demands. Several other Maori corroborated their tribesman's story. Kiri refused to serve Paul dinner that evening and even gentle Witi gave him the cold shoulder. Gerald, once again fall-down drunk, dismissed all of the house staff in a blind rage. Though Gwyneira had hoped that they would not take him seriously, neither Kiri nor Moana showed up for work the next day. The other Maori too stayed away from the stables and gardens. Only Marama tinkered ineptly in the kitchen.

"I can't cook very well," she apologized to Gwyneira, but she still managed to whip up Paul's favorite muffins for breakfast. By lunch, though, she had reached the limits of her abilities and served sweet potatoes and fish. In the evening, there were sweet potatoes and fish again, and at lunch the next day, fish and sweet potatoes.

Gerald stomped angrily in the direction of the Maori village on the afternoon of the second day. When he was only halfway there, he was met by a watch patrol, armed with spears. They could not let him through at the moment, the Maori explained gravely. Tonga was not in the village, and no one else had the authority to handle negotiations.

"This is war," one of the young watchmen said calmly. "Tonga says, war, starting now!"

"You're just going to have to look for new workers in Christchurch or Lyttelton," Andy McAran said to Gwyneira regretfully two days later. The work on the farm was running hopelessly behind schedule, but Gerald and Paul only reacted with rage when any of the men blamed the Maori's strike. "You won't catch a glimpse of the people from the village around here until the governor has decided this land business. And keep an eye on that son of yours, miss, for God's sake! Young Mr. Warden is about to explode. And Tonga is raging in the village. If one of them raises a hand against the other, there will be blood."

12

Howard O'Keefe was looking for money. He was angry, as he had not been in a long time. If he didn't get to go to the pub tonight, he would suffocate. Or beat Helen to death—though she really wasn't at fault this time. Gerald Warden was to blame for getting his Maori so riled up. As was Howard's ill-bred son, Ruben, who was fooling around who knew where instead of helping his father with the sheep shearing and herding up into the highlands.

Howard searched desperately through his wife's kitchen. Helen must surely be hiding money somewhere—her rainy day fund, as she called it. The devil only knew how she skimmed it from their meager household budget. No doubt it wasn't going to the right things. And besides, it was really his money. Everything here belonged to him.

Howard ripped open another cabinet, this time cursing George Greenwood, the wool trader having been the bearer of more bad news that day. The shearing gang that usually worked in this part of the Canterbury Plains, first visiting Kiward and O'Keefe Stations, would not be coming this year. The men wanted to go straight to Otago after they had finished their work at Reginald Beasley's. This was due in part to the many Maori who belonged to the crew who refused to work for the Wardens. Though they did not have anything against Howard personally, they had felt so unwelcome at his farm and had had to undertake so much supplemental work in the past that they had decided against making the detour.

"Spoiled brats!" Howard ranted, not entirely without reason—the sheep barons coddled their shearers, who viewed themselves as the most valuable of the farmworkers. The big farms outdid each other with prizes for the best shearing groups, offered first-class catering, and threw parties for completing the work. The piecework shearers did nothing but swing the knife: the farms' shepherds undertook the herding there and back, including gathering the animals to be sheared in the first place. Only Howard O'Keefe could not keep up. He had little help, which consisted entirely of young, inexperienced Maori from Helen's school; as a result, the sheep shearers had to help gather the sheep and then assign them to paddocks after the shearing to make room in the shearing sheds. Howard, however, paid only for the shearing itself and not for the rest of the work. He had also lowered their wages the year before since the quality of the fleece was not sufficiently high and he partially blamed this on the shearers. Today he was paying for that.

"You'll have to see if you can find help in Haldon," George said, shrugging. "The workers would be cheaper in Lyttelton, but half of them come from big cities and have never seen a sheep in their lives. By the time you've taught enough people what to do, summer will be over. And you'd better hurry. The Wardens will also be asking around in Haldon. But they at least have their usual number of farmworkers and all of them know how to shear. Sure they'll need three or four times longer to finish with the shearing, but Mrs. Warden will manage." Helen had suggested going herself to ask for helpers among the Maori. That was the best solution since many experienced shepherds were available because of Tonga's tribe's strike against the Wardens. Howard grumbled because he had not had the idea himself, but he did not say anything when Helen set off for the village. He was going to ride to Haldon—but he needed money first.

He rummaged through the third kitchen cabinet, breaking two cups and a plate in the process. Frustrated, he threw all the dishes in the last wall cupboard straight to the ground. Just chipped teacups anyway...but ho! Wait, there was something here. Howard eagerly removed the loose board on the rear wall of the cupboard. Well, all right, three dollars. Now content, he stuck the money in his pocket. But what else was Helen hiding here? Did she have any secrets?

Howard cast a glance at Ruben's drawing and the lock of hair; then he shoved them aside. Sentimental rubbish! But there—letters.

Howard reached deep into the hiding place and pulled out a packet of neatly bound letters.

He needed some light so that he could make out the script...damn it, it was so dark in this hut!

Howard carried the letters over to the table and held them under the paraffin lamp. Now, finally, he recognized the sender:

Ruben O'Keefe, O'Kay Warehouse, Main Street, Queenstown, Otago

He had him! And her! He had been right all along—Helen had been in contact with that ill-bred son of his all along. She had been deceiving him for five years. Well, she'd get what she deserved when she returned home!

Curiosity overcame Howard. What was Ruben doing in Queenstown? Howard hoped he was in rags—and didn't doubt that he was. Very few prospectors became wealthy, and Ruben certainly wasn't very capable. He eagerly ripped open the most recent letter.

Dear Mother,

It is my great joy to inform you of the birth of your first granddaughter. Little Elaine Florence first opened her eyes to the world on the twelfth of October. It was an easy birth, and Fleurette is doing well. The baby is so small and delicate that I can hardly believe that such a tiny thing can be not only alive but healthy. The midwife assures us that everything is completely fine, and if the volume Elaine achieves when screaming is any indication, I think it safe to assume she'll be taking after my beloved wife in strength of personality as much as delicacy of features. Little Stephen is completely enchanted by his sister and never tires of rocking her in her cradle. Fleurette is afraid he's going to rock the cradle all the way over, but Elaine seems to like the motion and only sings more happily the more wildly he rocks her.

There is only good news to report on the business. O'Kay Warehouse is flourishing, including and especially the women's clothing department. Fleurette was right to push for it back then. Queenstown keeps growing as a town, and the female population is steadily growing.

My work as justice of the peace takes up the rest of my time. Soon we will also be getting a police officer—the town is growing in every respect.

The only thing lacking in our happiness is contact with you and Fleurette's family. Perhaps the birth of our second child is a good excuse to finally let Father in. When he hears about our successful life in Queenstown he will have to see that I did the right thing leaving O'Keefe Station back then. The warehouse has long been bringing in much more profit than I ever could have generated with the farm. I understand that Father wants to stick to his fields, but he will accept that I prefer a different life. Fleurette would also like to visit you two for once. She thinks Gracie is hopelessly underworked since she only herds children these days and no longer sheep.

Greetings to you and possibly Father too,
your loving son Ruben, your daughter-in-law Fleurette,
and the children

Howard snorted with anger. A warehouse! So Ruben had not looked to him as an example but rather—and how could it be otherwise—his idol, Uncle George. George had probably offered him the seed money too—everything kept secret, everyone in the know but him. The Wardens were no doubt laughing at him too. They could be happy about their son-in-law in Queenstown who just happened to be named O'Keefe. After all, they had their heir!

Howard knocked the letters from the table and leaped to his feet. Tonight he would show Helen what he thought of her "loving son" and his "flourishing business." But first he would go to the pub. He had to see if he could find a few proper sheep shearers—and a drop of the good stuff. And if Warden was hanging around there…

Howard reached for the gun hanging next to the door. He'd show him. He'd show them all!

Gerald and Paul Warden sat at a corner table in the pub in Haldon, deep in negotiations with three young men who had advertised themselves as sheep shearers a few minutes earlier. Two were serious possibilities, and one of them had already worked for a shearing gang. The reason he was no longer welcome in it soon became clear: the man poured the whiskey down more quickly than Gerald did. In their present state of crisis, though, he was still worth the money; they would just have to watch him carefully. The second man had worked on various farms as a shepherd and learned shearing there. He was not fast but could still be of use. As for the third man, Paul wasn't sure. He spoke a great deal but couldn't produce any proof of his talents. Paul decided to offer the first two a fixed contract and take the third on probation. The two that he'd selected agreed at once when he made this suggestion. The third man, however, looked with interest in the direction of the bar.

There, Howard O'Keefe was just announcing that he was looking for sheep shearers. Paul shrugged. Fine, if the fellow didn't want probationary work on Kiward Station, Howard O'Keefe could have him.

Howard, however, had his eye on their first pick. Joe Triffles, the drinker. Evidently, the men knew each other. Howard ambled over to them and greeted Joe without so much as a glance at Paul or Gerald.

"Hey, Joe! I'm looking for a few good sheep shearers. Interested?"

Joe Triffles shrugged. "Any other time, but I just struck a deal. Good offer, four weeks steady pay and bonuses per shorn sheep."

Howard puffed himself up angrily in front of the table.

"I'll pay you more!" he declared.

Joe shook his head regretfully. "Too late, Howie, I gave my word. Didn't know there was going to be an auction here, or I would have waited."

"And would've been swindled!" Gerald laughed. "This fellow here talks big, but he couldn't even pay his shearers last year. That's why no one wants to help him this year. Besides, the rain gets into his shearing sheds."

"I'll want extra for that," remarked the third man, the one who had not yet signed on with Gerald. "That's how you get the rheumatism."

All the men laughed, and Howard frothed with rage.

"So, I can't pay, eh?" he roared. "It may be that my farm doesn't rake it in like the grand Kiward Station. But at least I didn't need to force the Butlers' heiress into my bed for it! Did she cry for me, Gerald? Did she tell you how happy she was with me? Did it turn you on?"

Gerald sprang to his feet and looked Howard over with derision. "Did she turn me on? Barbara, that crybaby? That colorless little gutless thing? Listen, Howard, you could have had her for all I cared. I wouldn't have touched her with a ten-foot pole. But you had to gamble the farm away. My money, Howard! My hard-earned money. And God help me, I preferred climbing on little Barbara to another whaler. And I couldn't care less who she was whining for on our wedding night."

Howard pounced on him. "She was engaged to me!" he screamed at Gerald. "She was mine!"

Gerald fended off his blows. He was already very drunk, but he still managed to duck Howard's wild punches. As he did so, he saw the necklace with the jade piece that Howard always wore around his neck. With one jerk he pulled it off and held it up high so that everyone in the pub could see it.

"So that's why you're still carrying her present," he scoffed. "How touching, Howie! A sign of eternal love! What does Mrs. *Helen* O'Keefe have to say about that?"

The men in the pub laughed. Howard reached in impotent rage for the memento, but Gerald did not plan to give it back.

"Barbara wasn't engaged to anyone," he went on. "No matter how many baubles you exchanged. Do you think Butler would have given her to a down-and-out gambler like you? You could have gone to jail for misappropriation of the money. But thanks to my and Butler's indulgence you got your farm; you had a chance. And what did you make of it? A rotten house and a few shabby sheep! Isn't the wife you ordered from England worth anything to you? No wonder your son ran away from you!"

"So you already know too!" O'Keefe exclaimed, swinging and landing a haymaker on Warden's nose. "Everyone knows about my wonderful son and his wonderful wife—were you the one who financed them, Warden? Just to get back at me?"

In his burning rage, anything seemed possible. Yes, that's how it must have gone down. The Wardens were behind the marriage that had estranged him from his son, behind the warehouse that made it so that Ruben could spit on Howard and his farm.

Howard ducked Gerald's right hook, lowered his head, and butted Gerald heavily in the stomach. Gerald doubled over. Howard used the opportunity to land an uppercut to the chin, and Gerald slid halfway across the pub. His skull landed on the edge of a table with a hideous crack.

A horrified silence came over the room as he sank to the ground.

Paul saw a thin trickle of blood flow from Gerald's ear.

"Grandfather! Grandfather, can you hear me?" Horror-struck, Paul crouched next to the groaning man. Gerald slowly opened his eyes, but he seemed to be looking through Paul and the entire scene in the bar. With great effort he tried to sit up.

"Gwyn," he whispered. His eyes became glassy.

"Grandfather!"

"Gerald! By God, I didn't mean to do that, Paul. I didn't mean to do that!"

Howard O'Keefe stood before Gerald Warden's corpse, scared to death. "Oh God, Gerald..."

The other men in the pub slowly began to stir. Someone called for the doctor. Most of them kept their eyes on Paul, who stood up slowly and fixed Howard with a cold, hard gaze.

"You killed him," Paul said quietly.

"But I..." Howard stepped back. The coldness and hatred in Paul's eyes were almost palpable. Howard did not know whether he had ever felt such fear before. He reached instinctively for the gun he had leaned on his chair earlier. But Paul was faster. Since the Maori revolt on Kiward Station he had taken to visibly carrying a revolver. He maintained it was for self-defense; after all, Tonga could launch an attack at any moment. Until that moment, though, Paul had never drawn the weapon. Even now he was not all that quick. He was no six-shooter hero out of the penny dreadfuls his mother had devoured as a young girl, just an ice-cold killer who slowly took his gun out of its holster, aimed, and shot. Howard O'Keefe did not have a chance. His eyes still reflected disbelief and fear as the bullet knocked him backward. He was dead before he hit the ground.

"Paul, for heaven's sake, what have you done!" George Greenwood had not entered the pub until after the brawl between Gerald and Howard was already underway. He wanted to intercede, but Paul pointed the weapon at him. His eyes flared.

"I...it was self-defense! You all saw! He was reaching for his gun!"

"Paul, put that gun away!" George just hoped to avoid further bloodshed. "You can tell it all to the officer. We're sending for Mr. Hanson."

Peaceful little Haldon still did not have its own officer of the law.

"Screw Hanson! It was self-defense. Everyone here can testify to that. And he killed my grandfather!" Paul knelt next to Gerald. "I avenged him! It was only fair. I avenged you, Grandfather!" Paul's shoulders bobbed in time with his sobs.

"Should we tie him up?" Clark, the owner of the pub, asked the group quietly.

Shocked, Richard Candler dissuaded him. "No way! Not while he has that gun...we're not that eager to die. Hanson will have to deal with him. First let's get a doctor in here." Haldon did have a doctor at its disposal, and he had already been informed. He appeared in the pub right then and quickly established Howard O'Keefe's death. He did not dare approach Gerald while Paul held his grandfather in his arms, sobbing.

"Can't you do anything to make him let go of the body?" Clark asked, turning to George Greenwood. He was obviously keen to have the corpses removed from his establishment as soon as possible. If possible, before closing time; the shooting would no doubt liven up his business.

George Greenwood shrugged. "Leave him. At least he's not shooting while he's crying. Just don't do anything to agitate him further. If he says it was self-defense, then that's what it was. What you tell the officer tomorrow is another matter."

Paul eventually got a hold of himself and allowed the doctor to examine his grandfather. With a last glimmer of hope, he watched as Dr. Miller listened for the old man's heartbeat.

Dr. Miller shook his head. "I'm sorry, Paul, there's nothing to be done. Fractured skull. He struck the table's edge. The blow to the chin didn't kill him; it was the unlucky fall. It was an accident, boy. I'm sorry." He patted Paul comfortingly on the shoulder. George wondered whether he knew that the boy had shot Howard.

"Let's take these two to the mortician. Hanson can look at them tomorrow," said the doctor. "Is there someone who can take the boy home?"

The citizens of Haldon appeared reluctant, so George Greenwood offered himself. People were not accustomed to shootings here; even bar fights were a rarity. Normally they would have separated the belligerents right away, but in this case the exchange between Gerald and Howard had been too riveting. Every man there was probably already looking forward to telling his wife what had been said. Tomorrow, George thought, sighing, it would be the talk of the town. But that was irrelevant. A Warden in a murder trial? Everything in George resisted the thought. There had to be some other way to settle the matter.

Gwyneira normally slept through Gerald and Paul's return from the pub. The last few months she had been even more exhausted in the evening than usual because, aside from the work on the farm, she was now responsible for the housework as well. Gerald had perforce consented to hiring white farm laborers, but not house servants. Thus only Marama still lent her a hand—and a rather clumsy one at that. Though the girl had helped her mother, Kiri, around the house since she was little, she had no talent for the work. Her skills lay in the artistic sphere; she was already regarded as a little *tohunga* by her tribe, instructing other girls in singing and dancing and telling imaginative blends of her people's sagas and the *pakeha*'s fairy tales. She could manage a Maori household, making fires and cooking meals on hot stones or in embers. However, she was not suited to polishing furniture, beating rugs, and serving dishes with discretion. Since the kitchen nevertheless remained important to Gerald, in order not to anger him Gwyneira and Marama had been attempting the late Barbara Warden's recipes themselves. Fortunately, Marama could read English fluently, so the Bible was no longer necessary in the kitchen.

That evening, however, Paul and Gerald had eaten in Haldon. Marama and Gwyneira had settled for bread and fruit for themselves. Afterward they sat together by the fire as a reward.

Gwyneira asked whether the Maori held her strike-breaking against her. Marama said they did not.

"Naturally, Tonga is mad," she said in her songlike voice. "He wants everyone to do as he says. But that's not our custom. We decide for ourselves, and I have not yet lain with him in the meeting hall, even though he thinks I will someday."

"Don't your mother and father have some say?" Gwyneira asked, still not entirely clear on the Maori custom. She simply could not comprehend that the girls chose their husbands themselves and often changed husbands several times.

Marama shook her head. "No. Mother only says that it would be strange if I were to lie with Paul because we were nursed at the same breast. It would be indecent if he were one of us, but he is *pakeha* and very different...he is certainly no member of the tribe."

Gwyneira almost choked on her sherry when Marama spoke so naturally of sleeping with her seventeen-year-old son. However, the suspicion now dawned on her that this was why Paul reacted so aggressively to the Maori. He wanted to be kicked out. So that he might sleep with Marama someday? Or simply no longer to have the reputation as "different" among the *pakeha* as well?

"So you like Paul better than Tonga?" Gwyneira asked carefully.

Marama nodded. "I love Paul," she said sincerely. "Like *rangi* loved *papa*."

"Why?" The question crossed Gwyneira's lips before she could stop it. Her cheeks reddened. She had finally admitted that she could not find anything to love in her own son. "I mean," she softened her tone, "Paul is difficult and..."

Marama nodded again. "Love is not simple either," she declared. "Paul is like a roaring river you have to wade through to get to the best fishing grounds. But it is a river of tears, miss. It must be calmed with love. Only then can he...can he become human."

Gwyneira had thought about the girl's words for a long time. As she so often was, she was ashamed of what she had done to Paul by not loving him. But of course she had little reason to be. While she tossed and turned in bed, Friday began to bark—which was strange. True, she heard men's voices coming from the ground floor, but normally the dog did not react to Gerald and Paul's return home. Had they brought a guest?

Gwyneira threw on a dressing gown and left her room. It was not yet late; perhaps the men were still sober enough to inform her of their success in finding sheep shearers. And if they had returned with some drinking companion, then at least she would know what awaited her in the morning.

In order that she might retreat without being seen if the men looked inclined to be troublesome, she crept noiselessly down the stairs—and was astonished to discover George Greenwood in the salon. He was just leading an exhausted-looking Paul into Gerald's study and lighting the lamps. Gwyneira followed them.

"Good evening, George...Paul," she announced herself. "Where's Gerald hiding? Has something happened?"

George Greenwood did not return her greeting. He had purposefully opened the display case and pulled out a bottle of brandy, which he preferred to the omnipresent whiskey, and filled three glasses.

"Here, drink, Paul. And you, Mrs. Warden, will also need a glass." He handed one to her. "Gerald is dead, Gwyneira. Howard O'Keefe beat him to death. And Paul killed Howard O'Keefe."

Gwyneira needed some time to take it all in. She drank her brandy slowly while George described to her what had happened.

"It was self-defense!" Paul declared again. He vacillated between sobbing and being stubbornly defensive.

Gwyneira looked inquiringly at George.

"You could look at it that way," George said hesitantly. "There's no doubt that O'Keefe was reaching for his weapon. But in reality it would have taken ages for him to raise the thing, release the safety, and pull the trigger. By then the other men would have long since disarmed him. Paul could have stopped him with a well aimed punch, or at least taken the gun from him. I'm afraid the witnesses will describe it that way as well."

"Then it was revenge!" Paul crowed, gulping down his brandy. "He drew blood first."

"There a difference between a punch with unfortunate consequences and a shot aimed at a man's chest," George replied, now a little riled up himself. He confiscated the brandy bottle before Paul could pour himself more. "O'Keefe would have been charged with manslaughter at most. If he was charged at all. Most of the people in the pub would testify that Gerald's death was an accident."

"And as far as I know, there's no such thing as the right to revenge." Gwyneira sighed. "What you've done, Paul, is taken the law into your own hands—and that's punishable."

"They can't lock me up!" Paul's voice cracked.

George nodded. "Oh yes they can. And I'm afraid that's exactly what the officer is going to do when he arrives tomorrow."

Gwyneira held her glass out to him for more. She could not remember ever having more than a sip of brandy, but tonight she needed it. "So, what now, George? Is there anything we can do?"

"I'm not staying here!" Paul announced. "I'll flee; I'll go into the highlands. I can live like the Maori! No one will ever find me."

"Don't talk such rot, Paul!" Gwyneira yelled at him.

George Greenwood turned his glass in his hands.

"Maybe he's not all that wrong, Gwyneira," he said. "There's probably nothing better for him to do than disappear, at least until a little grass has grown over the whole thing. In a year or so, the boys in the pub will have forgotten the incident. And between us, I hardly think that Helen O'Keefe will pursue the business with much vigor. When Paul returns, the whole thing will naturally come to trial. But then he can plead self-defense more credibly. You know how these people are, Gwyneira. Tomorrow, people will still remember that the one only had an old rifle and the other a revolver. In three months' time, they'll probably be saying they were both armed with canons."

Gwyneira nodded. "At least we'll save ourselves the commotion of a trial while this delicate business with the Maori is still going on. Tonga will have a field day with all of this...please pour me another brandy, George. I can't believe any of this. We're sitting here talking about what makes the most strategic sense, and two men have died!"

While George was filling her glass, Friday started barking again.

"The police!" Paul reached for his revolver, but George grabbed his arm.

"For God's sake, don't make things worse, boy! If you shoot someone else—or even threaten Hanson—they will hang you, Paul Warden. And even your name and all your fortune won't save you then."

"It can't be the police anyway," Gwyneira said, swaying slightly as she raised herself up. Even if the people in Haldon had sent a messenger to Lyttelton by night, Hanson could not have arrived before the next afternoon.

Instead, Helen O'Keefe stood in the doorway leading from the kitchen to the salon, shaking and soaked through by the rain. Confused by the voices in the study, she had not dared enter—and now looked uncertainly from Gwyneira to George Greenwood.

"George...what are you doing...? Never mind, Gwyn, you have to put me up somewhere tonight. I could even sleep in the stables if you just give me a few dry things. I'm soaked to the bone. Nepumuk is not very fast."

"But what are you doing here?" Gwyneira asked, putting her arm around her friend. Helen had never been to Kiward Station before.

"I...Howard found Ruben's letters...he threw them all over the house and smashed the dishes...Gwyn, if he comes home drunk tonight, he'll kill me!"

As Gwyneira told her friend about Howard's death, Helen displayed a great deal of calm. The tears she shed were for all the pain and suffering she had experienced and seen. Her love for her husband had faded long ago. She appeared more concerned that Paul could be put on trial for murder.

Gwyneira gathered all the money she could find in the house and directed Paul to go upstairs and pack his things. She knew that she should help him with that—the boy was confused and tired to the bone, and there was no way he could still think straight. As he stumbled up the steps, however, Marama came from the other direction with a bundle of items.

"I need your saddlebags, Paul," she said gently. "And then we need to go to the kitchen; we should take some provisions with us, don't you think?"

"We?" Paul asked reluctantly.

Marama nodded. "Of course. I'm coming with you. I'm here for you."

13

Officer Hanson was more than a little surprised when he discovered Helen O'Keefe instead of Paul Warden at Kiward Station the next day. Naturally, he did not look especially pleased with the situation.

"Mrs. Warden, there are people in Haldon accusing your son of murder. And now he's run away from the investigation. I don't know what I'm supposed to make of all this."

"I'm convinced he'll come back," Gwyneira explained. "Everything...his grandfather's death, and then Helen's sudden appearance here...he was terribly ashamed. It was all too much for him."

"Well, then we'll hope for the best. Don't take this business lightly, Mrs. Warden. The way it looks, he shot the man straight in the chest. And O'Keefe, the witnesses generally all agree, was practically unarmed."

"But he did provoke him," said Helen. "My husband, God rest his soul, knew how to provoke a person, Sheriff. And the boy was undoubtedly no longer sober."

"Perhaps the boy could not fully appreciate the situation," George Greenwood added. "The death of his grandfather had completely unmoored him. And when he saw Howard O'Keefe reaching for a gun..."

"You don't really mean to lay the blame on the victim!" the police chief reprimanded them sternly. "That old hunting rifle was hardly a threat."

"That's true," George conceded. "What I wanted to say was rather...well, they were highly unfortunate circumstances. This stupid bar fight, the horrible accident. We all should have interceded. But I think the investigation can wait until Paul comes back."

"*If* he comes back," Hanson barked. "I've got half a mind to send out a search party."

"I'm happy to put my men at your disposal," Gwyneira said. "Believe me—I too would prefer to see my son in your safekeeping than out there alone in the highlands. In addition, he can't expect to receive any help from the Maori."

She was certainly right about that. Although the sheriff delayed the investigation and did not make the mistake of pulling the sheep baron's workers away during sheep shearing season to form a search party, Tonga did not accept the situation so easily. Paul had Marama. Regardless of whether she had gone with him of her own free will or not, Paul had the girl Tonga wanted. And now, finally, the walls of the *pakeha* houses were no longer protecting him. They were no longer the rich livestock farmer and the Maori boy that no one took seriously. Now they were just two men in the highlands. Paul was fair game for Tonga. For now, he waited. He was not as dumb as the whites, setting off blindly after a fugitive. He would eventually learn where Paul and Marama were hiding. And then he would go after them.

Gwyneira and Helen buried Gerald Warden and Howard O'Keefe. Afterward, both resumed their lives, though little changed for Gwyneira. She organized the sheep shearing and made the Maori a peace offer.

With Reti as her interpreter, she strolled into the village and began negotiations.

"You will have the land your village stands on," she explained, smiling uneasily. Tonga stood across from her with a fixed expression, leaning on the Sacred Ax that was a symbol of his chieftain's status. "Beyond that, we will have to work something out. I do not have much in the way of paper money right now—after the sheep shearing, though, that will change for the better, and perhaps we can also sell some of our investments. I still have not finished going through Mr. Warden's assets. Otherwise...what would you think of the land between our fenced-in pastures and O'Keefe Station?"

Tonga raised an eyebrow. "Mrs. Warden, I appreciate your efforts, but I'm not stupid. I know very well that you are in no position to make any offers. You are not the inheritor of Kiward Station—in reality the farm belongs to your son, Paul. And you do not seriously mean to claim that he's authorized you to negotiate on his behalf?"

Gwyneira lowered her eyes. "No, he didn't. But, Tonga, we live here together. And we've always lived in peace."

"Your son broke that peace," Tonga said harshly. "He's insulted my people...moreover, Mr. Warden cheated my people. That was long ago, I know, but it took us a long time to find out. So far no apology has been made."

"I apologize!" said Gwyneira.

"You do not bear the Sacred Ax! I accept you completely, Mrs. Warden, as *tohunga*. You understand more about raising sheep than most of your men. But in the eyes of the law you are nothing and have nothing." He gestured to a little girl playing nearby. "Can this child speak for the Kai Tahu? No. So little do you speak, Mrs. Warden, for the Warden tribe."

"But what will we do, then?" Gwyn asked desperately.

"The same as before. We are in a state of war. We will not help you. On the contrary, we will harm you as much as we can. Don't you wonder why no one will shear your sheep? We did that. We will also close off your streets, block the transportation of your wool—we will not leave the Wardens alone, Mrs. Warden, until the governor has pronounced a judgment and your son is prepared to accept it."

"I do not know how long Paul will be away," Gwyneira said helplessly.

"Then we also do not know how long we will fight. I regret that, Mrs. Warden," Tonga concluded, turning away.

Gwyneira sighed. "Me too."

Over the next few weeks, Gwyneira tackled the sheep shearing, powerfully supported by her men and the two workers Gerald and Paul had contracted with back in Haldon. Joe Triffles had to be under constant surveillance, but when he could be kept away from alcohol, he did as much work as three ordinary shepherds. Helen, who still lacked any assistance, envied Gwyneira for having this capable man.

"I'd let him come over to your place," said Gwyneira, "but, believe me, you couldn't control him alone; you can only do that with a whole gang working together. But I'll send everyone to you as soon as we're done here anyway. It's just taking so miserably long. Can you keep the sheep fed that long?"

The pastures around the farms were mostly eaten away by shearing time, hence the reason for the sheep being driven into the highlands for the summer.

"Just barely," Helen murmured. "I'm giving them the fodder that was meant for the cattle. George sold them off in Christchurch; otherwise, I wouldn't even have been able to pay the burial costs. Eventually I'll have to sell the farm too. I'm not like you, Gwyn. I can't manage it alone. And to be honest, I don't even like sheep." Awkwardly, she stroked the young sheepdog that Gwyneira had given her first thing after Howard's death. The dog was fully trained and helped Helen out enormously with the farm work. However, Helen only had limited control of the dog. The only advantage she had over Gwyneira was that she was still on friendly terms with the Maori. Her students helped her with her farm work without being asked, and so at least Helen had vegetables out of the garden, milk, and eggs, and often fresh meat when the little boys helped hunt or their parents gave them fish as a present for their teacher.

"Have you written to Ruben yet?" Gwyneira asked.

Helen nodded. "But you know how long it takes. First the mail goes to Christchurch, then to Dunedin."

"Though soon the O'Kay Warehouse wagons will be able to take them," Gwyneira remarked. "Fleur wrote in her last letter that she's expecting a delivery in Lyttelton. So she has to send someone to pick it up. They're probably already on their way. But let's talk about my wool for a minute—the Maori are threatening to block the road we take to Christchurch, and I wouldn't put it past Tonga to simply steal the wool—as a little advance pay on the reparations the governor will award him. Well, I'm thinking of spoiling a bit of his fun. Would you be amenable to our bringing our wool to your farm to store in your cow barn until your shearing is done as well? Then we can take it all together by way of Haldon. We'll be a bit later to market than the other breeders, but there's nothing we can do about that."

Tonga was incensed, but Gwyneira's plan succeeded. While his men guarded the road, their enthusiasm for the task slowly ebbing, George Greenwood was receiving the wool from both Kiward Station and O'Keefe Station in Haldon. Tonga's people, whom he had promised ample remuneration, became impatient over the incident and objected that they were usually earning money from the *pakeha* around this time.

"Almost enough for the whole year!" Kiri's husband complained. "We'll now have to move around and hunt like before. Kiri is not looking forward to a winter in the highlands."

"Maybe she'll find her daughter there," Tonga retorted angrily. "And her *pakeha* husband. She can complain to him—after all, he's responsible."

Tonga still had not heard anything about Paul and Marama's whereabouts, but he was a patient man. He waited. Then a covered wagon fell into the clutches of his road blockade. However, it was coming from Christchurch, not Kiward Station, and contained women's clothing, not fleece, so really there was no justifiable reason to stop it. But Tonga's men were slowly getting out of control—and set more things in motion than Tonga could ever have imagined possible.

Leonard McDunn steered his heavy vehicle over the still rather bumpy road from Christchurch to Haldon. This was a detour, but his employer, Ruben O'Keefe, had charged him with dropping off a few letters in Haldon and having a look at a farm in the area.

"But without drawing attention to yourself, McDunn, please! If my father figures out that my mother is in contact with me, she'll be in a world of trouble. My wife thinks the risk is too great, but I have an uneasy feeling...I can't really believe that the farm is suddenly flourishing as my mother claims. It will probably be enough for you to ask around a bit in Haldon. Everyone knows everyone in that village, and the general store owner is very chatty."

McDunn had nodded amiably and, laughing, commented that he'd practice a tricky interrogation technique he knew. In the future, he thought happily, he might have need of it. This was his last trip as a driver for the O'Keefes. The population of Queenstown had recently elected him to police constable. Leonard McDunn, a quiet, squarely built man of about fifty, appreciated the honor and the sedentary nature of the position. He'd been driving for the O'Keefes for four years now, and that was enough.

At the moment, he was quite enjoying his trip to Christchurch, thanks to the pleasant company that had been sent along with him. On the coach box next to him sat Laurie to his right and Mary to his left—or vice versa; there was still no way he could tell the twins apart from each other, even now. Neither of them seemed to care though. One talked to him as cheerfully as the other, asking questions, always hungry to know more, and both gazed over the landscape with the same childlike curiosity. He knew that Mary and Laurie did invaluable work as purchasing agents and salesgirls for the O'Kay warehouse. They were polite and well-bred and could even read and write. Their disposition, however, was simple; they were easily influenced and easy to please but could slip into a state of prolonged moodiness if they were approached the wrong way. That rarely happened, though; usually they were both in high spirits.

"Shouldn't we stop soon, Mr. McDunn?" Mary asked blithely.

"We did some shopping for a picnic, Mr. McDunn! We even got grilled chicken legs from that Chinese business in Christchurch," twittered Laurie.

"It is chicken, isn't it, Mr. McDunn? Not dog? In the hotel they said people eat dog meat in China."

"Could you imagine someone eating Gracie, Mr. McDunn?"

McDunn smiled widely, his mouth watering. Mr. Lin, the Chinese man in Christchurch, would never pawn dog legs off as chicken.

"Sheepdogs like Gracie are far too valuable to eat," he said. "What else do you have in your baskets? You went to the baker's too, didn't you?"

"Oh yes, we visited Rosemary. Just imagine, Mr. McDunn, she came over to New Zealand on the same ship as us!"

"And now she's married to the baker in Christchurch. Isn't that exciting?"

McDunn did not think marrying a baker in Christchurch all that thrilling, but kept his thoughts to himself. Instead, he looked for a good spot to take a break. They were in no hurry. If he found an inviting place, he could leave the horses to eat and relax for a couple of hours.

But then something remarkable happened. The road made a hairpin turn, revealing a view of a small lake—and some sort of blockade. Someone had laid a tree trunk clear over the road, and it was being guarded by several Maori warriors. The men looked martial and fearsome. Their faces were completely covered with tattoos and war paint, their upper bodies were naked and gleaming, and they wore a sort of loincloth that ended just below the knees. They were armed with spears, which they now raised threateningly to Leonard.

"Crawl into the back, girls!" he called to Mary and Laurie, trying not to scare them.

Finally, he stopped.

"What you want on Kiward Station?" one of the Maori warriors asked menacingly.

Leonard shrugged. "Isn't this the way to Haldon? I'm on my way with wares for Queenstown."

"You lie!" the warrior exclaimed. "This way to Kiward Station, not to Wakatipu. You food for Wardens!"

Leonard rolled his eyes and exercised calm.

"I am most certainly not food for the Wardens, whoever they are. I don't even have a load of groceries, just women's clothing."

"Women's...?" The warrior frowned. "You show!"

In one quick motion, he sprang up onto the coach box and ripped open the cover. Mary and Laurie screeched in terror. The other warriors hooted approvingly.

"Easy now, easy!" cursed McDunn. "You're making a mess of everything! I'd be happy to open the wagon for you, but..."

The warrior had drawn a knife and cut the cover from its frame. To the amusement of his companions, the wagon bed now lay uncovered before him—as did the twins, who clung to each other, whimpering.

Now Leonard became seriously concerned. Fortunately, there were no weapons or any ironware that could be used as one. He had a gun himself, but the men would disarm him long before he could use it. Even drawing his knife would be far too risky. Besides, the boys did not look like professional highwaymen, but rather like shepherds playing at war. For the moment, they did not present any immediate danger.

Beneath the undergarments, which the Maori now pulled from the wagon and held in front of his chest, giggling, to the elation of his tribesmen, were more dangerous wares. If the men found the barrels of fine brandy and tried it for themselves right then and there, their situation could quickly become precarious. In the meantime, others had become curious about them. They must have been near a Maori village because a few adolescents and older men approached, the majority of them dressed in Western clothing and lacking tattoos. One of them lifted a crate of fine Beaujolais—Mr. O'Keefe's personal order—out from under a layer of corsets.

"You're coming with!" said one of the newcomers sternly. "This wine for Wardens. I once house servant; I know. We're taking you to the chief. Tonga will know what to do."

Leonard McDunn's enthusiasm at the prospect of being introduced to the high chief was tepid at best. Though he did not think his life was in danger, he knew that he could kiss his wares good-bye if he steered the wagon into the rebels' camp—probably the wagon and horses too.

"Follow me!" commanded the former house servant, stepping forward. McDunn cast an appraising glance at the landscape. It was predominantly flat. A few hundred yards back, the road had forked, and they had probably set off in the wrong direction. This was obviously a private path, and the Maori were in the midst of a feud with its owner. The fact that the approach to Kiward Station was better constructed than the public road had led Leonard to make a wrong turn. If he could break out straight through the bush to the left, he would have to intersect with the official road to Haldon...unfortunately, the Maori warrior was still standing before him, now posing with a brassiere on his head—with one leg on the box, and the other inside the wagon.

"It's your own fault if you get hurt," Leonard muttered as he set the wagon in motion. It took a while for the heavy shire horses to get going, but once they did, Leonard knew, they would fly. After the horses had taken their first steps, he cracked his whip at them and steered sharply to the left. The sudden trotting caused the warrior dancing with the underwear to lose his balance. He did not even have a chance to swing his spear before Leonard pushed him from the wagon. Laurie and Mary screamed. Leonard hoped the wagon did not run the man over.

"Duck, girls! And hold on tight!" he called back just as a hail of spears rained down on the cases of corsets. Well, the whaleboning would survive that. Both of the shires were now galloping, and their hooves made the earth tremble. On a riding horse, the Maori would easily have been able to overtake the wagon, but to Leonard's relief no one came after them.

"Are you all right, girls?" he called back to Mary and Laurie as he spurred the horses on to further exertion, praying that the land would not suddenly become uneven. These workhorses could not stop quickly, and a broken axle was the last thing he needed now. But the terrain remained flat, and another path soon came into view. Leonard did not know whether it was the road to Haldon; it looked too narrow and winding. But it was clearly navigable and showed traces of horse-drawn vehicles—though it looked more like the ruts of light buggies than covered wagons, whose drivers were not in danger of breaking an axle by riding on uneven ground. Regardless, he took it. Leonard urged his horses on further. Only when he thought he had left the Maori camp at least a mile behind them did he slow the team to an easy pace.

Laurie and Mary crawled to the front, sighing with relief.

"What was that, Mr. McDunn?"

"Did they want to do something to us?"

"Normally the natives are so peaceful."

"Yes, Rosemary says they're usually so nice."

Leonard began to breathe easy as the twins took up their cheerful chattering again. Everything seemed to have turned out all right. Now he just needed to figure out where this path led.

Now that they had survived their adventure, Mary and Laurie were hungry, but the three of them agreed that it would be wiser to enjoy the bread, chicken, and Rosemary's tasty cookies on the driving box. Leonard was still unsettled by the business with the Maori. He had heard of uprisings on the North Island. But here? In the middle of the peaceful Canterbury Plains?

The path wound its way to the west. It could hardly be a public road; it looked more like an unofficial path that had been carved out gradually by many years of use. Riders had gone around bushes and clumps of trees instead of cutting them down. And here was another stream.

Leonard sighed. The ford did not look dangerous and had surely been crossed recently. But perhaps not with a wagon as heavy as his. In the interest of safety, he had the girls get out first, then carefully maneuvered his team into the water. Then he stopped to let the twins back on—and jumped when he heard Mary scream.

"There, Mr. McDunn! Maori! They're up to something, there's no doubt about it!"

The girls crawled in a panic under the canvas that once again covered the wagon while McDunn scanned the area for warriors. All he saw were two children driving a cow in front of them.

They approached curiously when they saw the wagon.

McDunn smiled at them, and the children waved shyly. And then, to his surprise, they greeted him in very good English.

"Hello, sir."

"Can we help you, sir?"

"Mister, are you a traveling salesman? We've just been reading about tinkerers." Curious, the girls peeked out from under the provisionally secured canvas.

"Oh, come on, Kia, it's just more fleece from the Wardens'. Miss O'Keefe gave them permission to store everything in her barn," said the boy, while adeptly keeping the cow from escaping.

"Nonsense! The shearers were here a long time ago and brought everything with them. He's definitely a tinkerer. It's just the horses aren't dappled, is all."

Leonard smiled. "We are indeed traders, little lady, but not tinkerers," he said to the girl. "We wanted to take the road to Haldon, but I think we've gotten lost."

"Not badly," the girl reassured him.

"If you take the main road from the house, it's only two miles to Haldon," the boy explained more precisely. Then he looked at the twins, who had dared to show themselves again, in confusion. "Why do the women look the same?"

"Now that's good news," Leonard said without answering the boy's question. "Could you two tell me where I am anyway? It's not… what did they just call it? Kiward Station?"

The children giggled as though he had made a joke.

"No, this is O'Keefe Station. But Mr. O'Keefe is dead."

"Mr. Warden shot him dead!" the girl added.

As an officer of the law, Leonard thought amusedly, he couldn't have asked for more informative people. The people in Haldon certainly were chatty; Ruben had been right about that.

"And now he's in the highlands and Tonga is looking for him."

"Psst, Kia, you're not supposed to tell people that!"

"Mister, do you want to see Miss Helen O'Keefe? Should we go get her? She's either in the shearing shed or..."

"No, Matiu, she's in the house. Didn't you know? She said she had to cook for all the people."

"Helen?" Laurie squealed.

"Our Helen?" Mary echoed.

"Do you always say the same thing?" the boy asked, amazed.

"I think you'd better take us to this farm first," Leonard said finally. "The way it looks, we've found exactly what we were looking for."

And Mr. O'Keefe, he thought with a grim smile, would not be an obstacle anymore.

A half hour later, the horses had been unhitched and were standing in Helen's stables. Helen—hysterical with surprise and joy—had wrapped her arms around her charges from the *Dublin*, whom she had long believed lost to her. She still could hardly believe that the half-starved children from back then had grown into such cheerful, even rather buxom young women, who quite naturally took over the work in the kitchen for her.

"That's supposed to be enough for a whole company of shearers, miss?"

"Not even close, miss, we need to make it stretch."

"Are those supposed to be patties, miss? Then we'd better use more sweet potatoes and not so much meat."

"The men don't need it anyway, or else they'll get rowdy."

The twins giggled happily.

"And you can't knead bread like that, miss! Just wait, we'll make tea first."

Mary and Laurie had been cooking for the customers at Daphne's Hotel for years. Handling the catering for a sheep shearing gang was no problem for them. While they puttered around the kitchen, Helen sat with Leonard McDunn at the kitchen table. He recounted the strange Maori holdup that had led him to her and Helen reported the details of Howard's death.

"Naturally, I'm in mourning over my husband," she explained, smoothing the simple, navy-blue dress she had worn almost every day since Howard's funeral. There had not been enough money for black mourning attire. "But it's also something of a relief...excuse me, you must think me heartless."

Leonard shook his head. He thought Helen O'Keefe anything but heartless. On the contrary, he could hardly get enough of her joy earlier, when she had embraced the twins. With her shining brown hair, her narrow face, and her serene gray eyes, he found her rather attractive. She did, however, appear exhausted, worn out and pale beneath her sun-kissed skin. It was clear that her situation was pushing her beyond her limits. She was as ill-suited to kitchen work as to farm work and had been relieved when the Maori children had offered to milk her cow.

"Your son hinted that his father was not the easiest man to live with. What do you intend to do with the farm now? Sell it?"

Helen shrugged. "If someone wants to buy it. The simplest thing would be to incorporate it into Kiward Station. Howard would curse us from beyond the grave, of course, but I couldn't care less. As a one-person business, though, the farm is not profitable. There is plenty of land, but not enough for the animals to eat. To make it work, someone would need a great deal of know-how and investment capital. The farm has been run into the ground, Mr. McDunn. Unfortunately, that is the only way to put it."

"And your friend from Kiward Station...she is the mother of Fleurette O'Keefe, is that right?" Leonard asked. "Does she have any interest in taking it over?"

"Interest, yes...oh, thank you, Laurie, you're both simply wonderful! I don't know what I would have done without you!" Helen held out her cup to Laurie, who had just come to the table with freshly made tea.

Laurie filled her cup as skillfully as Helen had taught her on the ship.

"How can you tell that that's Laurie?" Leonard asked, astounded. "I don't know anyone who can tell them apart."

Helen laughed. "If you leave the twins to their own devices, Mary likes to set the table, and Laurie likes to serve. Just keep an eye out—Laurie is the more open of the pair, whereas Mary likes to take a backseat."

Leonard had never noticed that, but he admired Helen's gift of observation. "Now, what about your friend?"

"Well, Gwyneira has her own problems," Helen said. "In fact, you rode right into them yourself. This Maori chief is attempting to bring the Wardens to their knees, and she has no way of going over Paul's head to resolve it. Perhaps when the governor finally decides..."

"And the chances of this Paul fellow returning and resolving his own difficulties?" Leonard asked. It seemed rather unjust to leave these two women behind with all these troubles. Although he had not met Gwyneira Warden yet. If she was anything like her daughter, though, she could handle half a continent full of rebellious savages.

"Resolving difficulties is not exactly a strong suit of the male Wardens." Helen smiled crookedly. "As for Paul's return...the atmosphere in Haldon is slowly changing. George Greenwood was right about that. At first they would all have liked to lynch him, but now their sympathy for Gwyneira is winning out. They think she needs a man on the farm, and they're willing to overlook a few small details like murder to make that happen."

"How cynical of you, Mrs. O'Keefe!" Leonard admonished.

"I'm being honest. Paul shot an unarmed man in the chest without warning. In front of twenty witnesses. But I don't want to see him hanged either. What good would that do? In any case, when he returns, things are bound to escalate with the Maori chief. And then perhaps he'll hang for his next murder."

"The boy really seems to fancy the noose." Leonard sighed. "I—"

He was interrupted when someone knocked on the door. Laurie opened it. As soon as she did, a small dog shot between her legs. Panting, Friday reared up in front of Helen.

"Mary, come quick! I think it's Miss Silk...Warden! And Cleo! How is she still alive, miss?"

But Gwyneira did not notice the twins. She was so beside herself that she did not even recognize them.

"Helen," she exclaimed, "I'm going to kill Tonga! It was all I could do not to ride into the village with a gun! Andy says his people held up a covered wagon—heaven knows what it wanted with us, or where it is now. In the village, though, they're having great fun running around with brassieres and knickers...oh, pardon me, sir, I..." Gwyneira blushed when she saw that Helen was entertaining male company.

McDunn laughed. "Nothing to pardon, Mrs. Warden. I'm well schooled in ladies' undergarments: I'm the one who lost them. The wagon belongs to me. With your permission, Leonard McDunn of the O'Kay Warehouse."

"Why don't you just come to Queenstown?" Leonard asked a few hours later, looking at Helen.

Gwyneira had calmed down and helped Helen and the twins feed the hungry sheep shearers. She praised all of them for continuing the shearing, even though they were rather shocked at the quality of the wool. They had heard that O'Keefe produced a good deal of junk wool, but they had no idea the situation was so dire. Now Gwyneira sat with Helen and Leonard in front of the fireplace, opening one of the bottles of Beaujolais that had thankfully been rescued.

"To Ruben and his excellent taste!" she said with delight. "Where did he get that from, Helen? This must be the first bottle of wine to be uncorked in this house in years."

"In the works of Lord Bulwer-Lytton, Gwyn, which I like to read with my students, alcohol is occasionally consumed in cultivated company," Helen replied affectedly.

Leonard took a sip; then he made his suggestion about Queenstown: "Seriously, Mrs. O'Keefe, you do wish to see your son and your grandchildren, don't you? Now's your chance. We'll be there in a few days."

"Now, in the middle of the shearing?" Helen dismissed the notion.

Gwyneira laughed. "Helen, you don't seriously believe that my people will shear more sheep if you're standing there than if you're not. And you don't mean to herd the sheep into the highlands yourself, do you?"

"But...but someone has to feed the workers..." Helen was undecided. The offer had come so suddenly; she couldn't accept it. And yet it was so tempting!

"They fed themselves on my farm. O'Toole still makes better stew than Moana and I ever managed to. And let's not even get started on you. You're my dearest friend, Helen, but you're no chef."

Helen blushed. Normally she would not have thought twice about such a remark. But suddenly, in front of Leonard McDunn, it was embarrassing.

"Let the men slaughter a couple of sheep, and we'll leave them one of these barrels since I was the one to defend them with my life. It's a sin, really, because the brandy is too good for that lot, but after this they'll love you forever," McDunn suggested with composure.

Helen smiled. "I don't know..." she said coyly.

"But I do!" Gwyneira said resolutely. "I would love to go, but I'm indispensable at Kiward Station. So I'm hereby declaring you our mutual emissary. See that all is right in Queenstown. And woe to Fleurette if she didn't train that dog properly! Also, take a pony with you for our grandchildren. So they don't grow up to be lousy riders like you."

14

Helen loved Queenstown from the moment she laid eyes on the little town on the shores of the mighty, shimmering Lake Wakatipu. In the smooth surface of the lake she could see the reflections of the dapper new houses, and a little harbor was lined with colorful rowboats and sailboats. The snowcapped mountains framed the picturesque scene. Most importantly, Helen had gone half a day without seeing a single sheep.

"It's humbling," she confided to Leonard McDunn, to whom she had already revealed more about herself after eight days together on the coach box than she had to Howard during their whole marriage. "When I came to Christchurch years ago, I cried because the town had so little in common with London. Now I'm thrilled by this little town because I will be surrounded by people and not ruminants."

Leonard laughed. "Oh, Queenstown has quite a bit in common with London, you'll see. There's stuff happening here, Mrs. O'Keefe. You feel progress here, like you're on the frontier. Christchurch is nice, but there it's more about keeping up old customs and being more English than the English. Just look at the cathedral and the university. They think they're becoming an Oxford over there! But here everything is new; everything's on the up-and-up. The prospectors are a wild bunch, though, and raise a bit of rumpus. It's unthinkable that the nearest police station is forty miles away. But these boys bring gold and life to the town. You'll like it here, Mrs. O'Keefe, believe me."

Helen already liked it as the wagon rumbled down Main Street. It was unpaved just like in Haldon, but the street here was filled with people: a prospector was arguing with the postman because he had apparently opened a letter for him; two girls were giggling and peeking into the barber shop where a handsome young man was getting a haircut; the smith was shoeing horses; and two miners were talking shop about a mule. And the "hotel" was being repainted. A red-haired woman in an eye-catching green dress was overseeing the painters and cursing like a sailor.

"Daphne!" The twins squealed simultaneously, almost falling from the wagon. "Daphne, we brought Miss Dav...Mrs. O'Keefe!"

Daphne O'Rourke turned around, and Helen found herself staring into that familiar catlike face. Daphne looked older, maybe a little worse for wear, and was heavily made up. When she saw Helen on the coach box, their eyes met. Helen was touched to see that Daphne blushed.

"He...hello, Mrs. O'Keefe!"

Leonard could hardly believe it, but the ever-confident Daphne curtsied before her teacher like a little girl.

"Stop the horses, Mr. McDunn!" Helen called. She hardly waited for him to rein in the horses before she jumped down from the box and wrapped her arms around Daphne.

"No, really, Mrs. O'Keefe, if someone sees..." Daphne said. "You're a lady. You shouldn't be seen with someone like me." She lowered her eyes. "I'm sorry, Mrs. O'Keefe, for what I've become."

Helen laughed and embraced her again. "What have you become that's so horrible, Daphne? A businesswoman. A wonderful foster mother for the twins. No one could ask for a better student."

Daphne blushed again. "Perhaps no one has enlightened you as to my...line of business," she said softly.

Helen pulled her close. "Businesses work on supply and demand. I learned that from George Greenwood, another one of my children. And as for you...well, if there had been a demand for Bibles, I'm sure you would have sold those."

Daphne giggled. "With great pleasure, Mrs. O'Keefe."

While Daphne was greeting the twins, Leonard took Helen to the O'Kay Warehouse. As much as Helen had enjoyed seeing Daphne and the twins, she wanted more than anything to fling her arms around her own son, Fleurette, and her grandchildren.

Little Stephen hung on to her skirts right away, but Elaine displayed more enthusiasm when she saw the pony.

Helen looked down at her red hair and her lively eyes, already a deeper shade of blue than most babies'.

"Definitely Gwyn's granddaughter," Helen said. "She didn't get anything from me. Watch out, she'll be asking for a couple of sheep for her third birthday."

Leonard McDunn scrupulously went over the accounts from his last purchasing trip with Ruben O'Keefe before assuming his new duties. The police station had to be painted and the jail supplied with bars with help from Stuart Peters. Helen and Fleur helped furnish the cells decently with mattresses and sheets from the warehouse.

"Not going to put in any flower vases?" grumbled Leonard. Stuart was likewise impressed.

"I'm keeping a spare key," the smith teased. "In case I have guests in town."

"You can test it out right now, if you like," Leonard threatened. "But seriously now—I'm afraid we'll already be filled up tonight. Miss O'Rourke is planning an Irish evening. What do you bet half her customers end up beating up the other half?"

Helen frowned. "But it won't get dangerous, will it, Leonard? Watch out for yourself! I...we...we need our constable in one piece!"

Leonard beamed. He was exceptionally pleased that Helen was worried about him.

Hardly three weeks later, Leonard was confronted with a problem more serious than the usual brawls among the prospectors.

In need of help, he waited in the O'Kay warehouse until Ruben had time for him. Voices and laughter came from the building's back rooms, but Leonard did not want to intrude. After all, he was there on official business. It was not Leonard waiting for his friend but the police officer seeking the justice of the peace. He breathed easier when Ruben finally broke free and came out to see him in the front of the store.

"Leonard! Sorry to make you wait," Ruben said, evidently in good spirits. "But we have something to celebrate. It looks I'm going to be a father for the third time! But first, tell me, what's this all about? How can I help?"

"An official matter. And a sort of legal dilemma. A certain John Sideblossom just appeared in my office; he's a well-to-do farmer looking to invest in the gold mines. He was all worked up, said I had to arrest a man he saw in the prospectors' camp. A certain James McKenzie."

"James McKenzie?" Ruben asked. "The sheep thief?"

Leonard nodded. "The name rung a bell at once. He was caught a few years ago in the highlands and sentenced in Lyttelton to serve a term in prison."

Ruben nodded. "I know."

"Always had a good memory, Your Honor," Leonard said respectfully. "Did you also know they commuted McKenzie's sentence? Sideblossom says they sent him to Australia."

"They deported him," Ruben corrected him. "Australia was the closest place. The sheep and cattle barons would have preferred to see him in India or some far-off place like that. Most of all, they would have liked to see him in the belly of a tiger."

Leonard laughed. "That's exactly the impression this Sideblossom gave. Well, if he's right, McKenzie's back, even though he was exiled for life. That's why this Sideblossom fellow said I needed to arrest him. But what am I supposed to do with him? I can hardly lock him up for life. And five years in prison wouldn't make much sense either—strictly speaking, he already has those years behind him. Not to mention that I don't have space for him. Do you have any suggestions, Your Honor?"

Ruben pretended to think about it—though Leonard could not help seeing the joy reflected in his face. Was he against McKenzie? Or for him?

"See here, Leonard," Ruben finally said. "First, find out if this is really the McKenzie Sideblossom has in mind. Then lock him up for as long as this Sideblossom fellow is in town. Tell Sideblossom you're taking this man into protective custody. Sideblossom was menacing Mr. McKenzie, and you didn't want a rumpus."

Leonard grinned.

"But don't tell my wife anything about it," Ruben said urgently. "It should be a surprise. Oh yes, and before you lock him up, see that Mr. McKenzie gets a shave and a decent haircut if it proves necessary. He'll be receiving a lady visitor shortly after entering that grand hotel of yours."

During the first weeks of being pregnant, Fleurette was always close to tears, and so she cried her eyes out when she went to visit James in jail. Whether out of joy at their reunion or desperation over his renewed capture was hard to tell.

James McKenzie himself, on the other hand, hardly seemed upset. Until Fleurette burst into tears, he had been in high spirits. Now he held her in his arms and awkwardly rubbed her back.

"Now, now, don't cry, little one, nothing's going to happen to me here. It would be much more dangerous out there. I still have a bone to pick with Sideblossom!"

"Why did you have to run into him straightaway?" Fleurette sobbed. "What were you even doing in the goldfields? You weren't trying to stake a claim, were you?"

James shook his head. He did not look like one of the adventurers who set up camp on the old sheep farms close to the goldfields, and Leonard had neither needed to take him to the barber's for a shave and haircut, nor had to help him out with money. James McKenzie looked more like a well-off rancher on vacation. Judging by his clothing and cleanliness, he was indistinguishable from his old enemy Sideblossom.

"I've staked enough claims in my life and even earned plenty from this last one in Australia. The secret is not to spend all the gold you find right away by celebrating at an establishment like Daphne's." He laughed. "Naturally, in the goldfields here I was looking for your husband. Only to find out that he now lives on Main Street, throwing the book at harmless travelers." He winked at Fleurette. Before seeing his daughter, he had met with Ruben and was very pleased with his son-in-law.

"What's going to happen now?" Fleurette asked. "Will they send you back to Australia?"

James sighed. "I hope not. I could pay for the passage. That's no problem...now, now, don't give me that look, Ruben. I earned it all honestly! I swear. I didn't steal a single sheep over there. It would have been another waste of time. Of course I was going to come back with different papers. I won't go through something like I did with Sideblossom again. But I would have had to keep Gwyn waiting for so long if I had stayed in Australia. And I'm sure she's tired of waiting—just like I am."

"False papers aren't a solution, either," Ruben said. "They would be fine if you wanted to live in Queenstown, on the West Coast, or somewhere on the North Island. But if I'm understanding you correctly, you want to ride back to the Canterbury Plains to marry Gwyneira Warden. It's just that—every child knows you there!"

James shrugged. "Also true. I would have to abduct Gwyn. But I don't have any scruples about that!"

"It would be better to make you a legal citizen," Ruben said sternly. "I'll write to the governor."

"But Sideblossom will be doing that already!" Fleurette seemed to be on the verge of bursting into tears again. "Mr. McDunn already said he was raving like a madman because my father's being handled like a prince here."

John Sideblossom had come by the police station around midday when the twins had been in the midst of serving both the guard and the prisoner a glutton's feast. He was livid when he saw how the prisoner was being treated.

"Sideblossom is a rancher and an old scoundrel. If it's his word against mine, the governor will know what to do," Ruben said, appeasing her. "I will describe the situation to him in detail—including your father's secure financial situation, his family connections, and his marriage plans. In addition, I will stress his services and qualifications. So he stole a few sheep. He also discovered the McKenzie Highlands, where Sideblossom now pastures his sheep. He should be grateful to you, James, instead of planning your demise. And you're an experienced shepherd and sheep breeder, a definite gain for Kiward Station, especially now, after the death of Gerald Warden."

"We could also offer him a job," Helen joined in. "Would you like to be manager of O'Keefe Station, James? That would be an alternative, should dear Paul throw Gwyneira out on the street anytime soon."

"Or Tonga," Ruben remarked. He had studied Gwyneira's legal status in the conflict with the Maori and was not very optimistic. From a legal perspective, Tonga's demands were justified.

James McKenzie shrugged. "O'Keefe Station is as good as Kiward Station to me. It's all the same to me as long as I can be with Gwyneira—though I suspect that Friday will want a few sheep."

Ruben sent his letter off to the governor the next day, but no one expected a swift response. So James struggled with his boredom in jail while Helen spent a wonderful time in Queenstown. She played with her grandchildren, and watched, with an anxiously beating heart, as Fleurette set little Stephen on the pony for the first time. Helen, meanwhile, tried to comfort little Elaine, who cried in protest. Prepared for the worst, she inspected the little school that had just opened. Perhaps she could make herself useful there, so that she could stay in Queenstown forever. At the time, however, there were only ten students, and the young teacher, a likeable girl from Dunedin, handled them perfectly well on her own. There was not much for Helen to do in Ruben and Fleurette's shop either, and the twins fell all over themselves in their desire to keep their beloved former teacher from having to lift a finger. Helen finally heard Daphne's whole story.

She invited the young woman to tea, even though it might set the respectable women in Queenstown to gossiping.

"First thing after I had taken care of that brute, I went to Lyttelton," Daphne said of her flight from the lascivious Mr. Morrison. "I would have liked to take the next ship back to London, but of course that wasn't an option. No one would have taken a girl like me. I thought about Australia too. But God knows they have enough...ahem, women of easy virtue over there who could not find a job selling Bibles. And then I found the twins. They were headed the same place I was: away from here—and 'away' meant a ship."

"How exactly did they find each other again?" Helen inquired. "They were in completely different areas."

Daphne shrugged. "They're twins, after all. What the one thinks, the other thinks too. Believe me, I've had them with me for more than twenty years, and I still think it's uncanny. If I understood them correctly back then, they ran into each other on the Bridle Path. How they slogged all the way there, I have no idea. When I found them, they were running around the harbor, stealing their food together, and trying to stow themselves away on a boat. Utter nonsense; someone would have found them straightaway. So what was I supposed to do? I held onto them. I was a bit nice to a sailor, and he got me the papers of a girl who died on the way from Dublin to Lyttelton. Officially my name is Bridey O'Rourke. Everyone believed it too, with my red hair and all. But the twins kept calling me Daphne, naturally, so I kept my first name. It's a good name anyway for a...I mean, it's a Biblical name; it's not easy to let something like that go."

Helen laughed. "They'll canonize you someday!"

Daphne giggled, looking for a moment like the young girl from back then. "So then we left for the West Coast. We traveled around a bit at first, finally ending up in a broth...ahem, in the establishment of a certain Madame Jolanda. It was pretty run-down. First thing I did was clean the place up, which really caused business to pick up. That's where your friend Mr. Greenwood smoked me out, though I didn't leave because of him. It was rather that Jolanda was never satisfied. One day she told me that she wanted to start putting the girls to work the following Saturday. It was time, she said, that they were broken in…ahem, that they knew somebody, as it says in the Bible."

Helen had to laugh. "You really have your Bible memorized, Daphne," she said. "Next we'll have to test your knowledge of *David Copperfield*."

"So that Friday I really kicked up my heels one last time, and then we made off with the cash box. Naturally, that wasn't very ladylike."

"Let's just say—an eye for an eye, a tooth for a tooth," Helen remarked.

"And then we followed the 'scent of gold' here." Daphne grinned. "And we struck it big! I'd go so far as to say that seventy percent of the yield of all the gold mines in the area comes my way."

Ruben was confused, bordering on a little unsettled, when he received an official-looking envelope only six weeks after he had posted his letter to the governor. The postman handed him the missive almost ceremoniously.

"From Wellington!" he exclaimed importantly. "From the government! Are you being ennobled now, Rube? Is the queen coming by?"

Ruben laughed. "Not likely, Ethan, not in the least bit likely." He checked his desire to rip the envelope open immediately since Ethan was looking a little too curiously over his shoulder, and Ron from the rental stables was hanging around Ethan's shop.

"I'll see you two later, then," he said, trying to appear relaxed, but he was already playing with the envelope as he walked toward the warehouse. He had a change of plan as he walked past the police station. This was undoubtedly about James McKenzie, so he should be the first to find out what the governor had decided.

Soon Ruben, Leonard, and James were all bent eagerly over the missive. All of them moaned at the governor's long introduction, in which he stressed all the services Ruben had rendered for the blossoming young settlement of Queenstown. The governor finally came to the heart of the matter:

...we are happy to be able to grant your request for further clemency regarding the livestock thief James McKenzie, whose case you so illuminatingly represented, a positive response. We too are of the opinion that James McKenzie could be of use to the young community of the South Island, as long as he limits himself in the future to the legal exercise of his doubtlessly considerable talents. We also hope herewith and especially to serve the interest of Mrs. Gwyneira Warden whom we, in another case laid before us for our decision, must disappoint. Please maintain absolute silence with regard to this latter matter. The judgment has yet to be presented to the involved parties...

"Damn it, that's the business with the Maori." James sighed. "Poor Gwyn...and the way it sounds, she's still facing it all on her own. I should set out for Canterbury at once."

Leonard nodded. "I won't stand in your way," he said, grinning. "On the contrary, then I'll finally have a free room in the Grand Hotel!"

"I really should accompany you, James," Helen said with some regret. The zealous twins had just served the last course of a grand farewell meal. Fleurette had insisted on entertaining her father at least once before he disappeared to Canterbury, possibly for several years. Naturally, he had sworn to come visit them with Gwyneira as soon as possible, but Fleur knew how it was on large sheep farms: something always came up that made it impossible for the manager to leave.

"It was wonderful here, but I need to get back to caring for the farm. And I don't want to be a burden to you forever." Helen folded her napkin.

"You're not a burden to us," Fleurette said. "On the contrary! I don't know what we're going to do without you, Helen."

Helen laughed. "Don't lie, Fleur. You were never very good at it. Seriously, dear, as much as I like it here, I need to have something to occupy me again. I've taught my whole life. Just sitting around now, playing with the children occasionally, seems like wasted time."

Ruben and Fleurette looked at her. They seemed uncertain about how to respond. Finally, Ruben spoke.

"Very well, we didn't want to ask until later, when everything was settled," he said, looking at his mother. "But before you take off, we'd better just say it. Fleurette and I—and let's not forget Leonard McDunn—have already been thinking about what you could do here."

Helen shook her head. "I've already looked at the school, Ruben, the—"

"Forget the school, Helen!" said Fleur. "You've done that long enough. We were thinking...well, we were planning to buy a farm outside of town. Or rather a house, we haven't given much thought to the farm as a business. It's too loud here, too much traffic...I'd like the children to have more freedom. Can you imagine, Helen, Stephen's never seen a weta?"

Helen felt that her grandson would grow up just fine without this experience.

"In any event, we'll be moving out of this house," Ruben explained, taking in the sweet, two-story townhouse with a sweep of his hand. "The house was completed last year and we spared nothing on the furnishings. We could sell it, naturally. But then Fleurette thought it would be an ideal location for a hotel."

"A hotel?" Helen asked, confused.

"Yes!" Fleurette announced. "Look, it's got a great deal of room since we were always counting on a big family. If you were to live on the ground floor and rent out the rooms upstairs..."

"You want me to run a hotel?" Helen asked. "Have you lost your mind?"

"Think of it more like a bed and breakfast where people can stay longer if they like," Leonard said helpfully, looking at Helen encouragingly.

Fleurette nodded. "Don't misunderstand what we mean by hotel," she said quickly. "We mean for it to be a respectable hotel. Not a den of thieves like Daphne's, where bandits and loose women roost. No, I was thinking...when respectable people move to town, like a doctor or a banker, they have to live somewhere. And well...young women." Fleurette played with a newspaper that had been lying on the table as if by chance—the newsletter of the Anglican diocese of Christchurch.

"That's not what I think it is, is it?" Helen asked and took the thin gazette from her hand. It was opened to a page with a little advertisement.

Queenstown, Otago. Are you a Christian girl, strong in faith and animated by the pioneer spirit, interested in entering into marriage with a respectable, well-situated member of the community...

Helen shook her head. She did not know whether to laugh or cry. "Back then it was whalers; now it's prospectors! Do these respectable pastors' wives and pillars of the community really know what they're doing to these girls?"

"Well, it's Christchurch, Mother, not exactly London. If the girls don't like it, they're back home in three days," Ruben said in an attempt to appease her.

"And then people are supposed to take them at their word that they're just as virtuous and untouched as when they left," Helen scoffed.

"Not if they stay at Daphne's," said Fleurette. "Nothing against Daphne—but she tried to hire me on when I first got here years ago." She laughed. "However, if the girls were to stay in a clean, proper hotel, run by Helen O'Keefe, one of the town notables? Word gets around. People will point out to the girls and maybe even their parents that there's a respectable and wise chaperone with whom they can stay."

"And you'll have the opportunity to set the young things straight, Helen," Leonard commented, who seemed to think about as highly of mail-order brides as Helen. "They'll only see the nuggets the fiery-eyed swashbuckler has in his pocket that day—not the miserable hut she'll land in when he moves on to the next goldfield."

Helen looked grim. "You can be sure of that! I won't be witnessing at anybody's wedding after three days."

"So you'll manage the hotel?" Fleur asked fervently. "You think you can do it?"

Helen gave her an almost insulted gaze. "My dear Fleurette, in my life I've learned to read the Bible in Maori, to milk a cow, to slaughter chickens, and even to love a mule. I think I can manage to keep a small hotel running."

The others laughed, but then Leonard jingled his keys meaningfully, a sign that it was time to adjourn. Since Helen's hotel had not yet come into being, he had given his former prisoner permission to spend his last night in town in his old cell. No sinner, no matter how well recovered, could spend a night at Daphne's without backsliding.

Normally Helen would have accompanied Leonard to the door so that they could chat for a while on the porch, but this evening Leonard sought Fleurette's company. He turned somewhat bashfully to the young woman while James was saying good-bye to Helen and Ruben. "I...ahem, I don't want to be indiscreet, Mrs. O'Keefe, but... you know I'm interested in the elder Mrs. O'Keefe..."

Fleur listened to his stammering with a wrinkled brow. What in heaven's name did Leonard want? If this was supposed to be a marriage proposal, it would have been better to go straight to Helen.

Finally Leonard pulled himself together and got his question out. "Well...ahem, Mrs. O'Keefe: what the devil did Helen mean by 'mule'?"

15

Paul Warden had never felt so happy.

In fact, he did not know what had happened. After all, he had known Marama since childhood; she had always been part of his life—and often a nuisance. It was only with mixed feelings that he had allowed her to accompany him on his flight into the highlands—and on the first day he had been properly angry because her mule trotted so hopelessly slowly behind his horse. He had thought Marama to be a millstone around his neck and was confident that he didn't need her.

Now Paul was ashamed of everything he had said to her during their journey. But the girl had not listened; she never seemed to listen when Paul was cruel. Marama only saw his good side. She smiled when he was friendly and was silent when he got riled up. He got no satisfaction from taking his anger out on Marama. Paul had known that as a child, which was why she had never been the object of his pranks. And now...at some point over the last few months, Paul had found out that he loved Marama. Eventually, he realized that she was not patronizing him and not criticizing him, that she did not need to overcome any revulsion when she looked at him. Marama had helped him find a good hideout, far from the Canterbury Plains, in the newly discovered stretch of land they called the McKenzie Highlands—though it was not new to the Maori, Marama pointed out. She had been here with her tribe once before, as a little girl.

"Don't you remember how you cried, Paul?" Marama asked in her songlike voice. "We had always been together until then, and you called Kiri 'Mother,' just as I did. But then the yield was bad that year, and Mr. Warden drank more and would break out in a rage. There were not many men who wanted to work for him, and it was still a long time until the shearing."

Paul nodded. Gwyneira liked to give the Maori some advance pay in years like that to hold them over until the spring months when there was more work to do. That was risky, however: while some of the men remained and later remembered the money they had been paid, others took the money and disappeared, and still others forgot about the advance after the shearing and rudely demanded full payment. For that reason, Gerald and Paul had not permitted it the last few years. Let the Maori go. They would be back for the shearing, and if not, they could find other help. Paul had forgotten that he had once been a victim of this practice.

"Kiri laid you in your mother's arms, but you cried and screamed. And your mother said she didn't mind if you came with us, but Mr. Warden swore at her for that. I don't remember it all anymore, Paul, but Kiri told me about it later. She says you always held it against us that we left you behind. But what could we do? Mrs. Warden did not mean it like that either; she was fond of you."

"She never liked me," Paul said coldly.

Marama shook her head. "No. You were just two streams that did not flow together. Perhaps someday you'll find your way to each other. All streams eventually flow into the sea."

Paul only planned to make a simple camp, but Marama wanted a proper house.

"We don't have anything else to do, Paul," she said easily. "And you will have to stay away for a while. So why should we freeze?"

There was an ax in the heavy saddlebags Marama's mule carried, so Paul chopped down a few trees. With help from the patient mule, he dragged them to a clearing by a brook. Marama had chosen the place because several powerful rocks jutted up from the ground nearby. The spirits were happy here, she declared. And happy spirits were well disposed toward new settlers. She asked Paul to make a few carvings on their house so that it would look nice and *papa* would not feel insulted by it. When it finally met with her approval, she led Paul ceremoniously into the large, empty inner room.

"I now take you for my husband!" she announced seriously. "I'm lying with you in a sleeping lodge—even if the tribe is not present. A few of our ancestors will be here to witness it. I, Marama, descendent of those who came to Aotearoa in the *uruao*, take you, Paul Warden. Isn't that how your people say it?"

"It's a little more complicated than that," Paul said. He did not know what to think, but Marama was beautiful that day. She wore a colorful headband, had wound a sheet around her waist, and her breasts were bare. Paul had never seen her like this; she had always worn modest, Western clothing in the Wardens' household and at school. But now she stood before him, half-naked, with gleaming light brown skin, a soft fire in her eyes—and he looked at her as *papa* must have looked at *rangi*. She loved him. Unconditionally, regardless of what he was and what he had done.

Paul put his arms around her. He did not know whether the Maori kissed at such moments, but then she rubbed her nose lightly against his. Marama giggled when she had to sneeze afterward. Then she removed her sheet. Paul's breath caught as she stood fully naked before him. She was more delicately built than most of the women of her race, but her hips were wide, her breasts large, and her buttocks ample. Paul swallowed, but Marama serenely spread the blanket on the ground and pulled Paul down to her.

"You do want to be my husband, don't you?" she asked.

Paul would have to answer, without ever having thought about it. Until that moment, he had hardly given marriage a thought, and the few times he had, he had imagined himself in an arranged marriage with a white-skinned girl—maybe one of the Greenwoods' or Barringtons' daughters. That would be suitable. But what expression would he see in the eyes of a girl like that? Would she abhor him like his mother did? At the very least, she would have reservations. Especially now, after he had murdered Howard. Would she really be able to love him? Wouldn't he always be on his guard and suspicious?

To love Marama, on the other hand, was simple. She was there, willing and tender, fully submissive to him...no, that wasn't right. She had her own will. He would never have been able to force her to do something. Be he also would never have wanted to. Maybe that was the nature of love: it had to be given freely. A love forced on someone, like his mother's, wasn't worth anything.

So Paul nodded. But suddenly that did not strike him as good enough. It wasn't fair to confirm their love only according to her rituals. He wanted to acknowledge it according to his, as well.

Paul Warden tried to remember what little he knew of wedding vows.

"I, Paul, take you, Marama, before God and man...and the ancestors...to be my lawfully wedded wife..."

From this moment on, Paul was a happy man. He lived with Marama as though they were a Maori couple. He hunted and fished while she cooked and attempted to cultivate a garden. She had brought some seeds—there had been a reason that her heavily laden mule could not keep up with his horse—and Marama was as happy as a child when the seeds sprouted. In the evening, she entertained Paul with stories and songs. She told him about her ancestors who had come long, long ago in the *uruao* canoe to Aotearoa from Polynesia. Every Maori, she explained to Paul, was full of pride for the canoe on which his ancestors had come. At official events they used the name of this canoe as a part of their own names. Naturally, everyone knew the story of the discovery of the New Country. "We came from a land called Hawaiki," Marama explained, and her story sounded like a song. "At the time there was a man named Kupe who loved a woman named Kura-maro-tini. But he couldn't marry her because she had already lain with his cousin Hoturapa in the sleeping lodge."

Paul learned that Kupe drowned Hoturapa, and for that reason he had to flee his country. And how Kura-maro-tini, who had fled with him, saw a beautiful white cloud sitting on the sea, which revealed itself to be the country Aotearoa. Marama sang of dangerous fights with krakens and ghosts when they seized the land and of Kupe's return to Hawaiki.

"He told the people there of Aotearoa, but he never went back. He never went back."

"And Kura-maro-tini?" Paul asked. "Did Kupe just leave her?"

Marama nodded sadly.

"Yes. She remained alone...but she had two daughters. That might have comforted her. But Kupe was certainly not a nice fellow!"

With these last words, she sounded so much like Mrs. O'Keefe's little model student that Paul had to laugh. He pulled the girl into his arms.

"I will never leave you, Marama. Even if I haven't always been such a nice fellow."

Tonga learned about Paul and Marama from a boy fleeing from Lionel Station and John Sideblossom's hard regime. He had heard about Tonga's "uprising" against the Wardens and was eager to join the would-be guerillas in their fight against the *pakeha.*

"There's another one living over there in the highlands," he reported excitedly. "With a Maori wife. I mean, they were nice. The man is hospitable. He would share his food with us when we wandered by. And the girl is a singer. *Tohunga!* But I say: all *pakeha* are rotten. And they shouldn't have our women!"

Tonga nodded. "You are right," he said seriously. "No *pakeha* should defile our women. And you will be my guide and precede the Chieftain's Ax to avenge this wrong."

The boy beamed. First thing the next day, he led Tonga into the highlands.

Tonga and his guide encountered Paul in front of his house. The young man had been gathering wood and helping Marama to clear out a cooking pit. This was not common practice in her village, but they had both heard of this Maori custom and now wanted to try it for themselves. Marama happily gathered stones while Paul stuck his spade in the soil, still soft from the last rain.

Tonga stepped from behind the rocks that Marama believed pleased the gods.

"Whose grave are you digging, Warden? Have you shot another man?"

Paul spun around and held his spade out in front of him. Marama let out a quiet whimper of fear. She looked beautiful; once again she was wearing only her skirt and had her hair tied back with an embroidered headband. Her skin glistened from the work, and she had just been laughing. Paul stepped in front of her. He knew it was childish, but he didn't want anyone to see her so lightly dressed—even though he knew the Maori would find nothing offensive about it.

"What do you want, Tonga? You're scaring my wife. Get out of here; this isn't your land!"

"More mine than yours, *pakeha*! But if you want to know the truth—your Kiward Station won't belong to you much longer either. Your governor has decided in my favor. If you can't buy my share, then we'll have to split the land," Tonga declared, leaning casually on the Chieftain's Ax, which he had brought with him to make an appropriately grand entrance.

Marama stepped in between the two men. She recognized that Tonga was wearing warrior's jewelry, and he was not only wearing paint—the young chief had had himself tattooed in the traditional style over the last few months.

"Tonga, we will negotiate fairly," she said softly. "Kiward Station is big; everyone will receive his share. Paul does not want to be your enemy anymore. He is my husband; he belongs to me and my people. So he is also your brother. Make peace, Tonga!"

Tonga laughed. "Him? My brother? Then he should also live like my brother. We will take his land and level his house. The gods should reclaim the land on which the house stands. You two can live in our sleeping lodge, naturally." Tonga approached Marama, his gaze roaming salaciously over her bare breasts. "But then again you might want to share your bed with someone else. Nothing has been decided yet."

"You damned piece of shit!"

As Tonga reached his hand out to Marama, Paul pounced on him. A moment later, the two were rolling, brawling, screaming, and cursing on the ground. They punched and grappled at each other, scratched and bit, did whatever they could to harm the other. Marama observed the fight apathetically. She had lost count of how many times she had seen the two rivals in a similarly ignoble confrontation. Children, both of them.

"Stop it!" she finally screamed. "Tonga you're a chieftain! Think of your dignity. And you, Paul..."

But neither one of them listened to her. Instead, they stubbornly continued to strike each other. Marama would have to wait until one of them had pinned the other down, though both of them were about equally strong. Marama knew that the fortunes of battle hung in the balance—and she would wonder for the rest of her life whether everything would have turned out differently if fortune had not been on Paul's side, for Tonga finally found himself pinned down. Paul sat on him, out of breath, his face scratched and beaten bloody. But he had triumphed. Grinning, he raised his fist.

"Do you still want to question whether Marama is my wife, you bastard? Forever and always?" He shook Tonga.

Unlike Marama, the youth who had led the chieftain there watched the fight full of rage and consternation. For him, this was no petty fistfight but a power struggle between Maori and *pakeha*—tribal warrior versus oppressor. And the girl was right: this sort of fight did not befit a chieftain. Tonga could not tussle like a boy. And he had been beaten too. He was just about to lose his last shred of dignity...the boy could not allow that to happen. He raised his spear.

"No! No, boy, no! Paul!" Marama screamed and tried to seize the young Maori by the arm. But it was too late. Paul Warden, crouched over his pinned opponent, fell over, his chest pierced through by a spear.

16

James McKenzie whistled happily. The mission that lay before him was delicate, but there was nothing that could ruin his good mood today. He had been back in the Canterbury Plains for two days, and his reunion with Gwyneira had left no desire unfulfilled. It was as though all the misunderstandings and all the years that had passed since their then-young love affair had never existed. James smirked when he recalled how hard Gwyneira had worked to not ever talk about love back then. Now she did so openly, and there was no trace left of the Welsh princess's prudery.

Who was to make Gwyneira feel ashamed now? For the time being, the Wardens' manor belonged to them alone. It was strange to enter the house not as a barely tolerated employee but as someone taking possession of it—of the chairs in the salon, the crystal glasses, the whiskey, and Gerald Warden's first-class cigars. James still felt most at home in the kitchen and in the stables—which were, after all, where Gwyneira spent most of her time. There still was no Maori staff, and the white shepherds were too important and above all too proud to perform simple household tasks. So Gwyneira carried the water, harvested vegetables in the garden, and gathered eggs in the chicken coop. She rarely had fresh fish or meat anymore. Gwyneira did not have time to fish, and she could not bring herself to snap the chickens' necks. The menu expanded when James began living there. He was happy to make her life easier, even though he still felt like a guest in her feminine bedroom. Gwyneira had told him that Lucas had furnished the room for her. Although the playful lace curtains and the delicate furniture were not really Gwyneira's style, she kept them as mementos of her husband.

Lucas Warden must have been a strange man. Only now did James realize how little he had known him and how close the shepherds' mean-spirited remarks had come to the truth. But something in Gwyneira had really loved Lucas, or at least respected him. And Fleurette's memories of her would-be father were also full of warmth. James began to feel regret and sympathy for Lucas. He had been a good, if also a weak man, born in the wrong place at the wrong time.

James directed his horse toward the Maori village on the lake. He could have gone on foot, but he was here on an official mission, as Gwyneira's negotiator, so to speak, and felt safer—and above all, more important—on the four-legged status symbol of the *pakeha*. Besides, he liked the horse. Fleurette had given it to him: it was the son of her mare Niniane with a riding horse of Arab lineage.

McKenzie had been expecting to run into a blockade between Kiward Station and the Maori village. After all, Leonard McDunn had reported something to that effect, and Gwyneira was also aggravated by their attempts to cut her off from the road to Haldon.

James, however, entered the village unmolested. He was just passing the first buildings, and the great meeting hall was coming into view. But the mood in the camp was decidedly strange.

There was none of the antagonistic defensiveness and defiance that Gwyneira, but also Andy McAran and Poker Livingston, had spoken of. Most surprisingly, there was no sense of triumph over the governor's decision. Instead, James got the sense that they were tensely waiting for something. People did not crowd around him, amiably looking to chat as they had during his previous visits to the village, nor did they seem threatening. Though he did see the occasional man with warrior tattoos, they all wore shirts and pants, rather than traditional outfits and spears. A few women were taking care of the daily chores, trying hard not to make eye contact with the visitor.

Finally Kiri stepped out of one of the houses.

"Mr. James. I hear you here again," she said formally. "That is great joy for miss."

James smiled. He had always suspected that Kiri and Moana knew the truth.

But Kiri did not return his smile. Instead, she looked up at James earnestly as she began to speak again. She chose her words with care, almost caution. "And I want to say...I'm sorry. Moana also sorry and Witi. If peace now, we happy to come back to house. And we forgive Paul. He changed, Marama says. Good man. For me good son."

James nodded. "That's nice, Kiri. For Paul too. Mrs. Warden hopes he'll come back soon." He was surprised when Kiri turned away.

No one else spoke to him until James reached the chief's lodge. He dismounted. He was sure Tonga must have heard of his arrival, but the young chief was apparently going to make him beg.

James raised his voice. "Tonga! We need to talk. Mrs. Warden has received word from the governor. She would like to negotiate."

Tonga stepped slowly out of his lodge. He was wearing the outfit and tattoos of a warrior but not carrying a spear. Instead, he held the Sacred Ax of the chieftain. James recognized the traces of a brawl on his face. Was the young chief's position no longer definitive? Did he have rivals within his own tribe?

James held out his hand to him, but Tonga did not take it.

James shrugged. OK then. In his eyes Tonga was behaving like a child, but what else could you expect from such a young man? James decided not to play his game and to remain polite no matter what. Perhaps he could appeal to the man's sense of honor.

"Tonga, you are very young and yet already chief. That means your people regard you as a reasonable man. Mrs. O'Keefe also thinks highly of you, and what you've achieved with the governor is remarkable. You've shown courage and tenacity. But now we must come to an agreement. Since Mr. Warden isn't here, Mrs. Warden will negotiate in his stead. And she vows that he will stand behind whatever she agrees to. He will have to. After all, the governor has given his decision. So end this war, Tonga! For the sake of your own people as well." James held his hands out to the side. He was unarmed. Tonga must see that he came in peace.

The young chief stood up even straighter in his already tall frame, though he was still shorter than James. He had also been shorter than Paul, which had bothered him his entire adolescence. But now he carried the title of chief. He need not be ashamed of anything. Not even for Paul's killing.

"Inform Gwyneira Warden that we are ready to negotiate," he said coolly. "We entertain no doubts that her agreements will be kept. Mrs. Warden has been the voice of the Wardens since the last full moon. Paul Warden is dead."

"It wasn't Tonga," James said, holding Gwyneira in his arms as he told her of her son's death. Gwyneira heaved dry sobs. She found no tears and hated herself for that. Paul had been her son, but she could not cry for him.

Kiri silently set a pot of tea on the table for them. She and Moana had accompanied James to the house. As though it had been agreed upon, the women took possession once more of the kitchen and office rooms.

"You can't blame Tonga for it, or the negotiations might break down. I think he blames himself. As I understand it, one of his warriors lost control of himself. He saw the dignity of his chief under threat and stabbed Paul—from behind. Tonga must be ashamed to his core. The murderer did not even belong to Tonga's tribe. So Tonga had no control over him. That's why he wasn't punished. Tonga only sent him back to his people. If you want, you could have the incident investigated by the police. Tonga and Marama were witnesses and wouldn't lie in court." James poured tea and a good deal of sugar into a cup and tried to hand it to Gwyneira.

Gwyneira shook her head. "What would that change?" she asked quietly. "The warrior saw his people's honor threatened; Paul saw his wife threatened; Howard felt insulted…one thing leads to another, and it never ends. I'm so sick of it all, James." Her whole body trembled. "And I would have liked so much to tell Paul that I loved him."

James pulled her close. "He would have known you were lying," he said softly. "You can't change that, Gwyn."

She nodded. "I'll have to live with it, and I'll hate myself for it every day. Love is so strange. I couldn't feel anything for Paul, but Marama loved him…as naturally as she breathed air, and unconditionally, no matter what Paul did. She was his wife, you say? Where is she? Did Tonga do something to her?"

"I take it that she was officially Paul's wife. Tonga and Paul fought over her in any case. So for Paul, it was serious. Where she is now, I don't know. I don't know the Maori's mourning ceremonies. Probably she buried Paul and then withdrew. We'll have to ask Tonga or Kiri."

Gwyneira squared herself. Her hands were still trembling, but she managed now to warm her fingers on the teacup and to raise the cup to her mouth. "We need to find out. I won't let anything happen to the girl as well. I need to go to the village as soon as possible. I want to put all of this behind me. But not today. Not tonight. I want tonight to myself. I want to be alone, James…I need to think. Tomorrow, after sunrise, I'll talk to Tonga. I'm going to fight for Kiward Station, James. Tonga isn't going to get it!"

James took Gwyneira in his arms and carried her gently to her bedroom. "Whatever you want, Gwyn. But I won't leave you alone. I'll be there, tonight as well. You can cry or talk about Paul…there must also be some good memories. You must have been proud of him occasionally. Tell me about him and Marama. Or just let me hold you. You don't have to talk if you don't want to. But you're not alone."

Gwyneira wore a black dress when she met Tonga on the lakeshore between Kiward Station and the Maori village. Negotiations were not carried out in closed rooms. Gods, spirits, and the ancestors would act as witnesses. Behind Gwyneira stood James, Andy, Poker, Kiri, and Moana. Twenty warriors looked on grimly behind Tonga.

After a few formal greetings had been exchanged, the chief expressed his regret over the death of her son—in measured words and perfect English. Gwyneira could hear the traces of Helen's schooling. Tonga was a strange mixture of savage and gentleman.

"The governor has decided," Gwyneira said in a steady voice, "that the sale of the land now called Kiward Station did not correspond in every respect to the policies outlined in the Treaty of Waitangi."

Tonga laughed mockingly. "Not in every respect? The sale was against the law!"

Gwyneira shook her head. "No, it was not. It occurred before the ratification of the treaty that assured the Maori a minimum price for their land. One could not violate a treaty that did not yet exist—and that the Kai Tahu, moreover, never signed. Nevertheless, the governor finds that Gerald Warden cheated you when he bought the land." She took a deep breath. "And after a thorough examination of the documents, I have to agree with him. Gerald Warden paid you off with pocket money. You only received two-thirds of the minimum sum you were entitled to. The governor has now determined that we must either pay the rest of this sum or give back a corresponding portion of the land. The latter seems more just to me since the land will fetch a higher price today."

Tonga looked her over, leering. "We feel honored, Mrs. Warden," he remarked, and hinted at a bow. "You really mean to share your valuable Kiward Station with us?"

Gwyneira would have liked to give the arrogant brat an earful, but now was not the time. So she got a hold of herself and continued with as much composure as she had begun. "As reparation, I would like to offer you the farm known as O'Keefe Station. I know that you often wander across it, and the highlands there are richer in hunting and fishing grounds than Kiward Station. On the other hand, it's less suited to raising sheep. Thus we would all be served. In terms of area, O'Keefe Station is half as large as Kiward Station. You would thus receive more land than the governor granted you."

Gwyneira had formulated this plan almost as soon as she had heard the governor's decision. Helen wanted to sell it. She was going to stay in Queenstown, and Gwyneira could pay her for the farm in several installments. That way Kiward Station would not take a hit from the reparation payments, and no doubt it was more in keeping with the late Howard O'Keefe's desires, for the land would go to the Maori and not the hated Wardens.

The men behind Tonga whispered among themselves. It looked as though they took great interest in her suggestion. Tonga, however, shook his head.

"What grace, Mrs. Warden. A piece of less valuable land, a dilapidated farm—and the stupid Maori should feel lucky, eh?" He laughed. "No, I pictured things a little differently."

Gwyneira sighed. "What do you want?" she asked.

"What I want...what I really wanted...was the land on which we stand. From the road to Haldon to the dancing rocks." That was the area between the farm and the highlands that the Maori called the stone circle.

Gwyneira frowned. "But our house is on that land! That's impossible."

Tonga grinned. "I said that's what I wanted...but we owe you a certain blood debt, Mrs. Warden. Your son's death is my fault even if he did not die by my hand. I didn't want it, Mrs. Warden. I wanted to see him bleed, not for him to die. I wanted him to watch while I tore his house to the ground—or took up occupancy myself! With Marama as my wife. That would have caused him more pain than any spear. But so be it. I have decided to spare you. Keep your house, Mrs. Warden. But I want all the land from the dancing rocks to the stream that separates Kiward Station and O'Keefe Station." He looked at her presumptuously.

Gwyneira felt as though the ground was giving way from under her feet. She turned her gaze from Tonga and fixed it on James. Her eyes reflected confusion and desperation.

"Those are our best pastures," she said. "The three shearing sheds are there. It's almost all fenced in."

James stepped forward and put his arm around her. He looked at Tonga sternly.

"Maybe you two should take some time to think things over some more," he said calmly.

Gwyneira straightened. Her eyes sparked.

"If we give you what you want," she exclaimed, "we might as well just hand Kiward Station over to you. Maybe we should do it too! There won't be another heir. And you and I, James, we could just concentrate on Helen's farm."

Gwyneira breathed deeply and let her gaze wander over the land she had protected and taken care of.

"Everything will fall apart," she said as though to herself. "The breeding schedule, the sheep farm, the longhorns now too...and so much work has been put into them. We had the best animals in Canterbury, if not on the whole island. Damn it, Gerald Warden had his faults, but he did not deserve this!" She bit her lip to keep herself from crying. For the first time, she felt like she could cry for Gerald. For Gerald, Lucas, and Paul.

"No!" The voice was quiet but piercing. A songlike voice, the voice of a born storyteller and singer.

The group of warriors behind Tonga separated to make way for Marama. The girl stepped serenely between them.

Marama was not tattooed but had painted the symbols of her people on her skin that day: they decorated her chin and the skin between her mouth and nose, making her narrow face look like one of the gods' masks that Gwyneira recognized from Matahorua's house. Marama had tied her hair up, like adult women did when they dressed themselves for holiday celebrations. Her upper body was naked, though she wore a cloth around her shoulders and a wide white skirt Gwyneira had once given her.

"Do not dare to call me your wife, Tonga! I have never lain with you and I never will. I was and am Paul Warden's wife. And this was and is Paul Warden's land!" Marama had been speaking English so far; now she changed to her own language. No one in Tonga's retinue should misunderstand her. She spoke slowly enough that not a word should escape Gwyneira and James. Everyone on Kiward Station was to know what Marama Warden had to say.

"This is the Wardens' land, but it is also the Kai Tahu's. And now there is to be a child whose mother comes from the tribe of those who came to Aotearoa on the canoe *uruao*. And whose father from the tribe of the Wardens. Paul never told me what canoe his father's ancestors rowed, but our union was blessed by the ancestors of the Kai Tahu. The mothers and fathers of the *uruao* will welcome the child. And this will be his land."

The young woman laid her hands on her stomach and raised her arms in an all-encompassing gesture, as though she wanted to embrace the land and the mountains.

The warriors behind Tonga raised their voices. Approving voices. No one would fight over the land with Marama's child—especially not when all of the land of O'Keefe Station would fall to the Maori tribes.

Gwyneira smiled and composed herself for a response. She was a little dizzy, but more than that, she felt relieved; now she hoped that she chose the right words and that she spoke them correctly. It was her first speech in Maori that went beyond daily matters, and she wanted everyone to understand:

"Your child is from the tribe of those who came to Aotearoa on the *Dublin*. The family of this child's father will also welcome it. As heir of this farm called Kiward Station on the land of the Kai Tahu."

Gwyneira attempted to imitate Marama's gesture, but in her case, it was Marama and her unborn grandchild whom she held in her arms.

Acknowledgments

Many thanks to my editor, Melanie Blank-Schröder, who believed in this novel from the start, and most of all to my ingenious agent, Bastian Schlück.

Thanks to Heike, who put me in touch with Pawhiri, and to Pawhiri and Sigrid, who answered my endless questions about Maori culture. If I have still made errors in my depiction, the fault is mine alone.

Many thanks to Klara for a great deal of precise and specialized information on wool quality and sheep breeds, help with Internet research about immigrants to New Zealand in the nineteenth century, and professional "test reading."

Finally, thanks, of course, to the cobs who always galloped my head free—and to Cleo for thousands of adoring collie smiles.

Sarah Lark

About the Author

Photo © Gonzalo Perez, 2011

Sarah Lark, author of several bestselling historical fiction novels in Germany and Spain, was born in Germany's Ruhr region, where she discovered a love of animals—especially horses—early in life. She has worked as an elementary school teacher, travel guide, and commercial writer. She has also written numerous award-winning books about horses for adults and children, one of which was nominated for the Deutsche Jugendbuchpreis, Germany's distinguished prize for best children's book. Sarah currently lives with four dogs and a cat on her farm in Almería, Spain, where she cares for retired horses, plays guitar, and sings in her spare time.

About the Translator

Photo © Sanna Stegmaier, 2011

D. W. Lovett is a graduate of the University of Illinois Urbana-Champaign from which he received a degree in comparative literature and German as well as a certificate from the university's Center for Translation Studies. He has spent the last few years living in Europe.